No-Name Roundabout

NO-NAME ROUNDABOUT

PART 1

Michael Hulme

Copyright © 2023 Michael Hulme

The moral right of the author has been asserted.

Apart from any fair dealing for the purposes of research or private study, or criticism or review, as permitted under the Copyright, Designs and Patents Act 1988, this publication may only be reproduced, stored or transmitted, in any form or by any means, with the prior permission in writing of the publishers, or in the case of reprographic reproduction in accordance with the terms of licences issued by the Copyright Licensing Agency. Enquiries concerning reproduction outside those terms should be sent to the publishers.

This is a work of fiction. Names, characters, businesses, places, events and incidents are either the products of the author's imagination or used in a fictitious manner. Any resemblance to actual persons, living or dead, or actual events is purely coincidental.

Matador
9 Priory Business Park,
Wistow Road, Kibworth Beauchamp,
Leicestershire. LE8 0RX
Tel: 0116 279 2299
Email: books@troubador.co.uk
Web: www.troubador.co.uk/matador
Twitter: @matadorbooks

ISBN 9781803136622 (Part 1)
ISBN 9781803136875 (Part 2)

British Library Cataloguing in Publication Data.
A catalogue record for this book is available from the British Library.

Printed and bound by CPI Group (UK) Ltd, Croydon, CR0 4YY
Typeset in 11pt Minion Pro by Troubador Publishing Ltd, Leicester, UK

Matador is an imprint of Troubador Publishing Ltd

For my wife and daughters.

PUNCH

Stand here and we shall witness the start of something. Be patient. Simply wait, at the edge of the wood, sheltered in the lee of the great Hedge.

Hear that noise? It is gasping breath and the pounding feet of running men. Hazel, woodbine and ivy are too tightly woven to allow any view of the field beyond but what you hear are the sounds of ragged conflict. Ring of steel on steel, the flat 'popping' of flintlock pistols. This summer afternoon is being destroyed, by thievery, treachery and betrayal. Beyond the Hedge, ambush and murder are afoot.

That distant 'thwump,' is the sound of a small cannon firing. The echo dies away and only yards from where we stand, this stout English Hedge explodes. Hawthorn and ash snap, spindle-wood waves wildly, snaking withies of Guelder rose, old man's beard and bramble, all are blown adrift. Through the ruin comes flying the wearer of a ragged scarlet jacket, a fine tricorn hat and pants that are more hole than cloth. This unfortunate has just been blown through the Hedge backwards. Hurled through, complete with musket.

This is how it begins. First the strife from the field, followed by eerie silence. Then the explosion and here lies proof of something, a crazy red and black figure, stinking and steaming on the summer grass. The wreckage of his passage, scraps of branch, snakes of briar, crushed anemones, broken stalks of meadowsweet and bruised sorrels are strewn around him.

Punch, this being his one and only name lies, beaten to the ground. From hands, feet, through a great gash in his side, he bleeds, like a painted-plaster Christ, thrown down in iconoclastic fury. He hugs to his chest a thick vellum book, as if life was dependent upon it.

He cuts a crazy figure. The red jacket is filthy and torn, its last button dangling by a thread. Shredded gold epaulettes are unravelling from his shoulders. A patch pocket is adrift, any contents long gone. The cheap cloth trousers are as indecent from this side as they were from the rear and their cheapness contrasts badly with the sturdy leather belt that secures them. There are no shoes for the bloodied feet and the tricorn, once as noble an article as his belt, seems to avoid the blackened hand that makes crab-like forays for it, whenever his paw can bear to quit clutching the book of vellum.

Beyond the Hedge all sounds have ceased and as the drowsy day gathers itself, the vines and creepers that were hurled to the ground, recover themselves, pulling in their stems, stiffening, bracing their fronds. 'Nothing came to pass here,' is what they seem to say.

On the grass, Punch shifts a little and tries to raise his head. He fails, then, as his right hand is committed to the book and the whereabouts of the tricorn, he searches, unavailingly, with his left, for his musket.

This violent, near stillbirth, from an English hedge, is re-entering the living world. The odd groan, the spittle now flecking his lips, the final, ill-advised lurch upright, that provokes vomiting across legs, grass and shattered branch, all prove it.

"My God," groans Punch, wiping his lips as he sits forward. His eyes cast about and he spots a familiar strap lying in the grass. He hauls in a water flask and takes copious draughts. He splashes the palm of his hand, then with the wet and filthy paw, re-arranges the grime on his face.

Red and black he lies in the green sea, oddly aware of the quiet sounds around him. The afternoon conversation of the insect world is huge and continuous. The Hedge seems to speak, too, clicking, cracking and snapping as twigs are forced back under branches, while withies haul in errant shoots. Wild order is rebuilding itself. For a while Punch sleeps, as proven by a shattering snore that stuns the insect world. Amazed, tiny creatures freeze. Then, as the seconds tick away and no monster comes to trample the grass, their animated chatter resumes.

Were we to become skylarks for a while, we could rise and hover above the magical Hedge. We could see how it shimmers mistily, below, as if it was not yet firmly rooted. It and the small wood, the hollows and dells within, all have an air of sanctuary. They are places within a place, indifferent to the world outside.

Our bird's eye can also see the aftermath of the skirmish. Any survivors have long since fled. The slain body of the man whose book Punch coveted and stole, lies by the Hedge, his chest ruined by a small cannonball that, however feeble its force at the end of its flight, has smashed open his iron breastplate. It was that impact that arrested Punch in the act of murder, for it hurled him from his victim's back and through the Hedge.

There are other bodies, not many, for not many were there. But whatever this ambush was about, or by whom, we shall never know, nor will it warrant an entry in any county history. English legend admits of no conflict on its soil in the decade that concerns us and Punch, who may have been able to tell differently, will not. He will never speak of it and indeed, he cannot, for Punch is undergoing a change...

Way below, scavengers move into the field, local villains, chancers who, nevertheless, know only too well never to approach the Hedge too closely. It is an act of pure folly when Punch's erstwhile victim is dragged away by his heels to be plundered. A reckless move by a village braggart, who, before too long, will pay dearly for his arrogance, for the bold glance he threw at the dense, waving foliage of the Hedge.

We skylarks see that Punch still lies, concussed and abject, by now covered in evening dew, obliged to wait for the morning sun that will dry, warm and rouse him. During these night hours he will hang somewhere between life and death. Yet still he holds the pillaged book to his breast, while all around, insects consider his colossal wreck.

The scavengers move off, their cart barely laden. Any profits will come from the barrel of the cannon, which juts over the tailboard, from beneath a pile of clothing, the scant possessions that could be gathered. At twilight a few bold urchins arrive to play, to swarm on the empty gun carriage, to hurl stones at the privy parts of the piled, naked corpses and, perchance, to discover the odd coin, or button, overlooked by the pillagers. But these half savage creatures know better than any to avoid the Hedge.

This is not the only small enclosure in England where few enter and fewer leave. We skylarks know that. We ride upon the magical currents that rise up from such places, we own a secret that cannot be shared, except in the tongue of skylarks. Press your way into such places, on foot and you will be refused. Undergrowth will thwart you, sudden rills of water will spread out and deny you, your eyes will wander, turn elsewhere, your reason will become confused, nausea and migraines will defeat you. It is the same in all such places. The birds know it, the passaging insects know it, even rabbits, badgers, voles and stoats know it. This fox, loping in the lee of the Hedge is not only wary of man, he is wary of magic. Content to remain fox, he has no intention of pushing his way through to investigate the fallen body.

Punch, however, not wholly propelled there by wayward gunnery, is already deep in the grip of the wood's enchantments. He has lain, concussed, for seven hours and will lie another six. In that time the copse and Hedge will make him their own. Thereafter, only occasionally and exceptionally, will he be allowed to leave its depths. Even when he does, he will feel as if its boundaries follow him, in the manner of a child's pencil line drawn to describe the wanderings of an ant, on a sheet of paper.

Old Magic is peculiar magic. It has both great power and little power. Its business is with land, with the growing things rooted in it and with the rock that underlies it. Sinews and bones, ligaments laid down at the beginning of all things and living still. It has no interest in righting men's wrongs, unless they affect the ancient harmonies.

This is why Punch lies here now, one twist in the slenderest thread of that antique music.

He awakes with the most appalling headache. He closes his eyes against the sun. He tries to roll over but he is snared by bramble. He searches for obscenities, finds them but feels too abject to use them. He sinks back against the ground and curiously, finds great comfort in that.

Reflexively he feels for the book, still lodged on his chest. For the first time since seizing it, he raises it and with broken nails tries to undo the metal clasps of the cover. He knows that, secreted within is a shower of gold, but what comes tumbling out, after much fumbling with an inner latch, is a small rain of wooden whistles.

Such a hideous reversal propels him free of the briars, to the ruination of his calves and chest. He scrabbles at the book, shaking it violently, turning the pages, exploring the hollow of the spine, almost breaking the solid binding asunder.

"T'were meant to be..." he croaks, " a wealth o' gold coin! T'were meant t'be t'makin' o' a man's fortune..." and he picks up a wooden whistle, attempts a little trill upon it with parchment lips, dryer than the vellum itself. "Not these...but gold!" and Punch laughs maniacally, laughs and laughs for the sheer magnitude of the outrage. He is in no condition to note that a small squadron of bumblebees is gathering in the Hedge, busying themselves, for the moment with Guelder rose and foxgloves. He claws the whistles from the ground. He blows a note upon each. Again, he fails to witness the successive marshalling of earwigs, ants, beetles – large and small – all hurrying in his direction.

Punch is, strangely enough, literate but when he fumbles open the pages again, he finds that it has been so many years since he had cause to read, that he struggles to make out – 'A Boke of Bee and Insect Lore, rendered in the Tongue of Man and Beast.' Be damned to the author and his cursed name, though he warrants it was never Old Jolyon, whom he had been poised, ready to murder, not a day since. A waste of a plan and energy, as that weary cannonball had crashed into the old fool first and hurled him, Punch, hard man of taverns and gutters through this damnable hedge, backwards! All, it seems, without yield, except for this flagellation of his body. But, as we shall see, the betterment of his soul had also been included in the exchange and that would be for the good of many.

For all that Punch feels ruined, counting three or four cracked ribs, torn hands and feet, lacerated calves and chest, bruised back and battered pate, he also feels – different. For the first time in years he is conscious of the radiance of the sun, the nurture of the dew on the grass, the call of birds overhead and above them, the tiny white clouds that are dappling the sky, in those long furrows men call mackerel's belly. Punch feels oddly at peace, considering his disappointment at the gold-that-never-was.

He spies a fat bumblebee, struggling over the tussocky grass. Any time in the past he would have crushed it, wantonly, automatically, be it with bare foot, or boot. Partly what has restrained him is that he is still horizontal, prostrated with pain but for a while, he observes it and not without interest. Intuition tells him that it is seeking cover. He groans as he swivels on his hip but he has spotted an ideal location, a small, dark earthy hole cemented together by a covering lattice of grass roots. He directs its passage, gently, with a filthy finger and is boyishly thrilled when it hurries up the tiny slope, explores the recess, hurries in and is not seen again. Would that he could be so easily catered for!

He considers his situation. He has heard no racket of searchers. Whatever took place beyond the Hedge also finished there. He lies this side of that great, knotted barrier, battered, bruised but not wholly off his feet. For a man with limited ambition, such a beginning is not a bad start. The book, he admits, is a disappointment. It's a sorry business that Old Jolyon's prating – "truly my book of gold" – followed by a knowing wink, had to bring about his demise, albeit by amateur artillery fire. A matter totally out of Punch's hands, though he is forced to admit that one second later, he would have cut the old fool's throat, so bewitched was he by the scent of coin. Musing on the matter, now, he is forced to admit, albeit small consolation to the departed, that he is glad that he did not.

So, wither, Punch asks himself, next?

When was Punch ever short of a destination? Like the old dog he is, he's always headed somewhere. But not just yet. He sinks back into the grass and finds it welcoming. Then he considers his wounds. None are mortal but the gash in his side is deep.

His eyes rove about, indifferently at first but then more cautiously, more attentively. He realises he has shreds of his grandmother's herbal lore still locked away at the bottom of his mind. Here, tiny little thing, is eyebright…white florets touched with purple and in their heart, yellow eyes. He thinks. A handful of herb, brewed gently in a pint of spring water, cool and then wash the eyes carefully, clearing away scum and rheum. Do wonders for failing sight, especially that caused by long hours at the loom. Won't cure the blind but 'twill restore tired vision. Now, how would he remember that? He was no more than a child.

Turning his neck, he spies dwarf elder. Brew a massy handful to wash out women's privates! He laughs wryly… he must have learned that listening at closed doors.

He sits upright, swivels himself around, grunting with the night aches and day's pains. Here, by the edge of this rivulet is red dock. Now, this is good. He shuffles forwards to pick a plentiful quantity. Somehow he will pulp these over a warm coal or two and bind the mess, in a poultice, across his side. What's left he will rub into the briar stripes, for the healing power of red dock is well-known. He scuffles on a few more yards for daisy plants, these, too, he will include. When he has brewed this lot up, he'll have a potion fit to revive Old Jolyon. He subsides at the thought, finding none of the humour in it that he once would. Nevertheless, there's half a herbalist's stall within arm's reach and beyond, there must lie more. He scratches his head and ponders. He can remember half-a-dozen cures but the rest seem flown for now, no doubt drowned in tavern talk and beer.

His old Nan, who had the raising of him from the age of seven, knew a thing or two. She could set bone, pull a tooth. The recollection prompts his tongue to find a rotten socket and to poke at it. Not an action of much wisdom, he thinks sourly, as he sets off a long-lasting drum-roll of pain. She was midwife, wise-woman to the helpless and poor, as worthwhile with her lore as any so-called physician of the age.

He recalls himself, an awestruck child, gazing up at her jars of liquor in which, it seemed, swam adders, slow-worms, grass snakes and lizards, all pickled for their essence. How they fascinated and terrified him. The very threat of a draught of adder liquor was enough to bring him to heel for an entire day. Then there were the bundles of herbs that hung from every roof beam and scented the whole cottage. All had had to be gathered at the right phase of the moon, especially any destined to cure women's ailments. Then there were the greases she compounded, unguents the rich called them, herb decoctions locked into beeswax, lanolin, honey and the oils from fat seeds. These were to be smeared onto skin, cracked, riven or scrofulous. For boils, carbuncles and great, ugly spots she had her special grease, a secret mixture that only Punch knew the making of, now. It was no less than the fat rendered from a stray dog. Heaven help the cur that sniffed its way into Nan's kitchen. It would not see the light of day again. But that fat, which smelled so bad, would draw the pips from an apple, let alone the pus from a boil.

Lowly folk arrived humbly at her back door and were treated for free, or for the jar of milk, or rind of cheese they could spare. For the rich, whose coachmen summoned her, she would pack up her simples in a shawl, be driven away in secrecy and return with coin, small silver for gratitude.

Strangest things in the whole cottage, to the child Punch, were the earth-covered mandrake roots, which hung from strings on the back kitchen wall. Of what use they were, he could not recall but they had the form of scrawny devils, ugly little men and women. The men flaunted a great carrot between their thighs, whilst the women, a deep cleft. That the plants were male and female, there could be no doubting.

There were strange and ugly rumours about the gathering of mandrake root. Firstly was the tale that they only grew beneath the gallows' tree, where the ejaculate of the hanged had fallen to the ground. Secondly, to remove the root entire was vital. Were it to break underground, in its lifting, then the same injury would befall the digger. It was said that the wise-woman, for her gathering, should dig about the roots with a wooden knife, carefully loosening the mannikin body from its soil. Then, at some ungodly hour, she must tether a starving dog to the root at its thickest point. Firstly stopping her own ears with wax, she must now cast a scrap of meat some distance from the dog. It would be the hound's lunge for the meat that drew the mandrake from the ground, at which outrage it would utter a cry of such piercing fearfulness that all who heard it would die upon the spot…including, of course, the unfortunate mutt.

"Rubbish!" exclaimed Punch, loudly. He and Nan dug and drew mandrake wherever and whenever they found it. Certainly they took care to preserve the mannikins' form, which were indeed, uncanny and mysterious – not to mention valuable in the marketplace, but they had never been pursued by screams, only their own grunts and puffs, as they dug and teased around the shapes. The roots buried themselves deeply in the earth!

Despite himself, Punch recalled the old, fallen castle keep. There, in the damp, gloomy silence they could collect house leek, which grew defiantly between the great building stones, down which the rains now poured through shattered roof timbers. These they could sell in little earthenware pots, certain charms to thwart thunder and lightning strikes. More practically, macerated, they might be bound against swellings, stings and rashes. Punch's mood began to sour and sour badly. He remembered the old keep all too well. It was where his life had unravelled, despite his tender years.

He had been playing on stairs, which led only to a flooded hallway. But this he liked to gaze along and to imagine nobles and ladies, in their ermines and silks, freely passing to and fro. That fateful day a stray ray of light, passing some high point, cast a sharp pool of illumination into one dark corner. In the moment that it had lasted he had seen the unmistakeable glimpse of gold, shining up, through the trailing mats of duckweed and slime that coated the fallen stones. Undaunted by such, he had waded out and delved for whatever it had been that had shone so clearly. At length he had found it. A fat, heavy gold coin that nearly filled his small hand.

He had run, gleefully, home to Nan, clutching his treasure. She had hugged him, full and tight, called him her clever, darling boy but beneath that he had sensed that she was newly fearful and that the gold was the cause of it. In the evening, with the door locked, the shutters drawn and her seated by the fire, Punch at her side, she had explained to him. Gold, in the hands of such as them, an old woman herbalist and her orphaned grandson, was not easily explained. She prayed he would understand, that though he had done the cleverest thing, no-one must ever hear of it. It was to be their secret alone, for if the village bailiff should hear of it there would be no end of calamity. At the very best, the gold would be forfeit but the worst that could happen was too awful even to describe.

The old dame was shrewd. She took the gold far afield. She started one early morning and was gone one long night, during which Punch had shivered and shaken in his cot, certain he heard the mandrake on the stairs, come for his rag of a soul. The next evening, by twilight, she was home. Then she told him all. She had turned the gold into two cows, in calf. These she had stabled on the farm of a yeoman, far distant, whose wife, long while back, she had successfully delivered of stubborn twins. Both yeoman and Punch's clever nan did well from the arrangement. Nearer to home she had plans to purchase a brace of nanny goats and would hire the offices of a sire, when the time was ripe.

When that time came, Punch was much intrigued. It was also the subject of much discussion among the village youths. It seemed, his young ears heard, that for a beast to produce young, all that was required was the services of a willing male. The older boys assured him that this was always an exciting and rewarding venture. Emboldened he embarked on just such an operation as he had witnessed, with the most pliant of the nannies. It all went very ill. He bore the most painful bruises for weeks and not a word dare he breathe of his predicament.

Over the next few years, time and again, Nan would press on him the importance of never mentioning their wealth, or whence it arose. "Folks such as us don't have money and especially not gold. Ye talks out o' turn and a world o' care will fall on us. Remember that, if ye remember naught else. Now, get along to thy play!"

Punch, lying on damp turf, tying red dock and memories into his wounds, is now trying desperately to stop this fount of recollection before it's too late. But no, his mind will canter on to the final calamity.

He can no longer recall, clearly, what provoked him…some gibe about his ragged clothes, his scrap of food, his irregular attendance at the dame's school, oh how the hell should he be able to recall, for the tears are blinding him…But, to that overfed oaf of a bailiff's son he had bragged that his Nan could buy his fool of a father out twice over. That they had cattle and fields far off and were now rich as King Croesus, thanks to gold he had found!

The bailiff's men came for his Nan.

He cannot bear to think of it. He too was hauled before the so-called examining bench and made to witness what was done to her in the name of King, Church and Gentry.

He sits up, choking and finishes the memory in a rush. She was duly hung, for a witch. The land and the beasts went to the bailiff and he was thrown an orphan on the parish.

All of which was 30 more years past. Since then he has killed, or maimed, all those who played their part. Until today, revenge still ate at him like cancer. Could he find other innocents to ruin? Now all he wishes to do is weep and set the world back to how it was before blackness swallowed him.

"By the blackened mouth of God!" cries Punch, falling to his side, stuffing his mouth with stream clay and pebbles, in the wild hope that he will choke.

Punch, marooned here and haunted by the memory of his loving grandmother, her death brought about by his childish boasting, was in a place no one could envy. But now he has had done with the howling, with tearing at the earth, with breaking his head on roots and with swearing eternal vengeance on creatures he has long since destroyed.

At this moment, he is done with everything. He contemplates loading his musket and blowing what pass for his brains over the landscape. But as he casts an eye over the necessaries, he senses movement. Looking up, he sees a lonely figure struggling towards him. It is no less than a naked woman, her long hair in disarray, her eyes wide and round. Seeing his glance, she crouches and tries her best to conceal that which she can. Only yesterday Punch would have had none of that. He would have mounted a rescue that had ravishment as its logical outcome. But this new-born Punch, rising from the grass, is genuinely outraged, alarmed and distressed.

"Little maid…" is how he intends to begin but after nigh on 16 hours sucking air through an unconscious mouth, barely drinking, reviewing his life and deeds to date, all largely in the negative and with painful injuries, untreated, all he can achieve is – " Gah…"

But the 'Little Maid' can distinguish good from bad and she scuttles over to him, like an injured child to its parent. Fresh from his personal rememberings, this is all too poignant for Punch and fiercely defensive, he gathers her up against his filthy red coat and even filthier pants, praying that some inner light will shine through to convince her that she has docked at the right haven.

He summons enough spit for a gruff, fatherly voice. "What has't befallen thee, li'l maid?" he mumbles, seeking for tender tones in a repertoire that has, until now, encompassed only arrogance, derision and brutality.

"Sir," she cries, "they force me to their savagery, creatures of God though they purport to be. I swear, they are lower than wild beasts."

Punch, too confused to have cast a wary eye abroad, looks up to see that he is outgunned, outnumbered and outflanked by a handful of the heartiest looking thugs it has ever been his misfortune to fall amongst, armed with blunderbuss, pistols, pikestaff and a dog-catcher's pole and noose. If that were not enough, behind them are clustered gentry, of the court-bench and ecclesiastical variety. Uncomfortable though they may be in the country air, they still exude that air of self-righteous entitlement that has long goaded him to his worst excesses. Yet, against such odds as these and with his musket unloaded, he is forced into caution's arms. He takes a second glance, in time to see a woman, in the black habit of a nun, step forward from the group. It is not authority, spurious or otherwise, that she exudes but something far worse.

As he searches wildly for what foulness that might be, she takes confident paces towards him. Aloof and at the same time, far too close, she folds her arms with contempt and hisses – "release her, you bag of rags and be on your way."

Punch shudders with a rage so terrible that he might have attempted to kill every one of them, if they had not all vanished as summarily as they had arrived. One moment he was holding a sobbing girl and now he stands here alone, with only his filth, wounds and Brown Bess for company. This is not easy of explanation. Though Punch rarely errs on the side of reason in his explanations, he wonders what, in the benighted name of Father, Son and Piper Pan, just took place.

Caution on full alert, he draws out a paper cartridge from his pocket. He bites off the twist and empties the powder charge down the musket's barrel. He follows it with a patch, in which he has nestled the ball. This he packs down tightly with the ramrod. Time now to flick up the frizzen from the lock pan and blow away debris from his flight through the Hedge.

Punch takes time to prick clean the tiny flash hole with a pin – one he keeps for that very purpose, carefully secreted in his tricorn. He is not the man to risk a misfire on this, or any, unsettled patch of ground. From his private powder horn he sprinkles a tiny amount of gunpowder, the finest grind money can buy, into the pan. He cocks back the lock, checks the flint's alignment and finally restores the frizzen, to its seating. The old girl is ready.

Punch squats with the long gun across his thighs and quivers with thoughts, images and memories. 'How came they…how went they.?' is how he muses, over and over again. 'What form of creature was yon nun, for she fair unsettled me.?' Then, as the hours tick by and no answer has come, he rises up stiffly and goes in search of a stream, a pool, a spring…somewhere worthy of effecting his rebirth.

He paces a fair distance of the Hedge before he finds such a spot. But during his walk he also finds that the Hedge is a fine accumulator of items useful to castaways such as himself. Punch does not know this but the highway beyond the hedge has a poor reputation among travellers. Indeed it is well-known for petty villainy, as attested by the ruffians who made short pickings of yesterday's affair. Those very same scavengers, over the years, have set their traps thereabouts. What lies beneath the hedge are items abandoned in the heat of pursuit and also some that have arrived here by means which admit of no explanation. It is a fact that any stolen item that lies here will remain, abandoned both by the villain who flung it in the heat of pursuit, or any who might come a'following him, for all have a healthy respect for this haunted place. It is a forbidding line across the land, dourly enclosing no-man's land and now, sealed within its boundaries, Punch counts as no-man, not subject to any common sanction from without.

Merely strolling, he has found an excellent double-barrelled pistol, a saddle carbine, a large horn of powder, a small box of made-up cartridge suitable for Bess and a long knife, or short sword, depending on your opinion. Here is a good cast kettle, uncracked to his eye, that he will most certainly take. Punch has an eye for survival, a regular castaway he is always on the lookout for flotsam and jetsam. He wonders if a fine uniform might be forthcoming. The nun's taunt had stung him, it being all too warranted. One is not to be had, however, so for now he remains a scruffy, colourful man o' war. He searches hard for boots, for though his feet are currently horn and leather, a hard winter would soon find their weakness. Punch is a martyr to chilblains.

Weighted with freight, he casts about for a berth and finds that he stands on the edge of a sweet spot. A small circle of ash trees, no more than five, no, seven, have been cleverly drawn and pleached together at their crowns. Growing intermingled, doubtless to their intense irritation, they now provide a fine summer shelter. He stares up and recognises that, this last dozen years, the trees have had ideas of their own and are shooting up freely once again. Given the judicious use of a billhook and some twine, he reckons he could return them to the business of being a growing shelter… "savin' fer a brokken leg, mebbe…"

Punch is slowly coming to realise the magical nature of this ground. Is it not passing odd that none have pursued him here? Surely not all the irregulars were slain and what of the scavengers and rogues? What, too, might be the nature of a Hedge that collects useful items for its protegees? He casts another, circumspect, glance at the ash circle; he is not the first here, nor he conjectures will he be the last. Punch is led to conclude that he stands on ground where the sum of the parts give rise to a greater whole. Such a thought is both comforting and unnerving, for he cannot recall anything within his recent history that might warrant him receiving any such indulgence.

Processing these revelations, Punch, now slowing and weary, has been casting his eyes about the land. Mere yards away from the trees, in a dip, he finds the perfect bathing place, a pool formed among roots and refreshed by a spring. His body aches and though still wary of mischief, commonplace or alien, he begins to shed his rags, gingerly. He lays Bess within easy reach, together with the long knife. The pistol too, he sets hard-by, though he must see to the state of the barrels, before he risks loading ball and powder. Slowly he lowers his carcass of bone and sinew into the pool. The chill is stunning and to take his mind from it, he considers his form and concludes it would fetch only pence at a glue-makers. Settling against a convenient root, he eases himself back. The sensation is an odd one, unfamiliar, being biting, refreshing and despite this, oddly soporific. The fact is that Punch falls asleep. He only wakes when one of his outraged legs, indignant at being turned under him for support, throws a cramp and propels him, momentarily erect. Only then does it desert him, so that he crashes down to submerge completely. Mortified, he erupts from the pool like a gaffed fish, clambers ashore, falls on his back and howls, until he can grasp his toes to haul out the contracted muscle. "Dear Christ on the Cross!" he bellows, "Is this anyways to be rousing a man!?"

He hops and inches his way around the trees to where he abandoned the gunny sack he had collected his hedge treasures in. With the aid of this, together with handfuls of moss, he mops himself dry and sits blowing air, hard. A cynic and certainly a woman, would remark that Punch is almost dirtier than when he entered the innocent pool.

Rolling on the ground did nothing for his back. The gunny sack and moss were poor stand-ins for a dry cloth. Also, merely ducking his gunpowder-stained face in water was pointless. It remains as black as a toadstool's gills. Mercifully, there is neither cynic, nor woman, to hand.

Once suitably calm and dry Punch fastidiously reapplies his rags. The sack had contained a wrapping cloth which, on being shaken out, revealed itself to have been, originally, a pair of pants, marginally more decent than the pair he had been delivered in. There are at least a dozen fewer holes in them and therefore they can be worn with pride. He spends a little time recovering the deserting epaulette and is modestly pleased with the result. To crown all, as ever, he knocks back into shape the once-fine tricorn. He acknowledges that it lacks its cockade but a woodland like this should contain a dozen likely candidates. A fallen jay would be excellent. This hat he had from Blenheim and that many years ago. Four of them had sat out the heat of the battle in a farmyard chicken coop, playing cards. Punch had emerged richer, flea-ridden but importantly, unscathed and his sergeant dead – the battle, it seems, won without him. The hat had been just one of his spoils from the game.

As he dresses he recognises that his flesh wounds are healing with miraculous rapidity. He almost begins to feel himself fitted for some new and decent purpose. For decades his life has consisted of fights and flights, any actions to blot out the one memory he can never expunge. Suddenly he feels capable of facing it, redeeming it even. Did not the naked girl present such an opportunity? If only he could comprehend the mechanism of her miraculous appearance and disappearance, to say nothing of the simultaneous actions on the part of her captors. Where had they gone? He makes a few resolute strides, to demonstrate life's new found purpose, then sits down heavily, overcome by sudden weakness and the memory that he has not eaten for some days.

He casts about. Is there any livestock Bess might fell? He'd seen none and to tell the truth, the old girl was barely accurate at any range. It was the infantry volley that was to be feared, not the sniper's lone ball. Also he had a creeping reservation about wantonly discharging any firearm within this place. True enough, gunpowder was chasing away Robin Goodfellow and the Faeries but where he currently sat, this was assuredly Goodfellow territory. He had no intention of acting rashly. He pondered the quandary. If the Hedge provided hardware, might it also harbour some rations? He decides the idea is worthy of investigation.

He hauled himself to his feet and limped away, regaining strength with every stride, to the Hedge. Nodding to it, respectfully, he makes his way along its further edges and is rewarded, almost immediately, by discovering a fine brown hen, drowsy in broodiness, atop a nest of a dozen eggs. This happy discovery, however, presents a dilemma. Shall he murder the soon-to-be mother for a meal, with a dozen eggs for breakfast, or shall he, in some way, corral her territory and allow her to bring to term the first guests of a small-holding? His stomach rumbles while his head calculates – an ancient dilemma, if he had but known it. Should one think, or eat first?

For now, Punch moves on. The broody will sit fast and he has high hopes of finding some unhappy traveller's abandoned pack, perhaps containing the remnants of rations. Certain members of his small, irregular platoon carried such things.

The Hedge takes a great loop and following it, almost backwards in the direction he has come, he discovers a grove of ancient and decaying bee skeps, hollow logs and the like. All were once piled, no doubt for their protection, below a cliff-like jumble of rock. Now it seems, its crevices are inhabited by bees that have overflowed the original apiary. All has run wild and honeycomb hangs from rocks in tempting stalactites. The beekeeper has long since left. How, then, to acquire some honey? Without the aid of a passing and friendly bear, or protective wraps and choking clouds of smoke, Punch has no notion. It seems a grievous shame but this honey store is closed.

Or is it?

Projecting from a nearby skep, whose ruins perch atop a rock, dangles comb a good 18 inches long and enticingly fat. With every cell sealed, few bees attend it. Also, it hangs by the merest thread of wax.

Punch has a marksman's eye, if not a marksman's weapon. With this in mind he secures a solid firing platform and wedges Bess into place, using whatever rocks and creepers he can utilise. At 20 yards range he reckons he has a chance at the shot but to give himself some margin of safety, he fastens the length of twine he always carries about his person, round the trigger and runs it out as far as it will, maybe a further ten yards. Pull and run is what he intends. That and taking the shot as twilight thickens, seem the safest ploys. In the interim he will continue to scour the hedge. However, as his mind is pre-occupied by the plan, his eyes can focus on nothing. As a result he merely wanders aimlessly back and forth, spending the hours brooding on his fate. What is to befall him in this place?

Finally the evening light has thickened. As his palms sweat, Punch lies off in the grass and pulls the trigger, as gently as he can. The shot ploughs off into the unseen and loses itself. Nervously, he tip-toes forward, reloads, repositions the gun and takes what has to be his final shot. This time he hits the ancient skep square on, as disastrous a consequence as could have occurred.

Not even at Blenheim had Punch felt such terror as when he sees a black cloud spiralling out of the ruined straw, a spray of honey, wax and maddened bees. He takes to his heels in flight and abject prayer. No-one can outrun an angry hive but the darkness, the cover of the trees, all are colluding with Punch. He flails his tricorn desperately at sprinting, warrior bees as he leaps tree roots, re-discovering the meaning of fear. Not once dare he glance over his shoulder until he is far off. Finally exhausted, he collapses against a sturdy oak, where he can rub his back against the rough old bark and hopefully end the career of any hangers on. He thanks God, the one he doesn't believe in, for deliverance. Then with a groan, he remembers, he is still without food.

Water he could have by the gallon but he gazes miserably at the numerous little rills. Ale, by the firkin would suit, as would strong liquor. Not all of Punch is yet reformed. Then he be-thinks himself. If one broody hen has taken to the hedge to hatch her eggs, then it was more than likely there are others, in somewise protected from the night fox by this particular shelter. The light is almost too thick for search but luck is on his side. He finds a nest with two fine, warm eggs nestling within and their protector absent. These he takes possession of, knocking a hole in their ends and sucking out the contents. Then, ever artful, he finds two egg-sized stones, rounded pebbles and places them in the nest. They would dupe a broody hen and more eggs might yet be laid.

He straightened his back and was about to stride away, a tactical withdrawal to the sheltering ash trees, when he realised he was hard-by where he had fallen only a day earlier. Casting about, he could see plainly in the grass, Jolyon's book, wet with evening dew and shamefully abandoned.

Shocked, for he had been ready to kill to possess these pages, he gathered it up, wiping it dry on his rags and in particular, searching to secure all the tiny whistles he had scattered in his rage. Humbled by this mute accusation of character he made his way back, bearing the book, if not in triumph, then at least carefully. Then he sat, belly rumbling and considered very un-Punch-like thoughts. How might he make this place feel more like the home he had shared with his Nan and less like a careless bivouac?

Casting about for inspiration he picked up the book again, intending to examine it more carefully. Soon, he had lost himself in the very integrity of its construction. This was a craftsman-like volume, a careful gathering of hand-written, hand-stitched sections bound up in vellum stretched over heavy boards. The little drawer that held the whistles was cleverly tucked away within pages that had been cut to accommodate it.

Two nights ago, Punch would have hurled such a book away, to lie with its erstwhile owner, dead beneath the hedge. This emergent Punch, awkward, confused, felt the need for an apology and stumblingly, he muttered into the night air – "Jolyon, a'll try t' set things reet b' thee. A' swears a'll learn what b'more presh'us than gold. An' when a'ave, tha'll be 'membored wi' respeck." The night air said nothing and the silence was crushing. 'Oh aye,' said Punch witheringly, in his head, 'yon wer' a pretty speech. Don' ye start a' lyin', nor a'schemin' agin. On Nan's memory, don' ye be doin' o' it!'

Then, the combination of hunger, pain and growing remorse, pulled him down into sleep, where his dreams were vivid, varied and strange.

He found himself in a tavern, one like no other, though he couldn't say why. Old Jolyon was there, drinking but when Punch tapped him on the shoulder to apologise, he turned, dropped his ale and fled in terror. Punch chased him into the street but was accosted by the young girl he had encountered earlier. Now, however, she was a scarlet woman, louche in manners, looser in undress. He raised his hands to grasp soft white titties and woke with a start and a painful erection that had him cursing. "A' does not think o'her thataways! A' doesna' want to! She b' a good, sweet gal an' a'll hav' the saving of 'er. Now, get down tha' damned snake, or a'll 'ave thee in yon pool fer tha' wanton ways. Begone!" and he gave the instrument such a thwack that he almost yelped at the sting of it.

Sleep was fitful after that but shortly before dawn, he fell into another dream. He was walking a muddy thoroughfare between shuttered houses. Into the highway's filth some hand on high was pouring gold, while another was pouring chaff. The two were mixing in the mire, the gold being coated with mud, the chaff shining brightly. Invisible beings began to tramp the street, their boots crushing the coins down, out of sight. 'Tek care' he shrieked, 'th'art walkin' on gold. Stand steady, tha' fools!' But the boots ploughed on past, forcing him to plunge his hands into the filth. He was barged, bruised and finally bowled over, to lie helpless in the mud. Nan must have rescued him, for he was now standing, stark naked, on the kitchen tiles. She was washing the mud from him. Chaff and grime fell away but there was no sign of gold, except when he glanced in their broken fragment of mirror. Behind him, he could see gold, it was lying there, plain as day but he stood still and said nothing, though he did begin to cry.

That was how he woke, wet-eyed and empty bellied. He dragged a hand across his eyes and considered, with exhaustion, the condition of his guts. Something had to fill them and soon. He pondered afresh, then, in resignation, picked up his bayonet and approached the pool. Just beyond the outlet of the spring he found what he was seeking. A thick band of clay lay underwater, perhaps only visible to a searching eye. He scratched away the first inch of the ribbon and dug deep into its heart with the bayonet. He levered free a hand-sized portion and hauled it to the surface. Carefully he kneaded it on a flat stone and extracted every pebble, every particle of grit he could spy. Next he went in search of small sorrel, the smallest dandelion leaves, the seeding heads of fat hen, all the green edibles he could find. These he diced as finely as he could and worked the results into small balls he plucked from the wet clay. Solemnly he chewed them down, washing each bolus on its way with plentiful water. It calmed hunger, he had eaten it before, many times and though it made you hard at stool, he planned to counter that by eating fresh young hawthorn leaves, ones he would pick as he returned, cautiously, to the site of last night's honey raid.

His first aim was to rescue Bess. 'Tweren't her fault she'd bin made by 'eathens in far off Indy and shot so free,' he thought. A few bees were on patrol, circling the long brown barrel. Some had clustered by the open frizzen, finding something to their taste in the black detritus of burnt powder. Once he'd freed her from her bindings, he delicately brushed away the bees with a whisk of long-headed grasses plucked nearby. Then he made a grab for her forestock and tip-toed away.

Unbeknownst and unseen by him, however, one little fiend incarnate was lurking beneath, a brown body on brown wood. Warrior that she was, she sank her sting deep into the second joint of Punch's index finger as, fatefully, his grasp tightened on her. For a second Punch wondered if he'd been shot himself, so deep and sudden was the pain.

"Thou lil' de'il!" he shrieked, "hast thee ne'er 'eard o' quarter? God on 'is rocks, th'art p'ison itself!" and he danced about until common-sense caught up with him. Only then did he fall to carefully extracting the still pulsing barb and poison sac from his joint. Finding a convenient opening in the new pants he peed, rapidly as he could, on the site. "Or be thet fer waspsis?" he enquired of no-one in particular. Whether it was for wasps or bees, relief was momentary. Within minutes his hand was stiff, his thumb and forefinger were swelling in tandem, the whole falling to a deep, resolute pounding. "Tha' damned fool Punch!" he cursed, recalling last night's enterprise.

Limping back to the ash grove, he remembered that there was a leaf and earth poultice for just such accidents but as he could recall neither the leaf, nor the earth, all he could do was to wish he'd listened more carefully to Nan. He sat down miserably, wondering if he could distract himself from the pain by delving into Old Jolyon's text.

At least the handwriting was a plain, bold script, which Punch found he could read easily enough, now eye and brain had had time to remember what they had learned so many years past. It was a text by some Reverend fellow, which in itself elicited a long groan from him, divines not being among his intimates. Yet, this fellow was different from the pompous asses Punch had so far encountered. He had adopted an orphan of the Parish, whereof he held the Living, a young lad to whom he had given the name Ishmael. Punch warmed to the cleric as it emerged that, though the lad was mute, one of 'God's Children' as he put it and had few of the ordinary sensibilities suited to life, he loved him dearly. This book, he insisted was more of young Ishmael's doing than the his own. At which sentiment, Punch felt his attention begin to quicken.

The lad had been the butt of all the village and was a scared, broken creature when the reverend gentleman took him into his home. After months of gentle treatment and cautious observation, the Parson had observed that he was far from being devoid of wit and capacity. He understood a great deal and he had constructed a world suited to his faculties. He had a way with animals, befriending all, except birds and for those he had a distaste. This had perplexed his new father until, one day, he had intuited the boy was offended by their rapacious destruction of the insect world. The lad was a stalwart defender of that kingdom. "Truly the lowliest shall protest the abuse of those still lower..." wrote the author, ecstatically and piously

Left to his own devices, at the edge of the fields, where he could play peacefully and be entrusted with bird-scaring, Ishmael was a happy enough boy. He was assiduous, too, in his stone-throwing. The rooks soon learned which fields to abandon, once his diminutive silhouette became known to them. The boy passed his days contentedly and no longer harassed by his mocking peers, he blossomed.

One day he had presented the Parson with a little whistle he had formed from the stalk of an elder tree. He had gouged out the pithy centre and formed fingering holes in the soft wood, whereby a variety of reedy sounds could be piped. Obliging his 'father' had trilled a note or two but the lad had shaken his head wildly and quickly dragged the reverend gentleman to his own front door, pushing him forcibly into the street. He had been ready to protest when Ishmael had gestured, pointed and the parson had been astonished to see a swarm of bees approaching the cottage. The boy had seized back the little whistle and trilled a few strange, high notes of his own, whereupon the swarm had turned in mid-flight and promptly dispersed.

At first the Reverend had been shaken then, almost as quickly, dismissive…surely some coincidence of nature and art had been in play? But no, the lad then proved he could summon insects at will, with the aid of a pocketful of whistles he had formed. Each struck a different note and each summoned a different colony. For that was how they approached, by the colony. Not a few random insects mustered together but a formidable clustering.

All this Ishmael had discovered and by his own genius, no less. He knew how to 'speak' to the 'underworld' of wood and field, to the despised insects that lie beneath our boots and beneath our attention. The Reverend was forced to admit that, when they came flocking in their thousands, they made an awesome spectacle.

Leaning back against the master ash tree, Punch wondered when all this had taken place. When, let alone where, had this godly man defended his adopted son against the outside world and come to comprehend that he knew of a way to speak to the insect tribes?

A seemingly witless boy, alone in the world, stirred conflicting emotions in Punch. He, too, must have had a father but as he could barely remember his mother, recalling any long absent father was out of the question. All he had in his life that was decent, was his Nan and the most vivid memories he had of her were forever cursed, while the most tender were those that were fading fastest, the older he grew. Parsons had attended his Nan's death, so-called 'Godly' men had been complicit, authoritative. How close must this innocent child have come to being cursed as a sorcerer by his adoptive parent?

Punch knew how to curse and he did so now. He was vilely eloquent and his venom was, for a while, sweet to him. Then he fell morosely silent, contemplated the throbbing and swelling of his hand and reloaded Bess, for the comfort of having the means to kill.

After a while, he was to pick up the book again and read for the rest of the morning, until his eyes ached with the unaccustomed exercise. There was a deal of Christian cant that, had he had a quill and ink he might well have scored through. Either this parson had encountered a different God than Punch, or he had had the stature to rise above his own tribulations. Either notion made Punch uneasy but he read on, half-anguished to discover the fate of the lad, though given the existence of the book and its tray of whistles, things were unlikely to have turned out badly. As it happened the cleric had wrestled with his training, his conscience and his own sense of what was decent in the world. Fortunately, conscience and decency won the race – and by a fair head, Punch intuited, with an approving grunt or two. The Reverend's winning argument was that the child was God's work, as were his gifts. Therefore both were for the glory of the Lord and though the local peasantry might be blind to such, he was not. He was the boy's protector and was proud to be so. At this conclusion, Punch found his eyes were watering – "a 'ent used t' all this 'ere readin," he mumbled.

He ploughed on, through the soul-searching, the endless re-justifications of his wholly creditable desire to protect an innocent from the dangerous revelations he had unearthed. "Canna' a'bin easy," mumbled Punch. To live alone, with a gifted but blighted boy, in the midst of a superstitious and vicious peasantry.

At heart, though he didn't know it, Punch was a man of science. The Vicar, however, believed in the ineffable. What they held in common was the understanding that cause can remain invisible, only their reasoning as to why that should be so was different. When the Parson ascribed God's Will to the matter of the whistles, Punch knew that sound and vibration were at the heart of the affair. "If t' roarin' o' cannon cans't set mi' shekkin' in mi' boots, why's no'rra whistlin' stir up some bees? Meks sense t'me, though thet means nowt, a'll warrant!"

The Parson held an alternative view. In his opinion, if the bees came clustering, they did so instinctively, to praise the Lord. "Only the One God holds the answers and the answers are of the One God," was his piece of philosophising that Punch voted worthy of Old Nick himself.

Between all this fat, however, lay meat. Each insect tribe, it seemed possessed its own octave and each of Ishmael's clever whistles sounded a different one. The highest could order bees, the lowest, the woodlice. Punch had a soft spot for woodlice, 'busy lil' chaps', he thought affectionately. He was thrilled, however, to discover that the ladybugs also had an octave of their own. He blew a trill on the appropriate instrument and within seconds, two, three, then four and more were alighting on him. He complimented them on their uniforms, uncannily akin to his own but in better repair. Then he waited and for a while, more landed. But he blew no more notes and, in time, they lost interest and flew away.

What was at work here? He read on, eager to discover but separating God's Will from hard facts was tortuous work. All he could really glean – and by this stage his mind was reeling – was that each insect tribe was subject to a group mind and that this could be stimulated to readiness by sounding the lowest note of the appropriate octave. Once this mind was awakened, the individual insects could be expected to function as one.

This was the manner in which each tribe aroused itself. The low, menacing hum of one bee skep, was the drum-roll to all other skeps that they ready themselves for the defence of the realm. All too clearly, Punch understood the truth of that. The memory of that menacing rumble that had preceded last night's alarms was quite fresh…as was the throbbing of his hand. It was a note he would never be sounding by way of experiment.

Insects, he was informed, lived by commands. They were a commonwealth, a commonality, ordered by some greater whole. This revelation alone sparked pages of wonder in the Reverend's pen and breast, as he remarked similarities with our own mindless existence. "Are we not ordered by a greater Power? Is this not the essence of our Faith?" "Mebbe," grunted Punch unwillingly, remembering his own flight through the Hedge and subsequent events. The insects, then, existed in a state of mindless readiness, always primed for some new command from the group mind that would see them spring to attention.

The rest of the book was a dissertation on how to form different commands. It required great subtlety to modulate the whistles appropriately and there were staves of musical notation to absorb, a language utterly outside Punch's ken.

Befuddled, he laid the volume aside and allowed himself a digression. Old Jolyon had cried – "Ther' b'gold in these 'ere pages!" when he had first taken possession of the book, or something akin to that. All Punch had really heard, through his ale-fuddled ears, had been "Gold!" and a tell-tale rattling, as the old fool had shaken the volume over his head. It was that moment that had undone them both. Punch now knew that he had heard the rattle of wooden whistles which, no doubt, made him a fool – but at least, a living one. He pondered on that and the way he had manipulated events subsequently, so that matters ended as they had. Even so, for the new and apologetical life of him, he could not see how the ability to direct ladybirds, would ever be anything other than a charming accomplishment with which to amuse young ladies and children. Obviously Jolyon had been weak in the head and exalting his memory, as he had sworn to do, would be a hard task to accomplish.

Punch suddenly feels listless and unwell. He casts about as to why this should be so and realises soon enough that it's all matter of food, or rather its absence, that is unsettling him. He creaks unsteadily to his feet, rests against the tree to forestall dizziness, then slowly moves off, grasping Bess, to scour the Hedge afresh. The broody is still cemented to her eggs. With difficulty he persuades himself to leave her in peace and begins to probe among the dark recesses of the roots, desperate for any consumables he might have overlooked.

He was losing hope and the afternoon was nudging evening, when he heard squealing fit to freeze blood. He knew that sound, instantly. It was made by a rabbit, cornered by a stoat. In all likelihood, the stoat had just blinded the rabbit, facilitating its kill by pre-empting a chase. He had to locate this tragic drama, before it escaped from him. The obvious place was among a clump of violently waving tall grasses. He ran, dropping the long gun and plunged both hands into the grass, searching and grasping. Within a breath's space he had pinned to the ground a pregnant doe, blinded and gasping in pain, shock and terror. A second later he had dislocated her neck, an art learned, in company with every other urchin, at the warrens by his Nan's cottage.

Under ordinary circumstances, Punch could live off the land in such a manner, for months at a time. However there was nothing ordinary about this glade and he was uncertain of his status in it. There was also the matter of the disastrous skirmish he had provoked, the better to gain Jolyon's book. That seemed to have resulted in the death of every slovenly-marching man-jack of them, excepting himself. Punch was therefore, all too aware that roaming as far and free as casual self-sufficiency would require, was not an option.

The unhappy rabbit he prepared in minutes, opening up the still warm fur until he could pull it free of the meat beneath, as easily as peeling off a glove. Neatly opening the belly, he let the guts and the now-dying kits spill onto the waiting fur. For himself he preserved only the liver and heart. The bundled remains he dropped back into the undergrowth, where the stoat could find the remnants of the meal it had been anticipating.

He now cut and sharpened a strong green stick, which he ran through the doe from gullet to anus. He sought out a discreet hollow, where he could build up a long, slender fire line. This he kept fed with the driest kindling he could find. There was plenty. He replenished the line assiduously until he had a dependable supply of charred wood, dully glowing but hot, very hot. He cut two sturdy 'Y' forks from conveniently-shaped branches, sharpened the long descending arms and thrust them into the ground at either end of his charcoal line. Across these crooks he slung the stick on which he had impaled the rabbit and began his cooking. A rabbit killed in terror was never going to cook soft on a spit but nevertheless he turned it around and around, patiently biding his time, until he judged it cooked beyond a mere browning. He would be no more famished in 15 minutes than he was now. He could wait. The food was secure. Eventually he nodded approval and moved his meal to a litter of large leaves he had gathered to do service as a plate.

He let the meat cool, rather enjoying the anticipation, now the outcome was well-nigh certain. Then he chewed steadily, devouring the rabbit from head to tail, though conscious of ancient ceremony he saved a portion for Pan. This he rolled in a dock leaf, secured by a hawthorn pin and left it beneath an alder tree. He hoped Pan was not too hungry. Finally, he burned down to ash all evidence of his spit, grill and platter. He buried the lot, doused the plot with water and wagered weed would be growing there within a fortnight.

For all Punch's masterful dexterity, the sun was sliding into the horizon by the time he had completed his affairs. That he was now longing for a nightcap of ale, cider, brandy or port, went without saying and he was lost in such lush thoughts when he heard, from faraway, the sound of drunken song. He judged it to be cresting the hill that topped the common field, out beyond the Hedge. For certain it was coming closer and he loped back to the spot where he had first entered this place, the better to spy the land. Once there, nothing was to be seen, as yet but the racket was growing louder. He would wait, though what his intentions were he had not yet considered. Curiosity was uppermost in his mind. It was as if his fellow men were fast becoming unfamiliar subjects and already ones to be observed cautiously.

It was a good 15 minutes before he had plain sight, on the hill crest, where it was pierced by the track, of an ancient pony trap making its slow way towards him. Undoubtedly, the horse was in charge, heading patiently home to its stable, while its putative betters, still invisible on the boards of the trap, bellowed songs to the sky. They sang of fair maids, good ale, loose morals and fine times. In short, they were drunk – very drunk.

Punch watched the horse's progress. Down it came, carefully avoiding the slip to the gully, then taking the wide loop that led over the ford. Beyond was a tedious uphill haul and the old horse paused, mid-stream, to drink its fill.

The babble of the stream and the steady gulping of the horse had an effect on the still unseen songsters. Their song trailed off and both stood, unsteadily, dimly looking around, seized by an irresistible need to pee. Punch grinned, only to find that he was suddenly fighting the longings of his own bladder.

To accomplish their purpose, the two carters found it necessary to drop the tailgate of the trap to floor level, where it held steady on restraining chains. Then both stood proudly upon their deck, pissing into the cool night air – "pissing for King and Country" as Punch was wont to name it, every time he accomplished a particularly fine flow himself.

Punch could now see into the body of the cart and what he could see was… food! There was a fine round cheese, some hams wrapped tight in cheesecloth, stout crocks of preserves, sacks of flour and barrels of, no doubt, porter. In his mind Punch groaned. Meal of rabbit, or no meal of rabbit, his mouth was flowing with sweet juices. Then he groaned afresh. Had he not become a better man overnight? Also, wanting for a pair of pistols to hand, he was hindered from returning to a life of crime, should he so choose.

The younger man, no doubt the son of the older, tucked away his piece and without more ado slapped the horse on its rump: "git on theer…lest we be here all neet!" Reluctantly, the horse abandoned its drinking and began the haul up the hill. The cart lurched and the older man danced an ungainly jig in his efforts to stay upright. "Damn ye, boy! Will you not let a'man have the end o'is piss?"

The son cackled out loud – "git done wi'ye, faither. Thee's tekkin' longer 'n' longer. We shall 'ave t'ave thee cut fer t' stone afore long!"

"Tha' young ingrate, I should a'cut thy stones away at birthing, fer all thou'lt listen on thy own faither. Thee'd 'ave made a fine, fat porker by now!"

Obviously this was the funniest thing that had ever been said and father and son laughed immoderately. Such unusual merriment quickened the horse's pace, whether in equine endorsement of the abundant wit, or the desire to escape from it, we shall never know. But with the lurching of the cart came movement from the wheel of cheese, which was balanced perilously on its circumference. Much like the drunkards in charge of it, it went a little left, a little right, turned on a farthing then, obeying gravity in every respect, headed briskly down the cart bed and over the tailgate with one splendid bounce.

Once loose in the field, it scented freedom and took to its heels, gathering momentum.

"Stop ye cart, boy! Yon round o'cheddar is away, an' be rollicking down't'hill!"

Punch, crouched deep in the hedge, could almost taste cheese on toast – not that he had bread yet, but that was mere quibbling. The great wheel was accelerating towards him and he willed it on, like a man certain he has a winning horse in the steeplechase.

"Stop 'im, faither! 'E be mekkin' fer the 'aunted 'edge! Git ye after 'im!"

Father turned to berate son and son, indignant, hauled on the reins. The old horse nearly sat on its haunches, the cart wallowed and comestibles broke free in every direction. Lighter items vaulted the tail board and either followed the head start of the cheese or, according to their dimension, weight and profile, rolled right, or left, or adopted crazed routes to be finally arrested by thickets of gorse and bramble.

Punch, like God watching His sparrows, marked the fall of each and every one.

Meanwhile, the cheese, having weight, profile and momentum on its side, emulated Punch's flight of two days since and with a final high leap, hit the Hedge hard, edge on. Punch could never swear to this but he was almost sure that the Hedge, eased its snarls apart to accommodate the flying wheel. Whatever, there was a fine crash and a fair weight of cheddar was simply never going to appear again on the carters' side of the Hedge.

Darkness was already fallen but Punch eased back to even denser shadows as the now rapidly-sobering son, strode down the hill.

"Er's gone clear thro' t'edge, Pa…" he intoned, in shocked tones.

"Ow can 'er, boy ? Yon 'edge be thicker 'n' night 'erself. She'll be lodged at' foot, mark me. Fall t'lookin' fer 'er, tha' useless clod, 'afore night be on us, thick 'n' proper!"

"Pa, I dursn't gan' tae close, that 'edge be as 'aunted as t'wood be!"

"Away wi' yer stuff an' nonsense. Yon glades and trees mightn't well be 'aunted but yon 'edge be but an 'edge."

"No, Pa. Yon's an 'aunted 'edge and a' 'ent a touchin' nary a leaf nor a twig o' it," the son replied stoutly.

"Tha' flat tit's whelp! Then a'll gang theer, mi'self," said father, though to Punch's ears he sounded less than confident.

In that moment, Punch devised a plan. He waited until the grunting, shuffling and mumbling approached his hiding place and then, in piping, evil tones, enquired – "be a' able tae 'elp thee, maister? Be it gold 'ee be a' lookin' fer?"…and he snickered, making a knowing, insinuating question of it, asked by one willing to be complicit in all skulduggery.

"J'asus, Mary 'n' Joseph," wailed the carter to the thickening night and his boy, "look ye tae t'horse, boy! There be's a goblin in yon 'edge!"

"Nae, maister," squeaked Punch, "nary one, there be a dozen o' us, an' us all 'as gold! Will 'ee no tarry, tide a' whiles an' trade thy goods fer faery gold?" Then he clouted a branch or two, rustled the leaves and hurled a handful of earth into the dead litter of the Hedge bottom. Finally, for good measure, he chanted some lines of doggerel invented on the spot, to do service as a spell and finished up with a gurgling noise that even unsettled him.

Carter and son ran for their lives. The cart took off with a bound, as the old nag was cruelly whipped. More packages broke free and bounced wildly to earth. Then horse and man, each terrified in their own way, crested the rise and vanished.

The Goblin crawled out of the Hedge and brushed himself down. He had work to do and sleep would wait.

The moon rose and helped illuminate his spoils. It was when he had gathered them all, that he realised the extent of the problem. Much as he coveted this small mountain, it all had to be carried and stowed, far away from sight of man and scent of dog. That meant finding a hiding place downstream, wading through the brook some goodly distance, at night, while laden. Punch had a powerful fear of dogs. In an episode he didn't ever care to recall but could never erase, he had seen what dogs could do when they cornered a fleeing man. He was firmly of the opinion that, in the morning's light, the carter, his son and reinforcements, maybe with dogs, would return, looking for their spilled goods. No man likes to look a fool in his own eyes. Those two would be back, armed, angry and searching for their purchases.

He had to calculate clearly. What could he carry, what would keep? The cheese round had done him the favour of bouncing into captivity of its own accord. The roasted legs of ham and flitch of bacon he would carry off. So, too, half a sack of sweet apples, also an unbroken crock of pickled eggs, firmly sealed with a wooden plug and that caulked with wax. His final choice was a wrap of ship's biscuit, which would keep forever, under shelter. The other items, and they were many, he left lying – though he gathered them together neatly, as part of his greater plan.

Swiftly, he constructed what would be recognisable to any country lad, a faery house, a crude little shelter – on the lines of Baba Yaga's hen house, though sadly he could find no claws for the feet. Inside this he laid tokens, feathers, owl pellets, a badger turd, sundry berries. On top of which, to his utter mortification, he felt obliged to offer up his only golden guinea. Granted, he'd stolen the coin but over the years he had possessed it, he'd come to regard it as his own. He had developed a great fondness for it. Nevertheless, by his calculations, the goods he planned on sequestering could have been bought three times over for a guinea and that was all part of his greater scheme. He was hoping that the mortified duo would tear open the faery house, find the guinea, consider themselves well-paid and withdraw – discretion being the better part of valour.

However, if father and son brought reinforcements, they would be of the hard-headed variety, unmoved by faery houses, even ones with golden guineas inside them. Indeed, they would probably move to hunt down the owner of the guinea, to part him from any more he might possess. If so, Punch had a back-up plan. This pile of goods was perilously close to the wild bees. If necessary, he could stir them up with a long shot and sit out the consequences, at a safe distance. For now, though, he had work to do.

His task took the whole of the night. Dog-tired and with the sun rising, he trudged wearily upstream, back home, as he now thought of the ash grove. There he gathered the weapons he had, sufficient cartridges, powder and ball. He was about to stagger off, back to his vantage in the Hedge, when he bethought himself of the whistles in Jolyon's book. Deep notes on the bee octave, rapidly repeated, were said to rouse the hive mind to frenzy – at least, that is what he thought he had understood. The old Parson was nothing if not opaque, at times. Shrugging, he pocketed the tiny flute. What could it hurt?

He returned to the hedge, not exactly where had lain only hours previously but a little further out, from where he knew even a wayward shot would plough into the heart of the bee colony. There he made himself comfortable, appraised his lines of sight again, re-checked his munitions and settled down with a couple of apples and a huge slice of fat ham for company. Then he waited…and waited.

Their hangover must have delayed them. Punch was surprised. Had they been his possessions, as in a sense they were, he would have redeemed them at dawn. As it transpired, the sun had climbed well into the sky before the carter and his lad reappeared. Accompanying them were a pair of stout fellows to whom Punch took no liking at all.

As he had idled the hours away, dozing off and on, plaiting grasses and assembling little harvest dollies to amuse himself, Punch, in his half-awake state, could even imagine emerging from hiding, explaining everything to the old fellow, agreeing the guinea, declining any change and sharing tales of men in their cups. One glance at the hired help emptied his mind of all that. These were hard men, with black beetling brows, chests like barrels and arms that were harvest toughened.

The carter's son was the first to spot the faery house atop the piled goods. He fairly leapt over the side of the cart to tear it open.

"See you 'ere, Pa!" he gasped, "them 'ave paid their way wi' faery gold an' other impish tokens…" at which he held up a magpie's feather and the badger turd, the guinea glinting in his palm… "Them's paid us fair and square, let's be gone from 'ere!"

The carter gazed, uncertainty and amazement worrying his face. But while he dithered, one of the sturdy fellows jumped the side of the cart, took the guinea from the gawping lad and spat on the road.

"Faery gold my arse! Yon's a King's guinea, man's gold and where there' be man's gold, there be men."

He turned to his partner – "Harry, my lad, we'll take a scan beyond yon 'edge and settle this matter. The maister's tekken a shakin' an' some'un deserves a beatin'. Thee, too, young Crofton, dinna stand theer moon-faced 'n' pewlin, 'elp our 'Arry wi' them billhooks. We'll soon ha' cleared a way in."

Punch heard every word. Matters were demonstrably serious and escalating. The faery plan had done worse than backfire! Nor was he entirely sure which villain held his coin, should events fall to murder and with gold, they usually did. Bess was to hand and the double pistol, cleaned, pricked and primed. Yet the moment he fired, all subterfuge, all retreat and worst of all, secrecy, would be lost. All he could do was watch, appalled, as all four advanced on his Hedge, billhooks fresh from the shop and the grinding wheel. He couldn't bear to see the first blow fall. It would be a sacrilege, an insult, a calamity. His mind now a whirlwind of despair he drew Ishmael's tiny whistle from his vest pocket. Then, nerving himself, he blew four long, low, notes – was that enough ? He could barely hear them, they lay so low.

The besiegers heard nothing, for they were striking the first blow. A heavy, downward slash that opened 12 years of ash growth. Punch could have sworn that the Hedge recoiled in fury, bending on its roots. Then, above the grunting and crashing, he heard something sinister. It was a noise as if a whale had breached underground, rather than underwater. It spoke of ancient depths of anger and anguish at man's wanton assault on Eden. But most of all it expressed vengeance and Punch quailed.

It was the bees that had breached. Punch had never seen, nor heard, the like. At first all he could see was a vague greyness, as if an errant cloud had crossed the face of the sun. This grew darker, thickening swiftly. As it darkened it acquired volume, then vibration. Something terrible was unfolding.

The four men had stopped work. Not another blow would they strike. Even the two hard-headed brutes looked about, men searching for an unknown.

The swarm approached. Punch could sense the group mind. It was a brutal, crushing thing, devoid of all subtlety. It was still searching for what, for why, it had been roused. Of a sudden, Punch felt chilled to the bone. These whistles were not toys. They called to order the inchoate and gave it focus. This was power.

Punch felt the mind lock onto the waving, shining, billhooks. He pulled back his own ordnance, hiding it and himself beneath the rags and leaves he had pulled together, last night. He dug himself deep into the compost beneath, praying the bees had no attention left for him.

The wicked little creatures were corkscrewing out of the hollow by the million. A black cloud hung over the four. Then it simply fell upon them, savage hail on ripe corn.

Peeping through a hole in his camouflage, Punch had thought to find the spectacle amusing. The reality sickened his stomach. What defence can there be against bees in their millions? The four simply sank silently to their knees, until they fell prostrate upon the ground, crawled a little, then died.

Punch, horrified, terrified, could feel the blind hatred of the group mind as it searched for any further threat. The bees rose, circled and all too quickly, sighted upon the patient old horse, quietly standing between the shafts of the cart. They fell upon it, too. It writhed, imprisoned by harness, tried to gain the hill in flight but collapsed in a dark cloud of swirling, warrior bees. Where it fell, it died, blinded, poisoned, between the shafts. Punch felt an awful compassion choke him. He had not felt that for the carter, his son and men. He doubted they would have shown him any more mercy than the bees had granted them. But the poor, old nag? If anything proved the unthinking might of that ancient, hive mind, it was its total absence of feeling. It possessed all the clarity necessary for survival, for self-preservation. 'Learn from it,' urged a silent voice in his head. 'I cannot,' he answered it. 'I am a man'.

He lay beneath the still circling cloud, his face pressed into the decomposing matter. He could smell tannins. It smelled brown, already old. Old was where power lay. The group mind was old. Jolyon had not been weak in the head. It was he who had been slow to grasp what he had read, and read only yesterday. It was no book of party tricks, it was a book of power and as such, daunting in its implications.

He lay quite still until, of a sudden, he felt the group disband. It was as if the hoops had fallen from a barrel and the staves and contents were now free to continue with their business. He peeped out and witnessed the swarm swirling back into its stronghold, each bee seeking out its allotted place and task, once more about its daily affairs, all memory fled. Slowly, he eased himself free from cover, stood up and surveyed the wreckage. Danger gone, he pondered just how much guilt he should feel, at what he had brought about. He found that there was enough of the old Punch left for the affair to slide off him like water from a duck's back. Indeed so much so, that he found himself yearning for his golden guinea. He had some idea of whose pocket concealed it. There was also the question of the left-over comestibles.

The 'new' Punch then looked at the 'old' and found so much lacking, in every department, that he was amazed and faintly disgusted, that he had survived this long on earth. Old and New stared at each other across this divide and their owner smiled wryly. He was what he was, thought Punch and if that was changing, so be it.

Behind him the Hedge was making strange creaking noises. The wounded ash seemed to pull back, into the shade, while withies wound themselves across its former place. It seemed that the group mind of the Hedge was making its dispositions, too, compensating for the half-dozen blows that had fallen on it, before the black bees had ended the affair.

Punch was aware that, before long, village folk would arrive. They would find the ruined faery house, atop the goods he had left and eventually they would find his guinea. They would contrive an explanation for the bee-stung, bloated corpses and whatever reputation this corner of the field held now, it would be doubled before the day was over. They would risk no further meddling.

He was fairly certain that his refuge was safe. Some, no doubt, would bluster and bellow, demand the hedge be burned to the ground. Then others would ask who would dare set their hand to that, gesturing eloquently at the four who had so done. Sager heads would council withdrawal, leave the common land to lie as it was. Wild fires would bring the squire's men down upon them. Then there would be the matter of the guinea. Faery, or man's it was there to be drunk up at the tavern. Here was enough for all and they would withdraw, to drink and talk, according to their wit and comprehension, until the whole affair had fallen from mind.

Punch, turning away, now determined to make the ash grove his home. It seemed to hold no antipathy towards him, which was odd, considering his gory history. Not that he could know it but the old magical world was not wholly at peace with the new and it found no unforgivable sins in his ragged past. So feeling an urgent need to distance himself from the bloated ruins lying on the ground, he ducked back through the tightening Hedge, gathered up his ordnance and walked briskly away, vowing to explore the wider boundaries of the little wood.

It was only a little walk he intended, an innocent walk, one to scout the lie of the land, to see what lay downstream. Yet, gazing down the brook, beyond the ash trees, both land and water seemed to stretch into a vague, incoherent distance, as if they lay within the parameters of a dream, where the panoramas had only been hastily sketched, mere ideas to be bolstered if occasion demanded it.

He set off to walk and at first, the going was as he expected, marshy, awkward but generally commonplace. Then the grasses began to grow higher, rustling as high as his waist. Their roots were knotting around his ankles and underfoot. He found he was stumbling, catching his toes in unexpected snags and snares. The stream was still to his left but it had dropped from sight. He had the uneasy feeling it had grown broader, deeper, 'too wide, too still', a voice in his mind suggested. There were no trees, no fences in sight, just the endless swishing grass and the menacing flow of water that he couldn't even see.

'But this be England' thought Punch, 'land of tiny fields, hedges and trees – where in hell's name be they?' Unnerved, he turned sharply to his right, his only intention now, being to head back, away from whatever lay out there. Wildly, he looked back to where he had come from only minutes ago. There were his familiar trees and he nearly broke into a run to recover their blanketing shade. He leaned against a young oak, clutching the still smooth bark and resting his cheek, head bowed, against it. 'Dunna ye be doin' that t'me ag'in' he whispered, uncertain precisely what he meant but wholehearted in his conviction of it. He straightened, aware that his heart was pounding and in a manner that it rarely did. He felt lucky to be alive and it wasn't the bees that were troubling him. It was that grass and the unseen, viscous flow of water. "Tha' wer' in't Deadlands," he said solemnly and he felt the young oak rustling its leaves in agreement. "Don't ye be going theer agin!"

He moved deeper, back into unfamiliar dells and glades but there were none that held that rarified air that had so disturbed and haunted him earlier. Here he felt safe, if not precisely welcome then, at least, protected. "A' can do it," he protested to the spirit of the place. "A' can change. A' can be some…" he struggled for the right word, "…A' can b' some 'elp. Let me 'elp yon littl'un, fer her be sorry lost in summat bad." With which protestation he sank down, against a bank of dry moss and lapsed into a sleep of utter exhaustion.

How he dreamed. Of a wave that ran on forever but always returned to where it began. Of a loop, in the sky maybe, one you could enter at will but however far you travelled you returned to the beginning, time after time. There was nothing for him beyond this unending beginning and he grew heartily sick of it. 'Away with ye', he mumbled and sure enough, the wave and sky vanished. The dream span like a whirlpool and everything changed with it. Here was a Goddess brushing her hair and he was entangled in the ringlets! Her slender fingers gently plucked him free and set him down on green sward. "Now," said her vast but gentle voice in his head, "what was it you would do?"

Punch groaned awake, aware he was mumbling "A' dussn't know, a' dussn't know," over and over again. He felt tired and sick. For a while he sat, head in hands, elbows braced on his knees. He sat like that until the thought of food made him stumble upright, shake himself and head firmly back towards the dark, distant shadow of the Hedge.

His stores were safely sequestered where he had stowed them the night before. 'The night just gone?' he thought, incredulously. Some eternity had passed since then but the great wheel of cheddar said otherwise. He fell on it like a wolf but unlike a wolf, he was short on teeth and he found himself threatening the few survivors he had left as they became enmeshed in stout cheesecloth. "Be damned to ye," he complained, with a cackle of a laughter, as he conceded defeat, stood upright and walked to fetch the bayonet from the ash grove. Under that assault the muslin gave way, the rind was punctured and the dense, fragrant curds were free to work their magic on mind and stomach. "Eee, by 'eck," he sighed, addressing all who might care to hear, "there be nowt t'beat a chunk o'cheddar." Then there was the question of ham and cheddar to be settled, or whether ham, cheddar and a couple of apples were the actual antidote he was seeking?

At last requited, Punch considered his storage problems. Mother Nature's other children undoubtedly had yearnings as strong as his own. Somehow all this bounty had to be shielded from their attentions. Nets hung from trees were the answer, he decided. Sadly, he lacked nets. He could weave token webs with briars and withies but there was a month's work to make a fist of it. He didn't begrudge the time but it was likely that he'd have demolished the food in the interim. The flitch of bacon was well wrapped, reeked of smoke and that he trusted to see off insects. So he slung it across a pair of conveniently high branches, albeit after a mighty tussle. Then it was largely a question of the ham and the cheddar. After some pondering he developed what he thought to be an ingenious solution. In his bathing pool he built an island of rocks, the labour of the afternoon. On top of it he perched first the cheddar and astride that, the ham. True, he'd wasted all the night's effort of caching goods downstream, but he was now convinced that the villagers would not be pursuing hobgoblins into the haunted wood.

He was right. While he slept, the bodies had been recovered, the arguments held – just as he had forecast – and finally, the guinea had been discovered. As he built his watery larder the gold was being dissolved by ale, while more devious minds began the sympathetic seduction of two fine, wealthy widows. The world was moving on, as it must.

As ignorant as Crusoe of all that lay outside his Island, Punch began to build the outlines of a new life. With an eye to autumn, winter being too awful to contemplate, he set himself to weave hurdles. He gathered hazel rods, new growth from crowns that had been coppiced many years back, which he took to be yet another sign that he was not the first castaway to wash up here. The apiary builder had been before him and someone had pleached these ashes to their bower-like shape. He intended to build within their shelter, a tight, welcoming hogan in which he could keep himself as warm and dry as was possible. Consequently he took care to weave his hurdles as tightly as art could contrive. By the time he had finished he was an accomplished hurdle-maker and his hands were raw. Every hole and chink he stuffed with moss. Then, surveying his efforts he fell to gathering the longest grasses he could find, with a view to over-thatching what he had built. Reeds would have been better but there were none on the homely stretch of stream. Nothing would induce Punch to trespass further, though he was certain that the threatening water he had conjectured, beyond the invisible boundary, would be lined with them. He did his best with grass, after which he began to lay on clay and sods, until he feared that weight alone would bring his home about his ears.

This matter of weatherproofing weighed upon him, though. A steady downpour would melt his roof. As long as the weather held, sods, clay, grass and moss were proof against showers but he needed something more. As events turned out, he was to find the very item.

Beyond his own favoured watering hole, where his cheddar and ham occupied less and less space on the ersatz larder he had built, Punch was partial to visiting another watery spot. Here fallen trees made comfortable perches and a man might sit and think while idly contemplating the intricate web of waters. He supposed you might call it a marsh. Some weeks it brimmed with water, others it ran dry. It seemed to have purposes of its own. It had been his prime source of clay, when he was caulking and waterproofing his hutch. He was au fait with its twisting lines of high ground and the treacherous areas where a man might vanish up to his neck.

Taking a walk that way, one bright afternoon, he seated himself proprietorially on a favoured log. As he made an unconscious scan of its familiar, marshy outlines, he was surprised and offended to see that a large portion of the far bank had collapsed and that for no apparent reason. Interest piqued, he ambled round the headland and finally arrived at what turned out to be worse devastation than he had thought. The whole grassy rise had been pulverized under cloven hooves and the standing bank beaten back and then down into the water. Yards of turf were torn up, as if a drover's herd had passed that way and jostled one another for access to the water. Punch was reasonably certain that no such event had occurred. This wood was no highway, either for man, or beast. Also, after studying the marks carefully he came to the uncomfortable conclusion that this upheaval was the work of one animal. One set of hoof prints was discernible and although they overlapped, repeatedly, there was no indication that there was more than one. Yet, in the world of cloven-hoofed beasts, it must be a colossus, something from legend. He searched carefully and backtracked its spoor, Finally, in damp ground, he found indisputable evidence of its size. The front hooves were more than a cloth yard apart, the distance between hind and forefeet greater than the tallest man. Punch could lose his own foot in the impression of the hoof and where it had stood longest, that impression was sunk a hand's length into the ground.

Such a discovery unsettled him. It appeared he was not alone, nor was this unwarranted company likely to be amiable. Feeling he had little option, he returned home to collect Bess, lest he, or the beast happen, unexpectedly, one upon the other. He charged the musket carefully. He could risk no misfires. But if the brute left him alone, he would be delighted to return the compliment. Once armed he set off again and fell to wondering if there might be early mushrooms. His commissary was running low.

He took the same route and for all his wary alertness, his mind began to wander, amiably enough down familiar byways, most of which still ended in hospitable taverns. 'Now, where was it…The Peacock, o'course, where else! Belle Trowbridge, landlady and a lass who could hold her own in any company. She kept a fine cellar and served sterling food, which is why the bars spilled into the courtyard and the clamour of famished men could be heard a mile-off. He had been partial to her jugged hare, with a rich helping o'melted cheese and capers. Taken with a jug of dark porter, how the afternoon would slip away! There was always a good fire blazing and, My Lord, what if we has snow falling here? No use to fret about what can't be helped…but Lord again, he loved it here, like it were a part o'his insides new fed wi' jugged hare. He'd be scared to leave now, these trees knew of him and he weren't unwelcome, it seemed. Why on earth had he ever taken that King's shilling? To git out o'bad trouble by gettin' into worse. There were your answer, plain and simple. But if he 'ent taken the shilling, he'd not a'met Jolyon an' there'd be no book to wrinkle his brows over. Ach, but he felt bad about that. He'd a'murdered the old fool for a certainty, if Caleb's pop-gun o'a cannon hadn't taken the job from his hands. And what were those tracks by the water? Damned crittur' must be t'size o'a cottage…and yon book were worth gold, said Jolyon and Jolyon were right an' this 'ere Punch would a'slain a man who could see further than him, which made him feel small and sorry. Then the cheddar were running out and he was eatin' a deal o'mould, tho' it seemed to do no harm. But now the broody had hatched and she was raising up some fine lil' fellas. She was used to her crumb o'biscuit, she'd not stray far, bit like him an' Belle Trowbridge, he was forever goin' back just to sample that hare, or a saddle o'mutton. Would he ever eat in a tavern again? An' he wished the insect lore were not so deep, for he'd studied it hard but it would slip and slide from him. Too deep by far, his peepers not what they were and his old mind skatin' and shiverin' around and…Holy Mother o'Christ! There she were again, that hapless maid, cowering and naked under a cape, picking her way into the very heart of the swamp! Where in hell had the poor dear come from? Why, or from what, weer she fleeing, yet again?'

"Li'l Miss," he hissed across the water, "get ye back a'ways, get back…tha'rt going' in 'tae deep…turn yer s'en around afore 'tis too late!" But she turned her face to him, pleading and gestured in terror…and by The Trinity, he'd never seen the like!…silent as the mountain but steamin' on the bank, head tossin', the biggest bull he's ever seen in his whole life. It was, indeed, the size of a poor man's hovel and for some crazed reason, on a peaceful afternoon, wi' nary a cow in sight, its prick wer' trailing on't floor, gatherin' sticks an' leaves to its welt. An' thet wer' as thick as the python Punch had seen in Indy, sliding along t'maidan ditch when he'd been standin' a'sentryin'… 'Twas true enough, she couldna' turn back to that, yet another yard forrad an' she'd be bogged in roots an' sucking clay.

"Hold ye hard, just where you be, Missy! Not a word, not a step, whate'er I does next!"

He was not close enough but he unslung Bess from his shoulder. Checked the priming, checked the flint. Found himself a friendly branch and rested the long barrel on it. "Weel, Punch," he whispered to himself, "it 'ent like tha's nowt to tek' aim at…"

He was going to try and drill a hole right down the length of the brute. Whether to go in by chest or brain was the question. He settled on chest, there being more of it. He took a deep breath, exhaled slowly and pulled the trigger – just as the creature lowered its head, preparatory to making a mad charge into the water. The half-inch ball took it square between the eyes and ploughed on into its vitals. It was dead before its nose hit the ground. It came forwards like a tower falling and the weight of the brute, plus the depth of the water turned it, "arse over tit," as Punch would later congratulate himself, into the swamp.

He was half-way through reloading when he recalled he was saving naked maidens, not fighting a war. He dropped the gun and sped around the headland, once again to gather her up, to protect her from whatever new disaster was raining down.

She turned her tearful face up to his and it shone with gratitude. Punch felt his stomach turn over with paternal pride. She restored his faith in mankind with her trust in him, him of all people. "Wharr'on earth…" he began. But holding herself to him, not wantonly but fearlessly, she put a finger across his lips… "Go," she whispered, "they are coming, they will kill you and they have dogs. Go now!"

"Come wi' me, Li'l Missy," he protested. "I kin carry thee thro' yon swamp, I knows the paths."

"You cannot. I am a grown woman and too heavy for you. The dogs have my scent. So hide while you can. Soon I will be ready to leave. Trust me, the fabric is unwinding. Don't fret for me. I know what it is I do. I will come, I just await a little sign that the others are to hand. A little help is all I need."

"Then be a'namin' o'it!" cried Punch, torn between protectiveness and awkwardly aware of the well-nigh irresistible soft body pressed against his.

"Not yours to give," she said sadly. "That gift lies within the power of others and they are not yet here." With which she disentangled herself gently, stared scornfully at the half submerged corpse of the beast and proudly erect, stalked away down the track. As she rounded the bluff that blocked further sight, she turned, waved once, naively, as a child might, then vanished from sight. Alone by the swamp, Punch found he was choking at the thought that she might be gone forever from his life.

Winter came in hard. At first, Punch didn't care. The flayed hide of the slain bull now covered his igloo and had set over it like steel. Also, from its forelegs he had cleverly contrived to manufacture himself a pair of boots. They were great floppy affairs, that was true but once lined with coney skins, for warmth and then lashed around his lean shanks with fibres beaten and twisted from ropes of briar, were almost admirable. He had plans for improvements, once he could manufacture a dependable needle. The bayonet made for a passable awl but the best needle he had managed to make had the profile of a crochet hook. He could haul the briar fibres through the holes but the results were clumsy.

Punch was becoming curiously fastidious, despite his straitened circumstances and intended to become proud of his handicrafts. His greatest coup was that he no longer lacked for meat. Not only was the great corpse a fine larder of frozen beef but its head, severed early in the proceedings and casually left, long submerged, had eventually attracted the attentions of a large pike and a host of elvers. On discovering the pike he had summarily gaffed and eaten it. The head, however, he left where it had fallen, as bait. Eels kept arriving and he was delighted to supplement his diet with them. As for the body, he finally stored that safely on land, slung high in a tree. Precisely how he achieved that was a marvel of innovation and good fortune. It was a tale he was already mentally embroidering, so that it should make a fine fireside story, one he would be proud to tell, was he ever permitted to leave this place.

Within his igloo he had dug a firepit, which he kept burning, day and night. He also had Little Missy's cape. Tracing her retreat, the day after she had fled, he had found it neatly folded and laid upon a great rock. She had gone to meet her captors naked, the state he surmised, in which they had her enslaved. She had seen his need and had left the cloth for him to find, something to wrap himself in, some protection against the coming winter.

Punch's emotions ran high upon this subject. In his heart he had adopted the girl. She was his daughter, the child he had never had, a woman forever beyond the sexual horizon and all the more worshipped for that. These elevated emotions were quite alien to him. He had passed most of his life deliberately brutalising his experience. Now he had stumbled upon what might still prove to be a mirage of this perplexing place. Mirage or not, the young girl was reminding Punch of the days he had been a loving, open-hearted child. The vileness of the intervening years was being, if not expunged, then at least diluted. In some ways he felt a kinship with the Parson's religious ecstasies, expressed so tediously within the book of insect lore. The cleric found his passion in Christ, Punch looked for his own within the circle of something he had never had – his own family.

He was shy of expressing such ideas, particularly to himself but poring over the insect lore, driven half mad by the pious cant, he found he was longing for a son, who would stand beside his elusive daughter. A son who – clever lad – might translate these chapters into a language Punch could understand, a son who might read the staves of musical notation and pipe them up some honey to sweeten the bitter taste of winter herbs. All the instructions were there but try as he might, they slid out of Punch's mind as sinuously as the elvers slid from the bull's empty eye sockets. What a bright lad he would be, thought Punch and what a golden couple they would make, brother and sister, as they walked their old father, arm-in-arm, down the city streets.

"Owd faither," he mumbled morosely. "Owd murtherer, more likes." Poor, old Jolyon – fool that he had been. If his, Punch's hand, hadn't been the one to strike the blow, it was only because the cannon's had been swifter. In thought, in intention, he was guilty. He writhed inwardly at the irony of it. The honest fool is struck down, the lecherous, treacherous rogue is propelled into a magical kingdom, granted visions, provisions and the dream of a future.

The one hope Punch screwed his mind up against envisioning, tied it down more tightly than he wound his boot straps, was that he might find himself a decent, homely wife. Yet, why would he have a son and daughter without a wife? It was such a dream but it lay at the front and the back of his mind like a root he was forever stumbling over. He was growing bruised from his own dreams.

It was in such a mood, one that chewed him like a dog gnaws its bone, that he leapt to his feet one darkening afternoon and decided that, as he could neither hold to his reading and despised his very thinking, he would walk the long curve of the Hedge instead. Who knew what treasures might have washed up? His first find was a clay pipe, with the head of some Tom-fool cast as the bowl – 'per'aps it be our King?' he wondered. Anyway, he stuffed it in the capacious wallet he had made, lest he be lucky enough to find the tobacco pouch that should have lain with it. He wandered on poking and probing with a long stick but precious little emerged, 'chewed bits and pieces o'bone, mostways.' He moved out onto what was almost a pathway, in the lee of the ever-watchful Hedge and sauntered on. It was only because he cast his eyes up, to follow the flight of a bird that he spied a dame's shawl, snared on the topmost branches of a hawthorn tree.

This was the devil of an occurrence. It was also the very devil to recover and he almost abandoned the effort. But behind his exertion was the underlying worry that a shawl, waving atop a hedge, would be the equivalent of a flag on a tower and might attract attention where it was not wanted. Finally, with the aid of the longest pole he could cut and a bit of clambering, he brought it down. It was a well-knitted, capacious affair and made for a well-endowed dame. It wrapped around Punch in the most comforting way and he could feel himself growing warmer with every second. "Theer 'ent no-one t'see thee, Punch!" he gibed at himself and swaggered on, well-pleased to have recovered it and not half as cautioned by the strangeness of it all as he should have been.

Next – 'bless this Hedge, it never failed him!' – was a string net, abandoned with three grandsire potatoes and a pair of stout carrots. Granted, they all had their bit of rot but nought a sharp knife couldn't cure. Salt he still wanted and as yet, he had no answer for that. He had some tiny wild onion bulbs that sharpened the eating but they were powerful provokers of the bellyache.

He had walked a good distance and it was then that he noticed a change in the weather. What he had carelessly taken for early evening gloom when he set out, was a thickening in the sky that, he now realised, predicted snow, or sleet. Either would be bad tidings and he was about to turn on his heel for home. It was in that moment that he spotted the hat that matched the shawl he was wearing. A fine bonnet, bedecked with cheerful berries and leaves, cunningly modelled from paper and wax. He swept it up from the rutted ground, brushing the underside clean and faint disquiet swept across his stomach. He would risk walking on a little further, maybe discover what lay behind these matters.

Emotions being what they are, within a few paces he had shaken off unease and was appreciating the odd shapes that frozen leaves and grasses had adopted. Some lay like empty cockle shells on a tide-line, while the grassy bents copied the shapes he had made recently, when he tried to draw out his letters with a piece of charcoal. Suddenly he felt good about his son and daughter. They would teach him to write. He would live to know them and love them. Maybe they would love him back.

Entertaining these warming, new thoughts he walked on a little carelessly, not taking much care to disguise his coming. After all, it was twilight and this was his kingdom. It was then, as he stood on the brink of folly that, in the half-distance, he saw a familiar shape abandoned on disturbed ground. It was a long, woollen, sweeping skirt and with it a kirtle such as a respectable body, a mother, housewife or domestic might wear about their daily round. He loped closer to where they lay, crumpled, discarded. Like hat and shawl, they had absolutely no reason to be lying there and now the unease that had crossed the pit of his stomach earlier, returned with a vengeance. He began to feel sick with tension and awful forebodings. Despite the fact that he was here, behind 'his' Hedge, ostensibly cocooned and safe, something swift and malevolent had passed this way. What right of entry had it called upon? He intuited that there would have been none, so the very fact that it had and could pass this way, brought all his caution to the fore. He unslung Bess from his shoulder, checked the priming and cursed himself for not bringing the pistol. Nothing it seemed was forever, not even the sanctity of these hideaway groves, he thought bitterly. Whatever had happened here was ugly. That was now obvious and he took it as an affront to the unilateral peace he had unconsciously proclaimed.

He proceeded now with all the care of a military scout. He was inching around the bluff that obscured the view beyond the swamp when, under his ungainly boot and beneath the frozen leaves, a twig snapped. It echoed in his own ears but so did the pounding of his heart. He waited a while and heard nothing in response. So he took a step away from the litter at the base of the rock and moved on. He was hoping to gain a clear line of sight, something to give him leeway for thought, if action was required. What he saw almost stopped his heart.

In the far distance and against the fading light, where figures were pure silhouette, were the outlines of two powerful dogs. Dogs of the breed that would run you down in seconds and rip your throat out. They were on long leashes, thank God and motionless. Then, to his horror, they began to cast-about. Their heads went up, their ears pricked back and a restless twitching rippled along their spines – a minute movement but clear against the empty horizon. Any second, Punch thought and they would lock back onto that scent of skirt and shawl. Then he was done for. One dog only he could kill. Then the other would kill him. Where was the handler? Why wasn't he alert to his dogs?

The reason was awful. Raucous laughter split the silence and from the shadows of the woodland, a group of ruffians emerged, dragging the almost naked body of an older woman between them. The handler was among them, for he broke away to untie his dogs from some snag where he had them hooked. A coach and four moved into the scene, with two gentry on horseback accompanying it. An exchange of words but Punch could make out none of them, other than that they sounded harsh and villainous. The dogs, he knew for certain had his scent. They were straining back on their leashes. The handler, buttoning himself, cracked his whip, blind and indifferent to them and they cowered in fear. Punch's blood raced, his rage choking him. He sighted the musket on the largest knot of inhumanity he could see. He curled his finger around the trigger, fired and the little scene simply vanished. His shot ploughed into nowhere.

He dropped the gun. The net of food and the clothes he had been carrying, he abandoned where he had set them down at the first alert. Now he ran, as quickly as his awkward boots allowed, to the glade. The wheel tracks were there, the kicked up litter of frozen leaves and grass trampled by heavy boots, all were apparent. Horses had stood here, shod hooves had left their imprint. That was the story told by the road that led in to this place but nothing had left here by the road out. The road out was pristine in white frost. No coach, no riders, no ruffians or dogs had left this place, except by means magical. 'They fell through a hole in time,' said an agreeable voice in Punch's head and he found himself nodding a slow agreement. Then, suddenly aware and scared out of his wits, he wheeled about to see who had spoken to him. There was no-one. Nothing moved, man, beast nor bird.

Punch took several deep breaths. Then moving methodically he set off to explore what could be seen. The scene of the assault itself was clear enough and from it he removed one last garment which, tears blinding him, he folded carefully and stowed in his pouch. Numbed, he walked back to recover the musket, the food and the clothes.

He made his way home, cleaned the gun as best he could and lay down by his firepit, wrapped in Little Missy's cloak. For half the evening he barely moved, except to push more charcoal onto the coals. He stared into the embers and tried to think. All he got were images and they were muddled, vivid impressions of past and present chopped and diced, that then flared across the plane of his mind like showers of sparks. It all seemed to point to some revelation but all he could see through them was the upright figure of his long dead Nan. Somehow, positioned across her, was the tragic figure of the woman whose linen he had just folded so carefully. His intention was to keep it safe, until he could restore it to her. That would be after he had avenged her. Punch knew a thing or two about vengeance.

With the moon at its zenith he stirred himself. He was aware that he had made a decision, though what it was he didn't know. He felt curiously refreshed and ravenously hungry. He pulled the net of spoiled vegetables to him and carefully cut away the rotten bits. He raked the fire to one end of the pit and laid them on the burned earth. Then he raked back the coals and added fresh fuel. He waited peacefully. His mind turned but he didn't feel obliged to pursue any of its tracks. So, perhaps, after a while, it simply ceased trying to amuse him. When the pole star was high in the night sky, he raked back the wood and extricated his immolated vegetables. While he carefully peeled off the worst of the burn and ash, he flung a thick slice of the bull's rump on top of the charcoal and listened to it sizzle. Every so often he turned it and not being that choosey any longer, shortly declared it done. A split log served as a plate and on that he diced together rare beef and cooked vegetables, which made a dish, if not fit for a monarch, then adequate for a starving vagabond with a plan that was no-plan forming in his head.

Punch had fallen into a restless sleep filled with snatches of bickering dreams that jostled for his attention. First, he was drowning, then he was flying, next, falling. He was pursued, he was the pursuer. He walked along corridors, opening countless doors, staring into empty rooms that still vibrated with the echoes of departed conversation. He was always too late, for something. He grew tired and lay down, only to roll against some obstruction that would not give way. He pushed and pushed at it with all the weight he could muster but his legs began to burn and fret.

He woke bewildered and discovered that he actually was smouldering. He had slept so deeply, despite the deceitful dreams, that he had half-rolled across the hot ashes of his fire pit. His legs were badly scorched. His trousers, such as they had been, had totally betrayed him, burning away to nothing. A small mercy, then, that they had been more hole than cloth.

As he tried to sit up, the chill morning air attacked him. It sought out each patch of ruined skin and set it howling. Curses seemed irrelevant, as pain flooded through every nerve. He curled himself into a ball to try to deny the torment but that was no solution. Next he tried to think rationally. What can he do, what can he make? Is there anything that might ease this misery, because it threatens to unhinge his very mind?

He tries to imagine Nan's voice. She will help him, she always did, she always has. The truth is, he has no simples laid by, no dried leaf, no ointments. For a second he sees into the soul of womankind's selfless humility, their seeking, learning, storing, compounding, curing, seeking no reward other than the humble thanks of those they have helped. Now, here he lies, a helpless, violent male, undone by a set of burns such as a careless child could have earned whilst playing with fire. The rebuke stiffens his resolve. 'Think, Punch!' The land lies under frost, there is no aid to be looked for from hibernating plants. What has he to hand? He racks memory and remembers that somewhere in the coveted and stolen book, there was some passage that dealt with snails and the legless beings of the land. He seeks it out but it takes an eternity to rediscover, for it is tucked away amongst monstrous outpourings of religious sentiment. At last he has it, the common snail secretes a mucus that can seal the surface of a burn but the remedy is not without hazard. The snails must be purged for three days, so that their excrement is not introduced into the wounds. And with that the reverend's piety is unleashed…purges, excrement, hazard and final salvation, "even the most humble of the earth…" once started, the man was unstoppable!

Punch sheds the remnants of his pants, picking stray threads and ash from his parbraised thighs. Hobbling beneath Little Missy's cloak he hisses and clucks his way to the edge of the stream. He has brought the appropriate whistle with which he prays he can rouse dormant molluscs from their winter slumbers. Long, low tones, advises the book will summon them "but," it had continued, "allow the legless ones an adequate provision of time. Their progress is slow."

Indeed it was. Nevertheless, Punch was humbled as, one by one, from under rocks, fallen branches, out of hollow logs and knots of reedy growth, tight corners of every variety, a small army of newly awakened snails inched towards his low, whistling call. One by one he gathered them, positioned them, two and three to a burn and awaited whatever solace they could bring. At least, he consoled himself, fresh from hibernation, they were purged of excrement. His hope was that he would cause them no lasting harm and that they might render him some passing good. Even with a score or more of the little fellows to each leg, the treatment was less than speedy. It was, however, strangely consoling. The pain was ebbing under their combined ministrations and he began to feel indebted to creatures he could see no way to repay. They were blindly following the group mind, which had awakened them from slumber to send them searching for whatever directive that low tone might indicate. There was none of the drama of the bees, whose war-like instincts were only too familiar to man. Punch could think of no common platform he shared with these lowly creatures and the perplexity grew in him as to how he might discharge his debt.

His first task, he decided, after he had shivered under their ministrations for half the morning, was to return them to some safe abode. There was a hollow log to hand and one by one, he detached them from his legs and tucked them, as safely as he might, within its rotting fold. Then, with some embarrassment and an uncomfortable feeling that he was being watched, he essayed a short speech of gratitude. He took an oath never to harm one of their kind deliberately, in the future, though he had to allow, accidents did happen. Also, if he ever had the good fortune to gain a smallholding, by the beneficence of some lucky star, he would pluck them from his produce and ferry them to some safe place, far from harm. After that he stowed the log in a frost free pocket, high above any flood level he could discern and limped back to the comparative warmth of his bivouac.

For some days Punch did little except think, eat beef and wait for his legs to heal. He thought about two things – the mystery of the vanishing girl, the creatures that preyed on her and secondly, the question of his pants, or rather the lack of them. He came to an early conclusion, that new pants and the girl might be found conjoined, so-to-speak. He believed he had seen her three times, twice plainly and once by proxy, during the molestation of her domestic. Why he was certain of the latter connection he couldn't say but certain he was. He concluded that both were held, against their will, somewhere near this wood. He would not believe the wood played any part in that captivity, rather that it was using its powers to show him their predicament and provoke his assistance. The wood, he concluded, actually needed him. A sign signifying that matters were, indeed as he thought, would be appreciated but with, or without it, he was determined to proceed. Precisely how that would take place, without any pants, was distressing and implicitly farcical.

'How the devil,' mused Punch, 'can the lack of a pair of pants come between a man and his duty?' On that point he foundered. It could not be a problem but it was. As a diversionary tactic it might have something to commend it. The wild Scots were said to lift their kilts as they charged the enemy… There was his answer. A kilt. Slay a passing Scotsman, or cobble one together from the few skins and rags he had about the place. In a pinch some shift towards an apron would do. He didn't intend to retreat, whatever the odds. He could, the notion flitted across his mind, utilise the Good Wife's garments but he dismissed the idea. He had her clothing safely stowed and he intended, one day, to restore it to her, a silent apology for the bestiality of the male species.

So it was that Punch fell to sewing together the bird, coney and squirrel skins he possessed, the hides of every dead beast that his travels through the wood had presented to him these last long months. He had assiduously skinned them all and made a shift at tanning by soaking, rolling, part-drying and soaking again in urine, mushroom juices and whatever other concoctions he could conjure from imagination and memory. The results were only partially successful but the hides had at least retained both their fur and feathers. They even had some flexibility and withstood his awl and crochet approach to sewing. Latterly, he had taught himself how to roll out thread on his thighs and though it would be some time before he could do that again, he had a stock laid by, enough to make a shift at this apron.

His resolve hardened with every cobbled stitch and within the week, whatever week that might be, for any sense he had of calendar had long since fled, his garment was complete. He made it fast around his waist and it chafed less than he had dreaded. That was all the compliment he could bring himself bestow upon it.

He pleaded for a sign that he should set out but the wood said nothing. Silence seemed to have fallen over every glade. He waited a day longer, then shrugged and set out anyway. He took the carbine, for which he had had little use until now. It was a good weapon nevertheless, as was the double pistol, which would shortly be proving its worth, of that he was certain. Above all though, he relished weight of the short sword on his hip. The memory of the Goodwife's abuse that he had witnessed in the wood, was burning in his mind. He intended to wreak close quarters mayhem on the perpetrators. Such was his resolve as he set out down the stream.

He had not dared to trespass that way since he was first turned back, months ago. If he was allowed progress, beyond the invisible barrier, that would suffice as the sign he was seeking. If the wood turned him around, as it had before, then the time was not ripe.

His feet crunched iced grasses and frost devils stung his legs above the rude boots and below his kilt. He had greased his burns with a thick layer of ox-fat newly rendered from the haunch of meat that hung in his hovel. It kept the worst of the icy air out and eased the chafing of the skins. Nevertheless, he was soon forced to tie up the hem of his garment and there it would stay, for as long as there was no-one to gape at the murder of his legs and winter's shrinking of his privy parts.

He slipped along the edge of the stream in thoughtful and watchful mood. The alders here, at the edge of the wood, had their first catkins forming. He could almost sense the tension of Spring, coiled beneath the frozen ground. 'I'm walking South,' he told himself, though according to the sun, he was plainly headed west. But the word 'South' had a lift in it, it lent a bit of backbone to what was already a steadfast decision. 'South' was a part of the meaning of the Land, and the Land's purpose underlay his own, he was sure of it. Why else had the wood let him pass its 'Southern' boundary this time? Hell-bent though he was on his righteous venture, he believed he was just a mote in a greater landscape, a stitch in a tapestry. The whole idea, muddled though it might have been, lent him strength. 'Time's needle,' he told himself, 'that's me. An' a's come t' prick an unholy boil.'

The stream did widen but only by a foot or two. The grasses were taller but the frost had bowed their heads. At length he could step into an autumn-mown meadow and see his way clear across that to a hedge, an ordinary hedge with none of the brooding strength about it that he was used to, by now, in hedges. It seemed, in fact, that the wood was wide open from this 'southern' side and that puzzled him. Yet, as he stepped onto the short grass he had the certain sensation that he stepped from something very serious into somewhere very ordinary. He looked back, turned fully around but there was nothing that might strike one's eye as particular, or peculiar.

It would be wise, then, to attend to what lay in front. An open, too open, stretch of grass and bordering that the harmless hedge, that he now followed with his eye to the right. He warranted that it flanked a track and to judge by its zig-zagging progress, a track that led up to the far neck of his own domain, hard-by the arena where he had seen the phantom four-in-hand, on the day of the events he was plotting to avenge. "Weel, we'l," said Punch.

Walking into the field made him feel as exposed as a white hare on a ploughed acre. His body twitched with the expectation of a distant musket shot, or a belling of hounds. He was hideously visible, an invitation to scrutiny, assault and murder.

'Be calm, boy,' he told himself, 'not all are bent on mayhem.' Nevertheless, he should have scouted the land before he walked so brazenly into it. Had he come from the right, he could have hugged the hedge for cover and not risked this invitation to discovery.

A dozen more yards, to a high spot amid falling ground, gave him better vantage. Beyond this field, that lane beyond the hedge turned sharply downhill, heading for the tops of ancient trees above which rose a smudge of smoke. 'From chimbleys, a'll warrant,' he nodded to himself. There lay the Manor house, the seat of all the wickedness that plagued this corner of the land. He knew so as surely as he knew his own burns. He would root it out and destroy it. "Unless them destroys thee furst, Punch," he said out loud and the magnitude of his bravado washed over him for a moment, twisting his stomach with sudden anxiety.

He was about to press on when he noted that he was standing atop a tiny spring that leaked a thick red ooze onto the turf. Without really thinking, he stooped and thrust two fingers into the mess. They came away thick with pigment, a bright ferrous orange. He gave a wry smile and then smeared parallel lines on his cheeks, astride his nose and across his forehead. Above his ragged, black beard he was now an aboriginal, such as he had seen in Indy. "An' a fearful afreet they be!" he gurgled happily.

Swiftly now, he made his way to the hedge. He was well aware that he made a figure to be shunned but equally, he felt that his life hung in the balance of every step. The problem was, there was no height to the bushes, they had been well-laid in the autumn, cut-back, folded-over for thick growth, not height. He was no Gulliver in Lilliput but he overtopped it, head and shoulders.

On the other side, as he had thought, the roadway was sunken and despite the numerous drains cut along its edge, it had suffered in the autumn rains. Those had drummed wholly ineffectually on Punch's rooftop ox-hide but here they had cut great gouges in the roadway. For a second or two the comparison made him feel superior, until a particularly chill blast of wind parted the folds of his kilt and reminded him that he was wholly exposed and vulnerable, on every front.

He loped along the hedge, forced to travel totally in the wrong direction, away from the Manor. It was the cunning hedge-layers that were the undoing of him. The thorn bushes were impenetrable at that tight turn of the road and truth be told, there was little improvement hereabouts. He searched for some passage-way a fox might have scratched and eventually found one that sensibly ducked beneath a well-rubbed ash pole. He cast about for a stout flint and found a stone that would have to do. Then he set to work widening the fox-way to a Punch-way. God knows there was little enough of him but the last thing he wanted was to be caught like a beast in a deadfall with hounds on his heels. Eventually he had dug away enough sod and earth to permit passage. Then, looking at it, he fell to another round of scratching and gouging. He had wounds and ordnance about him. Neither were tolerant of tight squeezes.

He sat, recovering himself, on the edge of the field and considered matters. The sun was climbing to what would be its low zenith. Within the hour it would shine straight along the line of this road, right into the eyes of any who came riding, or coaching from the true north. Why though, should he assume trouble would come from outside, moving towards the Manor? It was morning, surely the inhabitants would be moving away from their haunts and it was with them that he desired conversation. 'No,' said the voice in his head. 'Look to the north.' So he did and it was from the north that they came.

It was the carriage with the four-in-hand. On the driver's bench, a driver and a guard, both stout-looking fellows, maybe the ones Punch had caught glimpse of at the end of the wood, though he thought not. Even though they had been mere, distant silhouettes, their cut and character were etched into his memory.

The carriage had a distance to come yet. The roadway was not straight, the bends were tight, the gradient marked at that north end and the matter of the autumn rains had distressed the going. He had time to observe.

What he observed was odd. Something was wrong about the whole event. Coach and landscape were not one. The coach seemed to flicker against its backdrop, at one moment too dark and massy, at the next almost translucent. Also it advanced in tiny hiccups of movement, very like to a caterpillar trying to balance on a drooping stem. The roadway was poor but not that poor. It was not merely a ragged surface that was the cause of the awkwardness, something was amiss with the whole affair, as if two scenarios from different plays, were being acted on one stage, with one troupe of actors unaware of the others. He was perplexed, he was also on cue. He either stood and challenged, or let the rig jolt its way forward to whatever fate awaited its passengers.

Action was Punch's strength. The horses were approaching, the sun was on the driver's bench and the guard was shielding his eyes against it. Punch rose upright, carbine across his chest, at the ready. His intention was to startle the horses and he succeeded. They shied, stumbling sideways, the lead horse that had had the full glory of his arising thrust upon it, shifting as far as it could from this motley figure.

The driver fought to recover his team. "Whoa, whoa!" he bellowed, hauling back on his reins. The guard was swift, far swifter than he had any right to be. Without a word he swung up the blunderbuss that had lain at rest across his thighs and as Punch hurled himself back, down onto the turf, it roared and the charge of old metal ripped through the dense weave of the hedge, making short work of branch and twig.

Punch leapt upright, aimed the carbine at the belly of the leading horse and shot it just behind the ribs. It collapsed, a gaping hole torn in the gleaming hide. The guard had been rising to his feet, struggling to free a pistol from his belt. As the horse went down, so did he, face first among flailing hooves. Punch leaned carefully over the hedge and shot him, precisely, through the ear. He turned to shoot the driver but the driver was gibbering with terror, his hands high in the air.

Punch seized his moment and went, feet first, through his crawl space, praying that he would emerge before the driver came to his senses and shot him. Mercifully the man was still frozen in terror and the sight of Punch's genitals, red-ochred – he had paused to pee using painterly fingers – seemed to have riveted him in place. Punch gave one final haul with his heels. He was through, upright and now able to use the dead guard's pistol. He ducked down to secure it. "Nae, nae…" babbled the driver, waving his hands in terror.

That was as well, because Punch could see that the fall had dislodged the primings from both barrels. He tried to think above the commotion but all he could focus on was the nerve-wracking sound of the horse, screaming in agony. That he would deal with as quickly as possible but he needed to be sure of the driver. There was only one option and he took it. The driver fell back, over the far side of the coach, shot through the chest. Now Punch was effectively unarmed, except for an unprimed pistol. He tore open the door of the coach, and presented himself, painted, kilted and stained with blood of man and horse.

Little Missy was fighting a fat man who wore the clerical weeds of a Bishop. His shovel headgear, much traumatised, rolled on the floor beside them. She was crouched on his chest like a panther, tearing at his face while he flailed at her with ring-studded hands. She had him down and was winning their battle. He was bellowing for assistance but it was slow in coming. What Punch took to be a curate-type was sliding about, dislodged by their flailing limbs, whilst trying to level a tiny pistol at the girl's head. The gun was so small and he so nerve-wracked that it slipped and skidded in his hand like a juggler's ball.

Punch leaned forward and plucked it from his fingers. For all its diminutive size, it had two barrels. In a spirit of experimentation, he fired once into the curate's shoulder. The man shrieked, so Punch supposed something positive must have happened. Consequently he thrust the barrel against the fat man's rump and pulled the second trigger. The result was much the same, a loud shriek. "A 'as theer attention," said Punch, to no-one in particular, while he slid the sword from his hip.

"I was winning," said the girl, turning around, panting but with a huge smile on her face.

"Indeeds ye wus," agreed Punch "but yon rascal might a'done fer ye!" and he displayed the tiny gun on the palm of his hand. "Do's a' kill 'em now?" he asked.

"Non, monsieur, the time is not now. We must wait still longer."

"Tis hard t' be 'unnerstannin' o' thet, Missy but a' be a'listenin t'ye."

"You creature, you vagabond, you ingrate!" roared the Archbishop, writhing on the floor. "You'll be dancing in chains over a slow fire when I have the measuring of you! You and this vixen!"

Punch leaned forward and knelt on the man's thighs. "B' that 'ow ye treats wi' a man wi' a knife at yer throat?" and he pulled the blade up under the double chins.

"T'ain't civil, t'ain't sensible. Think on, a'cares nowt fer' thee, nowt fer' thy God an' nowt fer' thy blather. Hurt ye a lock o'yon gal's hair an'a'll geld thee both. Thy reckonin' 'ent 'ere yet but tek this day as a warnin'…'tis approachin'"

Punch turned to the girl. "Can ye load pistols, Missy?"

"Of course, monsieur!"

"Then tek thyself off, outsides, an' load all ye find. If thou kin pur'an end t' yon unhappy beast, b'a doin' o' it, or twill 'ave ter wait on me." Punch handed her his powder horn and shot pouch and she scrambled out of the coach.

Once outside, Marie-Gabrielle fell to the task and skilfully. With the first barrel loaded she shot the suffering mare through the brain. Then she loaded and primed automatically. She knew her way around firearms, an accomplishment she had honed in the years she had doted on Denis Diderot. Terrified as he was of assassins, he left loaded pistols to hand in every room. But he never changed the primings, re-set the flints, or seated the balls properly on the charges. Silently, like the ghost she had been, she saw to the work when he slept and she could watch over him. Now her hands flew about the task automatically while her brain tried to understand what sign this eruption in the fabric indicated. This was the longest episode she had ever initiated, longer even than the catastrophic chapter that had led to the molestation of her darling Nounou. The very thought brought tears to her eyes and it was hard not to let the wild, nut-brown man have his way with murder.

Two piercing howls echoed from the coach but before she had had time to react, he was by her side. "Nowt t'fret on, lil'Missy," he assured her. "A reminder as theer t'be good t'thee an' thine. Now, a' 'as t'ask…'ow be thy maid? A' came upon t' end o'it but cud do nowt, an' a' fair frets o'er thet. Tell 'er, Missy, as 'er linen b' safe an' stored. When t'time be ripe, a'll be a' bringin' o' it to 'er."

"She is much changed, Monsieur and my heart is broken. I will never forgive myself. But I shall tell her your message, it will bring her hope that someone cares."

Punch looked at her sadly. "A' feared t'would be so. B' sure t'end this affair swiftly, lest more grief befall us all."

Marie-Gabrielle shook her head sadly. "Await a sign, Monsieur. Await a sign. Now, flee, for the shots will have been heard and they are many. This scene has its end but I cannot tell the moment of it." She stood on tiptoe and kissed his cheek. "Monsieur," she grinned, "you are un grand sauvage, terrible!" That was the moment Punch remembered his kilt was still tied up.

Atop a black gelding that he cut out from the team, he galloped back down the lane, in the direction the coach had come. He rode as far as the tip of the wood, dismounted, hazed the horse on its way and shouldering his weapons plodded warily and wearily into the wood.

It made not a sound but it closed around him. If he had turned to witness he would have seen a scurry and flurry on the woodland floor behind him. Foxes that criss-crossed the path, randomly spraying their musk across his every track. Unwitting small creatures that nudged and dragged leaves across footprints. Even the contours of the forest floor were being changed subtly but most effective screen of all was the icy ground mist that rose in his wake. That lay like a wall across the entrance to the wood and silently denying entry to all but the insanely reckless.

To Punch's pursuers, lacking all love for their masters, it reeked of sorcery and when they came, they rode on willingly. It was with great diligence, though, that they pursued the black gelding, ensuring that it led them all a merry dance until sundown.

Suddenly exhausted, his thighs rubbed and seeping blood, Punch barely had the energy to walk. "An' a' fergit'ed t'git mi'self some pants," he mumbled solemnly.

In time he came to the edge of the swamp and wondered vaguely why he had chosen this longer route. He was almost sure there had been a reason but he could not recall it. Finally, memory served. He sighed, indifferently, then fished in the breast of his ruinous jacket until he found what he was seeking. He drew forth the two ears he had severed. He contemplated them for a moment, then hurled them into the swamp. There, for a while, they floated like strange fungus, until they sank forever.

MARIE-GABRIELLE

Marie-Gabrielle is two-dimensional and sick of it.

She slips out of the book she lives in, peeling herself off the page more easily than a transfer glides from its mounting paper. It was some thousands of years ago, when she first realised that she was appearing everywhere, in graffiti and fresco, that she had felt exasperated enough to teach herself how to vanish from rock and plaster. Shortly after the innovation of machinery however, she had been obliged to finesse her ruse, to refine her method, so as to permit her to vanish from the printed page. Our heroine is a very clever young lady. She is also generous to a fault. She has taught lots of images how to free themselves since the printing revolution and at night the library is alive with man, beast and machine animatedly exchanging stories and exploring one another's pages.

Here, under the roof of the Manor – where the 'Archbishop,' fat and wet with summer sweat, lies windily snoring in his sty of a bed – anarchy is afoot. Were this self-titled Archbishop to visit the secret shelves of his library, at this late hour, he would be dismayed to find that the majority of his doe-eyed, 'girls-in-distress' had fled their leather bindings and were huddled at his lectern, busily plotting his downfall. Marie-Gabrielle is, without doubt, their de facto leader but this evening she wants to go visiting, by herself. She's discovered a fascinating book and she is intent on liberating its central character. Then she will initiate a very long conversation.

Being more or less pure thought in her two-dimensional form, she can travel almost anywhere, whenever she likes. However, she has found that the world beyond the library walls is a terrifying place. The arena is so vast, so overpoweringly 'open', that every time she has ventured out she has, just as quickly, hastened back home, to whichever library she was currently choosing to manifest in. That she can 'pop-up' wherever in the world she has been shelved is just one of the complex rules that govern her existence.

How to subvert these rules is what is concerning her at present. The agoraphobia she has experienced beyond the library has forced her to question what validity there could be in the parochial world of 'in-library' existence. Marie-Gabrielle has tried, many times, to play at being human but naivety being what it is, she has only just realised that, to really make the leap, it will mean her becoming three-dimensional.

"I want to feel things, I want to play 'house' in the real world," she explains to the exquisite and painstaking drawing of a Siberian shaman, she has just animated in his frame.

"Ah," exclaims the Shaman, "you must be talking to me. It's been a very long time since anyone did that. Tell me again what it is you were pursuing."

"I want to be real," Marie-Gabrielle repeats, a little sharply. She is used to being listened to, whenever she speaks. After all, she is the local heroine.

The Shaman laughs, a full-blooded sound that booms about the library.

"Silence, please!" hisses a chameleon, who is busily studying invertebrate morphology and has taken extensive notes which he finds he can't read, because as fast as he takes them, they disappear. Another unexpected problem of the animate, two-dimensional world.

"Apologies," says the Shaman breezily. "What's funny is that I spent most of my life trying to be unreal. It's only now that I'm experiencing it, unreality that is, I can see that I never really got the hang of it."

"Well, you have now," says Marie-Gabrielle, "you're floating in two-dimensions, like the rest of us. It doesn't seem to be bothering anyone else in here, as yet but it is bothering me. That's why I've switched you on, if you'll pardon the vulgarity of the expression and am talking to you. If you managed to become 'unreal' when you were 'real', you should know the way back to 'real' from here. I think that makes sense," she adds, uncertainly.

"I can quite see why you might think that," the Shaman said, apologetically, "but I'm afraid to say that that process was always quite automatic. I didn't actively do anything. As I say, I spent most of my time trying to stop it happening." The Shaman sees disappointment cloud Marie-Gabrielle's face and he feels terrible. "You've been so kind, freeing me from my page and now I've been a bit of a let-down. You wouldn't stay and talk a while, would you? It's been an age since I had an intelligent conversation… or any conversation at all, when I come to think about it. The very sound of words is quite emotional. It's been an age since anyone opened my book's pages."

"Of course I will," said Marie-Gabrielle "and don't be surprised you've never been opened. You're on the front shelf, you see, you're just for 'show'. That 'Dis-Grace' of an 'Archbishop' keeps his front shelves full of philosophies and religions of the world. But if you open that case over there," she said, pointing and forgetting that the Shaman couldn't yet move, or turn his neck to see, "it comes out on rollers and there's a secret room in which he keeps all his 'forbidden' books. That's where he spends his time. I live in there," she added, almost as an afterthought, "I'm on his 'favourites' shelf."

"Is that good?" asked the Shaman, innocently.

"No, it's absolutely awful. I've had enough of it, that's why I'm trying to escape. I can't manage without help though and I've been trying ever since I was invented."

"Invented, you said?"

"It's my polite way of putting it."

"Are you going to tell me more?"

Marie-Gabrielle pondered.

"Are you very, well, broad-minded?"

"I don't know," said the Shaman helplessly. "I lived in a very 'broad' sort of country but I don't think you mean that."

"No," said Marie-Gabrielle, "but I'm going to tell you anyway. Then you'll see why I'm trying to escape."

"That'll be interesting and you never know, I might have an idea or two.

Marie-Gabrielle sat down on the tundra, by the Shaman's feet and started her story.

"When the first people were born, life was very competitive. There was a lot of fighting, usually about women."

"Ah," said the Shaman, "I definitely recognise that story."

"Exactly. That meant that there were a lot of discontented men with black eyes and broken noses. Also a lot of cross women who were having to put up with one man to share.

"One day, one man picked up a piece of ochre that was lying about and drew a voluptuous looking girl on the cave wall where all these frustrated men lived. Do I have to go on?"

"Just a bit," said the Shaman, "I'm not as fast as I used to be."

"Hmm," snorted Marie-Gabrielle. "I'm that girl! Now do you see? I'm that girl and every other fantasy female that's ever been invented by angry, frustrated, young men. You'll find me in the caves of Lascaux, in the erotica room of the British Museum and a click and a half away on Porn Hub."

"You're losing me…no, you've lost me…"

"The British Museum is about to be invented and Porn Hub comes, oh, I can't do maths, about 250 years later. Do try to keep up!"

"I haven't done forwards, yet," said the Shaman, feeling a bit aggrieved.

"Nothing to it," said Marie-Gabrielle, "I'll show you how to unstick yourself in a bit and then we can go for a ride into the future – but it's not half as much fun as it sounds."

"Why on earth not?"

"It's very foggy. Stuff blows in your eyes all the time and you can lose your way. You have to stick to the path but because it's foggy, you can't. Also, it's incredibly noisy and not in a good way. All the paths have sounds, because they're competing and it makes navigating them very scary.

"Anyway, to get back to my dilemma. I'm what you might call 'an incorporated ideal' – I looked that up," she said proudly, "it means…"

"…that you're an icon," the Shaman finished for her.

"How did you know that?"

"Icons were very important in my dream worlds. They were how I navigated… 'here is earth, here lies water, now fire and overall is breath.' And I suppose in your case, 'here are universal, male, lustful feelings.'"

"Or 'Me', for short," said Marie-Gabrielle, glumly. "Do you know, it is flattering for a while, then it gets very tedious. If I'd just stayed asleep, like everyone else, it wouldn't really matter. But one day I woke up, enjoyed a few years of flattery and then arrived at tedious. Now I want out. I'm sure I'd enjoy lustful feelings in a real environment but I'm utterly fed-up with playing Scarlet Woman to the whole world. Also, I keep getting involved in niche products, a subject I don't think we should get into on first acquaintance but it's where I am, at present and for one reason or another, I think that indicates it could be a wise time to jump ship."

The Shaman thought deeply for a while.

"I absolutely hear what you are saying. Of course, you've contacted Earth Magic? Sorry, that was silly of me, obviously you have but it can do nothing? I have to say, I'm surprised by that. You are one of its own children, most odd…"

"Whoa," said Marie-Gabrielle, "back up a bit there. I may be very old but my education has been sorely neglected. Earth Magic…who, what, why and where is that?"

"Stick with 'what' is that," advised the Shaman. "Earth magic is the 'what' I spent most of my life pursuing."

"Are you saying that this isn't going to be easy?"

"Not a bit of it. It's nothing to worry about at all. It's not as is if you were asking for difficult, awkward things. You'll really just be asking to be remembered and helped. I suppose you might come as a bit of a surprise but that's likely to be an advantage. Earth Magic will be concerned that you got forgotten."

"My turn to be lost. Explain, please!"

"You couldn't get me off this page first, could you? I find I'm tired and I'd love to sit down."

Marie-Gabrielle clapped her hand to her mouth in dismay. "How appallingly rude of me! I'm so sorry. I was so anxious to talk to you that I didn't remember to show you how to float free. I'll talk you through it. I have to say it took me decades to perfect but once you know how, it's remarkably easy." And for the umpteenth time she explained the mental exercises necessary to animate an artist's line.

Meanwhile, overhead and all around, imagination's children drifted by, travelling serenely from shelf to shelf, visiting new friends, ancient relatives and experiencing life on tropical isles, or as it existed amid mountain ranges. Others wandered the strange, landlocked ruins of forgotten civilisations and heard the stone throats of forgotten gods calling for their devotees. In the forbidden room, the self-appointed Archbishop's inner sanctum, the girls clustered in menacing groups discussing what revenge they might wreak on the wretched creature whose peccadilloes had called them into existence.

"Oh," exclaimed the Shaman, suddenly, "this is most odd. I'd quite forgotten how it felt and yes, you're quite right, it's not really the same experience at all. I don't mean to sound ungrateful, I'm really very pleased and can't thank you enough but I understand why you've grown frustrated over all these centuries."

"It was falling in love that did it," said Marie-Gabrielle. "Until then, I'd been very happy floating about, just a sort of idea in the air and then I met Denis. I'm over it now but that's what did it. I wanted to be real for him and not unreal/real on scandalous pages. I'm not prudish, in fact I'm a very vigorous sort of girl but being one thing to all men became extremely irritating. Anyway, as I said, I'm over it now…Denis had a wife and two mistresses, far too much competition…but I would like to become human. I feel…forgotten. I'd like someone to be able to think about me and know I was there, if that makes sense."

"I'll be honest," said the Shaman, "I couldn't say. Not my area of expertise. I was never married. I spent most of my life sick, in bed."

"Oh, that doesn't sound much fun."

"It wasn't but that's how you know you're meant to become a Shaman. Well, it's one of the ways. The spirits torment you until you give in. Then you die 'the little death,' they rebuild your body and after that, you can communicate with them. That's it in a nutshell."

"I barely understand a word you are saying," confessed Marie-Gabrielle. "That's the crux of my problem. You were in the real world, the one I'm trying to peer into. I'm in the spirit world, or a sort of spirit world, peering out."

"No, no, no," protested the Shaman. "This is not the spirits' world. This is a much friendlier, lighter, brighter place. The spirits' world is very real, in the three-dimensional sense. Its problem is that there are at least six dimensions and some of those are not to be entertained by anything made of flesh and blood. I think your world has been imagination's world. Sadly, in your case, fevered imagination's world but if it hadn't been so febrile I suggest you'd never have found the energy to prise yourself away from the surfaces you were drawn and printed on. It might not be the beginning you'd have liked but it certainly won't have lacked for utilisable energy."

"What a strange idea," said Marie-Gabrielle, "I'd never have thought of it but I'm almost certain you're right. It appears, therefore, that I'm Onan's daughter!"

The Shaman roared with laughter and the chameleon fairly danced in fury. "Will you be quiet!" it hissed, "you're scaring my notes!"

"Oh shush yourself," said Marie-Gabrielle, "kindly recall who showed you how to get off that rock and better yourself in a library."

The chameleon flushed through a range of colours, pulled the book up around its ears and carried on reading, as though nothing had happened at all.

The Shaman sighed. "You know," he said, sadly, "you are all living a very happy life here. It might not seem so to you, thinking the way you are but being tethered to Mother Earth has serious downsides."

Marie-Gabrielle opened her mouth to speak but the Shaman held up his hand in a 'let me finish' way.

"You see, there are problems such as illness – I know a lot about that – hunger, that too, not to mention fear and anxiety. That's just four off the top of the pack."

"I hear all that," Marie-Gabrielle said impatiently, "but you try being at the whim of sadists, masochists, bondage fanatics, rubber fetishists and all the other niche employment opportunities."

"Not much call for those in 17th Century Siberia," agreed the Shaman, drily. "I've some catching up to do."

"Come to the secret room, someday, we can offer crash courses on sexual peccadilloes, past, present and future. There again, better not come, some of the ladies are quite cross."

"I'm rather old," said the Shaman, "better not, on that score, too!

"But I am serious about the real world. If Earth Magic decides to help you and I'm sure it will, you'll find it a very bumpy ride. You won't be able to control things. One minute you'll be real and the next minute you won't be. You might be able to influence matters a bit but I wouldn't count on it. I think Earth Magic will look after you, probably send you some help but the only way I can put this is that it will be like a dream – but the dream will be real, which is going to produce some very unpleasant interludes."

"You're not selling it," said Marie-Gabrielle "but Nounou says I'm a very determined, wilful girl and always get my own way."

"You don't see, do you?" the Shaman said gently. "And who is Nounou?"

"Nounou is my most precious person in the whole…whole…wherever we are. I'm taking her with me wherever I go, because I love her frantically and she's looked after me since I was small. She's called Marie-Claire and is very old, at least 50, so I have to be very gentle with her. No-one and nothing gets to hurt her!"

"Oh, merciful whatevers!" groaned the Shaman. "This is what I'm talking about. People could get hurt! It happens!"

"Not in my world," retorted Marie-Gabrielle.

The Shaman groaned again – "I see what Marie-Claire meant. You are – very 'determined.'

"I am," said Marie-Gabrielle proudly. "Now, are you going to help me?"

The Shaman sighed.

"Of course I am. You showed me how to get off this page, how could I not help you? I'll find a place to talk to Earth Magic but don't sit there expecting an answer. If it decides to help, things will begin to happen. I say again – you may not like them but once it starts, there'll be no turning back. I'll try to keep an eye on you, as far as is possible from this sort of place. By the way, am I right to sense that there are more of 'me', elsewhere ?"

"You are, it's called being 'editionised', which means there are as many of you as the printer printed." The Shaman looked perplexed. "Don't worry, you'll work it out but it means that you don't have to stay here in this freak's library, if you don't want to."

"I'll work on that," said the Shaman. "But I will try to look out for you all. There may be things I can do from time to time."

"Not 'all', just Nounou and I."

"Oh no," the Shaman shook his head. "There will be quite a few of you, in the end. That's how it will work. But can I make one last plea?"

"If you must."

"Don't do it!"

"Hmph!" said Marie-Gabrielle, "now tell me about Earth Magic, please."

"I want you to imagine an apple," said the Shaman, who knew he had met his match, "a big, delicious apple. An Adam and Eve one, with a big bite out of it!"

Marie-Gabrielle imagined but the taste of an apple was not something two-dimensionality allowed for. Maybe that wouldn't be important. So she nodded.

"Now although it's delicious, it's actually spun from tiny spider webs, from its very insides to its very outsides. These webs don't just lie one on top of the other, they're all interwoven by busy, busy spiders. Imagine all the junctions and connections, all the possible routes the spiders can travel by, if they wanted to! Expand the apple, it's at least as big as the planet, with all the atmosphere, the breath, that surrounds it. That is Earth Magic and it's both very simple and very complex at the same time. It's simple because it's all there is and complex because it's everything that is. Don't make the mistake of saying you understand, because you don't and neither do I. But Earth Magic does, it actually understands how it works. It knows about every living element of itself."

Marie-Gabrielle suddenly felt very shy. She looked at her invisible toes and wiggled them.

"Does Earth Magic know I'm like this, visible but invisible?"

"Of course it does."

She was about to ask more but was interrupted by the crashing of iron-shod hooves and wheels on the cobbled yard of the Manor."

"What under the all-seeing, all-knowing is that?" gasped the Shaman, who had totally forgotten about unexpected noises, during his long years on the page.

"Don't fret! That's his 'Dis-Grace's' four-in-hand coach being driven into the yard. For some reason and it won't be good, he must have an early start. Probably better if we all slip back into our books. We're not a secret that wants to be known!"

"How do I do that?" cried the Shaman, still shaken by the noise.

"Be calm. Just think yourself back onto the page, the way I showed you how to think yourself off. Nothing to it," I promise.

"The Shaman glided back, his coat of many symbols, thick with embroidered runes, slung with metal discs and incised bones, slipping easily into the perfect outline of his absent silhouette.

Marie-Gabrielle is being scolded. She doesn't mind. If her old nurse was not scolding her something would be terribly wrong.

"Why do you choose here, cherie? This is a terrible place, in a terrible land and that man is a monster. No good can happen here!"

Marie-Gabrielle pecks her nanny on the cheek affectionately. "This is the place, the country, even the man! And yes, he is a monster but I know this is where we escape. This is where we will find help. We cannot escape without help. It will find us here – elsewhere, we would be alone. And besides, this morning I began the avalanche. I set one little stone rolling and that stone will bring down a mountain…"

"On our heads, you miscreant child!" cried Marie-Claire, hugging her ward as closely as two-dimensions permit, which is as closely as the artist's drawing allows…

"Which is why you must sleep, Nounou. When you wake you worry so. Stay here in your chair, here you are safe." Marie-Gabrielle firmly believed this was so. The Shaman's warnings had swept through her mind, encountering all her pre-conceived certainties – and that had been the end of such cautions. How could those marvellously solid beings not enjoy a better existence than this floating, nebulous state of two dimensions? It was unthinkable. Therefore, she wouldn't think it.

"I am going for my bath," she declared regally.

"Whoever heard of a bath in a book!" snorted Marie-Claire. "You are a very strange girl. You always have been. Wilful and strange. You will bring that mountain down upon our dreaming heads, wicked one!"

"The beauty of the books," declaimed Marie-Gabrielle, "is that in a large library, there is everything one might want, ever. I have found the perfect bath and I am off to enjoy it. The fire is stoked and cosy, back to your dreams, you naughty Nounou." And with that, she skipped away towards the door. "After my bath, I may visit cannibals in Afrique."

"They will eat you!"

"Not if I eat them first, they won't."

Safe in his folio, the Shaman listened to the muting clatter of the departing coach and team. He remembered now, all the sounds of the world, from the winds across the taiga to the mewling of the newly born. He remembered touch, taste and smell. He remembered the beautiful and the foul. He had, despairingly, sought the freedom he had tasted only short hours ago all his life and it had consistently eluded him. He pondered the irony that the child who had brought it to him, viewed it as no more than a casual gift, worth less than a magician's sleight-of-hand. And that she, who had uncovered such a secret, yearned only to belong to the world of the grounded, tethered to the surface of the earth, no more than another ox yoked to the plough.

He had promised to help her, to help her gain the gift that would be no gift. Access to the real world. What, however, was real? That was the question. Was this Manor, with its squalid tenant, real? Did it have form in the real world? Or did it belong in those pornographic pages she had, eventually and unwillingly, described? Did the two blend into one, each taking a little from the other? Somewhere lay a shimmering line that divided real from unreal but for most of us that line was inscribed 'death', the all too real end of every life. But what then, beyond that line? Was it pure chance that, preserved on these pages, he had this floating world existence? Were others fallen into a void of non-being, or did they join some common communion unknown to him? Was he the lucky one, or the cursed?

Perhaps these were the enquiries of a fool. When he lived in that frozen land he knew what was real and there was no escape from it. There he had had no pages to slip between, no place of safety, where he could lie nursing a golden secret. He recalled the days of his dying and they had been arduous. Better than many, worse than some. How could she want that world, when she had this?

Only this morning he had described the apple of connections that made up Earth Magic. Within that labyrinthine construct, every possibility had its place. Either he believed that, or he did not. If he did believe it, he had no right to stand in the way of her choices. Also, he had promised her help.

In his coach the Archbishop tore at a freshly-roasted chicken with fat, be-ringed fingers. His lips, loose and indulgent, shone with grease. He was the very picture of insatiable greed and that is how his secretary, curate and artist was committing him to paper. Despite the lurching of the carriage he had wedged himself in an upholstered crevice and was producing passable aide-memoires for the drawings he would later work up in his garret of a studio. He was the author-designate of an uncensored and lavishly illustrated account of his employer's latest enterprise – a reformatory for young ladies who had fallen from the grace of the church, by a lamentable collapse of their previously high moral standard. It was to be the latest of a long line of such publications.

There was little love lost between the two but the Archbishop was in need of an artist and this artist was a committed voyeur, hungry to record his preferred subject matter. Unlovely couple as they were, each had discovered that he had a catalytic effect upon the other. When the Archbishop believed he had been daring in his undertaking the curate belittled his designs and suggested more outrageous scenarios, with the result that the other inevitably vowed to exceed all expectations. As a result of this indecent competitiveness they were constructing such a tale of sadism and misogyny that, if it was ever finished, it would undoubtedly become a classic of the genre. Today was the day that the Archbishop was 'opening the board' by extending an invitation to an old rival, an invitation that was to have fatal consequences – though those lay many years in the future. Such was the spiders' apple. It contained each and every possibility, good and bad.

This outrageous and ill-assorted couple were headed for a small estuary, some four hours distant. It was there that the Archbishop had arranged for a lady of his acquaintance, from the continent, to come ashore and join their humble menage. This woman, 'of peculiar and particular tastes', whom he had featured in many of his most successful books, had recently become something of a scandal-in-waiting in her own country and His Grace's invitation had arrived opportunely on her desk. With the connivance of 'People in High Places,' she would arrive on the noon tide, with little more baggage than a change of linen and a bar of gold to speed her on her way. It was in his more comely youth, many years distant, that the Archbishop and the lady had first met, under criminal circumstances. Subsequently, and largely to do with the exigencies of his publishing business they had maintained a correspondence, often enlivened for her delectation, by sketches from the artist's brush.

That they shared similar tastes was in no doubt but if truth be told, the Archbishop was somewhat overawed by his acquaintance's ruthlessness. Nevertheless, such reservations as he held he determined to ignore. After all, she would be his guest, at his latest enterprise, on his territory. She would be merely a physical addition to the household, rather than one licensed by art. All his niggling doubts he subsumed as unworthy and he contented himself with the demolition of the second chicken, as the carriage began the long descent towards the still-distant dock.

Had Marie-Gabrielle known of this assignation she might well have reconsidered her plans. A very dark cloud was headed towards the Manor, one she had never encountered, except as printer's ink. She had read many of the manuscripts that she and Nounou inhabited, from beginning to end and had pooh-poohed their vivid exaggerations. She little realised that those exaggerations were about to realise their physical form, courtesy of this feral guest

Therefore, carefree and relaxed, she was luxuriating in a magnificent malachite bath, once the property of Catherine the Great of Russia. She had perfumed the toasty-warm water with rare oriental scents and was trying to imagine herself as a great empress. What would be her very first command?

The Shaman couldn't settle in his folio. Such a short burst of freedom had been tantalising. Even the clatter of the outside world, now he had remembered its clamour, was seductive. He was already longing to slip beyond the boundaries of the library. Invisible, he could float, he could fly. Even if he sensed no access to those Higher

Realms he had so assiduously pursued all his short life, at least that floating form she had taught him, hung tantalisingly somewhere between the two. He was anxious to examine precisely how those parameters now looked. Also, he had a promise to keep, to the determined young lady.

Using her formula he slipped from the book and the shelf. For a while he roamed the stacks and found much to fascinate and intrigue him. Here was a book on 'Catherine, Empress of all the Russias.' He snorted with derision. 'What were Russians! Vile Cossacks more like' – he was Yakut! Then he paused to listen. He was sure he heard the sound of splashing. How could that be?

He was about to slide through a gaping crack in the window frame, when he remembered the secret room. Wouldn't it be wise to apprise himself of its contents? His young saviour counted herself as one of its actors and it would be sensible to see for himself what precisely she was fleeing from. He sailed easily through one of the many gaps and found himself facing a row of determined and initially hostile young ladies. An hour later and his education had been upgraded to the 21st century and beyond. Now he could understand why she eager to avoid the future. He fled, on a tide of fulsome apology for his sex's proclivities and expressing his determination to do what he could to halt that coming tsunami.

Once outside again, he wiped his brow – metaphorically – and considered what he must do. Some act of gallantry was called for and he decided to launch himself on a search for Earth Magic. True enough, Earth Magic pervaded all territories but some places were more magical than others, more certain conduits to the source than wishes casually cast upon the breeze would be. With that in mind he floated free of the window and rose up to the chimney pots that topped the mossy old roof. For a while he absorbed the daily clamour of the yard, the coming and going of livestock, the casual ribaldry of farmhands. People were familiar to him. They were much the same, it seemed, the world over. Where then, lay the oddity of this place? Was the secret book-room the beginning and end of the Archbishop's salacious empire, or was something more sinister concealed here?

He spent an eye-opening hour touring the Manor, after which he was in no doubt that grievous enterprise was underway in this very building. Somehow the world of two-dimensions and three had become entangled at this very node. The result was a local calamity but more seriously, a flaw in the fabric of the matrix of the whole, an infection in need of cauterisation. The Shaman knew precisely where his duty lay. He also knew that he owed his young friend a passport away from this catastrophe in the making.

He flew high. He rose until the Manor was a mere gathering of colours below. So this was flight! All those years spent ingesting the distillates of poisonous mushrooms, his weeks of starvation, of self-mutilation, all to achieve a poor imitation of this glorious freedom. How strange that one form of existence grants, so casually, the cravings of another. For the moment he had no need of the senses that Marie-Gabrielle longed for, real sight, sound, touch and taste. He had had those but he had never had this. He soared and circled for a while, for the sheer joy of it. Then he recalled that he had set himself a task.

There was a certain 'confusion' of the air he was looking for. It would be seen as a shimmering light, as if water vapours momentarily grouped and swirled before miraculously evaporating, only to shimmer and swirl again, then again. He had studied these places from his homelands, from the high places in the mountains that overlooked the plain. Long ago he had decided that they were vortices through which the great plateau of the earth breathed. Were a man to probe such he might discover a route to the levels of the world. The first level would be Hell, or such a hell as we might imagine. Below that, a place of waters but below that his imagination failed him. He had striven for further insight, to bring a little knowledge to his tribe's world but all he had ever found were the places of confused airs. The rest had been mere chaos, not even the way to Hell had been open – at least none that had a road back.

He circled and he found what he sought. Ridiculously, it lay hard by the Manor and he marvelled at such coincidence.

He floated down to the small wood and glided through it. It lay, drawn in upon itself, pure silence sleeping, if such a thing was possible. Lines of strength lay along the stream, along the great Hedge that rustled its leaves warily, even at his small presence. This place was watchful, even in sleep. From an ancient knoll – he sensed bones lay within – he could see the lie of the land. He was looking for some conduit to power, somewhere he could lie and let his message about the Earth Daughter trickle, like a tiny rill of water, to the heart of this place.

He considered the land carefully until he discovered a dell where bees rose and fell in their hundreds, each one a note in the harmony of the hive, each note forming the purpose of the whole. He was no obstacle to them, nor they to him. He found a fissure in a clay bank and within that a bulwarking of quartz. Though the clay ended there the rift ran on, down through the rock and deep underground. This was the place to lodge his message, in the perfect dark, where his eyes could now see as clearly as they did by daylight.

Insofar as he could, he pressed his head against a perfect crystal and wrote in it the story of a girl, born in a vivid scrawling of ochre, a plaything for desperate and despairing men, a girl who had raised herself to form and sensibility on that tide of abuse and now requested only her commonplace right of matter, of flesh, bone and blood within the world. She sought the right to pursue dignity, claimed it as a child of the Earth. 'Grant her a simple birthing to the lot of Everyman,' he prayed.

He lay there until he felt the Great Mind sigh far beneath him and felt its pulse probing for the place where a tiny flaw, no larger than pinprick, had once and that long ago, deformed the matrix. He could go now but for a time, he lay there among the quartz, reviewing the bones of his own, so-distant, life and death.

He had died alone, wondering what was truth and what was lies. In the moment of his dying he had realised that truth and lies were just aspects of the one thing, the consciousness of the whole, of that great wheeling band of pinpricked light that whorled overhead. There was nothing else, only 'the whole.' And then he had died, until some form of him was roused, centuries later, by a naive young girl. How strange. He was done with questions, which meant he was done with answers, too.

He slipped away, back into the world and for a moment or two he hung above the wood, riding on its breath, not thinking just drifting. He wondered whether he should just drift through the world alone, forever but the infinity of the prospect was daunting and he returned to the library, where the folio encased him, once again, like a glove.

Had he wished, had he even thought of it, he could have sought out the Archbishop's coach and four, where it stood alone, above the quayside of a provincial port.

On the high tide and still under sail, a cross-channel lugger is approaching the dock. For a little while she sails with the wind, a tiny white wave at her bow. Finally the mate bellows an order and canvas is struck. The ship loses way and with just a solitary jib-sail left to catch the breeze, glides serenely towards the harbour wall. Here harbourmen wait patiently for the leading lines to be thrown ashore. The light ropes fly through the air and are caught. Behind come the hawsers, dipping to the water, then rising inexorably to be made fast to the dockside bollards. Now the final business of securing the little craft tightly to its wharf is underway. That last, loose-flapping jib rattles down the fore-stay and the crew hurry to gather-up canvas before it strikes water. A moment's silence, until the hollow echoes from mauls reverberate around the dockside, as they hammer out the wedges that secure the holds.

Through this choreography of chaos strides the figure of a woman, dressed all in black. She strikes a straight path and all make way for her. She carries a small piece of luggage and no servant attends her. She strides up the boards of the companion way and speaks to no-one. If she made farewells they were performed below decks, for once upon the cobbles of the dockside she neither pauses for any backwards glance, or to orientate herself in any way. She walks stiffly, as if walking was an impediment and irritation, to the coach. The guard has scrambled from the box and servilely opens the door. He performs some imitation of a bow and she steps lightly into the interior, her step up and into the darkness being no cousin of her stiff-legged march from the dockside. Some contradiction exists here but not one that proposes its own solution. With the sharp "clack" of the door shutting behind her, a number of things occur, almost simultaneously, though life is not quite so ordered.

Marie-Gabrielle is arising from her imaginary bath, amid warm steam and with her hands resting lightly on the polished malachite. Of a sudden she feels the distant jerking of horses, as if she was among them and harnessed to some weight that was too great to bear. She looks up, from her place within the team and a small, dark cloud scuds briefly across the face of the sun. "How very odd," she says to herself and then falls to towelling herself dry, vigorously.

Within his folio, where he felt at peace, after his journey to the wood and the cleft within the quartz, the Shaman's mind drags him back to an image he saw in the secret room. It was not an image he had imagined or ever seen, before the moment it was revealed. Now, he knows, it is imprinted within his mind forever. He wishes it were not so but it is. Somehow he has become complicit with its existence. The thought darkens his mind. He broods on the nature of impressions, their perfidious ability to infiltrate and subvert what has been, prior to their incursion, one's peaceful accommodation with the condition of the world.

You can never know which impression will unsettle you. As a child he had witnessed the aftermath of village feuds, which were brief but bloody. Even now he could recall them in detail, yet remain at peace and that was how it had always been. Yet today he had been taken by surprise. He realised that, in many ways, he was a mere innocent, at sail on seas so treacherous they could threaten his very sanity.

Elsewhere, Punch has just stared into the face of a bee-slain man. It was thick with the still jerking bodies of bees and the pulsing remnants of their stings. Barely human, in purple and brown. Swollen, still swelling visibly, even after death. He had shaken his head, walked away but that particular shade of purple would remain forever in his mind. It had looked cold, cold as ancient porphyry.

Marie-Claire was the gentlest and most tolerant of women, which is why Marie-Gabrielle was so determined to protect her. That she loved her madly, with all her passionate, wilful nature, was also true. Therefore the step she was intent on taking, that of freeing them both into the arms of the real world, seemed singularly ill-judged, even reckless, given the nature of the book she was to launch them from. What she couldn't really admit, because it seemed so selfish, was that this was one of the few books in which she and Marie-Claire could be found together at a moment she judged ripe, one at which transformation could take place.

That such a transformation would occur was little more than pure guesswork and intuition. What else did she have to go on, however? Translating two people from two-dimensions to three, instantaneously, is not a widely reported phenomenon. She knew, she had scoured the literature in search of reports. The fact was, it had never been done. That it could be done, nevertheless, was self-evident. How else did engineers and architects realise their projects? They translated them from two dimensions to three. Granted, they worked in inert, seemingly lifeless materials… but those were exactly what she and Marie-Claire were at present, inert materials on a page!

The realisation of imagined projects was the story of man's tenure upon the earth. How else had she, Marie-Gabrielle, been awakened in the first place if it was not by the sheer weighty demand that she should do so, a demand made by millions of frustrated minds that imagined her living limbs, rather than the inert drawings of them? That was what had awakened her, Onan's child and that was the energy she intended to utilise for her next step forward.

But at this moment, Marie-Claire would have none of it.

"This is a bad place, petite mademoiselle. It is evil, I have heard, I have seen! No good can happen in this sewer. Why can we not escape from nice Monsieur Diderot's library? You loved him…non, don't deny it. I knew!"

"I thought you didn't like Denis, Nounou?" Marie-Gabrielle said, knowing full well that she was currently out of her depth and struggling. This was not a conversation she could win.

"Like – not-like, pooh! Monsieur Diderot may be no saint but he is the Archangel himself compared to this monster who titles himself 'Archbishop'. Archbishop, indeed! He is gutter trash! Non – the very gutters would spit him back. We shall come to great harm here!"

"Stop, Nounou, please stop! Have I not brought us this far? Trust me, this is the place. I know it and I am laying our path." 'If only I was,' she thought desperately. "Please, close your eyes, sleep, in the way I have shown you. When all is ready I shall carry you over, then, pff! we shall have arrived!"

"Pff, indeed! Sleep and leave petite mademoiselle alone? Never!"

Marie-Gabrielle hugged her as tightly as two dimensions permit and left it at that. There was no winning this particular battle.

What she really wished was that she was as confident as she tried to sound. She was attempting a manoeuvre for which there was no precedent. She had never heard of anyone 'crossing over,' if that's what it could be called. Her faith was based entirely on her own transformation from graffiti and print into a 'ghost,' one that now claimed self-determination. Her theory was that if enough minds were concentrated upon an image that image could become an actuality. The very naivety of the notion embarrassed her but she had some proof of it in her own existence. If she could only force an image into the real world she believed she could then subvert the story and make good their escape. It was all a question of how. If Earth Magic would help her, if Earth Magic even existed, then perhaps it would be possible?

The week that had just ended had been a bad one for Marie-Gabrielle. To begin with she had been forced to revise her plan. On re-reading the torrid story she had selected as an excellent point of departure, she had seen, immediately, that it was not a good jumping-off point at all. The very fact that the story already had a conclusion made her plan ridiculous. She and Marie-Claire might contrive to slip out of the tale but they would almost inevitably be dragged back into it. It was such an obvious point that she spent a whole day snarling at herself.

It quickly became obvious, she needed a work-in-progress. Library shelves, even secret ones, were no place to find one of those. At that she began to think and prowl. Along corridors, through keyholes, into secret rooms, down dripping cellar stairs to barrel-vaulted dungeons, then, in rapid flight, to attic rooms and finally, a makeshift artist's studio. There, on the unoccupied desk, was the work-in-progress she had been seeking. Here, in two dimensions, was the three dimensional world she recognised, this actual Manor where, seemingly, all players in the drama co-existed.

What troubled her was the artist's depraved imagination, the inevitable inclusion of that odious duo, Archbishop and curate in every scene and what she could infer about the outcome of the story. Also, there was this black malignancy on the paper, the woman from the boat, here dressed in the habit of a holy nun. She and Marie-Gabrielle had crossed paths before. This was yet another blasphemy and not one that must come to Marie-Claire's ears or eyes. Nevertheless, this was the springboard she sought. She knew that with a conviction and certainty she had never felt before. There again, she had never felt this scared before.

The imagination that animated these sketches was diseased. There was power here for certain but to tie oneself to it, with the intention of subverting it at some crucial moment, was an act beyond faith and one verging on folly. And to risk another's life…? For that she had no words but she had decided. Her mind was made up.

She went in search of the Shaman.

She found him in his folio, deep in thought but the moment he saw her, hovering, he smiled and slipped nimbly away from his outline.

"My little deliverer," he said, "what a pleasure to see you again."

"I have to get out of here," said Marie-Gabrielle, without further preamble. "We, Nounou and I, have to get out of here – soon!" Then she explained what she had found in the artist-curate's studio. "With help I can manipulate it," she explained, eagerness itself.

"Whose help would that be?" asked the Shaman, pointedly.

"Why, Earth Magic's, of course!" said Marie-Gabrielle with some exasperation. "Please tell me, you have told it?"

"I have done my very best," the Shaman said gently "but you remember the apple of spider's threads?"

"Of course."

"With affection and respect, you are but one pinprick somewhere deep within that matrix. When the time is ripe, perhaps today, perhaps within a week, perhaps not for thousands of years, your fate will be affected."

"Now!" cried Marie-Gabrielle, "it has to be now!"

"If Earth Magic wills it to be now, then it will begin as you wish. If it does not, then you will wait, here. Perhaps, from time to time, with me? I'm sure we have plenty to talk about."

"Oh!!" Marie-Gabrielle wailed, spinning round in a circle that accelerated rapidly to a blur. After a while she began to she slow down and when she stopped she said meekly – "what is the point of being in this world, if I am not of it?"

"Do you realise," said the Shaman, not entirely wisely, "that that is precisely the aim of most religions…at least, among their ascetic priesthoods?"

"What is?"

"To be in the world but not of it."

"Phooey!"

"Phooey or not, it's true. What they mean is that they should resist being caught up and compromised by worldly matters. Not to be hampered and side-tracked by desire, envy, those sorts of things."

Marie-Gabrielle pondered for a while. Eventually she asked – "what did you think of the world when you lived in it?"

The Shaman laughed ruefully – "I thought I'd rather be somewhere else, like here, where you can't be hurt, made miserable, experience hunger, thirst, fear, pain, all those sorts of things that embodied beings are subject to."

"But I already have those problems," explained Marie-Gabrielle. "The sort of books I'm in rather dwell on such things. It's very tedious when you wake-up in the middle of them."

"I'm sure it must be," said the Shaman, blushing.

"What's the matter?" asked Marie-Gabrielle. "You've gone a very funny colour."

"Yes, I'm sure I have. I took a trip to your secret room, only the other day and the young ladies gave me a guided tour. I had a lot to learn in half-an-hour and I'm not sure I'm better off because of it. So I sympathise. All I can say is that it's a good job you're all innocent of the real world in there. If you weren't you'd probably be feeling worse still. You see those books are really all about power and lust. A lot of their activities cater to people with serious illnesses of the soul. I do see why you want to leave but you won't be able to do it without Earth Magic's help. The power to move between dimensions is not available to the people trapped in them. I know what I'm talking about for once…" the Shaman trailed off.

"How do you know?" she demanded.

"Because, as I think I've already told you, I spent all my life trying to do just that – I was supposed to intervene, on behalf of my people, with the Spirit World. Some of them were very sick and I wanted to help them. I would have tried anything. But the old woman who taught me was able to tell me quite a lot about herbs, teeth and broken bones but when it came to Spirits, she fell back on toadstool broth and burning moss."

"Urghh!"

"Exactly. You drank one and inhaled the other. As a result you got terribly sick and had either wonderful visions or awful ones. You didn't get to choose. Sometimes you felt as if the answers were all there for the taking but when you crawled back to life, what had seemed wonderful was not. You thought you'd brought a cure back with you, or you'd intervened with a spirit but you hadn't. Of course, you had to lie about that. You see, you were the only hope people had. Sometimes they even got better, not because you'd done anything, they just did. The rest of the time, they died and you had to make up lies about why. As a result, half the people thought you were a powerful magician and the other half thought you were a liar. I was quite glad when it was time to die. I got very melancholy about not really knowing anything useful."

"But what's going to happen to Nounou and I? Look, just think again about my latest plan. I'm still working on some details but I know you'll approve, once you really understand."

The Shaman listened again, patiently.

"No! I don't approve at all!" he said. "Maybe, if you get a message from Earth Magic, you can risk such a gamble. Actually, it won't be your choice. Once Earth Magic intervenes it's a bit like finding yourself on horseback. Suddenly you find you're high up, the next second you're moving and the second after that, you're moving very quickly."

"I thought you never contacted any Spirits, well not really contacted?"

"Mm, you're mixing two things up. Earth Magic is not a Spirit. Earth Magic is everything there is. It's…what?…I suppose we could call it Life. Life is growing on this earth. I don't know if it grows anywhere else. I don't know why it grows here but it does. I know there's more than just our plot of earth and I'm not sure those other places are necessarily life-friendly.

"I've come to believe and this is pure guesswork, that Life is something like mould on cheese and harness leather. It shouldn't be there but it is. Anyway, you don't want to know about my ideas on that. But I do feel you can intervene with Life, at least I've reason to think you can. If you couldn't, things wouldn't be very slowly sorting themselves out for the better. Though there is still so much wrong, there is very slightly more that is right. At least, I believe that when I'm not melancholy. So if you ask Life, very politely, to look at a problem that's arisen, I think it sometimes finds a way to put it right. It's not always a straightforward way and sometimes other things get broken. I do believe, however, that it tries."

He paused and suddenly seemed a little hesitant, even anxious. "I don't know. I did ask, on your behalf and perhaps it heard. I'm actually scared it did hear and you're going to be whirled away into something you don't like half as much as you thought you would. Do you understand me, now?"

The Shaman looked particularly downcast and Marie-Gabrielle felt sad to be the cause of that.

"I understand," she sighed. "Things aren't always simple. So thank you for asking.

I shall just have to look for signs and take our chances. I'm determined to get us out of here."

"I am beginning to understand why," he said. "The young ladies rather opened my eyes, though they didn't seem to have your ambition to cross over to the 'real' world."

"I really have been around a long time, " said Marie-Gabrielle. "Many of the others just exist in one book and they haven't really understood about being 'incorporated ideals', or your 'icons'. They've not felt this sense of despair I have every time today repeats every other day that went before. Maybe they will, in time. Nounou and I are leaving and that's final."

"Then let's talk about something else but something I think you'll find relevant, or at least interesting," said the Shaman.

"And that would be?"

"The future. You remember you told me how difficult, noisy and foggy it was?"

"That's how it was for me."

"Me too but I found I could ignore a lot of the distractions, because I found some silvery threads. They floated in a pattern I thought I knew. I thought really hard about it and I had to conclude that it was the weave of Earth Magic, spinning a matrix for the future to fit into."

"Was I there?"

"No-one was there. That's why I became sure it was the future. But it wasn't empty, parts of it glowed, as if a door had been opened and the light had fallen through into a new room. The threads that ran through those parts were thicker and stronger looking. Did you notice them?"

Marie-Gabrielle tried to remember.

"This sounds silly but it's quite hard to recall. First of all I was scared. Then I had no idea what I was looking for. Also I kept feeling that the fog was nudging me and not exactly in a helpful way. All that got added to the 'scared' bit, so I ran back here as fast as I could. I must have sounded very boastful before. The fact is, 'scared,' just about covers it all."

"That's very honest and I understand why you'd feel that way. You may be very old, I don't doubt that story for one second but you've been handicapped by having to live the same few sensual years, over and over and over. That means you've never lived out a whole life, so you don't really know about futures, or pasts, just the same few years. You've been obliged to live a loop. Then you take all that trouble to wake up and you're as trapped as a bee in amber…"

"I'm very pleased you didn't say 'fly', or 'spider' just then," said Marie-Gabrielle. "A nice, stripy, furry bee is fine. A 'fly' would have been rude, a 'spider' out of the question! You just had a narrow escape."

"A perilous moment," agreed the Shaman. "What I'm working round to, though, is that I think you need to start imagining a very solid future for you both. You have to imagine that one of those rooms, with brighter lights and thicker threads, is your room. You start putting ideas and people in that room. What do you want, what do you need from the future? You're going to use the future. It's going to free you from your block of amber and pull you into the real world. Now, think! What do you really want to come true? Think of really solid things and I don't mean garden spades, or coronation jewels."

Marie-Gabrielle seized the idea and began to think furiously. Eventually she burst out – "I know what it is! I've got a really solid idea!"

"Excellent, are you going to tell me?"

"Yes, yes, I am! I'm going to imagine a lovely, gentle husband for Nounou. Then I want a brother and sister, for me. And as a real fantasy wish, I want a strong, quiet stranger, from a distant land, for my husband! How will that do?"

The Shaman smiled – "that's wonderful! You're wishing for a family. That's the strongest set of ties we humans can have. Really give some time to imagining this and you'll know when you've got it right."

"How will I know?"

"You'll be able to see them, clearly."

Marie-Gabrielle was so excited she skipped away to start her imaginings immediately. She had her own secret place, a dusty old room above the library. It had no door, just a hatch in the floor. There must have been a ladder at one time but that seemed to have vanished. For a two-dimensional girl, none of this was a problem. She slipped through the cracks and perched herself on an ancient stool that had a perfect view of the courtyard through the solitary window.

There were very old books in this room, far older than the volumes in the stacks below. Most seemed to have been hand-written but beautifully hand-written in different coloured inks, with ornamental borders. She couldn't read any of them, which was perplexing because language wasn't any barrier downstairs. There she could open any book and the language simply flowed into her mind. That was why the chameleon could read the books on insect morphology and why the Shaman, who had been quite illiterate when he was flesh and blood, could now read and converse with the two-dimensional world in any language at all. The seamless marvel of that was so absolute, that the wonder of it hadn't yet crossed his mind. So why such a powerful magic wouldn't work in the garret perplexed her. Occasionally she wondered if that made the room a safer space, or a more dangerous one. She could never decide.

Wriggling herself into what she thought would be a comfortable shape, when she had flesh and blood, was tricky on a stool but she tried. Only then did she pick up a favoured volume, one that had very few words but a great deal of beautiful ornament. These were largely vines and creepers that rolled and curled all over the pages, enclosing words and even solitary letters, making the whole into a wonderful, if inexplicable fairy story. 'But that,' Marie-Gabrielle thought to herself, 'is the perfect way to start my imagining.'

As she traced the path of the vines with her finger, she found that she was uncovering suggestions that tiny animals were there, hidden below leaves, behind fruits, or peeping shyly from behind the criss-crossings of branches. Here was a wet nose, there – in the darkness of a clump of blackberries – a pair of eyes, there was a tail vanishing behind that pruned stalk and she was certain there were paw marks in the dew that sparkled on the grass. The page was alive and yet she had never noticed that before. She looked up, to rest her eyes, to stare idly through the window and to reflect on what it all meant.

The courtyard bustled with the day's mundane activity. Women carried pails of water and jugs of milk from one building to another. A herdsman manoeuvred a cow and her new calf towards an open door in the stables. Lads carried firewood, or tried to look busy wielding brooms, whilst shying twigs and pebbles at their friends. It seemed an ordinary, English home farm, going about its business.

Just as Marie-Gabrielle was relaxing into its familiarity, a black-browed thug of a creature emerged from the buildings at far side of the yard. These were buildings without windows and only the one door. The effect was immediate. Even before he had commanded everyone's attention with three echoing, handclaps, all honest souls who had glimpsed his arrival were scurrying to safety through the nearest archway they could find. The sound of doors being hurled to, even bolted, sounded like the clacking of a bird-scarer's rattle, one slam rapidly following another. In seconds, that busy yard was deserted and silent.

The cause of this eclipse leered with grim satisfaction, then putting two fingers to his mouth gave a piercing whistle. Through the high double gates rattled a closed wagon, hauled by two heavy horses. The whistler indicated a circular approach, with a whirling motion of his hand. The driver nodded and having turned his cart across the yard, dismounted to urge the horses into a shuffling back-step that presented the rear of the wagon to the open door.

What happened next, Marie-Gabrielle could no longer see but she could hear.

The tailboard of the cart crashed against its chains. Someone issued an order – "get them moving." There was a faint blur of noise, as of muffled movement and finally, one sharp, high-pitched female cry, followed by the sound of what must have been a blow. In the wake of that, the heavy door was slammed shut.

The driver raised the tailgate, as if on any commonplace cart and led his horses away, iron-shod wheels and hooves ringing on the cobbles. As they made their exit, that was the signal for the courtyard to return to its commonplace, farmyard bustle. One by one, albeit chagrined and shamefaced, the domestics and labourers re-entered the yard.

Marie-Gabrielle was in no doubt about what she had just witnessed. Another group of unfortunates had entered the manor cellars. She knew what lay beneath that faceless block, with its solitary door and none of it was good. For a while she stared towards the horizon, seeing nothing but feeling, all over again, how imperative it was that she and Nounou take flight while they could. What she also felt was fresh horror at the idea her plan might fail.

When she returned to her book and slowly resumed tracing the vines out with her finger, she found that all the shy animals, peeping from the foliage, had vanished.

Rapidly she turned pages, one, two, three, four but she was slowing with every turn. When she finally re-focused her gaze she found she was staring at two blank sheets. Oversize pages had been folded inwards, to accommodate their extended width. Intrigued, she lifted the two inner leaves simultaneously.

She had opened a bird's eye panorama of a tangled piece of land. It was a virgin landscape, filled with trees, bushes, craggy mounts, low and higher hillocks, a swampy expanse and a flowing brook. The harder she stared, the more certain she became that the painting was a map, not a fantasy. Surrounding it all, at the top of the pages, was what must be a long and zig-zagging hedge. Even on paper it seemed a formidable barrier, while closer to her lap, on the lower margin, the land effectively dissolved, as if the map-maker was uncertain, or indifferent as to what lay there. The stream was the only constant. It ran out of the bottom of the page and for a second she thought she felt the chill of its water about her legs…which was a ridiculous notion.

The detail of the work was astounding and the bird's eye view was not fixed. As you moved your focus, so the view shifted with you. Here a tree tilts to the left, you can follow its trunk, steeply, to the ground. Move on and the same tree now inclines to the right and you can still allow your eyes to travel down its trunk. This was exceedingly strange.

Stranger still, however, was that if you stared at a particular spot it began to expand under your examination. Here's a hillock, a grassy knoll but with one side collapsed, cut away by the stream in the years before it meandered to the right, baulked, as it had been, by a huge crag of rock that underlay both clay and grass. Concentrate on the clay and the detail begins to expand. There are fissures in it and in the fissures there are stones and roots and here, in this root, is clutched the round head of… "Oh my," squeaked Marie-Gabrielle…the round head of a long thigh bone. This mound must have been a warrior's grave, once upon a time and here is evidence for it, the relics of the warrior himself. Her eyes could possibly wiggle into that hole but perhaps she won't, just yet.

She withdraws to a decent distance and starts to examine the winding paths that dissect the ancient woodland, instead. Here's a spot…that looks…familiar.? No, no, no, she's never been anywhere like this. Apart from the briefest of excursions, during her time with Denis and that cowardly trip into the future, she has rarely left the safety of libraries.

She leans against the bare poles of the stool back and returns her gaze to the cobbled court, which has become an innocent farmyard again. Idly, she follows the movements of random figures, still wondering about the book in her lap, the strangeness of the moving map. Then she remembers that she is here to think about the future, to forge a link that, with help, will pull them free of this snare.

A husband for Nounou is what she wants most of all, then a brother and sister for herself. Nounou's husband has to be very gentle, very strong too, someone who will protect her, whilst marvelling at what a wonderful person she is!

She thinks, very fiercely and in that split second of ferocious concentration, she has him and here he is, too! She's looking at the map, lying across her knees and he is there, walking one of those turning pathways through the knotted trees. He has a big hooked nose, set in a lean, sun-wrinkled face. He's carrying a long flintlock piece, a military weapon and he's dressed in… 'oh, this bad'…rags, absolute tatters. His red jacket is sun-bleached and falling apart. His pants…they're worthy of the secret book room! He has no shoes and his feet are black and horny. 'Oh no!' Nounou will be horrified. This is some renegade soldier, turned woodlander, living off the land and his wits. Then he turns up his face, as if to catch some glimpse of the eye that is watching him and he has the kindest, deepest, brown eyes she has ever seen. Beyond any doubt, this is Nounou's husband. Somehow she, Marie-Gabrielle, has to achieve the impossible and get him clean!

She tries to tell herself that this can't be so. She tears her eyes off the solitary, plodding figure, even slams the book shut but it's no use. Only one figure will come to her mind, now. He is as solid as a rock and she can feel the silver threads tightening across time and space. Something very strange is happening. She has found a husband for Nounou, a father for herself. She should be happy but instead, she is terrified – though not of him.

She is so frightened that she flees the garret and ignores the library. She tears her way back to the safe-book and page, the place where she demands Nounou remain. And, praise to some all-seeing power, there is Nounou, quietly sleeping, her knitting in her lap, always at the same stitch, the next loop never cast.

Relief suddenly, inexplicably, turns to rage. Without thinking she picks up the heavy glass paperweight from the table and hurls it through the bottle-glass pane of the tiny window. The shattering of glass is explosive in her ears, the pane flies outwards and that is the sound of falling shards.

It is all in her ears, for Nounou dozes on, undisturbed. She tiptoes to the window, feeling the chill influx of air, something she has never felt before. She looks out. There is the paperweight, broken into two, maybe more pieces. There are the shards of glass she heard fall. And she is breathing, not pretend breathing, something she does all the time in her mind but real breath is entering real lungs. She is feeling the thrill of cold air for the first time!

Then, just as quickly, she isn't. She is forcibly returned to her original place in the picture. The paperweight lies unbroken on the table. The window is whole. She is only breathing in her head, in her imagination. For a brief moment she finds she can't move. Hundreds of years of training frozen, she's rigid in a frame, an object once again.

'No!' she roars, silently. 'No-one does this to me!' She writhes convulsively, tears a huge hole in the picture, wrenches herself from the page. "No more floating, no more ghosts!" and she has seized the paperweight again. Seized and flung. The same satisfactory crash, the same aftermath of falling shards, the same chill air…the paperweight riven on the cobbles. In the distance she can hear clogs clattering and someone's hearty guffaw.

Whatever this Power is, it allows her the briefest moment but longer than before. Then she is back in her place. There is the paperweight, the pane is whole again and Nounou still slumbers.

She stands, then before risking another step, says – "I'm waking up."

For the third time she approaches the little table and picks up the weight. She has no intention of hurling it. She wants to feel the heft of it in her hand, to assess the texture and examine the intricate millefleurs design within the globe. She does so, turns the weight in her palm and admires the little coloured rods so artfully arranged to deceive the eye. Gently she restores it to its proper place and walks away.

"Oh my," she says delightedly, as she sits down, "I'm waking up! But how?"

She glances towards the paperweight. "I'm waking up," she tells it. "I'm sorry I threw you through the window. I won't do it again, I promise."

Marie-Claire is still peacefully asleep. She watches her fondly. Then her simple affection begins to tremble beneath a dreadful weight of responsibility, that eddies up from nowhere and envelops her. Somehow she has to extricate them from this place, break a dozen snares and chains, then tear a hole through the fabric of time and space.

She shrinks into her chair, gulping with anxiety. A small voice she can't silence begins to bleat – 'I want my papa!'- over and over again. "Where is the use of this?" she demands of the silence but the background wail of the lost child is an echo that reverberates. She screws her eyes shut, to lose herself in the darkness, to try to quiet the panic.

Unbidden, the figure of Nounou's ragged husband comes into sight. He is straightening up from a stooped position. He has been searching the hedge bottom and he holds something in his hands. "Those trousers!" she giggles, – to herself she is sure – but he reacts, to some simultaneous noise, with sharp glances cast left and right. Once again his eyes meet hers. There is the same kindness but outflanked, today, by exhaustion. 'There's your papa,' she tells the crying child, 'now you have one.'

Next week proved difficult. The promising beginnings of the paperweight and the brown woodland man seemed to be in abeyance. Marie-Gabrielle had to force herself to refrain from hurling the paperweight, just to shake things up. Things were exasperating.

She could no longer catch a glimpse of Nounou's husband. She could bring him to mind easily enough but he didn't move any more, as he had on the magical map. He was just a memory, a strong one to be sure but she craved movement, some indication to prove he was more than pure imagination.

The magical map in the book of vines and letters, had reverted to being an ordinary map. It no longer miniaturised, or magnified itself. There were no long bones in clay banks, no little creatures on paths. By the end of the week she was wondering if magic had left her world, or was it that her magical world was turning real? Either way, these were discomfiting thoughts and after entertaining them for ten unwholesome minutes she flew off in search of the Shaman, to see if he had some calming explanation. She scoured the library, peering into obscure volumes, even visiting the secret room – where the girls denied all knowledge of his whereabouts – until she was forced to conclude he had gone outside, into the real world. That raised the possibility that he might not be back for hours, days, weeks, months…ever!

"Gah!" she croaked in exasperation and in that instant, decided she would go for an imaginary bath in the malachite tub. It was only a whim but nevertheless, she hurled herself into it wholeheartedly.

She conjured up deep, warm water, admired the effect of the ripples over the malachite, then undressed and immersed herself almost up to her nose. And there she lay, perfectly content, until…someone, something, seemed to get into the bath with her. It was a big bath, there was definitely room for two but she hadn't issued any invitations. She'd also locked the door. Nevertheless, someone was sliding down into this water with her, because she was having to raise her head, so as not to drown.

"Hello?" she said, in a small voice.

There was a long silence but the water sort of wriggled, as if it was confused, or so it felt.

"Hello?" said an answering voice, "is somebody there?"

"Er, yes," said Marie-Gabrielle, "I'm here. I'm Marie-Gabrielle. I rather thought this was my bath. In fact, I'm sure it is. At least it was the last time I got in it."

"That's funny," replied the other voice. "I felt exactly the same way about my bath but now you seem to be in it, too. Anyway, pleased to meet you, I'm Evie and you say that you're Marie-Gabrielle?"

"That's right," agreed Marie-Gabrielle, cautiously. "The thing is, Evie, I can't see you but I can sort of feel you. Is there a reason for that?"

There was a bit of a pause.

"Probably," said Evie, "there's usually a reason for everything. I've got exactly the same problem at my end, I can't see anyone but I can feel something. How worried should we be?"

"I don't know," said Marie-Gabrielle, "we're probably over the worried bit by now but something very odd is going on."

"Let's agree on that," said Evie. "Do you mind me asking who, or what, you are?"

"I'm a picture in a vulgar book," said Marie-Gabrielle "and I'm trying to escape."

Evie must have done something because the water suddenly became agitated.

"Oh flip," said Evie, "I've dropped the soap. Has it scooted down your end?"

"I'll have a search," said Marie-Gabrielle and started to pat randomly at the bottom of the tub.

Two heads suddenly collided and each head said – "ow! Ooh, sorry, I can't see you!"

Then there was a bit of a strained silence, as each thought – 'ooh, ah, poof,'- and privately massaged their bumps.

"Agh, sorry about that," said Evie, eventually. "Look, I'll just get out. I've been in for hours. There's not enough room for two, especially when we can't see each other."

"Not your fault," managed Marie-Gabrielle, as the waters heaved and surged dramatically. She looked up, to smile forgivingly. Instead she shrieked but silently, because standing there was a man with large boobs and a big willy, or a girl with a big willy and large boobs.

"Oh my," she said in astonishment, "what are you, please?"

She was talking to herself. The person simply wasn't there anymore. "Hello, hello, hello?" she cried but there wasn't any answer forthcoming.

She sank back into the water and mentally turned the temperature up a few degrees. That was better. "Evie" had absorbed a lot of warmth. "It's not that I mind," said Marie-Gabrielle, to no-one in particular. "It was just a bit of a surprise. But, then, I suppose it's a very economical way to get a brother and sister in one package. Only one present on birthdays and at Christmas, which means more for me…oh," she faltered. "Did I just say? Yes, I did, didn't I."

She sank back into the water until she resembled a crocodile, just her nose and eyes above water. Submerged she began to think frantically. Nounou would have a complete fit. This whole family affair was going horribly astray…one vagabond husband, one brother and sister…as in ONE. 'Oh,' she protested, 'my very own man is probably going to be a…a…a…I don't know. Some sort of parrot with wheels for feet and a pole to push himself along with…I'm NEVER getting out of this bath, EVER. Out THERE is very dangerous for girls of delicate disposition and Nounou always said I was delicate.' Then being a fundamentally honest girl, she paused her thoughts for a second, sorted memories furiously and added – 'she might have done, I think she did…maybe, perhaps once?'

These were calming thoughts, of a sort and she fell to wondering if the two of them couldn't just become fish, brightly coloured fish on a tropical reef. In reply to which her imagination instantly conjured up a barracuda in a nun's robe, which forced them to dive in a desperate search for cover. She sat up and groaned.

She looked down the line of the bath and discovered that she was desperately missing Evie. Her first real friend, if you didn't count Nounou and the Shaman, which you couldn't really, because they were so much older…although, actually, she was older than any of them. Evie had been nice. Also, she must have scattered some rose petals in the bath. Might that mean she was a girl with bits, rather than a boy with bits? Because the last she knew about it, boys weren't that big on rose petals. But perhaps Evie had rose petal days and non-rose-petal-days? Things could get horribly complicated, very easily.

As she idly contemplated the petals, she realised that one was making a very determined passage towards her. She sat up a little higher and saw that it was being propelled by an ant. The tiny insect was making determined rushes from the prow of its craft to the rear, where it would leap up in the air and then descend on all six feet. The impact drove the leaf forwards and the repeated dashes were producing a respectable momentum.

What on earth was happening? This wasn't a real bath. This shouldn't be real water. There shouldn't be sea-faring ants in it, let alone ambivalent Evies. She studied the leaf, all the same. It was making a fair turn of speed and appeared to be heading from her toes towards her top end. How did one receive an ant in a rose petal? As she pondered diplomatic niceties the little boat was reaching the region of her elbow. Maybe he just wanted to get out of the water? In which case he was quite welcome to climb up her hair and onto the edge of the tub. Wherever he was going, however, there was a look of serious enterprise about it.

The closer he came, Marie-Gabrielle became certain she could hear a small and very cross voice directed towards her. She inclined her head gently, towards the coracle.

At first, all she could make out were the tiny noises associated with the " pitter-patter, pitter-patter, hop, skip, jump, crash" of the eccentric propulsion system. Finally, above that, she could make out a long litany of complaints… "shiver my timbers! Of all the stupid voyages on the face of the globe, I get landed with this one! Master mariner I may be but rose petals are inshore craft…a sight too fragile for these ocean voyages! Give me a sailing ship, snail shell packed with moss, caulked with beeswax, there's a vessel worth a tale! Pitter-patter, pitter-patter, hop, skip, jump, crash! Thick spider silk rigging, a butterfly wing sail…take you anywhere, rivers, rapids and fjords. This? Call this a vessel? Fit for a puddle! Huff, puff, pitter-patter, pitter-patter, hop, skip, jump, crash! Now, be that land on the loo'ward bow? By the legs of an earwig, I has that a'right! Ahoy there, Land! Ahoy!"

When nothing seemed to be happening, Marie-Gabrielle having been stunned into silence, the little ant stood on it hind legs, wriggled its feelers and bellowed at the top of its voice again – "Ahoy Land! Ahoy!"

"Ahoy yourself," whispered Marie-Gabrielle, barely daring to breathe, lest she overturn the petal.

"Agh" shrieked the ant, falling backwards, "no needs to shout so! Nothing wrong with my hearing! Pipe down there, Land!"

"Sorry. Some water in my ear. If you could speak up a little…"

"Nothing easier," squeaked the ant obligingly, conjuring a megaphone from the backpack it was wearing. "CAN YOU HEAR ME NOW?" it shrieked, putting down the megaphone and looking extremely pleased with itself.

"Thank you," said Marie-Gabrielle, "what can I do for you?'

"What can you do for me? The cheek of you, 'Land.' It's a question of what I can do for you!"

"Oh, I see. So, what can you do for me?"

The ant, swelling with self-importance, said – "I am to tell you, I am to tell you… tell you…tell you… Shiver my timbers! What was I to tell you?"

"I don't know," said Marie-Gabrielle. "What were you…"

"Don't interrupt!" shrieked the ant, seizing its megaphone, "I have it here, I have it here," and it rummaged desperately in its waistcoat pockets until it finally produced a scrap of leaf, nibbled at the edges. Swiftly scanning it, the ant struck an orator's pose and recited – "Folios 9 and 25, see your saviour come alive. Turn to 40, 1 and 2, here's a battle fought for you. Comes your end at 53 but turn the leaf for freedom's key!

"Phew," said the ant, almost out of breath. "Good, isn't it – the poetry that is? My own work, you see. It was the only way I could remember the numbers. If I'd just said: 9, 25, 40, 41, 42, 53, 54 to you, you wouldn't have remembered a thing now, would you?"

"Almost certainly not," Marie-Gabrielle agreed. "You don't have a copy of your excellent poem, do you, by any chance? One I could keep, as a family heirloom?"

"I can see why you'd want it," the ant confessed. It considered. "Keep the original," it said magnanimously. "I'm a natural artist, I'm sure those won't be my last words!"

But they were.

Something with savage teeth seized Marie-Gabrielle by her ankles and upended her. Her head went underwater, just as she took a great gulp of what she had expected to be air. Then, as swiftly as she had been inverted and half-drowned, she was out of the water, racketing upwards, hauled by her ankles towards a nest of pulleys that hung from a smoke-blackened ceiling. Below, she saw the whirlpool she had created as she was hauled from the water. She saw the rose petal coracle skating around its edges. She saw the tiny megaphone fly overboard and heard a last despairing cry – "Abandon ship!" Then the waters rushed and jostled. The nautical ant and his poem, vanished forever.

She looked away and realised in an instant where she was. She felt the pulley she hung from jerk sideways and now she was being lowered towards a flattened brazier of glowing charcoal. Her wet hair began to steam. She coughed and retched, looked desperately around her, only to see the black silhouette of the Nun, the woman from the quayside. Others were there, too, but that silhouette told her all she needed to know. This was from the pages of that depraved artist's book, which was growing longer day by day.

With all her willpower and that fuelled by shock, terror and rage, she dragged herself out of this unholy present and back, back to the sanctuary of the tiny room, where Nounou still snored gently in her chair. There, she collapsed into her own silhouette and pigments, with all the finality of the last piece in a jigsaw.

There she shuddered, trying to quiet her emotions. Was she still secure here, or had this haven been compromised? That was not a thought she dared to entertain. Nevertheless, it was a fact that she had almost been caught. Without that galvanic effort her life would no longer be developing, it would be well on the way to its conclusion. It would be being turned into a broken thing, just as in the picture she had seen, roughly sketched on the page. She allowed herself to sob quietly for a while. There could be no doubt, this was a dangerous game she was negotiating…

"…and the poor little ant," she allowed, as across time and space she heard his echoing cry – "Abandon ship!"

Then, she stiffened her resolve.

Marie-Gabrielle finally ran the Shaman to ground deep within a copy of Sir Thomas Browne's "Pseudodoxia Epidemica."

"So this is where you've been hiding!" she greeted him.

"I find it very soothing," he replied mildly, "but truthfully, I haven't been hiding, least of all from you."

"No, of course you haven't. That was very rude of me. I do apologise, I seem to be losing what little grip I had, I'm afraid. You see, things are happening to me. I can't just float away the way I used to, I think I'm becoming real."

"Oh dear," said the Shaman. "I know what that's like. I know what this is like and so I'm aware of the difference. I imagine you're terrified?"

"That sums it up," Marie-Gabrielle agreed. "You did warn me but I wouldn't listen."

"Too late to talk about that," said the Shaman. "We have to work out how to protect you, until you can make your escape. What precisely has been happening?"

She unfolded her story and he listened attentively.

"Well?" she demanded.

"Tell me more about this woman in black, the one you see dressed as a Nun."

"There are a series of books in which she and I are pitted against one another. I'm the innocent in white, she is the devil incarnate. By sheer good fortune I always survive. How, I can't imagine. I sustain more grievous bodily harm than any soldier might but all I ever register is pained distress above a sort of helpless winsomeness. It's almost amusing. Anyway, the curate-artist is hard at work on the next volume but the Nun is actually here, in the flesh, walking the corridors of the Manor! I've never seen her, incarnate, so-to-speak, before."

"I've seen her too," said the Shaman "and you're right, she's absolutely terrifying. I don't think she finds anything amusing about your joint antics."

"No, neither do I. If I'm going to 'come alive' on one of her pages, my goose is cooked. As I just told you, I was well on my way to being broiled, or roasted the other day. Also, I've looked into the dear little ant's poem and I think page nine is about to happen. What do you think I should do?"

"What happens on that page?"

"The silly thing is, nothing much. I get caught trying to run away and I'm surrounded by horrible people."

"No sign of a saviour?"

"None. Before you ask, he's drawn a lot more pages. On page 25 I seem to be stranded in a swamp and although there's a lot of awful things on other pages, I'm hoping I get to 'sleep' through those, because the poem doesn't mention them."

"I only hope you're right," said the Shaman, fervently.

"I still look alright in 41, 42, and 43. I'm even looking forward to those. The sketches aren't finished, so I can't be certain but it seems I cause a major upset. Or if I don't, someone else does. As for the two other pages, he's not drawn those yet but I peeped at 44 and 45 and 'she' is on those. Also, things look very bad indeed, so I'm terrified. I have to survive for 10 pages more. What on earth can I tell Nounou?"

"Nothing," said the Shaman. "You tell her nothing. She would be terrified. Anticipation is an awful thing, often worse than reality. Just insist she stays 'asleep', as you put it."

"What if Earth Magic starts to wake her up? At some point it's bound to!"

"Yes it will," said the Shaman, "no point in denying it. All I can say is that things are moving, far more rapidly than I thought they would and believe it or not, far more kindly. Earth Magic can be brutal. For some reason it's treating you very gently. Be grateful. The only reason for its acting this way that I can think of and it's not very consoling, is that you are both just part of a much bigger picture. When I mentioned you and your predicament, it's just possible that Earth Magic saw you as a way in to a deeper puzzle, one that might have been troubling it for a very long time."

"Should I feel honoured?"

"No. To be brutally honest, I'd feel scared."

Never before had Marie-Gabrielle wished that the world would stand still for her. For multiple life-times she had been trying to take control of her own time and space. Now time and space were taking control of her. What had the Shaman likened it to? Getting up on a horse. First you're high-up, then you're high-up and moving, the next moment you're moving far too quickly and all you can long for is for the horse to stop and let you back onto solid ground. In two dimensions it's difficult to feel fear, in three, it's very easy. Marie-Gabrielle was scared.

"I'm at a loss," said the Shaman. "I don't know how to protect you. I can try to sabotage things here, though that's difficult in two-dimensions. Also, I don't want to compromise either of you. What seems like a good idea can prove to be a catastrophe when things start to react to it. Not that I've got any good ideas, I hasten to add."

"I asked for this," groaned Marie-Gabrielle "but for some reason, vanity I suppose, I thought I'd be in control."

"We're never in control, if that's any consolation" said the Shaman. "We just think we are. Because things go the way we want them to, at least for a while, we think we have authority and our good luck will continue. 'Life' is the only authority and it has no interest in individuals, only the survival of the greatest diversity. Anything that threatens that will be thrust aside."

"Is this helping?" asked Marie-Gabrielle.

The Shaman blushed. "Er, not at all," he coughed. "I'm so sorry. It's easy to make sweeping statements when you don't have to survive them."

"Don't you have any magic of your own I could borrow?" asked Marie-Gabrielle. "I'm terrified for Nounou. I don't care about the world. I care about her!"

"Don't make me feel bad," groaned the Shaman. "There's no such thing as magic, only these minute alignments of time and space that Earth Magic can perform. They can cause an ant to drown, or a mountain to collapse. But Earth Magic knows what it does. It has no, how do we put it? It has no axe to grind. We implore it, that's all and sometimes that appeal triggers an adjustment. Your world is being adjusted. I don't know why but you can rest assured that it's not because we asked. It will be because it was necessary."

There was a long silence, in which both explored their innermost feelings and found little to reassure them.

At length the Shaman spoke. "I don't believe I shall see you again," he said. "I just want to say that you are the most delightful creature I've ever met. I feel certain that both you and Nounou will survive and become happy, or as happy as it's possible to be on this blood-soaked ground of ours. I wish you the greatest good fortune. Your family will pull you to safety, that much I can feel."

Marie-Gabrielle wanted to say something, anything…

Eventually she blurted out…"I'm just going to let go of the reins…"

…and that is why, when she ran from them, she clung to the ragged man – because she knew who he was!

…and it's why she wasn't scared when his long musket roared and shot a bolt of flame mere inches from her face. One which sent that foul beast flailing, head over heels into the swamp. And it's why she took off her cape and folded it neatly for him to find. For her poor papa was freezing to death…

…it's why she has the woodsmoke smell of him, lingering in her memory, for ever.

…but awful things still happen. 'And why, oh why, is that allowed, when I let go of the reins?'

JO-JO

Jo-Jo got back to where he began in 50 years, 3 months, 2 weeks, 4 days, 10 hours, 47 minutes and 32 seconds. His watch said so, or it did after he had furtively made a minor adjustment to the display. 'Journey complete' it bleated. Then the numerals froze. Jo-Jo looked at it with distaste.

"Is some discreet celebration indicated?" he enquired of the clouds, rocks, heather, grit and grasses. He waited and the never-ending wind plucked at his clothes like a petulant child. Eventually some white feathers flew by. "Ah, overwhelming," he said, to nothing in particular.

He began to circle the area cautiously. "Now, if memory serves…it's this one… or this one over here," he mumbled. Once he was certain he began to kick aside years of growth, the stubborn grasses and collected worm casts. There was little enough of either but that was not surprising, given the unrelenting winter climate. He laid bare a flat rock and this he pushed away with the tip of one boot. Below, was cached a grubby plastic box, of kitchenware variety. He stared at it glumly, then bent to free it from the surrounding earth. It was surprisingly difficult to extricate.

Jo-Jo walked stiffly to an accommodating rock, placed the box across his thighs and prised open the lid. "Still here," he said conversationally to the felt Rabbit inside. "Looks like it," replied the Rabbit, with an amateur dramatical yawn.

Rabbit pulled himself upright, sat for a while, yawning, then vaulted nimbly out of the box and onto the turf. Settling down together, man and rabbit contemplated the horizons, companionably enough, until the Rabbit, suddenly mindful of his former stature began to sprint about the grass, growing exponentially the while. By the time he stopped, he was almost Jo-Jo's height and weight.

"That's better," he confided. "I'd almost forgotten I'd been miniaturised!"

All around was rolling upland, sparse tussocky grasses, interspersed with large drifts of heather, occasional low channels of cropped turf sheltering between them. Dominating all, were crumbling dykes of black gritstone. These were rapidly eroding into flat plates of decaying rock that, if casually broken, revealed, unexpectedly, pink, mica-rich interiors, as startling as fresh wounds. This bitter landscape, with its hidden sloughs of damp peat, extended further than the eye could see in all directions, except one. There the eye was halted by an obstruction.

This obstruction was commonly known as 'The Wall.' It was a wholly inappropriate term, for 'wall' implies bricks, or stones. The word also comes loaded with the assumption that such objects will be arranged in accordance with the commonly accepted formats. This Wall fulfilled absolutely none of these.

Jo-Jo was now in a position to tell anyone who was interested – and no-one would be – that the Wall was in fact a cylinder, one that took rather too many years to circumnavigate, that it was made of some impermeable milky polymer, that never varied in aspect, that it stretched upwards as far as the eye could see and down at least as far as Jo-Jo had been prepared to dig. It had no joints, no abutments, its surface was unmarked, despite the grit-laden wind that played on it, nor could he dent, scratch, or defile it in any way. It also has to be recorded that this information would have been provided to any resident on the planet who chose to make the enquiry. The cylinder maintained an information and needs terminal in every abode, however humble. It had nothing to hide or, if it did, it hid it completely.

"Is it like that all the way round?" asked the Rabbit politely, adding, sotto voce – "I'm only asking so as to appear interested."

"Pretty much," replied Jo-Jo.

"Any the wiser?"

"Nope."

"Ah…so, to re-cap, pretty much the same, all the way round…?"

"Yep."

"Well, I'll be rewired!" said the Rabbit admiringly.

Jo-Jo swivelled to confront the object in question. The best description would be that of a curving sheet of milky glass dominating one entire horizon. On a clear day its width suggested it must cut the planet in two, while the impossible height produced the unpleasant feeling that it might be about to fall on one's head. Cloudy weather was preferable for then it appeared it might be simply a local, albeit Cyclopean, construct. But generally speaking, nobody gave it a second glance and certainly not the very few people who wandered these uplands.

To walk the circumference had been Jo-Jo's way of proving to himself that 'it' was, in fact, a rod. That this rod contained a life-form that interacted with the local population. Also, that it plunged through the core of the planet, rather after the fashion of a skewer in a kebab. Jo-Jo had the queasy feeling that, given the cosmic scale, it was planets that took the place of the more usual meat and vegetables.

He had known all this beforehand. It was a commonplace of living here, local knowledge, freely available. It was purely in a state of belligerence one day, that he had determined to prove the matter to his own satisfaction. Hence his intrepid expedition.

"How crushingly boring," opined the Rabbit. "Do you intend to publish?"

"The facts are certainly boring enough," Jo-Jo agreed. "There's very little to say, beyond the fact that it's there. You can't scratch it, smash it, bust it, reduce it in any way. As I was clean out of high explosive I skipped on that. It's definitely engineered – or it's an organic life-form of scary precision. Shapes move in it. In fact, in places, it's quite lively. As a source of speculation, it has a lot to offer, as a resource proffering information, it is a void."

"Mmm," mused the Rabbit, "did you try licking it, like an ice lolly?"

"Oddly enough, no."

"Aah!" said the Rabbit knowingly.

That made for an awkward moment. The wind pushed by them, irritated to be impeded, the cotton grass waved wildly, blown grits were accumulating against one side of Jo-Jo's boots.

"I could always bury you again," he said threateningly.

"Entirely your loss," said the Rabbit. "I'm a conversationalist of a high order."

"I have missed you," Jo-Jo said sentimentally, "but you'd have hated the travelling."

The Rabbit sulked. "I would have seen the World," he responded eventually. "Explored extraordinary things, witnessed different sunsets, devoured alternative cultures…"

"It's all the same! ALL THE WAY ROUND! I know! I've just been!"

The Rabbit shook its head sadly. "That could be you," it said. "It could be that you were the same, ALL THE WAY ROUND! Did you consider that the 'Wall' might have been hypnotising you, so that you only thought it was the same ALL THE WAY ROUND? If you'd taken me along, I'd have acted as a 'control' group."

"You're not a group, you're you, definitely a one-off."

"Unique, is the word you're struggling for," said the Rabbit tartly. "But my individuality is not the issue. It's your lack of foresight."

"Trust me, there were no pyramids, no camels. I saw no Eiffel Tower, devoured no croissants. Had I done so, I would have noticed."

"Mmm…you can't be sure…"

"This is amateur psychology, even worse philosophy, you have come adrift, loose from your moorings. It is the same ALL THE WAY ROUND."

"See what I mean?" the Rabbit said sadly. "Your Doctoral Thesis would have collapsed at the first enquiry."

"How utterly deflating," agreed Jo-Jo, caustically. "Where do I find myself?"

"Exactly where you started from. We, or rather you, have just wasted the last – 50 years, was it you said? You are a shocking example of aimlessness. Luckily my character remains undefiled."

"The time would have gone anyway. That's just one of the problems with time – it goes on, whatever else may be happening. I'm not even sure we are involved, or if we are, it's in a very peripheral way."

"That's got to be good thing," ventured the Rabbit. "Who would want their hand on the tiller of history? It will write itself without us putting our oars in."

"Oh, I don't disagree. I just felt that I wanted a peek over the parapet…you know, catch some meaningful glimpse of the field…which, of course, might not be there…it could all be fog…do you think?"

For a while, both were silent, either marshalling arguments, or dozing lightly.

"If you had a meaningful view," the Rabbit said at last, "then you would want to interfere. You'd glimpse some terrible, impending injustice and think – 'just one tweak on Fate's strings and I can put all that right and no-one will ever notice!' That's how it starts."

"How what starts? And anyway, would that be such a bad thing?"

"How disasters start," said the Rabbit, in a dismal, far-away voice. "Never volunteer."

"Why not?" asked Jo-Jo, largely to be awkward.

"Because," the Rabbit proposed, after a longish pause, "everything changes anyway. You don't want to take a side, or become some agent of change. Merciful Heavens! You might be held accountable, especially when you have no idea why you're doing what you're doing in the first place!"

"That rather bollockses the ideal of the Knight Errant!"

"Exactly!" said the Rabbit, in a tone intimating – 'Checkmate!'

"Now, I wish to change the subject. Tell me about The Wall, the Rod, the Pole, the Perch, or whatever it is, instead. Too much philosophy gives me flatulence and after 50 years – was it? – I have a lot in reserve."

Jo-Jo edged away.

"I performed a thorough investigation. I even tried digging down. At one point there was quite the excavation and I thought – 'maybe they stopped too soon. If I go on a few more inches, perhaps I'll find an inspection hatch…' So I did and it was just the same. Then I slipped in the hole and bashed my head on it. I can vouch for its being 'hard/soft' or 'soft/hard' if you prefer. Not in the sense that you could mark it in any way, cut it, dent it or scratch it but it doesn't knock your few remaining brain cells out when you accidentally headbutt it. It seems…" he searched for the right word… "forgiving, indulgent even. As if there was content in the contact. Content I was too thick to interpret it."

"Restrained contact, perhaps an 'affable' blow to the head?" tried the Rabbit.

"Dejecting, isn't it," observed Jo-Jo, who hadn't been listening. "Bit like having an intelligent friend you can't really talk to, because whatever you say, they're always waiting for you to catch up."

"Mmm," said the Rabbit. "I feel that way with you quite frequently."

"Oh, surely not? You don't have to!"

"Yes, I often wonder if you're up to the rigour of my conversation…"

"Should I bury you again?" asked Jo-Jo.

"You see what I mean…?" sighed the Rabbit. "Instant recourse to a futile physicality, all uttered without a flicker of intelligence, or wit."

They exchanged rueful glances.

Meanwhile, the wind, like time, continued to pass but the wind was making considerably more fuss about it than it had been doing. Standing upright was becoming a challenge and the Rabbit's ears were streaming.

"Shelter could be sought behind this bank," he observed, by way of proffering a peace-offering, also whilst making the first move. "I had every intention of asking about your boots. Fifty years is a lot of walking. Indeed, the wear and tear on all your garments – or is it 'raiment', given the quasi-mystical nature of your task? – must have been profound. We'll settle for boots as the exemplar, unless you'd rather discuss underwear…because I understand that 'lingerie-for-men' is become 'a thing,'" he finished hurriedly.

"Boots," said Jo-Jo. "I am prepared to discuss boots and you may extrapolate from them all you wish, provided you do so in silence."

"King Midas has Ass's lingerie," whispered the Rabbit to the wind, in a very tiny voice. What the Wind made of that up-date to the myth is not recorded.

"There was something of a mystery to that," said Jo-Jo. Once a year I would wake up and there, like a birthday present, would be a new pair of boots and etcetera's. Never a card though, never a 'Happy Birthday to you!"

There was a pregnant silence, in which only the moaning of the wind could be heard and to those who should have been listening, that had become threatening.

"On reflection," began the Rabbit and his tone was silky, "and how crass of me to forget – that would mean that you owe me 50 birthday presents. Quite a shocking quantity…"

"Me, me , me," said Jo-Jo briskly. "Could we stay on subject for once?"

"Pray continue."

"The Wall, the 'Thing,' the whatever-it-is, extrudes necessities and also, unseen, absorbs waste. But there was never any sign of irritation, or obligation, finger-tapping of any kind, quite unlike, shall we say, your good self."

"So cheap," reflected the Rabbit, "but can we continue to the heart of the matter, please? You stress the opaque, inert, apparently impenetrable nature of this membrane, yet it appears to be a watchful interface, ready and willing to oblige your needs. What on earth is going on here? You've actually had an escorted tour and yet you come back and all you can say is – 'nothing going on.' It may be that you are cretinous but I'll give you the benefit of the doubt and assume some mystery has manifested itself. So, for the third time, I think – 'what is it?'"

"In all honesty," said Jo-Jo, "I haven't clue. I hope never to see the thing again. It baffles all modest investigation and as regards speculation, my brain, such as it is, has collapsed under the strain. It could be anything, it appears to be everything, and nothing, to get worked up about, at one and the same time."

Both fell silent.

The wind, however, strengthened further. The pale pink grit skittered around the lee of their sheltering rock and began to pile up in neat windrows. Before them the grasses bent double, until their seed heads beat upon the ground and the contents were whirled away. Behind it all, the core, the Wall, the whatever-it-was, continued to radiate its dreamy, ice-cream shade of vanilla, through which darker movements could be observed. It was as though a vast aquarium lay ahead, through which gigantic sharks, rays and eels moved purposelessly. The observer was condemned to be baffled. Either one accepted it as a simple fact one was obliged to live with, or one went quietly and pointlessly mad.

"About this accumulation of birthday presents," said the Rabbit, after allowing some time to pass.

"You're not going to let that drop, are you?"

"I was thinking, maybe a trail bike?"

"You want a motorcycle?"

"A trail bike, it's not quite the same thing."

"They're awfully dangerous."

"I'm made of felt, I'll bounce."

Jo-Jo struggled.

"Are you absolutely sure that's what you want?"

"I've had 50 years considering the options."

"That's a fib," interrupted Jo-Jo, "you were turned off for the duration and miniaturised."

"…all right, if you must, I have spent the last hour considering the options carefully and a trail bike seems to tick all the boxes."

"OK," said Jo-Jo decisively, "we'll drop in on Moss and Shade, they're not far from here. Moss will build you something you'll like."

"Aah, I was hoping you'd say that," the Rabbit said, gleefully, "I like chatting to Shade."

"Oh, Gods!" wailed Jo-Jo, suddenly remembering. "She absolutely despises me…"

"Not precisely you, just your ideas."

"That's even worse!"

"Come on, then," said the Rabbit, "I'm raring to go!" He stood up, only to be promptly felled by the wind, which was roaring overhead. "Told you," he remarked brightly, "finest felt and silicone rubber inside! I bounce – you should be so lucky!"

Jo-Jo, forewarned, stood up cautiously. The gale clawed at him and he bent double. He extended a hand. "Hang on," he yelled, "we'll head down to the gullies."

They edged out from the sheltering rocks and the wind, affronted, tore at them.

"Have you seen that?" screeched the Rabbit, pointing.

A black wall was advancing rapidly from the western edge of the scarp. Laden with snow, if not ice, it was making straight for them. Outriders of the storm tore by, sudden flurries of hail laced with piercing crystals of ice. The two clawed their way across the bald expanse, heading as fast as was humanly and robotically possible, for any one of the hundreds of gullies that serrated these cap lands.

"WAS-IT-THIS-WINDY-UP-THERE?" shrieked the Rabbit. He had his volume turned to maximum but his words were perforated by the wind.

"FIVE-METRE-PROTECTION-ZONE-BY-CORE" Jo-Jo screeched. At times, snow had piled up as a one-sided, igloo-style tunnel, enabling his passage for mile after mile. Battling this wind now, made him grateful that it had.

"Pity, really," observed the Rabbit, taking advantage of a brief quietus, "they might have had to drag you inside. There again, you could have been blown straight through. Or ended up like a bug on a windscreen," he concluded thoughtfully.

"I think we should run," said Jo-Jo.

"If I had a trail bike…"

They ran, following one of the low runnels of turf, heading in a direction that eventually, must count as down.

"If we can just outflank that front," Jo-Jo panted.

"Turn me off, miniaturise me! Then you can carry me!" gasped the Rabbit.

"You feeble robotic…object! Run! It's not like you had lungs."

"I'm compromised, you forced me to walk upright. I'm an affront to Creation! This is what you get for messing with evolution. There again, if I had a trail bike…

"If you want to see another birthday," panted Jo-Jo, "I suggest you put a sock in it and concentrate on running for your electronic life. That cloud is nearly here!"

They zig-zagged furiously, tearing across the black face of the rushing storm, hoping against hope that a fissure would soon appear, marking the start of one of those infinitely long, knife cuts that sliced across the plateau. At least in that respect they were lucky. Only seconds after they were enveloped and lost in white-out they toppled into such a refuge.

Not that any of this wild panic mattered a jot. In his tiny backpack, Jo-Jo carried a small array of survival aids. One was a beacon that would summon a survival pod to any segment of the home planet. But it was a matter of pride to ignore the 'Nanny Core' and attempt survival on human terms, wherever one might be. Also, no-one died here. Immortality was the norm, though under what agency and for what reason, no-one knew. The Core, that enigmatic rod that skewered man and planets alike, had its reasons, no doubt.

A mile after first ducking and diving, the storm was above their heads. Yet it still raged and snow fell thickly enough, even in this comparatively quiet zone, to make further descent imperative. A good turn of speed was essential, before all signs of the safe path became obliterated. This they maintained, even managing the descent in mutual harmony.

Jo-Jo was a rim-dweller, as were Moss and Shade. Rim dwellers were the acknowledged eccentrics of this strange world and were naturally proud of the fact. There were very few of them. They had something of the Shaker ethos about them. Austere craftsmen, dedicated not to any God but to the pursuit of whatever particular genius inspired them. The rim was their haven, far from the doings of the lower regions. They imagined that the middle world was a hubbub of bustling productivity, a hive of normality. But no-one knew for certain, because no-one in living memory had ever been there. As memories here were long, 20,000 years was not unusual, reports about the middle world were little better than myths. Yet there were no rules enforcing this apartheid. Nor was there any overt enmity. There were such things as Tourist Trails, when adventurous middle-worlders would book Crawler Holidays that visited 'artists' outlets' and some of the more spectacular landscape projects that were 'open to the public…' albeit only by prior arrangement.

Moss, Jo-Jo's particular friend was engaged in building such a site. It was many hundreds of years from completion but the realisation of it, in Moss's head, was complete on the day he had first envisioned it.

That vision embraced the development of the lower part of a runnel, very similar to the one that Jo-Jo and Rabbit were now making their way along. Their runnel would eventually deepen to a gully. The gully would open into a ravine and the ravine would become a canyon. The canyon would then run for many hundreds of miles, before cascading whatever watery contents it had accumulated over the rim, either in spectacular Niagara fashion, or by mildly broadening and flattening itself, to thus sweep down in scenic obscurity.

Some ravines, however, had undergone traumatic, geomorphic events. Colossal land slumps occasionally occurred, caused by natural faults in the underlying strata, or where ancient rivers had formed great lakes which, on breaching, had carved away billions of tons of rock and soil, leaving great horseshoe-shaped crescents in the rim landscape. The upper plateau was terraced on its edges into spectacular, erratic forms.

It was one of these that had snared Moss's imagination, millennia since. An ancient river had carved a broad, deep gully through rock. It had carved a perfect 'U', the mouth of which broadened only slightly, before it fell again to lower levels. This upper valley ran for less than two miles and it faced due south, with the shadow and light interplay of east and west brought into theatrical brilliance by the natural transit of the sun. Moss had had an instant vision of his Task. He would create rows of gigantic, angelic figures along each face of the canyon and they would come together at the head of the cwm, where triumphant archangels, of colossal proportion, would set their seal on the project.

Moss could make anything, though his preferred medium was metal. Wood he treated as an inferior sort of metal, so that the home he had built for Shade, discreetly hidden behind the rim of the cwm, was an agony of precision-engineered joints, suffering under the rigours of winter and summer alike. Generally, though, the material world capitulated to Moss and behaved obligingly.

Shade was a few thousand years younger than Moss but not indecently so. Jo-Jo was younger than both. With Moss he was a relaxed equal while under Shade's disapproving eyes he quailed, like a child. At the moment, with the snow building around them, he would have welcomed the opportunity to quail – if it came with a hot and hearty stew.

"I think it's easing off," said the Rabbit.

Jo-Jo looked up and saw solid blackness, from which snow flurries still skittered. But the fact he could see blackness at all, suggested that this arm of the storm was lessening in ferocity.

"We might live to tell the tale," he agreed.

"If I had a trail bike," the Rabbit began, relentless, "I would ride heroically through the storm and fetch help. The rescuers would arrive, just as life was ebbing. As you were being carried away in a tinfoil blanket, you'd croak – 'glad I got you that bike, Big Guy…' Then the camera would pan back to me, wounded – possibly mortally? – I'll have to think about that and I'd raise a hand in brotherly salutation, secure in the knowledge that I alone – with the aid of my trail bike – had saved you. Then, as the ambulance doors closed, I'd collapse!"

Jo-Jo thought for a moment. "Big guy?" he asked, "you're really quite small."

The Rabbit made an exasperated noise. "Not that sort of Big. It's Big Guy in the sense of big-hearted, huge of spirit and courage."

"And, no doubt, fat of felted-head…" finished Jo-Jo.

"Romance is dead," the Rabbit observed.

"Totally. Start looking for the path, it can't be that far away."

But it was. They were to find it hours later and by that time the storm had renewed itself. Snow now twisted itself around them in malicious corkscrews. The trackway they had just found was rapidly vanishing, becoming a faceless and treacherous drift. Prospects were poor.

"I did not walk for 50 years to die in a local blizzard," said Jo-Jo. "Time to break out the life-saving technology." He glanced at the Rabbit, whose ears were streaming – blue, gold and red felt, crusty with snow. They nodded tacit agreement.

Jo-Jo unlocked his satellite phone and called Moss.

"Good heavens, you still alive?" asked his oldest friend.

"Seems so but possibly not for much longer."

"Then I suppose I'd better come and get you."

"Me, too!" squeaked the Rabbit.

"You there, too, old felt brain?"

"I am, ever his wise and faithful companion," said the Rabbit, in a wise and faithful voice.

"Well, then," said Moss's voice, addressing Shade, "we need room for two and dinner for one, My Lovely."

'Shade really does not like me,' thought Jo-Jo gloomily, as he tried hard to be a grateful, good and helpful guest. The realisation condemned him to the outer rings of some incredibly distant planet, at least in his own mind. If a genuinely good person didn't like you, what hope was there that you could ever start to like yourself? These were unnecessary thoughts but try as he might, they wouldn't go away.

Mercifully, Moss was rambling on about his flying angels project which, so far, had seen one cliff face with three tiers fixed in place. He was about to start work on the opposing wall, where the Core's robotic engineers had just finished excavating underground access tunnels.

His enthusiasm was boundless. He had been like a child with a new toy for the last 1000 years, at least. Shade indulged him in all his projects, had done for millennia. She was the most faithful and tolerant of companions – to the extent that she even accepted the tip of one angelic wing protruding into the living quarters through a half-demolished wall. To be fair, it had its uses. It was currently doubling as a supper table, from which they were consuming a delectable sausage and bean stew.

Jo-Jo was finding that he was torn between eating beans and staring at the surreal vision of snow piling higher and higher on 'the table,' a mere four feet away. That was a freak result of the screen-convection invention of Moss's that ensured the dining room was warm as toast, despite the roaring of the storm beyond.

Aware of his schizophrenic attention, Jo-Jo kept shooting helpless, apologetic glances at Shade. She torpedoed every effort he made. Each time she would pointedly turn to talk to the Rabbit, who was milking the situation mercilessly. He had even been given his own tiny, token plateful, despite Jo-Jo's well-meant explanation that he had no digestive system and was running on an atomic battery.

Shade had turned on him. "If you think I'm having him sitting at my table, sweet as pie and chatty as a little cricket, without pretend food for his little felt tummy, you can think again, young Jo-Jo!"

"Thank you, ma'am," the Rabbit had replied, with a winsome fluttering of eyelashes. "It's definitely a design flaw. After all, if I have a mouth for talking, I can't see why I couldn't use it for eating, even breathing, too. It would bolster my sense of self-worth," he finished shyly, whilst simultaneously managing to shoot an evil smirk at Jo-Jo.

"Good job my angels don't eat," Moss roared. "It'd take a bullock a day, hide and bones, too, for each and every one. Then I reckon it'd take more than God Almighty and an umbrella apiece to shield the congregation at bathroom time!"

"Moss!" warned Shade.

"Just saying, my love, as robots and icons are best left passive."

"Oh, I couldn't agree more," said Jo-Jo, shooting a venomous glance at the Rabbit, who smiled back, beatifically.

"Bless his little heart," cried Shade. "Will you two mind your language! Not like he doesn't have feelings."

"Oh, but he doesn't," explained Jo-Jo eagerly, only to curse himself as a fool with a foot in his mouth the next second.

The Rabbit simpered. "May I help to clear away, Ma'am?"

"You call me Shade, darling!"

"May I…do you think I…might I call you Aunty Shade?"

Jo-Jo kept his groan deep inside.

"Of course you may, darling. You come on with aunty. We're going to my kitchen. Leave these two brutes together."

"What…?" Moss gaped at the door, as it closed behind them.

"Sorry," said Jo-Jo, "the little fiend was wired by the Devil himself. Ignore him, tell me where you're up to?

Moss talked and Jo-Jo pretended to listen, punctuating the conversation with wise variants of – 'I see' and 'now I get you' with the odd, 'oh, now that is surprising – but I can quite see what you're driving at.' Meanwhile, within himself, he conducted a conversation based largely around 'should I jump off the cliff now, or later?' The trouble was, it wouldn't much matter when he jumped. No one was going to fret, at least not beyond a cursory – 'wonder why he did that? Young feller, had everything to live for. Still, always was a strange one.' Then they would nod knowingly and turn to a more interesting topic.

'I need a life,' he thought. 'A short, vigorous life. Not this long, drawn out passivity, this unending obsession with eternal verities. There are none. I've been searching for 4,000 years and I've spent far too many trailing round an object pregnant with meaning and utterly opaque to common enquiry. I'm a fraud, a fake in my own eyes and in everyone else's,' he added, recalling Shade's withering glance.

"So, are you up for it?" Moss was demanding, probably for the second time, to judge by the confused look on his face.

"What, precisely.?" said Jo-Jo, "do y'know, I think I drifted off there…all the good food, warmth, wine, your welcome…feel quite overcome…just backtrack a pace or two, would you? Sorry, old pal." He could feel himself blushing.

"I said," Moss spelled it out patiently, "we're lifting the first angel on the west wall, tomorrow. If I don't get this wing shifted out the house soon, I'm a dead man. Do you want to come?"

"Oh that," said Jo-Jo, "I thought you meant…yes, of course I want to come! Wouldn't miss it for the world! What about the snow, though?'

"We're underground," Moss explained. "It'll be the drones out in the snow and they don't care. Anyway, it'll have stopped by morning and be well on the melt."

"I suppose it will," Jo-Jo said limply. After a while, with the package of self-recrimination still whirling round at the back of his mind, he felt compelled to say – "you know, Moss, you really have been the best of friends to me. Always helped me. Always welcomed me. I've been able to rely on you and I just want to say 'thank you.' And thank you particularly for getting the crawler out tonight. I think we might have frozen, otherwise."

"Think nothing of it," said Moss, heartily, adding, ingenuously – "if anything happened to that little Rabbit, she'd have my guts for garters." Then, covered in confusion as he realised what he had said, roared towards the kitchen door – "now My Beauty, we got any coffee in this place and how about some of that cake of yours, I know I haven't eaten it all?"

"Cake!" came an answering roar, "Cake! After what's been happening to this poor little chap! How dare you mention CAKE!"

Moss turned white. Jo-Jo looked frantically for an exit, or any deliverance from his impending execution, on charges yet to be levelled

"What?" Moss managed to croak, mystified.

Metaphorically, the door blew off its hinges as Shade entered. An avenging angel cradling the Rabbit, who had miniaturised himself, everything that was except his ears, which drooped dramatically and pathetically.

"Buried alive for 50 years, in a plastic box!" she boomed. "How could you, Jo? How could you?"

Jo-Jo looked at Moss but Moss had already abandoned him, knowing a hopeless battle when he saw one. Instead of solidarity, there was a quizzical gaze creeping over his face.

"Buried alive, Ma?" he asked, ingratiatingly.

"Buried alive, I said!" Shade reiterated, in a low, dangerous tone.

The Rabbit gave a tubercular cough. "Perhaps he didn't know any better," he suggested weakly.

"Defending you, you monster! How could you! We'd have looked after him, wouldn't we, Moss?"

"We would,' Moss agreed righteously, having risen from his chair to sidle towards his wife, whilst slipping Jo-Jo a surreptitious wink.

"He meant no harm," the Rabbit said feebly. "I'm sure he didn't think." Then horribly aware his future was now under review, added – "he was kind enough to turn me off, first…but I had bad dreams…"

Jo-Jo, aware that he was facing complete and comprehensive defeat, went on the attack. "All he's bothered about are his accumulated birthday presents. He's added them all together and come up with this tom-fool notion that he wants a trail bike. This is his way of getting one. Beware of that Rabbit, he should come with a Bio-Hazard warning. You ingrate!" he finished. "Go on, kill me," he said to Shade, "I'm sure I deserve nothing less."

Perhaps a touch discomfited, Shade relaxed her fighting muscles and asked, in an almost reasonable tone – "why can't he have one?"

"I couldn't see the Core allowing him to belch two-stroke fumes over the landscape, while gouging great ruts in the ground. That's why."

"Just ask them," said Moss, "they'll come up with something…" and he gestured at the discreet letter-box on the wall.

"What's that?" asked the Rabbit innocently.

"As you know full well, that's your mother," said Jo-Jo, in evil tones. "When I was feeling lonely, when I needed an intellectual peer, a happy person to cheer me up, I posted my request…and I got you instead."

"We don't need much up here," explained Moss, "just the tools of life and that's how we request them. I post my plans in there and if they're approved, the Core send the materials, the robots, everything you've requested, usually. They're very accommodating. When I've finished with stuff, I tell them and they take it away."

"It's how I get my groceries, ducky," Shade explained in motherly terms.

"I don't see them approving a trail bike," said Jo-Jo crossly. "They do have standards and a long-eared maniac on a motorcycle won't wash."

"Wouldn't hurt to try," suggested Moss, sensing a escape route.

"I hate asking that thing for anything," growled Jo-Jo.

"Then I'll do your asking for you," said Shade, brusquely. "Come on, darling, we'll go next door and write a nice letter together. We'll tell them just what you want." She turned to Moss – "you two, get your own coffee and cake, you know where everything is!" With which she made her exit, still cradling the rabbit.

Jo-Jo collapsed back in his chair, making feeble noises.

"That was a close one," Moss nodded. "Still, all over now. Shape yourself, there's whisky on the side-table and you can pour me a double, too. I'll be back with the coffee."

Jo-Jo finally got himself upright and poured two serious tots, suitable for those wounded in action.

"You deserted me," he accused Moss, as he re-entered the room.

"Too right," agreed his oldest friend, "I live here. Do you think I'm mad?"

"No," Jo-Jo capitulated, "but when I get that spawn of Satan alone, I'll wire him up to the generator for the night."

"Are you crazy? He's under protection now. One word from him and you're cold meat, pressed and sliced."

Jo-Jo drained his whisky. "Can I have another one?" he begged.

"Just bring the bottle. Think of it as medicinal."

Jo-Jo woke the next morning to shrieks, whoops and peals of giggling. Blinding sun was inching round the edge of the curtains and when he swept them apart, all he could see was a sea of white, the snow having rolled and drifted over Moss's metal stockpiles, his small outbuildings, as well as gates, tracks and fences. They were definitively snowed-in, if not quite snowed under. Where thence and why, the whoops of glee?

He wandered off in search of explanation. The kitchen was deserted. The merriment was outside. Filching a mug of coffee, he headed for the forge.

If any snow had blown under these eaves, it had long since melted. The great altar of firebrick, topped with its ever glowing red heart, beneath a beaten copper cowling, inky with accumulated soot, blocked his view. He edged his way round anvils, irons and sledgehammers, was nearly snared in a jungle of welding equipment and finally discovered the source of the hilarity.

Overnight, the Rabbit's dream had come true in the form of a bright, red-felt, trail bike, with detailing precise as it was possible to achieve. Somehow, it was possessed of a silent motor that was allowing it to glide gracefully to and fro, across the modest and very flat terrain that lay under the lean-to roof.

"How the hell," Moss was mumbling, while scratching his great head, "have they made rims and spokes of felt strong enough to have them stand? Damned if I know the ways of it…" and he crossed his huge arms with almost proprietorial pride at such achievement.

Shade, with an arm that reached only halfway round his waist, was unashamedly crying with delight as the Rabbit, in miniature mode, glided to and fro.

"Again, again," she cried repeatedly, clapping her hand in delight.

Besieged by emotions, Jo-Jo edged closer.

Eventually he dared to shout – "is that what you wanted?"

"In every detail!" chirruped the Rabbit happily.

Jo-Jo had to turn away. He was welling-up, shamed by his own miserable, judgemental, pusillanimous attitude. Worse, he was wondering what on earth to do about it.

Over breakfast, he concluded that he was not much more welcome in Shade's home than he had been last night. He had a lot of lost ground to regain.

Consequently he turned-on his imitation of Popular Mechanics Man and directed his attention to Moss, where he was less likely to be scalded. He bowled questions about lifting capacity, aerial balance, fine adjustment and the robotic team necessary to ensure a smooth transition from forge to cliff face. As they downed the last cup of coffee, it became evident the charade had worked, or his host was simply hungry for a sacrificial observer.

"We'll show you," he boomed happily. "You'll see, it's easy as apple pie. The drones just slide them in. I get to work with the rag-bolts and overnight, the grouter works a bit of magic. In a day or so, you'll not see the difference between grout and cliff face.

"What you've got to imagine is three big horseshoe tunnels, lying right around the cliff, deep inside and laying above one another. Coming off these are crawl-ways. Those are what we slide the beams into. They look like cave openings in the cliff, when you see them from outside and below. The angels are built atop the beams and they rises up like jib sails from the bowsprit on an old-fashioned boat. The beams themselves, though, run way back. They're what gives us our fastening points. You get the idea?"

"Clear as mud," said Jo-Jo. "I'll get it when I see it. Still, that's a whole world of tunnels, Moss. A whole mountain of metal and a fleet of robots! How on earth…?"

"If they like your ideas, if your plans make sense, they don't quibble. They took a survey first, of course. Moved my lines a bit. There was something unstable, deep down in one pocket of rock they didn't like but the principle was sound. And you know, everything just turns up when you ask for it. It'd be a world of painful work for ten men, 20 or more but for them, it's nothing. They've cut those tunnels clean as you like. Not a scrap of waste and everything spot on, to the last centimetre. I think they built the robots just for this job. Once it's done, they'll be recycled – probably come back as felt motorcycles!" Moss roared happily at his own wit.

Daringly, Jo-Jo asked one of the forbidden questions. "Did no-one turn up to talk you through it? I mean, it's a huge project," he finished lamely.

He was immediately aware of the uncomfortable atmosphere he'd created. It simply wasn't the Rim-Dwellers' way to mention 'Them.' The facilitators of the Core were treated like embarrassing relatives – never mentioned. Why such an idiotic prohibition had arisen, Jo-Jo had no idea. It made no sense. Everyone living on the surface of this planet, be they Rim-Dweller, or Middle-Earther, was wholly dependent on the denizens of the Core. That they were never seen, never discussed and only tacitly acknowledged was mutually understood by all. Jo-Jo had transgressed – again.

"Come on, Jo," said Moss equably. "Of course no-one showed up. Why on earth would they? Anyway, we need to show up if this day's not to be wasted. Wrap up warm and get some heavy boots on your feet. They may be angels but they're heavyweights!" Then, turning to Shade, he asked – "you be all right, My Lovely?"

"I will," she said. "The little chap's staying with me and helping out."

The unspoken text would have filled a book.

Jo-Jo winced and went in search of suitable clothing.

Moss's latest angel was vast, more civil engineering project than art. For all of which she chafed to fly. Lightness had been worked into the expanse of metal, as if her sculptor's vision transcended the practical aspects of mass. But the theatre was equally vast, far grander, deeper and dramatic than Jo-Jo had remembered.

The angels already in place were neither dwarfed by their setting, nor did they dominate it. They soared from the cliff as if released by the folds of the strata. In the morning chill, melting icicles streamed from their wings and colour, refracting from the patinas worked onto the metal, winked and shivered under the ice, like the patterns in a kaleidoscope.

"They look like they're welcoming her," Jo-Jo said softly, more to himself than Moss.

"Just light on ice and metal," Moss replied gruffly but his eyes were moist.

"Say what you like but it was quite a vision you had that day. Then to go ahead and make a triumph of it. If it wasn't so cold, I'd doff my hat to you."

"Technical drawing, a lot of it and the Core has done all the calculating, checked my figures, altered this and that, bored the tunnels, devised the alloys, advised me about the patinas I wanted. I've felt like a spare part, at times."

"Never," said Jo-Jo stoutly. "A robot didn't think of this. Even if one dug the holes."

Holes there were in plenty. The western cliff resembled nothing so much as a giant dovecote, a socket prepared for every member of the angelic host. At this distance, as they rode the crawler to the service lift, Jo-Jo could block out each socket with the ends of two fingers held out before him. Meanwhile, Moss was assuring him that a short person could stand upright in any one of those holes and should he become overwhelmed by a desire to stretch his arms out sideways, would not feel unduly cramped when he did.

Arriving at the service lift, Moss presented Jo-Jo with a choice – "you can ride around, up and down with me, or you can go down the tunnel and watch the docking from the business end."

The stanchions that held the service lift jutted out, yards away from the edge of the cliff. Jo-Jo took one look over the edge and felt vertigo, breakfast and last night's whisky attack his stomach. He gestured to the land entrance to the tunnels, a safe 20 metres away. "I'll take the in-house trip," he said. "I'd like to see these holes the mice made in the cheese. It'll be like sex but with an inside view, for once."

Moss looked at him blankly. "What the hell you on about? Anyway, if you're going down, don't fall out of a hole – it's a long way to the bottom, with a hard landing." Then he was away, stepping across the void, into the lift, while barking instructions to the drones and crawlers.

Jo-Jo stepped back and heard the lift pulleys vibrate and sing, as Moss began the descent to wherever he was going. He walked across the broken rock of the surface, towards the inland access. Then he stopped. The robotic carrier was approaching.

The prostrate angel lay on her stomach with her wings outstretched, as she came lurching across the snow. It looked as if, with one galvanic thrust, she could defy gravity and thwart mortal plans. He watched as the universal lift-and-carry wheels locked and unlocked, pivoted, braked, released, bit and turned, humming and whirling with intent, until the invaluable cargo was anchored above laser-locators. The whole was an exercise in micro-precision needing no intervention by man. Utilising its own soulless electronics, the lifting drone descended from the sky to settle on the angelic back, with a barely audible "click". Small, self-locating, claw-carabiners scuttled to attachment points and locked into place.

Jo-Jo watched the process with fascination bordering on disgust. The descent of the drone, the skittering of the carabiners, all seemed to be intimations of some deadly, carnivorous insect, previously unknown on earth. Here were metal creatures preparing to devour one of man's sacred images.

He shook himself in mock indignation, flapping his hands against his biceps, though more for warmth, than for any real sense of impending calamity. But just to establish his mastery, he shouted – "shoo!" as the lifting drone rose silently into the sky, invisible micro-filaments taking the strain. It ignored him and rose peacefully.

Shunned, he scanned the horizon and from the east saw what he first took to be a small flock of birds approaching. As they came closer, he could see that they were tiny servo-tugs. They positioned themselves at strategic points along the angelic wingspan, against the draped, doubled legs, ready to nudge and stabilise any yaws or tremors caused by rogue gusts of wind. The whole affair was a tour-de-force of alien genius, all in the pursuit of one man's vision.

Jo-Jo shook his head and started down the stairs for the mid-way tunnels, far below.

Everything began simply enough – a descent by metal staircase. His boots made a hollow ringing noise on the openwork treads. Treads and handrails still shone with factory-fresh paint. Only Moss had ever trudged up and down these steps, if indeed he ever had. But they were here, because the Core had ordered that they should be, probably anticipating the time when the cliff lift would be taken away and these bright red stairs would be the only way down to perform whatever maintenance might prove necessary.

As he took the next step, he thought – 'the Core does our thinking. It probably made me think that – though why it would bother to do so defies my imagination. Logically, then, the next question is – are we extensions of the Core, or is the Core an extension of ourselves? Does that even mean anything?'

He took a deep, calming breath.

'It is well-known that these are useless, juvenile questions. Also, they are questions rarely entertained by decent people. Ergo, I am not a decent person. Good. I am an indecent person but none the happier for it.'

He took his next step and thought – 'things are as they are. Why would anyone wish to alter that? The Core has never hurt anyone. It has granted us eternal life. That we can't really see it, know it, or even begin to comprehend it, is beside the point. Ask it any question and it will answer, truthfully, helpfully. The only mystery to the Core is the mystery that we can't ask it anything that it can't answer.

'No, that's not right.'

He took another step and his boots rang. 'The Core is unknowable, only because of the paucity of our comprehension. Beside it, we feel shallow, diminished and therefore, nervous. Which is why these circular conversations, be they in your head, or around a kitchen table, are not smiled upon. Very few people enjoy being reminded that they are fools, incapable of understanding their own situation. Incapable of even framing a question that might, somehow, provoke an answer that would sweep away the mystery.'

It was a long way down to the mid-level and although there were only 17 steps to each course of the stair, each step provoked a fresh flurry of thought. Therefore, the conjectures arising from every zig-zag, 34 steps and a small half-landing, would have filled the pages of an indifferent philosophical dissertation. By the time he was four zig-zags deep he had awarded himself a doctorate in useless speculation and thereafter he was in post-doctoral realms.

Before he even reached the upper level, his mind had taken a pugnacious stance. Growling silently, he took the last flight and there he rested. He was growing aware that this was a strange, unknown realm and therefore a good partner for his baffled state-of-mind.

He leaned on the rock wall and stared first left, then right, down long, slightly curving, indistinguishable tunnels. They had probably been cut with whatever had superseded lasers – he must ask. In antique parlance, they had been cut with a knife, through butter. They were lit but with such lights as only appeared when his gaze was questing. If he merely 'looked', a short sequence of L.E.D's would wink on. If he sought an answer, such as – 'how does this tunnel curve?' bolder illumination came into play. Were he to take a meaningful step, in any direction, the tunnel became as bright as day.

"These damn lights are reading my mind," he said in disgust. "So, fuck off!" he roared and the lights went off obediently, leaving him standing in pitch blackness. He tolerated that for half-a-minute. Then he ventured an experiment. 'Ever onward!' he thought, and the lights were there, instantly. "You're reading my mind in the pitch dark," he groaned. "Have you any idea how helpless that makes me feel?" He waited, almost expectantly but there was no answer. There was no link to a vocal circuit. But, on reflection, Jo-Jo doubted he could have survived a conversation with a light bulb.

After that, every step was a descent into fresh, self-imposed anguish. 'How can there be any meaning in a world without doubts? If everything is unquestioned, perfect, what becomes of my judgement, my choices? I have limitless time and an ever-watchful protector. If I'd tried to freeze to death, last night, the Core probably wouldn't have let me. Has anyone ever died up here, on the Upper Rim? He couldn't recall but probably not. Why would they?'

He pondered Death for the length of three zig-zags. 'It should be a touchstone, an ominous reality in every life' he thought, 'always arriving too soon, when there was more to do. Without it, not only was life interminable, it was meaningless. There again, who could possibly want to die?' He reminded himself that he was young at 4,000 years. Death should be the last thing on his mind. His body was constantly renewing itself, with small improvements made from time to time. Certainly he found it useful to be strong, to have perfect vision, teeth, hearing. It was good that his internal organs worked faultlessly. He had no interest in exploring the physiological side of mortality. But this peculiar immortality that had been granted them all, unless you possessed the brain that could formulate a plan to occupy it meaningfully, was borderline disastrous. At least it was for him. Others, he had to admit, seemed perfectly content.

'The thing is,' he explained to himself, 'I'm not an artist, or a wife. I have neither creative vision, nor a supportive nature – at least, not in the sense that Shade possesses it, willing to find her meaning by caring for another who is busy pursuing his own, selfish vision.' With that thought he ground to a halt, half-way down, or half-way up one flight of treads. What, then, was he? What an appalling question to be stuck on.

"I wish I wasn't in a vertical tunnel, searching for the next horizontal way-out. I'm not a mole, I'm not a worm, I'm not even that keen on tunnels, or stairs. So why am I here? To watch the bum-end of a metal angel poke itself into a hole in a rock. I must be mad!" he said to the light-fittings and with that self-assessment, continued downwards.

'Think, think, think,' he told himself, but there was nothing worthwhile in his head. No skeleton on which to sling muscle, sinews and flesh. He felt devoid, not in a depressed, mournful manner but with a raging incandescence. How could his mind be so empty? It was a simple question – what are you living for?'

He stopped to press his head against cold metal and found his forehead was slick with sweat. This was not amusing. This was desperate. 'Could he not live for the moment?' He groaned. 'How many times had that old chestnut fallen from the fire? "The moment," which moment? This one…or that next one…oops, here comes another…and another…oh, gosh! I lived for them all! I was living in the moment but all I was doing was reciting "moment, moment, moment." No, no, this was too chaotic. Give me some simple rules, some baby steps, something I can follow…a Rule Book…I don't know, maybe some hints, too. Take me by the hand and lead me…oh, I don't know where. Somewhere, anywhere but here, where my mind is running amok. I have to stop this now!'

He couldn't stop. His wretched mind was skipping, going over the same groove again and again – 'what am I living for? What am I doing? Why am I doing it?'

"I don't fucking know!" he bellowed and was rewarded by some distant lights winking on below him. "You're having unreasonable expectations," he yelled to them. "You're expecting someone to arrive, which is my problem exactly…" he trailed off. That was his problem, he thought, he kept expecting to arrive, whole, sane and sensible in his own body. He shouldn't be orbiting himself, like some crazed comet describing eccentric parabolas around a black hole, wondering where the hell it was and what was going on.

"Sod this," he announced as he reached the mid-level. Time to get real. Time to be the intrigued and indulged guest. Time to be grateful and show it. Good.

"I'm going to see the Angel Lift," he announced to the chill air, in case such confidence inspired any robotic response. As it didn't, he plunged into the western tunnel and began the long walk under blazing lights. Everything about this tunnel was perfect. Any flaws, or cracks had been filled and in places, where the strata were tightly-packed, such rock had been highlighted by polishing. This was a geological outing if you wished it to be, if your fascination lay along such lines. That was the thoughtful, generous nature of the Core. It was indulgent, avuncular – maddening.

He stopped himself, just as his mind was gearing up for another rant. 'No, not that road,' he told himself sharply. 'You can take "the road less-travelled," if that's the approved phrase.'

He had a thought. "I'm a frog," he announced to the indifferent lights, the millennial strata. He crouched, bum on heels, arms to the front, fingertips barely touching the floor. "Ribbit!" he croaked exploding upwards. Down he came. "Ribbit! Ribbit! Ribbit!" 'Oh, this was fun!' Along the corridor he bounded, "Ribbit! Ribbit! and Ribbit!" A dozen bounds and he thought his hams would explode. 'One more,' ordered the Lunatic in the Driving Seat. "Ribbit!" and away he flew and down he came, not onto solid rock but into empty, black space, exactly like Alice.

His stomach writhed and his mind flared. In a split second he was aware this was no ordinary hole in rock and though that was good, it was also very, very bad. There would be no catastrophic impact but sooner or later, there would be…something, other. Something unlike anything that had happened before. 'If you thought this is what I wanted, that this was what I was craving,' he thought in panic, 'then you've misunderstood me completely. This is all a misunderstanding!'

He was screaming. He should stop that. It was stupid. This was no ordinary fall. There would be no-one to hear. No rescue. Some event was occurring, something that would have to be lived through. With a huge effort he tried to focus his eyes. He blinked, blinked again, eyes shut, eyes open. He was falling, effortlessly, lazily, past walls of snakeskin. Snakeskin on a huge scale. Black and red, at first blurred, then defined, as if each scale could not quite make its mind up what colour it was. It was a reptilian, alien colouration. It frightened him. Also, it was breathing – or at least, it was palpitating. Each scale was rippling across its face, as if it floated on agitated oil.

Then, directly opposite him, as he fell as lightly as a feather, a scale split. There was pain in that rupture, it was not the easy parting of an eyelid. A membrane had been brutally torn apart. Through the rupture appeared an agonised human face. A face that had been fighting its way through the opening but had now become trapped, by one final, gory membrane. Against this it thrust its features in such panic and distress, that Jo-Jo felt agonised kinship.

When the face drew back – and he knew it was only for a moment, the better to writhe its way forwards again – the ruptured scale mimicked the actions of a human eye. It blinked and wriggled, as if it had been fouled by grit. But these were not eyes and those tortured bodies were not grit. This was some scene either of terrifying escape, or monstrous birthing. Whatever lay beyond that palpitating screen of scales was evil and those struggling creatures were inhuman, harbingers of ruin from some poisoned kingdom.

Face after face appeared. Multiple ruptures punctured the skin. A solitary hand shot free and lunged. He span away in terror, now denying all kinship with that simulation of human despair, the longing to be saved, or to perish together. 'Not alone, don't leave us here alone…' each pleaded in the screaming silence. No! They were not human! They had no claim! He denied them all!

He floated, span, descended and saw scale after scale split. The same silent drama but every face different, every contortion an intimate, personal agony. He expected, any second to hear their voices, not to witness silent pleading but have a sudden, unbearable chorus of agony burst upon his ears. Not so. He twisted ever downwards, in pregnant silence.

One last scale, flickering black and red, tore itself apart. He was staring directly into a girl's eyes and though it was through the same veined, smoky membrane, their lustre mesmerised him. This one, alien though she might be, he had to save but that inflexible spiralling descent turned him about. Instantly she became nothing more than a memory. 'So soon?' questioned silent, taunting voices. She had become no more than a distant haunting from this place of savage birthings.

He fell faster now, until some matrix, rising up clutched his back, seized and supported him. To Jo-Jo it felt that he had fallen into a lake of viscous oil. Neither his hands or feet could penetrate it, nor could he gain any sense of what it might actually be. This was hideous entrapment, suspended on a sea which gave no hint of its being, its substance, its purpose. What else floated here? What swam beneath him? What might nuzzle at him, with white lips and pale lamps for eyes? He tried to lift, or turn his head and neck but he was held in position as certainly as if he had been trapped in amber, or pitch.

There was movement in the distance. He was floating towards light. He searched for any sense of scale, some indication of his predicament, or place. Was he large, or small within this drama? Slowly floating, turning inch by inch across this basin, or ocean, he had sight of a shore. It was a scene of carnage, of a battlefield. Severed limbs and heads, the broken bits of men, women and children. Here they lay in great harvest rows, in hills that were being trodden down by the implacable movement of beings so huge that all he could glimpse of them were the dripping soles of their colossal feet, feet that rose inexorably up and down. They were treading out the stuff of the living, as if they were no more than a harvest of grapes, to be rendered into a vintage of pulverised flesh, bone, brain and lung, all draining into this sea on which he was suspended. He was floating on the dead.

He opened his mouth to howl in despair but no sound emerged. Anguish consumed him. The rags of his sanity were unwinding, floating away on this sea. With a galvanic effort he summoned a memory of sun on grass. Then and as it flickered, pathetically on/off, useless as some failing filament, he saw, a mere ball's toss distant, a giant foot rise slowly in the air. He saw that crushed bone, shredded organs dangled, entwined, from its sole and he watched as it now began an implacable descent upon a new and pitiful mound of humanity.

Whatever grip held him, it thrust him against this awful shore and there, despite himself, he rose on unsteady feet. He looked around him wildly but everything was flesh, bone and blood. His feet sank into the ruin. There was no horizon, apart from an eerie glow above fractured lines. He could make no sense of the rising and falling feet…above their splashed calves they faded away into fog. He turned to the sea, the oily matrix that had held him. It, too, was shrouded in fog but within it he could hear distant splashing, coming closer.

"It is the new born," a voice whispered by his ear. "They come to ask why you would not save them. Why would you not?"

The figures from the honeycombed snakeskin were pursuing him. They had forced their way free, had fallen like him, into the oily morass and would have an accounting from him.

He turned to see who it was who spoke. A simple figure stood there. A man from the crowd. Not a man to be described. Neither young nor old, stout nor lean, neither welcoming or threatening. A man of every world and none, a man nevertheless.

"Who are you?" Jo-Jo quavered.

"Your guide."

"Then get me out of here! Get me back to where I was!"

"The place where you were content?"

"The place before this!"

His guide turned placid eyes on him.

"This is no place to make demands. Come and see."

It was an order and Jo-Jo abjectly followed, sinking in the mess of fluids and flesh, almost to his knees. His guide seemed to walk on some unseen path, neither bone nor rags of flesh touched him.

This must be a place of dreams, thought Jo-Jo. Because, from the beach of crushed bodies they were now walking among rocks, following a winding path and there seemed no incongruity in the shift. He felt hugely weary and leaned against a rock. It was soft to the touch and there were fingers within it. They clutched for his hand. 'At last, you have come for me,' sighed a voice in his head.

"They're alive!" Jo-Jo shrieked, dragging himself free of the embrace. Around him, all the rocks began to moan and sigh. They rippled, fissures ran down them and memories clawed at him, trying to pull him into their embrace.

"Don't touch the rocks," said his guide. "Hurry, they are waiting for us, Mortal Man."

Jo-Jo stumbled along the path, the rocks closing the way behind him. 'We cannot let you go,' their voices whispered silently. 'We love you. You are one of us.'

They were at the crest of a hill. A small amphitheatre was huddled in the hollow below.

"Not far," said the guide, in an encouraging voice.

Every seat was full. Everyone was speaking but there was no sound Jo-Jo could hear. It was a frantic, excitable audience, rude and vigorous but he could distinguish no faces, no smells and not a sound. The steps down which he was walking were steepening. This was a descent turning into a fall. He looked to steady himself but from behind – the guide was now behind! – all he received was a vigorous push, that sent him tottering, flailing frantically for balance down the last dozen steps. He landed on his feet but the forward rush floored him and he fell sprawling onto hands and knees. He turned his head to protest.

Now he could see faces. Here were citizens drawn by Bosch and Breughel. Those who came to mock at executions. His execution.

He was not the first. A heap of severed limbs and heads testified to that. There was a stone trough of entrails and the floor was black with blood. Here was the butcher's table, fresh scrubbed with salt and bristle. Here were the iron hoops for his wrists and ankles, a leather strap to control his heaving belly. A block for his neck and head, the better to view his own vivisection.

An executioner stepped forward. He was faceless but Jo-Jo knew him. He wore a white smock, over leathern trousers. He was blood-stained, no doubt a severed artery had caught him as he went, inexorably, about his work. He wore a belt of chain, from which hung cleavers, knives, saws and pincers. His gloves were of leather and chain mail, as was the shield that protected his groin. He beckoned, not unkindly, for Jo-Jo to come forward. It was Moss.

"So," he said, "you want to be a mortal man?"

"Never!" shrieked Jo-Jo, "never!"

"Never what, Jo? Never what? What are you gabbling about, old friend? What's been happening here? Did you miss the angel?"

Jo-Jo was lying on cold stone and all he could see was Moss's anxious face, haloed by one of the tunnel lights, as he knelt beside him. He flailed feebly, trying to sit up.

"Get me up, Moss, I'm freezing down here. I can't move!"

"You're all right, man. You're fine. Somehow you've cracked your head. You've got a bump the size of a pullet's egg on your noggin. But my, you've frightened the life out of me. It was one of the 'bots came and got me, just as we finished the lift. I came running and here you were, out cold on the tunnel floor, 200 metres from where you should have been. You saw nothing, did you?"

Jo-Jo groaned. "I saw plenty. I saw more than enough. I've never seen the like. Trust me, I saw." He was just about to add …'and I never want to see it again'…when he realised that they were talking at cross purposes. He was supposed to have seen one of Moss's angelic host lowered into place. He had not been scheduled to visit their cousins in the Nether Regions, if that was where he had been.

Suddenly he remembered details. "Gonna be sick…" he managed in warning and threw up spectacularly. Moss skittered away. "Sorry about your nice clean tunnel," he sighed. Then he did it again.

Moss had had to half-carry, half-drag him to the lift. Even Jo-Jo conceded stairs were out of the question. For a moment then, he hung in space as they crossed the gantry to the cage. He looked down and that colossal fall seemed welcoming. He'd fallen down worse and recently. Now they drifted up, defying all common laws, to the surface. Moss packed him into some auto-vehicle he'd summoned. It was warm, confined, welcoming. It had the smell of a new thing. It took him back to Shade.

He expected haughty indifference and instead fell into motherly care. Even the Rabbit seemed contrite, rushing about at Shade's behest to perform helpful tasks. Then he stood ruefully in a corner and twisted his hands together. "Are you all right?" he asked, in a very small voice.

"No, little fella," said Shade, "he's not all right. Look at that bump on his head and that eye's going to be black and blue by suppertime. Help me to put him to bed…can you grow a bit? Could be helpful, here."

'What a fuss,' thought Jo-Jo, nevertheless limp with gratitude, as the Rabbit, using a set of servos they'd never required before, carried him like a baby to his room.

"Pull the curtains, little chap," said Shade, indifferent to the Rabbit's metamorphosis. "He won't want light troubling him for a bit.

"Now, here's a basin if you need to be sick. Rabbit and I'll be in the kitchen and hopefully the noise will be soothing, even if you want to doze a while. You just call if you need us. Poor lad, you've had a nasty fall! What were you up to? It's smooth as an ironed sheet down those tunnels."

"I was…" began Jo-Jo, on the verge of confessing to his 'ribbit-jumps.'

"Not another word," said Shade. "Dozing'll be better than talking right now."

Jo-Jo managed a – "thank you so much"- and then faded away into dreamless dozing. For a second he was terrified of being swept back to that Other Place but exhaustion was more persuasive than terror. He slept and on the occasions when he did wake, Shade was right, the tinkling of pans, the laughter as she chattered with the Rabbit, the running water and finally the rich smells that floated down the corridor, were soothing.

He woke, in the sense of 'I'm-awake-now-I-better-get-up' only when he heard Moss booming the day's news and enquiring after his well-being.

He staggered to the kitchen, truly light-headed and unsteady on his feet and announced himself with a cheerful – "I'm alive, thank you all very much." Then he sat down in a bit of a rush. "At least I think I am."

"You are, you are," Moss assured him. "That was a Medic-Move brought you home. It had run all the checks by the time you got here. No bleeding, no bruising, well not on the inside, where it matters. You've got a lovely black eye, though. Quite the shiner. Haven't seen one of those for quite some time."

"I haven't seen it myself," Jo-Jo admitted.

"You look a bit like a pirate," said the Rabbit, awkwardly.

"I don't feel like one. Far too wobbly and weedy."

"Let me get some food in you," said Shade. She turned away from the oven, bearing a seriously large apple pie.

"Oh…oh…" said Jo-Jo, his senses suddenly on full-alert "is that…?"

"Apple pie!" said Shade triumphantly, "your favourite, or so the little fella' tells me. Did he tell the truth?" she demanded, suddenly recalling the never-ending sparring between the two.

"I wouldn't dare tell stories about that," squeaked the Rabbit. "Apple pie comes under the heading of Sacred Food – Chapter One, Page One, The End…if you follow."

"He speaks truth," said Jo-Jo. "I'm restored just by the sight and now I've caught the smell… If I hit myself on the head again, can I have two slices please?"

Shade even laughed. "No need to go that far. You're more than welcome."

Jo-Jo ate – and then he ate some more. He ate enough to amuse everyone and after a further slice they fell back on awe.

"Beyond perfection but not beyond praise," he warbled. "I swear that was life-saving and truly, I bless you for it. Also, Rabbit, if you're not eating yours, please push it round here. I abhor waste. Shade, if you still feel sorry for me tomorrow, please let me have the recipe. That is the best ever and I am a connoisseur."

"It's true," murmured the Rabbit, "he is. But he always steals my slice."

"I do," agreed Jo-Jo, "but look on the bright side, you'll never get fat."

The Rabbit sniffed. "A certain solidity lends an air of command. Isn't that Shakespeare's Fifth Age of Man, 'full round of belly?"

"My Lord," complained Jo-Jo, "the stuff they downloaded into your little felt noggin never fails to amaze me."

"And the Seventh Age," said the Rabbit, sensing an audience, "is sans eyes, sans teeth, sans everything!" Then, looking straight at Jo-Jo, he added – "so beware – Mortal Man!"

Now it was Jo-Jo's turn to stare hard at the Rabbit but the Rabbit looked back innocently.

"We don't do Seventh Ages here, " said Moss. "We go on until we're finished."

"When might you be finished, Mr Moss?" enquired the Rabbit, with engaging naivety.

"Sorry," apologised Jo-Jo, "I don't take him out enough."

Shade giggled. "That'll be when he's finished all them angels, sweetie. Though believe me, something new will pop into his head and we'll be off again. Moss won't stop."

"And you, Mrs Moss?" asked the Rabbit, exploiting his window-of-grace mercilessly.

"Ah, Gods' forbid…" interjected Jo-Jo, helplessly.

"When Moss is finished, you great fluff-ball!" she said happily.

"Then," said the Rabbit gravely, "anyone who wants to live forever should stick around here."

"That's the truth," Moss said, ending that particular conversation.

Jo-Jo was terrified that he would do something to banish Shade's mellow indulgence. So he tiptoed through coffee, mentally urging the Rabbit to fill in his blanks. Credit where credit is due, he did Jo-Jo proud, rippling with wit and repartee, while sprinting about performing ever more good and helpful deeds. 'Nauseating to behold,' thought Jo-Jo, proudly.

After one particular bout of successful ripostes and parries, Moss leaned over to Jo-Jo and whispered in his ear – "she be really taken with your Rabbit." And that was true, because the Rabbit made up to her shamelessly. Perhaps even robots enjoy being liked for themselves.

Now Jo-Jo lay in bed, battling both with an excess of thought and apple pie.

The mellowness induced by the latter was conflicting with rage provoked by the former. He was sure he had been roundly trumped by a practical joker and he hated practical jokes. Surely, that was what the performance in the tunnel had been about? A reminder of mortality from that Keeper of the Keys, the Core. 'Question our benevolence and see what could lie in store for you!' He must have been transmitting danger signals throughout his last dissatisfied millennium and some arbiter had decided to deliver a slap on the wrist of a dissenter, perhaps a defector? What else could that charade be about?

His mortification stemmed from the fact that he had been genuinely terrified. He had had no time to question the validity, the likeliness of such scenarios. He had been plunged into them with all the shocking immediacy of an ice-bath and hopeless romantic that he was, he had swallowed every Gothic trope.

Which might explain why he was now battling indigestion, as well as rage.

The indigestion was something of a triumph, in fact. The Core kept each and every one of its citizens in perfect balance. No gastric reflux was allowed on Earth II.

So it was quietly satisfying to know that not only was his mind rejecting benevolent dictatorship, so were his pH levels. But if this was victory, it was a Pyrrhic one, too. Stomach acid was dissolving him from the inside out!

Admitting defeat, he tiptoed to the sleeping kitchen and went in search of bicarbonate of soda. There would be no patent remedies to be found here, on this planet of perfect beings. He would have to fall back on ancient prescriptions.

He found bicarbonate… and he also found Shade's recipe book. Greatly daring but also calculating that as the bump on his head shrank, her indulgence of him would diminish proportionally, he stole a look at the apple pie recipe – lest it be unforthcoming thereafter. There was just one commonplace ingredient he had never used or, for that matter had never even heard of being used and he counted himself a cosmic expert on apple pie. As this evening's was the best he had ever eaten, he made a special place for it in his memory. Commonplace it might be but it was underlined in red. Then he swallowed the bicarbonate mix. It was quite disgusting but almost instantly, he felt his reflux abating.

Guilt-ridden about having transgressed every rule of propriety – for that personal recipe book would be the most sacred volume on Shade's shelves – he tiptoed back to bed, once he was certain he had restored everything to its rightful place. There he plotted. How might he use the day's events to his advantage? It might have flattered, or terrified him, had he realised that greater brains than his were also computing the potential of the day's actions. But eventually, incapable of advancing events in any way at all, he fell into another dreamless sleep.

When he woke it was with the certain knowledge of what he was going to do next. Such resolve was shocking. He genuinely felt faint. Therefore he groaned, pleaded an appalling headache and begged to be left in bed for the morning, when the Rabbit came to summon him for breakfast. He needed time to scrutinise his new-found dynamism, in case it turned out to be a temporary abreaction. But as the morning ticked by, his problem was that it seemed to be here to stay. He was going to confront the Core.

To even approach the Core, he had to quit the Rim and quitting the Rim was unheard of. Rim-dwellers were Rim-dwellers. They disdained the middle land, the low land, whatever might lie beyond the Edge. No-one actually knew what that was, because no-one in living memory had been even remotely inclined to investigate. As we have heard, a few hardy lowlanders penetrated to the Rim on adventurous excursions and that was sufficient to establish that they didn't have two-heads. What else was it necessary to know about them, or the doings of the Core?

What he was plotting was physical, moral and intellectual heresy. It was tantamount to questioning the credo of the Rim itself, it suggested there could be something worthwhile, over the Edge. Everyone knew that was not true. But, of course, his gravest sin would be the implicit suggestion that the Core was worthy of being interrogated by a Rim-dweller.

Haughty acceptance was the only attitude to be maintained in the face of the Core's omnipotence. That the Core was omnipotent was patently obvious, which was why polite society never discussed anything pertaining to such matters. There was an untruth to be maintained. An untruth on which the superiority of the Rim was founded. The untruth of the Rim's proud and rugged independence. This was their underlying myth. Woe betide a Rim-dweller who, in speech or by inference, acknowledged the dependency of the Clan. To go over the Edge, with the intention of interrogating the source of their rich independence would be…

'…absolutely,' thought Jo-Jo, it would be the ultimate betrayal – especially if he ever had any intention of returning, bearing the truth like some latter-day Prophet. That was the day the messenger would be shot. If he went over the Edge, it would be better never to come back.

The fact was, the moment he had woken up, he had known that he was going and would never be coming back. That was the heresy that he had needed time to interrogate. It deserved more than its split-second of revelation.

What part did yesterday's charade play in the whole affair? It had certainly been the catalyst. Primarily he was mortified at having been so easily traumatised but beneath his 'certainty' that it had been a dream, one induced to whip him into line, was a shred of doubt. 'What if it hadn't been a hypnotic interlude? What would that mean?' That was the goad, the gadfly, that was now driving him on. The age-old question – "what is real and what is not?" Like a first year philosophy student, he intended to interrogate the Core about the nature of reality. But unlike that student he would be doing it from a very different place. 'Yes, yes,' he could pop the question on a piece of paper, post it and get back an answer, probably within the hour. Questions, trail bikes, answers, all were to be had up here on the Rim. No need to go over the Edge.

"No," said Jo-Jo decisively, this question demanded its pilgrimage. After all, he was expecting the Core to admit to its intentions in eternally endorsing his continuing existence. That was a question too far, not one to be consigned to the in-house post.

That was his decision. He had made it, so lying here in bed was not going to further it. At the same time he wasn't quite ready to announce his plans. So he decided to steal out to the forge, where he knew Moss kept a supply of kitchen necessities and ponder the specifics of his mission, over a solitary breakfast. Just for the moment he wanted to avoid what would, no doubt, be Shade's withering comments.

The forge was a wonderful place. Dark, warm and secret, in the sense that no-one went there except on business. Not even Moss used it as a refuge. To him it was a functional space, not a magical one.

Moss was a visionary, or more accurately he had visions. He was not a romantic. Jo-Jo rarely had visions but he was an incurable romantic. To him the forge was a mysterious realm, filled with strange tools and the echoes of ancient gods who had occupied such workplaces. Celtic gods, Saxon, Greek and Norse, all had transformed metals, forged indestructible swords and terrible lances. All he would have on his travels, he reflected ruefully, would be a pen-knife. Whoever heard of a magical pen-knife?

Nursing a tin mug of jet-black coffee and chewing on a cereal bar he had stolen from Moss's cache, he stared out of the window to watch the Rabbit, gravely scooting up and down on his new machine. No wheelies, no skidding turns in the dirt, just the most decorous circuits with the occasional heroic foray over a bit of a bump at one end of the track, after essaying which he would glance for approval at Shade, who would wave encouragingly from the kitchen window.

Jo-Jo began to feel very emotional. His knockabout relationship with the Rabbit obviously ignored a whole raft of more sensitive feelings that had been written in the little creature's program. The phrase 'only a robot,' really didn't do justice to a creation that could have held its own with Socrates and yet delighted in delivering this child-like performance for Shade. Was that really all wiring? Jo-Jo hoped it was, otherwise the years in the Tupperware box must have been very bleak. Probably actionable under inter-galactic law…if there was such a set of relevant statutes.

That was how he allowed his resolution to drift all morning, back and forth, to and fro on an alternating ebb and flood of emotions. 'Not good, Jo-Jo, not good,' he kept lecturing himself but to be here, out-of-sight, detached from the realities of the day, whilst able to observe them, was a particular sweet form of self-indulgence and he soaked it up. Only hours later, when he was finally saturated, did he emerge and walk boldly to the kitchen, where he knew Shade and the Rabbit were hard at work preparing the evening meal.

"Can I help?' he asked breezily, halting both in their tracks.

Shade gave him a look suggesting that such a development would be highly unlikely.

Safe in her lee the Rabbit endorsed the glance.

"Glad to see you're mended," she said curtly. "Why don't you take Moss his lunch if you're up to that? I'll pack yours up too. You can be boys together, that way."

'Not a suggestion,' thought Jo-Jo but he smiled amiably anyway.

"What a good idea!" chirruped the Rabbit. "We're making supper!"

"Rabbit pie?" asked Jo-Jo, caustically. "Look out for the wiring!"

He found Moss in a new hangar, selecting metal. He had a whole sheaf of templates to fulfil and Jo-Jo judged he was finding things frustrating.

"You can help me here. I'm in need of a 'gopher' at the moment."

"Gopher I will be, then" said Jo-Jo.

From his point-of-view, Jo-Jo timed things properly that evening. He polished off the apple pie before making his bombshell announcement.

"You're going where?" demanded Moss, largely rhetorically.

"Over the Edge, off-Rim, via the Stair."

"The Stair!"

"The very same."

"And you think you know where it is, what it is, if it is?"

"I haven't got a clue but it's still where I'm going."

"And why was that, again?" asked Shade, incredulous.

"I've some stuff I want to ask the Core."

She gestured at the Post Box. "Then ask it!" she said aggressively.

"Face-to-face," said Jo-Jo.

There was a long silence, during which the Rabbit fiddled with his outline, going up, then down. Then up again.

"How do you know the Core has a face?" asked Moss, stumped for questions.

"I don't. I intend to find out. I mean to find out a lot. I'll let you both know."

"Not me," said Shade and left for her kitchen, where she crashed and banged to good effect. The Rabbit, dialling himself down, sneaked after her, edging away below table height.

"I've known you a long time Jo-Jo," said Moss "and you've done some daft things. As if walking round the ruddy thing wasn't rude enough, now you're going to go and bang on its front door! What for? What possible reason could you have? What sort of storm are you going to cause for the rest of us? Have you thought about that?"

"Why would anything I do, affect the rest of you?" asked Jo-Jo. "I'm no threat. I just want a few answers, a few things straightening out, a bit less mystery floating about."

"Don't you like what we've got, Jo-Jo? Don't you value it? Other folks do. Why risk messing it all up? Things have been this way a long time. Things work out nicely. We don't ask for too much and they don't begrudge the giving. Why endanger that?"

"Moss, old friend – 'we don't ask for much?' – have you looked at what they've given you? You've an asteroid-sized project underway here and they've never questioned it. Don't you wonder why?"

Moss stared at him in horror.

"You damn fool! Of course I wonder why! But I know better than to go round asking! This is you being petulant, arrogant, ungrateful! You should be ashamed!" … and Moss stormed into the kitchen too, where voices could be heard, rising and falling.

Jo-Jo felt like a teenager, finally routed by parents who had had too much. Taking his cue from such unfortunates, he crept away to his room to hide, until morning.

Leaving was a sad affair.

"You ready?" he asked the Rabbit.

They were all gathered outside, hostilities almost suspended. He had expressed thanks, obligation and deepest gratitude, then left it at that.

Now the Rabbit stood on one leg, hummed and hawed, clutched the handlebars of his little red bike and wriggled uncomfortably.

"That's looking like a 'No,'" said Jo-Jo.

"It's more of a 'do-we-have-to?'" replied the Rabbit.

"History and literature demand," said Jo-Jo, trying to keep things light-hearted, "that every Knight Errant have his trusty Esquire. Quixote had Sancho Panza, Crusoe had Man Friday and theoretically, I've got you."

"Look at this, " said the Rabbit eagerly and he cautiously accelerated his bike over a very modest bump that Moss had arranged for him in the turf, the evening before. "Bit hair-raising, don't you think? Imagine how good I'll be when you get back!"

After a long pause, Jo-Jo managed a fairly bright – "OK but only providing Shade and Moss don't mind."

The Rabbit looked appealingly to Shade, who had been surreptitiously dabbing her eyes.

"I love the little fella' like my own," she said emotionally. "He's a friend to chat to in my kitchen, what with Moss out all hours and weathers."

Moss carefully edged him to one side and whispered in his ear, conspiratorially.

"Sorry about last night," he said, humbly. "But thank you, you've made her really happy. Be off with you but careful now, no making a fool of yourself…and all of us!"

That had been leaving. The Rabbit rode part of the way with him, then declared it far too bumpy and had made off, back to safety.

Jo-Jo had turned and seen them all making their way indoors, the Rabbit hand-in-hand with Shade. 'Oh well,' he thought, 'you've got my Rabbit but I've got your recipe!' and a little of his 'thief-in-the-night' guilt drained away.

"Mortality, here I come!" Jo-Jo announced to indifferent surroundings and with Moss's place now lost to sight, set off in the direction of the Edge and the Stair.

'Which are where, precisely?' he asked himself, after the first few miles. To that question there was no precise answer. There was the Edge-proper, so-to-speak and then there were the other Edges. The Stair was located on the Edge-proper and the Edge-proper was distinguished by its being a vertical cliff of solid rock that plunged ever downwards, for some miles. It was not to be mistaken for the Edge-improper, which merely fell away in a treacherous fashion, leading the unwary into unstable landscapes liable to sudden collapse. Improper and proper edges probably alternated around the perimeter of the Rim, rather after the manner of a jawbone lacking a full set of sound teeth.

There were no maps, Rim-dwellers despised maps. They relied on local knowledge, personal experience and in the absence of those, were forced to fall back on myth. Consumed as they were by their various projects, this intense parochiality bothered them not one jot. They knew the way to their neighbours' properties, though these were often scores of miles distant. That fact alone gave them a comfortable feeling of being one with the landscape and as their neighbours' writ extended in precisely the same way, so local knowledge counted for a great deal in the end.

Jo-Jo had walked these Rim-lands for a very long time. He was rarely at home. In fact, he was uncomfortably aware that others spent more time in his cottage than he did. They always left things neat and clean, replaced what they had used and left him greetings. It was an arrangement of the Rim, rarely abused and one very much the norm amongst the roving individuals. Jo-Jo was not unique, there was a loose confederation of walkers who trudged the Rim, each describing their own peculiar orbits. He rarely used their homes, feeling slightly queasy about adopting other people's possessions as his own but he would occasionally bivouac in an outbuilding, to avoid heavy weather as a rule.

Thus he was in no doubt about the general location of the Edge. It was a very long way along the path he was now taking, far further than he had ever travelled before. Jo-Jo was a fan of circle-routes, not straight lines so he was at a slight disadvantage here. What he knew for certain was that Moss's place was a very good place to start if you were heading for the Edge. No-one in that vicinity looked at you oddly, should you casually mention the Edge. It was known to be a fact. The Edge lay – "in that direction" – and everyone would point the same way. Had he begun further in, say diametrically opposite Moss's homestead for argument's sake, mention of the Edge would have provoked stories that had more of myth about them than cartography. This had been a good place to start.

Days came and went and the terrain never varied. Gritstone, quartz-rich sands and cotton grasses underfoot, tussocks always ready to turn a walker's ankle, Just the occasional oases of bright green, cropped turf to suggest that things were slowly improving, that this steady downhill trudge was leading to marginally richer pastures.

Jo-Jo could walk very quickly and he did so, sleeping few hours, living off the emergency rations of his pack. Those could last him a year, if necessary. They were another beneficence of the Core, and would be quietly and efficiently provided at any domestic homestead in possession of the ubiquitous post-box, which in reality meant at every cottage.

Jo-Jo had always hoped that his walking would be a fine lubricant for metaphysics. The solitude, the rhythm of his lope, wouldn't these all add up to a flow of the richest thought? Sadly, that had never proved to be the case, which was why he had requested the Rabbit as a companion. Animatronic companions were a commonplace up here. Very few women had the taste for Rim life. It was a predominantly an enclave of solitary males but even artists and philosophers crave a little company. From time to time. Jo-Jo was used to meeting robotic wives. Most were very pleasant, which was why Shade was such a bracing corrective. Nevertheless, he had never craved a robotic female to share his life. Hence his Rabbit, a companion with a bit of backchat, though he might have over-stressed that option on the printed form. At least he'd never met another one, which was a point of pride for them both.

When he had made the ridiculous decision to turn the Rabbit off, for the duration of his walk around the great cylinder of the Core, it had been in the hope of catalysing some latent ability for philosophising while he walked. After all, it was not just one of his idle rambles, it had been a 'Walk with a Purpose' – to nail the mystery of the Core! That had failed, dismally. Also, after the first day and in the absence of an even slightly significant thought, he had been reduced to repeating a ridiculous mantra, simply to keep his legs going, on what he already knew would be a futile quest. It went – "Horsey, horsey – keep right on!"

That was the pinnacle of his achievement, his most masterly piece of creativity. It was mortifying, in retrospect, probably infantile. The fact was, he bitterly regretted not taking the Rabbit with him, just as he was already missing him on this trek. He would have been a superb Sancho Panza and they would have argued endlessly. That always made the time fly.

After his first few weeks he encountered a sort of tree. It was a twisted, flattened, juniper, half-buried in the hollow where it had seeded, probably centuries ago. It seemed desperate to burrow under the earth completely, to become the planet's first subterranean juniper. But of the weather that had driven it to such extremes, he saw nothing. No rain fell, blizzards were absent, wind didn't howl, nothing suggested that this was a relentlessly hostile place for man, beast or junipers.

He talked to some passing birds but they didn't stop. He had more luck conversing with beetles. One seemed so attentive that he lectured it for some miles, carrying it in the palm of his hand, so that he didn't have to stop but eventually, it unfolded its wing case, extended its wings and floated back the way they had come. "Did it know it had been going the wrong way?" he asked the world. It had seemed so.

He stayed for one night, with an elderly lady who had spent her life turning pond water into dragonflies. It was the distant shimmering of her dragonflies that had led him to her smallholding. She explained her mission to him and he failed, utterly, to grasp the sense of it but he nodded eagerly. Then he asked about the Edge.

It wasn't far, she said, maybe just a few weeks – thataways – and she indicated with a flourish of her hand a direction that could have meant anywhere on the visible horizon.

He had replenished his supplies, thanked her for his welcome and moved on. At least the Edge had been a solid reality for her, unlike her dragonflies. They were turned, every night, by the action of moonlight, back into pond water. It was the creating she enjoyed.

He met a boat-builder beside his clipper ship. He was quite certain where the Edge lay. "Her bowsprit points the way" he said proudly, "where else would I be sailing?"

Further on lived the maze-maker, whose creation now spanned acres, even delving deeply underground. He had been experimenting with corridors that would be held in the air. They were very beautiful but prone to collapse, not under moonlight but gravity. His corridor equations were complex but his directions to the Edge were explicit.

He wandered on through the same landscape, featureless by and large until, suddenly, rugged pines began to appear. "Now we're getting somewhere," said Jo-Jo.

He lay out under the stars that evening. His plan was to rest a while and then carry on, travel by moonlight.

As he lay dozing, he felt the ground tremble, distantly but too close for comfort. This was the clearest of messages. He was close to a section of improper-Edge. That trembling had been a portion of it giving way, carrying everything with it, turning life into a scree of jumbled earth and boulder. He jumped to his feet and could feel the shifting of the land under the soles of his feet. It was a sensation that took away every certainty you might hold.

Probably the Core was proof against such restless movement. Maybe the planet could collapse about it, tumbling about that impregnable, milky shaft with a cosmic thundering that would stun mere earthly Gods. But anything that clung to the surface of this sphere and felt that sickening movement, fled. Jo-Jo did just that. He scooped up his pack and loped away, as far as he could get from whatever was happy to hurl him into the void. Wherever the Stair might be, it was not likely to be hard by one of the unsettled places.

The cool night air suited his loping pace. Even though his path now lay slightly uphill, he felt no dragging at his lungs, no iron bands round his chest. Exertion eased his fear, blanked the atavistic terror that the trembling of the earth loosed in every living being. There was no more he could do. Every step took him farther away, made it less likely that some pent-up tension in the strata would rise, like forked lightning and surface beneath him.

He was running flat-out now but as he lengthened stride, pace drawn out of pace, he felt an empathy flowing around him, as if something was trying to say – 'not every hand is against you. I care for you.' Who, though, might that be?

That was a concept that engaged his attention fully. To have some Force of Nature place a reassuring hand on your shoulder would be an enormous boon in life. To come armed, as it were, to the fray would lift any individual head and shoulders above the pack. What a conceit! But, for a while he treasured it and the flood of endorphins it released.

Slowly it ebbed. Again he became a lone man, taking long strides across open country, whilst many miles behind him, the land lurched and heaved, casting things into ruin.

Dawn found him collapsed in the shade of another line of twisted pines. He had run all night. He was famished and dehydrated. His pack held answers to both problems and he just had the energy left to fall on them, as quickly as shaking hands would let him.

"Damn fool," he upbraided himself. What had all that been about? "I'm late, late for a very important date," he chanted, a memory from the Rabbit days. 'Happy days,' he thought, with a flood of nostalgia.

Then he thought about Shade and the probably colossal favour he had done her. After all, she could barely have asked Moss for an animatronic "other," male or female. She could have asked for a dog but dogs-proper lived such short lives, while dogs-improper went on far too long. Same problem with cats. It had taken him an age of brooding before he had come up with his talking Rabbit. "I should have patented you," he said to no one in particular. "Need sarcasm, irony, or whimsy in your life? Get Hot-Core Rabbit – hardcore wit, walking reference book, tells a good bed-time story, doesn't eat the wallpaper, or shit on the rugs. Comes in a variety of finishes, from Persian to Harlequin, with a new range in Steam Punk." Actually, there was a thought…if he ever got his Rabbit back he might get him a Steam Punk makeover. No, on second thoughts, bits would keep falling off and in the wrong weather, he might rust, or tarnish.

Nevertheless, as representatives of a colony of aspiring artists, the Rim's animatronics were dismally underwhelming. Complaisant girls with big boobs seemed to be the Gold Standard. True, there were a few Gay Icons cruising the territory but he had the feeling that whatever Gay Community might exist on this planet, it was likely to be found in the thriving lowlands, not philosophising, or obsessing over unique artworks up here. Not many of their tribe were confirmed solitaries – or was he stereotyping? Anyway, Shade should be very grateful to have his Rabbit in her life. He wondered if it had gone rogue yet. Its sarcasm circuits so underused that, one day, they would overload and the poor woman would drown in irony at her kitchen sink? Was it possible? – "I can only wish."

With a sudden rush of nausea, he realised he had to sleep, or doze, for a while. Only then could he consider the question of Edge and Stair. They were close. He could feel that.

Fitful dozing turned out to be the best he could manage by way of rest. Not ideal. But he must have slept more deeply than he thought, for when he did struggle back to the everyday world he discovered that, not only had a breeze got up but he had been acting as a litter-bin, of sorts. Flapping in the lee of his legs and wedged between his trunk and that of the tree were a dozen or so sheets of A5 paper. They were advertising flyers and never more aptly named, for the wind had brought them hither while he slept. As he scrambled up he grabbed a fistful, while the rest escaped.

All advertised the same wonder – 'BESPOKE LADDERS TO HEAVEN, sturdily constructed, finest materials, delivery 7 to 10 days. Competitive prices! Ten per cent discount on production of this flyer.' Underneath, in a fine italic script, was inscribed –

'by A. Abraham Esq.' 'I could get 50 per cent off,' thought Jo-Jo gaily, brandishing the five he'd captured. 'No, it won't work like that,' said the internal pessimist. 'You're probably right,' Jo-Jo agreed. It was always wise to defer to that personal kill-joy. Nevertheless 'Ladders to Heaven,' as a concept, was not a million miles away from a Stair to the middle-lands, low-lands, or whatever they called themselves. Jo-Jo speculated that A. Abraham had located his business hard by the Stair, hoping to capture any business that might ascend from the plains with the intention of proceeding further. Very enterprising, he thought. Maybe he also had a thriving business at the bottom of the Stair – 'Slippery Slides to Hell'…?

The question now was how to cross-examine an A5 advertising sheet? There was no address, which suggested a number of things – that Mr Abraham and his Ladders were well-known hereabouts, or that these flyers had blown from a place where directions would be available, or, or…? How old were the wretched things? Abraham and all his works could be dust by now. These could be wind-carried relics, circumnavigating the planet according to the seasonal weather patterns. No, not so, they were quite fresh but not so fresh that they might have been printed yesterday. They could be a year old, or was that the buffeting they'd received in transit from obstacles such as himself. The obvious thing to do was follow the paper trail.

What paper trail? He found two more flyers. One was sticking to the head of particularly unpleasant looking toadstool and the other was wedged in an animal burrow. They had led him no more than 300 yards. Nevertheless, it was a direction and insofar as he could, he followed it. Within a very short space of time he registered two important things, the wind was picking up and there was dampness in the air. He could translate those clues in two ways and the first was hopeful, the second, not so good.

There could be an approaching storm. They often occurred after earthquake and landslide. More hopefully, perhaps he was very close to the Edge. He would anticipate a sudden change of weather along a physical front as tremendous as legend suggested that the Edge was. Making the best provision for either outcome he changed his route, cutting into the pine break on a diagonal. That would take him even further away from any ripples of the earth tremor, while at the same time allowing him to approach the source of the damp air.

It proved to be a scant mile through the wood. At its exposed edge the trees were in little better shape than the stunted juniper he had encountered, weeks ago. They had been doubled over, their heads either jammed against their fellows in the rear, or bent to the scarified ground. Roots were exposed, arthritic knuckles that struggled to maintain any grip. Some trees were upended, the root ball flensed bone clean on the upper side, while the lower edges still clung on valiantly to whatever nurture was to be had. Behind those lowest threads huddled tiny wild flowers, so small as to appear little more than beads of dew among the sinewy grass. This was a hard place from which to cull a living wage.

Jo-Jo stared out from the comparative shelter of the inner tree line but he could see no Edge. What he could see was a great saucer of a plain. No, saucer was wrong. The great scoop of land ran on, left and right, as uniform as a feeding trough. There was a dive down from the tree-line, into the basin, then a long rise upwards. That ended abruptly, in a bland line of horizon that might be the crest of an Edge, or prove to be no more than the rim of a plateau. quite possibly the first of many descending steps, leading to an Edge achingly far away.

That moist wind told Jo-Jo otherwise. It was damp air, rising up from a rain blessed lowland, far below. He was convinced the Edge was that far line of bare-scraped rock. What, then, to do about it? To go in search of Abraham and his Ladders, or to explore whatever revelation lay beyond that rim?

He breakfasted, – or was it lunched? – maybe he even dined, in the shelter of the trees. He'd left his watch at Moss's place, dial frozen – until such time as he chose to release it. In the beginning of this expedition, he had been running by calendar days, now he seemed to be obeying circadian rhythms.

He straightened up. Brushed away crumbs for the ants and set out. Step by easy step he left the shelter of the trees. As soon as he did the wind began to test him, plucking at his sleeves, flattening clothes against his body, exploring the contours of the backpack. It was like a blind creature, recognising him by touch and feel. He leaned against it, moving down the slope into the dish of the trough.

When he thought he'd achieved a respectable distance he turned around, expecting to see the trees as specks on the horizon. He might have walked a mere 500 yards, for all the difference distance had made. There was nothing to measure yourself against. There had been sand, now there was grass, in the far distance lay rock. Nothing could be described as a feature, one zone was much the same as the next. Nothing grew higher than his ankles, no erratic boulders littered the ground, there was no sight of man, or beast.

He shrugged and moved on, aiming to register the defining moment, when down turned to up. It was definitely there but much of what had appeared to be irrefutable, definitive, contours were so spread out that it was a long time before his thighs registered 'up.' When he finally looked back, hours of walking seemed to have been compressed into landscape precis – the tree line seemed merely a large meadow's breadth away. Jo-Jo knew differently.

For the rest of the day, it seemed, he toiled uphill. It seemed an easy climb and as regards footholds, it was Sunday afternoon walking. But in terms of gradient, it was challenging. Jo-Jo was fit, lean and muscular. He was also panting, stopping to catch his breath, by the time he reached that final table of rock. But once there, what had appeared to be a slight lip, he could now see stretched for a mile at least. Equally unexpected was the fact that you had to scramble up on to it. It wasn't much of a climb but neither was the rock obligingly littered with hand and toeholds. In fact, it was a natural defence, convex, smooth and slick with lichens, greasy from the damp wind.

Jo-Jo plastered himself to that surface like a limpet and squirmed his way up, refusing to slide back. Every time he started to slither downhill, he imagined he was a rubber plunger and hugged every inch of stone that he could contact. Eventually, grazed and green with outraged lichen, he made it and forced himself into a hectic, slithering crawl away from the edge.

A yard or so higher and he found a grudging fissure he could wedge the blade of his penknife in, as a substitute for a piton. "Bloody hell," he allowed and idiotic though it might be, even as he spoke he sensed resentment at his presence in the rocks beneath him. Idiotic or not, it was sufficiently palpable to make him move on. He crawled, climbed and scrambled as rapidly as safety allowed. The further he got from that malicious frontal rock, the better he felt.

Eventually he allowed himself to stand. In reality it was more of a crouch but it sufficed to show him that the gradient eased at this point, that the rocks were dryer, easier of transit, with cracks and high points to grab hold of. More importantly he could see what must be the Edge. He could see an updraught of air. It shimmered and vibrated like a sheet of water, as if it had been tyrannised by rock for so long during its colossal ascent, that it had forgotten it was permitted to disperse, now that it had crested the cliff. There was nothing else out there except a faint line of clouds, the sort that align along an immeasurably distant horizon.

Perhaps there was an ocean too, but somehow he didn't think there was. In fact, as he moved towards it, he found himself arguing with his own, rational, self, that this might easily be the end of the world. Here, you might fall off, forever.

What began to trouble him more was that there were great fissures in the final section of rock crawl. Some were as much as a foot wide and they criss-crossed in a great mosaic, in which some pieces were the size of aircraft hangars and others worryingly small. Large or small, they all seemed keyed in such a way that any one, any section, might take umbrage at an expanding frost pocket, an alighting eagle, or a humble Jo-Jo, to abandon their post and topple unhesitatingly into whatever void lay below.

The closer he got, the lower he got. From a stoop, he descended to hands and knees. Then he abandoned his rucksack and decided to crawl. So he crawled, trying to gauge the integrity of the particular block he had ventured onto. Finally, he settled on a change of direction and inched his way sideways, towards a block that displayed great surface area and minimal fissuring. That it might be balanced on a pin head was a risk he obliged himself to take. He had to look over that edge and standing to do so was out of the question.

The wind, for all it surfaced like a shimmering sheet, hammered across every inch of that rocky platform. Confined for so long, it vented its fury on the leading edge of rock, once it rose above the ridge. Consequently those rocks had been bevelled like the edge of a kitchen knife but with a bevel in proportion to the majesty of the setting, which meant that four feet of rock sloped sharply down where rock met wind.

Jo-Jo gulped with terror but he had to see over the cliff. Was this the Edge, or was it just an edge, any edge, albeit one with pretensions?

He inched over the bevelled rock. Pinned himself out like a frog on a dissection board, feet and hands jammed into, or against, whatever he could find for support. Finally he extended his neck like a turtle's and craned forwards.

God in His Heaven! The rock simply fell away. A sheer face fell down and down, until it eventually vanished into mist and cloud. If it had been laid out horizontally, it would have taken him a day to reach that distant barrier of clouds.

Raising his eyes to scan the view he found that there was none. Below there was only the top of the cloud field. Yet, directly ahead of him was another armada of clouds, sitting atop a meteorological straight line that might have been drawn with a ruler. The peculiar and stomach-churning thing, was that the tops of the field below were shifting very slowly to his left, while the ruled line ahead was drifting to his right. How could that happen? Two weather systems must be in operation, one atop the other.

Feeling extremely small and vulnerable, Jo-Jo edged his way back, first from the bevelled knife's edge, then across the great hunk of mosaic he had chosen for safety's sake. Finally he made a mad dash for his backpack and finally abandoned the fractured rock field as quickly as he could. Wherever the Stair might be, it was not on this section of the Edge – unless mishap had carried it into the void, centuries since.

Logic dictated that it was not behind him, where the Edge collapsed into 'improper' form – collapsed being the operative word. The only way, then, was onward, That had such an heroic ring to it, he felt defeated before he began. "I shall amble on," he announced "in the manner of Proust, I shall take 'the Guermantes way' and no doubt be the better for it." Nothing responded to his elegant literary gambit and for a moment he felt very much alone. Had the Rabbit been here his Proustian aside would have been in shreds by now and he'd be feeling much the worse for wear. As yet unwithered, he began to slide cautiously down, towards the convex rock face he had so arduously scrambled up an hour or two earlier.

It was an ill-fated move. Within seconds his descent was completely out of control and he shot over the worst of the curve in a blur of arms and legs, hitting the ground with a disastrous thump.

He lay on his back, a tangle of limbs, eyes closed and breathing heavily. "Help," he said weakly. There was no response.

He straightened one leg and amazingly it moved. The other leg was twisted underneath him and he had serious concerns on its behalf. 'I'd rather it wasn't broken,' he thought desperately and set to work freeing it. The toe of his right boot had caught in a loop of the rucksack and in the manner of such an unlikelihood, was now well and truly snared. He struggled and that was proof enough that his arms still worked, though his left wrist seemed to be filing a complaint. Suddenly overcome by self-pity he flopped back onto his side and groaned loudly again – more for the pleasure of hearing the pathos in his voice than for any other reason – "Help."

"Porthos, Athos, swiftly mes braves!" came an answering cry. "Monsieur, how may we be of assistance, for behold, Le Chevalier d'Artagnan is here to serve!"

Jo-Jo opened one eye cautiously. A fine, black-faced Leicester ram, wearing a cockaded tricorn adorned with peacock feathers, stood in front of him.

Jo-Jo closed that eye and opened the other one. The extended field of vision now included two other sheep, similarly attired but carrying a staircase, which they were in the business of lowering to the ground.

"It seems we are arrived in time, Monsieur! Pray, where are the villains who have so distressed you?"

"Behind me," groaned Jo-Jo and swift as lightning the three had drawn wooden swords which they brandished over him. "Begone!" cried d'Artagnan, "he stands – sorry, my mistake – lies, within our protection. You have no further claim! Off with you!" and he shook the wooden rapier menacingly.

"Field mice," suggested the staircase carriers together. "Highly territorial, famously aggressive. Your very life must have hung by a thread!"

"Forever in your debt, messieurs," croaked Jo-Jo. "The actual fact of the matter seems to be that my toe is caught, within a loop of my rucksack…if you would be so kind as to unsnare me? Eternal obligation will fall upon me."

"Treacherous equipment," pronounced the two. "Have at it, mon brave!"

Together they advanced, rolled Jo-Jo onto his face and strained his foot out of the loop.

"Agh!" said the rescued one.

"We do not believe the limb is lost, Monsieur but the peril was grave."

Jo-Jo wriggled back against the treacherous rock face, sat up and surveyed the semi-circle of his rescuers.

"You excellent fellows wouldn't be connected with 'Abraham's Ladders' by any chance, would you?" He struggled in his pocket for a flyer and handed it to d'Artagnan.

"Jacob's Staircases, Monsieur," responded the black-faced Leicester, as he handed the flyer to Athos, or Porthos, who promptly began to eat it. "A recent change of ownership – a buyout, in fact. Trade war narrowly averted – the competition was fearsome!" and all three went 'en garde' with their wooden swords.

"Who'd have thought it," said Jo-Jo, slowly recovering his wind, while discovering that the right leg, if not exactly broken felt as if it should have been.

"Ah, Monsieur, our staircases are second to none! No-one climbs in vain. All are safely delivered. Competitive prices, exemplary craftsmanship, finest materials, prompt delivery… speaking of which, we dally, we delay, excuse our passage, Monsieur, duty calls…" and Athos and Porthos picked up their load and jogged lightly on the spot.

"Chevaliers!" cried Jo-Jo, "I exist within your debt," and he bowed as best he could while seated. D'Artagnan swept off his tricorn once more in acknowledgment. "One last boon, if I may be so forward. The way down…the Stair…do you know of it? Where it lies?"

"Down!" cried the trio. "Down! We are Jacob's flock, we elevate! We have no truck with 'Down.' Does Monsieur impugn our calling?" and their hands were on the hilts of their toy swords.

"Peace upon us all, Chevaliers!" cried Jo-Jo. "My sad lot is, I fear, with 'Down.' It is my fate, the call has come, I must make haste, I travel upon a Knight Errancy. Obstruct me at your peril!"

"Monsieur," explained d'Artagnan, "we are a traditional company. We cater for traditional tastes. The way of tradition is Up. We have no truck with Down. One arises to Heaven by means of a stair, a stair of the finest treads and risers. One is cast into Hell from the cliff itself…there is no stair, no ladder, the damned are not blessed with the excellence of hardwood joinery."

"But the cliff, the Edge," Jo-Jo insisted. "The Stair down the Edge? Surely that is not the route to Hell?"

The three looked at him and burst out in a chorus of bleating. "Ah-ha! The way down the Edge, the old Stair! Of course, why didn't you say so!"

"You know its whereabouts?" demanded Jo-Jo.

"But of course, Monsieur!"

"Then please, where is it?"

"Ah, cast down centuries ago, Monsieur. And now, adieux from Les Trois Musketeers!" and shouldering their burden, they made off swiftly.

"How do I get down?" shrieked Jo-Jo at their retreating, woolly backs.

"Why, Monsieur, by the elevator, bien sur!"

"And where is that?" he bellowed.

Very faintly the cry came back – "Onward!" but whether as a reply, or a goad to their own progress, he had no idea.

Where he sat was damp. Using the treacherous rock for support he stood up, slowly. Surprisingly, he found he was intact. He nodded thoughtfully, acknowledging fool's luck, limped to a warmer spot and sitting down again, rifled the rucksack for nutrition, then ate.

"It's not unheard of," he told the indifferent valley, "sheep were used as beasts of burden in Tibet, before the yak was domesticated. There again, they probably weren't in the joinery trade. Nor are they on record as having much to say for themselves." Having said which, he stood up and scanned the under-cliff carefully. Of the sheep, or their staircase, there was no sign. He sat down again, feeling dejected.

If the old Stair had fallen, what was this "elevator" likely to be? For some minutes he brooded. Then he remembered Moss and the ride up the cliff face. Not a good memory but it would have to do. "Onward," the Musketeers had cried, so "onward" it would have to be. Not, however until he had stolen some hours of sleep.

He woke very early, dew dampened, stiff and weary. After a scratch breakfast he made a reluctant start. For a while he indulged himself and limped, "onwards" theatrically, until he got fed up with that. There was no-one to see him, no-one to sympathise, so he settled for a less arduous, more accommodating lurch. His leg was not that bad…

It suddenly occurred to him that there were probably openings in the cliff lip. The sheep couldn't have vanished, last night. Even allowing that they had four legs and had been making a fair turn of speed, they couldn't have vanished from sight so quickly. Somewhere they had taken a turn into the cliff, into a narrow gully, occluded from where he had been standing but clear enough to the passer-by, or those with local knowledge.

That was a realisation that made him considerably less depressed. When he finally passed such a slot in the rock, one that plainly led somewhere, he felt much better indeed. It was, obviously someone's front door, because it had a large ship's bell hanging over the entrance. He stood and wavered for a while, wondering whether to make a social call. Proper food was a lure but finding the elevator, after all this time was more alluring still. Also, he had to admit, he'd lost the last traces of his taste for human contact. Such an effort would be needed to explain himself and it was likely he'd cause offence, even here on the Edge-proper, by expressing a need to go down, to the Middle-lands. So he lurched on, instead, into a long and weary day.

He hadn't found the elevator by nightfall, though he had passed many a front door. He slept out under a magnificent whorl of stars. Perhaps each one was in possession of a planet that had an elevator and a joinery firm run by sheep… Perhaps, on one of those planets he would be hailed as a quiet hero, instead of a local anxiety. He was absolutely sure he had hidden depths and he dived down into sleep to discover them.

To his vast relief, he found the elevator early the next morning, located exactly as he had guessed, down a gully in the rock and marked by a sign chipped into the stone itself – ELEVATOR, 3d (and Stair). To judge by the growth of moss, the accumulation of sand and the established grass, few, if any, travellers came this way.

He made his way in slowly, checking the cliffs, that very quickly began to soar above his head, for any sign of the cracked-toffee fissures he had been obliged to venture amongst, a day earlier, on the rim. There were none apparent.

How natural the gully was remained a moot question. It could have been cut by man, or machine and then weathered over millennia. Equally, it could be a natural joint, installed at the cooling of the planet, or following whatever sequence of subductions, reductions and reincarnations this particular promontory had been subjected to. Whichever it was, it looked solid, quite capable of taking the weight of a nervous adventurer.

It was a long and oddly lonely walk down that gully, which twisted and turned so arbitrarily that he concluded it must be a natural cleft after all. Sometimes the rising sun shone benignly along a section, then the passage would take an oblique turn and he'd enter a length that probably never saw sunlight at all. There he would begin to shiver and striding on, he would hope that the next turn would deliver him some modicum of warmth. Sometimes it did and as often, it didn't.

It was through one final, snaking twist that he was ejected at the head of the ELEVATOR (and Stair). He was the solitary occupant of a viewing platform and again, to judge by the bird lime, the small trees growing where they shouldn't be, not many people came this way.

The view was much the same as the one he had risked life and limb to see before. Today, however, the clouds beneath the vertiginous drop were a vigorous, jostling crowd. He looked away from them very quickly, because the clouds ahead were static, well-behaved, fluffy cumulus, much easier on a queasy stomach.

He searched around and discovered a bell to summon the elevator. There was a bird's nest on top of it, made of mud and stuck to the rock. Jo-Jo examined both and concluded that it was arguable which might be supporting which. Slowly he surveyed the rest of the structures. The guard rails had corroded into networks of metallic lace. The keeper track for the elevator was a mass of rust with the top bracket detached from the rock. The sign that advertised the long-defunct service was almost indecipherable. Finally, he managed to make out – 'ELEVATOR – 3d, pay in Gift Shop, at bottom.' What a tragic concept! Here he stood, on abraded and abused feet, half-way through an Arthurian quest to beard the mythic 'giant' of the Core, in its lair and he faced the humiliation of having to "exit via Gift Shop" when he reached the bottom… not to mention paying 3d for the privilege.

He sat on the top step of the Stair and asked himself – 'if I had sent a note to the Core saying – "Hi, I'm Jo-Jo, I'm sure you know of me, I'm on the payroll. I'm beginning to find this world perplexing and my own answers inadequate. Could I come to 'Mission Control' and have a chat with a member of staff, to try to straighten my head out a bit?' He might have got a letter back saying – "love to see you! We'll send a pod on Tuesday, 10.00 a.m. to Chez Moss. How does that suit? All best, Andrea" – or some such friendly name, and I wouldn't be sitting here searching for 3d, so that I can exit-via-the-gift-shop!'

He snorted derisively. Up here, thousands of feet above what was probably a teeming world of ordinary people below, some form of mass psychosis was in operation. We've all come to believe that the Core is an unapproachable mystery, something along the lines of a Godhead. It's probably just a massive quantum computer run by an enlightened despotism and based on advanced social engineering. That's why all the lunatics are perched up here on the Rim, out of harm's way, madly inventing myths about the Divine Nature of their grocery deliveries.

Jo-Jo pondered. Did he know too much, or too little? Too little, that was certain but he had the sinking feeling that should he suddenly find himself the repository of all human knowledge, the final question – 'What is the meaning of Life?' would remain as unanswerable to him as it was now. The meaning of Life was probably that it has no meaning but is trying to acquire one, now that it has the means of self-preservation under its belt. Man will prove to be no more than a note in its back catalogue. Suddenly he didn't think he had any questions worth asking. He should go back to wandering. Reclaim his Rabbit and draw aimless circles on the surface of this strange planet.

Instead he stood up and started off down the Stair.

'Hey, hey, hey!' his questions shouted after him, 'you've forgotten us!' 'No, I haven't,' he replied. 'I've just given up on you.'

The stairs were not in good condition. The pink sand, gritty and full of mica, so familiar to Jo-Jo from the Rim, clogged two thirds of every tread. Much of it supported the basics of life. Tiny drifts of greenstuff, not grass, not mould, not lichen, just greenstuff, grew across the most stable of the deposits, binding the particles together, sucking moisture from the air, converting energy from the sun. The cleverest, most humble things, were happening on these steps.

How does one admire a simple thing? He sat down beside one such enterprising clump and tried to tell it how marvellously clever it was. It wouldn't listen. It just kept on sucking moisture from the grit, flattening its tiny leaves to track the passage of the sun, overhead. Soon, the sun would pass behind that cliff edge and the immaculate leaves would fold together, to stop the evaporation of valuable water. But inside, out-of-sight, the micro-factories would churn on, sucking in passing molecules, excreting others. Photosynthesis would be orchestrating the most wonderful, magical tricks but he wouldn't see them, or ever understand them.

He hauled himself up, this improved model of sapiens sapientis and continued down. It was a very long way. He knew that because, after two-hours descent, he encountered a wind and grit-scoured sign that had once read – 'You haven't really started yet…turn back.' But he was a Pilgrim, so he continued.

He found he had a lot of questions he wanted to ask, such as – 'what is the place of ignorance within knowledge? What should be the posture of the knowledgeably ignorant?' But every question he framed, however much he tried to simplify it, would fall over its own cleverness and die. The only answer that came from the endless steps, the echo of his boots, the occasional howl of the wind and the pattering of rain as he walked into yet another cloud, was – "Humility. Be humble. Observe. Try not to speak. Be humble." It felt like such good advice that he wanted to talk and talk and talk about it.

These encroaching clouds, however, were a problem and one more immediate than the metaphysical. The steps were becoming treacherous. He was forced to walk on the outside edge of every flight, to avoid destroying the tiny green colonies of life. This meant he was perilously close to the void and was putting plant-life above his own. Not a point to dwell upon. The cloud obscured the view of the drop, which was decent of it, but the moisture-laden air was turning the soles of his boots into skates. One false step and he would be in the Gift Shop, with a vengeance and they'd have to sort through the wreckage for their 3d.

At some time in the deep, dark past there had been a handrail. It wasn't there now but the stout female receivers that had once secured the rail's uprights to the stone treads were only partly rusted away. Now, if he failed to spot one in time, failed to step neatly around it, he risked being capsized and lost with all hands… "aye, Jim lad…'tis so! Ye be a' markin' o' old John's words" he finished, adding the treacherous sea cook's legendary cackle and to good effect – because something large and black, a couple of flights above him, flew away with a croak and vanished into the mist. "Bloody hell," squawked Jo-Jo, pulse racing.

As if in answer, a shout came from far below – "Hello!"

"Hello yourself, where are you?"

"Somewhere down here, where are you?"

"Up here," said Jo-Jo, unless I passed you on the way down. I might have done, if you are very small."

"I'm very large," said the voice. "Do come down, I'm quite starved of conversation and customers."

"On my way," said Jo-Jo, and all caution thrown to the wind he positively scampered down increasingly treacherous stones.

He took a dozen flights in minutes and then bellowed – "do I sound closer?"

"Not really," said the voice, "best just keep coming. Take your time. I'd come up but I have to mind the shop."

Jo-Jo drew a breath and tried to behave like a rational being.

"What's the weather like down there?"

There was a long silence. Maybe the owner was engaged with a customer?

"Weather?" said the voice. "Remind me."

"You know – the atmosphere" said Jo-Jo, "weather – sun, wind, rain, snow, sleet, hail, sandstorms, tsunamis…no, not those last two, they're not weather."

"Yes, I've had all of those, time after time. Terrible stuff, weather, always one thing or another."

"Which terrible thing is it at the moment?" demanded Jo-Jo.

"The sun is shining."

"It's raining here, so I must be a long way away from you. I may be some little time!"

"Just so long as you're coming. I'm getting so excited," said the voice in flat tone.

"Not many customers, lately?" hazarded Jo-Jo.

There was a pause, probably for thought.

"I think I had one once but I could have been hallucinating."

"Oh well," said Jo-Jo, "I'm on my way, now. See you sometime soon."

That, however, was not to be the case. Weather of the bad variety, was closing in rank, damp and disturbing. Mist, wet and clinging as a fretful dog, closed about Jo-Jo. He could see three treads in front of him and if he bothered to turn, three behind. But beyond that, nothing. Only the wall at his right hand was a constant and even its huge mass was diminished to occasional glimpses of blackness, down which streamed erratic and tiny rivulets. Occasionally a spider web appeared in front of him spun across God alone knew what anchorages.

Walking in this strange world, from which all dimensions had been stolen, Jo-Jo began to hallucinate that the Stairs were flat. He became certain he was walking across corrugations, that he had to strike each folded edge, square on. He took his first such step and immediately skidded down six treads, in a blunder of arms, legs and backpack. He just retained sufficient wit to flail desperately to his right, thus crashing into the angle, at the bottom of the treads where direction reversed.

He clung to the slick wall like a child to its mother, pressing his forehead against cold stone, trying to calm his racing heart. 'Oh, God, that was close, that was close!' he told himself, over and over. He could be, should be, falling, head over heels through the void, through cloud, sun, not even an Icarus, just a clumsy walker who had fallen.

Sprawled in that unyielding, stony grasp, he found he had no desire at all to die. This was the same terror he'd experienced earlier, when his descent from the rim had spun out of control and he'd had to be rescued by the Three Ovine Musketeers. The farce of that had air-brushed away the terror. Here now, with nothing to distract him, he was alone with his fear and a wild desire never to tempt fate so foolishly again. He was going to sit here, in this dripping corner, until the cloud rolled away and he could see clearly.

Should he tell the shopkeeper? He'd seemed so eager to welcome a customer – or had he? He recalled the flat tone – "I'm getting so excited." Probably no more than an early model robotic, abandoned here and he'd nearly killed himself attempting to thrill its little electronic heartstrings. What irony that would have been.

The question now became one of how long was he going to be marooned on this step and how he should pass the time. Perhaps he should take out his penknife and inscribe the wall with a record of his passage – 'Jo-Jo woz 'ere,' or just 'Jo-Jo,' and maybe a date. Which date? Today's date was out of the question, as he had not the slightest idea what it might be. His birth date? That was tricky, too. When you're over 4,000 years-old birth dates slip away. How about a symbol? Which? There were lots.

Instead he rooted in his pack and found a snack to gnaw on. It was really rather good. He must order more of them, when he got to the bottom. Maybe the Gift Shop stocked them? Doubtful. There was never anything useful in gift shops. That was rather the point of them. Why was that? There must be a reason.

Finishing his snack he cupped his chin in his hands and sitting on his pack, stared into the mist. Funny, it was all tiny swirls. He'd always thought it was simply an opaque screen, akin to the milky translucency of the physical Core but it was made up of little, swirling eddies. How did they all…how did they all what? He hadn't really got a question.

Why did he make everything into a question? Questions weren't humble. They were something else entirely. They were intrusive. Perhaps the advice to self should be amended – "Observe and be Humble." Should he carve that into the rock wall? 'No,' said his wiser self, 'you would be carving a geophysical oxymoron. The very essence of that rock wall is observation with humility.' And, for just a split second he could see that. Then he was left with a jumble of words on his hands, all jostling to be included in the next question.

He must have sat for an hour or two, towards the end of which he found he was attending to the quiet sound of the mist. It had silenced every other living thing but it had a vibration all its own. He had no words for it but it possessed pressure, movement and coherence, in a mix that amounted to sound. Sound expressed on a scale he had no knowledge of. Which was probably a nonsense but he knew what he was driving at. What's more he knew it was lifting, because the timbre of that sound changed. The mist was packing up, it was on the move.

Within the half hour, so was he.

Sun now blazed on the steps and they steamed, their own skeins of mist spiralling up to vanish into the most cloudless of blue skies.

Jo-Jo bestirred himself, emerged from reverie, re-entered his world, such as it was.

Here he stood, wet and bedraggled, lately scared, within a keyway on the side of a precipice, that still sloped down, down, through further wreaths of clouds to the allurement of the Gift Shop. He was grateful for those lower clouds, especially now they'd stopped wriggling around and become sober representatives of their genre. He had no desire to see all the way down, the tops of those clouds was quite far enough.

"Hello," he shouted over the edge, "I'm on the move again!"

"Why, had you stopped?"

"Yes," said Jo-Jo. "Adverse weather conditions. See you soon."

"Doubt it," said the voice, lugubriously.

Not only were the steps as good as dry, they were freer from grit and its tenacious life forms. The winds that reached Rim must have still been watertight at this stage in their ascent from the plain. Barometrically considered, that could tell him a lot but the immediate positive was that he had more tread to step on. With that came less dread, so Jo-Jo positively pounded down flight after flight. An hour of that, however and his thighs were on fire, while something worryingly specific in his back was filing numerous complaints, in triplicate.

"Take it easy, idiot," he said to himself.

"I think you must be very close," said the voice. "I heard that quite clearly and it can't have been meant for me. I haven't moved for decades."

"Jolly good," shouted Jo-Jo, adding, sotto voce for his own consumption, "definitely a'bot."

It was just then that he caught sight of another abraded sign – 'STILL A VERY LONG WAY TO GO.' 'Truly, they knew how to encourage,' he thought. 'Makes me positively light-hearted by comparison.'

The next second he had a far more useful thought. 'That must mean I'm halfway down, because it might be read by someone coming up. Or even if it's not halfway, it will be a serious proportion, otherwise it wouldn't make a lot of sense.' Then he hummed and hawed about the likelihood that he was right and, as usual, decided he didn't really know. But it had been a good thought. Very encouraging, while it had lasted.

So, halting his helter-skelter descent, out of respect for his protesting parts, he proceeded sedately and after far too long, he came to what must be the mid-way viewing area.

Across the flagstones, on the opposite side from Jo-Jo, was a magnificent stag standing on its hind legs, in the manner of a supporter in an armorial crest. It wore the costume of an Elizabethan gentleman – to wit, white ruff, slashed velvet jerkin, pantaloons and black leather kneeboots, The jerkin, or tightly-fitted jacket more properly, as it had sleeves, was a sartorial triumph in hunting green, the slashes lined with anemone-pink silk. The pantaloons of a slubbed, stiffened-silk in black were decorated with gold buttons, each secured to mark the cardinal points of a diamond pattern, with some highlighting in gold embroidery, to guide the eye where necessary. The rack of antlers was truly impressive, a score or more of points, making the stag what was once known as an Imperial and the veritable Monarch of anybody's Glen. He had a haughty demeanour, appropriate to his dignified attire.

At his side stood a high wooden stool. On it was a square wicker basket. It was loosely packed with small envelopes, folded from handmade paper, the tongue of each sealed with a large blob of red wax and impressed by a signature too distant for Jo-Jo to make out. Each bulged invitingly, as if it held a cache of seeds, or dried herbs. It was a plain display but entirely in keeping with the medieval costuming.

"Unused history," intoned the Stag, sonorously, "each mixed with an element of chance. Only six pence each, three for one shilling. Try your luck, young sir?"

Jo-Jo was tediously familiar with this greeting and it irritated him. It grated against his vanity, it undermined his self-esteem. Yet nearly every newcomer he met used it. If he ever met a new-born, it would probably turn from its mother's breast and accost him with a lisping – "yungth, thirr!"

"I am 4000 years old," he said grimly.

"I can add a nought to that, perhaps two. I lose count.

"How far is Down now?"

"At least as far as it is Up."

Jo-Jo sighed. He had ruined his back jogging down a few thousand stairs in order to have this conversation. He had very nearly plummeted to his death. Now here he was, face to face with a Game Dealer's wet dream, who was treating him with the condescension due to a bit player in a period drama.

"Would that be your 'Up,' or mine?" asked Jo-Jo.

"I couldn't possibly comment," sniffed the Stag. "Your 'Up' is a closed book. This is as far as I got and it is far enough. I have never been further, 'Up,' as you put it, so vividly."

"Oh, you simply must," lied Jo-Jo, faking enthusiasm. "There are sheep selling Staircases to Heaven at the Top. You could triple your retail potential."

"It would mean more climbing," the Stag said mournfully. "I always felt that this was far enough. Pray young sir, do purchase an element of unused history, mixed with a soupcon of chance!"

"Why should I?" demanded Jo-Jo, "especially as you persist in calling me 'young sir'?"

"It would be gracious and I have not sold one for at least 1000 years. Yet, I was assured this was a prime site."

"For what?" Jo-Jo asked bluntly. "As a retail hub it leaves much to be desired."

"Really?" said the Stag anxiously. "You see room for improvement?"

"On the contrary, I see none."

The Stag took a moment to ponder.

"I think I grasp your drift," it began slowly. "You feel, perhaps, that this is a remote spot, incapable, shall we say, of becoming vibrant?"

"There is that and much else besides," Jo-Jo agreed.

"How about a sample pinch of powders?" tempted the Stag. "A chance to sample delights that might even see you avid for further experiment. Who knows where you might end up?"

Jo-Jo shook his head. "As a sales pitch, yours is less than enticing. In fact, I'm beginning to feel distinctly nervous."

"For which I have the very antidote!" the Stag segued elegantly. He offered Jo-Jo one of the fattest envelopes, double-sealed with the complex embossed signature in red wax. "Merely break the seal and inhale the aroma, young sir…transports of delight await!"

Jo-Jo pushed the package aside. "I can't mislead you…" he began.

But the Stag was about to bring the exchange to dramatic conclusion. "VERY YOUNG SIR!" he said caustically, "keep the lot! They're all yours! I'm gone!"

With which he turned gracefully on his heel, mounted the low wall that surrounded the platform and jumped into the void.

Croaking – "Stop!" Jo-Jo reached the edge in time to see and hear, the 'crack!' as a vast pair of wings unfolded from the Stag's back, just before he reached the top of the feathery cumulus below. Then with increasingly powerful beats from that colossal span, he drove himself on and ever outwards across the cloud ocean, until he vanished as a mote on the horizon.

"My God," appealed Jo-Jo, "what brought that on? It wasn't me, was it?" He looked around, as if there might be witnesses. But there was no-one, no other eyes and the fabric of the place was barely fractured. The Stag had simply never been. The only evidence he had ever existed, the tray of sealed packages.

Jo-Jo knelt and considered them. "Keep the lot!" those had been his words. You never knew when a tranche of unused history might come in handy, especially with a little bit of chance thrown in. He could barely leave them lying around, who knows where innocent passers-by might end up, were he to act so irresponsibly?

Carefully he wrapped them in the cloth from the wicker tray and stowed them in his backpack. He kept out one, largely because of the intriguing triple seal. He sat on the low wall, twisting it to and fro in the sunlight, trying to make out the imprint. It was definitely something more than a pleasing pattern but less than anything he recognised. A phrase drifted into his head…'the symbols at your door…' Now, where did that come from? He stared around, seeking inspiration and though the sun shone brightly, illuminating every cranny and corner, it took him a long time to see that there was a crack in the rock wall at the end of the platform. Above it was a sign and if he was not mistaken, it was the same sign as the one imprinted on this packet's seal.

He picked up his sack and idled the short distance. It was an oddly pleasing spot, this platform. It had a good feel to it. Now he was beginning to understand the Stag's belief that here had been a space where he might attract custom. 'Which goes to prove,' he thought, 'you should beware of your feelings.'

He looked up at the sign. It was the same sigil and as impenetrable writ large as it was imprinted small. He shrugged and peered into the gloom. He caught sight of a little sign – 'This way to the History Trip of a Lifetime' – an arrow pointed the way. There was a torch hanging below the sign. Surprisingly it worked.

'Can't hurt,' thought Jo-Jo and he followed the white light…

EVIE

Where to begin?

Here, in this Universe of peculiar and particular beginnings. So many of them.

My beginning goes like this ... I had the happiest childhood. I skipped, or danced, everywhere. I loved my little friends and I held my mother's hand eagerly, wherever she took me.

I was a little boy, Evan, until I was 11 and I woke every day, anxious to begin all over again.

At 12 it was judicious I become a little girl. My bosom was developing so quickly that all attempts to conceal it were doomed.

To become Eva, it was necessary that we moved away from where I had been a boy. I hope my maker saw and felt the unhappiness that brought to me. I was pierced through with pain I couldn't describe, because I had no words for it.

Years of concealment, all destined to be fruitless. What world would I have to have been born on, to find ease and friendship? I could imagine, or thought I could imagine, plenty of them but none seemed to exist.

Let me explain the next paragraph to you, before it arrives and grates uncomfortably on your sensibilities. Most of my early life was lived in the arena of four-letter words. Those will be the words I use here. Correct them as you will.

My prick grew as quickly as my tits. Behind my cock, where my balls should have been and from an unpromising indentation, I developed a perfect cunt. Yet I was free from all monthly curses and destined to be as sterile as a mule. No eggs, no sperm and little by way of either sex's orgasms.

"Poor, poor, pitiful me!"

Specialists marvelled. Papers were written. Under heavy disguise, I appear in several authoritative books. I should demand retrospective royalties, with accrued interest added

Only the nurses were kind, as they took me for scans and probes. They held my hand, they stroked my hair, they told me how pretty I was. All I could do was cry and cry. At first, I wanted to be a little boy again – and then, within a few years, I didn't know what I wanted to be. How about just – "Me"?

I grew up so quickly. The years are meant to last forever when you are young. Mine did not. They raced by, even when measured by interminable hospital and clinic appointments. I hated those but as everyone meant well, especially my mum, I went along with it all. Anyway, I was still too young to know how to be a rebel and when I finally thought that I did know enough, I made a terrible mess of it.

I'm going to start skipping years.

My first suicide attempt came when I was 16. I tried to cut my throat with a blunt, straight razor that I bought from a junk shop.

"For dad's birthday?" the old man behind the counter had smiled at me.

"Yes," I said. I didn't have a dad.

I was so scared that it might hurt but eventually, in front of the bathroom mirror, I cut. What did I know? I cut at the front, not at the side, where the big arteries lie. I remember the flesh opening. Then my nerve gave out. My fingers opened and the razor dropped, clattering into the sink. Big drops of blood fell on the ivory handle, splashed onto the edge of the basin.

"Mummy!" I wailed.

Everyone was so kind.

Even the policemen were kind.

It is so odd that even now, years later, I can recall everyone's particular scent but not their faces, names, or rank.

A year or so later, I tried pills. I knew I hadn't the courage for anything else.

People were not so kind this time. They were impatient. And I was tired, utterly exhausted and my throat was horribly sore. I can't recall anyone's scent, either.

My mother was in despair. She sold our house and took me away, one holiday after another. In retrospect, they were packed full of wonders. At the time, I thought I was bored and I behaved vilely. Anyway, when the money ran out we had to come home. Now, when it's too late to tell her how important those weeks actually were, I remember them, vividly.

Mum said we were lucky to be given even a rubbishy council house but seen through my self-centred eyes it didn't look very lucky at all. I was already beginning to be full of holiday memories and none of them included mould on every wall. My God, I can't believe how foul I was! I'm finding it pretty hard to confess now, even on paper.

Then I met a 'nice girl' and mum was thrilled that I had a friend at last. Unfortunately, she turned out to be a bit of a bad girl. Things went downhill rapidly.

For all of the colossal assets I had – big tits, heavy prick, sweet cunt, I didn't feel at all sexual. I felt blind and at the same time, driven. So I passed my time with the nice/bad girl and her stupid, mud-born friends.

That was a phrase that came to me from somewhere – "mud-born" – and in my arrogance I knew that I couldn't possibly be one of them.

Mud-born or not, I was certainly stupid. Because of our antics – each hectic session professionally recorded by "someone 'who knew' someone else" – I ended up in hospital with rips and tears. For all that I was in agony, sunk in misery and wrapped around with need, my arrogance was such that it would have taken a full-scale Crusade to have saved me from myself.

At least they gave me painkillers, probably to stop me howling the place down and the older ones seemed genuinely sorrowful that anyone so young was apparently hell-bent on self-destruction.

At least on opioids, I could close my eyes and my hospital bed, with me tangled in the sheets, would move off from its moorings as if it was a boat. We would slowly gather speed and glide along waterways, beneath grey steel bridges pustular with rivets but under which the reflection of dappled water, playing on the girders, made their filth inconsequential.

This particular day, we floated past black scows and lighters moored in blunt ranks, then slipped between gigantic tankers and freighters, all riding light and high in the water, while we drifted on with undefined purpose. I lay there drinking it all in – the huge underwater world of the deep-sea ships, those bulbous blind curving bows that look like the humps of whales when the boats ride high and their stems rise above the filthy dock. The light around their scabbed sides, how it danced and dazzled!

My bed, my boat, drifted into a flat, broad waterway. Here the water was still and grey and everything was silent, as if sound had not yet been invented. As the dawn slipped into the sky, it brought colour, blues, reds and golds. I could feel the monochrome dockland begin to groan under this onslaught. On every side black hulls flamed, as their oxide-red hulls were steadily illuminated. Wharf-side, a slim freighter in grey, its hatches high and twisted in the air, turned apple green, while stark cranes, dipping their jibs, flamed yellow as they swung palleted bales up and into the morning light. A black door in a faceless dockside block-house turned blue. The rusted bollards were white and black, beneath their throttling cables that ran up through bow hawseholes, onto braked winches.

As the sun rises silhouette-shadows stride across the world at impossible length. They masquerade as spindly limbs, spavined thighs and tortured ribs and arms. Yet all will resolve to the commonplace when the sun climbs higher. Barely a hint of human presence.

My boat has nudged against the stern of a white motor yacht. I climb a ladder, onto a scrubbed deck and now I can look back at the beauty of this desolate place, lit by the light of a new morning. Across the estuary an exquisite trellis-work of the banal is being steadily lit by the climbing sun. Fuel dumps, office blocks, Portakabins, overhead cabling, lights still burning futilely, tugs rocking at their berths, their blunt, business-like proportions touched with strange beauty.

A grey naval vessel catches the light and one by one the stubby ends of guns, arrogant in their bland revolving turrets, depth charge racks, acoustic dishes, the mess of radar and radio are etched crisply on the dawn. Remorseless daylight spills down her side to reveal, in vast black paint, F-26, her fleet designation. I grip the broad wooden rail that tops the yacht's steel sides. Wood, sun-split and varnished, split and varnished again until it glows, black and gold, like honey.

I stare so hard at these ruins, pegged-out against the clearest of blue skies, that I almost miss the slight movement of the most delicate girl. When I twist round to see her, she is turning away, in her white dress, as if I had failed some test by not noticing her earlier. I'm certain I may have caused her hurt and the thought of that is unbearable. I try to correct my mistakes, things must be right between us. For her I feel an unconditional love. She looks at me briefly and then I am gone from her eyes. Awkwardly she begins to climb a wooden ladder. She is crippled and I would offer her the sacrifice of my body. But I have no way to do that.

At the head of the ladder, she looks back briefly. Her eyes are filled with a liquid depth of meaning that I can't grasp. She opens a door and through a narrow way, is gone into the ship. I know that I lack all means by which I might follow her.

Despair overwhelms me as I turn away. The girl in the white dress is lost to me. My hands have become alien claws and I see them on the deck rail as two twisted, ugly talons.

By now the sun is risen higher. Merciless, it illuminates every knot, every rivet, every empty mortise, buckled plate and failing wire. The world is laid bare, every detail of its construction dissected. Not a creature moves, not a rat, a gull, nor the ripple of a harbour fish. I turn back to the steps where I had failed and see the narrowness of the door by which she had slipped within the vessel. My eyes drift upward. There, behind the vessel, is a slab of white building with no break in its fabric, not so much as a window or door, just pitiless white that rises higher than I can see and stretching far, far into a distant sky.

In despair, then, I opened my eyes and the polystyrene tiles of the ward's ceiling resolved into focus. It was against this banal background that a voice spoke to me, only the once -

> "When I stopped being a boy,
> I knew I had to atone,
> For the damage done
> To Eve by man's rib bone."

I lay on my hospital bed at five a.m. and this colossal phrase settled on me, gossamer hewn from granite.

Mum died. I know I did that and it will lie on my account for ever.

My fistulas were closed.

Still the clarity of that prophetic phrase rang all around me.

All other roads were closed.

Atone. I atoned. How I atoned.

I'd killed mum. If I died too, then it was no less than I deserved. I found the nice/bad girl and we started up again, seriously, professionally. The films we made, the scripts I wrote, were too outrageous. The Dark Web swallowed us, as I served myself up – raw meat. If I could only suffer enough, then I would have atoned. I would have set a wrong, right.

There's a compartment in my mind where, it seems, I'm obliged to store web addresses. They squat there, an indelible legion, charting a strange, futile cycle.

I can say that now. At the time, I was enjoying myself. No-one was compelling me and besides, I had a secret. I believed that one day, I would meet my mirror-image, coming the other way. On that day, everything would be set right, I would have corrected all the wrongs. If only that would happen, though I still don't know quite what I meant by it. But I refuse to say I was wrong. There was a wordless truth behind the idea. As regards what I was doing, it was what it was, it never lied, at least it never pretended to be 'art'. I could trust its outrageousness, totally.

That search went on for years and fruitlessly. Then one morning, I woke and swore I would never mix with the mud-born again. But I was still blind.

I buried myself in dead-end jobs. I took dead-end lovers and despised myself. I had no trace of self-belief. Precisely where my common-sense, my sensibilities had fled to, I have no idea. And still that phrase plagued me. I think I had a Messiah complex, together with zero self-respect. Fortunately, you're resilient when you're young. It takes an effort to kill yourself. (Or, if you're unlucky, none at all. Most things in life seem to come with that same disastrous, double-edged possibility.)

There were four roads out of our town, each unimaginatively named for the cardinal position they occupied on the face of the magnetic compass. At the time, even that seemed portentous, part and parcel of my mission of atonement.

I took the Western link first. The last bus left at nine p.m. It arrived where I wanted to be at ten p.m. For two hours then, I had to sit concealed at the edge of the woods, waiting for the 'shameless' hours. So there I sat, utterly terrified by what I was about to do, nailed in place by words I had heard in an opioid fog.

I was so beautifully dressed underneath mum's dowdy old coat. A white lace corselette, with white pants that left a couple of inches of soft belly on display. The bra top was too small, so my tits looked sluttish and my half erect cock bulged over the top of the pants. Long suspenders led to high white stockings and I'd even struggled into high heels. In those days I still had blonde hair in curling waves and I'd topped them with a rakish French beret.

At midnight and almost sick from the adrenalin pumping into my muscles, I teetered from the wood to the seedy neon of the bus stop. Mum's coat I had folded neatly and left in the embrace of a silver birch tree.

There I waited. I was cold beyond belief and most of me wanted to go home. But the inner voice said – "Atone."

A car, taking the roundabout exit suddenly veered as if to avoid a rabbit and I saw a woman's startled face, staring aghast at me from the passenger seat. When our eyes met, briefly, I came close to vomiting.

The driver of the second vehicle never saw me at all, I think. I began to wonder if I might even escape the Western road, for I'd set a time limit on this madness.

The third vehicle slowed, but speeded up when I put my hands on my hips and swayed provocatively.

The fourth was a grubby white van. 'Ideal for dismembering bodies in,' I remember thinking as it slowed. I pirouetted. The driver reversed up and the window came down.

"How much?"

"Depends what you're buying," I croaked.

"What you selling?"

I chittered off a list, as if I was a Pizza. "…extra salami? Fries with that? Stuffed crust?…"

We settled at £50. Ridiculous. With my body, my looks, my comparative youth, the way I was dressed, it could have been £2000, in Kensington. But that wasn't the mission I had launched myself on.

I climbed in, settling myself among takeaway empties, half-full milk cartons, boxes of screws, a plastic tray of various pop rivets and hardware catalogues. I nearly cried when I shifted a pile of newspaper and uncovered a battered copy of "The Gruffalo."

We were moving, now but he gave a half-glance and said – "leave that on top. She's lost it."

"It's good, isn't it," I said.

"Dunno, I never read it."

What a way to start! He was a squat, powerful man, with the hardest hands I'd ever encountered. But he was very gentle with them and seemed genuinely awestruck by my body.

"Is that all natural?" he asked.

I said it was, which was no more than the truth.

"Don't that make you – kind of special?" he asked.

I remember exactly what I said – "we're all special, honey. Come on. I don't bite."

He tried but he was at a bit of a loss. By that time, however, I liked him enough to try, too. I hope he had a nice time, because he was a very gentle, unhappy man. Sometimes we can't speak the words we want to say, or even believe that they could exist. I felt for him and I really tried to be 'worthy of my hire.'

He asked me where I wanted dropping and I said back at the bus stop. He took me there, in silence but as I got out he said – "be careful, there are some nasty fuckers out there."

"Well, you're not one of them," I said and gave him a peck on the cheek, which given the reaction I was having, internally, was no mean feat.

He flashed his hazard lights as he left and I waved to his mirrors.

I fled up the slope to mum's coat and sat and shuddered under it. Never have I felt so sick, so futile, stupid and deflated. "I know you don't want this, mum. Believe me, I know, But I have to do it. If I can just do it right, everything will be fixed."

That was West. I called a cab and went home. After paying for that, I was barely in profit and morally, I was bankrupt.

In some ways I couldn't have had a worse introduction to what I was undertaking. I'd come out of it unscathed. Nevertheless, it was weeks before I could summon the courage to go East.

That didn't go so well.

I was going to set out my wares in a lay-by but again, I had to wait for the witching hour. All that was available as a waiting room was a scrubby meadow, access via five-bar gate but at least its roadside fence was hidden behind a sea of brambles. It was also home to a small herd of cows. They were pleased to see me, as I toppled over the gate in patent leather. They crowded round, drooling but I don't think that was because I was particularly alluring.

I wedged myself behind a fence-side tree for safety and tried to pat their wet noses when they lumbered too close and they would dance skittishly away. Finally, they got bored, or tired and went off to lie down, grumbling about the traumas of a digestive system that comes in four parts.

I found a cow-pat free patch of grass and tried to wax philosophical under a three-quarters moon. 'We were all animals for hire and slaughter. Curiosity can kill. It's a bit unkind wearing leather in a field of cows. Hu-cows are a little known cul-de-sac in hard porn. 'Hu-cow' as in Human-cows…you can guess the rest. I wish I could talk 'cow. I would try to explain myself to them. But their focus is probably food and they wouldn't be interested. That makes me very much alone. I'd be worthless in an abattoir and they'd be worthless in a porn film, niche products excluded. I wish I had wider horizons. I used to have. I still read voraciously. It seems nothing, nothing, will displace this Biblical injunction to Atone.'

Time was up. I struggled to the lay-by. Hid mum's coat, my bag, in the brambles.

The cold did wonders for my nipples but my other bits prefer the Tropics. Half-an-hour spent shivering and fighting adrenalin rushes every time I heard a vehicle.

It was a large black BMW, a tank-like 4x4 and it positively stood on its nose with eagerness, as I flashed my array of straps and buckles.

"Darling!" cried an educated, ugly voice, "do get in."

There were two of them, overweight young executives aspiring to fleece the world and starve the poor. The car was thick with the sickly reek of dope.

"Tell us your tricks!" slurred the second, drunken voice.

"Depends on your kicks, guys," I parried.

"We'll soon be there," he drawled. "Then we'll show you a thing or two."

It turned out that 'there' was a motel court, as silent, grey and grim as three a.m. can contrive.

Inside things began to get awkward. If I'd been an "ordinary whore" they'd have known how to operate. A chick with a dick and a powerfully built one, at that, had them confused.

To buy themselves time, they raided the mini-bar and then tried to push one another into lewd scenarios, in which I would be the hapless victim. I recognised a situation that could deteriorate, quickly.

To divert them – and perhaps guide their impoverished imaginations – I directed them to one of my sites, where the nice/bad girl and I, together with some of her other friends had cavorted engagingly. I can still find parts of it raunchy, even now, sad sack that I am. Actually, that caper ended badly for me but two and a half hours is longer than most people can tolerate without collapsing from boredom.

It gave them some ideas. I went to work as gamely as I could, given that by now, I loathed them both. But after 20 futile minutes and still with limp pricks they started slapping me about, trying to recover some self-respect. Alcohol and dope had robbed them blind. Finally, they pushed me out of the door, stark naked and threw my clothes after me.

"Fuck off, you freak!" was their righteous dismissal.

My clothes, such as they were, landed in a puddle – including my innocent white beret. I felt sorrier for it, wet, gritty and filthy, than I did for myself.

I did my best and searching turned up a bicycle, which I commandeered. I contemplated keying their car with a flint. For some reason, I didn't. I'd been looking for humiliation, hadn't I? I'd had it in spades.

In comparison with the journey out, it seemed a long way when I was pedalling back to the lay-by. I was constantly terrified that cars would arrive, unexpectedly, behind me. None did. I rescued mum's coat, my bag and cycled to a distant bus stop. I hadn't even had the heart to explain myself to the cows.

I caught the last of the night buses home. The bicycle, 'fresh from my fragrant ass,' I leaned against the shelter. I hope it found its way home.

Home – I can't say it welcomed me. I'd become an alien. The tea towels looked strange, the chairs peculiar, a picture I must have seen 1000 times a year seemed downright odd. I felt a palpable hostility in the air.

As it wasn't time for the hot water to come on, I showered under cold. That knocked me sick rather than revitalising me. I crawled under the bedcovers, still wrapped in the wet towel and shivered, my feet just getting colder and colder. Eventually I gave up, got up and boiled a kettle. I sponged myself down, warmed my feet and tried bed again. This time it worked and I slept till mid-afternoon.

Later, sitting at the table, still surrounded by 'unfamiliar' things, I wondered what the hell I was playing at. Everything about last night had nauseated me and in the scales of atonement, I doubt I'd added one grain to my pan.

To be clear in my own mind, I spelled out my theory. I was half-a-man. That half-a-man was deliberately punishing himself to atone for the damage his species had wreaked upon his other half – the girl-half. But it seemed to me that the girl-half took the beating, every time and the man just looked on helplessly. Such efforts to atone were valueless, as valueless as I was.

So, wrapped in a cold fury, I went out in the middle of the night to the road south. There, everything blew up in my face.

Hard-by was a scrapyard, a grave for dead cars and a haven for spare parts. Maybe I found it symbolic. I hadn't been there more than 20 minutes when two hard lads in a huge, matt-black pick-up invited me to party with them. They held out to me, from the side window, a can of extra-strength cider as an inducement. My heart plummeted. This was going to be bad. Refusing would be worse still.

If you're interested, you'll find it on the web – though Google won't take you there. It gets a lot of hits. I'm told that the bit where they ram a beer bottle up my ass and let go of the neck is particularly LOL. With my tits tied up like the Sunday joint, purple and twice their normal size, my prick tied to the towbar by a long rope, I get to trot along behind the pick-up. The implicit message is that if I stop, my cock comes off. So I stumble along a country roads, tits flailing and begging for mercy in a masterpiece of cell-phone video. It's ugly. They piss on me, then take turns to knock me about, fists and boots. Finally – and this is the bit I hate most – one takes out a sheath knife and cuts off the great mass of blonde, curled hair I had back then, to leave it lying as gutter refuse, in the lay-by where they kindly dumped me.

The police found me, stark-naked, with a broken jaw and ribs. I was concussed, had a burst spleen and there's a list I don't care to recall of other injuries.

I got a blue-light ride to A&E Majors and spent a few hours in the operating theatre. It's a miracle but my fistula repairs had held up.

When I was semi-sentient the police took a statement, to add to the DNA they'd recovered. I gave a pretty clear description of everything, including the fact that the truck had no plates.

"Which means it's probably matt-red by now," said an unhappy detective-constable. "May I ask what you were actually doing?"

"You can ask," I said. "But I can't explain. Also, I don't care if you find them or not. It's my own stupid fault and I'm probably mad. I know you've got a job to do but as far as I'm concerned, you can leave it where it lies."

Worse, by far, was the lecture I got from the Registrar. 'What was the point of them sewing me up, wiring my jaw, saving my life, if I was going to go out and risk the same things happening again?'

"None," I said, "and I'm totally in your debt."

He was a truly nice man but he didn't have a granite injunction hanging round his neck – 'Atone.'

I lay in that hospital bed for what seemed a long time, asking – 'is this the colour and shape of atonement?' I got no answers. My mind had stopped answering.

I tried to find the girl in the white dress, the girl with the withered limb, the girl from my hallucinatory dream. I hadn't questions I wanted to ask, I just needed to look into her sad eyes and not have her look away. What did that signify?

Whatever road I was embarked upon, it was a lonely one. I'd found no companions, no kindred souls, not even a casual acquaintance. Is there anything more painful for the soul than trying to change but remaining the same, while all around you the flux of time and change seems to be conjuring butterflies from chrysalides? I felt hopelessly abandoned, worthless, discarded.

South had done for me, physically and mentally. I had been a stumble, a phrase away from death and not one ounce of understanding could I draw from any of it. I was still haunted by a phrase, a monster from my own psyche. I could gain no traction on it, achieve no freedom from it. It denied me the right to exist.

If I looked in a mirror, I couldn't recognise anything other than the contours of my face. What lay behind was blind mystery. I felt more fragile than bone china and simultaneously harder than a cast horseshoe. Why choose those analogies? I can't say.

I went nowhere for a year and that stretched out to two. I lived off my past immoral earnings. You see, unbelievably, I had royalties, paid from an offshore bank. It seems I was a film-star but I wasn't aware how that had occurred, or why anyone felt it incumbent upon them to be paying me.

I was in the depths of despair, one day and I was buying greengrocery, at the time.

"Hello, Eva," said a voice.

I turned around and saw a face from the hospital, a ward sister. She'd been a true friend, solid, reliable, friendly and encouraging. I'd quite worshipped her – the way you do when you're in a dependent state.

"Hello Meg," I said, genuinely pleased to see her. She was actually called Megumi. She was part Japanese and her full name meant beautiful waterway, or something akin to that. So I had, in the spirit of free association, tied her to the girl in the white dress, for my purposes.

I waited while she bought her salad stuff and then we went for a coffee – my treat. I insisted.

She wanted to know how I was doing now and I kind of shrugged.

I'd tried to explain the 'atonement' thing to her once but she'd said – "don't trust drug dreams. They trick you…" then she'd squeezed my hand and left. Of course, I wasn't having that. I was on a mission, not following a drug dream. I'd killed mum and I was atoning for that, as well as Adam's dirty deeds.

Today, after a comfortable silence, she said – "we saw you on the web. My friends and I. We liked you. Do you want to come and visit us sometime?"

"Oh," I said, "that's a bit of a blind-sider."

"Don't feel pressured," she said. "We all live a great big house and we have a lot of gentle fun. Nobody ever gets hurt and nothing would ever happen to you that you didn't want. We just thought you looked like our sort of friend – but we didn't like the others."

"Neither did I," I said with feeling. "Can I think about things? I'm in a bad place, recently and I don't want to bring a blight and a curse down on you all."

"That's why I'm asking," she said. "The Savoy cabbage and you both looked very lost."

"I think the cabbage is OK," I'd replied. "It's probably just concerned about me."

She giggled. "Here's our card," she said, "Call us if you want to. We have fun and we bake nice cakes, too."

That was how I passed another year, enjoying the company of the 'Order of Rubber Nuns,' of whom I shall not say another word, other than to assure you that every word Megumi had spoken was the truth. So it's very hard for me to understand why, then, on one particular day, I set out for the Northern link road.

To go North from our town now required great cunning. Once it had been simple, you drove north along a bit of tarmac and eventually you joined the Great North Road. But major arterial surgery had redrawn such a foolishly simple design. Our bit of the Great North Road had somehow vanished and with it, our link road. Now you had to drive doggedly south to go north.

Such action eventually precipitated you into a Gordian knot of roundabouts, each one of dramatic proportions. These, in turn, led to even larger roundabouts, which fed you into vehicle processing chicanes of such an awesome size that only military satellites could map their outcome with reasonable accuracy.

As yet there was no Damoclean sword designed that could simplify this unholy mess, which is lucky for anthropology, because there could be a tribe, or two, of modern ancient-Britons hunkered down behind the huge piles of broken concrete, tangled, rusting re-bar and thriving buddleia groves that cover much of the blind acreage within the circles.

Not that every Circle of this particular Hell is abandoned. Human beings work here, too, toiling in anonymous warehouses, with very strange addresses, between the hours of seven a.m. and eight p.m. Heavy goods move inwards and outwards – presumably escorted by pilots, especially trained by the Highways England equivalent of Trinity House.

These were Edgelands with a vengeance. At night the warehouse service roads were alive with sassy kids burning the rubber off the tyres of their Subarus, while their bored girlfriends shared influencer clips on their smartphones. Foxes slunk around the industrial waste bins, waiting to pounce on unwary rats. Rosebay willowherb proliferated and a few gnarled hawthorn trees kept watch.

My problem was that the last local bus to touch this benighted spot did so at 20.15. As any business I had with the link roads couldn't realistically begin until midnight, I would have had a long and tedious wait ahead of me, avoiding the Subaru cowboys and the illegal fly-tippers. A taxi was barely a proposition… "take me to the middle of nowhere and leave me there."

I concocted a plan. I would catch one of the inter-city buses, which were all condemned to twist their way through this spaghetti jungle and at a spot suitable for me, I'd ask the driver to stop… "aagh, I've left my passport on the table! Please let me off. I'll get a taxi back and just catch a later plane. Oh, thank you, you're a sweetheart!…". Actually, I hate lying – but it usually works.

At 22.00 hrs I was dropped on the asphalt outside the hardware supply depot, just beyond the road favoured by the Subaru lads.

I had two hours to pass. Mum's poor old coat and I were about nefarious business again. I don't know precisely why, even now, all these years later. Possibly it was because I was almost happy, being an honorary nun and Atonement was piqued at being sidelined. Actually, I think it was more to do with having some sort of death wish, despite my fervent prayers that I wouldn't soon be reliving the southern approaches.

The bus drew away into the night. The burn-up boys revved their engines and rubber howled in the distance. Adaptable material, rubber, I reflected. I picked my way into the broken concrete mountains, headed I wasn't entirely sure but away from here.

In the footwear department I was inadequately shod. I was wearing boots but not of a military specification. I needed something becoming, but with studs, cleats and ankle support, not patent leather with criss-cross lacing all the way up the thigh.

Overhead dirty-stop-out gulls were flying home, stuffed with the finest offal rubbish dumps can provide. Car noise, aircraft roar, distant music – other people's activities seemed so innocent compared to my intentions.

I rifled through the pockets of mum's coat. She always had a sweetie in her pocket, when I was young. I knew before I tried that there were none there now. Even if there had been they'd have been years old. What I did find was a collection of leaves. They mystified me for a moment, until I recalled my first trip of atonement.

I'd had the idea that, if the trip was successful, in any sense, I might somehow record it, in paint and collage. Lord, how reality overtakes naivety! I'd had a vision of my figure somehow parting a shimmering veil of leaves – an androgynous form wrapped protectively in beech, oak, hazel, hawthorn on its way…to what, to where? I had no idea but I'd shown a bit of promise at art school, until Pornocrates hi-jacked my soul. It was that remnant of me that thought a collection of dried, pressed leaves might provide inspiration. I really had no idea, did I? And apparently, I still didn't.

I did recall that collecting them had calmed me a little and I still think there's a painting to be had from them. Just not the one I imagined then. Nevertheless, finding them, provoked strange emotions in me. They were little more than dried fragments but if I'd had a 'medicine bag,' like the American Indians used to, I'd have poured them into it. As it was, I had to settle for my stomach turning over, feeling incredibly tired and wondering what on earth I was playing at.

My spirits sank so fast that I was about to abandon the plan and call a cab for a ride back to town. But while I thought about it, my kinky boots and I struggled up a slope of pulverized concrete and there, in a totally unexpected freak of landscape was a large hollowed dish, as if scooped out by the ice-cream scoop to end all ice-cream scoops. In it was a large, low building, a scattered collection of disparate vehicles and a clear neon sign reading "24-HOUR DINER". I hadn't anticipated anything so sophisticated. Maybe a small tribe of Crusties in a bender or two, with a few broken down vans but not food and neon, amalgamated in a legitimate venue.

Thank Heavens then, for mum's coat, for all I was wearing under it was a very sophisticated red and black corset, which was more of a multitude of criss-crossing straps than clothing, leather pants and above the boots, shiny black stockings held up by God knows how many suspenders. In certain situations I would have looked pretty hot. Currently, I was not in any one of them.

The climbing, memory lane and nerves all combined to make me anxious for a pee. So I nestled into a buddleia, thinking it might be grateful for the nourishment and while unloading my bladder, tried to map, by moon and neon, a path to the diner.

Bits tucked away, coat secured, I teetered off – ship launched. It was tricky going. Every gully was a scree of bottles, tins and sandwich wrappers. Each ditch was watery – at least the fluid looked a bit like water. But they were also hosting unwinding Pringles tubes, floating and drowned sandwich casings, indestructible crispy snack bags, as well as nameless objects. An 'Eye-Spy Litter' book just could be a winner.

I was picking my way along quite successfully when I became aware of a fellow tip-toer who was making heavier going than I, albeit along a vaguely parallel route.

"Fuck and damn it all!" was the most frequent protest, along with – "give me my time back! Give it back to me!" which was considerably more intriguing. For all the ferocity of delivery, it was not a frightening voice. It was old, tetchy and probably a bit drunk.

Eventually, against the night sky, I could make out a small shuffling shape – as I had thought, an elderly chap, in all probability bound in the same direction as myself and with a similar desire, to arrive there safely.

We had quite a few yards to go before we crossed paths but I decided to pre-empt any sudden surprises. In that way I would be able to make out what manner of man he might turn out to be.

"Good evening, sir!" I smiled, through a happy, welcoming voice.

The small figure paused, straightened up cautiously, ceased cursing and directed his gaze at me.

"Merciful judgement," croaked a ragged voice, "a lady! Madame, will you dine with me? These chances arise so infrequently that I force myself to be bold, in the vain hope that my offer may be construed as gallantry."

The little figure was unkempt and resembled nothing so much as an ill-wound ball of hairy twine. Nevertheless, he was wearing a suit, albeit one that under the moonlight shone with years of accumulated dirt and grease. In fact, I did him an injustice – I later found out that the shine was the result of accumulated linseed oil.

"I can make no pretence, Madame, to having more than the price of tea about my person – but that would be tea for two. Had you the price of bread and butter, we might dine royally. Is there anything in my proposal that might tempt you? I can barely bring myself to hope that there could be."

Why is it that one takes instantly to some people, yet others – who may nevertheless turn into lifelong friends – it takes an eternity to get to know?

I liked the little man, for all that the most awful smell emanated from the shiny, battered suit and the fact that he was clutching an empty bottle of sherry by the neck. It was 'La Ina,' a sherry so dry you could use it for sandpaper.

"If you have the price of tea," I agreed, "I may have the price of egg and chips for two."

"Egg and chips!" he said, ecstatically. "Merciful judgement, is this to be the day I regain my time?"

He glared up at the moon. There was obviously some issue between them, for he shied the empty bottle at it and to the sound of the shattering glass, declaimed – "let us waste no more of it! Forward!" and seizing my wrist, broke into a hobble, little more than a half-stride for me.

At this breakneck pace we entered a room of steam, forbidden cigarette smoke, bright lights, clamorous pans, cooking fumes and a modest tune from the juke box. Gathered, were lorry drivers, a couple of ladies of the night, a few bikers – medieval in their leathers – some of the older Subaru gang and two or three flight crew. We, on any social Richter scale, were not going to cause waves. Consequently we were ignored, until greeted by the Chef.

"A Lady and Harold," he said, with only a hint of chaffing and an immensely appealing, open affability. "Is it tea and bread, Harold? And what for the Lady?"

"Andrew," said Harold importantly, "tonight it is tea and bread and butter but also, Andrew, my love, it is egg and chips!" He turned to me, beaming, having invested 'egg and chips' with all the resonance and eloquence due to 'partridge and venison'. He did a little dance, which so enchanted me, that he had to nudge me to produce my purse.

"Might there be large portions available?" I asked. Andrew smiled and took a modest sum in exchange.

We found a side booth and sat opposite each other.

"I'm Eva," I said.

Harold reflected. He considered me. "Do I stink?" he asked.

"I'm trying to recall the smell, " I said.

"Boiled linseed oil," he said, "and dirt. I'm so sorry."

"No need to apologise, Harold. I don't have much sense of smell left, anyway." It was the truth, after the lads from the pick-up had finished with me.

"Allow me to take your cloak…may I make so bold?" he asked shyly, half-rising from his bench and releasing a fresh wave of linseed – and dirt.

Charmed and vaguely saddened, I said without thinking – "of course, how considerate of you…" until, in ghastly panic, I realised that that would reveal me in whore's lingerie under a paratrooper's beret. (I think mum had some sort of ex-military boy-friend, which is why I was in possession of a memento of Goose Green, not really to be sported atop a red and black corset and a bulging bosom. The nuns liked it though, which is why I was wearing it.)

I shed the coat and Harold trotted away with it, like a spaniel carrying a particularly dowdy pheasant. Mercifully, a few glances apart, no-one was that perturbed. One of the professional girls looked as though she might ask for the specialist boutique address, later.

Harold was quite unfazed.

He also sank into some sort of active reverie. The only words I can find that usefully describe it, was that a sort of great but awkward intelligence seemed to settle on him, as he stared past my cheek and shoulder. A very long time passed, during which the young lady cashier crept over, bearing a nice, light cardigan. This she folded over my shoulders, saying – "it can gets so cold on your neck, what with the door going all night. You know, people coming in and out…"

"You're a lifesaver," I said. "Let me tell you all about it, sometime."

"I'd love to listen," she smiled and left, leaving me to Harold's oblique concentration, which had continued, unrelenting and uninterrupted.

Finally he spoke, in a soft, clear voice.

"You are, of course, a God, a Goddess. You know that, don't you?"

That I wasn't expecting.

"I don't feel like one," was the best I could manage.

"Nevertheless, you are. You may not like it, you may not want it but you can't give it away, nor can you avoid its consequences."

Two mountains of egg and chips arrived and I smiled gratefully at the waitress cum cashier, whose cardigan I had buttoned, covering the raunchier regions. She grinned back.

Harold turned from contemplating Gods to egg and chips, which he ate like a starving man. First he ate his, then most of mine. Then he glanced around, cunningly.

"They used to serve tolerable apple pie here – with clotted cream," he added in a dreamy voice. Then he stared fiercely at the sagging fibreboard ceilings, as if such a dessert might be found lurking in its corners, unnoticed.

This was a dilemma. What length was the cardy? If it didn't make it past my bum, I was going to cause a ripple, even on these placid waters.

Eventually, Harold's unceasing hunt for the elusive dessert lurking in the ceiling, drove me to the counter, eyes locked on the chef's, alone.

"It's the apple pie, isn't it?" he said, "with clotted cream."

"It is," I said, "but given the state of my nerves, I'll stick to custard – rather a lot of it, if you don't mind."

"Cream, custard! What's up with you two? Try it with bitter marmalade and Calvados foam, sometime."

"Tempting," I agreed "but I'll leave it till I'm better dressed for fine dining. That sounds rather West End."

"I am West End," he said emphatically, with a flourish and a smile. "I used to have a Michelin Star, hence the Calvados foam but give me the diner every time! As for your 'dressed for,' don't fret. The cardy covers your very lovely bum. I promise that's not a come-on, just a soothing compliment from one Michelin Star to another."

"I couldn't cook a tin of beans," I protested.

"Don't pretend to be obtuse," he said. "There are Tin Stars for all sorts of things. Just like Nobel Prizes. You've got a Tin Star, you just don't believe it. Don't fret so. I'll bring those desserts in a minute. You relax."

Back at the table, Harold had begun emitting strange hoots and whistles, as if he was a bat, sizing up new accommodation. After a while I could tolerate it no longer and asked – "Harold, why are you making weird noises?"

He stopped abruptly and stared at me.

"Am I?"

"Hoots and whistles."

"Ah – any clicks?"

"Not so far."

"Good, good. That's good."

And he went back to hooting and whistling.

When we finally left I settled up for the apple pie but first I shed the cardigan, with profuse thanks. She shrugged into it right away, which I somehow found very sweet and trusting, the equivalent of not wiping the bottle's neck when you're passing round the rum. I buttoned up mum's coat, while Harold fidgeted and shuffled like a seven-year-old consumed with the urge to pee. On top, I perched my maroon beret.

"That's a paratrooper's beret, isn't it?" said the cashier. I agreed it was. "For what you're wearing underneath, which I think is stunning, by the way, this would be good." From under her desk she produced an obviously genuine montera, the Spanish matador's traditional hat, in Astrakhan lamb fleece.

"My little boy is Army mad and I was wondering, if you didn't have any particular connection with the beret, whether you'd consider a swop. I know that's a cheek but…"

I whipped off the beret and took the montera, commanding and handsome too, with its deep wrinkled surface, the wide brim and short crown. All I needed was the rapier.

"It's been a strange evening," I said. "Let's keep it that way."

She smiled and refused her tip, decisively.

Harold lived…I couldn't really say where…at the back of the diner, up an incline, along a furrow, across a headland and behind a mammoth wall of crushed concrete. There, down a short flight of steps and along a short alleyway, you took a decisive right turn and you were smack up against a very ordinary front door, complete with household Yale lock and letter-box.

"Harold," I asked, "do you get many letters?"

He gave me a haughty look.

"There have been Countesses, Princesses and Nobility in my life. I was not always in this reduced condition – before that monster, that poltroon, took control of my genius and sold it to the highest bidder! I was someone, I had a 'Name' in society… letters, indeed!

"Tell me, Countess," he asked suddenly, "that large and interesting bag of yours… which now holds the sainted Kirsty's montera…it wouldn't, by any chance, be home to a bottle, too?"

Before we'd left the diner, Andrew had sidled up to me and whispered – "don't let the old fool drink – whatever you do."

I whipped open the bag, graced my locks with the montera, thus revealing the remaining contents. Harold peered into every corner, suspiciously turning over a tissue or two.

He sighed. "Sorrow, sorrow, sorrow is man's lot. Nevertheless, let me welcome you to my humble abode."

Behind the Yale was a very large concrete silo that, towering ever upwards and criss-crossed by spidery walkways and platforms, brought back memories of the Mount Palomar Observatory. Not that I'd ever been but I had seen photographs.

A second glance revealed that these platforms seemed to double as rooms – rooms without walls. In the soft light of the doorway, it looked eccentric but serviceable. Then Harold turned to me to present a pair of dark glasses. "You'll need these," he said glumly and flicked a switch on the wall.

Dazzling LED's bathed the whole capsule in brilliant light. The industrial nature of the place was laid bare. Some process had been undertaken here that had needed light and plenty of it. Said process also seemed to have blown the roof off at some time, because the silo now ended, approximately, at the fourth storey in a ring of jagged concrete. The remnants of the roof lay on the ground floor, as a sea of heavy concrete chunks, complete with tangled re-bar. As a burglar trap it had much to commend it, as a reception hall for Harold's familiars, the Nobility, not a lot.

Harold turned right and started to climb a spiral stair that clung to the inner concrete skin. It looked secure and trustingly, I followed him to arrive in the first floor living quarters. There was an old-fashioned iron bed, a fairly clean mattress, a disgusting pile of sheets and two unspeakable pillows. Against the wall was a handbasin, on the edge of which hung a towel, obviously on loan from the biological warfare department at Porton Down. There was a rickety chair, with two surprisingly clean shirts, dangling on hangers, from the back. Three large cardboard boxes held the rest of his life essentials.

"I must show you the studio," he said and we carried on up the spiral stair which, thank God, had a hand-rail on its vertigo-side.

Here a certain element of genius had been in operation. A system of ropes and pulleys allowed him to raise and lower the theatre-sized flats on which he was currently working, one in front of the other. I guessed that the inspiration from one might lead to modification of the others, because as he hauled on the ropes and the huge paintings rose and fell, I could glimpse similarities of style, if not content. In those moments, before he spoke, I seemed to be looking at abstraction on a grand scale.

"Energies," he said, shyly. "I paint energies, or rather I try to paint them…when I'm not pissed."

That was blinding clarification… 'of course! Energies!…What's wrong with me?… Sweet Jesus, the man's a genius!…'

I gaped at him and said, stupidly – "Harold, you have no roof."

"That helps, when you're painting cosmic energy."

I had a sudden vision of cosmic energies, lining up to have their portraits painted for posterity, in a silo, just south of the Great North Road. Then, when I looked up, above the halogen light and gazed at the stars through the lens of the shattered concrete dome, I began to grasp what he meant when he'd said – "that helps…"

After a very long silence, that was beginning to feel awkward to me, he said – "you belong out there. You're an energy. I don't know how, or why but you are. It's very sad. It will destroy you and you'll never know why."

"I don't want to be destroyed," I said sadly.

"Then we must find you a way out," he said emphatically. "Let me start by making some tea." Oddly enough, he produced a passable brew, though I declined the savagely-opened tin of condensed milk, which he poured into his own cup until the combination took on the consistency of molten fudge.

"You know I have to paint you, don't you?" he said as he sipped.

"I didn't, no."

"Not now – and not those…things!…" he gestured savagely at a number of conventional easels that all held beautiful charcoal drawings of people unknown to me. In comparison with the great stage flats he had raised and lowered, however, they were insipid – and dwarfed.

"I shall command Andrew to speak with the Gallery. They will produce what I need. I shall see you again, in a week."

"Can we have egg and chips again?" I asked.

"We can," he said regally but before we dine, I want to explain something very special to you. So do come early. It's important."

After that, I concluded that I was dismissed. He began to fuss and mumble, re-arranging chaos inside his cardboard boxes, his back firmly presented to me.

Once outside and tip-toeing cautiously back to the diner, I contemplated my options. I no longer had the appetite for atonement, with its optional extras of being raped, or beaten. So I stood outside in the shadows, wondering whether to call a cab, or sit out the small hours with coffee and toast in the convivial warmth.

"Is a lift any use to you?" asked the cardigan-loaning cashier emerged from the shadows. I felt so pleased to be still wearing her hat. I hadn't taken it off in Harold's place, being wary of what wildlife it might attract.

"You going back to town?"

She nodded.

"That'll probably save my life. So, yes please."

We climbed into a beaten up Fiat 500 and took off, gingerly, across potholes and angry furrows ploughed up by articulated trucks and trailers.

"You know Harold?" she asked, as we made the approach road, jostled but still in one piece.

"Met him for the first time, tonight."

"He can be nice, when the drink's not in him. Mad as a hatter but a scrupulous, old-school gentleman. When he's drunk, stay clear. He can be nasty, stupid and aggressive."

"He wants to paint me."

"That's very unusual. He rarely paints people, in fact I can't remember him ever doing it. He does charcoal drawings, from memory and sells them in London, for booze money, to so-called friends."

"That would explain something," I said, remembering how viciously he'd dismissed his drawings.

"Andrew says he's a genius. He fixed him up with a gallery, about a year after he washed up here. He lives here for free – that's typical Andrew, he collects helpless souls, because he was born a soft touch. Anyway, the gallery fix him up with canvas, paint and shows. Sometimes he makes a lot of money. Andrew banks it for him and gives him an allowance, for which he gets nothing but abuse. They have terrible rows but at heart, Harold knows Andy's right to keep a tight rein on him. He'd drink himself to death, otherwise."

"Does Andrew own all this ?" I gestured at the huge blackness, now slipping astern.

"He does now. His brother did. He was a developer. This was a cement works and he bought everything, buildings, warehouses, piles of concrete, the land, the roads, the rusted-out lorries. He was busy demolishing the lot when he went down with a massive heart attack. At that she crossed herself and in empathy, the car tried to do the same. "Anyway, I'm Kirsty."

"I'm Eva," I responded, "who is very pleased to meet you."

"Can I ask…are you a working-girl?"

"I don't think so." I pondered. "I'm screwed up and they're pretty level-headed. I'm just trying to work something out and I've borrowed their tactics, it seems. Working-girls always seem pretty sorted to me. So far none of it's worked, which is why tonight was a bit of a miracle." I changed the subject. "I know you work at the diner, what else goes down in your life?"

"My little boy, that's Neil and I both live with my mum, since his loser of a dad scarpered and I'm trying to survive, while staying sane. Bit of a struggle, if I'm honest."

"I lived with my mum," I said. "This is her coat, though definitely not her undies. I really am pleased to meet you Kirsty. You seem like the nicest crew back there."

"We're tight," Kirsty agreed. Then she swung through the circuitry of roundabouts and we pitched off back to town, ending up pretty well the best of friends, exchanging telephone numbers, the lot.

A week later I rang Kirsty, to set a date on which she could take me up to the Diner.

"Portrait Day," I explained, "or so he said."

She told me to come over for midday and I said that would be great. Then I went into town and bought a complete change of bed linen in someone's never-ending 'Sale!' That was one thing that was happening, today – Harold's bed was being changed, come what may.

Back home I changed into the loosest, most shapeless grey tracksuit I possessed. Bitter experience had taught me that the outlines of bras and knickers take an eternity to fade and if they look naff on camera, they probably do on canvas as well. I topped off with a grey watch cap, tied up my hair and left home pure Patti Smith.

If I did heroes, she might be one of mine – though I think my swinging dick gets in the way of any real emulation, just as my other bits stop me sidling up alongside some of my male role models. Famous androgynes are thin on the ground.

I wondered how Patti would have coped with Harold. I bet she'd have envied me, understood what a privilege it was. Maybe she'd have written a poem, or a song.

At Kirsty's I met Neil, who was hurling himself about, clutching a plastic sub-machine gun and with my paratrooper's beret hanging over his eyes. I invented a couple of wild stories about the battles it had been in. Then I got to say "hi" to Kirsty's mum, who radiated frosty suspicion.

Finally, we set off.

"Don't mind mum, she's protective," Kirsty explained, once we were in the car.

"So would I be," I agreed. "Wounded daughter, delightful grandchild, plus new, dodgy friend – what could possibly go wrong?" In truth, though, I was upset. I wondered if my stupid experiments with life showed, had rubbed off on me, like Harold's dirt.

We arrived without incident, the little Fiat buzzing between the juggernauts on the roundabouts, like a pilot fish through a pod of sharks. They didn't seem to bother Kirsty. But as we filtered down the approach road, a rented panel van swung across us, the girl driver fighting the wheel as if she'd never driven a van before. Kirsty had to execute a sharp manoeuvre to avoid burying us in the broadside.

"That was neat driving," I gasped.

"That'll be Harold's paintings going up to Town, at a guess," she said easily. "I used to rally," she added, "before my world imploded. Those gallery girls are all tits and teeth, 'meeters and greeters,' more used to being driven around than driving – especially Luton vans." We drove around the back and cosied up to a buddleia bush. "I swear that thing grows six inches a day," she marvelled. "How does it do it on a diet of concrete and fox pee, with the occasional rainfall from heaven?"

I snorted appreciatively. " You should write songs."

"I do," she snorted back, obviously pleased I'd picked up on her rhythm.

Once out of the car, out of sight but not earshot, it became apparent that an unholy row was in progress. We could hear Harold's voice rising and falling, descant to an implacable bass line held down by Andy. We exchanged glances and walked round to the back door, where the bins were.

Harold was fairly dancing with fury, the less famous, demented eighth dwarf, while Andy, arms folded, countenance set, was stolidly repeating – "No."

"No, no and no, Harold. If I give you more money this week you'll just piss it up the wall. You'll make yourself ill. You'll get into trouble. I'll have to come and bail you out. You'll be that much closer to death and there's barely a cigarette paper between the two of you as it is."

"It's going in the bank with the rest of your money. When I think you can handle a night on the tiles, I'll bring the booze to you. That's how the rent free deal works, Harold. You know all this."

Harold accelerated his dance and then rounded on the bins. He gave one an almighty punt and a bouquet of cauliflower leaves showered across the yard.

"Usurer! Barabbas! Gaoler!" he wailed, arms flailing.

Andrew grinned at us. "Thank God," he said, "the cavalry. Do that magic that you do, Kirsty, in the name of Allah. Carl or I'll start up your shift and Lise says she'll cover for as long as it takes, God bless her!"

Kirsty was obviously no stranger to any of this. She linked the poor old boy's arm firmly in hers and walked him up and down the path, muttering in his ear and never once letting go of his filthy hand, while he wailed and wept, cursed and reviled all humanity.

Eventually she said – "and look Harold, see who came to see you, specially!"

For a panicky second, I wondered if he'd even remember.

"Eva," he wailed and tottered over. I took him to my bosom and only then wondered if the smell might linger forever – linseed, dirt and undeniably, shit.

"Dear old Harold," I cooed. "What's got you in this state? Don't fret, Kirsty and I are going to help, now."

"That catamite, that sodomist, that unnatural creation! He rapes me for my genius, robs me of my money, Eva!" And on he went, an extempore cursing of Andrew, first in Old English, then German, some languages I didn't recognise but finally in Russian, which really was a fine gravelly finish, possessing threat and gravitas in equal measure.

"Let's get you home," I said, when he finally fell silent.

The path was barely made for two-abreast but three-abreast was how we made it. I was impressed by the gaping holes, the tottering walls, largely held together by briars and bindweed. Every aspect of the landscape was a direct challenge to survival.

We tottered along.

One sheer drop gave a fine view of the Portakabins, where the two working-girls held court. The one who wasn't Lise was out sunning herself in her birthday suit, while her working undies skittered on the washing line overhead.

"Hi Harold – and friend. Hi Kirst!" she shouted.

"Save me, Penny," squeaked Harold. "These brutes are abducting me."

"I'm Eva," I shouted, "pleased to meet you."

Penny waved and went back to 'Hello' magazine.

So far, so ordinary, I guessed.

Harold's place was empty bottle heaven and the stench was appalling, despite the open roof. We went to work filling bin-liners, Kirsty having armed herself with a roll, from the kitchen. Harold sat on the floor and ranted while we worked. I dealt with the linen and barely stopped myself from throwing-up. Kirsty collected food waste, scrupulously rescuing the cafe's plates and cutlery. There were furred margarine tubs, cartons of solid milk and a sliced loaf, in shades of green worthy of a Farrow & Ball chart. I turned the mattress, then turned it back again, broke out my new sheets and condemned them to a living hell. Pillows too.

"Harold," said Kirsty, in a voice that brooked no disagreement. "Take off your clothes. Eva is going back to the cafe. We have time. To wash."

Harold whimpered, like a castigated child. "I'm so sorry, Kirsty," he said.

"Be sorry for Eva," said Kirsty adamantly, "she's come all this way, just to see you and here you are, a disgrace."

Harold wept piteously.

I actually couldn't bear it, so I loaded myself with multiple bin bags and took off.

I wandered slowly over the rubbish, wriggled my fingers at Penny and eventually came on Andrew, bowling along the path, carrying hefty buckets of scalding water, topped with foam.

"He's delicate," explained Andrew, "but so far and no further is my prescription for him. He can manage some work and some booze but he also needs rest. Galleries seem to think he's some sort of graphic designer. One day they'll tow him into town and it'll kill him. The man's a genius. He can 'see' cosmic energies. Imagine what that does to a mere mortal! Some of them want him painting to order. What blindness is that? By the time he's been charged for materials, transport, he's lucky to see £5000 out of every £20,000. If they won't let him rest, he'll be dead in a twelvemonth. That man's on earth to translate…the…the ineffable…!"

There he stood, fuming, Lord of this concrete jungle, a pair of Dettol-laced, steaming buckets his blazon. I shifted to one side to let him pass – me, a god, or goddess, carrying four bin-liners full of shit, bottles and mouldering food.

"Saving Harold it is, then!" I concurred.

"You have to try," he said softly. Then, with a change of voice like a change of gear, he said – "be a sweetie, dump the bags by the green bins would you, then see if Lise is coping, there's a good chap-ess!" And away he went, humming quietly to himself.

This afternoon was far from unfolding in any way that I had imagined. For a start, the idea of suddenly having to pitch in as cashier/waitress terrified me. I didn't much like people and to start handling the traffic of a busy cafe would undoubtedly bowl me over. For a few seconds, to my shame, I contemplated 'doing-a-runner' back to town, simply vanishing. Then it dawned on me that, for the first time in my life, I had been unhesitatingly "included in." Nice, good people were happy to have me around, so I hurried to the door, stomach fluttering, to see what I could do to help…

…nothing, as it happened. Lise and the chefs were equal to anything that might walk through the door, on a Tuesday afternoon. All that panic had been for nothing. Yet, as I wandered back, I felt curiously disappointed that I wasn't needed. The perversity of the creature!

I met Andrew again, at the halfway point. "I think you're 'on' now," he said wryly.

Harold was, literally, a changed man. My new sheets shone on the bed. The second-best suit was at least, as good as the dry-cleaners could get it. Under a frayed shirt collar, a tie was strangling his scraggy neck. His hand were almost clean, scrubbed to within an inch of bloodshed. I widened my eyes at Kirsty, as she rolled her own up to Heaven.

"Eva," he said in lordly tones, "do join Kirsty and I for afternoon tea."

We afternoon tea-ed – on a table improvised from boxes with a pallet fixed on top, inside a concrete silo with no roof, above a lower floor that looked as if heavy artillery had passed that way – aggressively. Nevertheless, like some belted earl, he dominated the conversation, sniggering at his own wit, ostensibly convinced he was the sole architect of his stunning transformation. We sipped our tea humbly, while exchanging knowing glances.

Eventually, Kirsty said – "Harold, I'm paid to work, so I'm off to it. Thank you for tea."

"Quite my pleasure," he said, rising unsteadily, to see her from the premises.

He returned with a weary sigh – "I thought she'd never go," he confided.

Poor Harold, he'll never know how close he came to death at that moment. But I took a deep breath, tried to grow up a couple of decades and continued to listen to his self-glorification. God knows, he had need of it.

"Eva, my dear," he said eventually, "I said I had something to show you and now is about the right time."

The right time appeared to be time that attends the thickening of twilight, just as the sun is giving up and long rays are magically transforming the ruin of an old cement works into a place of marvels and mysteries. We set off across that broken landscape in quite a different direction from the route to the diner. Here, banks of rosebay willowherb swayed in the evening breeze, pliant as flamingos. It grew in sheaves and lawns, by fallen pillars, or in colonies sprung from the fissures of an ancient floor. It was in competition with tall, swaying beds of nettle. Surprisingly, they still had their antidote thriving alongside them, broad-leaved docks, so many colonies of which have fallen victim to council-sprayed herbicide.

I keep a careful eye on weeds. It's not that I know anything about them, simply that I admire their tenacity and find them strangely beautiful, like the tiny purple flowers that ran along the rotten mortar joints of a brick wall, thriving on what? Presumably, lime, brick dust and Kirsty's 'occasional rainfall from heaven.'

We ducked through the cold and spooky skeleton of a low warehouse, which held a pile of ancient lorry tyres and not much else. Its sliding doors were welded open on their own wheels, rusted into running tracks now clogged with earth and oily water. I'd have expected a decaying mattress or two, a scattering of used condoms – a regular palace of atonement.

Beyond the far door we dropped to a more open segment of land. One strip still lay beneath recognisable, tarmacadam roadbed, which was finally breaking up into mussel-shell shaped fragments, under which grass was beginning to sprout.

Harold stopped. He was quite changed. All hint of the drunk was gone. Not a remnant of the afternoon-tea poseur remained. He seemed suddenly, very ordinary, very plain, as if recognising he was a broken man on earth.

"The Great North Road – lovely name don't you think, Eva – used to run down to here. Just up there was a great roundabout and where we are standing was a fuel depot, a primitive garage, the last one for miles."

We stood silently, companionably, for a while.

A flock of starlings, building steadily to that swirling mass dubbed a murmuration, passed overhead and we gazed after them until they dived into the horizon.

The last of the light then fell away rapidly. As if that had been the signal to begin, Harold seized my forearm with a grip like the Ancient Mariner's as he latches onto the wedding guest. Then, without looking at me even once, he launched into the strangest story.

"Imagine me. A child. Petrol pump boy. War over London. Bombs are falling. I can see the East End burning. My mother! My first job. Fourteen, I was 14. My first night alone. On my own, just the pumps, the fuel, the odd car. Boss is in the pub. His blonde doxy! Me, alone, on the Great North Road," he gestured, dramatically.

In that moment I could feel the ground shake as Legions marched North. I could hear the creak of the wain wheels, beneath the plague-encrypted woolsacks and I flinched as the King's Messenger, his portion of the quartered body of a traitor, bloody at his saddlebow, gallops by, bound for York. All players in their time, as we are in ours.

"I lock myself away, alone, with a pistol, a great revolver – heavy, heavy. Defend myself, defend us all, my mother under the bombs, defend her," Harold cackled wildly. "I can hear London's guns, see the searchlights. Engines overhead, low, droning, throbbing above. Cold, I shiver in the silence. A car, or two, tiny nightlights. Me, a boy, petrol pump boy, I sell them fuel. I take their coupons.

"Midnight. Great mass of dark lorries, a great trail, turning way back, one by one rolling onto the concrete. Bertram Mills Circus, heading North. Lurch and sway over oily concrete. Only the one diesel pump. I fall to work, my work. Glance up, look up to see huge men, broken-nosed men, behind cracked Bakelite steering wheels. They light cigarettes, cupped hands and their faces glow yellow, their teeth broken, brown stubs. I shiver and the van sides quake. Beasts move about. Lion roars and the diesel spills across my feet. Fumbling, fingers greasy. Van after van. Piss and straw leak from tailgates as they pull away, mix with the diesel. Never leave me, stink of piss and diesel. Revolver in my pocket. Huge, heavy. I pump and it bangs on my prick. Unmanned me for life. Never, no sex. Never. So scared. I see trucks of rounding boards, circus signs, bright colours dead in the night. Stepways, coils of cable, generators, great fuel drums. They all roll by. Pumping diesel and my arm, my arm! It won't flow faster. I feel men's eyes, bored, reckless. The elephant crashes in its truck and the boards creak, springs sag and lift. There are beasts everywhere, all around me. I smell them, they smell me, my fear. There are fires in the distance and engines overhead. The burning city and the living vans roll by, dainty lights behind lace, strong women in blue frocks. Strong as men. Ringmaster, still in top hat, tails. Clasps my shoulder – 'Bravo boy! Bravo!' Pushes coupons, money at me. White fivers. Something huge butts the headboard by my shoulder and I feel myself leak piss. They pull away, heading North. Fag ends flare out in the spill. So alone now, on the concrete, boots melting in the fuel. Lock myself away. Watch London burn and the night slip away. Morning, smoke and dust, night never happened."

We stand for a long time, where Harold's teenage epiphany played itself out, for better, or worse. Eventually I put my hand on his arm. "Come on, it's getting cold."

He let himself be led away, muttering phrases from his litany – "piss and diesel" – "I can see the match flare, reflected in his eyeball" – "well done boy! Bravo!"

It's hard to be given the key to someone's jewel-box, the combination to their life. On the one hand you can catch it up casually, like the small coins you sweep from the counter to pocket absent-mindedly, saying – "well, is that so Harold, what an adventure, what a night to remember!" On the other, you can lean into the omissions, that scent of fear, his teenage agony and feel the broken-backed promise of his life, blown away as certainly as the East End was that night of Blitzkrieg. Here, where there were lions, you felt yourself 'unequal to the task.' In some measure you failed and with that failure became superfluous to the world. The examiner, saddened, turned away and despite your truly having something to give, never came to view your genius again.

Just as I wished to atone – but could find no-one to record my atonement.

I led Harold back to the diner and restored him – or should that read – 'both of us?' – with eggs, chips, bread, butter, tea and apple pie. He, we, seemed much better after that.

"I was scared, Eva," he said eventually.

"I would have been scared, too, Harold," I said.

He looked at me for a long time. "No, I don't think you would have been."

"Harold," I said, "you're an artist. Not a roustabout, or whatever they're called. Tonight you will be able to draw whatever it is I am and can't see. I can't do that."

I had never seen anything quite like the transformation that had been effected in Harold's studio.

Neither Kirsty, nor I, had given it a glance earlier but when he urged me up there, a whole new world had been conjured. To begin with there was one colossal canvas, hanging in place like an over-tightened sail. In front of that, rigged from the spars in the rafters, some genius had devised a bosun's chair which, at the haul of a couple of ropes would allow limited vertical and lateral movement across its face.

"I can't climb ladders," he muttered crossly, taking off his suit jacket and flinging it down the stairs. "Told them. Got this. Eva, get ready."

I tried to cross-examine him but he was a changed man. Not another word could I prise out of him about the arrangements. I had to assume that the hire van that had nearly bowled us into the weeds earlier, had visited once again, this time packed with riggers and technicians behind the Chanel model who had been driving. There again, perhaps she was Wonder Woman?

He pointed and I was directed out into left field, too close to the edge for my taste.

"How do you want me standing?" I asked, politely.

"Silently," he snapped and taking up a huge cob of soft red ochre began to draw great swirling shapes, that terminated where the length of his arm ran out.

"Fucking, fucking, fucking…" he mumbled and clambered awkwardly into his bosun's chair. Once enthroned, however, he proved to be so adept at manoeuvring I realised this was not a new 'boy's toy' but an 'old reliable' called back into play. That explained a lot and I demoted Wonder Woman.

Swinging a few feet above the floor he joined up his swirls, curling them round to completion and grunted with satisfaction.

Grunts were all that were forthcoming from then on. He was deep into whatever it was he saw and although I could see, too, I couldn't see me. I hoped I was in there. It was horribly cold and I would have paid in gold for a huge mug of cocoa, with oodles of sugar. Something the very sight of which would rot your teeth. Oh, and an extra-large bowl of fudge cake, too. This fantasy grew as fast as Harold's swirls and I was nearly whimpering with greed when he stopped for a pee. He struggled out of his chair, unzipped and leaked, awkwardly and sporadically, into the void, muttering all the while. Naturally I had to follow. Nothing quite like the sound of water falling to stir a bladder into life. With nakedness and youth on my side, I had the advantage and I confess, peeing off the third floor landing had a certain 'je ne sais quoi' about it.

Whilst Harold still struggled with an obdurate prostate and an awkward zip, I managed a few warming press-ups, before he was ready to resume. But how to conjure the cocoa and fudge cake? I tried sending thought waves to Kirsty and Andy. Then I thought, if they got them they would probably think they were their own and simply indulge themselves on the spot! That was too awful to contemplate, so I ceased transmission.

It was a very long night and I'm surprised my vanity held out. I was close to chucking in the towel when Harold chucked his in, first. He sort of toppled down the spiral stair, gasping and landed face down on his crisp new bed. I stared down at him, tiny, frail, drained and wished I'd hung in there with my drawing classes, instead of sliding off for sex in public toilets. But this was now and that was then – the two rarely mix, or match.

I struggled into my clothes and hugged myself warm, while trying to find myself in the ochre work. Wherever I was and whatever it was, it was magnificent, however.

I stepped back, looked away and then span round, hoping to catch at least a glimpse of myself as some vague fleeting sprite, tossed on whirling energies. Then, of a sudden, 'I got it.' I wasn't consigned to the shadows, I was the entire canvas, billowing, booming, slicing, paring and carving-apart a great gulf in time and space. I saw it and it leapt at me like a tiger. I opened my arms, spread my legs, let loose a mighty howl and swallowed it whole, as if was a sheet of water I could drain from a cauldron that had burst under pressure.

That image etched itself into my mind and senses. I can conjure it even now, though its energy has spread out like the wave it was and will keep spreading out until time stops.

'God! Please don't let me have scared him to death with that shriek!' I thought wildly.

No, Harold was laid out like roadkill but snoring. I clonked down the stairs, covered him up as best as I could, prised the ochre out of his hand and stared at his reddened palm and fingers. 'Cave painter,' I thought, an immortal, like the artists of Lascaux. At that instant I loved him for what he had done for me. He'd placed me among the energies. How rare a gift can that be? I found myself pleading, to the God I thought I hated, to give him time to finish. Time to be able to crawl up the stairs, mix his paints and fall back into the trance he needed to finish such work. That just a shred of me should survive, a line from my truth, from my pain, from my desire to love the strangeness of my existence, before I drowned it forever in the crude ruck of my living days.

Who would buy this masterwork? Some oligarch. Would he see the torture under the skin, the yearning to serve a truth greater than itself? Would he hell. But at least I'd seen it.

I looked down at Harold, the little casement of ribs, barely flexing under the threadbare shirt and tears sprang to my eyes. What an agony to carry that level of seeing. Small wonder he drowned himself in alcohol, spat at and reviled the world. Andrew was right. He was a genius.

I grabbed my bag and moved out, back into the world, where the air rushed over me and my eyes blinked and blinked and blinked away tears of pity and of rage.

In the diner, Andrew stood in front of the grill, a priest at an altar.

"Sit," he said. "I know what you need."

I sat. A clock said it was five a.m. A few other beings sat at tables in different stages of life but no-one paid any attention to anyone.

What I needed was coffee, bright and bitter. Bacon, nearly burnt and fried bread. I don't know how he knew but that's what I got. After enough of that to feed a lumberjack, I got a slice of white home-made bread, thick with butter and thicker still with dark, bitter marmalade. I cut it into squares with a borrowed kitchen knife and ate each square with the reverence of a communicant.

"Divine," I said. "Your gran's recipe."

"How did you know that?"

"I'm having a seeing-hour. I'll be back to normal, shortly. Whatever, I sense your grandma was a wise woman."

"I loved her," said Andrew, "if that tells you anything."

"Let's hope it told her enough," I said.

He came over and joined me at the table.

"My gran's gran used to extract teeth, a bob a time, a shilling – five pence in your parlance. It was the going-rate, across the country. Because of that, they became known as bob-snatchers.

"Anyway, I know she operated at Barnes market, every Tuesday. She had two chaps to help. One was a drummer, the other the strong man. She stood there and as the drummer rolled his rat-a-tat-tat, the strong man bellowed out – ' Painless Pulling, or Your Bob Back. By Appointment to the Gentry…known and respected both sides of the river.'

Before long, some poor devil who couldn't bear the pain of his tooth any longer would struggle up onto her platform and sit himself down in the chair. He'd get a spoonful of laudanum, after she had inspected the problem and decided if she could deal with it. My gran said the old lady had paid to have a lesson from a famous surgeon, so she was no charlatan.

Once he was slipping off to join the fairies, the strong man would belt him in the chair, pull his jaw open and gran would, shall we say, get to the root of the matter. You push down hard, twist left and right and when you hear the crunch, you pull – out she flies! Meanwhile, the drummer has been rolling his sticks ever harder, drowning out whatever gargles and howls the poor devil is making. One triumphant rat-tat-tat and gran brandishes the fang at the crowd. 'Painless extractions,' yells the strongman, 'he slept like a baby!"

"You're embroidering," I said. "I can tell."

"Poetic licence," said Andrew, "I have a vivid imagination."

"Oh, so do I," I said with feeling. "At least two molars have started up since you burst into information-overload."

"I only charge a quid," he grinned.

"Don't," I said, "there goes another one."

"It's the marmalade," he said, "it seeks out the weaker vessels."

"It's come to the right place, then" I agreed.

"Anyway," he continued cheerfully, "the story continues thus…"

I held up a protesting paw.

"No, no, no more bloodshed. She was married to a blacksmith who had the knack of welding steel – this just at the height of the industrial revolution. They made so much money they retired at 35, fit, strong, wealthy – and very quickly bored.

"They bought a market garden and toiled therein, night and day."

"How did that turn out?"

"Dreadfully, they were eaten out of profit by slugs and snails."

"So, what did they do?"

"Do you know," Andrew grinned, "history does not record…"

It is now six a.m. I have just posed, nude, for seven hours in front of a mad old man, who has transformed me, by alchemy, into the creature I have longed to be, the creature who flies and not the animal that crawls. I am humbled and confused. I have also cleaned up shit, tried to understand pain in another and now I'm discussing dentistry and market gardening during the industrial revolution. I feel, justifiably I believe, wiped-out.

"Andrew – I love you but I'm off."

"Absolutely," he says, "Carl's going to give you a lift. You're on his way."

"I can get a taxi," I protest.

"Not easy, not cheap," he says. "Carl, my beauty," he bellows, "Eva's shot. Take her home mate, cop an early finish."

Carl comes out of the back, untying his apron.

"All right, Eva!!" he smiles, "see you later, Big Man."

Carl's wheels are better than Kirsty's but he only has two. Slung between them, is some giant pulsing device that imitates lions and might easily eat Evies.

As I fall asleep in my own bed, I thought I must have looked like one of those little animal backpacks that were all the rage once, for I clung to Carl's back like a comatose koala. I can't remember anything else, except the rough comfort of leather on my cheek and wind in my hair – because no-one had a spare lid I could borrow for the trip.

A couple of weeks went by. I came to a decision. I went into the town centre and bought the biggest box of decent chocolates I could find. I lugged it over to Kirsty's place and left it, gift-wrapped, with her mum – who was still giving me glances normally reserved for dangerous reptiles.

When I got the mystified phone call, I tried to explain why I wouldn't be going back to the diner. I felt that if I did, I'd never leave. I desperately wanted a family and I could have loved them all, recklessly. But I was trailing so many loose ends, had so much shit I didn't want to involve them in. That's what the chocolates were for, to say 'goodbye and I love you,' to everybody… could she understand where I was coming from?

She said she could and would try to explain to the others. Then she added that Andrew had given her the address of a gallery, in the City, with the suggestion that I go there and soon.

I said I was sure I would. But I wasn't sure at all.

In the end I went. I think vanity won. I don't know if I recognised myself or not. I know I wanted to, because whatever, or whoever, Harold had painted was magnificent. He was thunder and lightning, she was sun and moon. Both were tree and root. Down plunged the legs and were locked in rock, earth and water. Head and hair were woven into clouds and her breasts were alive with milk and blood. Where the cock hung at the groin were slung weapons of war, instruments of torture. From her hands fell seeds and at her back was a new dawn. I knew it, because I'd been there but the "art-lovers" were looking at 'an abstract exercise in the portrayal of energies' – because that's what it said in the glossy pamphlet.

My mum wouldn't have recognised me. This was no portrait, this was a military campaign in which energies fought under orders. Colour had a job to do, from the dripping fronds of yellow, to the blaze of vermilion, the bolts of greys, blues and those primary coils and swirls of ochre.

How had that strange, broken-down old man, seen such things in me? I was 25 feet tall and six feet wide – though the energies pulsed out still further than that. You could buy me for £140,000. Someone already had, before the opening day.

The tender, hard-handed man in the white van had had a bargain at £50 but what had this purchaser bought with their £140,000? Certainly not the creature I had just seen. Only I knew the true secrets of my anatomy and what they had become beneath Harold's brushes.

I left as I had entered, unnoticed, went to a coffee shop and brooded, stared through the glass at the world walking briskly by.

You set yourself a task – four roads, four directions to atonement. What you began was a blind whim, a shot in the dark, a rough idea, not even a wild card – which at least has a defined function in an established game. What happens next is that the mess you call your mind, that composite creature of the good, the bad and the ugly, begins to plot. It finds rules where there were none. It builds injunctions out of whimsy. It doesn't have a plan, it has – and I grapple for the right word – a vector and you are little more than the stone in its slingshot. How it develops its constructions is a source of endless fascination to me.

Against all my better judgement, whilst one part of the same apparatus is screaming – "No, No, No!" it has driven me out on ventures that have both humiliated and hospitalised me. Never believe that you are a free soul. You are a yoked ox, under the goad. I stumble to do its bidding. The wretched thing has the compulsion of an Old Testament prophet, biblical in its fundamentalism and righteous fury.

For weeks it has been watering bad seeds. Now one has sprouted, a tiny plantlet of self-castigation that lisps – "You-th didn'tth fini-ssth wha-tth you-th-thsst-arted!" then giggles, like some playground tormentor.

I never found atonement on the northern road. Instead, I found the Diner, with Harold, Kirsty, Andrew and Carl – actual friends, people I could have loved unconditionally. But this bad seed will have none of that. It tore me away, slashed at my new-grown umbilicus like some back-street abortionist and demanded that I continue to atone, with pain and humiliation.

It has been brooding but now it unfurls itself. Its leathery batwings scrape, restlessly, against all my better judgement Which is why I find myself at the bus terminal, studying timetables, mum's coat once again covering a whoreish exercise in impending, inevitable disaster.

My destination lies obliquely north and will have to do. An abandoned roadside cafe attracts an intrepid bunch of doggers to its car park, on weekend evenings. For some unfathomable reason I have decided that Friday evening might prove…more … what…decorous? Wasn't Friday named after a Goddess, Freya?

What delusional pap is that?

I look at times… 'no, not that one…nor that…aah, that one will do,' goes my mind, the clockwork oiled and turning, while on the stove hysteria is boiling over, screaming at its ignoble, hunch-backed brother to quit – NOW!

"Excuse me, lady," said a very polite and sub-continental voice, behind me.

"Hello," I said, turning.

A genuinely smiley face was peering out at me from the front seat of an old but immaculate-looking Nissan Micra, that must have ghosted up behind, because I never heard it approaching.

"Lady, do you know if it is the 17A bus that goes to…?" and he named a shabby town on the estuary.

"I do know and the answer is, yes, it does. But why, if you've got a car, do you want a bus?" I ask in friendly tones, only to think – 'idiot! One of them wants the bus. His friends have given him a lift to town.' That made me blush but not half so much as the blush that covered my face as one of those freak gusts of wind, those you get in forlorn places like bus stations, whooshed open my coat and revealed at least half of me, in pornographic splendour.

"Ah," said the smiley face, possibly smiling even more, "perhaps – and I ask with utmost respect – you are a Lady of Desire, available for hire? Are those the correct words, many apologies if not, we mean no offence."

'Fuck it,' I thought, coming over a bit Queen of Tarts. I took a step back, slipped the coat off my shoulders and gave the three guys the whole nine yards.

"Oh, my goodness," said smiley face and the driver stalled the car. Could a gal' ask for more appreciation than a stalled Nissan Micra in a deserted bus station, while the wind whirls rubbish around and clatters tinnies across the oily concrete? It all depends on your expectations.

Smiley recovered himself, though for what it's worth, backseat boy was risking spinal injury by craning his neck for a better eyeful.

The silly thing is and if I live to tell the tale, I should put this in one of Kirsty's country and Western songs, I'd already made up my mind to go along with whatever these guys want. That has to indicate a reckless naivety that is going to kill me, unless this insane driver in my mind lets go of the reins.

Be aware that, about now, I'm about to start skipping great chunks of narrative, because the next year was about to prove a little like listening to Wagner, some magnificent quarters of an hour but some soul-destroying 45 minutes.

The three little guys were brothers and basically formed the entire crew of a rust-bucket freighter that scraped its way to and from India, taking the long route via the coast of Africa. It was the merchant marine equivalent of a rural post-bus – dropping off bits of cargo here, collecting pallets there, making deep-water rendezvous with other post-buses and basically leading an under the radar existence across a very shady succession of worlds.

The true nature of all this multi-tasking only became clear when we cleared the coast of Spain. From then on, it became necessary that I should stay out of sight, whenever we were in sight of land. And once we'd rounded the Cape and were sailing into genuine pirate country, things got very frightening indeed.

"Eva, you stay here, behind bulkhead"… there was a steel box, coffin more like, artfully concealed from the casual glance… "if pirates come on board and find you, you end up on Dark Web as snuff movie. You not know? Oh, dear me, yes. Men pay to have you tortured, on web cam. Go on long time but never end good. So very quiet, yes. You be a good girl."

I'm sure my face went green and I can't describe how I felt, finding this out after two and a half months making friends with everyone, even the alcoholic captain and surly mate. My stomach filled with ice, my bowels quivered. I shook and cried. I've never been so scared in my life and I hope I never will be again. I took a lot of calming down.

However, skipping narrative or not, I am way ahead of myself. Let me backtrack.

The three guys wanted a communal wife for the voyage back to India – "although we all have wives at home," they were eager to explain. But their village wives didn't turn Western tricks and they were aching to emulate the pornography they downloaded to their satellite phone. That I came with additional equipment just excited them even more.

The reason that they had wanted the 17A was that they didn't know the way to the port. They were aiming to use the bus as a pilot. The Micra was going to India, too, as deck cargo. They'd bought it for £90, spent weeks doing it up at another brother's place in Luton and were still having furious debates about how they could turn the highest profit from it. Both mate and captain would have to be cut in on the profit, so their margin was getting thinner and thinner.

The owner of the vessel lived in one of the 'Stans and organised the dodgier cargoes that would be coming and going along the way. A Micra on deck was of no interest to him. If it kept the crew happy, pliant and silent, it paid its way in his eyes – or that's how I interpreted things. I never asked questions but I was intelligent enough to intuit answers.

Suicidal idiot that I was, I got in that car and embarked on a cruise of atonement – sans passport, sans plan, sans brain.

Sex at sea soon proved to be routine. They were all gentle guys at heart and once they had got to know me better, were reluctant to try out the crueller tricks of the internet porn they devoured unceasingly.

"This girl hungry for that, you see?" half-statement, half-question and one that came day after day, as they'd hold up the phone to show me the latest eye-opener they'd downloaded. I'd stop peeling carrots, or onions and say -"she probably likes the money. Sore for three days, rent paid for a month." They'd turn away glumly, pat me gently on the bottom and ask – "when dinner ready, Evie?"

I toured their bunks by a rota that soon became routine. I was offered, as a courtesy it appears, to the Mate but he was a bitter man. All he wanted from these voyages was money. To avoid becoming merchandise in his eyes, I made a point of flattering him and preparing his favourite foods. I hadn't by then, heard about the pirates, When I did I redoubled my efforts and made sure that First Mate regarded me as his non-existent, flesh and blood daughter.

It's going to be hard for you to believe that I had no endgame in mind. "WHAT?" when I got to India. "HOW?" would I be getting home, passport-less, moneyless – because for all the cash lures they had offered me, I quickly realised that I'd never see a penny of it.

I was learning slowly, like some very dull child, that I'd got this atonement business all wrong. The evils of the world since the expulsion from Eden, were not to be added to my charge sheet. The fluidity of my gender, the complexity of my antecedents had no bearing on the matter. The two were linked in no way at all. What arrogance I must have had to try and assume that burden, woman's sufferings at the hands of man.

I was beginning to learn a bit about it, too, on my own account. The only person on my conscience was my mum and though I have cried for her, mourned her, in the way you can only cry and mourn for the forever gone, I didn't wish to atone for her by being slowly tortured to death on the Dark Web. Maybe I deserved to be but self-preservation screamed otherwise.

Up and down the coasts of Africa we went. Hideous tropical nights, when I lay on my bunk and watched, impassively, as legions of cockroaches made their way along the overhead pipework from one bulkhead to another. Occasionally, before I was hustled below decks, I might catch a glimpse of a few battered motor launches and outboard-driven canoes emerging from the haze of the shore to head towards the ship, as she lay hove to, a mile or more off, in deep water. "Go, Eva, go! Very bad men!" A phrase guaranteed to send me scuttling for safety.

There was an illicit armoury on board. Four sub-machine guns and eight automatic pistols. They lived behind a steel panel that had to be removed before they could be retrieved. What frightened me most was the casual way my three 'husbands' knew their way around the wretched things. In every other way, they seemed such peaceful, gentle men.

Once we hit the Somalian coastline and after I'd been casually apprised of my potential on the Dark Web's darkest parts, I begged the Mate for the loan of a gun, before I was hustled into 'the safe space.' He spent an age considering it. Finally, he gave me a pistol with one round in the breech. "D'on' wan' you start no war, Evie girl. They come for you, put in mouth, point up, pull trigger. Boom, all gone.

"D'on' you worry. They wan' us carry their stuff. Need each other. Been here many time, no trouble. D'on you cry. I look out for you."

With everyone talking to me as if I was a girl and using me as one, I began to dress like one, feel like one. Before I'd been more ambivalent. I'd have boy's days and enjoy slouching around. Wandering into town and fooling most of the people, most of the time. Frequently I had been chosen to play 'boy' with the Nuns, too. Experience had taught them that the real thing was too disruptive by far.

Tits or no tits, the Captain always called me Mister. He was a functional alcoholic and I never saw, or heard him, make a fool of himself, or slur a word. But the amount of vodka he put away was prodigious.

I used to take him refills of ice, topping up the huge Thermos he kept on the bridge, five or six times a day. "God bless you, mister." Or, if I tried to tempt him with a tiny portion of food – "very kind, mister," before he'd push it away, absent-mindedly. I persisted, though and I swear he ate at least five big bites a month. On one memorable occasion, he even ate the whole plateful and that caused much concern among the crew, who wondered if he was ill.

Once we'd finished the Somalian encounter, we had very little business along the Arabian peninsula. The war in Yemen had made illicit trading offshore, far too risky. What it meant was that the journey was nearly at an end and I began to worry.

Two days before we were due to dock, in some utterly illicit sinkhole that I never could pronounce the name of, the brothers ushered me into the messroom for an afternoon tea which they had prepared. Somewhere, they had even found a flower, which sat alone, in a jam-jar of water in the centre of the table. I felt like it looked, confused and wary.

"Evie," said Sanjay, "we docking soon. You no have papers. Very risky you go ashore. But don' worry, we have plan. We get you ashore in Micra. But what you do then, eh?

"We go home, six months, see wives, children. We have money, so big men in village!" They all laughed insanely. "Now, you not welcome. Not Somalia but you not welcome…" and he grinned, probably imagining wives meeting the cruise whore.

Feebly, I grinned back – or tried to. Obviously they had a plan and after forcing a biscuit on me, they proceeded to unfold it.

"We have friend and he have friend who know lady run very high-class brothel. For boy/girl like you, blonde hair, white skin, people, important people, going to pay a lot of money. You not have to work much. You cost too much. Promise you, real high-class work. Only very beautiful, very refined, educated girls work there. You see doctor every week. You go on outings – theatre, cinema, shopping trip. This lady, she look after her girls. Most prestigious house in State – Government men, diplomats, Russian oligarchs – top flight stuff! No more poor boys from village!" and he giggled again.

I started to cry. "You're going to sell me! I don't want to be sold. I want to go home! I thought you were my friends."

They all tried to pat me at once, making coo-ing noises, as if I was a bawling baby.

I was actually playing for time to think. What the hell was the alternative? If I refused and things got ugly, they'd probably tie me to a bunk, leave me for the next crew to screw and then sell to pirates. While they were furloughed for six months, this apology of a ship would be making its way on some other trip and I could be sailing with it, or getting ashore. My choice was no choice at all.

"I don't want to be sold," I hiccuped.

"No, no, no! We not sell you! Never! We rent you!" cried Sanjay, obviously convinced he had devised the most wholesome of alternatives. "In six month, you come home to England with us – with lots of money you earn. Same friends – good deal, huh?"

'Fantastic, Sanjay,' I thought. 'Not sell! Rent! Rent-boy and whore, two for the price of one, I'm a deal, a steal, I'm the sale of the fucking century!'

I sniffed a lot. Dried my eyes, choked on a biscuit, was patted continually. After another round of thoughtful sniffing, I said – "Ok."

It wasn't much of a parting. I spent a day being hidden from the prying eyes of petty officialdom, which even in this oily backwater seemed ubiquitous. Then I went ashore in the boot of the Micra, swinging nauseatingly, at the end of an ancient jib crane that was old when it was scrapped by the builders of the pyramids. As I hung there in mid-air, describing stomach-churning circles, I could hear its decrepit engine misfiring and wondered if my fate was to be like that of the whore in 'Get Carter' who, locked in the boot of her car, is toppled into the dock. At least she got to die in a Sunbeam Alpine – who wants to cop out in a Nissan Micra?

The moment we hit land – hard – the boot sprang open. I was peeled out unceremoniously and bundled into the back seat of a vast BMW 4x4, with tinted windows. As the door slammed, I was shocked back to life by air-con set to Reykjavik. There was a blanket on the seat and I wrapped myself in it. Then I tried to follow what was happening to me.

What was happening that the car was negotiating muddy alleyways that turned right, left, right, right, left, left, right, left for what must have been 20 minutes or more. It needed more than Sat-Nav to negotiate that warren, probably some in-built sense of how things work in this part of the world, which was reasonable as the driver and his partner were both Indian.

We exited onto a broad and rapid freeway, forging – by divine right of a magisterial vehicle – to the centre of the lanes, which seemed to be largely interchangeable, as regards direction, across the whole stretch of tarmacadam. The whole business was terrifying and I gave up watching, as I was fast developing a paranoid sense of frying pans and fires.

It took hours to clear whatever city limits we were crossing but eventually the slums fell back, we cleared the tent cities and the dumps, then we competed with wildly decorated trucks for the privilege of the open road.

I didn't know but this journey was destined to last for two days. I tried questions but the passenger seat guy, turned, half-smiled and waved his finger in a 'no, no. no,' way. Occasionally, he'd pass back a water bottle, a bag of mixed fruit and nuts and when they deemed it necessary, they'd stop to pee. They pissed at the front of the car. When they'd finished, I was beckoned out to pee at the rear. I made a big thing of squatting, not wanting to share too many trade secrets with hard-looking, elective mutes.

You don't see a lot through tinted glass and what you do see looks like a reversed negative in blue tints. What I saw when I peed, was dust-brown fields, distant haystacks, perhaps a rickety barn or two and fields where colourful saris ducked up and down to the rhythm of their occupiers' labours.

As we travelled, I began to revise my expectations. I'd expected that I would have been sold as the white-skinned attraction in some small-town whorehouse. There I'd be shot-up with heroin and obliged to work my way through the local population, by the score, each and every day.

Thank God that was wrong. This very long ride, in an extremely expensive car began to give me reason to hope that Sanjay may not have lied. I started to stiffen my resolve, largely because my life depended on it and now was not the time for another chorus of – "Poor, poor, pitiful me…"

Physically, sexually, I was well-nigh unique. With the right cosmetics, the right clothes I could still look pretty good. Mentally, I had to accept I was a child, an obtuse, obstructive and defiant one at that. I had finally landed in the real world. (Obviously, A&E Departments in the UK had not been real enough.) All that adolescent stuff had to stop. So with one big heave, that entitled, teenage-plus rebel, Eva, was metaphorically jettisoned, somewhere near a crumbling temple – one now populated by goats. That seemed, somehow, appropriate.

I was hatching a plan that went like this… 'if you spend this much money on me, you want a reliable, equable package. Up to a point, that's for me to decide – I am holding most of the aces. It's how I play them that matters now.' At that point my stomach gave its first intimation that IBS was about to become my constant companion over the next few years.

"Stop the car," I screeched, pointing dramatically at my nether regions. The BMW stood on its nose and I hurtled behind a thicket of thorns, wondering about snakes – as if I didn't have enough anxieties. (All credit to the mutes, a packet of tissues came flying over the hedge-top.)

That first day ended in the late evening, at an anonymous concrete blockhouse in the middle of nowhere. I was shown to a room which had a simple bed, a chair, a wash basin, two jugs and a table. The other facilities comprised a hole in the floor, a bucket of water, a toilet brush and a pile of paper on top of a concrete block. An air-con unit sang on the wall and the place was as cold as a butcher's fridge.

I danced around slapping my arms and nearly missed the discreet tap at the – locked – door. "Come on in," I roared and a tiny girl, no more than nine or 10, all wreathed in smiles tottered into the room bearing a tray of food. Under her arm she also had a mosquito net. Outside I could see the shadow of one of the drivers, lurking – where did the idiots think I was going to run to?

The girl dumped the tray then, jumping up on the bed, nimbly rigged the net. Then she smiled and hopped down. I smiled back and started flapping my arms, as in 'I am freezing!' She twigged immediately and said – "Air-Con." in a very grave voice. "Too cold," I said and did my flapping wings routine again. She pointed to a dial, not quite on the ceiling but close. Then she made 'turning-down' gestures with her fingers. I made 'lifting-her-up' impressions and she grinned as in, 'up-for-it!'

So I picked her up, two-handed round her tiny hips and lifted her up to the ceiling, where she made adjustments, then wriggled her toes in an 'all-done-now' manner. I swung her round, in a playful swirl – she was featherlight – and she made a tiny squeak of glee. That proved enough to alert the sentry outside to peer around the door. I set her down and bowed my deepest 'namaste,' complete with pressed palms. As I didn't have even a rupee to my name, the matter of my wages having been deferred, I beckoned for her to wait and marched on the door. I jerked it open and eyeballed my minder. He was not the friendly one. Nevertheless I made the universal sign for money, pointing at the little girl and back to me, with empty hands. He cottoned on and signalled 'not necessary.' I signalled 'necessary' and glared. Angrily he produced a meagre-looking coin and greatly daring, I made a 'not enough' expression at which he looked furious. But it worked because he dug out a shabby bill, which I handed over immediately.

She scooted, undoubtedly to hide her ill-gotten gains, before he could retrieve them. Universal sign language almost expended, I acknowledged his munificence with a bow and stalked back to examine supper.

It was delicious though, rice apart, I have no idea what it was.

The second day was a repeat of the first. However, it ended in late afternoon at a sprawling villa, cum fort, cum palace, all half-hidden behind a curtain wall, which was probably modern but possibly ancient with recent repairs. The gate was opened, by remote and we swept up the most elegant drive, from which I caught an enticing glimpse of red sandstone battlements and towers rising above a modern entrance and extension that had been artfully designed to blend-in. Internally, I breathed a huge sigh of relief, this was not some cheap bordello. How well, though, could I play my cards?

That was the only impression I was to get, however, because as I was absorbing it, the car turned sharply away and ducked into an underground garage, where at least a dozen more luxury 4x4's stood in an obedient line.

The two drivers pointed me at an anonymous door and shooed me away. I'm pleased to report that I never saw them again.

Behind the door was a lift, which elevated me just the one stop.

The doors opened and in the lobby outside was a sari-ed, Indian lady, perhaps in her 60's who greeted me warmly.

"My poor dear! You are exhausted!"

I tried for a look of composure, underpinned with steel and radiating confidence.

"I am tired. Travel does not agree with me. Also, I am hungry and very thirsty. In the fullness of time and at your convenience, I would also relish a shower?"

"Nothing we cannot be providing," she replied confidently. "Do follow, please."

We walked a mile of carpeted corridors, more homely than a luxury hotel, with expensive antique sculpture displayed in alcoves and all cunningly lit. I was more intrigued by the body language of my guide, however.

She was an authority figure, for certain. The madame, I guessed but certainly not the owner. She had appeared far too inscrutable for that, as if she hid a multitude of compromises under her mask of bland affability. Her sari, though, was expensive and understated, in grey silk with seemingly modest, unpretentious hemming but touched with what looked like real-gold embroidery. It was a very clever compromise. Her mass of steel grey hair was gathered into an overflowing knot at the nape of her neck. She had strong hands and arms, possibly from a lifetime of work as a masseuse? She walked with her hands open, her back was straight and her stride confident. Walking behind, taking lessons from that gait, I decided never to become beholden to her. She would be a dangerous friend.

We arrived at a kitchen, though it cannot have been THE kitchen, because we'd passed enough residential doors for me to realise that THE kitchen would be a place of frenetic activity. This kitchen was a modern palace, cool and airy. Extensive marble worktops, large double-doored American fridges, at least two six-ring ceramic hobs, a fine central workplace and of cupboards, with unpretentious, wipeable doors, there were a plethora.

I chose to stride over to the windows above the multiple sinks and found that my view was of a modestly raised herb garden, that looked moist and inviting inside ancient sandstone walls.

"I hadn't realised what a vast country this is," I said calmly.

"We are a sub-continent, my dear. We have land, too many people, too much poverty but some of us have great wealth, fortunately."

I continued to peruse the herb garden, while behind me there was a bustling of servant feet and the inviting chink and clattering of plates and bowls on marble. When I deigned to turn around, the central work surface had been transformed into a smorgasbord of tiny dishes, filled with multi-coloured snacks and dips. Dominating, was a huge bowl of fluffy white rice. It looked mouth-watering. But more inviting still, were the pitchers of cold drinks, already clouded with beads of moisture.

"Please begin, my dear. There are no formalities to be observed. After all," she laughed without much humour, "I am not a client. I am the house-mother. All the girls call me Ma, for short, or Mother."

"I can't do that," I said bluntly, surprising myself. "I'll call you 'Muti,' if you don't object. It is the German equivalent."

"Muti it is, then," she said, easily enough but I sensed that the compromise was debited to my account.

Having regained some equilibrium, though I don't quite know how, I began to eat, seriously. Conscientiously, I rolled tiny cylinders of rice and seeing no cutlery of any variety, began dipping into sauces and sticky concoctions with gay abandon. Half way round the selection I located a spinach dhal, upon which some genius had effected a miracle. I decided to demolish it in its entirety. Finally attending to the fruit juices, I took on fluid like a dromedary fresh from the Gobi. Only then did I straighten up, stand back, square my shoulders and belch in Arabic appreciation.

Muti gave me a hard smile.

"Now darling, to business. Would you suck a dog's prick?"

"Not now, Muti. I'm completely full, thank you."

She laughed, without a trace of amusement and the lines at the corner of her mouth deepened.

"Of course not now, darling but in general, would you?"

"Muti," I asked, "do you know what I am?"

"Yes, darling, you're an uncut trans."

"No, Muti. I'm not."

There, in the kitchen I began to take off all my clothes. Trying to blend a certain amount of coyness with an anatomy lesson, I showed Muti precisely what I was.

She stared, then began a slow but appreciative handclap, her head tilting slowly from side to side as I swayed and pirouetted.

I could see her re-appraising matters when, suddenly and without turning round, she snarled – "be gone with you and run a bath, instantly!"

She looked at me with that compromised smile and added – "damn servants, darling. They have no wits."

Stark-naked, and trying to look as if this interview was an everyday occurrence, I forced myself to continue grazing, whilst sipping delicious, ice-cold almond milk, from tiny glasses. By the time Muti led the way to the bathroom, I was waddling behind her, looking four months pregnant.

I lowered myself into warm, clear water and allowed Muti to wash me. That was her discreet approach to a thorough examination of precisely what it was that she had bought. She was skilled and decorous, which was a major improvement on being served up in pieces on the dark side of the internet. Was it, however, anything to do with atonement? It wasn't, it was something else entirely. Something real and dangerous and happening to me, now.

Eventually she sat back, on her little stool and said – "you pretty special, Eva. I admit I never saw the like."

"I'm told I'm unique," I responded.

"Darling, you make so much money here!"

I slid beneath the waves, eyes closed and ran my fingers through my hair. I stayed under for 30 seconds and then surfaced abruptly, cascading water. I sat up further, insofar as my pregnancy allowed.

"You know Muti, I mean absolutely no disrespect to you but I want to say something. I'll only say it once, because I know I'm wasting my breath.

"I am a true androgyne and where I come from, I am a God. Here, on this blighted earth, I am no better than a fuck toy. All people want to do with me is screw me, film me, rent me out and have me suck animal pricks. No-one knows what to do with me, because I was called, by accident I believe, from somewhere else – where this condition is not rare at all. We androgynes could be healing balm among the divided sexes. But that means nothing to anyone because, on this planet, live an ignorant species who can see only as far as the limits of their ignorance. Too stupid to see that I may hold secrets beyond my body's strangeness, all they can think of doing with me is to fuck me, reduce me to their level. Do they never bother to think that there may be more here than meets the eye?"

Muti stared at me appraisingly, for quite some time.

"Quite a speech, darling."

"Don't worry, I told you it's a one-off and just for you. You won't ever hear it again."

She nodded slowly.

"We don't like cheeky girls here, you know that?"

"Muti, I'm not a boy and I'm not a girl. If you like I'll give you a web address and you can check out the crazy shit I've waded through, while grinning from ear-to-ear. So I'm not that scared of you. But don't worry, I'm not planning a war. I'm not a revolutionary. I know where I am and I'm pretty sure what I'll be doing. Like everybody else, I'm getting by. If this can turn into a good chapter in life, it'll beat the hell out of some of the rubbish I've lived through lately."

Muti went into herself for a long time. I idly splashed water around and trapped reservoirs between my curvy bits, for fun.

"Yes," she said finally, "you are pretty special. I think I almost hear what you' saying but sadly, we only sell one thing here, darling and that's sex. But you gonna' be so expensive, you not be run off your feet. That be some sort of respect. I like my girls – and boys – to be happy. You may not believe me but I'm a pretty religious person. I no want offend any god."

I stood up and stretched.

"You don't have to worry about me, Muti. I'm just one more god, lost in the land that invented gods. Let me give you that website, then you can see what they do to gods where I come from. It's pretty savage stuff and so was the surgery to put it right afterwards."

After this exchange, Muti treated me differently. It's just possible she was a little bit scared. Something in that speech had struck a chord. Sometimes she would say – "you pretty special person. I like you." But I knew better than to respond.

This brothel that I had been trafficked to could have been entered in the 'Top Ten Whorehouses of the World' and come in the top five – if I'm allowed so feeble a pun. It's not that I'm an expert, it's that the no-expenses spared aspect of it was staggering.

I don't know how many girls worked there. The whole acreage was broken into discreet units and there could have been a dozen units I never even knew about. In my own unit were about 15 to 20 girls. We knew each other, of course, but we only socialised in small groups. On days out our whole team did assemble but beyond polite little waves to one-another, we stayed with our personal friends. It would be the same in any factory, or office, anywhere in the world.

Every unit had its elite, girls whose particular attributes earned them the wealthiest clientele. Humbly, I admit I was in our elite – not that it afforded me any joy. I was in the company of a double-jointed athlete, who virtually turned herself inside out when performing tricks. A coal black Senegalese girl, who was teamed with a startlingly blonde Norwegian, so white she looked as if she was chiselled from marble. You couldn't hire one, you had to have both. Then there was our professional sadist, who was my 'bestie.' She was such a sweet-natured girl. She loved jig-saw puzzles, with really soppy themes. She always had one on the go in the common room and it was bizarre to see this vision in red and black leather, or latex, covered from head to toe, just eyes and a black pony tail to be seen, poring over puppies in a basket, little girls in frilly frocks picking roses, or kittens chasing balls of wool. (I always thought that raunchier shots from her sessions would make excellent niche jigsaws.)

Which remark leads me to reveal that it was an open secret, among us, that every encounter was filmed and recorded. I hope that revelation sends a chill down certain spines. Whoever owned that place meticulously maintained their insurance policy.

When I first turned up, I had to negotiate pecking rights with a very striking, uncut trans, with good quality implants and a decent-sized prick. He was petite and a total bitch. He thought I was there solely to de-throne him and consequently loathed me. Mercifully we only had to survive each other's company for six weeks, as his contract was coming to an end. Otherwise, one of us would have murdered the other.

The rest of the girls were conventional beauties, who came in different shapes, colours and sizes. They were mostly there to earn money – ten years conventional wages scooped in one.

Naturally, we were robbed blind. Our wage was sequestered, attached, held-back, accrued, whatever term you care to use for stolen. We paid for room and board at some phenomenal rate. Then we were obliged to buy clothes of the house style, to pay our cleaner and of course, the doctor. I never bothered to make the first enquiry about my income, as I thought it highly unlikely I would ever see it. Most girls however, kept scrupulous accounts, aching for the moment when they could walk away.

Of course, that suited 'the House,' which benefited from a regular changeover of staff. Occasionally a girl attracted the attentions of a rich suitor and would stay on, at his expense, in a separate unit, her body reserved solely for him. There were less than ten of these long-term relationships and how they ended, I can't say.

My time on the boat had made me deeply suspicious, despite my incurably romantic streak. I began to wonder how anyone ever left this place. The nearest town with a viable transport hub was 70 miles distant. To leave, you hired a driver and a 4x4. You, your tiny bag of belongings and your accumulated savings, in the form of a bank draft, were then transported across the desert and no-one ever heard another word about you. You were not allowed to call for a taxi, you were not allowed to write. No in-coming, or out-going communications were permitted. It was all in the contract. In my opinion, many girls simply died in the desert. Those drivers were all capable of murder. I tried not think about this.

Every six weeks we were offered a "day out" at the establishment's expense. They were actually very nice excursions, usually to places of touristy interest that boasted a decent array of shops. We were provided with excellent picnic lunches and snacks, we could debit our account for pocket money, allowed to withdraw a generous amount but not a fortune.

It was this caveat that set alarm bells ringing in my head, the first time I heard about it. I'd planned to make my own escape on one of these trips, once I'd accrued enough capital. But the fact was that at the end of the day, you had to hand back what you hadn't spent and produce receipts for what you had. This was to stop girls accumulating enough money to bribe the housekeepers to bring in drugs – or that was the House's explanation, along with some other tattle about the danger of clients stealing the girls' money, should it be left in our rooms.

To me, this just proved my paranoid theory that our domicile was another Hotel California. You could check out any time you liked but you could never leave.

Paranoia to one side, however, we all enjoyed our days out. The coach was modern, with two loos, air con, also a soft drinks bar. There was a strict no alcohol rule for we girls. Trust me, we had all signed a very detailed contract!

No-one wasted time on these trips. With beauticians and hairdressers provided in-house, each girl was hell-bent on raiding the jewellery quarter and spending her very last penny. I confess, I've never been one for modern jewellery but I do lust, indecently, over very old stones, crudely polished in hand-wrought settings. Tibetan necklaces and earrings bring out terrible cravings in me. I get over-excited by things such as the Staffordshire Hoard, with its exquisite garnet-set gold. As for gold torcs, I go all wobbly. The fatter and heavier they are, the better. Just writing about them makes my fingers start twitching – and just so everyone knows, I am open to bribes.

You won't find such things in a jewellery quarter, so on days out, I tended to go off on my own, hunting out little frequented antique bazaars. It was on one of these days, a few months in, that I wandered off and lost myself in the town's maze of alleys, among the steps, tanks, obliques, descents, ascents, blind ends, pocket courtyards of the old quarter.

I wandered into a handkerchief-sized 'park' – for want of a better name – that had a view over, I don't know, 1000 miles of field and desert, to distant blue mountains, foothills to the Himalaya, I guessed. What adventures had been played out there – by people who'd had the wit to plan their Friday nights properly!

I sat on a wall and stared, for an age. In my mind, I walked up those foothills. I came to Simla and stayed in an old colonial house. Then I pushed on, with my trusty companion, into aboriginal country, where the rains fell and the Himalaya cascaded down to the plain in a brown torrent of mud and broken timber, Joseph Dalton Hooker and I.

I shook myself back to the 21st century and scrambled to my feet. It was only then that I realised I had very nearly been resting my hooves on the headgear of an elderly gentleman, who had remained seated, imperturbable and at his ease, on the ragged grass beneath me. I flitted nimbly down the steps to apologise, in an ad hoc mix of English and Hindi.

As I babbled he sat and appraised me like a little bird, head first on one side, then cocked to the other. Having perused sufficiently, he gave a big smile, through 100 years' worth of wrinkles and patted the grass beside him, gently.

I was overcome with wholly unexpected emotion. So much so that I was welling-up with tears. I'd been bounced on by clients, turned like dough, pulled, parted, kneaded and impaled. A gentle gesture to share the grass beside a wrinkled old man, unsexed me, both girl and boy. I sat with an inelegant flounce, a thump and a sob. He patted my hand, tutted gently at my tearful face. Finally, he positioned his hand with his fingers on mine but barely touching. Together we stared at the distant mountains.

"Blue Remembered Hills," he said suddenly and in excellent English. "A.E Housman, I think. Fine poem, do you know it, young man?" And this to a girl in a sari, whose bodice is overtly ripe with intriguing anatomy.

I said that I didn't. He replied that I must. I said I would make a point of it and he hoped that I would. That seemed to agree with us both and I felt myself relaxing in great fits and starts, like some badly-packaged spring uncoiling.

"You cannot erase the past, young lady," he said eventually. "In fact, it is good we can recall it. Not in sorrow, celebration, or rage but as mere memory, simple marks we made upon a slate."

"All my memories are of mistakes," I blurted, crying again.

"Is this moment a mistake?" he asked, gently.

I sniffed… "Of course not…no, no."

"Now," he said, "I come from there and he pointed to the blue lines. Far beyond those hills we can see. High up," he nudged me conspiratorially, "where the ants mine gold!"

I hadn't wasted all my life. I'd read a lot. I still did.

"You're from Tibet," I exclaimed excitedly, "please tell me everything about it!"

He shook with repressed laughter and patted my hand again. While he was "hee, hee, hee-ing," he was also reaching into his robe with his other hand. Finally, after much of what I took for rib-scratching, he pulled out a ring with a ruby that was a wildness of natural crystal and ancient faceting. It bulged over a setting that probably was made from gold mined by ants and smelted over yak dung.

"Oh God!" I cried in a sudden ecstasy, "that is exquisite. Oh my God, oh my God! Can I touch it?"

He thrust it at me. "You hold it now."

I held it. Such antiquity flowed out of that massive setting, the natural-crystal facets and that look of having been found thus, bound in ancient rocks, rather than having been mined, cut, recut and assembled, that I burst into tears again. But these were joyful tears that such a treasure existed and that I was holding it.

The old man sprang up like a Jack-in-the-box. Fifty years fell away from him, which reduced him to the mere century mark.

He leaned into me, as if he was about to collide, forehead on forehead. Gently, he took the ring back and then, very swiftly – can one be forceful and temperate at the same time? – struck me on the forehead, squarely front-centre, with the ruby. The blow sank in, punctured the skin and I swear, touched bone. 'All hell is going to break loose when Muti sees the damage,' was my only thought.

I was also stunned. He sank to his knees and stared into my watering eyes. "Your ring now – you decide who will be next." Then he bobbed upright, beamed and boomed – "Blue Remembered Hills, eh! You'll remember them now, boy!" He span on his heel and walked away. As far as I could tell, he was merely strolling and even allowing for how woozy I felt, I was after him as fast as I could. Yet not one glimpse of him did I catch.

I sat down again, where I'd first perched. I felt triumphant, sick, happy and sad, all at the same time. I felt that no evil could befall me, now that I held the ring. (Good to know that my romantic side was still alive.) I clutched the ring, I kissed it passionately, what I couldn't do was look at it successfully. Somehow it kept skidding out of focus, refusing to be centre field. My eyes just rolled across and over it, as if it had become a part of me that was, more properly, invisible.

I dabbed my forehead with a less than mint handkerchief. It collected a juicy helping of Evie blood but what bothered me more was the bump, already the size of a quail's egg, that was gathering around the puncture.

'My ring now.' Really?

I stared at the blue hills. How, I wondered, would it even be possible to commit such simple, mysterious shapes to memory? Obviously, I knew that was not what the old man had meant but I would have liked to have engraved them on a brain cell, forever. They held all the promise of a musical keyboard. They even looked a little like one. All that would be necessary would be the ability to play the instrument and know the score.

On the coach 'home' I was inevitably the centre of attention, with a lump the size of the Koh-i-noor diamond on my forehead and it oozing blood. "I head-butted a wall," was all the information I was prepared to divulge, so eventually they left me alone.

Not, however, our S&M queen, who proprietorially sat next to me, tutting, fussing and 'kissing-it-better,' which she knows I like, because I'm a total softy. She mopped up the ooze with her own tissues. When they ran out she commandeered supplies from the rest of the girls, even the ones who, for girly reasons, hated me. No-one willingly crossed Jessica, she was that sort of girl.

"Which wall, Eva-Beaver?" she kept giggling. "Has it got a great big hole in it now?"

I leaned on her happily enough. She's a lovely girl and I'll be sorry when she's not in my life any more. To keep the repartee flowing, I kept saying – "I'll come and work with you, Jess. No-one will notice then."

"Mmm," she'd muse, as if considering the offer, "you'd need some more cuts and bruises if that was to be convincing, Evie-Beavie. What do you think, girls?" This latter to her two adoring subs, who were kneeling on the seats in front of us, gazing backwards so they could soak up my pain by proxy or, more likely, to be certain I didn't wheedle myself into their mistress's chamber. "We could go to work on her," they said enthusiastically.

"Oh, back in your cages, girls," I groaned.

What I really wanted was to be left alone, so that I could brood to myself about how and why 'stuff' goes round. All stuff, not just rings and paratrooper's berets, or paintings of an unemployable, earth-energy goddess. What about particles, plants and people?

We all go round. We are all broken down and our parts interchanged. We are all, therefore, theoretically looking 'for our moment in the park,' when we might seize the chance to transfer ourselves intact, like the ring, now warming in my bosom. But organic life doesn't get that chance. Its fate is messier.

Like my poor old kitten who'd gambolled into the road when I was nine. When I had finished weeping buckets, mum and I gave him a grand funeral. A shoe box, a sachet of cat food, nourishment for the journey to the afterlife. Arguably he was a finer construction than the ring but he couldn't hand himself on, intact – car or no car. No, he has to decay, rejoin the soil, his skeleton dealt with by time, or heartless gardeners. After God knows how many eons, he'll be returning as part of a flower, a potato…or maybe, as part of a ruby ring.

Everything goes round and round, call it recycling, resurrection or reincarnation. Just a few things cling to their original form more successfully, like carborundum when it has the smarts to disguise itself as ruby. It may last until the closing days of the planet. Will it be delighted, or has it made a huge mistake?

Let me jump a bit and say that, over the years I've occasionally wondered, 'how do I get myself into this ring?' Would I be making an egregious error? Is it better just to acquiesce in process and accept that everything has to go round? Even energy, or should that be – 'particularly energy?'

Disintegration, fragmentation, reincarnation are facts of life. Not reincarnation as peddled by charlatans selling tickets to 'your next life.' Reincarnation in the sense of our particles, shredded, blended into cosmic soup to be ladled out across the universe, again and again. 'Everything of you will endure…nothing of you will endure.' That's the sort of paradox that I live for, now…I find it commensurate with the paradox posed by my body.

But at the moment, I'm on the coach, being babied by a gentle, professional sadist and she is showing me her latest 5000 piece jigsaw. She ordered it the last time she was here, "and it had to come all the way from Germany, Beavie," she says in an awed voice, which suggests that 'Germany' is somewhere out in orbit, probably near Saturn.

She has chosen a marvellously ghastly theme – the ideal Tyrolean family at rest and play. Dirndl skirts, lederhosen, hats with feathers, flounced blouses, bulging bosoms, over-flowing steins and snow-capped Alps. Pure sodding 'Sound of Music.' I hate that film and I've never even seen it. I look at the half-timbered inn, with mein host telling a tale to the red-cheeked children, through the jungle of his Kaiser moustache, while mama and papa laugh gaily in the background. Sourly I think – 'Nazis, every one of them.'

"Isn't it wonderful, Beaver?" she croons. I say, "yes it is," and Jess slides it back into its bag with the reverence of a Rabbi replacing the Torah in the Ark. She smiles at her subs, fondly. "I'll take us all there, one day," she promises and they screw their faces up in delight. Then she turns back to dab at my forehead again and I swear she drops a tear on the end of my nose…but she swears she didn't.

Up front, someone kicks off a ribald song and we pound along the interminable, dusty road like the girls' wing of the All Blacks Supporters Club. Oh, so many verses and so-oo rude!

An hour later and we're "home" with Muti giving me all kinds of hell, as predicted. As it happens, it was much ado about nothing. By morning there was barely a scratch to be seen. Muti trumpeted the magical qualities of her salve – "heals silly girls who walk into walls, darling!"

I hold an alternative view.

I worked hard the next week. Probably I was using cross-grained logic but I felt I owed 'whatever-it-was-that-orchestrated-the-ring-business' some indication of my worthiness to be its current holder. That meant showing that I knew how to be the master of my situation, however much I might dislike it. I was currently a whore. Very well, I would be a good one. I wouldn't sell my soul but I would rent my body, provided I was offered the same sort of respect in return. I would aspire to be the master of my fate, not its victim.

I came to my last client just before my rest days were due to start.

Heaven help me, he was just a boy, a young Arab, probably barely 16.

He sat on my bed incapable of looking at me. Instead, he talked. He told me how many oil fields his father controlled, how many gold-plated Rolls Royce were lined-up in the family paddock, about the salukis with an Imperial bloodline, of cheetahs in the Royal mews. Then there were the summer palaces to describe, high among snow-capped mountains, the racing camels, the yachts, the falcons…finally, his voice petered out and he stared at the floor.

Poor boy was nearly dead with anxiety.

"Who sent you to me?" I asked him, gently.

"My brothers," he blurted. "They had heard of this man/woman and they said it would be the experience of my life, to lose my virginity with you. They said it would be a huge joke that I could tell all my life."

Finally, he looked at me. "I'm so scared, I don't know what to do!"

I went to him, covering myself up decently, took his hand and whispered in his ear.

"You have to trust me. I'm going to make a phone call. A young, pretty lady is going to come here and you are going to have the time of your life, because she's gentle, kind and fun. Also, she's just about your age – so you can be friends and that matters! Don't worry, you're going to fall in love but that's another story, for another day."

He stared at me with huge brown eyes.

"What can I tell my brothers? They'll laugh at me!"

"No they won't," I said. "This what you tell them, when they say – 'what was it like?' You're going to say – 'you'll never know, will you…!' and you're going to grin and roll your eyes. Then you'll say – 'honestly, she was the most awesome creature in the world…and now she's gone. Thanks guys, it was awesome but I don't want to talk about it.' That'll work, I promise. But I'm not right for you, in fact, I'm not even sure who I am right for. Still, you better look, so you don't have to invent things to tell your brothers."

With that I walked away, shook off my robe and turned around, god and goddess style, not whore style. "Where I come from," I said, "I'm part of a divinity. Try to look at me properly, try to see through to the other side."

Maybe I achieved something, for he was about to faint – or throw up!

"I'm making that call. You're taking all your clothes off and getting into that bed. I'll turn down the lights a bit and you are going to have a beautiful awakening. I promise. It will be special, she's a lovely, lovely girl and tonight, she's all yours."

I made the call. "I'm off for a bath," I said easily. "You won't see me again but I don't think you'll forget me either."

Within the minute Jaya had slipped into the room and 30 seconds later they had started giggling together. "My work here is done," I mimed to the mirror and awarded myself the Evie Good Deeds, Gold Star, 1st Class. Then I sank into the water in search of just reward.

I wasn't looking forward to three days off. Lounging around for 72 hours, nibbling, bathing, beautifying, ordering dresses and lingerie came low on my radar. Neither did I wish to go to the gym, jog round and round the inner walls, or do any one of the things I was able to do with perfect freedom. I'd infected myself with the "good whore" virus and though I had no wish to do any more "good whoring," I did want to do something real.

I had some excellent books stacked up to read but the very thought made my palms itch. I think my boy-bit wanted to break out and chop logs, build a wall, or get a project underway. I was longing for dirty hands, a sore back and a sense of time well spent. I could go and ingratiate myself with the gardener but it was frowned on as an activity. Also, I didn't much like flowers, they choked the weeds out.

My real problem was I felt very much alone and next door's giggling wasn't helping. The two of them were falling in love, because everyone fell in love with Jaya. Also, that was her own particular opium – falling in love, day after day, after day. She actually did. When the lad left, she'd be in floods of tears and she wouldn't be putting it on. Then the next forlorn virgin would turn up, scared witless and she'd be back in her element. It definitely kept her young. She was 30 and looked 16. There were probably only one or two Jayas in the entire world and this one was in the right job.

I wanted to talk with the old man from the scrappy little park. Ask him about the ring and about Tibet. That was the problem. There were no 'real' people here, only whores and their keepers. All the girls hid their souls from one-another, working through their contracts, focusing on a life beyond, where all this would be just a fading memory. No-one wanted to let down their guard and admit that they were helpless. A chippy, up-beat tone was the one we maintained and I would have given all my earnings to be able to visit the diner and talk idly to Kirsty, Carl, Andy – even crazy Harold. In fact, on consideration, particularly crazy Harold, if I could grab him at a moment when he wasn't drunk, or possessed by other demons.

I realised then, floating in this alien water, that no-one really cared if I lived or died. Harold had plucked out my insides and put them on canvas and subsequently, I had casually thrown the shell away.

The giggling was starting to drive me crazy. I was screwing up my face in irritation – but at what? Two kids enjoying themselves? Please, Eva! Get a grip!!

Just as I was grumping to myself, that was the moment when someone else got into the bath. I knew that because I was suddenly having to lift my head up, so as not to drown. Also, there was distinct movement at the other end. Then a small voice said – "Hello?"

I had heard that, hadn't I? I hadn't blown my main fuse?

"Hello," I whispered, "is somebody there?"

"Er, yes," said the voice. "I'm here, I'm Marie-Gabrielle. I rather thought this was my bath. In fact, I'm sure it was. At least it was the last time I got in it."

"That's funny," I said. "I felt exactly the same way about my bath but now you seem to be in it, too. Anyway, pleased to meet you, I'm Evie and you say that you're Marie-Gabrielle?"

Oh, this was very strange. There must have been "substances" in the evening meal, or I've got delayed concussion from my Tibetan ring.

"That's right," said the voice. "The thing is, Evie, I can't see you but I can sort of feel you. Is there a reason for that?"

"Probably," I said, a bit gloomily, "there's usually a reason for everything. I've got exactly the same problem my end, I can't see anyone but I can feel something. How worried should we be?"

"I don't know," said Marie-Gabrielle, "we're probably over the worried bit by now but something very odd is going on."

"We can agree on that," I said fervently, "do you mind me asking who, or what you are?"

I was not expecting her reply.

"I'm a picture in a vulgar book and I'm trying to escape."

I was so surprised the soap shot up in the air, as I squeezed my hand involuntarily and landed feet away, rapidly sinking to full fathom five.

"Oh flip, I've dropped the soap. Has it scooted down your end?"

I was thinking – 'you're in a vulgar book?! Try being a whore in a vulgar whorehouse

– then you'll realise you've got problems!' whilst patting for the soap. That was when our two heads suddenly collided.

"Sorry, ooh, aah, oh! Can't see you!" 'My God,' I whined to myself, 'that was right on my Tibetan wound. I may die! Ooh, ah, poof.'

"Agh," I managed eventually, "look, I'll just get out. I've been in here for hours. There's not enough room for two, especially when we can't see each other."

"Not your fault," was the last thing I heard, as I heaved myself upright. Then, there I was, dripping on the mats, staring around at the corners of the room, for the phantom of the bath, Marie-Gabrielle.

All I could think was that if she was an illustration in a dirty book, she might prove a bit elusive in the three-dimensional world. That was a pity. I'd been wanting a friend and on first acquaintance, she seemed just my sort. Nor could I feel, 'easy come, easy go.' I really wanted that friend.

"Hello," I tried cautiously, "anybody there?"

Not a peep. Outside, even the gigglers had screwed themselves to a standstill, or had scurried off to Jaya's room to get even better acquainted among her shoals of cuddly, stuffed toys. Of these there were now so many, they were becoming a serious threat to normal, planetary life. Certainly, the two of them would have to fight their way to the bed and then contest for possession of it. Jessica kept threatening to send round her very own Furry Toy Abattoir operatives, "that way you'll have room for more!" At which Jaya would squeal and run away, to check she'd locked the door safely.

Mercifully, they had gone, though my bed had been totally destroyed.

Nevertheless, 'the most awesome creature in the world,' managed to crawl into the middle of it and lie there, flattened.

For a long time I thought about nothing. I just let the static crackle between my ears. My eyes glazed and swam in the mirrored ceiling. Somewhere up there, or over there, or there, was a camera, or a dozen of them. I wondered if they edited the footage, or just retained it all on some private cloud, floating above the wilds of Uzbekistan in whatever fashion these clouds of memory exist…if they exist at all.

Did Marie-Gabrielle exist? I don't know. I hope she does. I don't want her to be a fantasy, or concussion, or something even worse. Not a bloody brain tumour. Mind you, if it is, there are worse things to be fantasising than a feisty, competent-sounding girl who doesn't get in a flap when strangers pop up in her bath.

I wonder 'where' she is, 'what' she is, 'how' she is, 'why' she is? All the great questions of the universe have suddenly descended on one lone girl in her bath. She's probably thinking the same about me and I'm sure there's a moral in there, somewhere. That's the trouble with morals, they get everywhere – 'like Jaya's wretched cuddly toys!' I thought, because something with legs was digging in my back. I fumbled around and, lo and behold, – a racoon! How very sweet. Must remember to give it back – unmolested. Jess once did a very terrible thing to a bear and has not yet been forgiven.

Moods are skittering over me like shoals of brightly-coloured fish, with the occasional shark pulsing through them, a swirl of blackness. It's all right the Zen crowd saying, 'watch them come and go. Don't attach yourself to any of them.' Not that easy, buster. There's one bearing down on me now and it's going to squash me into some strange and horrible shape…in which I'm thinking about Harold, on the Great North Road, when he was little more than a child.

London, under a bomber's moon and burning on the horizon. Somewhere under that dust and distant flame is his mother. Here, where he is, the dust is from the wheels of black lorries, and flame from the drivers' matches and fags, as he toils to pump diesel from under the earth. With his artist's eye he would feel the dissonance as fiercely as he felt the parallels. Counterpoint to both, the huge black pistol, swinging in his pants pocket, banging on his cock like the devil's own metronome.

What, in the name of the Almighty, was he meant to do with it? Such questions are intolerable, for what are we meant to do with any of the equipment we are gifted, endowed or abused with? We, who are freighted with pistols, pricks, brains and tits… WHAT ARE WE TO DO WITH THEM?

We are not born from some calm nuclear blueprint. We have emerged from raging universal chaos. Why would we, or any of our equipment, make sense?

When I was yet a little boy, still bouncy and lovable, I used to bamboozle my mum to take me to the local museum. I adored it there. The austere cabinets held the most alluring things I had ever seen in my short life. Flint spearheads and axes, broken clay beakers, burial urns and their cruelly-exposed bones, wincing from the sharp light. Red Samian ware, Roman coins, delicate green glass, full of air bubbles – bubbles that held the breath of ancient people. My mum told me that and I couldn't believe it. This was how the town validated its lineage, these jumbled remnants.

Away from the town's ancient history, were other cabinets. One held a collection of pristine, bleached fish skeletons, utterly alien to my eyes in their strange forms. First among these, to my child's eye, was the North Atlantic Stonefish, a creature who'd earned his alternative name of wolf-fish, maybe on looks alone. He seemed to be an excuse to bring together four sets of jaws, each successive one bracing its earlier brother. The whole fish was a swimming jaw. It lived by wrenching limpets from rocks, in the coastal seas off Iceland.

Ten-year-old me didn't really know what I was staring at. But I saw the wolf-fish and just stared and stared and stared. Every time I thought I'd had my fill, within a week the wolf-fish would start calling me and I'd have to concoct another excuse for a museum visit.

I suppose, back then, I was incoherently trying to frame the simple question 'why?' Why was he like this? Why this masterpiece of design? Simply to eat limpets? Did they need eating that badly? Had the planet been under threat from limpets?

How long did it live? I had no idea. "Maybe two years, maybe four…" suggested the equally ignorant but friendly attendant. Then it simply died? This miracle of engineering sank to the bottom of the sea, to rot?

Trying now, to connect with my ten-year-old self, did I intuit that I must be some sort of design, too. Was I intended for a particular task? Which was?

Evolution and its mysteries lay way ahead of my scholastic curriculum at that time. Which was a shame, for had some friendly teacher appeared at that point, to explain the processes by how the wolf-fish got to be the way it was, I would have followed that trail as far as it led. And, possibly, I would not be lying on a whore's bed, surrounded by mirrors, none of which can answer my questions.

Tonight then, I contemplate the fall of a newly-dead wolf-fish. The left-right spiralling motion, the implicit corkscrew, that helter-skelter of happenstance that has insinuated its way into every aspect of life, existence and experience. For when you stop to think about it, spirals are everywhere. They're a universal constant.

So, down it floats, to a final grounding in silt, mud and grit. There it will be picked-over by bottom-feeders, consumed, ground down, abraded, crushed and ultimately returned, by the great mechanical action of subduction, to the bowels of the earth. There it will vanish into the fury of the molten core. To be re-born as what? A pebble on a beach, part of a rich vein of bauxite, in a funnel of rare crystals? Perhaps it will strain upwards as part of those Blue Remembered Hills, the Himalaya. For all I know, some ancient wolf-fish, moving by the road less travelled, has ended up as part of this chick-with-a-dick…

I so, so want someone real in my life! I screw up my face and grind my fists into my eyes in an agony of summoning. And just for one micro-second I have the clearest vision of two real people I'm going to find – that feisty young girl is Marie-Gabrielle! So tell me, who is this darling, woodsmoke-tanned, old man, in military rags that are 300 years out-of-date?

The vision is so explicit, so ridiculous, so stunningly brief, so incommensurate with anything I might have imagined. But with it comes a frisson of total joy, an Hallelujah Chorus, swiftly followed by – 'now you know – don't ask again!'

This is crazy. I'm instantly in love with them both. As smitten as that wretched Arab child will be, by now, with Jaya. Something has granted me a sliver of the future, a microtoned slice from my life-to-come. This is joy.

The weeks go by, rest days come and go. We even have another exeat day, to a truly wonderful place, where ancient astronomical instruments were built, at the Rajah's command to record the movements of the planets and stars. Yet it was all in pursuit of a more accurate astrology. Strange, the way the two – astrology and astronomy – are so inextricably linked. It must be to the utter outrage of the astronomers. They must, at times, feel themselves betrayed, by the very stars they probe so assiduously.

What a paradox it is that the mechanics of the visible universe can be subverted to telling fortunes. I have begun to wonder if everything may be a bit like that… mechanical truth plagiarised by romantic interpretation. An outrageous example might be human beings, who can be free, or slaves, according to how they interpret themselves. Take me, an androgyne who works as a whore, something intriguing reduced to the ridiculous. Sold, by themselves, for 30 pieces of silver.

With such awkward thoughts pursuing me, ones that could cast me into depression, it's lucky that I now have a secret atomic battery to run on. I keep it buried, deep inside, where not even a probing pathologist could find it. I know to keep my secrets close. I have friends, in the Real World, for assuredly, this cannot be the real world – can it.?

I am, however, starting to feel tired. It's not lack of faith. It's the sense that I'm wasting valuable time. That a fuse has been lit and if I'm not careful, it will out-run me. I have to set things in motion. The free creature has to act, soon.

I'm not supposed to be working, today but nevertheless, the phone rings and it's an agitated Muti. "Darling, I know, I know but the Ranee would be pleased to see you now!"

The Ranee is my 'special client.' We have a relationship and it has evolved over time. Also, I know, that she knows that this is my rest day. I also know that she knows, that I know, that she knows this. So, this is rather sweet of her, I decide.

"Please, Muti, tell the Ranee that I shall, as always, be delighted to see her. I'll be down in a moment."

"Darling!" she hisses, "she's on her way up! You know what she's like!"

I think I'd like to be caught reading. I can at least try to look intelligent, whatever the truth may be. All I have on my side, is that it's a long way 'UP'.

In my eyes the Ranee is extremely beautiful. She's quite tiny and I can pick her up one-handed. She's very imperious, though it's hard to be imperious with no clothes on. So that's rather worn off, now. She's also had a rotten life.

An only child, brought up by grandparents, though she won't say why and finally married off, for her lineage, to a homosexual husband from a vastly wealthy commercial family. All very humiliating for her, poor little thing.

At first she was resentful, because she is a lusty girl. But fairly quickly they reached an accommodation of tastes. Their sexual lives were declared their own property, as were any emotional involvements – provided the social niceties were never breached. Once they had established those parameters, they had become very fond of one another. The ridiculous wealth was helpful, too. She had often groaned – "I have something very boring to do, tonight. Let's do something I can think about secretly, with a huge, huge grin. Something to keep me going!" And so we would.

Eventually, I gave up on the reading, mainly because she was an eternity and I'd chosen a very boring book. I went to wait for her in the corridor, where I hung over the banister, expecting her to scurry into sight. Finally, there she was. Scurrying, however, was out of the question because she had company, in the form of the biggest stuffed lion I have ever encountered. I think, if you stood it on its hind legs, it was at least six inches taller than she was. As I watched she plonked it down, to catch her breath.

"You can't leave that 'li-in' there!" I warbled.

"I know that one," she said. "Come down here and help. I'm puffed."

I arrived. "Can't we take it straight to Jaya's room?" I said.

"What do you mean, Jaya's room?"

"You've brought it for her, haven't you?" I asked.

"Are you serious? This is mine! I shot it."

"What are you talking about, woman? It's stuffed, it didn't need shooting. It's a toy."

"I know it's a toy, you idiot. I shot it, in the sense that I won it in a shooting competition. I'm taking it home for husband."

"So, if I may make so bold, why haven't you left it in the helicopter?"

"I wanted to show it you."

"Oh," I said, quite overwhelmed. "How very sweet. Let's take him upstairs."

"It's a SHE," she said.

"It's a HE."

"You're the last person I'm consulting on sexual differentiation," she said. "Have a squint. 'HE' hasn't got a dick. So, HE's a SHE."

"Stuffed toys never have dicks."

"They don't?"

"We can check with Jaya, if you like, she's the acknowledged world expert. But in my experience, no, they don't."

"Ridiculous," she said fiercely. "I shall write to someone. Anyway, take the front end, I'll push."

"OK," and off we went.

Later, we shut HIM/HER in the bathroom, because we found it awkward being observed by a very large cuddly toy.

In the evening and pinned down under my boyish side, Tulipa is musing, out loud, whether I might ever have had the pleasure of her husband's attentions.

"Not knowingly, I'm not very interesting to true homosexuals but boys do come and go. More men than boys, strictly speaking but their minds are all stuck at age 13, whether I like it or not."

"And do you like it?"

"On the face of it, Tee, that's a ridiculous question but I'll do you the honour of answering it. I prefer it. Then I know exactly where they are coming from. That makes my job easy."

After a pause, for some fairly vigorous fucking, Tulipa asks – "Where am I coming from, Eva?"

Ostensibly an ingenuous question but I'm not that easily duped. Danger lurks, like a snake in the grass. Never a good thing in sex.

I roll off my Ranee and feign exhaustion.

"Your turn, Tee. I'm an old woman, I'm whacked."

Out of nowhere and aware that I was pursuing a dangerous path, I said – "I think you're complex and capable of cruelty, a dangerous, lovable woman, who I'd rather be beside. Not on top of, or underneath, except for fun."

Tulipa arranged my limbs to her taste.

"I had a dream the other night," she said, languidly. "I actually have no brothers but in this dream, I killed them all. I don't know why but I never hesitated. If one could be said to enjoy anything, I enjoyed it."

She climbed up on top of me and rode up and down, holding my breasts together as she did so. "It was something I did in a dream…in a dream," she repeated with a laugh. She stared into one of the mirrors. "What do you make of that?"

"Nothing at all," I said, playing possum, "nothing at all…" whilst thinking 'the sooner this bitch comes, the better for us both. She's wound tight.'

"Are you my brother, my sister, my wife, my husband, or my lover…little Eva?"

My brain was now computing rapidly and cogently. 'NEVER LET YOURSELF BE THE UNDERDOG!' it said, in capital letters.

I am physically strong and I plucked the Ranee off my hips in one easy lift, turned her over in mid-air and crashed her down on the disarranged sheets. I grinned at her, devilishly, I hoped. Turned her on her stomach, lifted her belly with my left hand and with my right slid my considerable prick deep into her ass. She squirmed vigorously but I was too strong.

I gathered up a few yards of satin bedsheet, formed it into a hood, slid it over her head and drew it tightly around her neck. Then I fucked her vigorously, half on the bed, half in mid-air, The fingers of my left hand were already sliding each side of an already erect clitoris and I took care to keep plenty moisture flowing. My knees trapped her own. Basically she had become a rag doll, impaled on my cock and being tossed up and down.

It was damned hard work. Eventually, Tee came, in a languid writhing motion that died down to a gentle moulding of her hips, thrust up against my belly and hips.

I unwrapped her head and kissed her deeply, as she turned her head up towards mine.

"There's your answer, Tee," I said, "I'm none of the above, I'm your rapist."

Mercifully, Tulipa giggled.

"I shall be consulting my dream – again!"

It must have been a good dream, after all. A week or so later, on an evening during which I borrowed a few incisive moves from earlier exploits with the 'bad-girl' of my mis-spent youth, Tulipa lay exhausted on the bed.

After a while she squirmed into a position in which she could play with the weight of my tits, while languidly licking the length of my cock.

"That was scary," she said – long lick

"Good scary, bad scary?"

Heft of tits, short licks on the dick.

"Both," she said, in a satisfied voice. "I like you, Eva…you're a bit different."

"My God," I said, "'A' for observation, Randy Ranee Tee!"

"Idiot!" she replied and resumed her licking with some diligence. Then she paused, throttling all her hard work with both hands, sat up and asked – "Do you really want to go to London with me?"

I hummed and hawed… "it was more, oh ravished one, that I thought you might like to come to London with me and meet the Nuns for real. My stories and the videos have got you away often enough, how about the real thing? They're really nice people."

Tulipa scrambled onto my legs, flattening my abandoned prick and arranged my tits, one over each shoulder, which meant that the next sentence floated upwards, from under my chin.

"You must think I'm made of money!"

"I know you're made of money!"

"But, you evil, plotting girl – or are you an evil, plotting boy? – you haven't even got a passport."

"Then it's a good job you're made of money, isn't it?"

I lay back and rolled Tee to one side. I pushed her tiny left hand deep into my cunt, until it was buried up to the wrist. Her right I placed on my prick and moved it slowly up and down.

"Now try refusing me anything," I cackled, as I thrust my nipples towards her mouth.

She screwed her face up.

"Difficult," she agreed.

I lay back, after a while and wondered if I was enjoying this. Yes, but not yet outrageously so, I decided. I enjoyed our seductions, being strapped into, or enticed out of complicated lingerie. But my sex organs, despite being youthfully compliant, were not particularly sensitive.

My real motive was that I was driven to leave this place, and soon. But being poised on the cusp of achieving that was – and this is bizarre – making me regret the cosseted material world of silks, satins, leather and latex I would be walking away from. Some part of me had been seduced by what I had had to become, an institutionalised sex toy. At the same time, I knew I would give it all up in an instant, to be able to see Marie-Gabrielle and smell the woodsmoke on that wiry, tangled old man.

'But me no buts,' someone says. Yet life doesn't turn a page with the ease that the reader does. Some partings peel away like sticking plaster, necessarily with a rip. I'd been living as 'a good, hard-working whore,' and some of it had stuck. If I don't leave, though, I will die here. Probably unpleasantly.

For this plan to work I have to fake a double orgasm. Just occasionally my prick has the decency to simulate some modicum of ejaculate, though from what and where no-one has ever worked out. My cunt, I have a fair bit of control over. But I like Tulipa. I don't want this to be a charade, at the same time, I need her on board, now. So I grip her forearm with my pelvic muscles, more firmly than a badger trap, began gasping and – glory be! – ejaculate fulsomely enough to be convincing.

"Ooh," she cried, "this is a big day we're having!"

"Only for you, Tee…only with you!"

"Now, for God's sake, sod the sex and ring for tea and buns! I'm famished!"

Tee wants to join the mile-high club.

I said everyone had done that already.

She said she hadn't.

Which is why I find myself in this excruciating posture, perched in dubious fluids – maybe even solids – while she giggles with the abandon of a 12-year-old and squirms on my lap.

"You've the mental age of a schoolgirl," I say crossly.

"And you're an old grump," she says, pulling my boobs out of my top, knowing full well it'll take me an age to get them back in.

"Good grief, Tee," I manage, "when I get you into that hotel room, you really get it!"

"Promises, promises," she says gaily, sliding happily off my prick, pulling her dress down and unlocking the door before I've even started restoring my tits to their rightful abode, let alone covering up the rest of the family silver.

"Wash your hands," she says primly over her shoulder and leaving the concertina-door gaping wide open for the next contestant, away she sashays to our First Class recliners.

"We have to do it here, too," she whispers, when I finally return, red-faced with embarrassment, "when the lights go down."

"Jesus, Tee! You're going to get us arrested at Heathrow!"

"I know," she says. "It's the altitude. It makes me terribly reckless. What else do you think I might do? I should never be allowed to fly!"

1

COMING TOGETHER

"Good choice," says Eva of the Range Rover, as they bowl out of London, heading West. "You're a good driver."

"Really?" asks Tulipa, in a tone of true enquiry. "You're not just saying that to be polite?"

"No, truly, honestly."

"Wow! I've never driven a car in my life until now. But it's great fun. I suppose I must be a natural!"

Eva turns a strange ashen colour. "You showed the man your driving licence and insurance…"

"I know. When I had to get your passport, I thought 'I'm going to need a car, if we're going to travel,' so I got those done, too."

"Oh good grief," hiccups Eva. "Can we stop? I suddenly feel a bit poorly."

"No you don't. It's only terror. You'll soon get over it. I really am rather good at this."

Eva tries to make herself very small. Sometimes, truth is the last thing you need to hear. Nevertheless, as they bowl past roundabout after roundabout, it becomes clear that Tee either is a natural, or they are both under divine protection.

Jo-Jo is in the heart of the cave, led there by the torch whose beam had activated a succession of arrows inset in the floor, together with wall lights. It was all very tame, not at all frightening.

What was scary however, was the little pod that now sat squarely in front of him. It was the shape of a bullet and half of it seemed to be inserted into a borehole that, whichever way you rationalised it, looked exactly like the barrel of a gun. On the pod's dashboard were explicit instructions about what to do next. The thing was, did he want to?

He was supposed to be confronting the Core, not taking day trips back into Portions of Unused History – especially not ones salted with a dash of chance. And anyway, where had he got the idea that it was 'a day trip?' He could be gone some time.

Rebelliousness won the argument with a trump card – 'am I sick of doing the same damn thing over and over again?' The answer being what it was, he followed the instructions, lay flat, his survival pack behind his head, opened the triple-sealed packet and snorted a pinch.

There was no-one to wave him goodbye, which was probably as well, because the pod stayed exactly where it was – but Jo-Jo vanished, together with his pack.

Punch's thoughts will only run in one vein – 'why didn't he kill them when he had the chance?' That question leads to another – 'how were that young maid and her servant meant to survive the fury provoked by his cropping of those ears?' One final rider – 'what am I going to do about it?'

He knows what he's going to do but what he wants for is a sign that he should begin. The last 24 hours he has heard the tumult of dogs, men and horses, quartering the country about him. If something wasn't holding them back from this place, he'd be dead meat by now. But he isn't, so he waits for a sign that the time has come for him to sally forth. In the meanwhile he patches his clothes, elaborates his apron to something slightly more decent, cleans, re-cleans the weapons and eats slice after slice of ripe beef. His head pains him, his vision is wayward. Something is holding him in check. All he can do is to trust its judgement. It hasn't failed yet.

For Marie-Gabrielle and Marie-Claire, these are terrible times. The whole fury of the Manor's ugly crew surrounds them. Marie-Gabrielle can no longer control how they confront reality. More and more they are dragged into the daily dramas of the place. Already disaster has struck, with the wanton rape of Marie-Claire, something Marie-Gabrielle cannot bear to recall. Before that there had been the near-farcical incident with the bull, something so contrived as to be risible – if its disastrous conclusion had not nearly seen her trampled to death in a swamp. Now, the corridors ring with the screams of the Archbishop and his man, as the country vet sews and salves their wounds. But once those animals can think clearly again, she fears their days are numbered. All she can do is tend to Marie-Claire's anguish of mind, something she can never hope to heal in this setting.

Tulipa and Eva are now on the open road – if the M40 counts as such. Miraculously they are not pursued by Custodians of The Law and are only marginally exceeding the speed limit at 90mph, or so Tulipa insists.

"Do you know where you're going?" Eva asks, in as unconcerned a voice as she can muster.

"Of course," replies Tee, the haughty tone to be interpreted as, 'I-haven't-got-a-clue!'

"Good," says Eva, "why not take the next junction? We can have a pee, a cup of coffee and some cuddles on the back seat. This is an un-Christened car, you realise!"

"Excellent idea," agrees Tee.

At the end of the slip road there's a simple choice, left or right. Neither of them think that right is even vaguely welcoming, so left it is and Tee is now driving amiably, peacefully, through increasingly uninhabited and open English countryside.

"This is very beautiful," she says after a while. "Look at those trees up there, they sort of hang on their hilltop." She ponders. "It's not like a hat, or hair, it's more as if the earth was growing upwards but had taken another form."

"Beech hangers," says Eva, searching her memory. "I think that's what they're called. There's a famous painting of one particular clump, just let me dig for a few seconds, I might remember what it's called…"

"Anything?" asks Tee, after a decent pause.

"I think it's missing in action," says Eva.

"The name of the painting?"

"That particular brain cell."

"It'll come back," says Tee, confidently, "now it knows you want it."

"How about this for an idea. I stop this car and we go and investigate that particular clump? I sense great and exciting magic and I want to be part of it. Also, slightly more urgently, I need that pee."

"Ah, the bladder," agrees Eva, "it will not take 'no' for an answer, will it?"

Punch is on the move. The moment he woke, his hands were reaching for his weaponry, before he'd even realised what was afoot. His vision had cleared, his brain was in gear. Within minutes he was a lean and terrible fighting man. He had two double-barrelled pistols, his short sword, honed as sharp as stones from the brook could achieve and Bess cradled in his arms. On his back he had, bound and packaged, the good-woman's linen. He would restore these to her, even at the cost of his life.

In the days while Punch was still held 'captive in his bivouac,' with his head awry, his eyes near blinded and aching, at the Manor the Archbishop announced his design for simple murder. His Black Nun, fresh from the punishment cells, shrugged her contempt but his amanuensis, still as achingly sore as his master, was for once allied with His Grace.

"This is how I will have it, Chiara," he had rumbled, thrusting his finger at the latest drawing. "That vixen in the pillory, while her servant is hung on those gallows" and he had gestured through the diamond panes to the courtyard, where joiners were industriously hammering together the necessary beams. "After her flogging and only when that ancient crone has twitched her last, you may take the girl below and finish matters as you wish. For me, for us" he made an off-hand gesture of inclusiveness at the scribe, "this is business, something we will not alloy with our pleasures."

"Your loss," she had yawned indifferently. "Who would have thought the loss of an ear would have cost 'men' their wits into the bargain." And she had outstared the look of cold fury the Archbishop directed at her.

If Marie-Gabrielle had heard that conversation, witnessed those drawings, she would have fled, carrying her broken-hearted nanny, if necessary. But two-dimensions were now denied to them both. She could no longer seek out the Shaman for his comforting conversation, or slip between the covers of sheltering books. She was three-dimensional, exposed and vulnerable. She had wished for this terrible transformation and her wish had been granted.

Already, the cost had been appalling – she cradled its ruins in her arms. For weeks now, since that awful day, all Marie-Claire could do was to sob pitifully, not for herself but for fear of what might be about to befall her beloved Marie-Gabrielle.

Any thought of flight she might have harboured was already undone, with a stout lock on the outer door and a ruffian posted at the window.

Even if the Shaman had come to her – and for all she knew he already might have done – how could she have communicated with him? He would now be no more than his picture upon a page. The irony and misery of her situation was complete. The two-dimensional freedom she had discovered was no longer accessible, the freedom of three dimensions she had so hungered for was imprisoning them both. Where would help come from? Would it come at all?

Punch is at the top of the lane and he is bemused. Less than 100 yards distant is a busy home farm. But the great double gates are shut, there are no labourers in the fields, no wandering fowl busying themselves among the fallen leaves, no idling curs to announce his advance, musket at port-arms. Such a mystery makes him doubly wary.

What he can hear is a subdued murmur, as of a crowd gathered for some event about to unfold. Nor, as he tunes his ear, is this a festive crowd. It is a sullen one, gathered together under duress. He needs time to think but something tells him he has no time for thought, nothing more is needed – yet – than this steady advance.

Jo-Jo is advancing, too. He is hurtling through space and time, propelled by whatever force a small pinch of powder could possibly bestow upon a reckless traveller. His transit is painless but he has time for anxiety. What, precisely, has he done? Or undone? Has he traded the security of the Core for the truly unknown, or is he in the grip of some mind-altering substance? What he does have, is time to hope – and this most devoutly – that he does not end up in that mythological hell-hole he was propelled into by one too many 'ribbits.' Jo-Jo never wishes to see that place ever again and so he has to ask himself – 'why, oh why, did you inhale?' It is far too late to ask that.

Tulipa parks neatly on a flat prominence of grass, alongside a double-wide farm gate. She allows herself a cat's smile of self-congratulation and then beams at Evie.

"Didn't I do well,?" she crows happily.

"You were brilliant," agrees Eva, whose nerves collapsed somewhere near Heathrow.

Under these circumstances, 'She' has decided to die happily, because 'He' is in love. That realisation had come upon 'Him' suddenly, 50,000 feet over Kazakhstan and 'She' has been examining it, in amazement, ever since. It was something to do with being left flagrante delicto in the loo of the plane, or rather that had been the catalyst that drew out into the open the enormous protective pride the two of them – She and He – were assembling around the little Ranee. Her little Ranee. His very own Tee. This little Lupa thing that was smiling at them so openly.

"Come here," cries Evie and lifts Tee over the gap between the seats to smother her under a GBH of kisses and cuddles.

"Ooh," says Tulipa, coming up for air, "did I do something right?"

"Yes, yes, you did," says Eva and starts again, in case she missed some bits.

"Mmm," says Tee…then her face changes dramatically…

"What, wha-?"… Evie, suddenly fearful…

"Pee! Open the door, I've got to pee, now! I do! I do! I really do!"

"Yes, now you mention it…so do I!"

Two bodies fall out of the opening door in a calamity of giggles and flailing limbs.

"Over the gate, over the gate!" yells Evie, slamming the door.

"…and a pox on fancy undies," she swears, seconds later, trying to free herself from straps and fastenings.

"Ooh, sweet relief," sighs Tee, contentedly sharing the leftovers of her breakfast with an English field. "Take that, perfidious Albion!"

"We should have gone at the showroom," says Evie, mentally noting that she's obviously turning into her own mother.

"If I'd gone for the Humvee, it probably had an integral loo."

"And we'd also be jammed in that narrow bit we came through."

"Poo, I'd just have driven over it and anything else that got in the way. Tee the Unstoppable! Come on, I'll race you up that hill to the trees!"

"Lock the car," says Evie and steals a 10 yard start, while Tee fumbles to understand her lump of black plastic that does everything, or it did, back in the showroom.

"That is grossly unfair!" she shrieks and hurls herself in pursuit. "Where's your English sense of fair play?"

"Back in India," pants Evie, "with my wages. God, this hill's steep, or I'm fatter than I thought."

Together they reach the edge of the trees.

"You were right," says Evie, staring into the dappled light, then turning to look back down the hill in surprise, "this is a magical place."

"Yes, it is. You can feel it…just one step in and, phew, it's a whole different atmosphere. Quick, Evie, come in before I get swallowed-up by the magic things!"

Evie moves under the rustling canopy and looks around in awe. "Strange," she says, "it's so dignified and…strong. You feel that, too?"

Tee comes alongside and hand-in-hand they listen and watch as the wind stirs a steady heaving and rustling of the great, high branches overhead.

"Look," she says, "look back at the car, Evie…it's so little. Such a big car and now it's so small."

Punch has reached the great double gates and they are firmly shut. The crowd noise reaches him plain enough. He was right, this is a bitter, sullen gathering. Something beyond is seriously amiss. He tries the postern gate and it, too, is barred inside, though by no more than a bolt he'll warrant. Then some intuition flows through his veins and he takes up the great bar of timber used to lock the gates from without, should need ever arise. He lifts it, solid baulk of oak that it is and drops it in place across the iron brackets. It sits comfortably enough but loosely. Punch picks a loose flint from the road and wedges it, tightly.

He stalks around the Western wall. He was wary of the sun picking him out on the eastern edge and is grateful for the shadows here. Still he sees not one child at play, not one beast abroad It is uncanny and bodes nothing good.

Jo-Jo is convinced he is travelling through solid rock, that it is opening before him and closing after him. It is not an agreeable sensation and he's developing a claustrophobia based around the unpleasant notion that if this journey suddenly stops, he'll be sealed, fossilised at the centre of whatever mineral dimension he is transiting through. 'Enough, enough,' he protests silently. Evidently it is not enough, not yet. His journey hurtles on.

The day is underway and the Archbishop is seated in his papal balcony, high above the milling herd of domestics and farmhands he has commanded to attend this exhibition. The windows protect him against much of the murmured protest but the mutinous glances are plain to see.

Higher still, in his attic room, the curate, artist and amanuensis crawls from his sickbed, hungry to witness revenge. His wound is, of a sudden, infected and he is sick with fever. In his paranoia he is certain that the leech has poisoned the wound. The man is little more than a cretin, a veterinarian, with hands unwashed since lambing season.

He groans miserably, his head is as nauseous as his stomach and only with difficulty can he drag a heavy chair to his window. He tries to lift his pencil but he has no strength left. Memory will serve. He wishes the French bitch could be murdered a thousandfold and that this were some baying, drunken crowd, eager for death and punishment instead of these bovine cretins beneath, mutinous, treacherous. They have no sense of theatre, no lust for justice. This is entertainment worthy of a cathedral city

He looks with some relic of pride at the mise-en-scene he has devised. Before his fever set in, he had designed the most awful gallows, the most harrowing pillory. Their massive timbers speak of terrible justice and retribution. They will strike terror into the hearts of the condemned. The maidservant will be hung while the wench is a tethered witness to it. Only then, when her heart is broken, will she receive her 100 lashes, preparation for what lies in store below, in the company of the Black Nun. He prays he will have the strength to stagger there to witness it. She is inventive.

Tulipa and Evie have vanished under the trees, which rustle protectively overhead. A high wind stirs the top-most branches but between the trunks barely a breath of air pursues them.

Beech-mast, has been wind-gathered in hollows and troughs and Tulips kicks her way through one with evident delight. "Oooh," she cries, "I was born for this. I want to know these places, I want to grow among them. Evie, Evie, we've got to screw, now!"

"I see no problem in that," says Evie, inventing a rumbling, deep and ponderous voice. "Come here, little Indian wench and be ravished in the English way!"

"No!" squeaks Tee and tries to rush out of the harbour of beech-mast she has been playing in. Evidently Nature is on Evie's side, Tee can't move anything like quickly enough and is caught in a trice. The tree-tops race and nod their approval, the great rushing of the leaf song surrounds them and like every other pair of young lovers to struggle up this hill, they consummate a portion of themselves to Pan and his satyrs.

"Oh, Tee, I don't want to leave. Do you think we could stay for ever and live on the magic?"

Tulipa, staggers upright. Pulls up her pants and jeans, pulls down her bra and top, staggers amiably about. "I hear you," she says "but I want to explore too. Watch me sprint, I'm really fast!" And she is off, like a small, startled forest creature, winding through the trees until she is lost to sight.

"Gone," says Evie, "just when I wanted her to stay forever. Come back!" she shouts. "I can't see you and I'm about to be eaten by voles. They're massing for an attack. They love a tasty androgyne, when they can get one."

"Tough," says a distant voice, "get yourself over here, I've found a track, not a tractor thingy but a really old track. Quick, come and explore with me.

Eva lopes through the trees, tracking Tee by her squeaks and tiny exclamations. Every sound she hears produces a great surge of protectiveness in Him while, at the same time, She longs to join the squeaking and be protected and cherished. It's complicated. Eva comes up behind her friend and wraps her arms round the little body, which wriggles with pleasure.

"Love you, Tee."

Tulipa curls around to deliver a long, dreamy kiss. "Love the Beaver, too," she sighs, pulling gently at Eva's ears, while running her fingers into each complex of whorls and scrolls. Abruptly she jumps free and orders – "Quickly, down this path with me. I know it's important that we go."

Docile Eva trots obediently behind, following the darting creature with the mane of black hair, which is now beginning to lift and stream as they leave the shelter of the trees and the wind catches them.

They're on the edge of a headland and the track pulls free of the beech trees to veer off to the left, where it crests the shortest of rises and from this viewpoint, falls out of sight. Tee sprints ahead. "It goes down the hill. There's a big old house in the distance but it's a ruin. Got no roof, or has it? Can't tell. Keep up Beaves!"

"I'm in love," croaks Eva. "Can't run, too many endorphins weighing me down."

"No time for that," says Tee importantly. "Adventure first, sex later."

"I thought you were a sex maniac."

"I am. I'm an adventure maniac, too."

"Poo," pants Evie, "I was hoping for a quiet, bodily fluids sort of life."

"Keep up, Beaver, you're quite impossible at times. Try to concentrate."

Eva crests the short rise and feels her eyes pulled to the left, peeled away from the track Tee is following. She is looking across a field where, in the middle distance another, older-looking wood stands. It presents only a short side on this view but from that short side it spreads out, drawing a trailing arc back towards Tee's track, which it almost reaches, about a mile away.

Even at this distance, Eva can feel something ancient and forbidding emanating from those trees. 'Anarchic' is the word that finally comes to mind. That wood is beholden to no-one, it stands there in a placid landscape emanating a ruthless intent. Eva shakes her head. 'Get a grip! It's a wood. A wood in a field, not a king on a throne.'

"Tee, Tee! Have you seen!" she shouts after her Ranee-on-the-Run.

"What?"

"Come back a bit…over there," and she points, urgently.

Tulipa runs back uphill until finally, standing on tiptoe, she can see. Says softly – "how could I have missed that?"

"It's so powerful, do you feel that?" asks Eva, who has caught up by now.

"Can you see, on the left and I think, running back all the way, there's a hedge – and don't ask me why, or how – that's where the power's coming from. "It's sort of shimmering."

Entwined, the two stare and as they stare, some sense of kinship kindles between the wood and them. Pressure grows for them to be off, to begin, not to be shooed away but drawn closer to whatever lies in that valley, by the house with no roof.

Jo-Jo must have fallen asleep, because he wakes with a sudden start. A message glows on the pod dashboard – "You have arrived at your destination. For a tour booklet insert 3d in the console coin slot. Have a nice day!"

"What is it with these 3d's?" he demands. "Threepence to go down, probably 3d to come up and now 3d for a booklet! I thought this was uncharted territory?"

In a pique he throws open the cockpit and steps out, creaking in every folded joint. "Oh bugger!" he groans, "I'm getting old." The next second, his pack hurtles after him, like a faithful dog. He stares at it with amazement and as he bends to pick it up, the capsule simply vanishes.

Where he felt he had been standing, which was nowhere-in-particular, he now finds to be the cramped side-room of what he takes for a small library. Two things are immediately apparent, firstly, there is no door, secondly, books are flying off the shelves, unaided by human, or mechanical means. Jo-Jo is confused. He is also being buffeted by the passage of belligerent spectres, vaguely discernible forms, transparent figures. They seem to be mostly female but all of them are insubstantial, inconsequential – if it wasn't for the buffeting, which is all too real.

"Ladies, ladies," he protests, "I'm a newcomer here and a stranger to your ways. I mean you no harm! Could you return the compliment, please!?"

Looking around, he can see that the turmoil is a consequence of the rapidly flying books. These hurl themselves from the shelves, land upon a square and solid library table and there divest themselves of their illustrations. They simply peel off the pages – which open with great rapidity, one after another – grow to human proportion and then, by now in an unreal two-dimensional form, brush by him. He sees they are making for one particular corner of the room, where they slide through a crack at the end of a stack of shelving.

To try to rationalise, he studies the books as they land. They are all scandalous pornographic novels, more illustration than text. They are not bedroom romances. They are dungeon depravities and the young ladies are freeing themselves from racks, chains and cages, something he can well understand. His Moment of Unused History appears to be 'The Day the Victims Fought Back' – an event unrecorded in the annals of pornography.

'Not quite what I would have chosen,' thinks Jo-Jo, as a particularly well-endowed young lady nearly sends him flying. He is also in danger from airborne books. Folios are whizzing past his ears and if one of those catches him, it will be a blow to remember. He ducks down and heads towards the corner the escapees are favouring, still clutching his survival pack.

The shelving proves to be an ill-concealed door, as revealed by metal wheel tracks etched into the wooden floor. He struggles, momentarily, to free the latch, then exits into the library proper. Here the chaos ends. The books are on their shelves, there are no scholars at the desks. In fact, the place is eerily deserted.

He turns about and sees that the newly-liberated images are all pouring through what must be the library door, behind him. Something dramatic is afoot and half-hesitant, half-intrigued, he follows the crowd. They are in full cry down the long corridor but the further they get from the library, the more insubstantial become their forms. Now they are at a point where, if he didn't know they existed, he would be unable to see them. Some vital ingredient is missing from this revolution.

The corridor leads to a kitchen. So far, however, he has not seen one living soul. Here, in the kitchen of a large house, all is deserted, despite the simmering pans and smell of roasting meats. If it wasn't for the murmur of a large crowd, just beyond that wall, he'd be ready to assume that Unused History was a deserted continent.

Jo-Jo is not feeling confident, or perhaps it is not so much a lack of confidence as the growing sense of unease, a foreboding that things here are not at all right. Jo-Jo has a well-developed sense of life's proprieties and has, on occasion, found himself fearless in their defence. Up till now, this defence has largely been theoretical but as he steps through the outer door of the kitchen, he finds himself staring over the heads of a muttering crowd at a scene that makes his blood boil.

"No!" he bellows, from lungs of leather – "Stop!"

Punch, cautiously advancing along the west wall, has had a revelation. He suddenly comprehends Group Mind, something that has baffled him every time he has tripped over the phrase in Jolyon's book. He has seen it in action, with the bees. He has used it with the snails and he played with it, summoning the ladybirds. Now, finally and comprehensively, he understands it.

He, the way he is moving, in obedience to an unheard order, is a manifestation of Group Mind in action. He suddenly knows, beyond any shadow of doubt, that there are others – unseen others – directed, just as he has been, towards resolving this unknown crisis.

Emboldened, he quickens his pace and comes, at last to the outer door of a shed, which seems ajar. He opens it, senses no danger and steps in. Almost immediately, a little voice speaks up – "Sir, are you come to save the ladies?"

He neatly avoids jumping out of his skin, recognising a child's voice and one, it seems, right to the point. He glances about the gloom and sees two ragged figures sharing a perch on the top of a hogshead. In them he sees himself and his playmates of nigh on 50 years gone.

"A' be thet, littl' uns, a's come. Show me 'ow a' gits theer. Shall us b'swift to business? No time to waste."

"No sir," pipes the smallest voice, "my dear old lady be at the gallows!"

Punch's blood chills and his knuckles whiten in the gloom.

"Tek us theer," he says.

They have come for Marie-Gabrielle and Marie-Claire. Rudely torn them apart and though Marie-Gabrielle would walk, they have forced her into a dog-catcher's steel collar at the end of a long pole, so that they can drag her along in a humiliating stumble.

The Archbishop has thought through every evil detail.

Marie-Claire, terrified by the fate of her heart's own child, has had to be carried, dragged, bundled along, a weeping sack of torn dress and petticoat, the most pitiful sight and one at which the murmur of the crowd rises. Sympathy, mounting towards open insurrection.

"Silence," roars the bailiff ordering the proceedings, a colossus of a beast standing atop the gallows platform, adjusting his rope and stool. This monstrous creature is well-known for his casual brutality, indifferently meted out to animal and man alike. He is roundly hated but feared even more. This crowd is not made up of fighting folk, they are domestics, field hands and dairymaids. They are used to submitting to oppression, not in resisting it.

Marie-Gabrielle is dragged to the pillory and held fast, by neck and wrists. But by far the more pitiful sight is that of Marie-Claire, bundled up the gallows steps and forced to stand upon a stool, while noose and rope are made taut about her neck.

No amount of bellowing from the ruffian sentries can quiet the murmuring of the spectators. Mothers drag their children into their skirts, the few menfolk shoot rueful, terrified glances at one another. What are they to do against armed thugs who will not hesitate to shoot down the innocent, let alone the dissident?

On his balcony, the Archbishop can feel his rage mounting. He will not be bilked of his revenge by a horde of muttering dairymaids. He is minded to have his men pluck out the ringleaders and have them made examples of. They can join those unfortunates he has incarcerated in the cellars, those currently receiving the attentions of his Black Nun. She has spurned today's offering, feeling it a waste of good meat that would have been better served up slowly. 'His Grace' is beginning to wish he'd never invited her to his demesne, her orders are beginning to eclipse his own. He feels his authority is ebbing.

Above him, the artist stares at his composition in the courtyard and wonders if it was not all a mistake. Perhaps the Black Nun had been right. The privacy of the cellars was the right venue for these dramas. Played out before a resentful populace they are losing their savour and constitute a real danger to their continuing activities. Then as his fever soared, clarity vanished, sweat poured from him and he cried feebly for the manservant to bring him water.

"We must hurry," says Tulipa and starts off towards the dark wood, across the open field.

"No, no, no" cries Evie, "not that way! Down the track, it's happening down the track. Hurry, hurry, I can feel it pulling at me. It's really strange, Tee, it's like a hook through my tummy button, pulling, pulling. I actually daren't stand still. Grab my hand."

Together they jog down the lane, trying not to turn an ankle in the ancient ruts, so overgrown now with ragged couch grass.

"What do you think it is?" asks Tee.

"I just don't know. Something I've never felt before." But what Evie can feel is the weight of her ruby ring. It seems to be shifting about, 'aligning itself' is the phrase that springs to mind. "My ring is moving around. It's as though it's come alive."

"This is a very strange morning," pants Tee. "What do you think the afternoon's going to be like?"

"Dramatic."

The two children lead Punch through a little maze of tunnel runs, once built to shelter piglets, to separate them from the sows. At one time he wouldn't have made it but now he can, starved to the bone as he is. It's the dragging of Bess behind that takes time. Then, at last, the shoat-run is over and he can stand again.

They have reached the main farm's stables. All the gates have been barred, explain the little pair. Every soul commanded to attend. These orphans had decided they would rather hide.

"We likes the ladies," they explain, as they guide Punch through the dark. "We sneaks in to see 'em and they's kind to us."

"We mun' mek' 'aste," is Punch's reply. "Yon noise, beyon', troubles mi."

They reach a hayloft, overlooking the yard. The lower planks of the door are split away and make a perfect vantage point. 'Or firing port,' thinks Punch. He squints out and winces in dismay. He checks Bess has not shed her priming and by some miracle she has not.

"Set thy legs across yon 'ole," he whispers, "put ye fingers in thine ears and dinna' twitch a muscle. One shot an' a'll needs a way down from 'ere, sharp like! B' reddy, littl' uns!"

Marie-Gabrielle is in no immediate danger, despite her dress being torn from her back. Marie-Claire will be dead in minutes. Only the taut noose holds her upright. The scoundrel just awaits his signal to kick away her stool and she will strangle slowly, as Marie-Gabrielle watches.

Punch, suddenly and awfully remembering his nan's execution, is taking aim on the centre of the black executioner's torso. The children's legs give him just the cushioned rest he needs. "Stop yer ears!" he hisses and as the little hands press inward, he squeezes the trigger. He sees the jet of flame from the barrel and the next moment the blast in the closed space deafens him. He has a hit, for the brute has spun round as though kicked by a horse.

As he pulls back the barrel he realises that he just took his last shot with Bess. Here she'll lie, until he is dead, or fled.

"Get mi' down," he says to the gleeful children, as he hears the mounting roar of the crowd. They sprint away, Punch trailing in their wake.

It's a short flight of stairs and he's out at the back of the milling crowd.

A second after Jo-Jo bellowed his – "No! Stop!" Punch's shot had split the courtyard. He had seen the executioner spin round where he stood but his shout had been directed at the villain tearing the dress from Marie-Gabrielle's back.

He could sense fury all around him. His intuition was that it flowed from the transparent figures he had followed from the library. It could be they were here now, but beyond fuelling a mood, what purpose they could serve eluded his best guess.

People had turned at his cry. Rather than waste that energy he ran in among the crowd – "drag them all down, revenge yourselves!" he shouted, hoping that made some sense. "Come on," he cried, seizing a burly creature by the arm, "we can take them."

But it was the women who rose up first. The first to dare the pillory steps was shot down but the villain who fired was bowled over, his legs hooked away by a shepherd's crook. Dragged into the crowd, he was clawed to death.

Across the courtyard Jo-Jo could hear another voice exhorting the crowd to rise up.

"Kill 'em all, kill 'em all!"

There was another guard on the pillory. His pistol misfired as Jo-Jo pressed forward. "Pull them down, pull them down!" he howled, suddenly realising that he really meant it. He and the man he had roused surged forwards, as women swept up the steps before them. The last guard went down among their shrieks of fury.

Elsewhere, pistols were being fired and screams from the wounded began to ring out.

Punch, the children in tow, is rushing forward to save Marie-Claire. She is teetering on the edge of the stool, which has begun to gyrate with the pressure of the crowd surging against the platform.

He screams his war cry – "Kill 'em all! Kill 'em all!" and is providentially presented with the retreating form of one guard, struggling against a waving mass of women's arms. He comes up hard behind him and his short sword slips effortlessly into the side of the man's gut, just below the ribs. He pulls it free in an arc and opens his belly. Yards of gut begin to spill out.

He sidesteps the women. The children vanish in the melee. He reaches the scaffold just as Marie-Claire loses her balance and the stool spills from under her. He looks up in horror and locks eyes with the Archbishop. He can sense his hunger. The madman is determined to wring at least one moment of triumph from this fast unfolding disaster.

"Never!" howls Punch and he finds it easy climbing up the elaborate timbering, that by-product of an artist's eye, with its own fantasies of domination.

He rolls across the staging. Standing he can seize her by her lower legs. He lifts and feels his shoulders take weight. But now he is helpless. His pistols are at his waist. His sword thrust back in his belt. He stands desperately alone and the next head he sees is that of the beetle-browed dog-handler, the creature he saw, months since, down that long channel of frosted grass within the wood. Then he had fired and the ball had flared into nothingness.

Now the animal is at the top of the stairs. For a moment, it seems he will have to choose.

But Punch has not lost the children. "Sir, sir!" eager voices at his knee, a pistol butt thrust at him. God reward them! They have cocked the hammers. One-handed he shoots the beast in the face and a double-handful of brain-matter flies backwards.

"Littl' uns" cries Punch, "tek me sword! Climb up mi! Cut yon rope!"

These children have a better idea. They pull his sword and rush to the belay, where the hangman secured his rope. They saw furiously, tiny arms tense with effort. The rope parts and Punch collapses under the uneven rush of weight.

Marie-Claire is breathing, raggedly but breathing.

Punch seizes the children by their shoulders. "Th'art best chillun' on earth!" he cries. "See her safe wi' t' women, but don' ye be strayin' far. A' 'as business wi' 'im," – he gestures overhead – "first o' all. One o' ye' needs see mi' into t' Manor."

One of his little guides, he finally realises it is a girl, beckons and they rush the steps. "Up, up!" screams Punch at a gaggle of women, who are rising, blooded, from another fallen guard they have slaughtered. He gestures to the scaffold. They stream away. He catches up the guard's blunderbuss and races after his scout. She is beckoning impatiently from a distant doorway.

Jo-Jo's war is proceeding well. With little cost to the onlookers, four guards have been torn down and killed. Men have armed themselves with their weapons. Emboldened they are hunting others. Jo-Jo is left to climb the scaffold and release the struggling girl who is screaming in rage – "Get me out! Get me out! Nounou! Nounou!"

"Hold still," he roars, for her frantic shaking has jammed the bolt tightly.

"Idiot!" she screams, "Set me free!"

"Idiot yourself! You've jammed the bolt! Hold still will you?"

"My nurse, my nana! Nounou!"

The girl is wild, driven near hysterical by fear for her nurse.

Jo-Jo roars at her – "hold still – or we all die!"

He employs all his strength – which is more than merely considerable – and tears the bolt off the wooden headpiece, in one final surge of power.

"Now!" he gasps, "run to your Nounou, Mademoiselle…"

"Monsieur!" she cries and is gone. One leap from the edge of the platform and she is cutting a line across the courtyard.

Jo-Jo takes the steps. At the bottom lies the unrecognisable ruin of the pillory master, his whip handle thrust down his throat. Below the waist, he is a mass of gore. Jo-Jo winces, not that he feels an ounce of sympathy.

Suddenly he hears a great cry from the high gable across the courtyard. "Stand clear below!" He looks up and across. Struggling in the air, just below the roof tiles, is a writhing body, clad in bed-linen, squirming against the grip that holds him suspended in mid-air. Jo-Jo has no way of knowing but this is the hapless artist, curate and amanuensis. Shocked from his fever by his manservant, who was to have brought water, he is offering a fatal flight to the cobbles below, instead.

The crowd, roused to bloodlust, begin to chant – "Throw him! Throw him! Throw him!"

"I cannot hear ye!" shouts the unseen captor's voice.

'This is turning ugly,' thinks Jo-Jo suddenly, 'very ugly.'

"Throw him!" a great collective bellowing and stamping of clogs on cobbles.

With a high-pitched squeal of terror, the artist is pitched forward. His body contorts and plunges down the short arc. He lands, with an awful thud, a blood sacrifice at the foot of the gallows he so lovingly designed.

A fitting end but one that sickens Jo-Jo. All he can do now, he thinks, is to secure the young woman and her nanny. He begins to shoulder his way across the yard. Behind him, looting has begun and smoke is rising from a stable.

Evie and Tulipa, still jog-trotting towards the old manor, are about to experience the unprecedented. The collapsing old ruin, that had been so clearly in sight, roofless, walls thick with ivy, has suddenly gained a roof and chimneys. The chimneys even have peaceful, domestic smoke trickling from them. A gate and entrance wall have sprung up and the gate is visibly barred from the outside. Behind it, however, is the sound of violent, non-domestic conflict and at this peaceful, lunchtime hour the sound is, at the very least, surreal.

Both grind to a halt to stare at each-other.

"What happened?" cries Tulipa.

"I don't know," says Evie. "Is it a film set? Some sort of projection? "

"Are we frightened?" asks Tulipa, quite earnestly.

Evie considers. "No," she says finally. "We're perplexed."

"What do we do?"

"We hold hands," says Evie, grasping, "and we wait, a while."

Punch has followed the girl upstairs and through the corridors. Silently, she points to a heavy oak portal.

"Get ye gone," whispers Punch. "Tis all mine, now. Bless thee, lil' childer," and he kisses his fingertips and pats them to her cheek.

She hides behind him. He readies the fat blunderbuss, aims at the lockplate and fires. The door bursts back, swinging from its frame. Punch, sidestepping, waits and the shot he anticipated thuds uselessly into the plaster of the hall.

Now he swerves, quick and low, into the room. The second shot is wild and wide.

The Archbishop, at bay, holds a struggling whore to his breast with one arm, his empty pistol dangling uselessly.

Punches advances on them. He surveys the whore without compassion.

"Thou 'elps an' aids 'im."

"E meks me!" she cries.

Punch shoots her through the heart and the ball ploughs on, into the Archbishop's ample belly. He shrieks and falls to the floor, writhing.

"Man of God! I am a man of God! A pillar of Mother Church! Christ aids me! Murder me, thou murderest thine own God!"

"That's al'reet," says Punch calmly. "Tis good t'hear thee confess," and with his short sword he cuts cleanly and deeply inwards, under the left ear, down to the windpipe.

"A'd a'rather stabbed thee through tha' balls," he reflects, 'but a' finds I 'ent t'stomach fer it. Rot in Hell, y'pestilence!"

Punch stands and glances through the window. In the middle distance he can see two horsemen galloping away. They are away to raise the alarm, to rouse the militia. Time is now very limited.

Jo-Jo, Punch, and Marie-Gabrielle have clustered about Marie-Claire. All are sheltering from the storm that has erupted outside. The house is being looted. Fires are rising from the stables, glass is breaking, shards showering into the courtyard. The guards are bloody remnants, the artist hangs from his own crossbeam and soon the Archbishop will be hurled from his casement. The mood of the crowd is verging upon madness.

Jo-Jo speaks across the women, directly to Punch – "is there a way out? We have to get the women out of here. This has turned ugly."

"Worse," says Punch, instantly recognising an ally, "Militia b'ere afore long. We'll 'ave t'carry yon dear owd soul."

"I can do that – trust me."

"Then do it. Lil' miss, we b'away, all o'us."

Marie-Gabrielle knows when to trust.

Jo-Jo finds Marie-Claire a modest weight as he scoops her from the ground. He follows Punch, who leads the way through the madness, navigating scenes of primitive rage, turning aside wild-faces by issuing orders, as though he still directed his old platoon. No-one thinks of questioning his authority.

They make the front gate, buffeted and breathing hard. As Punch had wagered earlier, the postern was bolted but not locked. He draws the bolts and the little group stumbles away from the chaos, into the light and air of an ordinary day.

Evie and Tulipa see them emerge but can do nothing but gape.

"It must be a film set," says Tulipa, uncertainly, clutching Evie's hand a little more tightly.

"It's … not…" said Evie. "It's … something else … something very strange is happening. My head is hurting and the ruby is… just…burning me. Oh Tee, I feel sick as a dog!"

"Mek' off up t'lane," yells Punch. "A'm minded to jam this 'ere door behind us."

Jo-Jo sets off, carrying Marie-Claire, trying not to jolt and jar her. "Can you keep her head up, do you think?" he begs Marie-Gabrielle. "I'm bothered about her neck."

"Oui, Monsieur, oui!" and she trots alongside, obedient, anxious.

Casting around for suitable wedges, Punch can only find an old scythe blade, rusting by the wall, with which to jam the handle. He thrusts it through the iron ring and hammers its point into the door frame with the butt of his pistol.

He's about to turn away, up the lane, when a radical option presents itself. Fleeing unarmed, they might just stay the wrath of the Militia, which will be about their ears all too soon. They could claim that they themselves fled the mob. Thus, with a wry grin, he rams home the pistol as a secondary wedge. Finally, he hurls into the long grass his remaining weapons, powder horn and cartridge pouch. It's only when he pauses to rub his bloodied hands on the kilt of animal skins, that he grins ruefully and addressing no-one in particular, remark – "theer agin, mebbe not…" And away he jogs, up the road, to join his fellows.

Jo-Jo looks questioningly at him. "Up t'track," he says, "then we mun cut int' t'woods, yonder. Safe then, 'appen."

Marie-Gabrielle looks at him, tears in her eyes – "you saved Nounou."

"An' it wer' this 'ere stout fella' as saved thee," says Punch, equably.

"I think we need to move from here," said Jo-Jo, who can smell and see smoke rising in thickening clouds.

"Lad's reet," says Punch. "Theer b' a ways to go afore us b'safe."

They stumble up the lane, newly aware of exhaustion, terror and a new-born, desperate desire not to die now, having come this far.

Evie is retching on an empty stomach. In despair at her nausea, she has turned away to hide behind the little bank of grass they had been standing on.

"So sorry, Tee," she gasps. "I'm not sick, really. It's my head, it's bursting. I don't know what's wrong."

Tee crouches by her. "Sweetie, sweetie, it's OK. It's a migraine, I'm sure. I'll look after you. Don't fret, I'm here."

"No, no," says Evie, "I have to do something. It's the farm, the Manor. I have to do something. I just don't know…ow! Oh, it hurts, Tee!"

Tee feels frantic. She feels Evie's forehead and truly, she's burning up. But her pulse is solid, slow and steady. Her pupils are dilated and Tee can see into them. It's as though she was staring into the darkest of tunnels, down into some immeasurable depths.

"Get me up, Tee!" Evie is shouting suddenly. "Get me up! It's vital! Get me up!"

"No! – no … OK, ok, ok … don't scream so! I'm getting you up, darling! It's me, it's me, it's Lupa."

"Get me up this bank. Help me up. It's so important! You can't know how important!"

Under orders, Tee drags and heaves and Evie struggles against the pain in her forehead. She is unsteady on the grass but by grasping tussocks and hauling, with Tee pushing, pulling, half-crying, half-laughing, she staggers up to where they were less than a minute earlier.

"Better, better!" gasps Evie. "This is right. See, down there!"

Tee can see the little group of actors – they have to be actors – three are in period dress, for Heaven's sake! Besides, when she looks up, over the top of the burning house she can see a group of horsemen. This must be the rest of the scene they are shooting – these people are being hunted by the riders!

"Oooh, it's exciting Evie! We're in a movie. I hope we're not spoiling their shot!"

"Not a movie…" gasps Evie. "This is real."

Punch moves to the front and urges the group on. "Us 'as t'git runnin' – tha' can 'ear 'osses, 'tis t'militia. Us b'done fer, if us don' git ter yon wood! Can thee still carry yon dear soul?" Punch asks Jo-Jo.

"All day, if needs be. Trust me."

"Now, our lass," Punch says to Marie-Gabrielle, "run up theer, up this 'ere lane, see what's t'be seen. What's a' comin' our ways?"

She sets off at a sprint, just as Evie and Tee rear themselves upright on the grass bank.

"Papa!" she shrieks and points.

Punch and Jo-Jo look up. The taller of the two figures, less than 100 yards distant, is waving wildly, a universal 'come on, come on!' At the same time, she seems to be swaying, having to be held upright by a smaller woman.

Punch makes an incoherent yelp, perhaps dismay, maybe elation. But Jo-Jo gives a great roar of recognition. "I know that!" he cries. "That's a Third Eye trance. You don't see them much, any more. But, believe me, if we can just get into her range, we're safe! Start running…" and he breaks into a lope.

Punch runs a few yards, hesitates and looks back. He can plainly see mounted militia and equally plainly, the militia have seen them. Half of the troop are peeling off, coming round the western flank of the house, where Punch had made his way earlier. It's not far enough. Half-a-mile for well-fed, thoroughbred horses versus 100 uphill yards, for four struggling refugees and one of them half-dead in another's arms. Punch can see riders pulling carbines from saddle holsters.

On the rise ahead, the swaying girl is trying to steady herself, while the little, dark-haired one is desperately trying to keep her upright.

"They're almost close enough, Lupa," says Evie through dry lips. "Keep me upright."

"I'm trying, I'm trying! If we get out of this alive, you're going on a diet!"

This is no film. Tee is suddenly and acutely aware that they are in real danger, in an unprecedented situation that is not subject to discussion.

"Do you know what you have to do?" she asks Evie.

"Just keep me upright!"

"I will, I will…"

The little group is closer. The girl in the torn dress keeps circling, running forwards, running back, then towards them again, as if by sheer will-power she was trying to pull them together.

"Tha's-Marie-Gabrielle…" Evie slurs and then begins to shudder. "Shout-to-them-Tee-shout…"

"Come on, come on!" shrieks Tee. "Run!!"

The Militia are at the side of the house but their horses are already foam-flecked. Beneath their hooves the ground is suddenly wet and sticky. They slow, visibly but as they do, one or two riders rise on their stirrups and fire their carbines. One ball hits a flint in the track and sparks fly, ten yards behind the fugitives.

"Just get closer, closer in," pants Jo-Jo, who is beginning to find this track steeper than it looked.

"Fer what?" yells Punch, bitterly regretting the decision to shed his weapons.

"You'll see," yells Jo-Jo and even manages a wild grin.

"Papa, papa, monsieur, monsieur! Vite, vite! Les cavaliers!"

"What's our lass jabberin' about in Froggy?"

"Them!" Jo-Jo throws a nod of his head backwards.

Punch looks round as another carbine is fired. "Out o'range an' firin' wild. Squire's fat lads on 'osses," he says contemptuously. "A'd gi' a gowd guinea fer' t'ave Bess!"

'Everyone,' thinks Jo-Jo, on the verge of hysterical laughter, 'is talking in tongues!'

A second shot ploughs into the roadbed but Punch was right, it is yards short. The horses are still struggling across the boggy ground.

"I have them!" says Evie, "got them, got them! Got them, Tee! They're safe, we're safe!" and she slides down to the grass, to sit laughing hysterically.

Jo-Jo spins round for a final glance. The leading horseman's mount has cleared the sticky ground and is surging towards them, as if released on starter's orders. The rider, no 'squire's fat lad' but a lean, hungry figure in a black and gold jacket, topped by a rakish hat with a feathered plume, rises in his stirrups, draws a sabre in a forwards flourish – and vanishes… as do the gate, the walls and roof of the manor. No peaceful smoke, no wild noise of insurrection.

All that is left is four figures, one still being carried and two young women crouched on the grass, slowly coming together in a group.

The skylarks who witnessed Punch bowled through the Hedge, seemingly so long ago, see him now. He takes slow paces and moves to the front of his little group, whilst Marie-Gabrielle slips back to croon comforting nonsense to her nanny. She leans against the stranger and tucks her arm under his. She glances up, Jo-Jo glances down. Something deep and wonderful in their World, turns over silently. But Punch, whose head was drooping with weariness as he trudged uphill, now begins to straighten, as if he heard a distant music. He stares at the blonde girl, slumped on her hams and sensing that glance, she looks up…

"Our lad," he says awkwardly, stuttering a little. "Yon b'mi boy…" Then, with a great shout, he bellows – "our lass, 'tis our boy!" and the blonde girl comes upright, like a rising sun hailing a miracle and taking a pace forward, gasps – "Pa, sis, is that you?"

The skylarks swirl overhead as the two little groups come together. Punch, Evie and Marie-Gabrielle in one hugging, weeping pile. While Jo-Jo and Tee are left to smile, apologetically over their huddled heads, to one another.

Tee, rarely at a loss, assumes her BIG VOICE – "HELLO, I'M TULIPA AND I'M VERY PLEASED TO MEET YOU"

"I'm Jo-Jo," he replies, holding out as much hand as he can spare from supporting Marie-Claire.

"My best friend Evie, seems very busy with your friends…so, in the meantime, who is the poor, poor lady you are carrying. She looks very… scared and alone."

"This is Marie-Claire," says Jo-Jo. "We've only just met, I'm afraid to say under rather awful circumstances. I'm sure she'll be delighted to meet you when she feels a little better."

"Bonjour, Marie-Claire," booms Tee, searching desperately for her schoolgirl French, "mon nom est Tulipa – comment t'allez vous?"

"Tres bon," says a feeble voice, "enchante."

Tee looks again at the three huggers and decides the situation is beyond her immediate control.

"Jo-Jo," she ventures, "I have a very large car over that hill. It's one of those vehicles that climbs trees and mountains. Do you think we can leave this dear lady in the care of these lunatics, while we go and get it?"

"That is at least a plan," says Jo-Jo, "we've been singularly short of those so far…" and he stoops to lie Marie-Claire on a dry and sunny patch of turf, making certain he has drawn Marie-Gabrielle's attention to the fact.

"BEAVER!!" bellows Tee, relying on BIG VOICE once again: "WE HAVE GONE FOR THE CAR!!"

2

HEADING HOME

The management of the 'Les Trois Vents Boutique Hotel' are equal to the foibles of their most demanding patrons and very rarely does it happen that they will be politely requested to seek alternative accommodation…but it can happen…

"Well, I used to know somewhere," I say. "If it's still there and they remember me."

We drive, or rather Tee does and after more practicing of her circles than the infant Giotto, she says crossly – "this roundabout sucks! Everyone's going the wrong way, except me!"

"It's over there," I say desperately, above the blaring horns, "behind the buddleias and nettles. No surrender, Tee!"

"These cars," Tulipa explains comfortably to her passengers as she takes the decision to drive, as it were, off-piste, "are built to go over rough ground." And all is going well until, with one final, despairing lurch, the Range Rover grinds to a halt, atop a particularly treacherous erratic of concrete. There it sticks, like a child's toy snagged on the shag-pile, at Christmas, all drive-wheels whirling.

"We're here," says Tulipa, confidently. "Everybody out and form search parties. We're looking for what, precisely, Beaver?"

"Squat, ugly, wood buildings with neon lighting and a rather nice smell of cooking…"

"Eva, baby! Where have you been?!"

Here I am with my motley crew. Whatever I was expecting it was not a happy yelp from a wheelchair-bound Andrew, marooned more or less, in the centre of the room, surrounded by empty tables. I grin and wave but then have to turn to field – "Oh, Eva!" from an exhausted and harassed-looking Kirsty. I'd seen the 'last-legs' Fiat outside and now it seems they are both barely alive.

"Ho! Eva!" – from Carl, unchanged, behind the grill and the most solid body in the room.

The five or so customers barely raise their heads.

"Oh guys," I cry, "what on earth's happening?" Then I remember – as if I could forget and no more would I want to – "guys, guys, … this is my family. I promise you, they're all lovely. We had nowhere to go, until I thought of here and then I thought it would be a bit of a liberty.

"Whoa, I'm so confused! How many of you can I kiss at once? But come on here guys, you've got to tell me what's happening – what's gone wrong!"

"Kisses are for me first!" shouts Andrew, "I'm the one on the wheelchair! I get everything first!"

So I do.

Then Kirsty, who weeps a bit on my shoulder and wants to cling on.

Back of the counter to Carl. "Hey, Carl, remember me, a koala bear on your back, that night?"

"Never forget it, honey," he shouts cheerfully, flipping an egg. Two big soft boobies hugging my back and me as gay as a Maypole. What a waste of a journey!"

"She nearly turned you, boy!" mocks Andrew.

"In your dreams, big man…you're the only one for me."

This is information overload, right there – and everywhere else. Give me time, I need to catch-up, give me some hints, help me out here!

I turn to my guys, open my hands, semaphoring – 'go on, people, you know how!'

Which means that within two minutes, Marie-Gabrielle is scurrying round Andrew's chair, introducing him to -"Papa, fresh and bloody still, from Blenheim. Imagine, a national hero!" Then adding, sotto voce – "I know about the missing 300 years but Papa hasn't caught up with that just yet."

Tee, bless her tiny hands and giant heart, is helping Kirsty cash-up a lean night and making huge, "no, really!!" sounds, interspersed with – "you poor thing! But your mama will get better, yes?" Helping her with her coat … "don't worry, we are here now!"

Jo-Jo, still the quiet man, is helping Marie-Claire to a table, holding both her hands and somehow conjuring a tissane of lime leaves, not by magic but by Carl. Then he listens very seriously to her lamentations, only releasing her hand to allow her to sip her tea.

The customers, perhaps they feel unwanted, leave one by one.

Thank God.

This is some sort of Heaven…albeit, possibly on a handcart to the other place.

I rush madly round everyone again, kissing wildly. Even Carl, who pretends to hide, can't escape. "I am half a boy!" I pant, in hot pursuit, "hold still!"

"But Kirsty, Kirsty, what's wrong sweetie?"

"Oh things are not good, Eva. Neil's got to that awkward age all of a sudden. Mum's had a stroke, not as bad as poor old Andrew's but it's going to take time. I'm nearly out of my head with worry. That wreck of a car's got something wrong. Carl's mate will fix it but it still costs money. This place has fallen apart since Andrew… well, we were closed for three months and that drove everyone away. Penny and Lise had to go – no tricks, no waitressing."

All I could do was to hug her, whilst making extravagant promises that everything would be all right now.

"Why don't you go home and just come in tomorrow when you feel up to it? We'll finish up here and open up. I'm sure I know how… if Carl gives me some nods in the right direction."

"Are you sure? I hate leaving Andrew but I feel awful leaving mum on her own…"

"Of course I'm sure…"

Sure? Sure…what was I sure about? Where was Lupa?

Here, with Andrew and she is saying in her lady-like voice – "of course, we were all staying in my suite at the 'Les Trois Vents' but there was a minor disagreement…about open fires in one of the rooms…" and she giggles, helplessly.

He roars with laughter and says – "you're all welcome to stay. This place has gone to Hell and now it needs all the demons it can get!"

Jo-Jo interrupts us – "Marie-Claire simply has to lie down and I really think she needs a doctor."

"What time is it?" says Andrew. "Ah, a mere 9.30. Phone my man, Frank. He'll come. On my bill. Just ask Carl to set the wheels in motion. Poor old girl, what's the problem?"

"Put simply," says Jo-Jo, "she's been beaten and raped. But I think the damage is to her soul, her self-worth, rather than anything purely physical."

"Oh Christ," says Andrew, propelling himself to her side, where she sits sobbing quietly, Marie-Gabrielle gently stroking her hair. "Whatever it takes," he murmurs, staring at her beleaguered face with compassion.

Jo-Jo returns and clasps her hands again. "He's on his way," he tells the little group.

Meanwhile, Punch is examining the place minutely, trying to make sense of it all, I think.

"Pa," I ask, "are you ok?"

"A's awl reet, son. 'Tis just thet theer's bin some changes goin' on, since a' bin in mi' wood. A's a spot o' catchin' up to do. A'll b' awl reet, boy – just gimme a squeeze, now an' then, t'b' sure we's both 'ere, like. An' while we's at it, son, – weer's yon gal o'mine?"

"Just over there, Pa. It's all to do with Marie-Claire and sis' is trying to keep everything calm until the doctor can get here."

"Poor ol' gal's 'ad t'worst o' it," says Punch. "Men's evil, it allus falls on't' women. A' aims to protect 'er from thet, from hereon in. No more o'thet!"

I look around for Tee and can't find her. Finally I run her to ground outside, sharing a cigarette with Carl and knowledgeably discussing motorbikes.

Later, much later, in bed, she explains to me – "Husband Dear, is motorbike mad – as in he has about 150!" We spend a bit of silent time together, me vaguely pondering how anyone has 150 of anything that size. Then I can't bear the suspense, the not-knowing, any longer.

"Tee," I implore, "this is all right, isn't it? What I've dragged you into? Please say it is. I didn't realise how much I loved this crowd until we got here. And suddenly we all seem such a perfect fit. But I promise, I love you more."

She gives me a huge kiss and all my worries flow out of my toes.

"I was actually just thinking how happy I feel. You see, it's family and Indians adore family. I haven't got one. It's so funny really! You and I went out, just for a walk and found half a family. Then you brought us here and we found all its missing bits! It's one great, big family – all ready-made. I love it!"

"But Tee, it's going to be chaos, not elegant touring."

"I like chaos and I'm really good at causing it."

"Don't go, Tee. I couldn't bear it."

"Not going anywhere, Beaver, promise. You, me and the rest of this crazy gang against the world."

3

'SIFT THE INGREDIENTS TOGETHER...'

We'll never really know why and how we all washed up here. Marie-Gabrielle believes it's all to her credit – but that's just Marie-Gabrielle and you never know if she's serious or not. There was a hell of a lot to sort out and we all came at it in our own ways, over weeks that turned into months. We had early starts, late finishes, no pay but free food, a lot of fun. We tried to patch one-another up, in our various ways...

...JJ is sipping tea, out the back with Andrew, who's fallen asleep in his chair...

'I'm not Jo-Jo anymore,' he thinks. 'My friends have re-christened me JJ. Gives me a sort of warm feeling, that they care enough to bother and it's also odd, because I've had those O's for a long time.

'I've tried to explain to them why I'm tormented by questions but no-one can really grasp it. Here I am, a 4000-year-old man, in the body of a late 40-year-old and I haven't aged, backwards or forwards, for as long as I can remember, which isn't very far – about 40 years, in fact.

'Where do I come from? Oddly enough a planet called Earth but pretty obviously not this one. I can't help but think, though, that there's a connection. I feel as if I might have started here, once, but up on Earth II – which is what I shall call it – our memories have been cleaned out and we run by endlessly reiterating some solitary theme that was established in our past. Doesn't make much sense, does it? But that's all that my self-interrogation has produced. Nothing, really.

'I was talking to Carl about his mum and dad, who died when he was small, leaving him to be brought up by his grandparents. Did he remember his parents? "Not really, JJ, they're sort of shadows, with bits I've bolted on from what gran and grandad told me." That's what my memory is like, a mass of shadows surrounding a few years of my ever-repeating present.

'Now that was nice, Marie-Gabrielle just came out with freshly-made scones for us both. She gave Andrew a soft peck on the cheek but he didn't wake-up.

'Then she danced over to me – she dances everywhere, just like little kids skip everywhere – and I got two scones and a peck on the cheek. I held her hand, to stop her dancing away and asked – "Marie, what's going on? Why do I feel that everything is so 'unknowable' at present, that everything is questions and no answers?"

"It's only questions if you want it to be, JJ," she answers lightly. "One day, I just rolled out of my book. I didn't want to be ink on paper – and certainly not that sort! Here I am, with a papa and a brother – even if he has got the biggest boobs I've ever seen! – and lots of friends and adventures. I find it all wonderful and I don't care how it happened, or why. You shouldn't fret so. We all love you and all you have to do is love us back. It's really easy, I promise."

"Marie," I said, "I saw those books being scraped clean in the library and that was one thing. But on my planet, I feel that we, the people, are being scraped clean, not books, and that's something else. I've been scraped down to a disgruntled, questioning misanthrope and accommodated as such. Why would the 'Core' do that? Why would it help me sharpen myself to that questioning, grumpy point? Doesn't that bear thinking about?"

"Ways of thinking, JJ, whys of thinking... You have to beware of thinking. It's insidious. If you don't take care, thinking does you, rather than you doing it. Thinking should be a tool, not an end in itself. Not all thinking deserves a gold star.

"I'm a girl made of pigment. I could get very anxious about that. I used to and I tried my best to escape my origins. But nothing I did, or anyone else did mattered a fig in the end. Things came together because they did and we're all very joyous because that suited us. But it would be a big mistake to assume it was necessarily about us. We were, we are, just cogs in a great big devising and whatever has happened to you, or me, or Marie-Claire was all to do with a much bigger whole that's still unwinding, influencing other things. Amazingly the future doesn't unwind to accommodate us. We pretend it does. We'd like to think it did, but it doesn't.

"Imagine a really, really vast mechanical machine, something as big as a planet and made of tiny, tiny cogs and springs, escapements and what have you. Somewhere in the middle is a cog asking 'why did this happen to me?' and a cog a few miles away is thinking 'this happened because of me.' But all the time, for all of their lives, both of them were just back-up, in case, thousands of miles away, something went wrong and they were suddenly required. It's pointless to ask deep questions, or think deep thoughts, about personal events.

"Be happy, grow more memories, if you feel you're short of some, be fond of your Rabbit, Moss and Shade. Refuse to be sharpened, like a pencil, by your thinking. You're so much more than grudging questions."

'I couldn't really follow her but I made an effort. "You're a miracle, Marie. Love you. Don't worry about the scones going cold. I'll eat them if Andrew doesn't wake up."

"Don't you dare!" and with a playful slap, she danced away.

'I went back to my brooding. "Don't ask why, just be!" – the best advice in the world and the most useless to someone like me. Something, something in or beyond the Core, has an interest in me. It has maintained me in prime physical condition and allowed me to roll up here, one more oddball on an island of weirdos. Why? Why the new set of parameters? Why are we all the way we are and why are we here?

'Take poor old Evie, a son, a brother, a lover and a beautiful woman, to boot. Plumbed "incorrectly" but working just fine. What's all that about? Why is she condemned to fret about Atonement, some Delphic dream wished on her by morphine? It's nearly destroyed her. It seems that, contrary to all common-sense, hot and cold, good and bad can be channelled through one tap – but the complexity of that, the thinking behind it – or, far worse, the lack of thinking – unnerves me. She believes her life is about one set of things but the portion she is destined to play in the unfolding of the cosmos, may be about quite other matters. Which is exactly what Marie was saying. Stuff-personal and stuff-primordial becomes tangled together in space and time, then you mistake one for the other.

'If, like Marie, you start every day from where you are and go forwards, everything is just fine. But I want to ask Marie – what if Punch hadn't turned up, if I hadn't arrived, if poor, dear, sweet Marie-Claire had been murdered in front of you, what then?

'Are those questions just vindictive, because they didn't happen? Some things do end badly, Marie. What of those things? Why can't we speak of them usefully?'

Andrew, were he to wake up with a start, might reply – "Because the present has no traction in the past, JJ. I was a seemingly healthy guy on the Monday. I had a partner who, dare I say it, loved me. I absolutely worshipped him, even if he is a kid of 32 and I'm an ancient of 48. Then, you better believe it, on Tuesday I was leaving here behind blue-flashing lights, an old man of 148.

"And, damn me, my partner still loved me, loves me. What does that do? Fortifies me, upsets me? It does a lot of things. It changes history. I know what this place was, look at it now! Down the pan, more of a nursing home than a tranny caff."

'I hate sympathy but my God, I need it. Or, if not sympathy, someone to talk to who didn't know me before, has no memories from the past. That why I've come to love the old man so much. Old Man Punch. Together, the two of us tried to calculate it once and worked out that he's actually 47, which makes him younger than me if you don't allow him his +300. But he looks 147. Wood magic, Earth Magic, whatever it was that harboured him in that wood, pickled him in walnut juice. He looks like a gnarled old root, something that's been growing for generations.

'Day One, we had to find him some pants! That kilt he'd made was one of the scariest things I've ever seen. I've got it, folded away in a secret place. He wanted to throw it. No way, not on my watch, not in my bins. That thing is serious voodoo. Never know when we might need it again!

'For some reason he seems to have taken to me, which I count as one hell of an honour. He drags a chair over to my wheelie, parks himself alongside, grabs this useless right hand between both of his and just sits smiling at me, or over my shoulder, or following the antics of his two kids, with such liquid love in his eyes, I just feel like weeping – tears of joy and celebration at the miracles in life.

'Ye gods, how he loves them. 'My boy, my girl,' he'll whisper under his breath, if they happen by together…Marie doing that dance step she does everywhere, Beaver sporting the crazy new hair she's got. It's a sort of double Mohican, black on one side and tall but mid-blue on the other and shorter. It's shaved high on the neck but not on the sides, those taper into long bangs hanging down her cheeks. Once you're over the shock of the blonde who left here, one morning and came back like that mid-afternoon, it looks pretty good.

'Tee took her off to this crazy salon she'd found on one of her expeditions and this is what happened – the double Mohican and the skinhead. Yep, Tee had the lot off, simply acres of fabulous, silky, long black hair, all carefully saved and pinned in a box. She's going to grow it three more times, then plans to have it mounted together with a huge silver moon and sun face she's commissioned from a jeweller. It's meant to be a symbol of her mystical union with Evie, a personal fetish.

'Oh, don't ask me but I like new, crazy things and this is bat-shit crazy. Carl went totally rogue when she came back like that. Gay he may be but how he loved her hair. He'd spend half-an-hour brushing it, arranging it, before appealing to me – "Look, Andy, isn't she the picture of a princess?!" And Tee would say, in her best haughty voice – "That's because I am a princess, you peasant!"

'Anyway, he was so mad after she had it cut, that he chased her all around the estate, threatening 'heaven-knows-what' when he caught her. They were like a pair of tweenies, brother and sister. She was squealing in mock terror but eventually, she let him catch her – because, boy, she's fast – and he carried her home, piggy-back. Then he dropped her in the Beaver's lap and said – "All yours!" Evie said – "I tried to stop her but you know what she's like."

'I knew she'd had a secret plan, which I proceeded to leak. "She was going to save you a great big plait, in a little silver mount, as a thank-you for all the brushing. Now you feel a prat, don't you!"

'Tee, doubled up on Beaver's lap, sticks out her tongue at Carl and says – "see-ee-eeee!! Who says I didn't care!"

'Talking of presents, I've got one for the old guy. Should be here by the end of the week. It's a genuine, re-proofed, India pattern Brown Bess. He'd been telling me all about her, how her last shot had been her best, how he'd had to leave her behind on the stable floor and how she probably went up in flames. There were tears in his eyes. It's costing a fortune but then I'm lucky, I've got one and Carl thinks it's a cool, sweet idea.

'So, here we sit together, as if we'd been planted to model an Edwardian kissing couch, holding hands. His is as solid as a river stone, mine as slack as marzipan. What a weird pair we make and I guess I should just leave it at that. In reality, my life is in ruin and all I have are anxieties…but I'll take a leaf from Marie-Gabrielle's book, refuse to play that game and start from here.'

Carl is watching Marie-Gabrielle do one of her dances through the kitchen. She gives him a wicked smirk and pretends to steal a cake, then swirls away with him in pretend pursuit.

'Do you know,' he thinks, 'she could steal anything of mine – except Andrew – and I'd count myself blessed. She could even nick the bike and that's saying something. Can't really see her on it, though. She should be riding one of those push-along rabbits, or bears, while wearing a kid's party dress and with a ribbon in her hair. That's how she makes me feel, innocent and about six, or seven years old. She's very tiny, too. Tee is small but Marie is petite – the word was invented for her alone. Despite which, she's stacked. That makes two of them, Marie and Evie, outright winners of the bosoms of the year award.

'So glad to see Eva again. I didn't think I was that bothered. Then I found Kirsty in tears, one day and got it out of her that she was missing Evie, like missing a big sister. I fell to thinking…do you know, I feel much the same! Yet she's younger than both of us. It's not even as if she was around that much but when she went there was this huge hole. Andy and I talked about it, a pair of gays sad about a missing chick. Odd but not that odd, I suppose. Plenty gays love having women around. We're human first, before the sex, Anyway, if we needed an excuse, Eva was half-a-boy. That made me really sad for her. She only got to play boy with girls, so I don't know how she felt about the boy/boy thing. Cool, certainly but whether she hooked up to it, or not, I dunno. Why am I fixating on bedroom rubbish?

'Then Andy went down with a thump and that floored me. God, he fought me off like a man battling an octopus… "Go! Don't waste your life here…you're a young guy don't tie yourself to a cripple…I don't need you, I've got money, I can buy nurses… he gave it the whole nine yards. I just kept flipping him the finger and eventually, he cottoned on. That's when he started crying and I honestly didn't know one human being could hold that many tears. He just cried, silently, for days – or it seemed like days. It was as if he was melting, from frozen.

'It was one of those nights that finished Kirsty. Neil had been giving her grief, for weeks, like teenage brats do. While fielding that she was trying to sort out carers for her mum. Next thing to explode in her life, her 'big rock,' Andy, falls down. Add to that, her junk-heap car starts playing-up. All her walls fell in. When Andy started weeping on her, one night, she started weeping back. I needed a mop and bucket that evening.

'With one thing and another, we had to shut up shop. Kirsty was hanging by a thread.

Lise and Penny saw the bedroom work was drying up, along with any waitressing, so they moved up to Town. I reckon they're too embarrassed to come back – not that anyone holds a grudge. They were working girls without work, why wouldn't they skip? Why should they hang themselves out to dry? Crazy thing is, we now find out poor old Eva was working as an unpaid 'wife' on a slow boat to China, or wherever, all because of some crazy mantra she has ruining her life. And here were we, all thinking she'd just forgotten us.

'At least she met Tee. Tee is full-on amazing. She's a force of nature. She even knows about bikes. In fact, she reckons she can get me an old wreck of a Villiers, because her other half, actually I mean her husband, because Evie's her other half, is desperate for some Norton spares I can lay my hands on.

'Makes me happy to see how Punch has kind of adopted Andy. He sits down and picks his hand up in a very particular sort of way. Then he starts transfusing him with essence of ancient tree root. Tree roots are what he reminds us both of. I can just imagine him at night, resting in the forest with all the other trees, his toes shooting roots down through soil, clay and quartz, soaking up some essence we know nothing about. He seems so old and not really in years, something deeper. He still carries that faint smell of woodsmoke, despite all Marie-Claire's scrubbing.

'If I was still at art school, I'd try and find a big old root ball…maybe I could find one where contractors are digging out a road and have felled a bunch of old trees? Hose out the clay and rocks, or a lot of them, leave the interesting ones. Then start cutting in the places where I can see faces are already peeping out. Eventually I bet the whole gang of us would be there, even Tee's hair, flowing along some long vein…Lord, but I will make her pay for that! Though, if she's giving me a plait of my own, maybe I'll let her live just a bit longer, at least until she's given it me.'

'Owdin' on t'Andrew's hand? A' thinks as it 'elps us both. When e's awake, we talks but 'e sleeps a lot, same as a' do, it seems. But grappling 'ands, 'tis kinda like talkin' wi'out words.

'A' feels that bad 'bout losin' owd Jolyon's book. Ishmael and the Reverend's work, all them lil' flutes e'd carved t'enchant t'people o' t' lil' world. A' thinks missen melancholy 'bout that, which is 'alf why a' sits wi' Andrew. A' thinks we's both carryin' guilt. See oursen' as murderers. God knows it, A's killed plenty but t'only one I regrets is Jolyon. T' b' fair, thet weren't me anyways, thet were Caleb, firin' of thet damned rusty owd piece we towed about wi' us. Andrew, he reckons as 'e 'as 'is brother on 'is conscience. An' fer both on us, ther' ain't no reasonin' wi' conscience.

'Damn it though, thet book should ne'er a' bin lost and not by one who'd learnt from it, bin led by it t'find 'is boy an' 'is lass.

'A' bin too 'shamed t'tell anyone other than our Marie. She wonders if she cud git Earth Magic t'trace it. It were thet 'as unravelled 'er from them unseemly pages 'as she were trappit in. She dunno but she says she'll gi' it a go, once she gits a idee' 'ow t'proceed.

'A' don' like t'ask t' boy. E's got thet many problems o' 'is own. A' just tries t'gi' 'im love, like a' does wi' Andrew, but different.

'Funny, 'ent it…say "love" t'me any time this last 40 year an' a'd 'ave laughed in thy face. Now a' sees 'tis t'only portion o'us worth 'avin.

'Boy's found 'isself one fine woman in yon Tulipa. A' wonders if 'e's thet bit shy o' tellin' 'er 'ow 'e feels? Mebbe, mebbe not. She's a real Princess but 'tis like she ne'er knowed just 'ow t'shine 'til now. 'Tis a fact, she's startin' t'shine, from t'inside out, wi' a sort o' Princess light – whate'er thet mebbe. A's talkin' rubbish! Tae much gud food be addlin' mi' brains!

'Fact is, a's mi' own love affair tae fret o'er. Yon Marie-Claire, 'er be thet much better now. Yon doctor left 'er wi' lil' pills 'n creams but she's still terrible shook up 'n' shy. So, t'other day, a 'as a lil' ceremony like. A' gi'es 'er 'er clothes back, them thet she'd shed in't wood. A' got our Marie fer t'do translating. "Just t'tell 'ere 'ow a'd found 'em, washed 'em, pressed 'em flat wi' a smooth stone, packed 'em up wi' some sweet smelling' 'erbs a'd found and then wrapped up all togethers." A 'ent sure 'ow all thet went, fer she goes a bit pink, then a bit pale, an' our Marie 'as some fast Froggy fer t'be speakin. After a'wiles she gi'es me a bit o'a nod, 'n' a curtsey. A' says t'our girl, "tell 'er a' likes 'er. A 'ent no fancy Lord, a's as common as muck on shoes but a' does like 'er, proper like." Then they both trot off, like a pair o'geese an' a'm left t'wonder 'n' worrit 'ow thet went.

'T'weer in't' evenin,' a's a sittin' wi' Andrew an' up she come an' presents mi' wi' a lil' pie she's med, wi' 'er own 'ands, reet theer in Carl's kitchin.' So up a' gits, does mi' bobs 'n' blushes 'n' off she do scuttle, leavin' mi' stannin' theer like some lovesick bullock. Anyways, t'judge b'Drew's gigglin' a' reckons a's theers reason fer 'ope in thet department.

'Then theer's this business wi' time. A's not in't same place as a' was afore a' gits blowed through yon 'edge. Then theer's t'business o't' 'Edge…powerful strange stuff. Marie sez best not t'think on it. Easy t'overcook yer' brains, them as yer might 'ave. Tek' poor owd JJ 'e be fair torturin' 'imself wi' worritin 'bout things 'e canna fix.

'Yet, a' as t'sort thet theer book out, afor long. Willy-nilly, b'wha' may, 'tis weighin' on me sorrowful 'ard.'

'Petite Mademoiselle has somehow saved us. Also she tells us all she has found her papa. Yet the good Monsieur Punch is not her papa. This I know, for was I not there? Her mama and papa are dead, yet this little story delights her so and anything that makes petite mademoiselle happy, makes me happy, too. Also, Monsieur Punch is a good man and one who saved my life. When all was lost, it was he who held me aloft until the children could cut that evil rope. For all that he cursed and killed, there was great kindness in his eyes. If he had not been there, assuredly I should be dead. That day is a great confusion to my head and to even think of it makes me shake with shame and sickness. I owe so much, to so many. To Monsieur Jo-Jo, who carried me from that field of killing, to Monsieur Andrew who sent for his own personal physician to attend me, to the little children I shall never see again.

'To Monsieur Punch, however, I owe more than I can repay. Throughout that terrible day he had carried on his back, the clothes that were ripped from my back by those thieves, torturers and murderers. These he had cleaned and pressed with a stone he had sought from the river. How can he have done this, living as he was, in the depths of a wood? What kind and gentle nature attends such an act?

'And now, I think, he finds himself bemused, for he sits all day with poor, invalid Monsieur Andrew. I think he senses that they have both lost their lives, in different ways. Both have lost their meaning, as it were, for they have lost control. Control is what men are born to, raised for, exercised in and contracted to. It is a cruelty we women wish upon them for, once, we led and know what a perilous lonely place it is. Better by far to follow, than to lead. The followers can smooth the path the leaders gouge. We women place flowers, cloths, embroideries in the houses that men raise for us. Then, eating our food from the table they made, they tell us we have made a home and forget that they built it. It is not the whole story but it is a part of it.

'This is a strange world we have been conjured to and I do not understand it. Yet, if I can make this funny place a home, if I can make Monsieur Punch and Monsieur Andrew happy, I shall be happy, too. If petite Marie skips about, I have nothing to fear.

'Then there is the Princesse Tulipa – who could not feel happy to see her swooping comings and goings? Her heart is as warm as a hearthstone and she is as lively as the cricket that alighted on it. Yet, God in His Heaven, now she has cut all her hair off, her hair that Monsieur Carl would spend an hour brushing! And he would say – "Now, does not she shine like a Princess?"

'Now she looks more like a boy than does her boy-friend Monsieur Eva. Now, I know that this is a strange world we are conjured to, have I not just said this, but Monsieur Evie has the biggest bosom I have seen on a young person and these are usually found on girls. But Princess Tee, Mademoiselle Marie and Monsieur Punch are quite certain that she is a boy! Petite Mademoiselle says, just to shock me: "… and I have seen the evidence, maman!" Shock me! The births and deaths that I have attended…including my own, if it were not for brave Monsieur Punch.

'Princess Tee – hee, hee! That's me! Someone's let me out of my box and I'm never going back in. I was born to raise hell here! I love everything – I even love the rain, because it makes everybody miserable, so I can rush around cheering them all up. Then I get puffed and so they all fuss over me! What fun!

'Carl, the sweetie, used to fuss over my hair. He'd spend hours brushing it and it did make me happy. We all love being groomed by our friends. The excellent Mr Darwin said it's like being a monkey again and having your nits combed away. But the hair had to go. I had a plan and nothing holds up one of my plans.

'I think I may be a supercharged bumble-bee, or an atomic mole. The terrifying, terrible Mole-Bee! Buzz-burrow-buzz-burrow, burrow, buzz, buzz…phew! Exhausting. I think Carl might just have forgiven me for the hair thing, because he says he can get my car down. It's still stuck up in the air and it looks really sad. Also, it's a bit of a waste.

'He knows some people who specialise in getting trains back on the tracks, when they've fallen off. They have EQUIPMENT, of a very special sort. They don't want paying, what they want is a slap-up Indian curry cooked for them by a real-life Indian Princess. That is such awful racial stereotyping, I don't know where to start complaining. But Carl says they're very decent, simple souls who don't know about racial stereotyping and are just terribly excited by the idea of a genuine Princess cooking a curry.

'I have, very patiently, explained to him that I've never cooked a thing in my life. That I'm a Princess and Princesses don't cook. Also I'm a mole-bee and mole-bees don't cook, either. But he was totally unimpressed and said – "do you want your car, back or not?"

'I said, very humbly, "yes please." But I have another plan. This is going to be a cannabis curry, with added chilli – in a form I shall REVEAL LATER. The hairdresser, after he'd 'done' Evie and I, must have thought we were kindred spirits, for he said that if we ever needed 'fixing-up' with some 'gear,' he was the man to see. So I shall be seeing him, very soon, as well as taking a trip to the supermarket for a couple of dozen curries. I promise, this will be an EVENT!

'Once I get my car back there's the question of Punch's wood to be explored – if we ever get any time off from cleaning, cooking and waitressing. I've told the Beaver that we have to go back but for some reason, he's got cold flippers – or whatever beavers use to paddle with. I've explained it's all going to be very simple and easy. Apparently the Manor was rebuilt about a quarter of a mile away, a couple of hundred years later. A colony of artists lived there on some sort of tontine arrangement and the last one standing gifted the place to the 'Heart of England Foundation.' The woodland, that's Punch's woodland, is part of the gift and there are walks, official walks, that go sort of round it but not into it. Too swampy, or something and the trees are unsafe, whatever. Anyway, I don't do rules, so we can go and investigate for FREE if I join the Foundation as Princess Tulipa and Mr Beaver. I think it would be fantastic having little cards with those names on. Also, I bet there's wild magic on other Foundation sites, so I'm up for it. Beaver just says – "my third eye says NO." He's being very macho about it.

'My fault, I've been turning him into a boy while I have a daft, frou-frou, dangereuse five minutes, investigating my inner Marie-Gabrielle. She doesn't have an inner-boy. I told her so the other day and she got very upset about it. As a result, she mascara-ed a moustache on for the rest of the day. The customers loved it. "Customers?" you ask. Oh yes, and with a vengeance. The Beaver will explain, when I've finished my chapter.

In the meantime, we're begging Kirsty to come back. Andrew says he'll sub her a new car, so the Fiat can die in peace. But I think Kirsty's burnt-out and I'm only just getting going.

'Apart from all this fun stuff, there are serious topics on the agenda. Why is JJ 4000 years old and how did he get here? Why is Marie-Gabrielle seven when she should be 21, at least! (That's just me being catty.) Why has Beavie got a Third Eye and I haven't? Also, why won't he let me try the ring out? I'd be double-super responsible with it. But he says I've gone a bit crazy since flying and thinks I might crash my astral body. I've never crashed anything! Well, there is the little matter of the car but that's just because the concrete thingy got in the way. Anyway, crashing your astral body? What a lame excuse! That's why I had my hair cut off. If he can have a magical talisman, so can I. Then we'll have two, an old one and a new one. Even talismans – talismen? – have to start somewhere. I'm working on its myth at the moment…it starts with this tantric Indian Princess who…I don't know what, really…anyway, she did some tasty stuff.

'What on earth has happened to me? I used to be a bit spiteful, hurtful and wary. The Beaver gnawed through all that. Then I embarrassed him six ways for Sunday on the plane and we nearly got arrested and nothing's been quite the same since. I think it's oxygen starvation and altitude that did it. Everybody else seemed OK, but I'm convinced that's what it was. It doesn't show much sign of wearing off, though.

'Oh, memo to self! Get that bike shipped over for Carl and get those parts shipped out to Husband Dear, who really is a dear husband and one whom I hope never to see again, in the nicest possible way. I'm sure he feels exactly the same way about me, too.

'I'm exhausted! I yammer on so much, I tire myself!

'Then with everyone seeming to acquire mamas and papas, as if was Special Offer Week on them, Carl and I got to feeling a bit left out, both of us having been brought up by nanas and grandads. So we took ourselves off to ask Marie-Claire if she'd be an honorary mama to us both. (My school French broke-down and we had to send out a 999 call for Marie-Gabrielle to get the point across.) I don't know what she asked her, because it seemed to take ages but eventually she said "yes" and we both instantly felt better for it. As Carl said – "if we graze our knees, it's good to know where to go for a plaster…"

'Funny things, groups, they have a life of their own. You can feel them consolidating themselves, if they decide they want to come alive. They're not like formal clubs, or tribes, they're living things in their own right and they have techniques all their own. For a start, they're elastic. JJ is "in" our group, whether he likes it or not and the fact is, he does like it, despite not being an "in" sort of person. But the group won't let him be "out" – it needs him "in." Also, Andrew is de facto leader, however crippled he may be. For starters, it's his place and more importantly, he's the only one who could be described as "a responsible adult." At the same time, the leadership is a bit like a crown on a round table. You pick it up and put it on, or people put it on you, according to what's going on.

'You'll have to excuse, I'm about to get ahead of events but I'm allowed, because I'm a Princess and I've probably let loads of cats out of their bags already.

'Back to JJ – he should be leader, if age counts for anything but he says his Rabbit would make a better job of it. He's taken to cooking and for 4000 years, he hasn't. So that's a turn up for the books. His speciality, it seems, is apple pie. Every day he makes two huge apple pie bakes, with oceans of yukky custard – much to Beaver's delight. Being a Princess, I have to have cream. The thing is, people come for miles for it. My theory is that he adds a secret ingredient from his Planet Zog and we'll all become slaves to the Apple Pie God. The whole thing has been a cunning plot!

'JJ wants to talk seriously about things – the situation on his planet, parallels with and dissimilarities from life here. But no-one wants to. How can you discuss something you know absolutely nothing about? (Easily, I do it all the time!) But this is different. It's so outside everybody's experience of what counts as possible, that there's actually nothing to be said. So, JJ comes from another planet, Punch and the two Maries got whirled across 300 years by Beaver's magical Third Eye and MG made herself real because she was fed-up with being vulgar graffiti. Either everybody's telling terrible stories, or that's the truth as far as we can understand it. Nothing more to be said, you find you simply dry up if you try to rationalise it. It isn't rational – but we're all here.

'Marie-Gabrielle probably knows more about it than anybody else but she absolutely refuses to discuss any of it. "Live now!" she says and puts a tiny fingertip on the table… "from this point…" stabs the finger, "this way," drags her finger forwards. "Never backwards, never sideways, only forwards…" That's actually great wisdom but it's too simple for JJ. He wants to understand mechanisms, motives – those particularly – and then chew them over.

'Just once, Marie gave in. She got what ranks as cross, by her standards. "You still don't get it, do you? Listen carefully – the cosmos is winding itself in, even if it is travelling outwards. It's winding itself backwards, if you like, that's called entropy. Life is winding itself out, it's going forwards, or it's trying to. The two are in conflict. Only one can win. Life is a parasite. We are parasitic upon the cosmos. We oppose its natural direction. Conflict is the key and no right thinking person wants it to be. All you can do is to be a part of it. Everything else you can discount. Some of it's fun, some of it isn't. I only learned this recently." Then she danced off, singing and everyone who'd heard sat around looking stunned. After that, if anyone so much as mentioned metaphysics, she ran away.

'Poor Beavie got very upset that night: "Where does that leave redemption and atonement, Tee?"

'I tried my best – "Buggered if I know."

'And she hit me with the pillow…'

4
END OF THE ROAD

Beaver was thinking that she'd come round in a great spiral – 'like the ones Harold painted into my portrait.

'Poor Harold is dead. He made a mint when my picture sold and as usual, Andrew put it all in the bank for him. Kirsty told me that Harold went crazy, even by his standards, when he found out. He raged into the caff, started throwing things, breaking stuff and then began smashing up cars, outside. Andy cracked. He picked him up by the collar, carried him to the till, opened it up and stuffed £200 in his pockets. Then he took him outside, gave him a shove down the road and told him never to come back. "Contact me via solicitors only. They write to me over your signature, I release your money to them. Now go and don't come back." It never got to that, though.

'Harold took the bus to town and went to Soho. That had changed a bit in 40 years. He got paralytically drunk and threw up in some bar he'd crept into. The bouncers bounced him and he staggered off into the night. Two days later the refuse cleaners found him, cut to shreds in one of those street bottle banks. Cold, dead and a feast for rats. That was all Kirsty knew.

'Andy filled in some blanks. Pathologists couldn't decide if it had been the cirrhosis, a fall, or a punch that had opened up his liver. Everything conspiring together was the best guess. Either way, booze had killed him – the kid with the pistol on the Great North Road. Of course, he had no Will that dealt with his estate. It turned out that no-one knew that much about him. The funeral was scratch, in the sense that only the diner crew and a girl from the Gallery turned up. All she really wanted was to find out if there were any paintings or drawings in the studio. Andy had said "No, there weren't" and "No, she wasn't free to look."

'He had had no idea what was there. Going through all that crap, he told me, was the saddest thing he'd ever done. The only memorable thing he'd found was a tiny A5 book of pen sketches, not energies but of the diner crew – Andy, Carl, Penny, Lise and "one of you, Evie." He got Carl to show me and they are sad little bits of genius. Every one of us is laid bare. I was really ashamed at how lost I looked but at least I looked gentle. After seeing them, all I could think was what a tragedy he wasn't here to draw Punch, Tee, our two Maries and JJ.

'Oh, I wished he could have drawn Tee. He'd have adored her and he so needed things and people to love. I would have been able to show him my ring and maybe he would have understood, being a familiar of energies and the like. Why do we betray ourselves, when being true would be so easy?

'It was only a few weeks later that Andy came unstuck. He'd gone to the loo and didn't come back. After a bunch of wisecracks, Kirsty and Carl got anxious and went out on a recce. There he was, one monumental stroke and then a series of mini-strokes that just shut him down, one centre after another. All he was left with was the ability to think and speak. A bit of neck and left shoulder movement, a hint that life was flickering on and off in his left hand and arm. As he put it – "takes me to be right-handed."

'The crew tried to carry the place but the life had gone out of everything. How could they care for Andy, (he had no family left) and deal with up to 400 covers a day? So, saying it was a temporary move, they shut up shop. Andy appointed Carl as his attorney – whereby hangs the story of how we come to have more living vans out the back than we used to.

'No-one had quite realised how much this place was Andy's life – the crew and the diner. He was a very reserved guy, affable to one and all but only sharing hopes and fears with Carl and Kirsty. To understand him, you had to look at what he'd done. He'd saved Harold from a dozen early graves and he'd made sure that Penny and Lise had safe places to work. He'd built himself a family and now it had taken a direct hit. Kirsty's domestic situation couldn't be squared with working and with the caff shut down, Penny and Lise couldn't afford the luxury of sticking around.

'You might have thought that was it but Andy fixated on a plan to re-build. He asked Carl to source some static vans, have some services plumbed in, pour a few concrete pads and make the place a secret little village. Carl couldn't work out if he was crazy or not. But given that the man was a multi-millionaire and that he loved him, he went ahead and none of it cost a fortune. What did cost a fortune, in the end, was that while the contractors were all over the place, the diner stayed shut. When everything was finished and they re-opened, it was too late. All the punters had found other places to go. Thirty covers a day now counted as good. Then we arrived, just as everyone had agreed to throw in the towel.

'That was a shed-load to take on board, especially when I was trying to sort my own back catalogue. But it presented one of those moments – somehow we had to hook-up our two operations, though I'm not exactly sure that our motley was an operation.

5
EYES THEY HAVE THAT SEE NOT…

Thus-It-Came-To-Be that, one night, I found myself trying to consult my Third Eye for inspiration – that's how out of my depth I felt. I was sitting on the bed, gazing at the moon through the ring, feeling five per cent seer and 95 per cent idiot, when Tee crept up on me. She grabbed me round the boobs and went – "Worrah, worrah, worrah!" in my ear. (Carl has been educating her and we've just got to Winnie-the-Pooh. She's totally obsessed and has tried out all the characters in turn, finally settling on Tigger as the best fit. She's not wrong.) So, "worrah, worrah, worrah! What are you doing?" she demands, whilst doing all sorts of advanced-Tiggerish things to my boobs…

"I'm consulting my Third Eye," I said, fighting to control the situation and to salvage an ounce of dignity.

"Eeek!" she screeched and froze.

"What?" I demand, dragging my top back into place.

"I've just had a message from the Beyond," she said, in a mesmerised voice, "and it says…"

"Yes?" I ask, crossly.

"Absolutely nothing at all. But I do have a brilliant idea. Should we start again, from the beginning, starting with 'what is the problem we are trying to solve?' Just a thought."

I started to giggle and the next 20 minutes were an intellectual write-off.

"I was trying," I said finally, "to work out how we get this place back on its feet."

"Ah," says Tee, "definitely a three-pipe problem, Watson." (Conan Doyle is on Carl's syllabus, too.)

"Topless waitresses?"

We agreed that would work. But who wants to live with bare tits all around, forever? Also, hot fat and boobs don't mix. Furthermore, having just emerged from my own round of exploitation I didn't fancy enslaving the sisters – however brain-washed and eager they might be.

Thinking like that also knocked Friday night mud-wrestling on the head, too… "though," I said, surprising myself, "I vaguely fancy a go at that…"

"Impossible," pronounceth the Tee, "what if your boy bits popped out?"

Gloomily, I had to agree that she had a point.

"I don't think," said Tee, "that you and I are that magical. Consulting the runes, the bones the Tarot, the Ouija board, or the Things that Go Bump in the Night, won't help us, But we do, after all, have a resident magician."

"Who?"

"Marie-Gabrielle, of course!"

"Why is she a magician and I'm not? I've got a Third Eye, like Tuesday Lobsang Rampa – or was he called Thursday? Anyway, I've got one and may I remind you it's pulled us out of the poo once already."

"Hmph!" commented Tee. "I've got a stretch Range-Rover but I don't know how it works. It's got us out of trouble a few times, too but now it's stranded on that Kilimanjaro of a concrete block, waving its wheels in the air."

"And your point is?"

"That we may be proud possessors of very clever devices but we are not educated in their complexities, or uses."

There was a long silence.

"Do you want to try my ring on?" I offered, lamely, apologetically.

"Thank you, I was wondering when and if you might ask."

"Now."

Feigning indifference but convulsed with mad desire – maybe? – she slipped it on her finger.

"Anything?"

"Not a glimmer."

"Not even postcard scenes of Tibet?"

"Not even one of those."

"Oh."

"You may well say 'oh' but as I remarked, some short while ago, we are blessed with a magician in our midst."

"Marie-Gabrielle."

"Marie-Gabrielle indeed. Consider. She cooked up a plan to free herself and a whole host of victims of pornography, from two-dimensional bondage. She translated discreet portions of those fantasised events into actual time and space, real-world events. She encountered you, 5000 miles away in your bath and poor old Punch about half-a-mile down the road, cooking himself in his camp fire – have you seen those burns? She then micro-managed said scenarios to the split-second. Consider, had I been slower pulling my pants up on that hill top, or if you had been seized by one of your ungovernable outbreaks of IBS, we'd have been late going down the hill and the Militia would have kebabbed them all."

"Pa would have fought them off!" I protested.

"He'd abandoned his arms and was shagged-out anyway."

"True."

"Timing like that is… I mean, dammit, she collected us from the other side of the planet and interim, I nearly had us arrested a dozen times. Timing like that is spooky-plus."

"Also," I added, "let us not forget dear old JJ, wrenched from his Rabbit and collected from a few light-years away. You're right, you're always right. She's a magician. She'll know how to save this place. Let's have a contemplative sexual interlude and then go and capture her. We'll tickle her till she confesses!"

"Now that's a plan!"

We had just completed our modest ritual when there was a discreet knock at the door. A little voice said – "Hello."

"Come in, come in," I warbled, hauling up the sheets.

"You were planning to capture me?" enquired Marie-Gabrielle. "I thought I'd save you the trouble."

"Absolutely," said Tee, "you knew this through…Third Eye, Tarot, Sixth Sense, casting bones, divination, a skrying bowl?"

"Umm, the walls are quite thin and when passing, hearing my name taken in vain, so-to-speak, I decided to surrender, rather than be hunted down, captured and tickled."

"Oh," said Tee, in a deflated sort of voice.

I explained our problem.

"Ah…" said Marie-Gabrielle.

"You have the answer?"

"Of course," she said.

"What is it?" we demanded in unison.

"UFO's" she said. "After supper JJ and I will tell you all about it."

6

TIME FOR SUPPER

Supper was a delicious beef stew. So delicious that Punch declared – "D'ye know tha's t'best bit o' beef a've 'ad, since a' cut down yon beast in't'wood. A' near ate off 'im for a six month."

"Papa," said Marie-Gabrielle, looking slightly pink around the gills, "this could be an indelicate story."

"Be it? 'Ows thet then, lil'un?" Punch seemed genuinely perplexed.

"Papa, people would wish to know what the beast was doing in your wood!"

"An' wor' of it, girl? 'E were a'untin thee as a' recalls it."

"Oui, it was and if we start from there, please to tell your story. But don't anyone to ask what had taken place earlier, please, or Marie and I will be mortified."

"Womens!" exclaimed Punch, baffled. "Well, short b' short. A' shoots it, clear through its browbone an' reet down 'is spine wi' a ball from my Bess. 'T'were a lucky shot, a' admits it. A' were aimin' fer its chest an' as a' pulls yon trigger, 'e lowers down 'is 'ead t'tek a run reet across t'swamp. As a' said, short b' short. Bang! Down 'e goes, knees bucklin, 'ead first into an' under t' water. So a' butchers 'im, 'angs 'im up 'igh in a tree an' cuts off a 'andy slice ever' day fer mi' supper. An' d'ye know, t'owder it gets, richer it tasted. My but 't'were a size o'a brute!"

Both Maries relaxed visibly.

"En realitie, Papa, how did you get it out of the swamp, for as I recall, it was as good as underwater?"

"Eh, but a'm glad tha's ask't mi' thet! Fer a' were thet proud o'missen an' a've allus wanted fer t'tell thet tale – fer theer's a funny endin' t'it."

Everyone rapped the table in encouragement. Punch rarely spoke at length, so we were all only too happy to listen.

"It took some thinkin' an' a bit o' engineerin'. A've told thee all as 'ow yon 'edge were allus findin' things fer mi. One day, it delivers mi' a fine coil o'rope. Must a' rolled off a wagon, same as yon round o'cheese thet a'as spoke of. No man sniffs at a coil o'rope, such a fine length 'as t'come in 'andy, one day. Now thet day were wi'mi, at last!

"A' wades into t'water, meks an 'ole thro' them girt great legs wi' mi bayonet, passes t' rope an' teks a good few turns t'tie things off, firm like. Next, a' as t'be findin' a tough owd branch as'll tek t'weight and gimme height, when yon monster comes clear o' t'water. A' finds one, 20 foot off ground an' thick as mi' thigh. T'git rope over, a'teks a length o'twine an'ties it tae a'rock. O'er goes t'rock, o'er goes twine an' a' gets t'aul in mi' rope – d'y'see?"

We all nodded. We could follow this.

"A' tell thee, it took a fair few 'eaves o'thet rock, afore a'could pull it o'er!" Punch chortled, hopefully with glee at his own cleverness, for he was usually reticence personified when it came to self-promotion.

"What a'needs now be an 'eavy owd tree, near t'end o'its days an' in line wi't'beast an' wi't'branch. 'Tis a tall orderin' an' it weren't no skill o'mine as found one. Must a'been growin' theer special, fer't'last 100 years. Anyways, t'ows an' whys o'why it were theer 'ave engaged me in much perplexity o' contemplation, on them long neets unner't stars." Such a sentence dried up more than Punch's vocal apparatus and he hid his head in his tankard for a long moment, as much to recover his composure, as for refreshment.

"Mi'plan, such as it be, tha' sees, is t'fell yon master tree. As 'e falls back, 'is weight should be enuff as t'drag yon sides o'beef clear'o't'water – tree bein' made fast ter mi' rope, y'ken?"

We kenned.

For some reason, Punch shot a hasty look at me, half-conspiratorial, half-apologetic? It was hard to tell. Whatever, I nodded encouragement back.

"T'keep mi' tale short, all this plannin' teks a week o'work an' a'm sore, an' fair weary. But at t'end o' it all, a' as mi' rope all in place an' a' can starts t'choppin' at t'owd, girt tree. A' chops all day, an'all t'next, an' am fair winded. A' were hurryin' miself along for two reasonings. First were, thet theer swamp water weren't good fer t'meat, second, theer's a big owd pike swimming around in theer an' 'e's got 'is teeth int' beast's 'ead an'tongue an' a' reckons 'e's a'minded t'start chewin on other parts, soonest 'e can.

"A've cut mi'self a big birdsmouth int' trunk o'tree, at back, so's t'be a'directing wheer she's got t'fall, like. Now a'starts on t'front, an' think on, all this 'ere choppin' is done wi' mi' lil' sword. A'm so weary, a'sets a fire t'burn, at t'front, fer t'elp me out a bit. A' keeps it well stoked wi' wood chips an' it burns good and proper. But wha' appens? A' falls asleep. Some good soul looks after drunks n'fools, fer in t'middle o't' neet, theer's this 'ell o'a bang an' a crash…beggin yer pardon, Madame Marie…"

Marie-Claire, who has been all ears, thanks to Marie-Gabrielle's sturdy translating, smiles with indulgence and approval, having heard no doubt a suitably Bowdlerised version.

Emboldened, Punch continued apace – "Up a'jumps, fair out o'mi' skin wi' t'shock an' surprise. But a'canna see a thing, fer 'tis pitchy-dark, nae moon, nae stars. A' looks around an' what does a'see?"

"What, Papa!?" squeaks Marie-Gabrielle, on cue.

"A' sees summat' rare an' strange. Theer be t'bull, 'angin just as a'wanted 'im but 'e's a'glowin' in t'dark, like 'is 'ide is runnin' wi' thet St. Elmo's fire, what sailors do tell of, as runs all o'er riggin an' metalwork o'a' vessel. Summat in yon swampy water is fer 'avin a reac-shion-isation-ing wi' t'bull's hide, an' 'e's a glowin' in t'dark, like 'e were one o' owd Nick's personal 'erd – allowin' 'e keeps a few bullocks in 'ell!

"Now a'm a'gettin t'it" – and again Pa shoots me the apology cum conspiracy look, so again I nod approval, albeit I am in utter ignorance of what it might be that I'm approving.

"So, what else does a'see?" – and Punch glances around the table, making sure he has our attention, which he certainly does – "what a'sees is yon damned owd pike, a'holding fast to t'bull's nose an' 'im 'angin down a good four foot! Well, weren't 'e just askin' fer trouble? Yon owd chap ends up rolled in clay and set t'bake in t'embers o't' fire a'set. A' goes back t'mi sleep an in t'mornin' a'digs 'im out and a's got mi'self an 'ole pike fer breakfast. But, by 'eck, it were some bait a'd a'needed fer t'catch 'im!"

A huge round of applause greeted Punch's tale and he flushed bright red, beneath his coppered skin. "A' says thankee kindly. A'bin a purgin' t'tell yon tale fer some time – 'bout 'ow thee catches a pike, usin' an whole bull as bait!"

It was a lot later that Punch sidled over to me and whispered – "A' were fibbin' a bit, our lad. Y'don't think they noticed? A'd had thet pike a week earlier and a' sawed t'head off fer t'leave in't water as bait fer eelsies. But after a'd pulled t'beast out, as a'said, an'wer' a' eatin' o'him, a'thinks t'would be a grand tale if a'told it t'way a' just did. It weren't wrong, wer' it, lad?"

"Oh Pa," I said, "never let the truth get in the way of a good story! We can agree on that and your secret is safe with me. My lips are sealed, forever!"

"Tis a good tale, ent it," he cackled quietly. "Most on it 'tis truth…God's own, an' a bit o' mine, thrown in fer t'saltin,' like."

7

JO-JO'S MODEST PLAN

Earlier however, Marie-Gabrielle, while still clapping her hands, had stood up to make her own announcement over the general mirth.

"Everybodies! Just as Papa's bull was glowing in the dark, we need something to make 'Andy's Place' glow in the dark again. JJ and I have had a bit of a 'heads-together' and we have a plan. Actually, it is mostly JJ's plan, because all I said to him was – 'if we could have a UFO sighting here, like this one in the silly newspaper, this place would soon be famous again.' And what did you say to me JJ?"

Jo-Jo blushed.

"I think I said – 'I might be able to help there, Marie."

"That is absolument what you said and now you're going to tell us your genius plan!"

Jo-Jo went a deeper shade of red, something he tried to conceal by bending down to recover, from under the table, the modest rucksack he had been carrying throughout his travels.

Without ceremony he now upended it and a collection of small packages fell out. "This little pile," he said, "is what is called a 'Core' survival kit."

We all stared. Nothing was familiar. No flashlight, no Kendal Mint Cake, or chocolate, no satellite phone, compass, first aid kit. In fact nothing that should be a commonplace in the serious traveller's rucksack.

"I think you've all suffered my endless musings about 'the Core.' It's an artery, a cosmic artery that, I suspect, connects planet to planet, throughout myriad solar systems. To what end, I have racked my brains. Finally, I might have come up with an interesting theory but that would be digression. If anyone wants to discuss it, we can do so later – and I would love to, by the way. OK, ok, Marie…I know, I promised," he grinned.

"What may act as a catalyst to revive 'Andy's Place' is one of these little chaps," and he indicated a plain box, little larger than a regular block of butter. Out of it tumbled 12 metal cubes, each apparently without any distinguishing feature. He passed one around and we all looked suitably bemused. Examining it, I found it to have a shallow concavity on one face, thumbprint-sized.

"You've all noticed the indentation. That's because they are all keyed, for want of a better word, to my Metabolic-DNA signature, which it reads from my thumb. In short, they will only work for me and only if I am alive, hence the 'metabolic' proviso. They are locator beacons. It's quite easy to get lost on our planet, especially on the Upper Rim, where I come from. There are no maps, because there's nothing really to map. We Rim nomads know our way around thousands of square miles. I don't know quite how but we do. It's not something I've had to think about before. Just occasionally, however, we can get lost – usually by risking a short cut, or our genetically implanted map breaks down. These things have gone off maybe twice in my entire life – not mine, I hasten to add but other people's.

"Right, like the excellent Punch, I'll try to keep it short. Let's say you're sick, injured or lost, you activate one of these. It sends out a signal and the Core responds, by dispatching a rescue module. These are unmanned drones. You explain your problem to it, your needs, whatever and it buzzes off to organise whatever is necessary. It carries on-board basics, which frequently suffice I'm told. Also, at a pinch, you could crawl inside. So I guess it's not that small, really. Perhaps the size of a quad bike? It has a lot of interfaces you can utilise in many ways. It's a very clever and ingenious emergency service. Also, it makes quite a song and dance when it lands, so it can be seen and heard in some of the fogs and blizzards we get. That's the aspect of it that might get us back on the map, if you follow my thinking…

"…phew," he added suddenly, looking red and rattled. "I think I might need one any minute now!"

"Non, non!" said Marie-Gabrielle, "we are all ears, truly."

We nodded encouragingly.

"Right, thank you. There is an obvious caveat – this is an in-planet resource. Has it ever been used across light years? I have no idea. Will it work under those conditions? Will the drone be able to respond, to travel as I did? Again, I have no idea. All I can suggest is that we put it to the test," he finished humbly.

Marie-Gabrielle clapped her hands in delight.

"JJ's is the most wonderful idea!"

"Only if it works," Jo-Jo interjected.

"Of course it will work," she said in the assured tones of female certainty.

"So who," I ask, "can rouse the Press, the TV, the loonies and tin-foil hat brigades?"

"I can," said Carl. "But JJ, you have destroyed one of my most cherished ambitions – which was to see an alien UFO! Also, Eva-Beaver, see me after school to discuss the politically incorrect use of the word 'loonies…'"

"Oh," I said and felt myself going a fetching shade of finest John West's.

"Hold on to your faith, love of my life," said Andy, "this would still be an alien UFO, wouldn't it?"

"How so?" asked Carl, warily.

"JJ and no offence here, JJ, is actually an alien and his rescue craft will thus be pure alien UFO. Although, I suppose, as we're in the know, it would be an IFO – an Identified Flying Object, instead. Would that still do?"

"How can JJ be an alien?" asked Carl. "He's a mate of mine…who happens to come from another solar system…" he trailed off. "Yes, I suppose an IFO would do, after all. Hm, that's good – though you're still in direst doggy do-do's, Eva-Beaver."

I tried to look ashamed but failed.

Marie-Gabrielle clapped her hands. "Let JJ finish!"

"Nearly done," he said. "You get three goes with one of these beacons. The drone flies in, then it beeps, squeaks, honks and strobes, off-and-on, for about 10 minutes. That's how long you have to access it. If you don't, it zooms off back to base and tries again, 25 hours later – we have a slightly longer day than you guys, also a couple of pounds more gravity and two moons."

Carl looked as if he was about to faint from sheer joy.

"You get three goes, all-in-all and if you haven't accessed it by then well, to be honest, I'm not sure what happens. I guess, if we go ahead, we're going to find out. Let's hope they don't send a battle cruiser…"

Carl's eyes widened.

"Sort of a joke," said Jo-Jo, lamely. "Look, the biggest unknown is will it operate inter-galactically? The drone I do not doubt. Anything I can do, or have done to me, it will be able to emulate and probably enhance. My doubts centre on the beacon, which was undoubtedly designed for in-planet use, or so pessimism insists I must assume. Optimistically I would say 'yes, we're on,' while pessimistically I would have to caution 'no, we're out of range.' Anyway, details aside, which I'm happy to discuss with anyone, there you have it."

"From pike-fishing with bulls as bait, to alien drones in one meal," I whispered to Tee, "this is Bizarre Miracle Night at the Palladium."

Tee's reaction was dynamic.

She made a very loud – "worrah, worrah, worrah-ing" noise. That proved to be preparation for springing onto the table with one startling, vertical leap. "I'm an alien spaceship," she howled, "beep, beep, peep, peep, bleeeep!! Bleeeep! Where's MY PUDDING? I WANT IT NOW!! I'VE BEEN WAITING FOREVER!!"

JJ, grinning from ear-to-ear, got up and produced one of the famous apple pies, with a small jug of cream for Royalty and a pitcher-full of custard for we plebs.

8

WHAT'S ON THE MENU?

As the Bible says – "and so it came to pass…"
And a good job it did, for we'd bet the bank on everything working as planned. Andy and Tee, having the souls of gamblers, had dug into their deposit accounts. The first tranche of their small fortunes had been spent on groundworks. Concrete lorry stands, with state of the art access and exit roads were laid. Next came new loos, a paint and furnishings make-over, a couple of new ovens. The final bill was simply colossal.

Only when the smell of new paint had died away did JJ venture out one afternoon to activate one of his cubes. He'd calculated, from what he could recall of his own transit, just when the drone should arrive and amazingly he was less than an hour out…though that became one of the longest hours any of us had spent.

Carl had the worst time of all. He was perched on a chalk cliff, about a mile away, with members of the local UFO Society, each equipped with night vision goggles and their cameras loaded with infra-red film. He'd fibbed so successfully he was now half-convinced that he really had seen an alien drone the night before, just when he was knocking off shift. But an hour is a long time to spend with a fib, in the cold, the dark and the damp.

Feet were getting restless, a few cameras were coming off their stands, when The Core's Rescue Mission arrived, seemingly from nowhere but certainly to our eternal gratitude. It had the decency to do it again the next night – then, stunningly, on the third. By then there was barely standing room on the clifftop.

"It's working to a 25-hour period," Carl pronounced solemnly, as he was now Group Guru and his every utterance was golden. "Also, for what it's worth guys, we've a special on the early birds' breakfast and I can get us discount off that!"

'Andy's Place' got publicity you couldn't have bought.

As the owner he was interviewed ad nauseam. "You should be talking to my sous chef," he would laugh. "He's a fervent believer. I'm more inclined to think the local youths have hatched a very convincing spoof." But, he did concede that there had been previous sightings and strange events reported in the past. Certainly, he admitted, the videos were very compelling and yes, it was odd that it had happened three nights in succession, which would have been hard to fake for ten minutes at a time.

Professionals were welcome to come and look around but we couldn't have just anybody wandering over the site, it was far too dangerous. There were concealed deadfalls and unsafe structures. Simply walking around was to invite a broken ankle. "Yes, it's true, we've had to hire a security firm – until the fuss dies down. Our insurers insisted."

"No, I didn't know there was footage on the BBC…well, I guess that's hard to argue with. But I'm still betting it's all a hoax. It'll come out, eventually – just like Piltdown did."

"Did he think he'd ever served an alien in the cafe?"

"You never know…we've had some funny customers! As it's the last old-fashioned tranny caff for miles, perhaps they know a good place when they spot one? Whatever, I'm flattered they'd think it was worthwhile coming from another galaxy. Maybe they've only just heard about my old Michelin star? I guess news can travel slowly across the light years…"

That did the trick, one of the Red Tops splashed – "Aliens land on a Michelin Star!"

After that, the cash register kept on ringing, night and day.

9

SEQUINS GET EVERYWHERE

Princess Tulipa's car, which had also found itself in an alien environment – thin air – was recovered in a manoeuvre that owed nothing at all to aliens, Houston Control, NASA, or the Apollo Programme.

Five very powerful, capable-looking men arrived in a beaten up crew-bus.

"Fucking hell," said the leader of the gang, respectfully, "how'd she geddit up there?"

Then they set to, amiably, swiftly and efficiently, with powerful-looking jacks, scaffolding poles and planks. Eventually, down she came, back onto Terra Firma once again.

Remarkably little damage, declared the mechanic of the group and nothing he couldn't fix here and now.

So, a great deal of tea was drunk and much cake scoffed, as we all sat around his legs that projected from the side of the car. It was a scene at first suggestive of some ghastly accident, and at which we were the attendant ghouls. In fact, we were solicitous waiters, trolleying under his share of the tea and cake to grunts of – "Ta very much!" After which there would usually follow thunderous hammerings.

Then it was time for the requested and promised, curry-fest. We used the back stairs and the private dining room, so mercifully there were no witnesses. Had there been, we might have had to assassinate them.

The five were ushered to their seats and Princess Tulipa herself appeared to thank and welcome the workers. She was wearing an outfit conjured by Bollywood and Madonna, out of a particularly vulgar dream. Baggy see-through harem pants and no knickers – what a cheer went up! – a conical bra top, floating veils and some sort of headdress that reprised themes from Star Wars and Indiana Jones. "I designed it myself," she'd announced proudly, during my sneak preview. "Thank God," I'd replied. "That means there aren't any more roaming loose in the world."

That saw me pushed out of the door, so I'd sauntered off to join the gentle corralling of Punch and Marie-Claire, far from the action. We had unanimously decided it was unfit for the morals of their century and age group. Thoughtfully we had provided a very toothsome hamper of food, to be taken with delicious, sleepy wines. The sun shone on our little picnic subterfuge, too – which I thought was decent of it.

Meanwhile, at the main event, the Princess was whisking away a golden cloth to reveal silver tureens of supermarket curries, vibrating with extra chillies and heavily enriched with cannabis resin.

Earlier, Carl had sniffed, nibbled and declared it – "A1 gear." The rest of us were too pathetically stolid to have any experience of assessing junk. So we stood around uselessly. Then he turned his back, as he said later – "only to go to the loo" – but in that time Tee had grated all two ounces into the curry. "That should be enough," she said. "But there's some oil in the dhals, just in case."

The next surprise was the arrival of a mini-bus out of which trooped five working girls, each of whom was to become the allotted waitress – and 'companion' – to a member of the team. They were led away by Princess Tee to be equipped with versions of her own sartorial splendour. They took that in their stride. They were experienced girls, each one vouched for by that former crew member, Penny. "It's sorta' like sumffin' outa 'It Ain't 'alf Hot, Mum,' innit?" commented one, as they got into character. Then they were off, to fawn over and feed the working males.

The 'added ingredient' got to work pretty quickly, too, as did the lager, at which point, moulting sequins and veils, Princess T floated away, never to be seen again. Looking very ordinary she turned up to join our discreet picnic, drowning in a pair of baggy jeans and a huge sweatshirt – "I borrowed yours, Beavie."

Her handmaidens were running the store and what precisely went on, no-one really knows – most certainly not those on the receiving end. The engineers subsequently admitted to Carl that their memories seemed to be lacking several vital hours. As for the girls, it was just another day at the office.

It had to be admitted, it was a masterpiece of organisation and that was probably because most of it was down to Carl. The mini-bus that had brought the girls now dropped the men off, returning later for the ladies. Carl drove the crew-bus away, loading his bike in the back, all ready for his return trip.

What little remained of the food – and they had certainly eaten heartily – rated as 'Haz-Chem,' in my opinion, not to mention 'Evidence' and I disposed of it down one of the many gaping holes that perforate the wasteland. I hope it made the underground creatures happy.

"All very successful," declared Princess Tulipa, still picking sequins out of her cleavage six hours later, as I laboured to remove remnants of her headdress from the glue that held it in place. "A crane might have been cheaper but not half as much fun."

"I'm running out of solvent, up here," I said grumpily. "We may have to take this to the hospital – they've got special stuff."

"Hmm," she mused, "would that be the hospital where they laboured to take the beer bottle out of your bum? Do you think we'll meet anyone you remember?"

I redoubled my efforts.

Outside, purely from the goodness of their hearts, JJ and Carl waxed and polished the Range Rover.

"I can't believe it," groaned Carl, "a whole two ounces and a capful of oil? I only went for a pee!"

"Seems she's a very fast grater," nodded JJ.

10
DRIVING LESSONS

With the car back in service, Tee decided she needed lessons. Not driving lessons, which might have been sensible but homing lessons, as if she had become a pigeon. Wide-eyed and innocent, she put it to Carl a bit like this – "your lovely friends have rescued my car, so it's only sensible to start using it. But we are stranded in the middle of an insane traffic management system that no sensible human being could be expected to understand, without having been born here. Obviously it has to be imprinted on the genetic code and I have not been so enabled. Thus, I do not understand this mayhem. A little lesson or two would help me grasp just how, having once left the security of 'Andy's Place,' the hell I'm ever expected to get back! Out there I feel like water going down a plughole the wrong way. Also, I do not want to have to come in the back way again! It was very expensive. Plee--eese – a lesson or two?"

Off they went, only to be back within five minutes.

"Carl needs the loo," she said airily, examining her nails.

After 20 minutes I pretended to be a boy and went in search.

"What are you doing?"

"Has she gone away?" His voice was terminally lonely.

"Oh, she'll never give up."

"Oh God," he groaned. "I'm terrified. She's terrifying."

"She's good on straight bits," I offered.

"What use is that? These are roundabouts and they're all curves."

"Why don't you pilot, on the motorbike?" I suggested. "You ride in front, she follows."

"That could be a quicker death," he conceded. "Promise me you'll look after Andy if anything happens…"

"God, that's a bit O.T.T. isn't it?"

"Some of those trucks out there weigh up to 40 tons. I weigh 11 stones!"

"Really?" I said with interest. "You look a bit more than that."

"O.K. twelve and a half stones."

"Ah, that's more what I'm seeing."

"It still won't stop me dying."

"Think Jason Bourne thoughts!"

"I'm not Jason Bourne. I'm me."

"Oh man up and wipe your bum! Get out here and meet your maker. 'Come back – with your shield, or on it!"

That invocation was met with an inordinately long fart.

Way too much detail, I decided and retreated.

Out in the fresh air, Tee was tapping her toes in a very threatening way.

"What's keeping him?"

"Terror and bowels, working in sync."

"Really?"

"Absolutely."

"Is that what you get?"

"You know I do. Try saying 'boo!' by way of an experiment, while we're waiting."

"Boo!!"

We gave it a while.

"That's unusual, I'm OK so far," I reported.

Carl emerged, wan but defiant.

"Let's do it!" he said grittily.

"Did you wash your hands?" demanded Tee.

"I'm a cook," he said haughtily. "Of course I washed my hands."

This time they lasted 45 minutes and as I heard no horrendous bangs, no sirens, saw no blue flashing lights, or medi-copters rotoring in, I took it that meant everything was OK.

In fact, they stepped from the car wreathed in smiles.

"I think she's got it," said Carl.

"He's over it now," explained Tee. "It was just first time nerves."

"Really quite exciting," he burbled, "like the old days on the dirt track."

"Come here," I beckoned Carl. "Uh huh, pupils dilated." I took a quick pulse. "Easily 200 and rising. Get him inside, nurse. Easy chair, alcohol. Sweet stuff."

"I can walk," said Carl, swaying slightly. "Thank you Tee," he turned and inclined graciously. "That really took me back."

"Oh, where to?" she asked, smiling.

"The dawn of the universe," he said, staggering to the door. "The Big Bang."

11

AN EYE IN THE DARK

Marie-Claire was ruefully examining her generation gap, or more precisely the 300 years she had vaulted, from that hideous manor to this strange place in the middle of…where, precisely? Oh well, she supposed, that didn't matter. Wherever it was, everyone was very kind and petite mademoiselle was safe, chirping like a little bird.

She and Monsieur Punch are safe, too and that gives her a warm glow, every time she remembers that it has actually happened. Something good came from the worst day of her life. Today, they are having a little picnic, here on the new turf, at the edge of the big vegetable plot that Monsieur Andrew has had dug for them.

She stands in the shelter of a wall of colossal concrete blocks, misshapen blocks to be sure, that the men have told her are called caltrops. Apparently they were to be used to block roads in the time of a great war. But the great war came and went and now the blocks have ended up here. Monsieur Andrew's brother was paid to break them up and there are thousands upon thousands of them.

She had been telling herself a fairy story, that they were left-overs from a game played by giants. They had a competition to see who could build the longest and highest, by lunchtime. Then, when lunchtime came, off they clomped, wiping dirty hands on their hairy thighs and forgot all about the game. So that's how the walls, 12 feet high and 100 yards long are still standing, on either side of the new garden.

What a strange affair digging the vegetable plot had been. When Monsieur Andrew had first suggested it, she wondered how she and Monsieur Punch could ever manage it. It would take them forever! The rest of their lives…but if they started slowly, who knows?

Then Monsieur Andrew had smiled and promised it would take a week – at the very longest! 'Which was when I must have started imagining giants,' she thought, wryly to herself.

The first giant was yellow and it looked like the most monstrous bird, ever created – or maybe it was part of a bridge that had broken itself up so it could begin walking. This giant rolled onto their plot of land and started picking up the caltrop blocks, as if they were feathers, piling them into a new wall which, when it was finished, would make their garden a private space. Then, with no further ado, it began to dig up all the ground in between. All the rubble, the weeds, the broken bottles, tins and little wiry bushes, the concrete slabs, fallen walls and broken doors…it just picked them up and dropped them – with huge bangs – into the backs of lorries which were waiting to take the rubbish away…somewhere. Some very big hole in the ground, she supposed.

It had been so exciting to watch. She had insisted that Monsieur Punch take her there every day. Even though the machine terrified her, it was a good sort of fright, like a Christmas ghost story that ends well. She sat in a safe place and Monsieur Punch jumped up and down from the machine to tell the driver what he was to do next.

Eventually they had a very long, wide trench, with not very good-looking soil. She didn't think they would grow much in it but she couldn't bring herself to say so. A good job she hadn't, she smiled to herself, laying down her rugs. For now, the same lorries came back, filled to their tops with rich brown soil. Then, just like farm carts unloading manure, they tipped up their backs and poured the soil onto the ground.

The yellow giant was called a 'digger,' which made sense because it had done a lot of digging. Now it did a lot of raking. Where there had been foul earth, it pulled over the good soil and it patted it down into place. It was so very quick. Months of work for 100 men, armed with mattocks and baskets, was over in days.

Marie-Claire knew the world had moved on. She had understood that on that very first afternoon, in the back of Princess Tulipa's huge car. But the big machines were a surprise. What surprised her most was that at the end of a working day, they just stopped roaring and seemed to die. In fact, the first time it happened she thought they had died!

Maybe she would have preferred the old earth-moving machines, the placid Percheron horses, slowly moving back to their stables after a day in the field. Her brothers and she would pick great armfuls of grass from the roadside, then scampering into the farmyard, hold up the sweet-smelling bouquets to those noble heads. The horses would lean over the gates to pull at the sheaves, tearing them with blunt yellow teeth, snorting and sneezing. She could remember both smell of hay and horse. The strange mixture had lingered on her hands for hours. The smell of the resting yellow giant, was altogether different, sweet and rather sickly.

After the vegetable patch had been dug, more yellow giants arrived to swarm all over the place. It had been an invasion and she had watched it all, half-scared, half-fascinated. They were going to bring new life back to the sad little cafe and to do it, everyone said, an awful lot of work had to be done. Marie-Clair was rather glad things had started slowly for her, one giant and its lorries. When there had been a dozen giants at work, she had found it all a bit too much and was very glad when it was over.

One day, hoping to get away from the roar and noise, she had taken herself off to neaten up the edges of the vegetable garden, before they started their autumn sowing.

She was well out of sight, behind one of the caltrop walls, digging quietly, when her spade hit something hard. A stone, she thought, then a clod of earth broke away and as she pulled back the blade, there was something shining through the soil. She stooped, loosened soil with her fingers and was able to pull free a shining metal disc, perhaps six inches in diameter and two inches thick. It was completely without features, except for a thumbprint-sized depression on one side, which held something like a little window of black glass.

As she turned it in her hands, it caught the morning sun and Marie-Claire was almost sure that something flickered, like an eyelid across an eye. But the next moment it was still and inert, merely a beautiful plain object, surprisingly light and warm for metal. It had a perfectly friendly feel about it, so she brushed it clear of soil, wrapped it in her cardigan and when she had finished digging, took it back to her room. There she wrapped it in paper and stowed it at the bottom of a clothes drawer. 'I will ask Monsieur JJ if he has ever seen the like,' she thought and promptly forgot all about it.

12

STARGAZING

Some weeks earlier I had begun to have a problem with the stars, or to be more accurate with what seemed to be one particular star. It consistently peered through our caravan window. It peeped through the annoying "V" that formed at the top of the curtains once they had been futilely hauled together, every night. It had begun to rouse a certain kind of paranoia in me and this particular night I was trying to analyse the phenomenon away, by sweet and reasonable internal arguments – such as 'how do you know it's the same star?' or 'since when did stars spy on people?' and 'stars don't have eyes…do they?'

Unaware and inevitably indifferent to my train of thought, Tee was pondering aloud – "do you think, if I was to buy us a really old showman's living van, all mahogany trim and cut glass, Andy would be upset if I brought it on site – providing I paid for all the hard-standing, connections and what have you? I'm such a snob and this Essex-girl, trashy-trailer living – or do I mean trailer-trash? – is getting to me."

"We have a muddled metaphor problem," I'd replied. "I," – pointing at my chest – "am trailer-trash, this," I said, with an expansive gesture, "is a trashy trailer."

"So-oo," she said slowly, "I am a Princess living with trailer-trash in a trashy trailer?"

"Correct!" I'd saluted.

"T T, T T," she'd stuttered, "anyway, do you think he'd mind?"

"I reckon that if you could find enough showman's vans to replace all the Portakabins, double-wides and towables, he'd be thrilled. The place would start to look positively boutique, not quite-so 'Traveller Approved,'" – excuse my bigoted snobbery!

"Besides, we'd then be in a position, if the Indians came – the Red Indians, of course, or does that have to be Native Americans, these days? – to 'circle the wagons,' which is always something I've wanted to be involved in."

"No chance," Tee had retorted, "you need Conestoga wagons to do that properly. Won't work otherwise. The Indians would just ride off in disgust."

"That's rather flattening. Are you quite sure?"

"Positive." And when she said it like that, I knew there'd be no negotiating.

"However," her ladyship continued, "if I may elide to matters serious, cosmically serious, I wish to bring to your attention the fact that we are being spied on by one particular star." And she had pointed.

"I'm delighted you have mentioned that, because you are right. I'd come to the same conclusion but was, this very minute, trying to dismiss it from my mind as cosmic paranoia."

"You undoubtedly are paranoid," Tee had agreed. "However, as I am always right, I have concluded that star is spying on our sex life. I can think of no other explanation."

And at the time, that had rather flattened things.

Tonight, that same star was peeping again. Tee was right. I was paranoid but it kept doing it. Therefore, as I couldn't sleep and to the tune of Tee rumbling cosily alongside me, I thought I'd stare it down with my Third Eye.

I stared and it stared and neither of us gave an inch. Then, the next moment I looked, for I must have dozed off, the star had been replaced by an actual eye. 'My God,' I squeaked internally, 'a Poking Tom.' Then I got in a muddle correcting myself, 'Peeping Tom, get it right!' Such a muddle that I found I was waving at it. 'Idiot, why did you wave? You don't encourage them, you fool!'

It was a good job that I had, though, because now there was a hiss at the door that said – "it's JJ, are you available?" 'Available for what?' was the reasonable answer but it seemed insane to start a conversation through the keyhole of a trashy trailer.

I rolled quietly out of bed and hissed back – "wait there." Then I went in silent search of a thick pullover and jeans. Wellies I picked up as I tiptoed to the door. The squeaky handle was a problem but I stifled it successfully. Then I was outside and JJ was doing a 'quick, no time to lose' signal as he led the way into the night.

I paused to pull on the boots. I was not the equal of the gravel path, unshod. Pink Panther-like, I followed.

We sped past all the vans. A light was on in Punch and Marie-Claire's twin abodes but they often played cards until late, for the sheer comfort and pleasure of each other's company.

"What time is it?" I dared, as we crossed open ground. "Nearly 1.00 am," said JJ, not even turning round. "I need you to witness something. You're the only person I can ask."

That did nothing to improve my apprehension. I've never been good with surprises, whatever form they take.

We were approaching the vegetable garden. There, JJ started to scramble to the top of the highest pile of caltrops – Tank Trap Mountain, I'd mentally Christened it. "For now, until I've introduced you, it's got to be here," he whispered, "not some random spot."

"Stop talking in tongues," I whispered back. "You'll bring on my IBS and I can't scramble down these things fast enough to cope with that."

There proved to be a bit of a cat's cradle at the top and we settled into it comfortably enough, at first. Then it grew awkward. Thereafter, purgatorial.

"This had better be good," I whispered.

"Oh, it's better than good. You've never seen the like, before."

From inside his anorak he produced a small hand-towel that proved to be protecting a shiny metal disc. It was the same object that Marie-Claire had unearthed, weeks earlier, though that part of the story was to emerge later. He handed it to me. Like Marie, I found it surprisingly light for its size.

"Turn it over."

I did so and found that I was staring into an eye. It was an eye so deep, so black, so bottomless, that I very quickly flipped it back over again, preferring to confront anonymous metal.

"OK," said JJ, "I can see you've got it. Now point the 'eye' at that star."

I shifted myself to sight along his finger and although he could have been staring at any one of 100 stars, I was pretty certain I knew which one he meant. In any case, I had no doubt at all that the eye in the disc would know exactly where to look. All of which constituted a whole pile of assumptions in a very short space of time.

I scrupulously avoided glancing at the black eye but I pointed it towards the relevant patch of sky. As I heard some distant clock strike, I swear I felt the disc realign itself minutely within my grasp. There was a slight shift, a hint of pressure. I grew still. I was suddenly very scared. Also I was frozen to the spot by the certainty that the eye was now open, aligned to one particular star and that that star and this eye were communicating.

"Poo, poo, poo and poo, again…" I mumbled to myself.

JJ simply sat stock still, apparently ignoring me.

Eventually he relaxed and spoke.

"I knew it. You're the catalyst it needed. That's the first time it's been able to 'speak' properly. When I try the communication starts up, then it just fades away. It's over now, you can wrap it up. It only takes a few seconds."

I wrapped the disc and made to hand it to him. As far as you can, on top of a pile of tank traps, he backed away.

"Keep it," he said. "It's meant for you. Or if it's not meant for you personally, it's meant for people like you."

"People like me?"

"Third Eye people."

"Oh bottomless hells," I groaned. "That was so incredible when it happened and now it's starting to haunt me with a horrible sense of failure."

"You didn't 'fail' just then," said JJ.

"That puts me on the same level as a light switch. Flick me down and 'let there be light.' Flick me up and 'darkness shall cover the earth.' In either case I'm not even a go-between. I'm part of some sort of circuit."

"Exactly," said JJ, "you've hit the nail squarely on the head. You're part of a circuit. Because of you, that disc has been enabled for the first time in years. Not thousands of years, certainly not. Maybe less than 100. It wasn't lying deep underground, Marie-Claire said."

JJ told me the tale then, as it had unravelled for Marie-Claire. She'd never told anyone about it, not even her darling girl, nor Punch. She couldn't explain why, even to herself but to top that off, she'd completely forgotten that she was actually storing it at all. What had reminded her was when she dug deeply into a drawer, to find a very old sprig of herbs, the ones Punch had folded into her clothes. She'd wanted to see if she could rescue some seed from them, wondering if they might still be viable in her little herb garden. Then it had bumped against her fingertips and in that instant she had remembered her intention of showing it to JJ.

"I don't want any more of this stuff laying on me," I whined. "First, voices in my head, then old men with Blue Remembered Hills, now an agreeably-tempered alien, sitting atop a pile of tank traps, at a tranny caff on the Great North Road, is pressing Star Wars hardware on me. Sorry JJ, I'm closed for that sort of business. I've had an awful decade and now I'm happy, for the first time in ages."

"Look," JJ appealed, 'I don't believe that this device is in any way malevolent. It fits, very well, in a theory I've been brewing. Sadly, it seems you fit with it too. If it makes you feel any better, then let me tell you I'm a part of this 'circuit' just as much as you are.

"Just take your time with it. One year, five, 20 however long it takes – stick it at the back of your sock drawer," (JJ would never say 'knicker drawer,' I thought). Until then, forget it. Sadly, you'll find that when this sort of stuff is laid on you, you don't get to walk away from it. It will track you down. I once told you how Death put his hand on my shoulder, to show me stuff. That was all Halloween dressing, wrapped around an underlying message. This stuff comes to us in the guises we can recognise at the time. I was ripe to be 'ghouled' you were ready to be 'little old man-ed.' We were both needed in circuits. This is a vast intelligence that is sifting basic particles to see what it can utilise in its own dawning consciousness."

"JJ," I groaned. "Please, it's 2.00 am – can we not do this some other time?"

"No Evie, we can't. You have to listen to me now.

"You are special. You've been told that. You know that. Not only are the signs all over your person, you're also a magnet for unique particles. Think about Punch and Marie-Gabrielle, how they've gravitated to you. Think how incredible it is that you were gifted Tee. That's like being given a top-of-the-range Ferrari.

"OK, you feel like a shipwrecked sailor in all this. I get that. Your boat sank but you've scrambled up on a broken plank. Wet-through and sobbing, maybe. Now a huge wave – what do surfers call it? – a bomb! A bomb has lifted you and you are hurtling towards new, dry land. New revelations, new understanding of yourself, of the cosmos, of time, of everything. You are part of that chain!"

"JJ," I said, "it's now 2.30 am. I'm really impressed with your passion and I will talk theories with you soon, just not now. I'm actually not impressed by being a part of anything's chain. All I want to do is understand some very basic 'whys.' Such as – 'Why did I put myself through all my garbage and for what?' Then I want to be left alone, hopefully to get old and fat with Tee."

JJ smiled. "OK, I'll hang on to it for now but don't say I didn't try to help you. The next nudge you get might not be half so delicate as mine. What we're all involved in here is far more than a tranny caff run by a bunch of eccentrics. This is a nerve node and it won't let you go, because you're a key ingredient. You might think you have self-determination but you don't."

"I could blow my brains out," I said sulkily.

"If you did, it would be because it was part of its plan. Besides – all over Tee?"

I felt tears welling up.

"Let me go back to bed, JJ. Please."

He looked at me and his fervour collapsed beneath chagrin.

"Of course, Evie, of course. Let me help you down."

He did, with huge tenderness. Once again I couldn't fail but note that he was as strong as an ox – for I'm a tall, powerful person and he lifted me down like a baby.

"I'm sorry, Evie. You get back to bed."

"Thanks, JJ. I won't pretend it's not been interesting but it's too much, too soon." I gave him a peck on the cheek and shuffled off.

It was not to be. Morpheus had banished me from his kingdom for that night. As I made to leave, I saw Punch, planted squarely on one of the two old benches he'd rescued from somewhere and had installed in a sun trap. I hadn't seen him when we came in because of the peculiar nature of the allotment entrance. It was through a chicane, made by overlapping two walls of tank traps into a sort of twisted alleyway. It forced you to keep your eyes-left, when entering and eyes right when leaving…which means that you didn't automatically scan the allotment. It made for a bit of privacy and it also meant that I was more likely to see Pa on the way out rather than on the way in. Don't worry… doesn't really matter…

It was dark but under the moonlight and stars his face and hands were shining like burnished copper. He looked for all the world, like a bronze cast of an ancient Hindu God, pure on one face, tricksy on the other. So, making my crossing by means of raised paths, hammered flat under walls of shattered caissons, tank traps and anonymous, concrete cast-offs, I circulated towards his seat.

"Ello boy," he greeted me, as I was half-way across, "canna' sleep?"

"Bit more complicated than that," I answered ruefully.

"Wan't' talk 'bout it?"

"Probably," I said, sitting down and leaning on him, "but for the moment I'm thinking – or maybe trying not to think. And anyway, why's the light on in your trailer, if you're out here?"

"Marie'll be in theer an' she's scared o't' dark. She finds my place company, e'en if am not theer.

"Now look, while thee's thinking, 'appen tha' cud do some listenin' as well. A's a tale to tell t'neet an' theer's none 'ere to tell it to but thee. Don' b' set t' fretting, it calls fer nowt, fer theer's nowt can b' done 'bout it, now."

"Tell away," I said drowsily "but I can't promise I'll be awake."

"Thee nod off," he said easily, "a'll 'ave unburdened missen, w'ate'er."

Pa told me the tale of Jolyon's book. The short, vicious outbreak of savagery he had provoked when his greed was sparked by imaginary gold. How he came to be blown backwards through a hedge into a new world. His reading, done by light of sun, moon and stars. His falling asleep, into his night fire. How he summoned snails to soothe and seal his burns. How woodlice came to be his partners in understanding the group mind – at least that's what I thought he said because, as he was elaborating, I became aware there was a small mound of bedclothes underneath and behind us. I turned, for a better view and a tiny hand emerged from them, to wave, in a sleepy sort of way. So I waved back.

"Oh, don' thee worry ab'at thy sister. She an' a' often weathers our nights out 'ere. It don' troubl' no-one an' it soothes summat in us. We both like fer t'look at t'stars an' think as they're a' lookin' back at us." He laughed, gently, contentedly and took a draw on his unlit, broken 'old clay' – "as gi'en t'me by t' 'edge, boy!"

"Me, a' regrets thet book bitter, a'does," he sighed. "Theer's things as can be lost an' things as should never b' misplaced and yon book were one o' them."

As he talked on I began to feel almost unwell. His words seemed to be coded. In my mind, through my ears, I was hearing the same message that JJ had been trying to implant in me on Tank Trap Mountain, an hour earlier. Cue after cue was repeating itself, sleepless nights, the observant stars, the necessity of continuing. Everything was implying a job half-done. Somewhere, a cosmic finger was tapping a table, tapping, waiting…waiting for me to catch up, to cotton-on.

"Why me?" I suddenly burst out, interrupting Pa's ruminations and startling a stirring under the bedclothes, complete with the emergence of a cold-looking nose and a huge pair of bush baby eyes.

Punch laughed and it was a rueful, repentant sound.

"Why thee, son? 'Cos t' rest o' us 'as done all us can. Thee is just gettin' started and wi' our 'elp tha' can go a ways further. Our 'elp an' all t'elp yon lovely Princess can gi' thee. 'Ow many 'eroes get t' ave t' Princess from t' second chapter? En't thee t' lucky un?"

"Bother and be-blast you all!" I raged. "I never asked anything from any of you. I helped! Why is everything now coming to my door? Why is it suddenly 'my turn'? I don't want any more, I've had enough already. Don't lean on me. Whatever it is, it's not for me to do! Do it yourselves! Why me?"

"Ssh, ssh lad. Boy, boy, calm 'ee down now. Thee were a'yearnin' t' belong, t'be a part o' somethin' bigger, summat wi' meanin' for thee. Gi' it time. It'll show its face afore long. An' we are 'ere t'elp thee. We're a'all tae willin' t'kep things steady for thee. So 'ere we all are. Good folks and willin' folks all around thee. Ther' 'ent no anger pursuin', ther' 'ent no evil shown 'is face. Thou 'as time t' prepare. Why does thee tek on so?"

"Because I'm scared," I sobbed. "You just lost a book and you're doubled over about it. I as good as killed my mum and then I went on to sell the better part of myself. Now 'something' wants me in charge of not losing whatever it is that comes next. I thought I was done when I got us here. I thought I'd landed us all in a happy place. Now, like that idiot Odysseus, 'something' is pushing me to set sail again. I don't want to!"

"That's not wrong, son," agreed Punch, "but thee'll not b' sailin' blind this time. Tha's as solid a family as tha'll ever get. Tha's a beautiful bride and none threatens you with evil – not like it were for yer sister, an' me."

I stood and paced, to and fro like a romantic poet possessed by a baleful muse, wandering beneath the weird shapes of wrecking ball concrete, still mysterious in their wraps of shade and shadow, half-concealed under night. Dawn would break the spell shortly. Like Nosferatu, the vampire, I felt the need to flee the morning light. It should be bringing me absolution but I felt that its first rays would undo me completely.

So I fled and as I fled, I heard Punch whisper -"let 'im go, girl, let 'im go. 'E loves you and 'e loves me. 'E loves everyone, 'cept isself."

That gentle remark landed like Jolyon's cannonball and wondering what else might be heaped on my shoulders, I flew back to the safety of our plastic-box caravan. I crashed through the door, as though pursued by bears and flung myself full-length on the bed.

"Jabberwocky!" shrieked Tee, shooting up like a Jack-in-the-box. Then recovering herself and seeing the ruin that currently passed for my face, growled – "who did this to you? I'll kill 'em!"

"Oh Tee," I wailed. "I did it to myself."

"Tell me everything," she demanded. "Then I'll kill you."

So I did. And she didn't.

13

INTERSTELLAR WIND...

Tee had been uttering soothing words, calming me down since 5.00 am and despite the depression that had settled on me, together with the 'I-am-thinking-very-hard, VERY HARD!' look that had frozen on Tee's phiz, we both found we were insanely ravenous by six. Consequently we trudged over to the diner for breakfast.

Everyone else had succumbed, too. All the crew were there, far earlier than usual. Carl's early morning team were perfectly up to the job, so sensing 'war council,' he joined us in his whites.

"What's afoot?" he asked innocently.

"We're helping the cosmos redesign itself," said JJ. "It's sick of doing it the same old way, over and over again, so it's developing new neuro-pathways designed to utilise incipiently entropic materials."

"Of course it is," said Carl, easing himself out of his chair. "Damn... it's a pity but I sense I'm needed over there, so..."

"Hey, best buddy," Andy chimed in, 'you've been knocking my clock around with UFO mysteries for years. This is the real McCoy, so stick around, listen and maybe, learn."

Carl sat down again.

Large platters of eggs, sausages, beans, bacon, hash browns and fried bread arrived in front of us.

"Dig in," said Andy. "Who's next for a stroke?"

We ate, dangerously.

Then JJ began.

His opening sentences were - "the Universe is not yet fully conscious. In other words, it is not autonomous. True consciousness implies autonomy. True consciousness may be able to circumvent entropy. At least, I believe so and it appears the Universe thinks the same way."

That much I remember verbatim. The rest I reconstructed later, with Tee's help.

He said that the universe is not all that there is. There is an unseen and arguably, unseeable totality that we would call "Nothingness." But using nothingness in this sense requires a hyphen – "No-thingness." There is in No-thingness, no place for things. It's that simple.

Think of it, he said, as the most perfectly blended, homogenous soup. This soup is the sum and total of every universe that ever existed, except the one – or many – that are currently in existence. When these finally rundown, like so many clocks and simply stop, that is when entropy has gobbled up every last particle, they will have been returned, across the barrier of the quantum vacuum, to the soup. There they mix and therefore homogenise with the existing soup, adding whatever new information they may have acquired, in their existence as independent universes. The soup is being enriched in this way, constantly.

Now, he continued, you have to imagine that after a while, the vessel holding the soup springs a leak. This is what we locals have Christened the Big Bang moment. Now it could be that this wholly imaginary vessel is as leaky as a colander and universes are being born, as well as re-absorbed, in their billions, all the time. But it's easier for our brains to stick with one leak, one Big Bang and one universe – ours.

In miniature this process applies to every life-form. It comes into being by some quasi-magical event that we can almost describe but not quite. And it exits by reabsorption into the whole. Everything goes round, in the short term, in the long term and in the exceedingly long.

Life, as we know it, is not particularly thrilled by this process. Most of us, by the time we reach old age, are complaining that just as we were getting the hang of things here, on earth, it's suddenly time to leave. Probably all life-forms feel much the same way. My suggestion, said JJ, would be that there is developing amongst the universes a similar dissatisfaction at being attacked by entropy – 'just as we were getting going!'

Until now, life has been largely parasitic on the surface of the universe. As Marie-Gabrielle so memorably put it in this room – "life is going that -> way, the cosmos is going <- that," or, he gestured wildly, she used words to that effect. The Universe is starting to wake up to its predicament and it sees that the fix it is in is very similar, if not identical, to the problem that all short-term life faces. Therefore there are energies at work within the Universe that are seeking to tap the experience of 'base-life,' to see if there is any knowledge within transitory life-forms that could give hints on how to dodge the inevitability of annihilation via the processes of entropy.

These energies have, therefore, been busy creating innovative life-forms that tap the unusual, the inexplicable and the unexplored in Life. They already draw on a vast range of life experiences but they are currently getting more, how can one put it, creative and humane in their enquiries.

I believe that my planet and the others linked to it by the Core, is one such 'designer' experiment. I think certain human beings are being relocated to a place they can still think of as Earth, to live out eternal lives along one chord of their being. The hope is that some element within each individual quirkiness will shine a light on the mystery of survival, as it might manifest itself within 'obsessiveness' – again, for lack of a better word!

The Core itself, I believe, is a miniature version of the 'No-thing multiverse,' the crock of soup. It's a stab at, an imitation of, the real McCoy and is composed of all the likely bits and pieces these searching energies have discovered over eons of time. The Core represents one deliberately cultured consciousness drawn from this, our Universe. It intends to defy Process, to avoid entropic digestion and annihilation back into the universal, 'No-thing soup.' It's seeking to avoid the inevitable and for this moment, it wants our help. Not 'needs' but 'wants' – 'would like.'

If I have to validate what I've said, I would say look at its influence parochially, here within our time and history. Even within such a minute timescale its imprint is visible. The entire history of esoteric enquiry is a by-product of its needling our developing consciousness. Let's not make the mistake of thinking that we are conscious. We are struggling low-life. It is astonishing that cosmic consciousness has deigned to involve us at any level. It could ignore us with the same indifference that we ignore life-forms lower than our own. Life on earth is an experiment, an indulgence of a line of cosmic enquiry. Life on Earth II is the equivalent of molecular engineering, only so infinitely more refined that it's almost inhumane in concept.

That was it and JJ sat down with a thump. There was total silence. The legendary pin would not have dared to fall, despite the crashing of the caff all around us.

Marie-Claire had fallen asleep on Punch's shoulder early in the proceedings. She now shifted comfortably in her sleep and let fly the loudest, longest and most-echoing fart the world has ever heard. On and on it ran, changing key, invoking vibrato, until finally dying out in a crash worthy of the 1812 Overture.

Punch, instantly and wildly defensive, made furious 'don't-you-dare faces and fingers' at us all. Andy tried to play the Responsible Adult but started to cry, silently and hysterically. Marie-Gabrielle looked around wildly for assistance but could only find two sausages to stuff in her mouth – sideways. JJ simply heaved in his chair, like a ship in the grip of a miniature tornado. Tee and I buried ourselves in each-other's bosom, while Carl fled for the kitchen where he could be heard making distant ululations, akin to the Muezzin's Call to Prayer. Then, just as we had steadied ourselves and were pretending to be grown-up, she let fly with another one.

This time it was hopeless, even Punch gave up and started braying like a donkey, Andrew howled, Marie-Gabrielle got hiccups and giggles, while Tee and I went into schoolgirl hysterics. Carl was heard reprising his calls to the faithful. JJ managed to stay silent but fell off his chair and rolled around under the table.

Not surprisingly, Marie-Claire woke with a start. But instead of looking around indignantly, or hiding her face in her apron – two regular recourses, for I should have mentioned earlier, she has a tendency to violent flatulence – she stared straight across the room, towards the door, with a face stricken by horror and amazement.

14

THERE MUST BE A NAME FOR IT

We were silenced and every head turned to follow her gaze. Advancing across the floor, with an attitude both agreeable and open, was a seven-foot tall rabbit, walking on its hind legs. Its forelegs were most definitely to be recognised as arms. It wasn't wearing fur. It was wearing a seamless, skin-tight, harlequin suit, made from diamond-shaped, coloured felts. In some manner, as if lit from within, it glowed.

The diner's patrons, a sophisticated crowd, medics and paramedics coming off shift, cleaners and night-workers on their way home, executives on their way in, gave it a handsome round of applause, which it acknowledged with a faint bow. But we, who remained frozen in our seats, mouths open and hands paralysed in our laps, simply stared in shock and awe.

It approached.

"Good morning. I wonder if any of you excellent people are acquainted with a gentleman who goes by the name of Jo-Jo?"

From the darkness beneath our communal table came a hollow voice – "how the hell did you get here?"

"Ah, there he is," said the Rabbit delicately. "Alack and alas. You keep him as some sort of floor-level pet, I gather? May I tempt him out with a sausage? He was always very partial to them."

"No, you blithering idiot," protested Jo-Jo, slowly emerging. "I was down there… shall we say…by choice."

"Oh my, things have deteriorated. Obviously you've missed me."

Then, addressing the company, the Rabbit pleaded – "Do let him sit among you. He has several prestigious degrees. Well, at least one, I believe in media studies…?"

"JJ," said Andy, "we're at a disadvantage even greater than yours. Do introduce us to your friend."

"Certainly," said JJ, by now in full recovery mode. "Rabbit, may I introduce the last speaker, Mr Andrew, owner of this prestigious establishment. On his right, Sergeant Punch, a veteran of Blenheim and under his protection, Madame Marie-Claire. To her right, her putative ward, Mademoiselle Marie-Gabrielle. On this side of the table, at the head, sits Miss Eva while beside her is her friend, companion and it is fair to say, partner, Her Very Royal Highness, the Princess Tulipa Agnethuram, of Sikhim. The two place settings currently absented belonged, one, to me – you idiot – and the second to Mr Carl, currently engaged in calling the Faithful to Prayer, in the kitchen – as you can, no doubt, hear.

"Ah, how I love such devotional ritual," the Rabbit rhapsodised. "We have so little on our threadbare apology of a planet."

There was a slightly awkward silence, finally broken by Andy, enquiring if the Rabbit might take breakfast. "You see the ruins of ours," he indicated. "I'm sure the kitchen can rustle up some greenery, a grated carrot or two?"

"Too kind," observed the Rabbit, inclining slightly, "I have a lifetime's supply of radioactive lithium in my stomach. It suffices, I find."

"I take it," said Andrew, "you have private business with JJ, the moniker by which we have befriended him. Perhaps you are unaware that among friends, a shortening of the Christian name, or very occasionally extending it, is a common sign of inclusion and affection among us? Such a diminutive is in no way offensive. Jo-Jo had little to lose, nevertheless we reduced him to JJ. I'm afraid to admit he had no say in the matter. Perhaps seen through your eyes, it could be interpreted seen as rudeness on our parts? Not the case at all, I assure you."

"So," said the Rabbit, showing an interest, "were I to be befriended, I might become Rabbi?"

"Ah," said Andy, "there's a clash of nouns there that you may be unaware of. We would be more likely to hail you as 'Rab,' or 'Con,' or 'Bun.' I regret to say you would not be consulted."

"Oh my goodness," said the Rabbit. "Such a situation as mine now becomes more serious than I could ever have imagined. You see, I always told him that I should have a proper name! Being the 'Rabbit,' or even, 'The Rabbit,' is barely acceptable, even when there are generally only two of you and that on a sparsely populated planet."

The Rabbit turned a baleful, censoring eye on Jo-Jo – "did I not always beg for a name, a Moniker, as your friends so interestingly fashion it?"

"You were tedious on the subject," Jo-Jo admitted, dusting himself down after his sojourn under the table. "By the way guys," he added wickedly, "that corner down there is a perfect paradise of dust bunnies."

"Now that is just plain hurtful," said the Rabbit, "and typical of the cheap repartee I tolerated for millennia. I should never have let myself be persuaded to take this mission. I was perfectly happy trail-biking round the cwm and chatting with Shade – who was never, ever, unkind…"

An awkward moment, innocently saved by Carl who had been lured from his self-imposed exile to investigate this latest UFO. "Ah, another dirt bike freak?" he interjected, hopefully.

"Don't go there, Carl," warned JJ. "All is not as it sounds."

But the Rabbit's attention was focused on our very own 'Alice-in-Wonderland,' as Tee had gleefully tagged Marie-Gabrielle, some weeks ago. She, sensing an awkward silence, had taken the opportunity to ask sweetly – "what would you like to have been called?"

"Privileged to meet you, Marie-Gabrielle," said the Rabbit, bowing graciously. "I have longed, over millennia, to be known as Rufus – as in… 'Rufus-the-Rabbit!'" And he made a flamboyant gesture, as if to sign his name in copperplate, on the morning sky.

Jo-Jo made a throwing-up noise.

Marie-Gabrielle slapped him on the arm.

"Then," she beamed, "henceforth you shall be known among us as Rufus!"

I had to admit it was a very 'Alice' performance – indeed, she should have clapped her hands with delight. Instead, she delivered an absolute roundhouse of a punch to Jo-Jo's left bicep, when he persisted with his gargling noises.

"Ow! That hurt!" he yelped.

"This elegant person SHALL be Rufus," she commanded. "Rufus! – not Roo, or Fuzz – but Rufus. He has come a very long way to see us, it's the least we can do by way of a courteous welcome. Behave yourself, JJ!"

"Crikey," mumbled Jo-Jo, "it cost me two O's to join…he gets five letters free…"

"Don't be petty," said Marie-Gabrielle, "you know you don't miss them."

"Rufus, darling, if you'd like to come with me, I could show you around."

"Enchante," said Rufus the Rabbit. "Perhaps I could book an interview with 'JJ' later? When, perhaps, you have sufficiently recovered yourself," he finished, sardonically.

"Enchante, RR," said JJ. "Can't wait." And he skipped nimbly away from Marie-Gabrielle, a second before she could deliver a second, fatal, knockout blow.

15

TACTICAL RETREAT

"Do you know," I said to Tee, "I feel the pressure of a business trip, one long-arranged, coming-on. Care to join me on my tedious excursion?"

"Delighted, darling. Would I be correct in assuming that you plan to travel by means of my automobile, yours truly at the helm, ever willing to extend the helping hand to a partner caught, as it were, short?"

"Such had been my assumption, implied I admit but your recapitulation has reassured me that I made no egregious error in my planning."

"Then ponder no more, Sweet Leaf of Tea, we shall depart upon the instant!"

"Guys," said Andy, "why are you talking like that?"

"Like what?" we chirruped in unison.

"Like the Rabbit?"

"My God!" exclaimed Tee, spinning round, clutching her temples. "We've been infected! It's like myxomatosis. We're going to swell up and die from a superfluity of conversational elegance."

"I've been pierced by vowels," I groaned, doubling over. "Save me!"

"Can't," gasped Tee, "I've been ambushed by a subjunctive."

"Oh shut up," said Andy. "Can Carl and I come, too? This place has gone to the… I was going to say dogs…but it appears to have gone to the rabbits, instead."

"Certainly," said Tee, "your hoist awaits…as in 'car-hoist'…not a vocal exaggeration of 'host'…agh, I'm still in the grip of it."

"You're all crazed," vowed Carl. "I'm driving."

"I think you better," groaned Tee. "I'm quite overcome."

"Let us to our boudoirs repair," said I. "The better to prepare for overnight revelry. One hour, shall we say, till we meet again, by the vehicle? Meantimes, farewell!"

"I think you're bucking it," Tee observed. "Parts of that were pretty clumsy."

"You, I observe, are still very unwell. I'll soothe you, as we bowl along the carriageways of England, with peppermint drops."

"Now you're talking," said Tee.

It was quite a different experience being driven by Carl. We stopped at traffic lights, gave way at roundabouts, paused politely at zebra crossings.

"Run 'em down," ordered Tee from the backseat, "their lives are over. Do them a favour!"

"Good grief," said Andy, "she's worse back here than she is behind the wheel."

I turned round. "Open!" I said.

Tee obediently opened her mouth, like a baby gannet and I popped in a peppermint gobstopper.

"Y'um…lights…mm…advisory…slurp…only…um…yum…"

"How many of those have you got?" asked Carl.

"Hundreds, I buy wholesale."

"Praise be!"

He drove on calmly and we toured the industrial ringworld, before bowling along the M40 at a sedate 70 mph.

"It…'ll…go… fa…st…er…" slurped Tee. "Some…bod…y…tell…h…im…"

We rolled on, beautifully, sedately, accurately.

"Stop at the services," I said. "We're going to have to let her drive. She's going into withdrawal. Don't worry, this thing's got multiple air bags."

So we stopped. Pees all round and then personal refuelling. We all had black Americanos and pain au raisin. I remember that distinctly, because it started a tradition. Also it seemed unbelievably redeeming, whatever I might mean by that.

When we made a move to leave, prompted by some deep-seated seed of devilment, Tee spent an eternity negotiating discount for double-glazing, with a sweet, innocent salesgirl doomed to stand by the exit for her sins. Having finally agreed some complicated deal she proffered an address in Madhya Pradesh, which she insisted on writing out carefully and then swept away, queenly and imperious. We, her fumbling retainers, trundled in her wake, one on wheels, two on barely functioning legs.

She then drove like an angel. I swear, if she had spotted such an unlikely phenomenon as a pedestrian on the M40, she'd have stopped for them and painted zebra markings across the carriageways. After silently relishing this merciful intermission for several miles, I described my scheme to everyone.

We were going in search of Pa's book or, more properly, Old Jolyon's book. Firstly because it was important to him, secondly because it sounded important on every level. Communication is the handmaid of progress and progress marks the development of intelligence, or so I am assured. This book was a manual describing how higher and lower life-forms could communicate on the everyday level. Its insights might indicate how we, as lesser life-forms, might expect communications to arrive from the cosmic intelligentsia. That, at least, was the sum total of my theorising. It seemed that I had, unintentionally, scrambled aboard JJ's ship of discovery.

"You mean," said Carl, after my laborious exposition, "they might give us a whistle?"

"Death can arrive in many forms…so beware," I said, mystically wrapping myself in invisible guru robes, proof against the slings and arrows of the uninitiated.

My immediate plan was that Tee and I were going to reprise the walk that had begun this entire chapter of our lives. Andy and Carl were going to drop us by the beech hanger, where we'd parked before. Then they were going to go and make a call on the custodians of the Manor and book themselves a visitor's slot touring the more modern building. There they would snoop, paying particular attention to the library.

I had a theory that, 300 years ago, the Militia, thwarted when their quarry evaporated into thin air, would have scoured the woodland searching for Punch's hideout. I doubted Earth Magic would have had any reason to resist their intrusion, once Punch had completed his task. It would have made a tactical withdrawal.

When they found his camp, they would have found the book. I hoped, fervently, that incunabula were not so commonplace as to be kicked aside, even then. The book could, over time, have found its way to the library of the new house. I had to admit, especially the further we drove, that this was a thread so thin as to be almost imaginary. But there might be indications as to its whereabouts, even after all these years. It was a long shot but one worth taking, I hoped. At least it had got us out of Rabbitsburg.

We could all stay in touch, assuming cell phones had any writ in this part of the world. Tee and I could make our way back to the drop-off, or even down to the Manor. Punch had indicated it was less than a mile's stroll.

It was a plan, at least.

What I didn't let on was that in my little day sack, I had Marie-Claire and Jo-Jo's shining metal eye. My intention was to see if it had any interest in the beech hanger, or in Pa's old magical wood. I also wanted to scour the Hedge-line, to see if I could find any token from his past. He'd been dragged into the 21st Century from the 18th and never once had he protested. As a born survivor, he'd quietly adapted. I doubted I would have coped as well, moving forwards or backwards across time. If I could find him some small talisman of his past – like his 'old clay'- it might be a welcome touchstone and keepsake.

Amazingly, everyone agreed. Even the sun and tiny clouds seemed to smile on the idea.

16
OLD HAUNTS REVISITED

The Range Rover pulled away smoothly and we waved after it.

"It's a fabulous car you bought, sweetie," I said gently. She'd looked so sad to see it glide away without her. "You know Carl will drive really carefully."

"Worrah, worrah, worrah," she said softly, in a very sad, downbeat voice.

"Come on, little Tigger. We can do this."

"Worrah…"

I turned and inhaled English hedgerow smells. Meadowsweet and fractured soil, other scents more elusive and some I probably imagined. But the rough, worn, top rail of the fence we clambered over left a green mould smell on my hands, and more likely still, a green mould stain on my jeans.

For all that I tried to snare Tee with English sights and smells, with interesting stones, or empty snail shells, all I could prise loose was the odd "worrah," or "worrah, worrah" as we steadily climbed the now ploughed field along its far headland. This new approach was forced on us, because the old way had been blocked. Today, behind the gate, had been a life-endangering, muddy flood that had collected below the furrows.

The closer we got to the hanger, the more Tee's mood lifted. She straightened up, 'sharpened' herself and stopped the mournful "worrah-ing."

As we made the last sharp climb, she opened up a fraction and said – "this really is a place and a half, Beavie." She stood, wind tugging at the neck-length hair that had grown back, faint echo of the superb mane she'd shaved away. Her half-hair matched the half-lost expression she still wore. Some itch remained unscratched.

"What's wrong, Tee?"

She pondered.

"Until last night, you weren't going anywhere. Now you are. You're casting for a scent, like a dog. You're not going to leave me to go after it, are you?"

"God, Tee, no! I'm not going anywhere if you won't come. I'm not courageous. You're the adventurer. You're the one with the big heart. I'm just a truffle-hound. I'm on a scent, that's true enough but not without you I'm not."

She was still looking at me, sadly.

"We've got to trust each other, Tee. Come on, let's move into the trees, for I've something to show you and it's not safe out here."

She brightened a bit and said – "Tiggers love surprises and secrets."

We found our old trysting place – I think we assumed we had squatters' rights on the place – and settled back against the friendly tree. Once again the canopy danced and sighed overhead, great branches executing turns and pirouettes that must have inspired the choreographers who gave birth to ballet.

I handed her the towel. "I don't think it's delicate. It was turned up from under a yard of London clay but, well, see for your dear old self. It's all yours…"

She smiled. Still a bit sadly. Ecstatic "worrahs!" had gone right out of her. I prayed that they'd be back.

She stared into the black lens and it stared back. "Nothing," she said glumly.

I took it back and stared for a while. "Nor me," I agreed. "I don't think it works that way, though. Last night, when I pointed it at the star group JJ showed me, I felt it twitch and come alive. Then, I think something flowed through me. Maybe it came from the star but where it was going to, that's a total mystery. I just don't know. JJ said I was like a switch, an on/off node in a circuit but what switches me on and off, I have no idea.

"Let me tell you, Tee, that 'don't know' and 'I have no idea' are the most overworked phrases in my vocabulary. I didn't want any more occasions to use them but JJ just dumped this one on me and somehow, it's sunk its teeth into my bum. You saw how miserable I was, I wasn't faking but despite that, I'd still like to know about some of the big things in life. Is the Universe learning to think and might it really need our help? I find that a seductive idea – even though it'll probably need us the way we need doormats."

"That wouldn't be so good, would it?" said Tee. She was pointing the eye at the trees, at the waving branches, the sky, the ground, her feet, the view – everything and anything she could think of. Then she nodded and wrapped it up carefully.

"I feel like a kid who's unwrapped an exciting toy, at Christmas. But the mysterious uncle who sent it me, didn't put any batteries in. Now I've got to wait and there's a sort of hole of expectation in my little life that'll never be filled by what it actually does when the batteries finally go in."

"Yes," I agreed, "it's a peculiar business that you always expect more from the unknown than it can possibly deliver. Managing expectations, especially on this level, is pretty, what do we say, 'challenging.' Yet everything that's going-to-be will finally arrive, sometime in the future. It's just that we'll never know if we were useful, or causative in any way. And even if we did, we'd just be disappointed, because our expectations had been so huge."

"If the Universe feels the same way," Tee said slowly, "it must have a monstrous headache or, even worse, heartache."

As our ruminations grew ever more speculative, ever more deeply subjective, there came a huge tearing, splitting wrenching sound. We leapt to our feet and in the distance, though closer than was comfortable, were witnesses to a large tree executing the last throes of falling. We saw, heard and then felt it pound onto the ground – a ripple that penetrated the soles of our feet. Then a little dust blew our way, followed by silence. We looked at each other.

"Did we bore it to death?" asked Tee.

"It's entirely possible," I agreed. "Do you think we should go over and apologise?"

"We could at least take a respectful look."

Despite an underlying sense of misgiving, we approached the deadfall. In its rush to the ground it had brought other large branches down. 'Collateral damage,' as the Yanks have it. Even as we walked, one last innocent victim plummeted down, whatever strings and ligaments had held it until then, finally parting.

"Look up, look up!" warned Tee, "there may be more of those scary persons hanging by a thread up there…"

"Too, too true…" I agreed nervously.

We worked our way round to the root plate. It was a flat network of underground branches that had had enough. There was some rot but for the most part, the wood seemed sound. There were great, ivory coloured rips and tears that had an oily feel to my fingertips and smelled of sap.

It didn't seem to have made much of a hole in the forest floor but when I jumped in, it was deeper than I had thought. All there was, though, was dust and stones that hadn't seen daylight for a while. No iron-bound chests, no gold coins, no warrior's bones.

"Was that a message?" asked Tee. "Say – 'something has to give way before anything new can start?' Because if it was, believe it or not, it's scared me."

"I'm with you 100 per cent," I said. "Messages on a postcard, please, not via 30-ton forest giants. It's bad enough having to decode symbols. It's a whole different ballgame when their interpretation becomes downright dangerous, too. I suddenly feel very, very small and startlingly irrelevant. May we press on?"

"Too right we can," said Tee. "I'm leading the cowards' retreat to open country, where the worst thing that can fall on you is bird poo." With which she turned and walked briskly away.

I threw a blank and desperate look at the wreckage but I was too obtuse to deduce any messages.

"Wait for me!" I squeaked. "I'm coming, I'm coming, I'm coming!"

Not getting it…or, more simply, not knowing when you should know, is the very devil. I think it's one of the reasons that I hate quizzes, be they pub or the Uni' Chall' variety. Instantly you're back at school, not knowing what you should have learned in last night's homework and what's even worse, being convinced that you HAD learnt it. The teachers roll their eyes up to heaven, your own name slips from your mind, you're plumb-dumb and empty, blank paper, tabula rasa, the freshly-scraped palimpsest.

We burst out of the wood-of-not-knowing like a pair of terrified gnomes. The forest giants, nodded, waved and roared at us, as we fled in search of a sheltering toadstool.

"What's got into us?" I gasped. "This is already a very freaky experience and I didn't think it was even supposed to have started yet."

"Can we stop running?" begged Tee. "I'm not half as fit as I look and I don't look that fit to begin with."

"If there's nothing in pursuit of us, wearing vivid colours, a scaly tail and uncertainty as to where its mouth might be, I reckon we could ease back a fraction, yes."

Tee stopped dead.

"You haven't seen anything like that recently, have you?"

"Not since I was about eight and chewed my way through a whole pack of cola sweets, no."

"Thank God! I'll take a quick look astern."

"Anything?"

"A cow."

"Natural or unnatural?"

"Looks normal, leg at each corner, black and white and it's eating grass."

"Could be a disguise."

"No. It's just done one of those enormous pees. Not even the worst ghouls pee."

"You're right, they don't. That's probably a very important observation, though where to file it, I haven't a clue. So, shall we proceed, 'dignified and stately?"

Which is what we did, until we came to the long line of trimmed hedge that would lead, in its turn, to the unkempt, unruly Hedge that flanked Punch's one-time abode.

There we stood, shuffling, turning around, pulling at leaves and generally feeling weak-of-bladder.

"Why in hell are we so nervy, Tee?"

"I honestly have no idea, Beavie but I'm as skittish as a mouse in a basket of kittens."

"Shall we try a trundle alongside this trimmed hedge? I don't think flail-cut hedges fight back. They've had all the magic battered out of them."

17

ANCIENT BONES

After a 20-minute walk we ran out of shattered hedge and there, at a stile, were confronted with its big brother, the huge, silent buttress that a rogue cannonball had once punched my soul-father clean through, backwards.

There was a nicely cut signpost that read – 'To the Manor.' Its other arm, pointing whence we had just come, bore the legend – 'Deadman's Copse.'

"That could explain a lot," I said, pointing. "Dead things have never been my forte, especially dead Beavers."

"Agreed but last time it was so warm and welcoming. I mean you remember too, it was a pants-down, equipment-out sort of place."

"Absolutely true…maybe there are different strands of magic there, trailing like spider fishing line and it all depends which one snags you."

"Oddly, I don't find that at all comforting."

"I feel we need to do some serious reading up but whether we should be reading physics, or magic, baffles me."

"How about both?" said Tee. "I mean you're forever banging on about McGilchrist and the way you tell it, that's half mysterious and half very real."

"That's how it feels to me. Right brain is mysterious, a bit Jungian archetypes and Goethian holism. Left brain makes lists and ticks things off them. Neither hacks it, there has to be a conciliation between the two – who, or what, though is the mysterious conciliator and how does he, she, it, promulgate their conclusions?

"All the important stuff starts where words give out, where they simply curl up and die, spluttering. Left and right, good and bad, black and white…that division into two absolutes is flawed, badly off kilter. The annoying thing is, it can work and then people forget to look any further. Science does have answers and in the long run, it will have all of them. But we're never 'in the long run.' We're always 'here,' which is where a mystical approach can give a clue…not an answer, a clue. Think about it, so much of what we take for granted now, would have been seen as airy-fairy, mystical ravings at one time. Atoms, black holes and big bangs come into that category.

"Techno-science is such an arrogant absolute. It needs fringe thinkers to be drawing it out into uncharted territory, otherwise it spends too much time making more stuff we don't need.

"I like reading scientists who still believe in God, or who have gone 'dangerously mystical.' There's loads of them, Lothar Schafer, Ervin Laszlo, David Peat, Rupert Sheldrake, David Bohm. These guys poke at the place where words start to give up. They actually dare to lapse into the realms of 'what if…?' Science so hates that but it's actually how science proceeds, pursuing leads that are suggested by 'what ifs…'

"Hans Vaihinger, who's more or less forgotten now, wrote a whole philosophy around 'what ifs…?' He described them as useful fictions. There was an early review that really put it in a nutshell…"

"I wish you could," muttered Tee, who'd been looking bored but was now beginning to look rebellious.

"Unfair," I pleaded. "Just give me two minutes, I'm on a roll here."

"Hmph," said Tee. "After two minutes I'm charging, by the second."

"I used to charge from the start," I dared.

"You mean Muti did."

"Don't remind me, I'm owed millions!

"ANYWAY, I was really struck by something I read, about a bunch of anthropologists driven mad by ants in some village they were working in. There was an old boy there who had made a deal with the ants. They could go as far as his knees, but no further. The field workers were reliant on bug sprays so toxic that they were melting their watches. What the old guy's secret was, I don't know. Maybe it was something he smeared on his thighs, maybe he really did have a deal with the ants. Science wouldn't dream of investigating the old boy, only how to wipe-out ants.

"Why won't we take the whole world of alternative possibilities more seriously? Much of it will be mumbo-jumbo but something will emerge that isn't and that something will advance things."

"Be honest, are you getting anywhere with this?" asked Tee, batting at a fly.

"I guess the whole point is 'no, I'm not.' I'm not a scientist and I'm not a mystic. But I do get that there are other ways of processing and understanding information, so that you don't arrive at the 'same-old' conclusions that you normally would."

"And this helps us, how? Because, I confess, I was trying but I lost you some while back."

"If I could say it straight out, I would. What I'm trying to say is that if we remained open in front of phenomena we've not encountered before, we might learn something."

"That's straight-forward enough. Now all you've got to do is persuade the scientific establishment that you're right and they're wrong. But as we're currently imperilling our health by overdosing on fresh-air, in the middle of nowhere, I suggest you put that on hold and follow me. Try whittling your theories down to postcard size, as we proceed. I shall be doing the proceeding…you will be theorising. I suggest you could distil a whole philosophy from that simple fact, O Great One."

"Harsh," I muttered.

We set off and I cast a wary eye to the rear – checking for the coloured creature with the elusive mouth, then followed her over the stile.

After a while Tee said – "Do we know exactly where he got blown through? Because this hedge and wood seem to have done some growing, latterly. The wood now seems to be on both sides and that's not how Punch describes it."

I pondered for a while.

"If the Manor is that way," I waved to our right, "then he came through from our left and judging from what he said, at the other end. Also, don't you find it odd that here we have a hedge, running through a wood? You'd think that woods trumped hedges, sort of."

"Which proves," said Tee, "that this is The Hedge, because it still has attitude."

"Is that good?" I enquired nervously.

"I doubt my opinion counts."

Despite crossing the stile and encountering the Hedge, we had yet to push into the wood. There was a deep ditch between the rough old meadow we were in and the wood-proper. It was an effective barrier, steep-sided and obviously swampy. Eventually it petered-out and we could cross it, with a scramble. However, we then had to walk back and the closer we got to where we had wanted to be, the more obstructive the vegetation became. What had looked to be easy passage, to a casual glance from the other side, now proved to be chicane after chicane of hazel-breaks, fallen birch trees, bramble mounds and pathways surfaced in treacherous, ankle-snaring ivy.

It was like playing snakes and ladders with a rigged board. And that is an unfortunate metaphor to spring to mind when your ankle is being grabbed by ivy. I gulped, I should have asked Pa if there were any.

"What, ladders?" sniggered Tee, turning round and stopping.

"No snakes, idiot," I said and then stopped dead in my tracks. "How did you know what I was thinking?" I demanded.

"I didn't. You were mumbling. You're always mumbling."

"I was not mumbling. I was tight-lipped and anxious. Also, I am not always mumbling."

"You were mumbling about it being like snakes and ladders with a rigged board and you should have asked Punch if there were any snakes. How else would I have known?"

"Exactly!" I said. "I wasn't talking out loud. I was thinking. Somehow or other you read my mind."

"How could I?" demanded Tee. "How could I read the mind of an associative lunatic? You being you, were just as likely to be thinking about…parrot cages and cashew nuts. So, you were obviously talking about snakes and ladders…which is why I said, sardonically – 'ladders?' You were just not keeping up with yourself, which also goes to prove the fact that you're deeply troubled."

"I'm deeply troubled that you're reading my mind!" I squawked. "It's private."

"What, from little me?"

"Especially from little you. I'm not having you snooping into my seedy past. You'll go right off me."

Tee sniffed. "You were mumbling. You always mumble."

"I do not. I was not. You read my mind. This wood is playing games. I hate games. Stop it, now."

"Me, or the wood?"

"Both of you."

"How will I know? It's a reasonable question. How do I know if you said it, or the wood gave me a prompt?"

I gave that some thought.

"I'll be totally silent for 10 minutes, so if you get anything – it's the wood."

"OK."

We pushed on but what had been obstruction now turned to blockade. Larger trees were supporting canopies of trailing vine, mostly old man's beard and this had woven itself into well-nigh impenetrable mattresses between the coppiced hazels. Underfoot, the ground was suddenly less accommodating. Rocks pierced the surface and clinging to them, thin mats of moss gave way treacherously beneath your shoes.

"Jesus!" yelled Tee. "Punch lived in this lot for a year? I take my hat off to him. I also give notice that if it's like this all the way, I'm giving up, until we come back with bill hooks or our own portable cannon."

"You know where bill hooks will get you," I replied.

"Did you say that, or didn't you?"

"What?"

"Did you say – 'It's not far, only a little bit further'? Did you, or did you not?"

"Oh, bloody hell," I said. "Did not say it…I actually said – 'you know where bill hooks will get you.' Sorry, I broke my 10 minute embargo but that's what I actually said."

"Not what I heard," said Tee with a shrug.

"Oh dear," I said. "This wood, or this Hedge is messing with us. There again, on second thoughts," I paused, "…maybe it's got a sense of humour and your information, 'as-not-received-from-me,' was right…" Putting intuition to the test, I shoulder-charged a mattress of tangled vines and hazel and found that, with one arm at least, I had broken through into a quite different world.

Peering through the rent I had made, I could see into a peaceful glade of well-spaced, older growth trees, with grassed dells and paths, lined by moss covered rock.

"Help me sort out this tangle," I said. "Then we have a way through, I think. Try not to do too much damage. I suspect we're here on sufferance only."

Tee sidled closer, while at the same time giving me a look of the gravest suspicion. "If you've gone all fey on me," she said, "then I am definitely getting spooked. Should you feel you're growing horns, or developing hooves, let me know and we'll head for the nearest veterinary surgeon's."

"I'll be sure to," I said, running an exploratory hand over the thatch I called hair.

Once we were through, the turf was springy and dry underfoot. Had I had hooves, I'd have felt quite at home. Boldly, I headed towards where the Hedge should be. The going was good, the air was fresh, even the flies, which had been pestilential at one stage, had backed off. And at least the Hedge hadn't vanished. It lay exactly where it should and it was both dense and dark.

"No pun intended but you'd actually need a cannonball to 'punch' through that lot," said Tee.

She was right. The trees Pa had known were gone and it was their grandchild-saplings that were now standing as solid, old growth, growing in a double line between which was interwoven every type of shrub and bush ever listed as native to an English hedgerow. Ubiquitous vines clung to everything, offering themselves up as swatches of dark green ivy, rakes of grey and silver lace, and even the occasional wedding bouquet of wild, pink roses. Suddenly, I felt very humbled, stirred, even honoured, to be standing here. I wished there was some way of saying that but as it appeared the Hedge, or wood, could read my mind, there wasn't much point.

I let my eyes rove along the long, snaking line of it and was reminded of Jo-Jo's description of his journey round the Core, that he'd unfolded to us one evening. He'd talked about the "safe" zone, the few yards alongside the milky barrier, where wind, rain and snow could not penetrate. The Hedge seemed to have a similar selvedge, along its inner face, in which nothing grew, other than scraggy grasses and traces of cowslip clumps. Somehow, I would have been reluctant to use it as a path, though it must have been by walking along there that Punch scoured the Hedge bottom for jetsam.

I ran my eyes down its length once more and at the very end of my useful sight, I saw something lean and white, idling in whatever airs might stir along the Hedge-line.

"What is that?" I asked, in a strained voice, while grabbing Tee's arm. "Your eyes are better than mine."

"Stop watching porn on your phone," she said flippantly, "it's ruining your…oh, my Lord, I think it's a bone."

"That's what I thought. What do we do?"

"We go and investigate, at once, of course!"

"What if it lurches at us?" I whimpered.

"Oh, you baby! Bones don't lurch, they swivel and clatter…and now and then, skulls rattle and chatter!"

"That's all tacitly summed up in 'lurch,'" I said defensively.

"You may have a point. Anyway, follow me, I've got my inner Tigger back!"

"Thank God!" I muttered, painfully aware that my 'outer Beaver' would probably prove useless, should a Halloween-themed drama intrude.

We walked swiftly, blessed with the same springy turf we had already encountered. Meeting a few tiny rivulets, we leapt over them, easily. We scrambled the odd scree of gravel and stones, that clicked and clacked in protest and eventually came to a more uneven stretch of land of ups and downs, as if mining spoil had been laid out in tailings, been forgotten and then grass had grown over them.

The white object caught in the woodbine was now, identifiably, a bone and at a guess, a long, curving rib bone. As it certainly wasn't human, the latent menace ebbed from it.

As we got closer, leaping more and more rivulets, that were turning to tiny streams, I suddenly realised where we were. This was what was left of Marie-Gabrielle's swamp.

"It's a bone from Pa's bull. Maybe there'll be a pile of them nearby, or this is a lone one carried off, donkeys' years ago, snagged on the vine to be drawn up year after year."

Tee was ahead of me, being a superior brook-leaper. "You're right," she shouted, "there are other bones over here. That one has just strayed into the air and probably like you said."

You didn't need to be a forensic archaeologist to describe the scene, though it certainly was an advantage to have heard Punch's account of it.

High above where a small mess of bones lay on the ground and secure in a very old tree, the eye of faith could make out a yard or two of rope. Below that, woven in a dense twist of vines, segments of backbone. The rope was frayed to mere wisps but you could recreate where it had been crossed over a branch to haul up the great beast. The very fact that the vines grew so densely at that point, suggested they had swarmed over the lower leg bones. Perhaps, in winter, they shone whitely through the old growth, when the leaves fell.

I looked around and realised that the swamp Punch had described had shrunk enormously. The ridges we were standing on, the rivulets we had been jumping, all suggested we were actually within its old perimeter. This hard ground would once have been mud and Marie-Gabrielle would have been teetering in it, up to her knees in muddy water, while the bull snorted and tossed its head in rage only yards away.

This mud might have tiny Alice footprints impressed somewhere in its depths, slowly fossilizing for posterity. And elsewhere would be the half-inch lead ball that ploughed its way through the great head and on into the backbone. Now that would be a find to take home for Pa!

"We have to take him a souvenir, Beavie!" Tee was shouting enthusiastically, waving segments of backbone at me, from the haul she had discovered. "How about this vertebra, it's as clean as a whistle? Come on, choose one, he'll be tickled pink!"

I wasn't so certain. I think Punch's memories of this place were forever mingled with remorse about the death of Old Jolyon. We were probably wrong to be here, wrong to have come. I was beginning to feel I'd made a huge mistake, innocently but naively.

However, it is very hard to resist a Tigger in full cry.

She was now searching for evidence of where he had clay-baked the mammoth pike.

Embarrassingly, I knew the truth of that but when she happened upon a particularly lush growth of weed, at the side of an ancient and almost totally decayed tree, I hadn't the heart to say anything. Certainly, you could convince yourself that the tree had been crudely felled and equally certainly, rank weeds can indicate a burning.

"I reckon," I volunteered, "that if I think carefully I can work out how to backtrack to Pa's bivouac. Not that we're going to find the book there. In fact, I hope we don't. Because if we do it'll be in the form of mouse turds."

"Clever old you," said Tee. "But I thought we were going to investigate what the Hedge had caught for him in the interim?"

"We were but I've suddenly got a bit windy. Scared stiff, to be precise. I don't want you to mistake my meaning."

"Fair enough," said Tee, "but I'm not. I'm going for a recce. It's not much of a wander. I want to see if there's a Blue Plaque, 'Punch's Hedgerow Epiphany 1734' or whenever it was."

"You think I'm staying here? I shall follow in your wake. But if we get Jabberwocked, my last words were, just in case I can't get them out at the time – 'I told you so!'"

"I shall snicker-snack it," crowed Tee.

"You haven't got your vorpal sword."

"Details, details, always making with the details…come on!"

Tee was now on a high. She fairly fled through the wood, as if she had some map stored in her head, a key to Punch's secret places. For some of the time we followed the Hedge, at others we swooped out in a great loop but always on a course that was true to my reading of where Pa had passed his solitary life. Precisely how she was navigating was a total mystery to me.

Every time we approached the Hedge the worse I felt. It was neither good, nor bad but it was powerful and it was creating an ugly commotion in my bowels.

Tee, however, seemed immune to whatever I was experiencing. She was now eagerly crawling about in the undergrowth, turning over leaf mould.

I couldn't get closer to her than 10 clear yards. Move beyond that and some pressure weighed me down to the ground, my head began to spin, my sight to fail, my ears to roar.

But she would not give up. She was grubbing among the roots with great diligence. Only after a full 20 minutes of this belly to ground crawling did she give a triumphant yelp and slowly back her way out. She scampered over, cackling – "this is what I was looking for! Pound to a penny, this is the ball that carried your Pa through that Hedge!" She held up for viewing a battered, fist-sized, round of lead that was carrying the imprint of what might well have been the rolled, decorated edge of an ancient breastplate.

"That was incredibly clever of you," I said. "Please can we go now, before that Hedge takes a pound of flesh from me in part-exchange? Also, I'm about to pee and crap myself."

"Can't we have a jolly photo-snap, a nice selfie?" she begged.

"Lupa, if you take a selfie, I swear I'm dead meat. That Hedge is turning me inside out. I don't know why but it hates me"

She finally realised I was serious. Probably I'd turned green. She grabbed my hand and dragged me. I made it a scant 50 yards, to a patch of shrubbery, where I broke away to duck down. There I voided the world, together with its seven wonders. After that, I started on the planets.

"Wow, Beaver," said Tee, wide-eyed and I hope, a little awed. "That's a really irritable bowel you've got."

"My bowel," I said gasping for breath, rising and hauling up my jeans, "is not merely Irritable. It is Angry. Mostly I have IBS. That was an assault by full-blown ABS – Angry Bowel Syndrome, just to be clear. You might also have heard that my bladder loves to join in, too. All-in-all I believe I could win a prize, or a competition, were such a fete-noir to exist."

"To think," said Tee, "that you are my companion in life. It makes me weak with, I'm not sure what…"

"Hysterical laughter? Helpless mirth? Incredulous jealousy? Frenzied admiration?"

"I'll get back to you on all of those," she said, tossing the cannonball easily from hand-to-hand, "in the meanwhile, are you fit to resume the search for Punch's bivouac?"

"Provided that Hedge keeps its roots out of my intestines, yes. What I don't understand is why you're completely unaffected by it."

"Different Gods," said Tee, "that's all I can think of."

"You're not licensed to accept converts, are you?"

"Don't be flippant."

"Me, flippant? ME! You were the one digging in its private parts. I tried to stop you. I'm the innocent victim here. I was full of respect…now look at me…an empty vessel."

"Certainly making enough noise," Tee agreed.

We found what was left of the bivouac, which was nothing, except the hollow of the fire pit, now thick with weed, together with the slight impressions in the ground, left by the slender posts that had supported the ox-hide shelter. If we hadn't known, we'd not have guessed. We combed the area for archaeology but nothing remained, no trace of Punch at all. That was quite depressing, I'd expected some sense of him to haunt the place.

Somewhat listlessly we moved out into the field that lay below the wood. Unlike Punch on the two occasions he had marched out, we were not full of purpose. We were devoid of any. Forging a connection across 300 years seemed outside our abilities.

To be fair, that describes my own condition. Tee had the cannonball which, as she didn't know the whole sad story, she felt righteously gleeful about. I hadn't the heart to tell her it could turn out to be the most poisoned of chalices. For my portion, I was taking away a small bone from the beast's tail. Albeit faintly macabre, it had seemed the most innocent item I could find, record of a triumph, not a memorandum recording a disaster.

By the hedge, above the lane, where so much drama had occurred, where Punch had hi-jacked the coach and cropped the clerics, Tee went full Sherlock on me.

"Watson," she thundered. "This is a layered hedge. It is, therefore, like a bonsai tree – much age, much growth in a very small compass. Look at the thickness of these hawthorn stumps if you doubt me – quite 18 inches in circumference, representing very slow growth. Somewhere along here we are going to find exactly where the guard opened fire and nearly blasted a hole through your beloved Pa."

Then she went to work, scurrying along the bottom of the hedge like a demented mouse. "Could be here…or here…or here. No, maybe here…or this, perhaps. No, wrong growth. I have it, I'm certain. No, maybe not…just up a bit, back a bit…no, yes, no…could be, could be…I sense a presence…agh! Oh Beelzebub! Bloody hell! Ouch, oh, nurse! Urgh, dying… Ooh, poo, toads! A pox and a blight on English hedgerows and their keepers! Ow!"

"What have you done?" I enquired.

"I, that would be me, the Princess, have knelt upon a hawthorn spiky thingy and it has penetrated me cruelly in the knee. It is the dolorous blow. Like King Pelly-whatsit, I shall die, very slowly and be recorded in myth and song."

"May I see?" I asked.

"Sight-seeing, or first-aiding?"

"Bit of both, I suppose."

"OK, have a gander. I daren't look, there'll be oceans of blood."

"Then pull your jeans up, or down."

"It'll have to be down. I'm also a victim of fashion."

A bit of a struggle ensued.

"Ah, I see. There's a bit still in. Do you want me to pull it out?"

"It's not in an artery is it?"

"No."

"Oh, go on then."

"Don't scream."

"Why ever not?"

"Heart of England Foundation property. It's against the bye-laws."

"I protest. Who do I write to?"

"I'd start with The Times, of London."

"Maybe. I'll give that some thought. So, go on, operate. I can take it. I'll bite on the cannonball."

"Don't do that."

"Why not?"

"I've already operated and the cannonball's lead."

"Oh. Thanks."

"Don't mention it. You can pull your pants up, now."

"I was very brave."

"Incredibly."

"I've always been brave. Famous for it."

"I can believe that."

18

ON SUCH A NIGHT AS THIS…

We spent the evening sipping pints, around an open fire in the Fox and Hounds, after a meal that even Carl grudgingly described as memorable. He had taken himself off to the kitchen to discuss with the chef the ins and outs of a sauce we had just consumed which, he believed, he had the perfect partner to, by way of balance.

As a result, Andy was taking the opportunity to explain certain things. He was talking rapidly, because Carl's pint, half-full or half-empty, take your pick, awaited his return.

"In his tearaway days, Carl was a rather good burglar and he still can't help 'conning a joint' – if you'll excuse my outdated slang. If he visits a stately home, an office, a warehouse, he's looking at what standard of security they've invested in, location of equipment, wiring, cameras etc. In his casual opinion, the Manor security is outdated, dysfunctional and easily disabled.

"The point of this is that the book is there, on the library shelves, as plain as day. It's not even in a cabinet. The only security is a fixed camera and a waist-level, laser light beam behind the roped off bit. As for the bookcase, it just has a wooden bar across each shelf which you release by undoing a wing nut, either end. Twirl a knob, lift the book, replace it with one from the table – or something you've mocked up – and Bob's your uncle.

"Now I wouldn't dream of asking Carl to reprise his past. But he's full of it. As he said, the books are never touched, the dust proves that. The rest of the shelves are filled with bound copies of Gardeners' Weekly, a definitely-not-antique Mrs Beeton, Readers United titles and John Buchan adventure thrillers. It's a morgue for dead books. Also, this is not the 'real' library, that's next door!

"The selling point of the tour is that the Archbishop famously abhorred pornography. So he had all the popular titles of the era bound up as plain paper. This was on show to his house guests as a denunciation of the vogue for Gentlemen's Libraries. So there, in the next room, you have this cabinet – obviously the surviving relic of Marie-Gabrielle's secret library and ostensibly denouncing vulgarity – but we know differently, do we not?

"The real history of the original house never gets a mention. Maybe it was suppressed, back in the day. All that's mentioned is that it was partially burned down and rebuilt on an adjoining site as an artists' community. As no-one's ever heard of any of the artists, they don't get much foot traffic. As a result, the whole place runs on a minimal grant from the Foundation…and it shows. As regards the book, Punch's book, I don't think they understand what they've got. It's just been assessed, by whoever does their valuing, as the handwritten sermonising of some reverend gentleman obsessed with insects. Eccentric self-publishing, circa 1600.

"We got a bit carried away, over tea and scones – they can do that to you – and we hatched a plan. Obviously we do nothing now. An eight-wheel Rangie – or is it six? – with a crip in an electric wheelchair and two highly attractive young women, sorry Beaves, is likely to be remembered around these sleepy parts for some time. If we did anything tonight and it was noticed, it would be tied to us by pure weight of coincidence.

"Tomorrow, we toddle off, tipping exactly 10 per cent. The young ladies are serious and demure…sorry Tee, I know it'll be a stretch but take one for the team. We make a fuss about flying back to, I don't know, Singapore and we go.

"In a couple of months, we send a bike gang of crusties through here – Carl's leather and dreads mates. They make a modest display, not that they'll have to try. Busty babes, big bikes and dreadlocks'll hack that. Carl does the job. We'll have a mock-up made – I snatched a phone shot. Bingo. Anyone twigs, it'll be down to the gang. What do you think?"

Tee was all enthusiasm but then she always is, second thoughts not being her strong point. (She gets over-excited by first ones.) I was completely hung-up about it. I didn't want Carl caught, or reprising his ancient and dishonourable past. I knew a thing or two about dishonourable pasts. I hated the idea of theft, per se and the tacit insult it would be to all the volunteers and trustees. Also I was a coward and even at a distance I didn't want to be involved. So that evening, I left it lying on the table – "I'll give it some thought," was my best offer.

In bed, I said to Tee – "I didn't realise I'd developed so many scruples but I tell you what's really haunting me – why do we need the wretched book in the first place?

"I know it was all my plan but I'm good on bright ideas. I am sorry for Pa, particularly about the guilt he's carrying but just being able to tell him that the book is safe should quieten that a bit. I know the book's an eccentric wonder. A lonely cleric and a touched orphan learn how to talk to the insects. It's important stuff, sure enough but we're not the people to unpick it. In local terms, it should be lodged at Reading University. In honest truth it ought to go to an Institute of Anthropological Studies, in Europe, where they take things more seriously than on this Isle of Ignorance. Sorry, I'm ranting.

"In all likelihood, the whistles are lost. They were the key. We know it's all to do with octave and notes, or it was. For all we know, it wouldn't work now. And why do we want it? I keep coming back to that? Are we exploring insect lore – because you can count me out. I'm scared of spiders and I don't like big moths, either."

"That's our Indian holiday shot," said Tee, giggling, "moths as big as soup plates."

"Yuk. Anyway, our little group is just our little group. It's not doing anything. I don't want it to do anything. Can't we just be happy being us?"

"You're flailing, Beavie," warned Tee. "Why are you carrying a lump of metal with an eye in it, round the wilds of England? Why did your eyes light up like saucers when JJ was spouting this morning? I was nearly dead with boredom. Why did you lecture me for hours about the watershed point of magic, philosophy and science, this afternoon? Why was your bowel turned inside out by a Hedge, when I was the one exploring its undercarriage? You are hooked Ms Beaver, on the occult. Like it or not."

"Poo," I said. "You're right, you're always right. But in all truth, I don't believe that book is ours to take, nor do I have any idea how, or why, we might use it. I'm feeling guilty before the act. If we actually stole it, I'd end up walking to Canterbury with dried peas in my shoes."

"Why?" squeaked Tee, "is that a thing?"

"It was 800 years ago," I said defensively. "They didn't have frozen peas back then. In all honesty, what do you think about it?"

Tee went into thoughtful mode and contemplated her toes. She turned them up, then down. Then she twiddled them. First randomly, then in alignment. From the absorbed way she was studying them, she might never have seen them before. Eventually she sneezed, violently, grabbed my hand, squeezed it and divested herself of a long and thoughtful "worr-a-a-h…!

"I think you're probably right," she said. "It's a diversion. It's also hard to ignore when we came looking for it and found it. I'm not a saucer-eyed, occult bunny like you are but I am fascinated by how Punch's old Earth Magic might tie to Jo-Jo's Core. I can't believe the two are not connected in some way, though what that means, or even what I mean by that, I'm not sure.

"I'm incredibly reluctant to think I can assess anything outside my very limited sphere of knowledge and just because I 'see' a connection doesn't mean there is one. You possibly died of funk, this afternoon. You've absorbed everything Punch has said and believed every word, not that I think he'd fib, not for a moment. But what protected him might be far more Core-like than actually goes with his century. Every age might see the Core in a different set of clothes, if you follow me."

"You mean same-Core, different apprehensions thereof? That's what I'm hearing."

"Exactly so. The only bit of Jo-Jo's monologue that intrigued me was when he suggested, implicitly, I think, that Life might be a Core experiment…"

And that is when, with pencil and paper we settled down to reconstruct exactly what he had said, because we were already putting different emphases on the same words. And Tee was only half-right, Jo-Jo hadn't said that Life was a Core experiment just that it was seeking to explore aspects of Life's experience. Interpreting it the Lupa way, would make the Core a far-more serious proposition, indeed.

After a couple of hours spent reconstructing the morning's words, we were wide-awake.

"Fancy a walk? "I asked, "We could take the eye. It's black as pitch round here, so we should have a good star show. Maybe it'll start pumping out the theme to 'Close Encounters.'"

"What could possibly go wrong?" asked Tee.

So off we went.

There was a choice, left or right. The Manor was left, so we chose the right. We wandered down the tiny country road and listened to the life in the hedgerows. They were motorways of scuttling, clicking and clacking.

"Do you think they're all in the employ of the Core?" I asked, not entirely jokingly.

"I think life's a seed-bomb, those balls of clay you make with loads of seed inside. You lob them into derelict sites and some of the seeds make it. Most don't. Read meteorites, asteroids, for seed bombs and on a parochial level, solar system level, that's how we got going. Universe-wide, it's all above my pay-grade. There are too many possibilities. Until some credible science gets laid down you might as well pick theories out of a hat.

"Reading between Jo-Jo's lines the Core is Universe-based. Possibly it's checking on its seed bombs. It's more than likely we're dealing with delegated authority – wrong phrase – on the universal scale, which is why we're being entertained with puppet shows of the Rabbit variety. We're a very long way down the command profile."

"Oh," I said. "You're streaks ahead of me. Do you think you could see to my education?"

"If you take me to meet the Nuns…you did promise."

"Never," I said. "They'd steal you. I'm not risking it. You're all I've got. All I want."

"Still want to meet the Nuns."

"You've seen the films."

"Wannameetem!"

"Oooh look, an open gate…follow me."

I boldly and briskly, led the way to the crown of the field.

"That was a diversionary ploy," gasped Tee.

I had set a cracking pace, it's true. "Never," I said brightly. "What a fabulous array of stars, where do you think we should point it?"

"I have no idea," said Tee. "How did Jo-Jo know where to point it?"

"I never asked. I was on the point of IBS."

"Not ABS, the Angry one?"

"IBS is induced, involuntarily, by the sufferer. ABS is enemy action.

"But when we get back, I'll have to ask him that," I said. "It's a good point."

"If we ever get back," said Tee thoughtfully.

"What do you mean – if?"

"Take a look behind – there are about 20 pairs of eyes looking at us."

I turned round. She was right, there were. Also, as fast as one pair winked out, another set winked on. They weren't cows, they were too close to the ground. But they were diffident. I tried an authoritative "shoo!" and they wheeled and regrouped.

"Oh, it's nothing," I said.

Upon which came a horrid, gargling cough. Probably the sort Blind Pew made on his deathbed. And then another.

"Disconcerting," suggested Tee, as her grip on my hand threatened to break bones.

Then a set of eyes did something I recognised.

"Oh, bugger. They're just sheep. Jacob's sheep, at that."

"How come you know Jacob and his sheep?" asked Tee, in an interested voice.

"Ah, information deficit detected! Jacob's sheep are a breed, like Southdown, Herdwick, Border Leicester. They're supposed to have descended from Jacob's biblical flock."

"Do they bite?"

"Only grass."

"It's just that one's nuzzling my bum."

"Shall we find another field?"

We shut the gate carefully and discussed why it had been open in the first place, while we searched for an uninhabited pasture.

The next meadow held cows.

"Don't like cows," said Tee, "they wee too much."

"Too much as in too frequently, or too much in one go?"

"Too much in one go."

"Strange prejudice."

"Don't like ducks, either.

"You can't see them wee."

"Cold, webbed feet."

"Ah, when I was being sliced and diced in hospital, one time, as a red-hot androgyne misfit, there was a girl there with webbed toes."

"Wouldn't have liked her."

"She might have been a really nice person."

"Was she?"

"As it happens, no."

"See…?"

We walked on, while I silently but frantically, reconsidered the whole business of webbed feet. When I had realised I didn't like the girl with webbed toes, I had automatically disliked her webbed feet, too. Might I now therefore, be predisposed to dislike persons with webbed anything? Had fate brought me a partner with a similar passion and if so, why had we only just discovered such a fundamental bond… I know. My excuse is that I was very short of sleep, with little prospect of catching up on any.

"How about this one?" Tee was asking.

We agreed that it was nicely mown, apparently untenanted and as neither of us was inclined to walk any further, we shimmied over the gate to search for a point of vantage.

"I suppose," I said, "you can admire the stars as well from a ditch, as from a mountaintop. Though ditches come with a poor reputation. Mountaintops come with built-in purity. Utter landscape snobbery. I'll bet Holland has some five star ditches, though barely a mountain to its credit."

"Would that make Holland short on star-worshippers?" wondered Tee.

"They'd feel disadvantaged. They could develop neuroses. But here's a cheering thought – one day, all the ditches will be mountains and all the mountains ditches. Let me finish this one, then I'll shut up forever. I learnt this in General Studies and it's my BEST FACT. The Himalayas are actually ditches! Their strata are all in the form of synclines, the anticlines have all been eroded!"

There was a bit of a silence, which I hoped was an awed one, because that business about the Himalayas was one of my most cherished pieces of information, which is odd really, coming from the former star of numerous quadruple X-rated sex tapes, on the internet. How one's mental deck of cards re-arranges itself, year on year!

"Quite done?" asked Tee.

"Completely emptied out."

"Excellent."

We settled down and I gave Tee the towel. Ceremoniously she unwrapped it and traversed the thickest part of the stellar field.

"Feeling anything?"

"Can't say I am. Do you want to try?"

"I'll try, I'll do the other side."

I settled myself and passed the eye across the drift of stars. Now, for the second time, I felt the twitch as the disc aligned itself, fractionally, between my fingers.

"Oh Lord, it's doing it again."

Tee scrambled up. "Worrah, worrah, worrah! Me too! Me too!"

"Stand behind me, lean over, hold the backs of my hands and just go with me."

Dutifully, Tee leaned on my back and stretched her arms down to reach my hands.

"Keep quite still and wait for it."

I panned from right to left and again, the quiver.

"Did you feel that?"

"Yes! Yes, I did! Do it again!"

"OK, I don't think it's meant to be a game, but I'll do one more time, left to right. Suck this one up and make do."

I went again and felt the familiar tremble of fine alignment.

"What do you think?" I asked.

Tee considered for at least a minute. "It's not spooky. It's more, I don't know how to put this, it's sort of 'grown-up' as if it was securing a link, fulfilling a purpose, almost saying 'thank you, together we've got this covered.' Do you feel anything of that?"

"I've not really verbalised it to that extent but yes, I know what you mean. You become aligned with it, perhaps in the same way that it aligns itself with the star it's reporting to. After the initial excitement, you calm down, become serious."

I wrapped the disc up and popped it back in my shoulder bag. Silently Tee pulled me upright and I dusted my jeans off.

"Curiouser and curiouser, said Alice," she recited softly.

We wandered back to the pub, stopping for a chat with the Jacobs, who were all clustered by their gate. We breathed in their steamy, woolly, pee-heavy odour.

"Any of you guys big on alternative reality continua?" Tee enquired politely.

A few shifted their feet anxiously.

"I'm taking that as a 'no' – especially at this time of night." I said.

"It could easily have been a 'yes' and it's us who don't parlez le foot shuffling."

"Either way," I said, "the acreage of my ignorance increases daily. I'm beyond being humbled by it. I am amoebic in intelligence."

"You were amoebic in dysentry, earlier – so you've a matching pair."

"I shall write a song…
>
> "My unicellular plighted troth,
> "Is amoeba-like but we can't be both,
> "One of us will have to go,
> "Or say farewell to our unicell…"

I came to a halt. "I don't know what comes next."

"That's because you're an amoeba."

We let ourselves in with the night key. Crept upstairs on stockinged feet. Made amoebic love and fell fast asleep.

19
'I HAVE A BETTER IDEA'

"Well?" demanded the boys, in unison, as we crawled towards the breakfast table.

"No," I said. "It's all very Raffles but there's an easier approach by far.

"Today, we return home, conquering heroes. You guys most of all. You spotted the book. We lady amoebas will now swing into action with our Plan B."

"What's with the 'Lady Amoebas' thing?" asked Andy.

"It's sex stuff," said Tee. "Far better left upstairs."

"What sort of answer's that?" grumbled Carl.

"Shush all! Here is Plan B…we will be writing to the custodians of the Manor, under the letterhead of a famous Indian University, explaining that the Princess Tulipa Agnethuram is currently completing her post-doctoral publication, 'Medieval Anthropomorphism and the Insectivora.' Her researcher has recently learned that a very quaint volume, germane to her theme, lies within the Manor's collection. The Princess would deeply appreciate a one-day study loan of said volume, under supervision, of course and on Manor premises. She would be privileged to make a generous donation to the upkeep of the House. She would also anticipate being allowed to copy salient sections by digi-cam, a method wholly approved by the Society of Archivists and requiring no special lighting or straining of the book's fabric. Her supervising Professor, Dr. Yet-to-be-Invented, wishes himself to be remembered to all at the Manor, having been so kindly received himself, albeit many years in the past.

Yours kindly, fondly, ingratiatingly, grovellingly, A Very Small Amoeba."

"Oh," said the boys, again in perfect harmony.

Andy sighed. "I rather saw myself as that guy in the Bond films, the one with the cats and the scar, dropping people into the piranha pool…don't tell me! Blofeld."

"Ah," said Carl, "I rather saw myself breaching a suspended sentence and taking five years for the team. That was after I started thinking and stopped fantasising. Sorry, Blofeld but I'd miss changing your poo and pee bags. So I was wondering how I was going to break it that I'd be staying on the straight and narrow, despite yesterday's improvisation on the criminal banjo. A big 'thank you' to the Amoebas, great and small. I shall definitely be reading your book Princess T."

Tee gave us all a worried look. "What is 'Anthropomorphism and the Insectivora' precisely?'

"Cockroach love," said Andy, "niche but not to be missed!"

"Urgh!!"

The drive home was uneventful. Tee spent most of the time musing out loud about how exotic she could make herself appear. A resurrection of the Curry House Goddess seemed on the cards, as the miles ticked by.

"If you took the Rabbit as your researcher," said Andy, "you'd both blend nicely."

I intervened. "You will be wearing a severely cut woollen suit, in black. The skirt will be below the knee. Your blouse will be plain, white, high-necked and definitely not see-through. Your hair will be respectable, non-cohabiting dyke. You will have no jewellery except plain silver studs and your accessories will be voluminous, of the many-notebooks variety. You will look like a news reader on North Korean TV announcing 'Death of Beloved Leader.' Get the idea?"

"Then I shan't wear any knickers," she grumped. "And you can't make me!"

"Accomplish this mission and you may have the reward of your heart, dear one."

"OK – pizza at Wycombe Services and enough high-octane coke to send me hyper. How about that?"

"Only if Carl drives."

"Grr! Why does no-one want fun anymore?"

20

UNPLEASANT TRUTHS

The Rabbit and JJ are having a serious conversation.

The Rabbit has dimmed his lightshow effect and has shrunk himself, so that he is once again the accommodating soul Jo-Jo left behind and has been quietly mourning, ever since.

"It's actually good to see you," says Jo-Jo, "though I have to say the grand entry was distinctly OTT and heavy on ham."

"Granted," agreed the Rabbit. "I was nervous about what sort of welcome I might get."

"I assume this visit is all down to the locator beacons?"

"Absolutely. I wouldn't go so far as to say that the Core was piqued…but twice?… what do they say here… 'that was taking the piss…' Is that right?"

"That's exactly what they say. But needs must, I fear. We have formed a uniquely bonded group and odd though it may seem to you, this Diner, Transport Caff, 'Andy's Place,' is our life support system. It was going under and we'd have gone with it. So it wasn't such a phoney call as it might have seemed. There was method in the madness, even if the Core detected madness in the method. Anyway, since when did the Core get cross?"

"Did I say they were cross?" asked the Rabbit. "I did not, nor did I mean to imply it. I'd go so far as to say that their concerns centre on a prodigal son. And before you ask, yes, they've 'interfered with me,' as we might have said, coarsely, in the old days. I'm no longer slap to your stick. Wouldn't say I was autonomous but I get by. Which is not to say I don't recall all our old affection for one another and value it. After all, you're the only parent I've got… 'Daddy'…" hammed the Rabbit.

"Don't," Jo-Jo winced, "please!"

They sat and stared, questioningly and affectionately at one another.

After a longish pause, the Rabbit said gently – "you have realised that Marie-Gabrielle is dying?"

"I hadn't verbalised it, even internally," said Jo-Jo, with a sigh, "but now you've said it, yes, I know. Also, Punch and Marie-Claire are ageing, far too rapidly. They were fit, late 40's, when I first met them. Granted, Marie-Claire was in a state but Punch was fighting like a young Cuchulainn.

"Yet, when Tee gave him that cannonball, this morning, you could see that, along with amazement, there was bewilderment, the sort that comes from memory files having been archived. To Punch, it truly feels nearer 300 years than a mere two since he was thrown through that Hedge. He first used to tell me that story as part jolly jape, followed by epiphany. But, whatever, he had written the story. Now, in some peculiar way, the story has written him…and, no, I'm not sure what I mean by that…"

"I suggest you are talking about control," said the Rabbit. "When we are young we think we are writing our own story. As we age, we realise that our story wrote us. We were not the controlling agency, we had always ceded control to circumstance, happenstance, whim and time, all acting on matter. As individuals, we never really existed.

"But to get back to Marie-Gabrielle. Simulacrum I may be but I'm the best the Core can contrive and I've enough empathy to feel sad to see 'Alice,' – if that is what Tee calls her, – slipping away. So much gentleness, happiness and girlish glee at finally being alive. You'd not want to connive at the death of a child would you?"

"Whoa! That is heavy."

"Yes. It's called getting to the point. Unless we get Marie-Gabrielle back to the Core, where they can substantiate her, she's lost."

"Then you take her, you've formed a bond," said Jo-Jo.

"You think she'd leave Marie-Claire, Punch, Evie, all her new friends?"

"Probably not and that goes some way to undermining your argument. I think you'd agree that Marie-Claire and Punch are happy to stay here and slip away, gently, together. Drag them to the Core, stabilise, revivify them…I don't know. Maybe everyone wants to live forever, until they actually start to do so. I don't know any more."

"Let me try another track," said the Rabbit. "Had you realised that you are now ageing? You may have 40 years in you, in local terms but that's all."

Jo-Jo tightened his lips and stared at the wall.

"I hadn't realised that, no. As it's no doubt the truth, it undercuts every argument, every point I've been pushing at you. Live for ever, you want to die. Start to die, you long to live. Yes, I'll concede that's a trump card, of sorts."

"The simple fact is," said the Rabbit, pushing home his advantage, "that vulgar run-in you had with 'Death' in Moss's tunnels was just a medieval interpretation of what awaits you here. One of your days on Earth will, inevitably, be your last."

Jo-Jo laughed wryly.

"You used to have an 'off' switch. I don't suppose you do, any longer."

"Not one that's accessible to you, no."

"Pity, you're punching above your weight, in my opinion."

"Not much fun, being overtaken by your own straight man, is it?" asked the Rabbit, bitterly.

"Did I treat you that badly?"

"No, but you never really cared. And I could mention 50 years in a plastic box."

"So how do you find the travelling these days?" asked Jo-Jo, archly.

"Dreadful."

"Told you. Anyway, I would have you know that when I first arrived here, I felt distinctly damp-eyed at times. I really missed you. Not to mention the fact that it was you who declined to come along."

"Circumstances," countered the Rabbit. "I was happy at the time."

"You were always happy. That's what I asked for and that's what I got. Someone who'd be good to chat to and would be a foil to my wretched misanthropy. As I didn't want a sex doll, I asked for a Rabbit. But they've built a new resentment into you, so that you don't change sides, would be my guess."

"That's entirely possible," the Rabbit agreed. "But the bottom line is that if you stick around here, you're going to die and so is everyone else. You're all in need of a bit of an upgrade and those can't be initiated here."

"OK, accepted. Tell me why the Core cares? Four thousand years of misanthropy. They must have sieved the pearls out of that by now. They can't be hungry for another 4000 years of bile."

"I am just the messenger. Come back and visit us. All is forgiven – not that it was ever unforgiven. Bring a friend, bring seven. Tea and biscuits, free, on arrival."

Jo-Jo took a deep breath. "I'm off to have a chat with a friend. I'll have a deal worked out for you in a day or two. I'll tell you now, you won't like it. What's more, the Core will hate it. But they'll do it. There are things here that they want and my way is the only way they've got a chance of getting them."

The Rabbit, sighing at such stubborn ingratitude, stood shaking its head dolefully, then abruptly shot up in size, restoring colour saturation to full Tokyo neon. It made for a colourful exit – and one without a parting word.

"Manners, manners maketh not the Rabbit…" muttered Jo-Jo.

Then he went in search of Tee.

Finding her in a public thoroughfare, he led her to a dark corner.

"Oooh," she said, "is this an attempted seduction? How utterly exciting."

"Only of your mind."

"Oh, how unexciting. Can we sit down nicely, then? As in coffee?"

"Must we?"

"We absolutely must. Coffee lubricates my mind and seduction always works better with assorted lubricants. You wouldn't wish to be thought inefficient."

They walked towards the diner, managing to collect Eva and Marie-Gabrielle, in separate swoops, nimbly performed by Tee.

"JJ's buying coffee, buns too, now I think about it. Tag along, he wants to seduce our minds."

Just like 'Three Little Maids from School,' thought Evie, who was much given to finding Gilbertian parallels in everything, as they toddled obediently along behind.

While he laboured at the counter, he could hear footwear problems being hammered out at high volume and cross purposes – "oh, you meant there!"… "no, what I really meant was"… "what I wanted to say, if I'm given half a chance"… "really? You can get them there?"

"STOP," said JJ, sitting down at last. "My treat, my chat!"

Awkwardly he tried to deal out plates and saucers Immediately three little pairs of hands shot out and made effortless work of his fumbling. Then three inquisitive, friendly pairs of eyes turned gently on his scarlet face and Tee said – "but…"

"No," said Jo-Jo, "definitely not one of your buts."

Now all three were looking at him with eyes like saucers, expectant saucers, which was unnerving, as he had prepared his pitch for one set of ears only and certainly not for eyes.

Clearing his throat he began, an octave too high – "Marie-Gabrielle, you are…" and conveniently choked on a crumb.

"Dying?" she said sweetly, patting his back affectionately.

"Exactly," said Jo-Jo, red in the face again.

Eva and Tee looked appalled.

"What of? Why?" they chorused.

"Defective translation," she said. "Perhaps it would be better to say inadequate translation. I came off the page, how shall I put it…too thinly. In my current state I'll last another two years but I'll be fading all the time. That's really why Papa and I sleep outside on clear nights. We like to think the moon strengthens me. I think it strengthens both of us, because Papa is dying, too. Marie-Claire doesn't care that much about dying. At the moment she remembers too much about living to want to go on forever."

"This is too, too appalling," muttered Tee.

"Which is why I wanted to do this one by one," said Jo-Jo, "now I've got three of you in a state."

"I'm not in a state," said Marie-Gabrielle, brightly. "I want to live forever. And I'm going to make sure Marie-Claire does, too. And when she does, Papa will too."

"Yes," said Jo-Jo. "I see Rufus has been whispering in your ear. But take him with a pinch of salt. Meanwhile what do I do with these two?" – he pointed at Evie and Tee.

"Ask them," said Marie-Gabrielle. "It's a simple question."

"Marie says this is a simple question. Would you like to live forever?"

The twins stared at him. He thought of them as twins, despite the fact that they looked nothing like one another and had totally different temperaments. They stared, like pandas, like lemurs, like bush babies and probably like koalas with burnt paws. A hugely sad and moving sight.

"Simple question, eh? Tricky to answer. Here are the bare bones, do you want to die, conventionally, on your planet, of old age, or whatever else may be in store for you? Or will you risk travelling to where the Core can tamper with your bits? All I can promise is that it will be non-intrusive, painless and you'll effectively never know a thing about it. So to answer this 'simple question,' you might like to apply lubricant, in the form of this Japanese saying, which goes something like – 'matters of great importance should be decided now, small affairs may be considered at length.' Is that any help?"

"Oh dear," said Marie-Gabrielle, "I think they're lost."

"What do I do?" asked Jo-Jo.

"You could prod one."

"I daren't. You do it."

Marie-Gabrielle leaned over and took a huge bite out of Tee's cake. They both waited for the roar. Not a squeak.

"Hm," she said.

Greatly daring she twanged Evie's bra-strap, the one act absolutely guaranteed to turn her into a raging monster.

"Uh…don't do that, Alice…" she muttered absently.

"Oh come on guys," said Jo-Jo, finishing off Tee's cake. "Die tomorrow, or live forever?"

"How 'tomorrow' is tomorrow?" Evie managed, in a small voice.

"Couldn't say precisely. It'll fall between the usual parameters. Anywhere within the next ten seconds and 70 years."

"Put like that," mumbled Tee, "we'd probably have to go for 'forever.' You could always take a powder if it got too much."

"You reckon?" asked Evie.

"Sort of," nodded Tee.

"OK," said Evie, "we'll sign-up for forever."

"Did I eat my cake?" asked Tee. "Did anyone see?"

Jo-Jo had a similar conversation with Andy and Carl, though indecision was not their problem.

"Can they fix me?" asked Andy.

"Undoubtedly."

"Would they?"

"I'll include it in the terms and conditions. In fact, I've just had a huge idea…" and he half rose from his seat.

"Will I be coming too?" asked Carl.

"That's taken for granted," said Jo-Jo and shot out of the door.

The Rabbit was sunning himself by the tank traps, or perhaps he was idly competing with the sun for which of them should be the dominant light source.

"Could you turn yourself down a bit?" asked Jo-Jo.

"Of course," said the Rabbit, obligingly. "I've been thinking, I could be RR, as in Rufus Rabbit."

"You could," said JJ, "but it's not that easy. If you want to be RR then you have to be in 'our gang.' Currently you are very much viewed as being in 'their gang' and therefore, somewhat flying under false colours."

"Mm," said the wannabee RR. "By the way," and he gestured at the concrete caltrops, "what are these?"

"Tank traps."

"Why do you want to trap tanks? Is there a war on?"

"Not that anyone's noticed, locally. But be prepared and all that. They caught Tee's car on its way in."

"But this is not the way in…"

"Exactly. Now listen, I've had a bright idea and everyone is going to love it – I hope."

21

PERIPHERAL VISION

In a sense Andy's Place as good as ran itself these days. In the early days we had laboured like Trojans, after the UFO's had done their bit. We had cooked, cleaned, played at being waitresses and cashiers. And slowly that huge investment of faith and money that Andy and Tee had poured in had been justified. Not one of us could bear to see it fail and it didn't.

Over the year, though, Andy and Carl had been steadily recruiting and training a cool crew from outside, who could now keep things running 24/7, without our input. Nevertheless we still liked to pitch in, each in our own way. It was, primarily Andy's Place, but everyone felt proprietorial about it and Andy was gracious and mature enough to indulge us all in joint ownership.

Small things helped in big ways. Marie-Claire might get a sudden urge, one day, to cook her mother's recipe for mutton pies. Marie-Gabrielle would tell the world about it, on social media and the afficionados would pour in, salivating like Pavlov's doggies. JJ's apple pies got similar publicity and 'following us' became a pretty trendy thing to do. Then there was the matter of Punch's beef sauce, so rich and rare that cattle lined up for the honour of swimming in it. Maybe not…

I liked to pitch in at a very humble level…cover a shift for a mum who needed to take her child to the doc's, mop the floor industriously and for some reason I've never worked out, I loved clearing tables. I wasn't much of a cook, though I could hold my own making toast. Tee, despite having so much money invested, operated as a sort of universal oil can. She had huge empathy and a larger heart. Teamed up with Marie-Gabrielle, who simply made everyone happy by being consistently radiant herself, they house-mothered the entire floor staff. We wanted to make the wage-packet crew feel like family, because we were so tightly knit ourselves.

Our group chemistry was a bit of a mystery and one I frequently pondered. We weren't under each other's feet, or crammed into any individual pocket but we meshed like a finely-tuned gear train. We were a functioning hive. Who the Queen was, I have absolutely no idea. Something was producing queen substance, the pheromone that ties a colony of honey bees together in useful harmony. Ours seemed to be coming from the group itself. No individual was dominant but take any one of us away, then the connection would stutter, momentarily. Normally, we would manage, make an adjustment and bridge the gap. Take two of us away, though and unless there was certainty as to when they would return, the group was wounded. Three down and the special connectivity fell apart.

Eight people made up our group and it was more than the sum of its parts. We were a syncytium, a mass of nuclei contained in one cell membrane and we perforce, were symbiotic and altruistic into the bargain. What I couldn't get over was the random collisions that had produced it all and the uneasy question…how random had they been? If they hadn't been that random, who, or what, had done the selecting and on what basis?

If we weren't working in-house, one or two of us would inevitably be there drinking coffee, having a group lunch, or inviting one-another to afternoon tea. So it's fair to say that we knew the pulse rate, blood pressure and oxygen saturation of the place. We were not absentee landlords, living off the labours of others. Andy was pretty much a fixture, from opening to night shift, or from night shift through to lunch. He rarely intruded and he could keep himself to himself, as there was a balcony cum mezzanine floor, an extension of his domestic space, that jutted into the caff proper.

His own place was a ramshackle double-storey, hooked on to the back of the diner. Since the stroke, he lived largely upstairs and he could rumble out on his wheels, onto the mezzanine and benignly survey the action and the troops below. He wasn't spying and no-one felt he was. Cheery waves were the order of the day, whenever eyes crossed.

I was down below, contentedly sipping a large, and particularly rich Americano, one rainy morning, when I heard the rumble of wheels, 'Andy moving onto his bridge,' I thought. I looked up and waved. He waved back.

"Evie, you busy?" he shouted.

"Only busy drinking coffee."

"You reckon it would taste as good up here?"

"Can but try. I will ascend, pronto."

Which I did and joined him at his long table.

He gave me a sideways look, like a particularly canny bird."

"A few weeks ago, did you and JJ have a conversation which ended with you voting 'yes' for eternal life?"

"Now why would you be asking that?"

"Because he had a chat with Carl and I that went that way."

"OK then, he did with we three gals, too."

"Right, that's all I needed to know. Now look."

I watched and he raised his right arm six inches from his lap and wriggled his fingers."

I jumped up, rushed round, squeaking and kissed him.

"Oh, Andy, that's amazing!"

"Be seated Sweet Pea and listen."

Something about his mood wasn't right. I'd have been expecting him to be whooping with joy – calling Clan McAndy to come and bear witness. Pleased as he was, his priority was obviously something else. That much was apparent. I had no idea what. So I sat and paid attention.

He grinned at me. "Love you, Evie."

"Back at you," I chirruped.

"Right, – an experiment. On the count of three, look back over your left shoulder, as fast as you can turn your head."

"Can it be my right shoulder? Something went wrong with the left side of my neck during my dark days and I turn pretty slowly that way. If you ever want to mug me, creep up quietly on my left!"

His face darkened. I think he was imagining some non-consensual depravity gone awry and he now incapable of avenging it. Pointless, but sweet for all that. Finally he regained his affable grin.

"Left, right, it makes no odds. So, do it on three. Ready?"

"Ready."

"One…two…three!'

I whipped my head round, knowing I should see the counter, the grill, the queue and the first line of tables. For just a micro-second, they weren't there. It wasn't that they were fuzzy, or tricksy from the rapid turn. Nothing was there…trust me, there's a difference.

"…what the…" I said and promptly did it again. Everything was as it should be.

"Forget it," he said, "you won't fool it again. Not today, not tomorrow."

"What is 'it'," I asked, perplexed. "What was that?"

"I'm not sure anymore," he said. "I thought I was, then I thought I wasn't. Then I thought I should just shut up. When I saw you though, I couldn't resist trying it out.

"To put it bluntly, I think we've been tampered with. Possibly we've been rewired, internally. Or it could be that we're being dreamed, or we're dreaming ourselves…a bit like Marie-Gabrielle. She thought, or dreamed, her way off graffitied rock, then became adept at peeling herself out of printed books. Which world does she exist in? How do you know…"

I think my face must have been displaying – 'Evie is Out, – please leave a message.'

"Let me try another tack," he said, struggling for single-syllable words. "I think we're already on another planet but to keep us sane, we've been wrapped in a dream of the familiar, a dream we can even participate in, apparently as usual. No?

"Go back to Marie-Gabrielle. Doesn't she look well? She has a sheen like a fresh peach, as crisp as an apple. Not a hint of her dwindling. In fact, everyone's particularly bright-eyed and bushy-tailed."

"Duh?" I enquired.

"Go away and think about it. Keep it to yourself, though. Oh, and do finish your coffee. Isn't it particularly good this morning – and still warm! Not even a new blend."

22

RABBIT WISDOM

I did think about it. All the way back to our van. There, Tee was doing her face.

"Why are you doing your face? You never do your face, In fact, it's you who says – 'art can't improve on nature, at least not in my case!' So why are you…"

She swung round.

"Oh, Saints preserve us! Who are you? Cruella de Vil, or Elizabeth Bathory?"

"I'm the insect-sex lady, you moron. Today's the day of your idiotic plan. So where have you been, when my need was greatest?"

"Trying to find you a pet woodlouse…? No, that's a lie. I've been drinking coffee and thinking you were idling in bed. My shame is total. When does your chauffeur attend?"

"Immediately, so scurry off and give me a peck before you do, somewhere unpainted would be preferable."

I searched, found a portion of neck that hadn't been horror-movied and dutifully pecked.

"This may sound strange but as you are being driven, keep flashing glances at the far horizon."

"Why?"

"Because I say so. Tell you more later. Promise."

"Agh! I hate not-knowing. Tell me! Now!"

"Can't, it's not a surprise thing. Well I suppose it is but it won't work if you know. Just be a good insect-sex lover and keep your eyes on distant vistas."

"I might," Tee said haughtily. "Anyway, anthropomorphism is nothing to do with sex. You've all lied to me. I looked it up."

"Yes but you like sex, you'd hate identifying with flies. You'd be miserable all day, imagining yourself with wings and going 'buzz.' You'll carry-off being an insect-sex fiend really well, for sheer perversity's sake."

"When I get back," said Tee menacingly, "I'm going to invent a sex niche all of my own and none of you will be allowed to join. So YOU can go forth and multiply – only you can't, so there! Also, I'm late!"

I left, whistling a jaunty air. When it comes to sexual niches, I'm in a league of my own. Unchallengeable – and she knows it. Then I remembered that I might be being dreamed and got quite embarrassed.

My major problem now was that having been sworn to secrecy, who could I find to blab to, Tee being absent on a mission? I ended up in Pa's vegetable garden. It was a magnet for loafers, thinkers and not surprisingly, I suppose, Rabbits.

"Morning, Double-R, how are you?"

"Very well," His Highness replied. "Double-R…I like that. I shall run that past 'Alice' and see if she thinks it might stick. R,R, is proving a bit awkward…Double-R is definitely easier on the tongue…and ear."

"Here's a question for you Double-R – if you weren't here harassing JJ, where would you be?"

"Oh, that's an easy one. I'd be on Earth-II, 'pootling,' as JJ terms it, around Moss and Shade's place on my bike."

"That sounds a very innocent pursuit for such an important emissary."

"I'm not important. I sometimes think I might be a detailer, at best. If you think of Earth-II as being an unfinished drawing, requiring infinite detail, I attempt to supply verisimilitude to, shall we say, one sugar cube's volume of the colossal whole. I don't even know how I supply it, none of us do, we are just endlessly downloaded, humans and simulacra alike. It's not something you can fail at."

"Earth-II sounds a strange place."

"No, really it isn't. It's just a work in progress. At one and the same time it's a simulacrum of a whole and a deconstruction of the same. The 'intelligent-energy,' poor choice of phrase, that controls Earth-II, deals largely in particles, nothing bigger. So its appetite for detail is effectively infinite. It is trying to build perfection without having to go back to the zero point."

"The cosmic soup being the zero point?"

"Precisely Miss Eva! That translation into 'soup,' as my dearest friend JJ has termed it, wastes colossal quantities of energy and time. Breaking down particles is incredibly wasteful in so many ways. Much of the information load they carry is irretrievably lost. Earth-II, and other planets, are being built, not from soup but from existing energy modules that are pristine enough to have no need of further reduction."

I had a sudden, flaring, visceral understanding. "You mean that this controlling energy is trying to emulate natural process but is removing chance from the equation? It wants to start the cosmic clock a couple of hours into the day. Is that vaguely right?"

"That's certainly how I understand things," agreed Double-R. "But do be aware, I know no more than I can know. It's not that anything is secret, it's merely beyond our comprehension at our 'specialised,' solid-body level. But it's very hard to express 'what-is-going-on' adequately, without invoking notions of secret knowledge, arcane lore, hidden mysteries. The very fact that intelligence is, inevitably, hierarchical, produces enormous difficulties in comprehension for many people."

"Because they take it personally?"

"Precisely! They won't understand that, to a very great degree, form limits the possibility of comprehension.

I stared down the neat rows of vegetables and focused on Punch and Marie-Claire. Marie-Claire with her wicker basket, picking mange-touts. Punch, armed with a hoe, upturning weeds that had dared to stray into his furrows. I choked up and could barely keep back tears. Most certainly I couldn't speak.

What was it? Their worn, browned bodies, slow and certain beneath the sun. The sense that their time was on the ebb, yet mine was not fully at the flood? The obscenities we'd all had to survive to be here, today, now? And all this 'truth' might be no more than a dream, as real as pixels, no more. What would be the point of that? What could be gained from it? Surely reality must be real?

I stared at the sun, then at shadows, back and forth, to and fro,' until Punch and Marie-Claire were no more than vague transparencies among a surfeit of green light. There…just like that…I'd done it…reduced them to nothing real, with my own eyes, in my own brain!

"What's the point?" I blurted.

"Of what?" asked the Rabbit.

"Of this fateful copy, accurate to every particle."

"To improve upon the original, I believe. To gently improve upon it. You've already seen Andrew's right-hand, he showed it to you this morning."

I couldn't even be bothered to pretend I was surprised. I felt so fate-saturated, nothing could surprise me.

"The hand is not some fake. Circuits are being restored. Many, many things you cannot see, things you don't know of, are being tweaked and improved. But with respect, Andrew's paralysis is not the point, nor will his attaining freedom from it be, either. The reconstruction we were talking about, will be undertaken a million miles back down the track and as a result certain things will not occur, strokes being one of them. As you said yourself, 'chance' is being removed from the equation. But do understand, this is not genetic engineering, this engineering is taking place in worlds where genes will not arise for eons of time, if indeed they arise at all. You'll have to take what I say on trust, that there is no malice in this enterprise, only strangeness."

"What's the old magic, then, Earth Magic, which Marie talks about?"

"Earth Magic, Old Magic, title it as you will, is a manifestation of energies generated on this planet in the ancient past. It is capable of malice. You know that to your own cost, do you not ? When you revisited the beech hanger and Punch's old wood, Earth Magic played fast and loose with you for no better reason than that it could. That's why the old Shamans had so many cautionary tales about their magic, it was capricious. One day gold, the next day, disease. It's that very flaw in its nature that is slowly robbing it of its power. The people within its sway see it as awesomely immortal – it knows full well that it is as mortal as man. It arose from chaos, not from the calm beneath chaos.

"But it has done some very beautiful things. No-one can take that from it. It is capable of great altruism and generosity. Think what it did for Punch! It drew him through that Hedge and then it unpicked him, poisoned cell by poisoned cell. A great evil settled upon him on the day he could not save his beloved grandmother…"

I must have looked baffled, because the Rabbit looked at me sharply – "you don't know about that? Then never, ever ask. Take it as Gospel, however, that for many years Punch was an avenging angel, or more accurately, devil. He was red in tooth and claw. For which he had his reasons.

"As I said, Earth Magic transformed that. It gave him a crusade, something he wished to embark on and something for which he had to purge himself of all baseness. For at the end of it lay his very own Grail, a desire he had stifled through all his murderous years – the gift of a wife, a son and a daughter, a family on which he could pour out all his betrayed, unconditional love. And, if I'm not much mistaken, that is the same emotion it generated in all of you, Marie-Gabrielle, Marie-Claire and yourself?

"That was Earth Magic at its finest. An achievement that drained the resources of a whole woodland and one that sat atop a very ancient and powerful site. Earth Magic was painting with a broad brush, you see. The intelligence behind the Core project and Earth II looks to remodel events at the particle level, so that such wasteful corruptions never arise in the first place."

The Rabbit considered the vegetable garden, the wreckage of broken concrete, the ruined buildings in the middle distance and the hum and buzz from the diner to our right.

"This is a peculiarly interesting place," he said mildly. "Did you chose it, or did it chose you?"

I tried to think properly about that, blinking wildly, trying to correct the dazzling perspectives I'd induced earlier. I needed my vision back, to do this abused-ground justice.

"I think," I began slowly, "that this place chooses its people, though I don't sense any desire in it to become power-possessing. It's not like Punch's wood but neither is it impotent. I think and this has only just come to me, that it's a navel point, an omphalos, though of what, or for whom, I have no idea."

We both stared afresh at the curious sprawl of ruins and waste. It was a place between worlds I always felt, a liminal spot, an edgeland, neither one thing nor the other. I found it marvellously non-judgemental, a habitat equal to hosting saints and sinners alike. Double-R must have read my mind.

"I wouldn't," said the Rabbit, "like you to think that there was anything sanctimonious about the intelligence we've mentioned. It's not moralising, or possessed of missionary zeal. It does have ideas about wasted energy, however and that may, in the long run, result in the achievement of certain ends. Ends that, today, could look like opinions. But we live in a black and white age, I don't think the future will be willing to be so easily polarised."

"Take the burden you carry on your own soul – oh yes, the Intelligence has no problem with souls, 'no soul, no life' – your need to atone for sins you never committed. I don't think that could arise again, in the vision that we have been speaking about. I'm not sure it can save you from carrying your cross, it being so integral to your nature but I don't believe such a thing could arise in its time, when it arrives. But perhaps I speak out of turn. I shouldn't try to interpret what I can't comprehend."

I took a huge breath.

"You strayed above my pay grade several Biblical utterances ago. But if anything could adjust my burden to a more comfortable yoke, or something I can understand, I would be greatly indebted to you, to Earth II and the Intelligences beyond."

The Rabbit bowed from the waist. No mean feat while wedged among tank traps. I nodded my farewells, climbed down and went in search of a deserted place to think. But what my thoughts would be about, only Earth II knew, for I certainly did not.

23

CALTROP COUNTRY

'Andy's Place' stands off centre, on 'No-Name Roundabout.' Truly, that's what it's called. The actual genesis of the diner remains a bit of a mystery and I've never felt inclined to ask the leading questions that would establish its pedigree.

'No-Name' is absolutely huge, acre upon acre of derelict land, pushed together by the creation of bigger and therefore 'better' ring roads, access freeways, industrial estates and warehouse parks. Everything that was left over from them got dumped here.

A long time ago, someone bought the site for a song and opened a concrete-casting plant there. That went bust and Andy's brother bought it, ironically for concrete-crushing – a story already told by Kirsty, if you've been paying attention.

What I'm so awkwardly working my way towards here, is the intriguing fact that 'No-Name' possesses thousands upon thousands of the concrete caltrops we residents familiarly call 'tank traps.' They only really become traps when they're cunningly arranged in serried ranks, in hidden hollows, or at beach-heads. Anyway, as they're ours, we can call them what we like.

Why are they here? Because Andy's bro' secured an MOD contract to remove and break them up, from the airfield where they'd been gathered together after WW II.

They paid him pretty handsomely as they were very hard to break-up, being tank-resistant and all that. Rather than waste energy smashing them to pieces, he ringed No-Name with them, piled five, six deep and let nature do the rest. That saw off the Traveller incursions that had been interrupting his business but it didn't polish off the caltrops. There were lots left-over, with more coming in daily. So all over the place he was obliged to build towering defensive walls and miniature alps.

Slowly the crushing business started chewing them back into aggregate but entrepreneur that he was, bro' found that, left intact, they had re-sale value to landscape architects, seeking to create a 'new brutalism' in their jaded clients' gardens. Forthwith, the crushing stopped and they became a niche product. Very desirable and his monopoly. Then he died and the niche died, not precisely with him, but at much the same time. So, for the moment they're staying where they fell, years ago. As I count some of them as personal friends, this makes me very happy.

There was one particularly friendly trap that overlooked an ugly expanse of ruined asphalt and concrete. It was perched near the top of its own alp and I scrambled up to sit in its mossy angle, minutes after I left Double-R.

Out there, something once deemed useful, had risen above ground level. When it finally lost its utility it was demolished, down to pockets of asphalt and cracked concrete pavement, together with a few low walls, some of brick, others in block but all now crumbling back into the earth.

For some reason, there are pebbles up here – (maybe a Pleistocene sea got its timings all wrong and swept over the land, very briefly, in the last 25 years… No?) I picked up a good-sized one and shied it out, towards the heart of the whole affair. It fell pathetically short and landed instead in the regiment of fireweed, the rosebay willowherb, that has sprung up just at the foot of my alp.

Its vanguard platoons are strung out across the territory, following the ruptures in the foundations and every year, broadening those veins and arteries a little further, remorseless in its persistent heaving against constraint. Currently, it was marvellously pink and the flowers ducked, bent and swept in the push of the wind. Another month or so and snowstorms of seed would be released, colossal amounts, lighter than thistledown. They would float over suburbia and bring rage to the heart of every proud gardener.

Growing from a pavement crack no larger than the edge of my hand, a large buddleia is mimicking the fireweed ballet, its straggly branches, heavy with purple cones, bowing gracefully up and down, a multi-limbed Hindu deity at its yoga. There were hundreds of these bushes, sprouting from cracks, eschewing pockets of open land, seeming to prefer a hard living between brick joints, poking from under the edges of slabs, or emerging from deep within the caltrop alps, by way of preference.

There was a mongrel glory of weeds everywhere, an impure, riotous assembly, taking advantage of every ray of sun and drop of rain.

Sometime in the past, along had come a bulldozer and sliced off their heads, more ruthlessly than any guillotine. Then the formwork team had arrived to lay the foundations for walls, the slab for the floor. A 24 inch bucket mounted on the front of a JCB, dug trenches for foundations, after the bulldozer had flattened the opposition. No gradients to worry about now.

Up rolled the ready-mix truck and out poured a slurry of concrete into the trench, along the line of the walls. A couple of days later blocks and bricks were being laid, while inside the form-workers industriously set out their sheets of metal grid to reinforce the floor. Rafts of floating, rusty steel, from which projected, here and there, the vertical reinforcing rods that would form the pillars to carry the roof.

With everything braced to 90 degrees against the horizontal, the great ballet of cement lorries can begin. Some concrete pours down chutes, wetter mixes are pumped into the arena through pulsating hoses. A scene to be painted in Paynes grey and burnt umber. A wet and sticky couple of days.

The mix settles, levelled by a crude thumping from the edge of a crusty scaffolding board. Slowly, pools of filmy water gather here and there, forming foggy mirrors on the surface. Perhaps 10 inches of concrete sits atop buddleia roots, fireweed seeds, all of which yawn and settle down to sleep a while – perchance to dream?

For a few years industry booms overhead. Goods come and go. The bald tyres of forklift trucks skid around on the 10 inches of concrete, leaving streaks of black rubber in a meaningless graffiti of diligence. Then the order book falls apart, an export tariff has trebled, a demand fell off, a commodity price has risen, the business is overdrawn, a good idea founders. Who can say?

Now it's the turn of the second-raters, the patchers of broken windows with polythene, the bodgers and dodgers exploiting an end-of-lease bargain, the hopeful amateurs, the car-engine tweakers, the scrap brigade. The end is in sight. Eventually it arrives. The vandals move in, the windows disappear. A section of blocked gutter means a roof begins to decay, a column is rotting from the inside out, its reinforcing bars exploding in rust, protesting the rainwater that oozes down them, day after day.

The site is sold, the wrecking teams arrive. The building vanishes. The four seasons get to work on 10 inches of concrete. Nothing is forever. The weak patch, where too much sand gathered, cracks apart. A seed sees the light of day.

A few years later, I sit here and watch the fireweed ballet and wonder if, as an honest androgyne, I could have seeds of my own? Better still, little pods of Evie-peas. Evie plants would grow, year after year and children would collect my pods and shell little harvests of Evie-peas. "Can we collect Evie-peas, mum?" I could be an alternative to blackberrying, or feeding the ducks.

What would I look like, if I was a plant? Most people would opt for the head of a rose, a dahlia, or a sunflower. I don't really want a head. I want pods, full of Evie-peas that people have to chase around on their plates, or stick to their knives with honey. Winnie-the-Pooh, armed with his jar of the sticky stuff, would come and eat Evie-peas. A little bit of green veg. Just the thing for a bear of little brain. Then Tigger would arrive and accidentally jump over everything.

"Worrah! Worrah! Worrah! Sorry, squash, sorry, squash!"

I dug out my apology for a phone.

"Where are you Tiggs?"

"Grinding along in third gear, somewhere after Heathrow. Fog everywhere. Not a horizon to be seen. What are you doing?"

"Planting myself. I'm going to sprout and be a pea. You know…a little green pea."

There was pregnant silence, immediately followed by a high-octane Tigger shriek – "Oh God! Why did you say that?! Carl, we've got to stop. I'm going to wet myself. Pull over, pull over. I don't care about trees. I can pee anywhere."

Quite fascinating, all this drama on one little cell-phone. I try to visualise and oh, the sweetheart! She's left it on…slipped it into her pocket. I can just make out, above the roar, the ping, pong, ping, pong, of the door, or maybe the hazard lights?

Muffled – "Tee! You can't get out on a motorway. It's against the law!" Oh, poor old Carl. He's got no chance.

"It's against my laws to pee my pants. Don't be so uptight. You're only 32."

My thought – 'but she isn't wearing any pants!' A Tiggerish protest against not being allowed to reprise the Curry House Goddess. Either way, that was pants down, or skirt up and oh, My Lord, nothing wrong with that girl's bladder or kidneys. My fault, I should have told her to go! I usually do. Forgot my 'mum' routine – "have you been? Then go now. Go anyway!"

Oops! There goes an appreciative horn. Oh wow! Quite the fan club building up now. She'll be viral on social media by mid-morning. Difficult to be elegant in a crouch but she'll manage it. Oh boy! There go my ear drums! That was a full set of air horns – 40 tons of love and affection? A bellowed – "FUCK YOU!!" Mmm! apparently not… that's my girl. Proud of you Tiggs!

Car door 'bongs,' followed by – 'clunk.'

"You still there, Beaver?" says a happy, relaxed, empty-bladdered voice.

"Yep."

"You'd think they'd never seen a woman pee before."

"They probably haven't, on the hard-shoulder of the M25, or whichever stretch of hell you're on. Shall I tell the world you're a Princess, or just your nickname? Which do you prefer – 'Tee's pee' or, 'the Princess and the pee'? You're going to get so many 'likes' you could become an influencer. 'My hot knickers for that roadside simply-must-moment. You could get rich."

"I'm already rich."

"I'm not. You can give it to me."

"OK, love you, bye."

"Love you too. Bye."

24
A TIGGER MOST EXCELLENT

Princess Tigger had excelled herself. Consequently she was preening, enunciating a soliloquy attended to by no-one other than herself.

"I could have a P- ee added to my T- ee," she was saying. "Thus I would become PT, which is quite snappy, as the trend round here seems to be towards snappy monikers. PT! Whaddya think, guys?"

No-one answers. Everyone is drooling over the high definition glossy 10 x 8's, that had been so meticulously photographed. Not that PT had actually done that.

She had delegated, to a humble, acned, youth, a lowly volunteer, the gruelling task of photographing 180 double-page spreads, while she whisked away the Manor's manager to the restaurant of his dreams for lunch. On the love-struck youth she had laid the full majesty of her ancestry, while her soft little hand lay atop his. Her brown, dew-filled eyes, the casual thrust of her bosom against his upper arm, had his hormones in turmoil. A gentle peck on the cheek, a promise to return with the takeaway of his choice, were all that it had taken.

As the manager and PT gourmandised their way through turbot and venison, having begun with the excellent soup and concluded firmly in the sticky heart of the dessert trolley, this hapless boy, testosterone raging through his veins, photographed with the utmost care every wretched page.

His reward was another flutter of the kohl-blackened eyelids, a gentle arm linked through his, as she snuggled up tightly – "for a selfie with you, so I never forget how wonderful a man I met!" As for the humble takeaway he had requested, she had doubled his ration at a superior venue, and bought three litres of petrolhead cola – one for her, one for the youth and one for the manager – "because everyone likes cola, don't they!"

Mercifully, the youth had concluded his "little task" by the time they returned, because when the 'Princess' pressed a litre of cola on the man who had selected Chateau Mouton Rothschild to go with his free lunch he, intolerable snob that he was, began to doubt both her genealogy and her credentials.

The youth, blushing crimson, had confessed that cola and he did not agree. So relieving him of his cup and adding the manager's reject to her personal supply, mi'lady was left, waving her goodbyes, with three litres of high octane fuel on which to refresh herself, during the journey home.

"So we took the back roads," Carl yawned. "No more motorway potty moments for me."

They had, however, detoured via a megastore, to have the photo prints run-off and for PT to consume her promised pizza-reward in the caff, washed down with "just a little more cola."

"Another litre," said Carl bluntly. "Then she got two more for the road – in case we got lost."

Hyperactivity cut in quite suddenly, as did the need to pee – frequently. "Got rather out of hand" – was Carl's phrase. When not peeing, Tee had started crawling round the hire-car looking "for that secret way out of the boot that they always have in films…do you think it matters if I go the other way…into the boot, from the car?"

"We stopped eight times," he said, wonderingly "and she still drank the back-up ration." With that he had crawled off to bed, aged before his time.

I was left with a hyper-toxic Princess who couldn't stop peeing and asking me if we could go and see the Latex Nuns NOW, because this really was their thing, wasn't it? Then she wanted to act out the entire cycle of the Mahabharata, with no clothes on and she wondered if there was a way of unzipping my willy, so Ganesh could have a trunk, because she didn't have a willy, though she wouldn't have minded one.

At 3.00 am she was munching some sort of E-numbers snack – "just to top-up, Beaves, 'cos I'll crash, otherwise and that would be dangerous," when she finally did crash.

"I did well, didn't I Beaver?" she demanded, through smeared make-up that was, by now, more Joker than Princessa. I gave her a huge plonk of a kiss on the end of her nose. She sneezed violently and fell asleep, clutching my hand in a vice-like grip. At which moment I decided I'd never loved anyone so deeply, desperately and unconditionally.

I'd come a long way from the Machiavelli I'd been, trapped on Muti's Farm, in India. Then my lovely Princess had been a means to an end. Those calculations would remain a knife in my conscience, forever. I'd have given a great deal to be able to wash their stain away. Guilty memories, however, are my strong point. When they cut me open on the pathologists' table, that guilt will flood out like a bucketful of squid ink.

Have you ever heard happy wood-wrenching at 5.00 am? It's quite unlike anything else. It's jubilant – "crack!" Joyous – "crunch!" Ecstatic! – "sound of nails giving way under wrecking bar." Triumphant! – "noise of packing case finally disintegrating."

"Oh God, what's that?" asked Tee, poking her nose out from under the duvet I'd covered us with at 4.00 am. "Is it the end of the world, or am I pooing the bed?"

"I have a theory…" I began, ponderously. Then the door of our trashy trailer burst open and hideously cold air invaded the van. Carl followed it, apparently rejuvenated.

He was waving a very ugly piece of rusty metal. He flew across the, admittedly, limited space and fell on the bed between us.

"I love you, I love you, I love you!" he warbled, brandishing his piece of rust.

"Get off! Get off!" roared the Princess. "I haven't even gone to bed yet!"

"Oh, you darling!" he cried. "You utter sweetheart! You masterpiece! You utter one-off! You adorable lunatic! God, how I love you!"

"Sorry, Eva!" he yelled. "I love you too! See ya' both!" And he fled, complete with rusty thing, though he left the fresh air. I tried to find it revitalising but it remained stubbornly cold.

"I hate him," gibbered the Princess. "I'm going to call down a 40,000 year curse on him, his friends and family. Where's my bra?"

"Why do you need your bra?"

"Because I curse best when I'm Ganesh and to do Ganesh I need a bra, for the ears. In fact, one of yours would be better – bigger ears."

"Could you curse him later?" I enquired. "After breakfast, say?"

"I could, but it'll take better now, while I'm worked up."

"Tell you what, you roll over and I'll rub your back."

"Oh, OK."

After that we had a good snooze till nine.

"What did Carl want earlier?" asked Tee, enthusiastically billowing toothpaste foam.

"To say 'thank you' for the old bike your husband sent. But he couldn't quite get it out."

"Oh, I'm glad he likes it. I love him to bits."

Before we toddle off for late breakfast, I sit Tee on the side of the bed and squat cross-legged on the floor in front of her.

"What are you doing?" she asks suspiciously.

"I'm arranging something."

"What?"

"A strangeness."

"Why do we want a strangeness?"

"Because I'm about to talk about something strange."

"Well get on with it, because I'm incredibly hungry."

"OK, here comes something strange. I don't think we're here."

"Where are we then?"

"Earth II, I think."

"That place JJ and the wretched Rabbit come from?"

"The very same – and why is it 'the wretched Rabbit,' may I enquire?"

"Because I'm the shiny, glitzy one around here and I'm not used to being upstaged."

"He's all surface show. No-one really notices. Don't worry, they recognise a real nutter when they meet one."

"I hope so. I put a lot of effort into my persona. I'm not used to being ignored."

"If you really think things are deteriorating, you could always blow something up."

"Like terrorists do?"

"Freedom fighters, please."

"What would I be fighting for?"

"The inalienable right of Princess Tulipa to be acknowledged as the Premier Zany of this roundabout and not some hi-jacker from outer space."

"You're right. I'll plot an explosion. What do you think I should blow-up?"

"Oh, I dunno…Pa's garden?"

"Beaver! That'd be evil. Marie-Claire would be heartbroken. So would Pa. How could you have such an awful thought?"

"I didn't. You're right. I'm withdrawing it from circulation. One which basis, Sweet Pea, I think we should stand the whole Freedom Fighter thingy down."

"Why?"

"Cos you're not a convincing terrorist! You can't bear hurting people and anyway, you haven't even got a gun."

"I could borrow your Pa's Black Beauty, whatever-it-is, that Andrew got for him. He's desperate to show me how to shoot it."

"It's called Brown Bess, not Black Beauty – that was a horse."

"Same thing."

"Tee! You can't lead the revolution with a musket – or a horse."

"I could, if it was 1704."

"But it's not, it's now."

"I don't want to lead a revolution, anyway. I just want that Rabbit out of my premier loony spot."

"You could get a glow-in-the-dark suit like his."

"Do you reckon that would swing it?"

"No, it'd look as if you were copying – with the added danger of looking like an idiot."

"So why suggest it?"

"Because I was subtly trying to get us back on track."

"Which was?"

"What if we're not where we think we are?"

"I think I'm in a trashy trailer, being provoked by a self-confessed piece of trailer-trash."

"Yes, you are – BUT WHERE?"

"God! On a derelict roundabout at the back-end of nowhere!"

"Look…do you remember the crazy thoughts you had when you were a kid? You'd just been to the circus, or the fun-fair, then your nan took you home and you couldn't hear the music, see the lights anymore and you thought 'does the fair really exist? Is it really there? Or is it only there when I'm there?"

"Of course."

"And what conclusion did you come to?"

"That it was only real when I was there. And, might I add, that conclusion has served me faithfully ever since. Life is only real where I am."

"Lucifer! My girl-friend is Bishop Berkeley!"

"Yum, can I have the Bishop-y outfit? That'd show the Rabbit who's top loony."

"Knock yourself out! Don't forget the crozier, Very useful for poking things at a distance."

"Are we done?"

"Oh absolutely. I'll wind up with something really simple. We're not on Planet Earth – we're somewhere else!"

"Can you still get breakfast there?"

"You could yesterday."

"That's all right then. Oh, here's a thought – are they real breakfasts? I mean, we don't just think that we're eating them?"

"How should I know?"

"I thought you were the brains in this partnership. I'm the loony with the cheque-book."

"Try this one then…how are your bowels?"

"Number one, or two?"

"Two."

"Clockwork."

"Then the meals are real."

"I'm really glad to hear that. By the way, how are your bowels?"

"Awful."

"Excellent! They've always been awful. If they'd suddenly gone clockwork, I'd suspect alien interference."

"No such luck."

"S-P-L-E-N-D-I-D!!" roared Tee in her best Tigger voice and off we went to breakfast, somewhere in the cosmos.

25

A GRAND DAY OUT

Tee was eating sausages in what can only be described as a dedicated way, when the Rabbit came in, carnival lights on full.

"God!" she spluttered, spraying offal, "turn yourself down, you're like a stripper-gram from a horror movie."

"Apologies," said the Rabbit, dimming his wattage to the barely visible, "may I join you?"

"Hop aboard," I said, instantly offering up a silent prayer that my unconscious punning would pass unnoticed. It's a verbal tic I have. Striking a pun about someone's particularity and then dying of embarrassment because they might think I'm taking the mickey. I'm not. In fact, I think I'm being subconsciously empathetic but that would take some explaining and would probably only make matters worse.

"What's on your mind, Double-R?" I asked.

"Locality," he replied.

"What a coincidence. That's been on our minds, too."

"Fundamentally," said the Rabbit, "materiality is very simple. Add enough particles together, in the right way, under the right conditions and you have an inert material."

"Like this sausage?" asked Tee.

"Nothing like your breakfast chipolata, Princess. No, nothing like that at all. To get to your choice of breakfast meat, materials have to be combined in endless complex, innovative ways, given the spark of life – as batteries are not included…apologies, just my silly joke – so that they can become pigs, be fattened, killed, processed and end up on your plate. Let's stay with the simple end of things…"

"Uh, huh," interrupted Tee, "let's not. I need to take a business trip to Delhi, to see my husband, to endorse a new business venture. Voila, my trusty phone," which she flourished, and proceeded to make a First Class reservation at the top of her voice.

This was news to me and I was spinning my wheels trying to catch-up.

Double-R sat there patiently and in my opinion, mentally tapping his finger on the table.

The flicker of a smile passed across his face, a totally disconcerting imitation of the human temporarily displacing the animal.

"Ms Eva," he said politely, "would you care for a trip anywhere? Into Town, to shop? A trip to the country to visit a fine historical property? For obvious reasons I can't accompany you but I'm sure I can secure you a driver and car. If the Princess is forced to abandon you, I'm mortified by the prospect of your loneliness."

Tee gave him her full-burst, twin-laser treatment. I almost fainted on his behalf.

Double-R just inclined his head, politely.

"I was, actually, here to invite you all on an Earth II outing, to meet our friends, Moss and Shade. Jo-Jo will be driving the crawler and the cwm, with its angels, is spectacular. Moss and Shade are also the most lovely, welcoming people. Everyone else is coming."

"Everyone else?" I gasped.

"Everyone. Your newly adopted Papa and Mama, Punch and Marie-Claire, are particularly excited by the idea of there being other worlds, other people, other ideas."

"Jabberwocky," said Tee, in a very downbeat voice. "I wouldn't have thought they even knew about planets." Then, in a different tone, she said – "I thought I had you there Double-R, fair and square."

"Do you want to come?" asked the Rabbit, gently, "or are you compelled to be in Delhi?

"Ms Eva…where do you find yourself?"

I looked at Tee. "Come on Tiggs, let's play with the grown-ups."

"OK," she grunted. "But no hard-boiled eggs in the picnic, Whiskers. They give me awful wind."

Once again, the Rabbit inclined his head politely. Standing, he said – "outside, in one hour shall we say?" Then away he strode, accompanied by a smattering of local applause, as he turned up his lights.

"That was a bit rude," I giggled. "Whiskers!"

"Just let me cancel this plane," muttered Tee, "I really thought I had him there."

Marie-Claire linked arms with Tee and Marie-Gabrielle. "Look mes petites," she said, "it's got caterpillar tracks for wheels, just like the big digging machine had in our garden. Do you really think we'll be safe? I am so excited!"

"Tee and I will protect you, maman," said Marie-Gabrielle. Admiringly, I watched as Tee turned off her grump and turned on the glee. It was as seamless a performance as was the planetary chicanery now being played out on the forecourt of Andy's Place.

For some reason I'd ended up as the wallflower for this outing. Tee was tied to Alice and Maman. Pa was up front with JJ, bouncing about like a child allowed in the front seat of the family car for the first time. Andy and Carl, the latter still showing signs of ancient Villiers rust, were side-by-side and hand-in-hand. That left me with Double-R. But he had greater tasks to perform than the squiring of wallflowers to the Ball. He had a comms-panel to play with and from the look of it, it was considerably more complex than the average "can you hear me at the back?" affair. In fact, I've seen simpler flight decks.

I was quite happy to wallflower. I was trying to get my brain to work out what, on or off Earth, could possibly be going on. Also I wanted to spot 'the join,' the moment we segued from Andy's Place to Earth II. That, at least, might provide some traction to help edit my confusion.

Eventually, as I sat waiting for some mighty diesel to growl into life, we began to glide away from the Diner in total silence. For a moment I was convinced that the diner was moving and that we were static. But then we were on the exit curve, ready to hit the roundabout.

A red and black articulated truck was swinging into the caff on the approach road. Exit and entrance roads run parallel, almost side-by-side for a short distance and then each curves away. I was able to scrutinise the driver's face. I intended to remember every detail of his perfectly ordinary, middle-European phiz. My question was, would he be in the cafe when we got back? Would this all prove to be a trick in time, an affair of smoke and mirrors?

As the cab pulled past me the trailer swung into view. It was carrying twin containers. First came one in maroon and rust, stencilled MAERSK, no memorable detail there. But container two was decorated with explicit graffiti. On a background of grubby ivory, in green spray paint, was painted… 'the Rabbit sucks.' Inter-galactic irony?

I turned from the side-splitting graffito, to try and concentrate on the exit road. Stomach and brain executed a slow forward roll. It was of beaten rock between never-ending moorland. I could hear the crunching of the crawler's tracks, feel the rapid adjustment of intelligent springs and stabilisers, as we climbed an unending hillside, without the slightest sign of life on either side.

Near me, the Rabbit's hands were a blur at the control panel. As I gawped, he half-turned to give me a conspiratorial grin, another loan from his gallery of human emojis. Weakling that I am, I smirked by return. Why I didn't just stand up shrieking – 'WHAT THE HELL!?' I have no idea.

"Welcome to the Rim, ladies and gentlemen," says Jo-Jo on microphone. "You OK at the back there, Evie?" I give a cheerful wave and am gratified when Tee looks anxiously over her shoulder. Hopefully she was checking that that exchange was no more than casual camaraderie between friends.

"Did any of you spot the join?" he asks and I can hear Alice whisper "I did" but no-one else seems to hear, either the question or her answer.

"This is my world," says Jo-Jo brightly, "as you can see, there's not much to it, though we are heading towards one place that's quite different. It's a wanderers' world, or a series of isolations, artistic oases very often, joined by nomad trails. Up here we never question its point, why it exists, or even how. The fact that it does is good enough for us. But it must look strange to you, seeing it for the first time. It's a physical location, sure enough, with winds, rain, snow-by-the-blizzard-full but it's also a construct of the group mind, for want of a better phrase.

"I've been reading Punch's book, Jolyon's book I should say and though I can't articulate what I felt, I sensed a similarity, a parallel, between what exists here and what the author struggled to describe when he spoke of group mind in the insect world. Not the most comfortable thought but one worth chewing on, perhaps."

'Please tell me when,' I thought, 'you had time to read Jolyon's Book, JJ? Has someone really messed with Time?'

I don't like the sensation I get when my mind spins its wheels, when I'm presented with the unprecedented and am forced to accept that it is happening. Every touchstone of reality has been overturned and yet I can breathe, smell, see, touch and probably taste. I can definitely hear, Jo-Jo's familiar voice, speaking English.

'Please tell me what is happening?' I groaned inwardly. Nothing spoke up.

I decided it must be to do with particles. Something could do tricks with materiality and mind. I could probably be moved around the cosmos, like a chess piece – albeit the humblest of pawns. I could be taken to pieces and reassembled elsewhere. It must be all to do with complementarity, every particle has an equal and opposite particle…

'Oh, a blight upon it. I can't even get within question distance. I have no idea what to ask. The enormity of it and yet, the utter tedium of this landscape. Why isn't this an Eden, why is it a kissing cousin of Ilkley Moor, with or without the obligatory hat?'

We drove for hours and the terrain barely changed. Rugged moorland, with an occasional hint of life in a distant farmhouse. What were they doing here? What was the 'great intelligence' building? 'A copy,' the Rabbit had said, with the bad bits taken out. This didn't look like that. This looked more like a Year One Psych experiment, writ large and that was not a comforting thought. 'Hello Rats, welcome to your maze!'

'What was the common denominator here? If I could just alight on that I might get a clue.'

I wracked my brains. All I could dream up was that 'something' was studying 'tenacity,' the refusal to stop. What drives you on if Death is taken out of the equation? Given that Death is the engine that drives the human race, or rather fear of the certainty of Death, what happens when you take it away? Here, it seemed, an intelligence was interrogating that. First, it froze the ageing process and fortified the bodywork. Then it left the mind to determine why it wanted to carry on living, providing it with a planet that could offer you everything you needed to make the most of immortality.

Jo-Jo had endured 4000 years of his own misanthropy, a repetitive recycling of negative thoughts had been sufficient to carry him through four millennia – together with his Rabbit.

That was peculiar. This Grand Inquisitor allowed you a companion. It must have discovered that without a partner, human beings gave up very quickly. Some would tough it out for a while but in general, a human being without feedback was a dead human being. There'll never be 'a last man, or woman, on earth.' They'll just turn off their light and join the dead.

This 'great intelligence' must have worked that one out very quickly. If it wanted to study solitary existence, it should have created a planet for wolf spiders. ('Maybe it had! – note to Super Intelligence – I don't want to visit it!')

So-oo, what was being interrogated here? Jo-Jo had suggested that most of the rim dwellers were artists of one kind or another. They had 'visions' they were keen to work out. The Core enabled them. It was the ultimate artists' supply warehouse.

Artists were forever trying to stitch another dimension onto life – the dimension of their 'vision.' Of course they could never get it down on paper, or cast it in bronze as precisely as they had seen it. They were, therefore, forever pursuing the ineffable 'vision,' the one that escaped them again, and again, and again.

Next came the question of their partners, all those Marthas, cleaning up after the Marys. That was a two-part conundrum worthy of examination. A visionary needs an audience. The vision itself is only enough for a little while. But the heart of the conundrum is that Martha never sees what Mary sees. However much she wants to, tries to, she can only pretend to.

'So, what are we seeing here? That Life endures, in the absence of death, by lying? What a peculiar finding that would be…that Life is a lie…or, life has to lie…surely not?'

"Interesting thoughts," said an avuncular voice in my head, "yet very stark conclusions. I think that's a problem you should examine. Stark conclusions. Often misleading. Pint-half-empty ideas, don't you think?"

I do not like voices in my head. I have been badly misled by them. I say them. I mean one. The one that floated down upon me in hospital. I have no intention of being crippled by any other pop-up salesmen of mantras, who elbow their way in between my ears. Good, or bad, they are banned.

'I am not here for this,' I thought. 'I am not here to listen to the reasonable voice of reasonable thoughts, broadcasting its propaganda in my head.'

"Oh, why not?" asked the voice, in hurt but kind tone – or was I imagining everything now?

'Because between my ears is private space, clearly marked – "No Entry." Occasional broadcasts and blogs may exit via my mouth. But what goes in, goes through my filters, so bog off and stay out!'

"Oops, got it," said the voice agreeably.

I pushed back against my seat and shrank myself down into its upholstery. If I'd had the Rabbit's technology, I'd have made myself about six inches tall and reconfigured my outline, to a featureless titanium ball.

We were really crawling, now. You could hear the treads grinding, having to haul at the pounded surface for purchase, no more agreeable click-clacking over a decent bit of road. It was the sort of climb that comes before the giddying descent of a Big Dipper ride. First the ascent, next the brief horizontal respite and finally the sickening plunge, down towards the centre of the earth. I hoped we weren't in for one of those.

I pretty soon discovered that we were negotiating hairpins We took turn after turn and climbed higher and higher. JJ had talked about an Upper, higher, Rim. We must be working our way there. To lapse into my vernacular, we were climbing the nipple on the tit.

"There's only about 3000 feet in it ," JJ was saying, "but to we Rim dwellers, this is where the High Rim starts, not down in the valley – where we left Andy's Place…" he ended with a rueful laugh.

I shifted irritably on my seat, convinced that the inner voice was still present and silently laughing its socks off at my childish behaviour.

If I hadn't told it to 'bog-off', I could have asked it if Andy's Place was still there, in the valley, in some kind of limbo until we returned, or if I was being hopelessly naive in insisting on the primacy of my familiar material forms above all others. If you accepted the hypothesis of multiple universes, then slipping between them, as easily as Alice might have changed pages inside one of her books, was entirely possible.

These theories had existed for years and no one had proved or disproved them, yet. More to the point, what did it matter? I was here, in some form or other and we were probably going to be restored to Andy's Place without anyone really having missed us. Didn't matter how impossible it was. It was happening. I didn't believe it but I was here.

I sat back and stared at the back of Punch's head, catching an occasional glimpse of his raptor's profile. He was a bit shy of 350 years old. The guy driving was 4000 years old. The 'little girl' behind them had peeled herself off a rock before civilisation had really got going. Now all of them were dying and for all that this was, ostensibly a sight-seeing trip, it was also a pilgrimage to a cosmic Lourdes.

Tee and I were going to become immortal. Well, I didn't believe that for a start. An immortal Beaver? Too stupid for words. I had nothing to add to the cosmic conversation – despite a ravening hunger to comprehend it at some level. Why bestow immortality on me? Any random dip into humanity's pot would be more likely to turn up a better candidate.

We were going to meet Moss and he was at least 10,000 years old, according to JJ. But death had been removed from his equation, so time no longer had any meaning. His body stabilised, his brain in some way protected, entropy refuted.

'Is that what this is all about?' I suddenly thought. 'They can do all this mechanical maintenance but they need some particular fuel from a living human to make it work? They can't isolate the life spark, so they keep some of us ticking over to provide it? A little like early man probably kept a fire burning continuously, because he didn't know how to start one himself. There's that little bit of Life that is obstinately elusive, that won't be isolated, described or artificially induced. They've got the lot but not that final fraction. And without it, nothing will work, except robotically.

'Otherwise, what can we possibly provide that they want?'

It must be something to do with the group because even I know our group is more than the sum of its parts. And a group like ours is not any old group…in fact, it's probably unique. None of us really understand how it assembled. At one stage Alice (I'm going to keep calling her Alice, because she's less Marie-Gabrielle-ish every day and a lot more Alice-y) thought she'd done it, by unleashing the Shaman. But then she'd realised that most of the players were already in place. Also, it had been the best part of two years earlier that I'd made the acquaintance of Andy and Carl and without the diner, there'd be no group. Just as there'd be no diner without the Core's rescue beacons.

I couldn't find a vantage where I might be able to get a clear view of the situation. Did my androgyny have any part to play? If it did, then things began so much earlier?

I remember when mum was trying to 'rescue me' with our year of holidays, we took a cheap flight to Sicily. As we crossed the Alps I had a God's eye view of the terrain below. At cruising height, looking down, it had seemed that it would be the simplest thing in the world to walk across them. That black slot led to that valley, a bit of a scramble up that slope presented you with a wide path around the peak, then over that shoulder, dodge the snowfield on your right, down to the river valley and keep going.

Then I'd forced myself to think properly. About boulders the size of houses, about snow covered crevasses, traverses on scree at 70 degrees to the perpendicular, raging torrents falling on needle-sharp black rocks, translucent under ice. I almost started to shiver, to feel fatal weakness in my ankles, the failing grip of my frozen hands, one vertical ascent after another, my eyelids glued together with frost.

Terrified, I'd pulled myself back into the little aluminium tube and concentrated on my peanuts.

Leaving Sicily, from Catania, provided another aerial epiphany. Maybe all the planes take off in the same great arc but ours dipped its starboard wing and banked over an arc of volcanic islands. Some were no more than eroded blocks of tufa but the largest were lush with greenery and boasted the odd house. The last but one island was the largest and in the eroded cone of the old volcano, there was a farm. The farmer's wife had hung her washing out to dry. White sheets against the most intense green I've ever seen. The white and green against the black throat of the collapsing cone. It was such a strangely moving sight and I can't say why. Too many variables to select any single one. Fire from the centre of the earth had once erupted from that cone, now human mice lived in it and pegged out their washing to dry.

Everything is relative. Everything depends on where you are standing. How close, how far away. What is time doing? Is it moving quickly here and slowly there? Do these rules apply over there, what is it we can't see? Where are the unknown, unknowns? When did anything begin, when will anything end? There are no constants, everything is change, everything is chance – but only under certain conditions of relativity. From here the volcano is a spectacle of wonder, from there – a disaster.

How much does the informing intelligence of the cosmos see? More importantly, what does it feel? What can it control, what can it not? Somewhere, a metronome is ticking…tick, tock, tick, tock. That is not the sound of time, it's the sound of entropy.

Who sees our little group? What do they see? Do they see flawed human personalities, or little pulses of energy, flaring and fading? Are they looking through an electron microscope at the barely visible, or are we, in some unfathomable way, larger than life? I wish I knew something.

"I promise I won't do this again," says the voice in my head, "but you simply have to look up and out, Eva."

Despite myself, I looked up and out and decided that this once, I'd forgive the voice.

26

VALLEY OF THE ANGELS

The entrance to this cwm, as JJ called it, would have more in common with a cross-section of the Grand Canyon, than of some sunken Welsh horseshoe, covered in the greenest of grass. It was wide, sheer-sided and ideally suited to the miracle that had been worked upon it.

You could have parked 50 or more Princess Tee Range Rovers, nose to tail, across its entrance, so it was no geomorphological slouch. It was strata-slump on a fine scale, after which the river had been doing a sterling job of excavation, smoothing, polishing and removing the general litter of millennia. But it was the angels streaming out of the cliffs, like so many doves leaving their cote, in a flurry of wings against the morning sun, that pulled the valley together with threads of light. They were vast but the interplay of scale simply messed with your perception. At one second it seemed you might hold the whole scene in the palm of your hand, as in a snow dome, the next, the little globe billowed outwards and a dazzling light, reflected from angelic wings, filled the entire horizon.

I don't calculate size easily and there was nothing to gauge the scale by. That was why I was mentally parking Tee's car here and there, to try and corral some sense and proportion into the vista.

Each angel must have been three cars-length and the wing-spans seemed wider than that. They were hurtling towards the spectator, each on an upward trajectory, outwards from their respective cliff-face to form up as a golden-echelon that would soar towards the sun, to join in it in celebration of light and life.

Whatever they were made of, it must have been some new lightweight alloy, for they had nothing of the cast-steel brutality, typical of large-scale, metal artworks. They looked as though they might have been spun, like so much candyfloss but that was a trick of the patinas surfacing the alloy.

They had something of the Rabbit's luminescence but in considerably better taste. These angels were not forming up for a Harlequinade, they were divine emissaries, departing on some task beyond our understanding.

They came out of the cliffs in ranks of three, their wall anchorages cleverly cranked to avoid any sense of regimentation, or linear alignment. The result was that the mouth of the cwm, was simply ablaze with colour and form, which only slowly resolved itself into the recognisable. It was an epic tour-de-force, an artistic masterpiece, landscape harnessed to a vision and transformed by it.

The river below, played its part, too. It virtually filled the canyon floor, though there were wide-enough pathways, either side, to accommodate a dozen, and more, pedestrians abreast. But at the margins it flowed and swirled slowly, forming dark pools which reflected the overhead radiance in more thoughtful tones. Only mid-channel did the water rush, building white peaks that advanced almost menacingly towards the parapet-less bridge on which we had parked. But before it could crash into us, it simply vanished without sound, down the widest of sluices, where hundreds of feet below, JJ was explaining, it generated whatever the local equivalent was of hydro-electricity.

What, I asked myself, were Moss's angels proclaiming? The Second Coming? The End of the World? Whatever it was, many of them were doing it by trumpet. These flared out, like the blossoming spathes of Calla lilies, from pouted lips. Heads were thrown back in celebration and golden hair streamed over their shoulders, flowing down their backs to dance among the vast feathers of their spread wings.

Moss had built everything, designed everything, to exploit the perfect light he had here. The metallic patination was causing the sunlight to splinter and refract into all the glorious possibilities laid bare by chromatics. This is where Goethe's spectrum met the aurora and both blazed in brilliance. Newton could eat his heart out, he hadn't had the 'sympatico' to get past seven colours.

JJ was rattling off statistics…each angel could take fifteen years of work, some improbable number would be needed to fill the cwm. Each one would be different. Millennia would be needed to finish the work and millennia had already passed since its conception.

Moss freely admitted that he had stolen the idea of his tiered angels. He had read, by chance, about the churches of East Anglia, on dear old Earth I. In a village called March, the vision of mounting angels on the projecting timbers of the hammerbeam roofs had, in his opinion, achieved its finest realisation. This cwm was his homage to those long-dead artisans. Men who had used their hands and the basic technologies of the day, to raise miracles in glorification of their church.

Tee came tottering up behind me, doing her 'I-need-unconditional-love' walk and tried to put her arms over my shoulders and rest her chin on my head, which was a deranged move, as I was at least 12 inches taller. So I hauled her round in front and did it to her, which had been her intention all along.

"I knew there was a way it worked," she said comfortably and smugly, wriggling happily against me, until she felt confident enough to finally settle back at ease.

"This is all a bit – 'bloody hell!' – 'bloody hell!' – 'bloody hell!' – isn't it," she puzzled, as much to herself as to me.

"It's worthy of something," I said. "Though I can't think what deserves it. Certainly not religion, even if it is their iconography he's pinched. Frankly, it makes religion look outdated."

Jo-Jo joined us. It had been peculiar, the way he'd started to get his twin O's back, the moment we'd driven away from Andy's Place. He hugged us both, which for a small, if stocky, guy was an ambitious move, when we're in a symbiotic knot to begin with. But we got the message.

"It seems like an eternity ago but Moss and I used to sit up there," he gestured to the far end of the cwm, "where he has his farm and workshops. We'd sit on whichever bit of angel he was fabricating and eat potatoes we'd baked at the edge of the forge, at least we did when Shade was away and dinner was not happening. They were always baked like bricks on one side and sweet and soft on the other. We never remembered to turn them round – too busy yakking."

"Can't be that long ago," ventured Tee, from where she was still tightly glued to my front.

"Thousand years, or so, maybe more. There were only a score or so installed when I was last here. Also, that river was half the size and ran over this lip where we're standing, right down the new crawler road. No sluice back then.

Tee peeped out, a cautious cuckoo from a dodgy clock. "You're messing with my head," she said accusingly. "Old three-eyes here might have zapped you up 300 years or so, along with Punch and friends, but how did we arrive at 1000?"

"The Minister of My Interior, makes a good point," I said, pulling her back into position, where she settled quite happily. "I've been cross-examining the time-scale thing, while you were driving but I have to confess, it blew my fuses every time I tried, so I gave up."

"I could get the Rabbit to explain," offered Jo-Jo.

"No!" protested a muffled voice. "Anything but Whiskers!"

"I think I'll leave it in peace, on the inexplicable pile," I said. "But you and Moss will still be friends?"

"Oh, as if it was yesterday," Jo-Jo smiled. "Time is of very little importance here. In fact, zero importance. People vanish all the time. They take themselves off to study their art, fabric technology, choreography, light-works, whatever it may be and they come back after centuries, millennia. I spent one millennium with the stoics, when I was young and no-one seemed to notice at all."

"Do you any good?" asked the muffled voice.

"Actually, it was very revealing."

"Oh, good grief! Don't try to explain. It would start my hiccups off."

"In that case, I'll skip to the end," said Jo-Jo equably. "The plan is to walk up the river. It's the best way to get the full effect. There'll be a picnic at the top."

"Which side do we have to take?" I asked.

"You get to choose," said Jo-Jo. "The light is good on either side, for an hour or more and that's all it takes."

"Which side will Whiskers be on?" asked Tee, emerging ruffled from her nestbox.

"He's up the top already. Helping Shade arrange the picnic."

"Left then," she said. And so we went on the left bank.

27

CAKE-WALK

Punch, Marie-Claire and Marie-Gabrielle, chose to walk on the right-hand side.

The path was cunningly engineered. It appeared rugged, as if chewed out of the cliffs by the river's unending, swirling waters but robot-surveyors had been along here, sheering off obstacles, laying a path that wouldn't break ankles but would avoid humiliating walkers in search of the wild. By any measure they had been successful but to Punch, recalling his year in the wilderness, he could feel the absence of what should have been a presence. That made him rueful.

"Now, watch 'ow tha' goes, t'two o'ye bein' t'most precious things in my 'owd life."

"Papa, we are fine. We are not made of spun sugar."

"T'me thou art – delicate enough fer a weddin' cake!"

He laughed out loud at a sudden remembrance and promptly launched into a story.

When he been very young, he, Susanny and Johnno, were best friends and being the three youngest in the village, apart from the babies, stuck together, for adventure and misadventure alike.

On days when they were feeling particularly bold – and particularly hungry – in the hope of the heel of a loaf, or even a spoonful of jam each, they would sneak down the alley that led to the slop-house door, of the Old Stag Inn.

"Now, hard by t'slophouse wer t'kitchen, o'course an' if we cud just slide in through yon door, which were allus open, on account o't'heat, well let me tell youse…

"Cook wer' a dear owd thing who on account o' having no chillun o'er own, loved ever'n' else's chillun as if them b'er own. So, sometime we'd get bread an' jam and sometimes we'd be sweppit out by a maid wi' a broom!"

"And quite rights, too," declared Marie-Claire. "I would have shooed you all away!"

"Nae, tha' wouldna. Ye'd 'ave 'ad us on yer lap, probable all at once, a'eatin o' white bread an' butter – and thou knows it!"

"Never!" protested Marie-Claire.

"Yes, Papa, you are right. She would. When I was little, there were always sweets for me and my little friends, hidden in her apron."

"Anyways," said Punch forcefully, taking back control of his narrative. "Wot' we see'd this particular day wer' something marvellous. T' wer' this big 'ere cake, tiers on tiers o' it such as Johnno said it reachit-ed reet up to 'eaven, an' Susanny said indeed it must, fer ther wer' an angel on't'top! An' so ther' wer', or so it seemed to us. It wer spun sugar work around some kinda' biscuit, a'reckons now. In yon dark owd' kitchen, it all shone, just like these 'ere angels is a' shinin' now.

"Wh'n we snuck in, theer wer' cookie, our favourite, a'stannin' on a stool, wi' a big jar o'honey, which she b'a drippin' down t'sides o't'cake. An' as it runs down, it catches t'light, too.

"She sees us an' she puts 'er fingers to 'er lips, as in 'b'quiet an' stay back,' all serious an' urgent, like. Tis' th'n we sees why. Theer's two girt footmen theer, all in livery they was, just waitin' fer t'carry yon cake thro' t'dinin' room – fer it wer' a reet posh do! Now, if they's set an eye t'us, we'd a' 'ad such a kickin' owt thet kitchen, thro't slophouse an int' t'lane. Boxed ears, too, a' shudna' wonder. So we cowers down like lil' mousies.

"She gets off 'er stool, bit stiff like, an' reaches fer a flagon as is a' warmin o'er a candleflame. She pours some liquor 'round t' bottom o't'cake an' o'er t'layers wheer t'honey ent drippit down to, yet.

"We 'ad no idea what wer' t'come next, fer now she's a' sprinklin' o' lil' flecks o' gold o'er t'honey."

Punch paused for effect and glanced around and above, where the light show played, in all its kaleidoscopic glory and reflected in the still pools by the path side. He nodded, with respect then, smiling, continued.

"She teks a taper, lights it on t'range an' tells yon footmen t'b'ready, sharpish an' t'brace 'emselves either end o't'trencher yon cake wer' on.

"Wh'n I've lighted it," she sez, "tha' picks it up an' teks it through – careful!"

"Weel, we three kitchin-mice wer all eyes and expectings – I dunno what. But we stays as tiny as we cud and as quiet as weeds."

"Then she sets 'er taper t'brandy, fer thet wer worrit was. It all lit up, wi' snakes o'blue fire, a flickerin' an' a' catchin on t'gold shreds.

"Git goin' yer dummies," she sez "an' don' ye dare fer t'put them flames owt!"

"Yes, ma'am," says they – an' they's tremblin' an fair a'freeted of 'er! 'Twere a marvel t'see, fer us, thet young.

"Off goes them footmen, at a gentle clip and we 'ears a great cheerin' an' a bangin' o'pots on't table, a'floatin' down't'hall.

"Ol' cookie crosses her sen,' in relief a's a'reckonin' now, turns t'us an' sez… 'off wi' ye, fer now. Come ye back in a longish while an' a'll 'ave t'scraps fer thee, a' shouldna' wonder. But, fer now, away wi youse, God b' blessin' thy grubby lil' faces!'

"We 'adn't ev'r seen t'like. A' settin' fire t'a'reet gud cake, an' it wi' honey an' angels all oe'r it. So's we runs t'our owd barn – we pretends it wer ours – creeps int't' hay and climbs up fer t'ave a reet gud discussin' o' matters.

"Susanny said it were magic.

"Johnno said 'e 'adn't seen t'like afore an' that wer'plain.

"A' didn't say owt. So it wer'nt much n'a'discuss at all but we did fall t'wondering what might b'left fer us. Fer cook 'ad as gud as promised.

"We passet time a'rollin' down t'hay an' thet wud a'got us a reet skelpin' if owd George's boys 'ad caught us. Anyhows, up an' down we goes, 'appy as lil' rats…"

"Papa," said Marie-Claire, "you are straying from your story."

"A'ent, Ma! Tis all entirely relevant, at least t'mi mind it be and a's a'tellin' t'tale."

In which manner, they happily bickered along the path, with the great angels overhead craning an ear for the next stanza of Punch's saga – or it would have been nice to believe that they did, he thought. In fact, it was left to Marie-Gabrielle to request the finishing touches. "Come on Pa, what happened when you went back?" And she hung so heavily on his bony old arm, face upturned, gleefully, that he nearly fell over.

"Let up gal, tha's as 'eavy as a bag o'spuds. Tha's a' overfeedin' o'er, Ma!"

"I am not. She is starvation thin and you know it!"

"I knows nowt o't'sort but a' does love every inch."

"So, tell, tell, tell!" squeals the far from portly one.

"Ther's nowt much t'tell, girl. Nowt wi' a surprise t'it."

"We sneaks back, an cookie's waitin' on us. She sets us down by't'bread trough, fer it be just the reet 'ite fer lil' folk. Then she brings out t'ruins o't'cake. My, 'ad they bin at it! Whoe'er they bin, 't weer a reet mess. She pours it in t't'trough, like we wuz lil' pigs, an' lil' pigs is what we wer, fer we stuffit oursen' 'til our lil' bellies wer' a'burstin'. If we'd 'ad buttons. they'd 'ave flown 'cross t'floor. Then she brings out big cups o'buttermilk an'we drains 'em. So she fills 'em up ag'in – an' we drinks them, too!

"Whiles we cud still walk, she shoos us oot o't'kitchin, wi' a pat t'our lil' mucky 'eads. Fer Susanny, she gi'es t'angel, from t' top o'cake. It wer' a bit broke, but what wer broke t'us?

"So, we legs it t'our privit place an' we puts t'angel safe, up in a tree, like. No ground beasts cud gerrit theer! But just like me, 40 year on, we's fergettin' 'bout t'birds.

"Next mornin', up we pants, thet 'ungry t'see t'angel agin and she's all 'et up! Didn'a e'en leave a crumb!

"Thet neet 'afore, we'd stood theer, lookin' an' marvellin', like t'lil frien's we wus an' solemnly pledged as we 'adn't seen anythin' that beautiful. We pledges as we's t'tell no-one, fer they'd b'wantin' t'steal t'glory, o'it. No, 'twer t'be jest fer us. Mebbe, it'd be our talisman an' set us Quests an' t'like. First time we'd 'ad t'luxury o'thinkin' lek theet. Normal, we'd 'ave jest gobbled 'er up, 'alf starved as we wus. But cook-y stuffed us thet full o'good fare, we 'ad time t'think different, like. Y'canna expect starvelin's t'think. Ye needs some fat t'yer bones t'do thet.

"Ye'd a'thought a'd a'learned but nay, all them years on, a'raises up mi' cheddar in t'watter and thinks it be safe as 'ouses. Along comes jacky-daw an' 'is friends, pecks their big 'oles an' topples 'er int' t'watter, fer' t'fishes.

"Now, theer be's a moral t'all this. A 'ad it clear in mi 'ead when a'starts, but wi' thee two a mitherin' an' slappin' o'me," – and Punch fondly pulled both Maries closer – "an' mi' gerrin' lost in mi' childhood, a's quite fergettin' o'it."

The three smile together and walk on under the flaming, protective swords of the warrior angels, guardians of man and all his foibles. If they heard his homely tale, they give no sign.

Punch glances upwards and wonders at the skill and artifice. 'B' thet's all t'is,' he thinks. They may look as if they were raised by unknown, unearthly beings but they are devices from the mind and hand of man. The idea behind them was old before Christ was even born.

"Theer's nowt new in t'world, 'owever shiny it be," he mumbles contentedly. But his women have had enough of his talk and they walk on, wondering if fabrics exist that might mirror the angelic spectrum? For, if they do, they will be first and second in the queue to purchase them. Punch they leave, happily propped against a warm rock, half-sitting, half-leaning and gazing upstream at the restless tumble of water.

"A remembers mi' moral now," he says to himself, "it 'ent t'idea, it 'ent t'finishin' o'it, or t'startin' or t'fettlin' o'it. Tis bein' able fer t'see it in t'first place. Ther's awl types o'seein' and ther's a world o' difference between a gud many o'em. This 'ere Moss fella, 'e saw into t'guts an' soul o' this 'ere place and we visitors, we just comes along easy street an' sees t'clothin' on't top o' it. When us wer lil' childer, we crept in an' saw t' wonderment in yon sweet cake, b't them as 'ad t'eatin of o'it, they saw nowt but a rowdy bit o'pastry, t'round off a fat day's dinin' – j'ist summat they 'ad 'afore and wud b'avin' agin. Tis awl abawt ways o' seein.

"Ah, tha's better now. A'likes things straight in mi'ead. Now, wheer's mi gals an' wheer's yon boy o' mine, fer 'e 'as a seein' eye a'layin' on 'im?"

28
MOONLIGHTING

The 'boy' with the seeing-eye has spotted Carl and Andy, only a few hundred yards ahead of them. He nudges Tee – "that looks like a very serious conversation going on up there. Do we gate-crash it, lighten the moment with kazoos and pigs' bladders on sticks, or exercise our discretion and hang back?"

Tee shakes her head, black hair flies. "I swear, Beaver of Mine Own Lodge, some days thou talkest in tongues. I would not have it any other way, because you wouldn't be the same Beaver if you didn't. But what are you braying about, to put it bluntly?"

"I said – Carl and Andy – serious chat – we interrupt? – be discreet? – options – discuss."

"Oh, need you ask, Beavie? You know me, discretion every time!"

Standing in the middle of the path, legs akimbo, she opened up her larynx and beneath the silent wings of the angelic horde, let fly with – "hold hard, guys! Major annoyance approaching from astern!" Then she thrust out her hand at me and bellowed – "come on Beaver, run!"

Thus we arrived, panting like breathless idiots.

"Ah-ha," Andy greeted us, "one unstoppable Force of Nature, one tow-along Beaver. When not present, you are sorely missed."

"See!" said the Princessa, "Told you!"

"Told me what?" I protested.

"That we should gate-crash their serious conversation, of course."

"You got the last bit right," said Carl. "This useless pudding wants to die."

Tee stared, dangerously.

"If you can duck, I'd do it now," I advised, mildly.

"No-one dies on my watch," she thundered, " and certainly not voluntarily. I may murder you, with hideous tortures I have yet to devise but voluntary exits are N-O-T O-N.

"Tell me why you wish to expire?"

"Did you see The Times, this morning?" Andy enquired.

"Certainly not," Tee replied haughtily. "What do you think I am? I have embarked on a programme of Anglo-Saxon Comprehension. This means that I look at pictures and headlines in The Sun, then the Beaver explains them to me. In this way I am developing a flawless understanding of mindless English stupidity. I am on the cusp of grasping precisely what propels this clapped-out apology for a country. Why on earth would you read The Times? Do you wish to be misled?"

"It's not all bad," said Carl. "It had a very nice picture of Daisy Edgar-Jones the other day."

"Prompt me, Beaver."

"The tiny tit action in 'Normal People.' Highly protectable, wounded spaniel, could be next gay icon…any memories coming back yet?"

"Possibly. Anyway, why do gays do that, Carl?" asked Tee.

"Do what?"

"Select girls to be gay icons?"

"It's complicated."

"Try me, later. Am currently resolving Boss Man's intellectual error and emotional crisis."

"In a nutshell," Carl explains, "The Times has picture of Iranian mum in Calais refugee hovel, with tiny, innocent, adorable daughter. Her husband has been rejected by her family, hence they are hoping for asylum in UK. Is threatening to kill herself if not accepted as asylum seeker. Implication, tot dies, too. Boss man much stricken with sadness. Feels if he was dead, there'd be space for them."

"Oh, I see," hammed Tee, "that's how it works! I bump you two off and I get to choose two replacement refugees of my choice? Good scheme!"

Andy grunted, through thinly-veiled rage. "With the greatest respect, Tee, you can't half play the tediously irritating idiot, at times."

"At times," she agreed, " I can, indeed. But this is not one of them. You are suffering from 'poor, poor, pitiful me' syndrome and totally understandably. If I could give my billion quid to have you back, upright and firing on all cylinders, I'd do it and the B. and I, thus for ever impoverished, would – 'live-in-a-paper-bag-in't-middl'-o-t'road,' we finished rowdily and admirably in synch.

"Thing is Andy, you're showing improvements already. You've almost got enough use in your right arm to engage in some physiotherapy. And there's nothing more agonisingly stressful than waiting to see if the rest of the old bod is going to follow along behind. I'm not surprised you're overwrought.

"Now, you and I know, that we're in the middle of some colossal mind-fuck. Something has us in a petri-dish of its own devising. Call it Earth II, a dream, a hypnotic trance, a parallel universe – I don't care. But it's pretty obvious that it's studying our reaction to stimulus. And the more toxic the stimulus, the more interesting is your reaction. In your current condition you're as much use as a hand-crocheted dachsund is for badger hunting but you still crave life. Whatever it is you contrive to wring from your awful predicament, whatever it is that drives you on, is what they are focused on.

This vast intelligence can't yet prise these pieces of grit, of determination, free from the individual that owns them. This is the area that still defeats them. They can't isolate this particular will o'the wisp. Why do you think they chose our crew? Because we're all dying different deaths, for different reasons and none of us want to! You show even a shred of giving-up, of shutting down, of handing over your reins, they're likely to turn their attention elsewhere.

"This intelligence is super-canny, it's way beyond our wildest dreams. What form it takes, what dynamic it expresses itself by…completely unknowable to us. What do we see when we try to look back up the microscope, to peer into its eye? Sweet F.A. But for some reason and my guess may be wrong, it's interested in us and that in itself is fascinating. I'm certain it doesn't need us, that it could turn its attention elsewhere in the blink of an eye. You, wishing to die, is not interesting.

"This 'Thing' said it would rebuild you, that it would give Punch, Marie-Claire and our very own Alice the means to be with us, to stay in our gang. Our gang, I repeat, half of whom are dying but are longing to live. Our gang, you recidivist! You, the boss, Carl, your adjutant. Punch and Marie-Claire, our god-parents. Beaver and Marie-Gabrielle, everyone's brother and sister. The joker in the deck – Moi! And last, but very far from least, Jo-Jo, our very own JJ, the hanged man who came from the Tarot of outer space.

"You do not get to renege on that! Kill yourself? I'll murder you first! We're a tribe, a unit. That's how we roll.

"Now," she skipped around on the path and presented her be-jeaned backside to his face, distorted as it was by tears and laughter. Dropping her pants and revealing, only briefly thank God, a very cheap pair of knickers, she wiggled her bare bum and danced off down the path, butt sashaying very acceptably, trilling – "follow the moony, you loony!"

"Wait for me, bare bum!" I yelled.

"Catch me if you can!" floated back, as she danced away, under the beneficent gaze of angels.

29
COMING DOWN TO EARTH

"I'm thinking about thoughts, Beavie."

This floats out from behind the half-closed door of the en-suite.

"While you're poo-ing?"

"Yep. It's a very good time to examine them. Have you noticed that they never stop, that they just rattle on endlessly? A totally unconscious stream."

"What might happen if they stopped, do you think?" I asked casually.

There was dead silence from the loo. Until, slowly and in a voice that made me sit up a little straighter, pay a little more attention, she said – "I think we'd stop."

I tried, I really tried, for a semi-intelligent reply.

"Isn't that the aim of meditation? To try and stop your thoughts?"

"That's certainly on the project agenda."

"So, when people get to that level… they kinda' stop?"

"Yes."

"In what way?"

"I think they fall free of the information highway, or at least stand to one side of it."

"I'm not up to speed, Tee. What do you mean by the information highway?"

"All the world's thoughts, all the non-material activity of the great mass of humanity. Imagine a huge co-axial cable, frayed out at one end, a strand goes to every living, thinking thing. As long as that thing lives, it thinks according to its abilities and that information, no matter what it is, flows along, or vibrates within the cable."

"Where does this cable go?"

"Somewhere."

"Does that mean that you don't know?"

"I certainly don't know but I think I do."

Tee was still using her serious voice, so I tried desperately to keep my end afloat.

"That sounds as if there's a third option, when there should only be two."

"Exactly, Beavie, exactly! Go on!"

Go on – ? I could barely recall what I'd just said, let alone 'go on.'

I tried for telepathy. After all, we were symbionts but all I got was static.

"I had something, Tee but it's done a runner. Give me a minute."

She granted my minute and I staggered into action.

"Your 'I don't know' and 'I think I know,' are two different places, two points, essentially two. My inferring from that that there must be three therefore, was just me riffing off your back – now, what the hell do I mean by it? I mean that whatever answer would satisfy you, is neither of the two that are currently in your in-tray – that is 'I don't know' and 'I think I know.' Somehow, from that I'm deducing that information is only ostensibly a closed system – it's actually a system that strives for the possibility of closure, whilst never actually wishing to attain it."

"Yes! Yes! Yes!"

Tee staggers from the loo, hauling up her jeans, this morning's very commonplace knickers, as exposed in her moony, all askew.

"Sweetheart, those knickers are awful!"

"I know, I know, I know! If you can nail this, I promise I'll present an 'Asian Babes Lingerie Special."

High stakes indeed are now upon the table.

"We are in an information swirl. Oh, I don't know, some sort of Mobius ribbon that feeds through an analyser, a converter…We're constantly being consumed and regurgitated. It's what JJ said, 'Implicate and Explicate,' the Bohm thing and these Daleks who run Earth II have interposed something between the two and that's where we are. We are feeding through, being fed through I mean, a closed, probably inferior system. That's why they're keeping some people going for thousands and thousands of years. They're like high-yield dairy cattle, you can't allow them to die and be recycled through the universal system. These characters are looking to operate their own system and we've opted to join it."

I sank back on the bed, exhausted.

"That's done for me. I'm destroyed. I have no idea what any of it means but in principle, I sense I'm right. Someone, something, is messing with the implicate/explicate interface. The natural order is being messed with – possibly on that universal political principle – 'we are the Party that can give you more' or, 'we know better.' That is super-dangerous territory, Tiggers and Beavers beware!"

I lay there blowing mental bubbles, my little brain circuits fused. 'And so what?' said my own internal voice, 'someone's always messing with something.' After another few minutes of frothing, impotently, I sat up with a jerk – "Oh God, they'll have heard everything and they'll kill us!"

Tee, wiggling into something interestingly evil-looking, in black and red, with lots of intriguing straps, paused – "don't be daft. In the first place 'who' is listening and in the second place, who gives a toss what we think? We're probably wrong. You're suffering from delusions of grandeur and I shall slowly and sexually erode those, in about 10 minutes time."

You may be asking if this titillating experience is about to occur on Earth II. Do

'THEY' provide wardrobes of bondage-style lingerie in Moss's old farmhouse, just in case visitors 'get-the-urge'? One, I don't think Shade would tolerate it and two, 'no, they don't.'

I'd been puffing and blowing by the time I'd caught up with Tee. And that was only when she'd stopped running, in order to pull up her pants. After which, in companionable silence, we'd ridden the elevator to the top of the cwm.

There, waiting to greet us was… "Whiskers! Excellent to see you. The blonde bimbo here and I have to return home for urgent business of a depraved nature, of which I am unwilling to share details. Would you, please, arrange our departure within the hour, preferably the half-hour, otherwise I shall start making an inordinate fuss. And please – and that's the last 'please' you get out of me, today – let's not discuss the matter further."

'Whiskers' had turned full-robotic. He had inclined his head, without allowing the least flicker of emotion to cross his face, turned and walked away.

Within 15 minutes a small craft had arrived, something akin to a two-man, side-by-side, enclosed jet-ski, if there is such a machine. We had climbed aboard, stated our destination and in total darkness, were transported home within the hour.

"That was awfully rude," I said as we scrambled out of the pod, just below the rows of winter peas, in Punch's garden.

"I thought so," said Tee, "dropping us off alongside the peas, is definitely a pun too far."

We were talking to ourselves. The pod had simply winked out of existence, vanished into thin air the second we left it.

"I meant…" I began.

"I know what you meant, dear heart but I think that little trip just proves that it was all smoke and mirrors."

"Really?" I said. "Take a look at this."

From my pocket I produced a metal dome nut, rippling with ever-changing iridescent, translucent colours. I'd found it trodden into the gravel, just beyond the elevator.

"Poo," said Tee and led the walk back to our caravan.

"When I was quite little," said Tee, "I had a revelation one day. It was quite an unusual discovery for a little girl. Dada-ji and Dadi-ji – that's grandad and nanny to you, had taken me for a day-out to the sea-side. The sun was shining, the sea would be warm, there were coconut sellers offering chilled milk and coconut ice, there were men with monkeys, there was a whole host of happy things. We would have deckchairs, an umbrella, a nice spot to sit – all these good things were on offer and would come to pass. I was so happy, I could have burst.

"Then I said to Dada-ji – 'Dada-ji, where is my bucket and spade?' I'd suddenly thought I had better build some castles quickly, in case any bandits came by. Dada-ji puts his hand to his mouth and says – 'oh, Lupa, sweetie, Dada has forgotten them! I'm so sorry…' – and I could see him preparing to weather the usual Princess Lupa meltdown. I was quite famous for them. A perfected art-form you could say. Anyway, I was just about to suck in my breath, close my eyes, clench my fists, maybe roll on the ground and batter it with my heels, a good full-blown tanty, when I had a thought.

"This thought arrived in block capital letters, the sort I was learning to read off the blackboard. And it said something which I didn't exactly read, I either inhaled it, or it did an Alice and climbed off the page, ran up my nose and into my brain."

I lay on my side, naked on the bed and listened to Tee's childhood confessional with something approaching mother-love. She never talked about her childhood, except to say that it had been enjoyable, that her nan and grandad had loved her and that she had loved them. But for some reason those early years were private property. So this confidence was a special privilege.

Tee, with no clothes on either, was sitting cross-legged, leaning against the padded headboard of the divan and I had my head resting between her tummy and her thigh. She was absent-mindedly grooming my hair, as if she was searching for nits and I was soaking up the attention and the story.

"What ran up my nose, in capital letters, was – 'WHEN YOU RANT AND RAVE YOU SEND EVERYTHING ELSE AWAY'. The implication was that the sea would vanish, along with the coconut-ice man, the monkey, the sand, our deckchairs and umbrella – everything, whoosh, GONE! So I made this great big snort, a sort of 'achoo!!' and said – 'don't worry, Dada-ji, we could always buy another one, or I can do without and use my hands.' As I said that, the sun came out, the sea started rolling again, the monkey chattered and my poor old grandad nearly fainted, before Dadi-ji made him walk nearly half-a-mile to buy another bucket and spade.

"I don't recall I ever had any more temper tantrums after that."

She cracked a few more non-existent nits, pulled my nose gently and said – "what about you, Beavie; did you have mean tantrums?"

I wriggled gently.

"Can't remember down here. Swop over and I'll have a think. I'll do your hair for a while. Once ensconced against the headboard and when Tee had manoeuvred into position, I tried to think. Blank evasion was what I encountered. Then, rolling into my mind came one of those recollections that you know you're going to have to tell, no side-stepping, no convenient shelving 'for another day.'

I think she must have felt my body tone change, because I could feel her muscles flex. She was becoming attentive, ready to rescue whatever wreck might ensue, pump some oil onto choppy waters…

"I can't pretend to be proud of any of this. I'm afraid to say that this is a confession and you're the priest. Saying that is meant to make it jokey and actually, it's not funny at all.

"I told you I was brought up as a boy, until these boobs started to run away with the story. When I was obliged to be a girl, I was very sulky about it. I really didn't understand.

"My gran was living with us by then. When I was a little boy I'd adored my gran. I spent lots of weekends at her house, which wasn't that far from ours. Every morning I woke up there, I crawled into her bed and we told make-believe stories. They were a sort of running saga, with characters who we had voices for. I really wish I could remember some of it. It got very complicated but we always knew where we were up to. I guess my surly teens just stopped all that.

"Anyway, despite being a girl I had absolutely refused to surrender my bow and arrows. It was a good bow. It wasn't just an ash pole and a bit of string. It was a proper lemonwood stave, with animal horn nocks at either end to take the bow string.

"To string the stave, you'd already fastened the end of the bowstring to one of the nocks with a special knot. The other end was a pre-formed loop that would slide up and down the wood. You put your left knee on the inside face of the stave, towards the secure knot end and with whichever hand you found easiest, you pulled the top end of the stave towards you, while your right foot held the bottom of the bow against your pull. Push with your knee, pull with your hand, trap with your foot, that's how you formed the curve.

"The fiddly bit was sliding the loop up the stave and over the notch in the nock. When you'd finally got it there, you eased the pressure and voila, one strung bow. You were ready to fire arrows at the enemy.

"I was so self-important about all this. I wanted everyone to believe that I was deft and knowledgeable. Vigorous…manly … hah! I was awfully proud that my bow had horn nocks, real horn, not plastic and certainly not slots cut in the wood. I've always been a detail snob."

I fell silent, reflecting for a moment and remembering details through my fingers, even as I sorted Tee's hair with them.

"Did you have a bow and arrow?"

"Nope. The old palace was full of swords and spears and daggers. For some reason or other, I was allowed to charge around with them, spearing sofas and the like. Well, only one particular sofa, actually. But it was enormous fun and very dangerous. Those things were for real and they were sharp!

"But go on with your story – I told you mine."

"I used to shoot my bow in the back garden. The garden was so small the arrows went all the way. I had a target but no stand, so I used to prop it against the back wall of the house. Stupid idea but no one said not to.

"My sweet old gran was washing up the tea-time pots at the kitchen sink, which was right under a window. We waved to one another. Then I let fly an arrow and it went straight through the kitchen window, right in the corner of the lower left hand pane.

Had it gone all the way through, rather than jamming, it would have missed her but not by a lot.

"Anyway, I was terrified. I'd broken a window! Expensive repairs, caused by me. All hell was going to break loose! I ran up the garden. Gran shouted – 'don't worry, I'm all right.' I replied – 'I'm not worried about you, it's the window I'm bothered about!' And it was.

"I can't remember a thing after that. But when I was miles older, long, long after gran had died, I remembered it all one day. It came back in a horrible rush. I nearly died of shame, on the spot. I can never take it back. I said it and I meant it. To me, it shines this pure, cold light on my character. Every time I recall it, a bit more of me cringes and dies. I'll never be free of it.

"Isn't that funny – you opened up your world, I shut mine down?"

"What a terrible person you are, Evie. I really shouldn't associate with you," said Tee in a languid voice.

For the split second that I thought she meant it, I was about to die of terror and in agony.

"I like you as a boy," she murmured, "however awful boys like you are and I like you as a girl, too," she whispered "and we both know how awful girls can be."

"My trouble, Teazle, is that I don't know what boys, or girls, are like. I'd like to but I don't."

I don't know how long we remained locked together in this confessional embrace but it was interrupted by a soft knock at the door.

Tee grimaced at me and we slid apart – "if that's anyone other than Alice, pee off, even though we really love you. If it is Alice, come in."

It was Alice and she came in like a wraith, around the door.

"Hi," she whispered, "please may I come under your duvet?"

I was ready to die but Tee was totally relaxed. I could feel that from the beautiful anatomy that lay against mine.

"Snuggle in," said Tee, "it's nice and warm."

Alice kicked off her shoes and clambered up, snaking under the duvet still in her jeans and jumper. "Hi," she said to us both.

"Hi, Marie," I croaked – managing, "are you OK?" a little more fluently. I'd made an arm for her to tuck under, so it seems my body was up to speed with what was necessary but as usual, my mind was bringing up the rear.

"No, she's not," said Tee.

"I feel papery and thin," said Marie-Gabrielle. "I'm turning back into a story and I don't want to, especially that sort of story."

"You're OK," said Tee. "You're just a bit panicky. It's the first time you've been alone."

"I know. I'm terrified. I want Marie-Claire to be happy with Punch but who will love me?"

"We will," I said stoutly. "We do loving packages, don't we, Tee? Do you want our top range – that's the exclusive designer one, or the discount basement offer?"

"Is the designer package very expensive?" she whispered.

"Nope!" said Tee, "it's free, providing we can come on your next adventure."

"Oh, you don't want to come," she exclaimed. "I never seem to end up in nice places." "You will when there's three of us," said Tee. "We'll turn things inside out, like pairs of socks!"

"Are you sure?" asked Marie.

"Absolutely," I said confidently, though the two of them seemed to know something I didn't. "Now, if you shed your clothes, we'll be able to restore you to warm flesh and blood in no time at all."

"Is that all right? You don't mind me interrupting?"

"Do we look like we mind?" growled Tee, as she folded us, one under each paw, like a tigress with cubs.

Alice was icy. She must have been standing outside in the night air, scared to interrupt our rituals. Body warmth came back slowly but once it had, it radiated. "Wow," marvelled Tee, "We've turned her into a sauna!"

"Shush, she's fast asleep."

"I know. She won't mind us talking."

"She's a really sweet, gentle little thing, isn't she?" I mumbled. "I feel such a clodhopper in comparison."

"Are you?" asked Tee, in surprise. "I thought I was the turner-over of clods."

"Makes us sound like an extension of the Planets Suite, doesn't it?" I said. "Mars, bringer of war; Venus, peace; Mercury the Messenger; Tee, the turner-over of clods. What are the rest, I always forget them? I know Saturn is old age; Jupiter is jollity – though that's never sounded right to me. Uranus, of all the dumb names to give a planet, what was he? Don't answer that. One more…help me here…"

"Pluto?" Tee suggested.

"No, there's another one."

"I know," she said, "the fishy fellow…trident…crown."

"Brilliant! Neptune, he was the mystic, which sounds a bit of a contrived effort. Should we add Pluto, the popper of zits?"

"Bit more realistic," cackled Tee. " So, which am I?"

"Mercury, maybe," I said eventually but half-heartedly. "They're hopeless tags, aren't they really? Was life simpler back then? Had people not begun being multi-faceted, or something? You should be 'The Kaleidoscope,' or 'the laser show.' I'm sticking to being 'the Androgyne', that's complex enough, or so it seems so far. Bah! I can't be bothered, smug small town labels. We're better than labels. Everyone's better than a label.

"You're not 'The Kaleidoscope', you're Tee. Everyone knows what 'Tee' means, everyone who matters. You can't be summed up with the equivalent of a pub sign.

"The whole crew knows 'The Tee,' if you went round as Mercury, they'd be floundering for a toehold. You only have to say 'worrah!' and everybody knows."

"Worrah!" Tee whispered to Alice, who moved peacefully between us.

"See, Alice knows, even when she's asleep."

"Maybe she does," said Tee thoughtfully, "but you never recognise yourself, do you?"

"Never," I agreed, "I think that was part of what I was trying to say – and failing."

"Sometimes," Tee pondered, "I wonder if we actually exist, other than as collections of different sorts of cells, vaguely co-operating to hunt down the secret of eternal life. The way we do that best, is to allow ourselves to be fooled by the intelligence lurking behind self-preservation, into believing that we really have a self, an 'I,' a pilot at the wheel. That notion stops the cells squabbling about who is really top dog. 'I,' is top dog. All the cells can agree on that. That leaves one question – 'Who the hell is I?'"

"Why are we hunting eternal life anyway?" I asked.

"In a nutshell: because we're terrified of eternal death. Consciousness, ordinary consciousness, cannot abide the possibility, the inevitability, of unconsciousness.

"It's like our lovely sleepyhead here said, a while or so ago. Life is a parasite and it's going in the opposite direction to the entity that it is parasitic upon. The cosmos is, ultimately, winding down. 'Life,' is never going to bet on that pony. 'Upward and onward,' says life.

"Why?" I ask, playing Tee's straight-man.

"Because it can't do anything else. That's the way that it's been constructed, written, coded. The very essence of its being is to persist."

"So what is death?"

"Death is a pain in the butt – at least, that's what 'I's' think. But sneakily, death is Life's trump card, its winning play. 'Lives-enduring' couldn't win in the long run. Death allows new Life room to breathe. Reproduction in multiple, way beyond necessity, is Life's gameplay. Every tsunami of birth has to unleash an avalanche of death. But because births aren't regulated and arrive in all sorts of shapes and sizes, for every billion losers, a handful will get through and be winners.

"At some level, Life and Death know this all too well, that they need each other, like an atomic nucleus needs an electron or two to zoom around it. They are utterly compatible but when Life starts to build complex structures, especially those that develop aspects of consciousness, that's when the going gets sticky.

"Consciousness has done Life a lot of favours, it's helped to stabilise it, to allow it to draw breath and give it a chance to creep up on entropy. But in its ego form, consciousness is prickly to handle. It has to be soothed, preened. Life keeps us pliant, acquiescent, by pretending that we are its ultimate aim, 'I'm doing it all for you!' So it pretends that one day, Tulipa, Evie and Alice will develop enough skills to live forever. If that ever happened, it would be an unmitigated disaster, because the Universe has to self-annihilate, be subducted back into the mother world of the Implicate. In that way, all the changes implicit in re-birth are assured – 'Life' can't just be 'carrying-on-as-you-were-before."

"You've been reading up," I accused Tee. "Anyway, weren't we promised eternal life by Earth II's Rabbit King?"

"I don't think we were there long enough before I threw my tanty. Anyway, did you get to see the small print?"

"I never even saw the big print," I admitted, " but I don't feel very eternalised."

"I'm not sure I want to be. I get pretty bored and irritated by myself as it is."

"Me too. But I don't want to die and lose you. I'm so scared of that."

"And you think I'm not?"

"I don't know. Bold, brave Tiggers aren't scared of anything, are they?"

"Only of the truth leaking out that they're not bold brave Tiggers."

"So what does that make them?"

"Scared Tulipas from Amsterdam?"

That made for a long and mutually-agreed silence.

"What could we do that would be really scandalous but wouldn't hurt any of our friends?" I asked eventually.

"Where did that fly-in from?"

"Oh, it's a bastard child of the desire to say 'ME' in capital letters and a cringing lack of self-belief in anything I embark on."

"Something bad, or something good?" Tee asked.

"I'm pretending I'd like bad but I'd much prefer good. I just want to scandalise Clan Grundy and say I don't care."

"I'd have thought your life to date had belted that particular nail particularly hard."

"It has but I'm too ashamed of it."

"Then I'll have to give it some thought."

"Is that the best you can do?"

"Afraid so. It's late. Night-night."

"Night-night, try not to wake the baby!"

30

SAINT CHIPOLATA

At breakfast, the next morning, Alice did something remarkable. She ate 10 slices of toast and butter. Ten!

"Another one," coaxed Tee, "the day stretches ahead."

"You'll need all your strength," I said encouragingly.

"Are we doing something special?" she asked excitedly.

"No," groaned Tee, "absolutely nothing beckons. I'm clean out of ideas. Beavie's brain is redundant and yours has just been wiped out by toast. Do have another slice. It can't do any harm, now."

"Why don't we explore?" volunteered Alice, brightly.

"What, as in Darkest Africa?" I enquired warily.

"No, not exactly. As in uncharted bits of the roundabout. We could make a map."

"It could be dangerous," I said. "This roundabout and I have history."

"What sort of history?" asked Alice.

"The sort I don't care to revisit."

"But you met me!" said Tee indignantly.

"That was a year later and cannot be laid at the door of the roundabout. Only by the longest stretch."

"There's a very deep hole," said Alice, "with rungs you can climb down."

"Really?" said Tee, in her 'take-me-there-now' voice.

"Really," said Alice, " I went down 20 rungs once. Then I got scared and came up."

"No," I moaned, "I'm scared already. Beavers don't do heights. They are valley creatures and lovers of flat pools of water. They like certainty, not rusty rungs."

"These rungs are quite new and shiny."

"That's even more worrying!"

"Why?" demanded Tee.

"Ancient, rusty rungs equals disused access shaft. Bright and shiny rungs suggest recent climbers whose agenda involves bottom of said hole and a 'not-pleased-to-meet-you' attitude, quite possibly. At least, that's what they suggest to nervous Beavers."

"Oh well then, maybe one more slice won't hurt."

"OMG!" squeaked Tee, "if we let her destroy herself with toast, what's Marie-Claire going to say?"

"Something pained in pidgin-English," I said. "If you eat any more toast, you'll swell up like Pooh in Rabbit's hole. We'll go down that hole and due to decompression, or the bends, or whatever happens 20 rungs down, you'll swell up with yeast, get stuck and the monster will come and eat your legs and bum."

"Ugh," said Tee, "you reckon that's inevitable?"

"Totally," I said. "Look, if we're after a Grail-like quest, why don't we try taking the 27A bus to its last stop?"

"My God, Beaver, you certainly were born to conquer," Tee said, shaking her head sorrowfully.

"That was unnecessarily hurtful. I've just explained, Beavers are peaceful creatures of slow, aquatic habit. The top deck of the 27A is as exciting as I want things to get, these days. As it happens, I normally sit downstairs. Upstairs would be stretching my envelope."

That's why I've been elected to stay at the top of the hole, in charge of a long rope, while Tee and Alice venture down the very shiny-looking rungs, clipped to the very same rope with carabiners. Apparently Alice was a girl-guide in one of her books. I am 'paying-the-rope-out' as it's called. Its nether end is anchored to a sturdy-looking piece of concrete that would probably counterweight Alice, her toast, Tee and a whole colony of more adventurous beavers, should any care to apply. I suspect that the very idea would see them all barricaded in their lodges.

To entertain myself, while manning my 'belaying point' – whatever that may be – I have been contemplating what they might find at the bottom. Water seems the most likely. A shopping trolley is a racing certainty. Little dead cats and dogs…a suitcase with human body parts…?

I felt dejected. No good could come of this. I had not realised that Alice's persona incorporated that of an Isabella Bird. After all, I was the one with the dick (and the balls of a mouse) or, to be anatomically precise, no balls at all. I was definitely feeling cowarded, despite having made my position, vis-a-vis adventure, clear to all.

"Anything?" I shouted.

"No," cried Tee.

"You coming up?" I asked hopefully.

"We've only just started going down! You can still see the top of my head."

It was a fact, I could.

"Remind me why we're doing this?" I asked the hole.

"We're having an adventure!" Alice's voice floated up.

"I'm not," I confided quietly to the rosebay willowherb, ironically my 'weedy' confidante. 'Ha, ha… geddit?'

I paid out the rope, via the belaying point as instructed, made certain no stones hurled themselves down the hole and kept a lookout for strangers, policemen and bats. Alice had admitted she was scared of bats. A surprise that, for I was fast coming to the conclusion that Alice wasn't scared of much. It was probably because she'd been exposed to ingenious engines of torture, for most of her post-pubescent life and survived them all.

Idly, I watched the cab roofs of the juggernauts, as they circled and skirted No-Name Roundabout. They looked like predatory blocks of watercolour paint, moving in for a makeover of our greys and greens. I hadn't fully realised that No-Name was raised up quite so high, perched as we were, on the demolition and excavation waste from other projects, great undertakings that had once been deemed worthy, in the past.

Given that I could only see slices of each lorry-load, I began another game – 'Guess my Purpose?' There go newsprint rolls, coils of aluminium, on their way to be roller-formed into useful profiles, Portakabins, tractors, containers, a pleasure boat, a backwards facing lorry and lots of things wrapped, Christo-like, in tarpaulin. This is not proving much of a game, really.

A convoy of ancient double-decker buses stutter sedately by – en route where? Had to be a vintage transport fair, somewhere, because a traction engine has just gone round on a low-loader, together with a static engine sprouting an oversize funnel. Now I'm interested, I've got a boy-bit that loves traction engines and there goes another one! I wonder if Tee would take me, if I can find out where it is? There's a Foden lorry and a tiny flotilla of old grocery vans, then something extremely weird and wonderful, roped down under canvas and with a profile like a part-opened multi-tool.

Ooops! something large and aggressive met a low-flying pigeon. Absolutely no contest. Scoreline – Pigeon 0, Lorry 1. Feathers start to flutter by. Out of boredom, I snatch at two or three and redirect them down the hole.

A minute later a startled – "Jabberwocky!" – floats up, considerably faster than the feathers went down. 'Agh,' I thought, 'this calls for discretion … not my fault a dozy pigeon gets murdered and some feathers flutter down the hole … sort of …' Deniability is everything. 'Oh Lord, though, what if the love of my shabby life had fallen off, surprised by a ghostly tickles to the nape of her neck? Beaver, get a grip! This is a serious job. You'd never have made a Girl Guide, you buffoon.'

"Everything OK?" I yell, giving a gentle tug to the rope, as arranged.

"Fine… feather… floating… surprised… don't worry!"

"OK!" Phew, saved again. 'Come on Time, pass. Tell me a story, or something. You must have the world's greatest story books, filed in your archives!'

Oh, the loneliness of the lookout…and the lookout has just spotted what, precisely? In among the roots and dying stems of the willowherb, lies something large, black, round and iron-y looking. I'm pretty certain that it is a grille.

Two yanks is STOP. I give two yanks.

"What?" floats up.

"Just wait," I shout down. "Wait…a…minute."

I tie the rope off, as instructed and wade into the rosebay, kicking, pushing, flattening. 'Oh yes, it is.' It's a great round iron grille. Very obviously the stopper of this bottle. Which makes perfect sense, because who would be insane enough to leave a hole of this dimension and depth, gaping and open? This sort of hole is an 'owned,' hole, an 'administered' hole, a hole with a pedigree.

There's a nameplate, or some such, welded to its face. I scrape away snails, bird poo and vegetable life and can read – 'Keep Out. Danger. Museum of London. Romano-British Dept. Emergency telephone' etc.

Beavers are not necessarily dull of brain just because they prefer the peaceful plateaus of life. I get it right away. Down that hole, buried under a century's civil engineering waste and two millennia of worm casts and natural compost, is an archaeological site, no doubt of special interest. But not that interesting because, although fireweed is no slouch at growing, it still doesn't come up four feet overnight.

Back at the hole I yell down – "you're in a dig!"

"Pig?"

"DIG!"

"Big?"

Lungs and invention fail me.

"Come up."

"No, you come down."

"No, I'm scared."

"Don't be a baby."

I give up.

"Forget it. Take your time. It'll keep."

I can feel the shrug through the rope.

"OK," floats back, distantly.

I sit down to review my situation. I'm far too scared to go down. Without doubt there'll be a monster, even if it's only a spider. I'm a coward who doesn't like adventures because I've had too many. But who can take the middle road through life with Tee? And who wants to lose a Tee, when they've just found one? What a bind. 'Don't go without me Tee – I'll wait for you.'

Oh dear, I've embarked on the road to instant melancholy. I must think of something that Beavers can do and that Tiggers are scared of, then do lots of it. Probably eating custard is top of the list. Beavers are excellent custard consumers and the thicker it is, the better. Tiggers don't precisely run away from it but they do get very supercilious and ask for cream instead.

I sit on a piece of concrete that has surrendered its identity and watch a cabbage white butterfly take charge of its day. A clumsy pass at a mare's nest of bindweed, a pointless touchdown on the couch grass, then with rapid, climbing wing beats, up into a wildwood of broken and stunted hawthorn.

If I half-close my eyes and relax the focus, images simply pour out of that hawthorn break. There's a dog-like creature in a black cloak, with half a head and beside him a gurning buffoon, whose nose has bulged up so far, it's forced his eyes onto the plane of his corrugated forehead. There are lots of mouths, pursed lips, blubbery lips, crooked smiles and awkward grimaces. I can see a very long creature, whose body is the length of a fence rail. At this end his head is a coronet of leaves, with a wicked, fearsome eye. But there's a competing head at the other end, impish and wrinkled.

I abandon the hawthorn creatures to listen to the snarl and changing notes of the traffic. What would you think that noise was, if you had no reference points at all, other than the natural world? Animals, a crowd of savages, a river flooded with boulders and trees, an avalanche? You'd have to peep, however scared you were and what would you make of it? Best guess would be that they were animals of some sort. But don't animals come in herds that all look the same, like wildebeest, or bison? These creatures are all different.

No reference points…that's a big thing, isn't it? When you're devoid of prior knowledge, explanatory words, comparatives, received wisdom, when you're thrown back on your own resources, entirely…you're really stuck…

Lost in conjecture, I suddenly noticed that the rope had gone slack. They'd untied themselves and gone exploring. Fair enough, I was exploring boredom and so far, it was precisely that – boring.

How did mystics deal with it? They must have such iron self-control, not to be endlessly goaded by their inner idiot squealing – 'I'm bored! Bored! BORED!' Drive him out with a mantra, drive him down, until he's smaller than an electron. But he'd still be there, wouldn't he? I know he would, because that little voice never leaves, he just learns how to hide in the compost of your new-won sensibility. To be honest, I prefer him in his everyday garments, not his guru weeds, pretending to be something he can never be. "Hello, I'm Nirvana. I used to be a gossip but all that's behind me now. Let me tell you how I won my inner peace…"

I liked the poet fools of ancient China, when I read about them. Han-Shan, his buddies Shi-de and Feng-Gan, scrawling their graffiti on the rocks of Cold Mountain. But my question is, what would have become of them if someone hadn't recorded their few cracked lines and antics, immortalised them on scrolls, in books, awarded them posthumous accolades? What if they'd died under their rocks, unknown, un-mourned, unrecorded, their bones hauled away and scattered by hungry beasts? They would say that that was what they had wanted. But they wouldn't have had an audience to say that to.

When I was in India, I read lots of books about the solitary Tibetan mystics, who had rejected even the society of the lamasery. Some faithful acolyte would wall them up in a cubbyhole of a cave, remove a rock once a day, to pass in a portion of food and remove the holy piss and poo. For years and years this fragile symbiosis would drag on.

If the acolyte could write, or spin a yarn…if he had the ear of a neighbourhood monastery, his solitary master might achieve acclaim. His every utterance recorded, miraculous events attributed, pilgrims rewarded with portions of dried poo, to grate over their dinner, like Perigord truffle. That was one way they MIGHT acquire fame but only if their acolyte's P.R. skills were up to scratch – "The famous solitary hermit…" The contradiction is obvious, isn't it?

I used to wonder if there were little knots of bone, sand-covered remnants, tucked under sheltering rocks on the high plateau, the remains of solitaries who truly had lived alone. Forgotten, unrecorded stoics. The thought chilled me then and chills me now. Had they died cursing the world they had denied, or were they ecstatic, aligned with whatever illusion they cherished, as they lay gasping for water and died, eyes glazing 'beneath the vast indifference of heaven,' as Warren Zevon wrote?

I could do the same here, become the Hermit of No-Name Roundabout.

For a second or two, the idea was amusing, then it began to make me thoughtful and sad. I tried to draw it out so that I could examine it properly, as a narrative in progress. Eva, ending her days here. No Lupa, no Alice, no Andy, no Punch. Just the circling traffic, the waving buddleias, the willowherb, the cabbage whites, the mysterious hole in the ground, which wasn't actually that mysterious any more – though, God knows, they were taking their time over it.

I doubted that I could sit it out even for 24 hours. Anyway, which dumb acolyte would be willing to bring me a sausage sandwich a day and haul away whatever is left of sausage sandwiches, after the sacred digestive system has had its evil way with them?

The Unity, the 'One,' must be available here just as much as it is in the Taklamaklan desert. But no-one would give a toss, would they? "Nutter walls himself up on an abandoned roundabout and dies of slow sausage poisoning." St. Sausage, St. Chipolata – doesn't really cut it, does it? And yet I'm not really joking, I mean it. 'Truth' must be as available here as anywhere, hidden deep inside oneself and why shouldn't this rubble-strewn wasteland be as good a place as any to excavate it?

I have a fierce love for this little wasteland. I told Andy that once and was happy, when I saw that he was pleased to hear me say so. "Yeah, I like it, too. If I ever get out of this pram, you and I'll go and explore it, inch-by-inch, like Burton, in Araby, or wherever he was."

"I'd really like that," I'd replied. "When I think about it, so much of my life was decided here – even if it happened elsewhere. I want it to stay like this, it's magic."

31

WHEN IN ROME

I do know, however, that that was a Tee bellow from the bottom of the mine. "Oi! Where are you, Beaver Bright?"

I crawled back to the hole and could see their torches shining up.

"I'm coming up," yells Alice, "to lower you down. There are things you have to see for yourself." As I can hear her, loud and clear, it's obvious that she is, indeed, coming up.

"Now," says Alice, in a very no-nonsense voice, as she appears at the rim. "Tiggs says that you're to be a b-b-brave Beaver and that there'll be a reward."

It's obvious that they're determined. I could run but disobligingly, my legs have turned to jelly. My legs are in the pay of the enemy. Utter treachery – don't they know who feeds them?

I'll spare you the procrastination.

I went down very slowly. First, I recognised the Cretaceous. Six rungs later I probably hit the Jurassic. The Carboniferous was a blur and I missed the Cambrian completely, because I had my eyes shut. But then a creature sprang out of the Devonian, grabbed my bum and in familiar tones said – "open your eyes, you idiot. You're down. It's ME!"

"Who's ME?" I demanded, craftily. (The Devonian/Silurian is a disputed boundary and you can't be too careful.)

"Tiggs," said Tiggs.

"Where's Alice?"

"Standing on your head if you don't shift out of the way quickly!"

"Hang on, Alice. She won't open her eyes yet."

There was solid ground under my feet, so I could be 'down,' it's true.

"Where's my reward?" That was my masterstroke, because if 'Tiggs' turned out to be a monster, imitating Tiggs, it wouldn't know about the reward.

"Open," said the Tiggs/Monster.

"Yum. A large peppermint."

I opened my eyes. Two lemurs were staring back at me.

"Oh," I said, "I think I may have recovered myself. So, can I have another mint for later, please? P-L-E-A-S-E?! I was very, very brave. I made no fuss at all and I am not at my best, with heights or depths."

"Evie!" protested Tiggs, "If you look up, you can see the top. A kangaroo could probably hop out of here."

"Are there kangaroos down here?" I asked, as I thought cleverly, but I'd fallen into a trap.

"No," said Tiggs triumphantly, "which goes to prove my point. So stop being a baby."

"I like being a baby!" I said defiantly. "It's time for my nappy change, too."

"Is she always like this?" asked Alice.

"Holes, high places, spiders, snakes, sudden shocks, they all bring it on," Tee admitted.

"You're scared of cow wee and ducks," I countered.

"I'm not 'scared of them," said Tee, with careful emphasis. "I simply don't like them."

"What's the deal with the cow wee?" asked Alice, intrigued.

"She thinks they do too much."

"I got milked like a cow in one of my books," said Alice proudly.

"Did you have to wee?" asked Tiggs.

"No-oo, they missed a trick there."

"Did you have to have a calf first?" I enquired.

"That was how the whole affair with the bull started. The bull Pa shot. When he started that yarn, I thought he was going to go back to the embarrassing bit. Then I realised he didn't know it."

"Wow," Tee exclaimed, "that must have been an event!"

"I was mortified when I realised it was unravelling from the page and that I couldn't stop it. But it was an unmitigated disaster, total farce. The whole set-up collapsed. The bull and I escaped to the marsh – but with quite different ambitions."

"So you never…er…?" I said.

"No," said Alice, "and I've always been intrigued by the Greek myths. But I can't see how it could possibly work."

"Mm," Tee pondered. "I'm more a Xenia – Warrior Princess fan, myself. Funny, there's acres of porn about that. Some of it's even a bit of a turn-on."

"I haven't got any fantasies left," I said gloomily. "Either somebody gets hurt, or the whole shebang is too stupid and ugly to contemplate. On that wretched boat, the boys were always trotting into the galley, when I was up to my elbows in onion skins and saying – 'Evie, look, this chick really enjoys this…couldn't we…?' And I always had to trot out my speech – 'she's grinning like an idiot, because she's being paid quite well to do so. Do you think any girl would enjoy that? Why would they?' And off they'd go, totally downcast."

"I know just what you mean," said Alice. "The books I've been in! I should have emerged like minced beef at the end, instead of which I'm grinning like the cat that got the cream."

"All over your face, no doubt," drawled Tee.

"Exactly so!"

"I appear to be back," I announced suddenly. "Capsule Evie has returned to earth. Porn and peppermints, guarantors of reality a la 21st century, or wherever we are these days. So, in the words of the Prophet, – 'where do we find ourselves?'"

Alice smiled. "Rome," she said.

"Wow," I said. "It's changed."

"Oh dear," said Tee patiently, "not yet. You have to crawl into our new home. But apart from that, it could grace the pages of 'Hello' magazine."

I was supposed to be brave now, so I crawled. It helped that I could see Tiggs stand up, just a couple of yards ahead.

I rose up but by muted torchlight, nothing seemed that wonderful. Bits of colour, bits of wall, a basin or two, maybe. Then Alice flicked a switch on the wall and an array of photo-floods burst into light. By the time I'd blinked my way back to normality, I was indeed, in Rome.

"Oh my goodness," I gaped. "How real is all this?"

"Very real," said Tee, "this is just the first of a series of huge villas. Hidden away though and I'm guessing it's from an earlier settlement, is an actual Mithraic temple. In technical terms, that's rarer than rocking horse poo – at least, one in this condition is."

"We're talking bulls again, aren't we?" asked Alice.

"We certainly are," Tee agreed. "I bet Punch would get automatic honorary membership. But I don't think women were allowed in."

"Really?" wailed Alice. "I've designed a really sophisticated, leather-covered, steel frame for the main event. And, if I'm honest, I'm quite keen to try it out." She paused for a moment, then said glumly – "I'm mad, aren't I? I've been in too many lewd books and drawings. I've been infected."

"Alice," I giggled, "we saved you from all that!"

"I know and thank you all very much. The creatures I was involved with were ugly and idiotic – and I'm not slandering the bull. I'd just been wondering if there was such a thing as consensual bestiality, one to do with female power, not female subjugation. Or am I afflicted and need emergency psychiatric help?"

"Shouldn't worry about it," said Tee. "It's been an unsettling time. Stress always squeezes up fantasies, like spots. Come and see things that are already amazing!"

They truly were.

Whole rooms had been preserved – with actual ceilings, surely that's unheard of? Mosaics of the finest quality, Leda and the Swan, Zeus as a Cloud, Narcissus gazing into what would have been an actual pool, once. There was a plunge bath, tiled with dolphins, whales, strange-looking fish, crabs, lobsters, anemones and star fish. There was also a very robust-looking sturgeon, which gave me the odd feeling that I was peering into an era of quite different sensibilities. I would not have wanted all these whelks, oysters and lobsters crawling round my jacuzzi.

"Tiggs, do you think it would be nice if we had a hot tub, or a whirlpool?"

"No. It would get frogs."

"Oh."

"Pay attention, Beaver. There might be a little quiz at the end."

"I do hope not. That'd be really humiliating. The more I circulate among extraordinary objects, the duller I feel myself becoming. It's an inverse relationships. If I went round the Hermitage, I'd have to be wheeled out in a basket."

"Stop babbling! You're starting to leak!"

"Oh, sorry."

Room after room of it. In fact, as my reprimanded brain reset itself and I realised that I actually was seeing villa after villa, I began to excavate my own ancient memories. All this reminded me of something I'd seen before… What had it been, what was it…?

"Perugia!" I finally bleated.

"It was in Perugia…" I added.

"What was, Beaver?" coaxed Tee.

"This was," I said. "But this is a hundred times better. A buried city, under another city. In Perugia, they cut the top off the medieval city and used it as foundations for a new Renaissance style plaza and palace. Not as building-rubble foundations but using the buildings as foundations. The old-style fortified torres, towers, got sliced off at the knees and Joe's pizza shop – joke!- had its roof taken off and so on, until they'd levelled out the old city on the hill to be the underpinning for the new build. It's quite a phenomenal piece of visionary vandalism."

"I've never heard of it," said Alice.

"Nor me," said Tee.

"It got some lurid headlines, ages back. A rather nasty murder, involving students. Arguably a botched police job and a wayward sort of trial. Pretty student acquitted. Cynics would say 'another Italian job.' Whatever, far from appetising events. Somebody with their life ahead of them actually died, which seems to have been forgotten. Why are murder victims always forgotten and murderers remembered? It's the same everywhere – unless you're famous to begin with, then everyone remembers the assassinated and not the assassin…"

"Beaver," warned Tee, "you're starting to ramble…"

"Yes I am but it wouldn't be me if I didn't, would it?

"Anyway, my point was, someone took a scythe to medieval Perugia and cut it off at Renaissance level.

It's such a surprise to the coaches-full of trusty tourists – mum and me – because the guides file you in at the old, low-level. Then you take escalators up to the modern streets. If you haven't read up about it you're gobsmacked, because you drift through this dusty, abandoned ruin of a town, everything chopped off, or simply fallen down. It looks like a plague swept through the place, all the people blown away, as if they'd been no more than printed bits of paper…

"Oh, Marie! I'm sorry! You're the latest victim of the Beaver empathy-pun – let me explain." And I rambled through my five-minute explanation of the incredible empathy that leads me to pun on people's particularities – such as Alice's tendency to end up on the printed page.

"I hadn't actually noticed," she said, when I finished, which was a bit flattening. Then she and Tee wandered off, as I tried to resume my tale about Perugia and the chocolate factory and the awful fact that I'd missed the tour because I kept going up and down the escalators, fascinated by the ruined city. When I finally realised I was only talking to Roman remains, I sniffed, to salvage some dignity and determined I would keep my best story – about the road to Gubbio – for another day. Then I scampered after them, whinnying – "wait for me!"

They were only two villas ahead, which was obviously where the excavation ran out, because there was nothing more than a wall of compacted outer-London crap, on top of clay and a set of stairs, going down. I pointed, mutely and Tee said – "a steel door, with an extremely serious-looking lock on it. Maybe it's still being excavated, perhaps down in the Neolithic regions."

"Actually," said a quiet voice behind us, "it leads to a Secure Regional Seat of Government."

Terror and confusion fell upon us, though to be fair, we all reacted differently.

"Oh," said Tee, "you can explain what one of those is, while I de-fibrillate my former companions. If you've terminally injured my Beaver you're in dire trouble."

"And what about me?" demanded Alice indignantly.

"One terrible revenge at a time," said Tee placidly.

"Sorry," apologised JJ, emerging from the gloom of a Roman-something and vaulting a low wall to join us by the stairs. "I just couldn't resist."

"Phew," said Alice, clutching her bosom, "just like I can't resist this!" With which she started pummelling JJ's torso with considerable gusto.

"You might as well take it out on a post box, Ally," I gasped, as I hauled in oxygen by the cubic litre. "He's made in the same factory and on the same principles, as Pa's bull – solidly."

"I know," she said, panting, "but I find it's very satisfying. Anyone else want a go? There are lots of bits left."

"Leave me a square foot, or so," said Tee, "but do tell – what is a Secure Seat of Regional Government, before you die?"

JJ gently folded one hand around both of Alice's wrists and pulled her into an embrace which she quite willingly accommodated herself to.

I glanced at Tee in indignation.

"Wake up, Beaver! It's been obvious for ages!" she replied.

"Nobody told me and I'm supposed to be her brother! You might have asked, JJ, family jewels and all that."

"I like bull-like creatures," giggled Alice, "I've been telling you. As for you bro, I've seriously embraced female liberation, so you can stand-down."

JJ went the colour of the baked terracotta tiles.

"Thing is," said Tee "if it's all top-secret Government rubbish, why aren't we surrounded by men in black jump suits, shouting – 'Get down on the mosaics, NOW!"

"Because someone, or something, has very cleverly convinced all the sensors that no-one is here," said JJ.

"Now, who would do that?" I asked, in an 'I-know' voice.

"Tell us, then. Who?" demanded Tee.

"Whiskers! We've found his Rabbit-hole. He's been here for absolutely ages!"

"You're spot-on," agreed JJ. "My old pal, the Rabbit, has been living the life of a Patrician bunny, AD 34-ish for some time now. Did none of you notice the hinges on the grill?"

"I did! These two didn't even notice the grille. They're three inch steel and something has lasered through them, hot-knife-through-butter style."

"Quite so," JJ agreed. "It's no use, Tee, hand-over the Sherlock Badge to Beaver, you're demoted to Watson."

"No! Don't do that to her!" I implored. "She'll go all miserable and upset. A sad Tigger is a truly appalling sight, very affecting. Strong men have wept."

The 'affecting-sight,' gave a supplicatory 'worrah?' and held her paws up, appealingly. Everyone's heart melted.

"OK, this time then," said JJ "but no more missed clues!"

"Worrah!" chirped Tee, temporarily reprieved.

"More properly called a Regional Seat of Government, these are secure bunkers, relics of the Cold Wars and nuclear stand-offs of the last century," JJ explained in tour-guide mode. "The West anticipated a Russian attack and these things were bomb shelters where the Great and Good could hole-up, while the riff-raff died, outside. Once the radiation had faded, the Queen, the Prime Minister and the Lord Mayor would emerge – anticipating joyous acclaim."

"…more likely the guillotine," said Alice, knowingly.

"Precisely," JJ agreed. "Most of them have been sold off, now that some sense of proportion has returned to Government thinking. But some are still Top Secret and this must be one of them. How it was installed is a mystery that probably died with whoever Andy's brother bought this site from and how it came to be sold is an even bigger mystery. I'm sure it'll have a lot to do with bureaucratic cock-ups, then subsequent cover-ups of same.

"But I am totally flummoxed as to why it was installed alongside such an outstanding piece of archaeology. That makes zero sense. This should be a premier tourist spot but though it's been excavated, it's sealed off. That's one for the Baker St. gals to solve!

"I found this place when I was planting the beacon. Pootling around, I literally stumbled across the grid, which was still attached at that time, so obviously I never went down. Just to be discreet, I planted the beacon a long way off. After all the fuss had died down, I had another look and the grille had been lasered and lifted out. So I started keeping watch. What do I see one night but a perfectly ordinary rabbit hopping towards it. When it gets there, however, with a sort of quiver, it becomes a large, multi-coloured Rabbit and vanishes down Alice's hole, if you'll pardon the expression."

"I don't," said Alice primly. "See me later, after school."

"Let me guess," I said, "that carnival appearance months later, the day Marie-Claire made her memorable commentary on your cosmic thesis, was a bit of a taradiddle. He'd been keeping an eye on us and reporting back all that time."

"It would seem so," said JJ. "Which leads to the question – 'why?' What did 'they' see here that 'they' wanted, or could use, something that 'they' couldn't just take?"

"Who are 'they'?" asked Tee.

"Yes, I'm sorry about that. I'm forced to say 'they' because I don't have an adequate alternative. I'm certain there are no individuals per se, no Mr Big, no Fat Controller, no Mekon, no brain in a bell-jar. There must be a low grade chain authorising the Rabbit but it won't have any executive function. That'll be found within the series of interfaces that are forever collating cross-cosmos data. A shred of something that they've come across here, among us, has initiated the stream of events we've been involved in.

"The poor old Rabbit is just our facilitator and we've all tested his patience above and beyond what's reasonable. We've been trying to force some sort of disclosure out of him, about what is really going on but I suspect he doesn't know. Or, if he does, he's not going to crack. As a messenger, he's top rate."

"You've got to tell them," said Alice.

"Tell us what?" we chorused.

"That I've been blackmailing Rufus Rabbit from Day One of his spectacular entry. I told him that unless he started treating my friends with utmost respect and initiating the necessary rebuilds for Alice here, Punch, Marie and Andy, I'd blow the whistle on his eavesdropping from way back and he could kiss goodbye to whatever cooperative venture he was trying to facilitate on behalf of the mysterious 'they'.

"The thing is, he just rolled over for that, as if it had already been agreed. I thought I was engaged in ruthless blackmail but pretty obviously I'd missed the main point by a mile.

"Don't get me wrong, he was embarrassed. He didn't want to lose your trust. That bit of blackmail was effective enough but I could have asked for a lot more. Thing is, I didn't know what to ask for. I still don't. My brain, dare I say 'our brains' aren't of the order that can call-out a cosmic intelligence and confound it.

"These mega-intelligences probably have the ability to see a number of future scenarios and one that they favour, will be abetted by our continued existence as a group, which is probably why they've glued us all together with the off-planet excursion. Because that's what that was, glue. I can see that now. At the time I demanded it, I thought I was being very clever. That it would blow the Rabbit's circuits. Now, I think he'd actually been angling for it.

"I'm beginning to wonder if I've done you all a massive disservice. The time we spent rebuilding the Diner, the time I was wondering what the Rabbit was up to, we could have been running for the hills and hiding. Because something very large is coming our way and I have absolutely no idea what it could be."

"Do you think scattering and running might have been the way to go?" I asked.

"Possibly. Equally, I think we're in a 'you can run but you can't hide' situation. They'd have rounded us up, if they'd wanted us."

"Maybe we've nothing to fret about at all," I said. "Who's read Vonnegut's 'The Sirens of Titan'? Nobody, good. I'll paraphrase…"

"You've got one minute, Beaver," said Tee, threateningly. "Do NOT pursue tangents."

"And to think I pleaded for your Sherlock badge!"

"That was 20 seconds you wasted."

"Alien space craft breaks down. Spare part needed. Child has 'lucky' piece of metal he scrounges on a school trip to a factory. Circumstances see child deliver said sliver of metal to alien craft, many years later. Revealed that all our great civilisations were just signs to alert alien craft that help was on its way. Pyramids meant – 'Got you!' Stonehenge meant – 'Nearly there!' Ooh, can't remember, er, Twin Towers meant – 'On our way!' Something like that, anyway."

"You mean that all earth's civilised history was just a ploy to get a spare part to a stranded space craft?" asked Tee.

"Yes."

"Well why didn't you just say so?"

"I am so-oo misunderstood and under-valued," I groaned. "I even brought string, in case we had an emergency. I bet neither of you thought of that!"

"I would not be without you," said JJ stoutly.

"Thank you. I appreciate that."

Everyone now perches on their own section of Roman wall. We look like a bunch of maquettes for Rodin's 'Thinker' each one brooding, in their own way, on what might or might not, have been laid bare by JJ's revelations.

I can't get my head around the micro/macro interface that is implied here. I would not have thought that a motley bunch of friends, running a tranny caff on some bomb-site of a roundabout, north of London, with its members much given to communing among the willowherb, broken concrete and dandelions, could ever register on the wish-list of a cosmic intelligence.

As I understand it, we are engaged with something that consumes planets – and by extrapolation, solar systems – and operates on the inter-galactic scale. Its 'seeing' us, is as likely as my spotting a pinprick on the face of Neptune and being able to recognise what it might be. What could we possibly have that it could possibly want and why can't it simply take it?

"I feel wobbly all over," I announced. "Like a jelly that's been introduced to a benevolent volcano. I'm not certain that it knows just how fragile I am."

"Hmph," said Tee. "Tiggers aren't scared of anything." She paused. "They're probably too thick to understand the implications but I simply don't care. And the Beaver, the one that's a bit wobbly at present, is under my protection. Beavers think too much. Tiggers act."

"I feel just the same about Alice-Marie, here," said JJ. "Anything comes near her, I shall be all tooth and claw."

"Thank you," said Alice, looping an arm across his back. "If you think about it, Carl and Andy feel just the same way about each other and so do Punch and Marie-Claire."

I hiccupped. I do that when I'm scared.

"I feel very country mouse," I explained "but I believe this thing, this intelligence, is trying to explore the nature of what we call 'love.' I had a conversation with the Rabbit, ages ago, in the vegetable garden as it happens and he said that the governing intelligence of Earth II had no problem with souls. 'No soul, no life,' was exactly what he said. I didn't make much of it at the time, because it just sounded like a concession – 'oh, let them keep their totem poles, they do no harm,' that sort of thing.

"My mind extrapolates love from soul. Maybe that's just me but JJ's planet is a bit of an object study in love – all these women, like Shade, devoted to husbands, who are pursuing their soul's longing through creating objects of veneration, things like Moss's angels. I know Moss and Shade were the only people we met but it's sort of what I heard you describing on the way up there. The solitaries, too, on their walks are searching for love, aren't they? Or have I made it all up, because I don't really know where all that came from?"

Then for some reason I felt completely overcome and shuffled down my bit of wall to collapse onto Tee.

JJ looked as miserable as a man who's just pressed the wrong button and started an atomic war. "I hope I've not brought this lot down on your heads," he said. "My planet is a weird place, governed by a weirder intelligence and you guys were happily busy with your own business."

"Don't be silly," said Alice, poking him gently with her forefinger. "You're the architect who's gifted everyone eternal life, not to mention organising a rebuild for Andy and we paper-waifs. We're all tied together more tightly than we know and I think Evie's right, love is the glue. You thought they glued us. Not so. We were already glued."

"I never have ideas," said Tee, "they waste my time. But here goes, I'll sacrifice five minutes. This 'so-called' intelligence is playing truant. It's trying to run its very own mini-universe. As Whiskers told Evie, that dive back into the Implicate Zone, the dive a universe is forced to make when entropy finally shuts it down, is massively wasteful. Firstly it wastes valuable energy but more importantly, all control is lost.

"In the Implicate Zone, everything is mixed, ostensibly to a homogenous 'soup.' Any cook will tell you that's not the case. No soup, however blended it may be, can be homogenous. So what emerges from the Implicate Zone will be slightly different, every time. Every new universe will have a slightly different mix. What this truant wants is to control the recipe. It doesn't want pot luck, it wants a rigged deck and the best way to get that is never to duck behind the Implicate curtain. Send your rubbish back, by all means but it wants to keep its aces and picture cards.

"Trouble is, although it can separate everything out just the way it wants to, it can't fire up its materials again. It's lacking a catalyst. I suggest that it's combing through all the discards, to see if it can spot where it lost the secret of Life.

"Because our little group generates energies that weren't there before we all came together, it's suddenly very interested in us – or perhaps I underestimate it and it's put this little experiment together all by itself. Fact is, who knows? All our brains combined couldn't hold a candle to this thing's laundry list but for some reason, it's indulging us.

"My suggestion is – taking a leaf from its book, we indulge ourselves! Come on everybody, let's roll off back to the diner and make sausage and mash, with Punch's beef gravy. I shall steal that from the freezer! I also authorise the Beaver to poach the fattest, roundest, crinkliest Savoy cabbage from the allotment, which we shall steam and chop with butter. JJ will produce a magical apple pie, with gallons of custard and a jug of cream. We will all become instantly happy and probably quite farty, later on, too."

With that Tee led what was either a strategic retreat, a triumphant re-entry, or an elegant segue into a very late lunch.

32

BLOWOUTS AND BARGAINS

Whatever that meal was, it was a triumph. We raided all the forbidden stores and would be in terrible trouble when Andy and Carl got back…

…in itself, that sudden realisation occasioned a very shaky moment, not the store-raid per se but the 'when they got back…' bit.

"When do you think they'll do that?" Tee aimed her question squarely at JJ.

JJ raised his hands, signifying both bafflement and 'why ask me?'

"When they choose to 'dream' themselves back," he said. "Or when they see that they have no choice other than to be here? When they 'demand,' or 'request' their return? How should I know? I can't verbalise it. I don't have the capacity to process what precisely happens, how much is voluntary, what is actioned on your behalf, what precisely is the nature of the material translation. I can't even phrase the questions, let alone deal with the answers."

"Do you think Rufus knows?" asked Alice. "He was so sweet and helpful to me. I'll tell you sometime.

"Grrr!" growled Tee, "Whiskers is a 'bot. He can do what he's programmed to do – no more."

"Peace," begged JJ, hands up again, palms out, "no war over my Rabbit. I'm very fond of him, even if he has become a 'tad hyper-extended for his boots, recently.

"Don't forget, Tee, this Intelligence – which you most certainly can't out-Tigger…" Tee growled her disagreement. "… is searching for the sparks that initiate autonomy and life in clustered particles. You said so yourself. RR, Rufus, Double-R, Whiskers – he's got more AKA's than John Dillinger! – will be full to the brim with all its latest ideas. Also, he'll just be one of billions, maybe, of experimental interfaces, combing through the inter-action of emotions. For yourself, for ourselves, think – amoeba."

"Amoebas are very small."

I said that very quietly, so I don't think anyone heard me.

We ate and drank so much, we could barely move. After we'd waddled back to our van, Tee lay on the bed and announced that she was pregnant. She undid her jeans, to prove it and certainly something very large had taken up residence in her tummy.

"Too high," I pronounced. "That's definitely cabbage, mashed potato, sausage, a very rich sauce and a gallon or so of that superlative red you produced. Not to mention apple pie in multiple helpings, the contents of your double-cream jug and a glass of two of Tokay."

"No," she groaned, "it's a refrigerator, or maybe a hi-fi system. Sausages have nothing to do with it. My stomach is chipolata-trained, it shrugs them off."

"Sausages have everything to do with it. How many did you have?"

"Er…six?"

"Don't be silly," I said patiently.

"Maybe…eight?"

"Up!"

"Not nine…?"

"Ten. I counted and I might have missed one."

"Ten?! Jabberwocky! I'm a marvel. Someone get me on the Internet!"

"You're already there – remember 'The Princess and the PEE?"

"So what? This trumps all previous entries."

"No evidence," I said. "You ate it."

"There's this," she slapped her palm on the expanded anatomy and a hollow 'thwack' vibrated round the van.

"Purely circumstantial."

"It won't be in a bit. You wait till I go full Veronica Moser. They'll be queuing up!"

"They won't have to. That's the point of the Internet, you don't have to queue."

"Well, they will for this." And to endorse the point, she vented a truly odious fart, which contained the promise of more to come.

"Princess Tulipa," I said, "that was uncalled for. I can call the Nuns if you like but cut the farting."

"Oh, I don't feel even vaguely up to the Enclosed Order of the Toilet," groaned Tee. "I want bowel relief, not scatological games."

"Don't the Nuns combine both?"

"Don't be so pedantic, you know full well it's totally different."

"True," I admitted, "why not go and perch on the throne – you've done some of your best thinking there."

Tee lay morosely on the bed, staring blackly at the gap at the top of the curtains. "Twinkle, twinkle, twinkle, Little Star – I'll fart in your eye, that'll entropise you dead!" with which salvo she rolled off the bed and groaned her way to the loo.

After five minutes or so, during which I'd pinched the curtains together with a clothes peg, because it was a very intrusive star and wafted the outer door to clear the still-lingering smell, I heard another animal roar echo from Tee's bum. This one actually shook the van.

I fell on the bed and started to howl with laughter.

"What's so funny?" her voice floated from the loo.

"You thinking," I gasped, "it sounds exactly like farting to me."

"If you only knew the relief that brought, you wouldn't mock it. And anyway, I am thinking."

"What?" I cackled.

"Very deep thoughts. Far too deep to share with a moron like you."

"Go on, try me."

"I'm considering exactly where death comes in all this."

"Eh?" I sat up on the bed. "You're not contemplating death by farting, are you?"

Tee groaned. "I knew you wouldn't get it. You've been ruined by scatology. I however, can bend my bowels to my ends, in yogic fashion."

"You mean there's a yoga of farting?"

"There is now. I'm a very inventive person. When I was five, I invented the spear."

"Hang on a minute. I thought your ancestral pile was full of spears, swords and the like?"

"So it was but not one invented by ME. There's a difference."

"There is?"

"Absolutely. As it happens, mine wasn't very good. The idea was good in principle. It was the bread knife, tied to the yard broom handle with sticky tape. But I couldn't get the brushy bit off the pole and by mistake, I taped up the sharp bit and not the handle."

"So it wouldn't have speared anyone?"

"No. Mine was the very first safety spear. I told you, I'm a very inventive girl." Which boast was followed by another thunderous fart.

"Have you been taking lessons with Marie-Claire?" I asked politely.

"Good heavens, no. These farts are my own. Can't you tell the difference between an Indian yogic fart and a French peasant one?"

"Oddly enough, I can't."

"Good grief," Tee muttered, "have I ever fallen among savages!"

"Anyway, Mighty Yogi of the Sphincter, dilate, I pray thee on death and farting."

"Hang on a minute, just let me get my farts in line. OK, I'm ready now – what was the question?"

"Death?"

"Ah yes. Hang on, I had it a minute ago but you will keep going off at a tangent."

I gave Tee another minute to get her thoughts and flatulence marshalled and stared at a patch on the ceiling I hadn't seen before. I really couldn't take to it. It looked like a failed attempt to wash poo out of a Terrycloth nappy.

"Do you know," I said, "this is just like consulting the Pythoness at Delphi."

"Really?"

"Truly. You see the questioners couldn't enter the sacred cave. They had to scribble their question on a fig leaf, or whatever and hand it to the Pythia. The Pythia then strolled off, suitably bribed and handed the enquiry to the Pythoness. The Pythoness puts down her knitting and goes off to steam her brains over a fissure at the back of the cave that emits noxious fumes.

"When she's quite overcome and gaga, she considers the question and whatever comes to her by way of inspiration, passes for the answer. She hands that over to the Pythia, who puts on a suitably grave face and returns to the supplicant, who's busy reading the illustrated magazines in the waiting room and delivers the pronouncement.

"I imagine the size of the bribe determined the quality of the answer but I could be being cynical.

"It's just like you on the loo. I ask questions. You utter thunderous farts, which choke you with awful fumes and wild prophecies fly from your lips to the benefit of mankind."

"But you haven't asked me any questions."

"I did. I said – 'death?' quite recently. That was 'death' with a question mark."

"What about it?"

"You said, ages ago – 'where does death come in all this?' – remember?"

"I did?"

"You did."

"Blimey, that was deep."

"Exactly my point. Squeeze off another one and try for an answer."

"I can't, they've dried up."

"Never! You looked like a pregnant hippo when you went in there."

"Did you know that hippos are terribly beset by flatulence?"

"I did not. Pray expound."

"Nothing to tell, really. They sit at the bottom of ponds all day, eating water grass and the result is awful wind. That's what makes them tetchy."

"What, having wind?"

"Absolutely. I mean, if you were the size of a hippo and you're not far off, for a baby one, imagine having gripes and not being able to rip one off!"

"Excuse me! That was quite hurtful and entirely uncalled for. I'm exactly the same weight that I was when we first met."

"I know. That was one of your selling points. Muti first described you to me as having a prick like a stallion and tits the size of baby hippos."

"Baby hippos don't have tits."

"No, they don't. Baby hippos descriptive, not baby hippos possessive."

"Good grief woman! All this time I've assumed I was described in terms of mystery and imagination! Something from Greek myth, say or 'The 1001 Nights.' Perhaps I was the 1002nd Night, or kin to one of your more androgynous Hindu gods and thus exotic and mysterious."

"Nope. Stallion prick, hippo tits."

"Which of those lured you in?"

"Oh, that was the discount."

"What!?" I yelped.

"You were marked down that night, for some reason or other and you know I love a bargain."

"This is awful!" I wailed.

"I know," said Tee. "I think I may be managing a poo at last, which puts the kibosh on yogic interpretation."

"No, no, no, no!" I yelled, "you don't get to leave that Oracular Throne before you've dilated on death and if you've any sense, apologised about 'tits like hippos'- I'm deeply wounded."

"It wasn't me that said it," wheedled Tee, "it was Muti."

"It's still wretchedly impolite to mention it, especially when you're usually all over them and as for bringing in 'discount' as well. You sound like you were buying by the pound!"

"Well exactly!" Tee agreed. "That was the selling point. Huge objets d'art at bargain basement prices. More bang for my buck…that's quite funny, if you think about it – 'more bang…'"

"This is awful and you will pay a terrible price," I said in my deadliest voice. "But for now, having started, I find I can't stop. How much was I, per pound, that night?"

"Oh, you were still hideously expensive," said Tee calmly. "That was another point, too. Even with 25 per cent off, no-one could afford you. Which is why I did. I always have to have the best but I do relish a bargain."

How mollified was I? I was musing on this, in tandem consideration with acts of terrible revenge I might wreak in the months ahead, when another cataclysmic fart shook the van.

"Gotcha!" I squawked. "Death! Dilate!"

"OK," groaned Tee. "Phew, that really smells. Augh! It's awful!"

"You ate it. In fact, it was you who suggested the menu."

"Good, wasn't it?"

"Excellent. Now – death."

"Ah, phew… I wonder the Pythoness ever got any work done at all. She must have had an air freshener fitted somewhere. You can't work in this. It's quite outside anything tolerated by the Health and Safety elves."

"Death," I thundered. "Get on with it, before the dam breaks."

"OK, ok, ok, you win…"

"Everything dies. Everything that dies is eaten – from pork sausages to mountains. Everything is 'food' for something else – agreed?"

"Agreed."

"You can't short-change that cycle because, vicious and ugly though it sounds, that is the creative cycle at bottom. You keep getting new lamps for old.

"This Intelligence is hoping to subvert that and create a self-perpetuating landscape – I use the term figuratively – in which automatic-death is exiled for its chosen lifeforms. In doing this it will, inevitably, be denying some Higher Intelligence still, its food. What that might lead to, I cannot imagine.

"One Intelligence is trying to rewrite the death, digestion and rebirth cycle. But my death is something else's birth. That's how stuff works, how the system works. We don't know what 'eats' us but something released by our deaths, will be consumed by something else. Just because we can't imagine what that might be, or how it will eat us, means nothing.

"That's how, in my very limited way, I understand Implicate and Explicate might work. Explicate universes, like ours are wound back into the great pool of No-Thing. After a thorough mixing, with a very big whisk, random re-births occur. No-Thing spurts out and begins the process of becoming Some-Thing.

"It's not so much that you can't break that cycle, it's that you mustn't. If you do, you'll end up like the Hapsburgs, weird chins…you know, the infamous Hapsburg jaw?"

There was the sound of toilet paper flying off the spindle, to a heartfelt – "Hallelujah!"

If I was ever to write a book, the title of this chapter would definitely be 'Wisdom from the Dunghill' and I'd really like each chapter to have one of those precis-headings that the Edwardians were so fond of – 'in which Princess Tulipa has a poo – the cyclic nature of the universe is revealed – Eva is weighed in the balance – and found she was wanted.'

33

GOING HOME

Carl wasn't precisely miserable but it was breaking Andy's heart to see him trying so hard to disguise his unhappiness.

"I think we'll go back, Caz," he said quietly.

Carl looked up from the hub he was stripping down for Moss. "Have you gone crazy?"

"No, I'm not crazy. I'm just like you. I'm homesick.

"I want to hear the big rigs growling in and out of the stand. I look forward to the Leather Boys turning up, late on Friday nights. Me, wheeling myself out, so they can show me the latest slab of chrome they've managed to bolt onto the Harley.

"I miss the unholy twins, Evie and Tee. Did I ever tell you I had to up the chipolata order, just to keep the Princess improperly fed? God, but she's a love, isn't she? Like a really haughty Good Fairy, she turns up with presents for people when they're least expecting anything and stalks off before they can get a 'thank-you' out. Then there's Evie, like a mummy bumblebee, if there is such a creature. I think it's the bosom that does it. Then she swings off into the gents to pee a stream like a stallion.

"I miss all that. I miss Alice and JJ, who are most definitely having it off. I know, I can spy, with my little eye, when people are… 'enjoying each other's company…'"

"Yes. But. And," said Carl. "You're working again, down to the waist-ish. It's a flat-out miracle. Now I don't care if your cock works or not. But I would like to see you back on your pins – then you can empty your own bloody bags! But joking apart – and that was joking, because you know I'll empty them till Kingdom come – I want to see you up and about before we go."

"I know you do, mate. Look, I've chatted to the Rabbit and he swears blind they'll carry on re-wiring me, wherever we're living. So, let's go home. I want to see you breathing life into that Villiers. I know you and Mossy are building something but you've got Villiers' rust in your veins now. Being here is keeping you from it."

Carl spread his oily hand on the workbench. "You know I'd chop that off for you, don't you?"

"Yeah, I know it. Just don't ever do it, or like Tee says – 'I'll have to kill you myself.'"

They grinned, personal memories of the soft-hearted warrior Princess surfacing for both of them.

Carl moved to sit on the floor, his back to the wall, knees up, staring into space, until he eventually fell to talking and thinking at the same time.

"This is strange but I actually miss the new crew. All the stuff you taught me, I've been teaching them and I love to see when they've picked up on why we're doing it. Little stuff, y'know, flattening the bacon, getting a fried egg into a fat circle, swirling them onto the plate of some guy who doesn't seem to notice but deep down, it's why he keeps coming back, why he tells his mates. I miss the whole diner thing. I miss having a fag by the bins and knowing you'll bollock me for smoking. I miss seeing Punch in his bits of uniform, polishing that musket till the walnut glows, sitting by you, holding your hand.

"Until it wasn't there any more, I didn't realise what we had. It's priceless. Sure I want to get back to rebuilding the Villiers, trawling eBay for parts. I even like writing to Vikky, in India, about his collection, what I might be able to find for him in the way of spares – and you know how much I hate writing, worse than sewing!"

"You're good at sewing!"

"Prison can do that for you…" Carl took a deep breath. "Apart from you, Moss is the straightest guy I ever met. He's a miracle worker in metal. He's shown me how to make dies and fettle the castings. He's even taught me a bit about how he conjures up those magical patinas…so you see I'm not going to spray the Villiers, any more…" – Andy smiled to himself, he could sense the building enthusiasm – "…I'm going to turn her brown, like the barrel of Punch's musket. But gun browning wears off. Moss's doesn't, ever. He showed me a piece he did, centuries ago. He cut it all wrong, so it's been lying out there in every kind of weather, catching a suntan, or buried under snow. Whatever its been through, it's still as crisp as a conker out of its shell, that unbeatable, slick, chestnut brown.

"I like the nights in my wreck of a caravan, listening to the rain on the roof, or curling up with you on the verandah, in summer, when we've had to rig the mosquito net. You know, listening to the growl of the traffic dying down, until it's just the odd drift of wheels. Then maybe a big rig will crawl in, hiss of air-brakes, then the diesel shuts down, cab door slams and you know some solitary soul is going to crawl in for coffee and beans on toast.

"I wish our working girls would come back. Strange thing to say but I thought they gave the place a bit of class. I used to love to watch them, sashaying past the bins, down the walkway, off to the Portakabins wiggling their butts, some shame-faced loon tagging along behind.

"I dunno Andy, everything was there when nothing much seemed to be there.

"I like to wander up to the old cement works. Evie likes it up there, too. She's got a thing going with the willowherb. Talks to it, tells it stuff. When it was seeding once, she ran through it, backwards and forwards till she was covered in white down. Then she went home to show Tee! All hell broke loose! 'Look at you! What have you been doing?

You lunatic. Do not come in here! Take your clothes off now, now! Yes, outside and put them in this bin-liner!' So, big shrug and off come all her clothes. Standing there in her bra and pants. 'Can I come in now, Tee?' Door opens a crack. 'That's better – oh my, you do look nice! Do come in!' Guess the rest…"

Andy grins. "It's all in the little details, you're not wrong. I've got a lot of memories of Harold and I'm gutted it ended the way it did. It was inevitable, I guess but what a waste!

"When I could still wander around the place, I used to feel it was more than just the ruin it seems to be. I don't know what I mean by that but I feel it's some sort of energy bank. When he wasn't out-of-it, Harold could see energies. I think he saw that Evie is some sort of conduit for them, a lightning rod if you like. That's why she sits up there in the fireweed. There's something up there, where the Great North Road petered out, donkeys' years ago. Evie and Harold were wired into it – Evie still is.

"Then there's Punch and Marie-Claire in that allotment. I can see them from the back of my place and I find them pure magic. So slow, so sure, they don't waste energy. Neither of them are more than 50 but they come on like two old Zen masters. They have that centred gravity, certainty. I keep expecting them to shoot branches and roots. If they do, big rosy apples will be hanging off the boughs and they'll be the sweetest, juiciest apples you ever tasted. They're the mum and dad I could never find. There, you don't get much soppier than that!"

Both stare into the rueful middle distance, until Andy says – "I think we agree, we're going back, aren't we, Caz?"

Carl examines his hands, then sticks them under his backside, uncertain where they live it seems. "Provided the Rabbit is solid on your re-build, that'd be good. You see, I can do the Villiers, but I can't rebuild you, however good you'd look in nut brown.

"Do you think Punch and Marie-Claire will drift back, too? I'd hate to lose them here, they're like the other nan and grandad I never knew."

"I'm sure of it. They love those two kids, Alice and Evie. I hope they love us, too but it is their choice, at the end of the day.

"I'll throw something else in, too. I think that whatever brought us here, wants we lab rats back in our maze. Whatever this Intelligence may be, has had a look at us, downloaded our blueprints and shaken its head in despair. Now it wants us to keep buggering-on, aboard our little traffic island, till it can figure out what exactly it is that it needs from us. That's pure conjecture but I don't think I'm wrong."

"You're really are sure they'll rewire you? That they'll help Alice and Marie-Claire lay down enough substance to make it off their pages for good? Because I tell you what, Andy, I don't think we'll ever make it back here, if we up and leave. This trip, whatever sort of 'trip' it was, was a one-off."

Andy took his time. Tried to remember that he had a lot riding on the outcome of what was little more than hunch, conjecture and emotion, those prime drivers of human actions.

"I've got the same voice in my head that, I assume, everyone else has? He says it's cool to split. We shouldn't see things as gifts, or a favours. Bodywork is just something they can do, so why wouldn't they?

"He makes no bones about it, something in our little group interests them. So, obviously we don't see things the same way that they – whoever 'they' are – do. In fact, my voice tells me, we're misleading ourselves when we think of materialised entities. What we should be thinking about, as far as we can, is energy interfaces.

"I don't get it. As in I just haven't a clue how to think about it, let alone what to think about. So I've given up fretting. If this 'thing' says it'll do something, I've no option except to assume that it will. If it bails, I'll be gutted but I'll still be a damn sight better off than I was. On balance, though, I trust it. My gut says we go home."

Punch and Marie-Claire knew where their hearts lay, too.

"Papa," she whispered.

"Oui," he replied quietly, his brown hand on her shoulder, her head of grey hair resting in the crook of his arm.

"It is beautiful here, non?"

He stared down the valley of the angels. They had the best room in the new guest house and their picture window gave the finest view.

"Tis fairyland, maman."

They breathed in unison and she snuggled closer.

A light mist was forming in the cwm. It touched the angelic wings and for seconds they would be eclipsed, until they re-appeared in a gathering of refracted colours, morning light passing through a bowl of glass marbles.

"Th'art reet," Punch said, "as allus, th'art reet. We's mek our way 'ome, tomorra, like. A' misses 'em, just like tha' does an' God knows wot nonesense thet boy o'mine is up to. E's not fit out by 'isself. 'Tis a gud job e's got yon Princess t'sort 'im, or e'd be in all manner o'pickle."

"You may talk, papa! What of my petite mademoiselle?! Une petite folle, more like! How do you say 'folle,' in your barbarous tongue?"

"A cud'na say, Ma, but trust me, yon lass is no-one's 'folle,' whate'er it may mean!"

At which they both started giggling together.

34
GET TO THE POINT

If Eva could have heard, he would have been roundly affronted. Currently in efficient, no-nonsense male-mode, he was starting to extract a splinter from Tee's bum.

"Where," he demanded severely, "did you get this? Because this is not the first time you've needed my skilled, medical attention. Recall the affair of the thorn in the knee?"

"No, I don't. You're just angling for promotion – as my personal paramedic. Ouch!! Be careful you animal! Alice and I were sliding down the bannisters."

"Never forget who is wielding the needle, little Tigger… Also, which bannisters? I wasn't aware we had any."

"We don't," said a muffled voice from the head buried in the pillow, "but Andy does, from his upstairs to his downstairs. It's a really good, long straight run."

"What were you two doing in Andy and Carl's place?"

"Cleaning, putting out some flowers, what else? They'll be back tomorrow…

"…ow,ow, OW! Stop, stop, stop! That really hurts, honestly."

"Sorry! How do you know they'll be back tomorrow?"

"Alice has ESP."

"You mean JJ told her, because the Rabbit told him?"

"Exactly, ESP."

"E.S.P. stands for extra-sensory perception."

"Exactly."

"So how does that correlate with the Rabbit telling JJ and JJ then telling Alice?"

"It just does, it's obvious. Don't be so male. Just because you think you're Doctor McDreamy. Ow!!"

"Shut up. It's in really deeply. I need tweezers. Or if you want I can go and get some drawing ointment and slap a plaster on it. That might coax it up a bit."

"And what am I supposed to sleep on tonight?"

"You've got two other sides and a tummy."

"Yes but in turning over it'll be unbearable, mind-blowing, searing, white-hot agony."

"That sounds a bit OTT but I'll concede, at the wrong angle, it could be uncomfortable."

"It's not in your bum, is it?"

"Thankfully, no."

"All right then."

"Right," said Eva, "I'm going to bung a load of numbing cream on, give it five minutes, then really go after it."

"Oh murder, that sounds awful!"

"Try turning it into a fantasy."

"Fantasies don't hurt and splinters aren't even remotely sexy."

"Trust me, some fantasies hurt but I'll concede the splinter. Try a bit of Zen detachment, you know, it's not your body, it's just a body and the pain is not your pain, it's just pain."

"Fuck off."

"Never worked for me, either. Anyway, does that feel any more numb?"

"Any more numb than what?"

"Number than it was before, of course."

"A bit."

"Good. Just try and relax. You could think about sausages and gravy – but do not, under any circumstances, dare to fart!"

"Then I better not think about sausages."

"You are the worst patient in the world. Will you shut up and stay still? I'm going in. 'Nurse! Scalpel!"

Tee wriggled over like a turtle threatened with a soup tureen.

"What!? You are not taking a scalpel to my bum!"

"I know I'm not. I was getting into character, for pity's sake. Turn back over."

"So stay out of character and pull the ruddy splinter."

"Did Alice get a splinter?"

"Yes, she did and it was bigger than mine."

"How did that end?"

"I pulled it for her, 'cos the end was sticking out."

"I bet she didn't make this much fuss."

"She said some startlingly vulgar words."

"Woe is me," said Evie, staring at the operation site. "Do we actually possess tweezers?"

"In the cutlery drawer, with the spoon."

"As an operating theatre, this place leaves much to be desired…" mumbled Evie, shuffling round the end of the bed and rattling the jammed cutlery drawer…

"Yuk! They're disgusting. I'll sterilize them."

"What with?"

"Water, dishcloth, gas ring, gin bottle – in that order."

"Give me some gin. It's pain killer."

"If you're brave, you get pain-killer later."

"It's my gin!"

"And I'm the doctor."

"Oh stop procrastinating, just dig it out for me."

"Right. I'm going in. Needle first, then tweezers. I'll try not to hurt but it's bound to. Try and bear it. If you can't, we'll have to rely on some drawing ointment."

"OK," Tee said philosophically, "just go for it." She buried her head in the pillow and clutched its edges.

Evie dug.

Eventually the black end moved a fraction.

"It's on the move Tiggs. Be super brave, I'll have the little devil in a second or two."

He dug and coaxed, until triumphantly, the tweezers gained a grip and a portion of Andy's banister slid clear.

"Coo, Tiggs, that was really deep and really long. Roll over and have a look."

Tee turned, eyes watering and breathing hard.

"Oh poo, oh poo, oh poo…" she said. "Show me."

Evie laid it in her palm and after a moment's contemplation she treated it to a volley of Hindi, that required no translation at all.

"You've been super-brave. I'll pour you that gin."

"Plerff," groaned Tee. "Too late. Dying now."

35

TOO COMPLICATED BY FAR

"What are the profits like these days?" asked Carl.

He had his feet wedged up, under the mantelpiece, warming the backs of his thighs at the open fire. The rest of him was swallowed by the depths of an old armchair that might have seen better days but had the appearance of being a comfortable, trusted, old friend.

Andy was similarly contained by the chair's twin but he was more conventionally secured, wedged in position with pillows and cushions.

"As modest as they always have been. Any particular reason for asking?"

"Footfall and covers are up, that's all. I wondered if we might be bound for glory."

"You are quite correct, with the exception of the glory. Unfortunately, overheads have risen disproportionately. More in, true enough but more out, also."

"It was pure idle interest. Just glad we're not sinking and that there's a bit in reserve. I think it's that I get fonder of the place every day and I couldn't bear to see it crashing again, the way it was before the UFO's came to the rescue."

"Ah yes, our friends from outer space. Wasn't there a book of that title, once?"

"Could be," said Carl "but it obviously passed me by, so whether it was relevant to our interesting situation, or not, I cannot say. I'll tell you a title that is, though. Clifford Simak's 'Way Station.'"

"Oh yes, what's the story.?"

"Ah, tricky – this'll have to be using the broadest brush, because I read it when I was a teenager. It was one of the books I used to help myself grow up, so I have feelings for it. That's not the best recipe for a precis.

"There's an old boy, Enoch Wallace, who is so like Punch but as we're in the USA, he's a survivor of the Battle of Gettysburg, not Blenheim. Neither he, nor his farmhouse, get any older, because they have become an inter-galactic B & B, for aliens obliged to pass by earth, en route elsewhere.

"What's lovely about it, is that it's a thoroughly homely book. As I recall, Enoch only has one alien at a time and he has a special room that's been adapted to hold any sort of atmosphere to accommodate them. He dials up the appropriate gases and in float the visitors. But while they're waiting for their flight connections, he likes to shoot the breeze with these strangers, maybe offer them sweet corncakes and coffee.

"He has one particular mate, a routes supervisor, whom he really has a deep relationship with. When this guy sends him a note – 'put the coffee on!' – that makes his day. Anyway, regulars pass through and as they get to know him, they bring little presents from their worlds.

"It gets around the galaxy that what he really likes are lumps of strange wood, suitable for carving. I think I've got that right, certainly wood and carving come into it. Anyway, it's the way the book feels – coffee, cake, wood for carving and sitting around gossiping together, in front of an open fire, just like we are now.

"Simak spun a lovely tale out of it, despite having to graft on a daft plot. It's a book with a sense of timeless place and of being content with not very much."

Carl stared into the fire and some changing configuration of logs and flame prompted him to add – "I just remembered, every day Enoch takes the same walk, his rifle hooked in the crook of his arm. It's not because he's into killing but for male kinship. While he walks he's actually drinking in the green of the trees, the spring of the grass.

"I've been feeling this echo of what's happened here, yet apart from suddenly clueing to the fact that Enoch is Punch, I'd be hard-pressed to say why. It's just what I feel about it, some sort of parallel."

"We haven't any aliens passing through, have we?" asked Andy, lightly.

"Oh, my ageing and obviously senile friend, what would you call JJ…if I may make so bold as to turn the tables on you, as you once did to me!"

"I did, didn't I," says Andy, grinning feebly. "Yes, well, umm, hmm, I suppose… but he hasn't got any aerials on his head and he doesn't breathe hydrogen cyanide. All excellent points in his favour. Also, he did not arrive bearing gifts of timber. And, as I recall you saying, equally feebly – 'he's my mate!'"

"Oh, stop procrastinating, prevaricating and whatever else begins with 'P' and means dodging the bullet."

"Very ruthless of you, dear boy. You're not one to force an advantage, as a rule."

"I very rarely have one, hence my enthusiasm for this particular specimen."

"I suppose he is an alien. But he makes apple pie and custard with miracle ingredients!"

"A-L-I-E-N ingredients," ululated Carl, in his best Boris Karloff voice.

"I haven't noticed you holding back on second helpings!"

"Why would I, they're incredible puddings and he's my mate, too. I'd defend him to the last drop of custard!"

"Beware! The last drop belongs to Tribe Beaver."

"True."

They relaxed in amicable silence, relishing the odd crackle from the fire, the distant hiss of tyres on the tarmac of the roundabout. Carl idly walked his feet back up towards the mantelpiece. As they ascended, he sank lower in the chair until, to an unaccustomed eye, he might have resembled one of the alien lifeforms so recently considered, as his torso and hips had vanished behind worn upholstery with only limbs and head protruding.

"I wish you'd take your shoes off before you do that. You're wearing a path up my Grade X, 1940's fireplace, as rescued from big bro's scrapheap."

"Exactly. It was ancient before I could even walk. Now I'm re-walking it, keeping it legally open for ramblers and armchair loungers alike. Otherwise, you know, unscrupulous landlords shut down access, deny freedoms fought for over generations…"

"I'm not unscrupulous!" Andy protested indignantly.

"List me your scruples."

"I will never, wittingly, run down a hedgehog – assuming I ever drive again. I am kind to aliens and persons of dubious sexuality. In fact, the only thing I will not tolerate, under any circumstances is 'Authority,' in whatever guise it presents itself. The very word is a red rag to a bull."

"Not much 'Bull' in you these days, lover boy! Bullshit a'plenty but 'Bull,' you're cleaned out! Bankrupt!" Carl cackled.

A crutch flew across the room – with maximum intent but zero accuracy.

"You realise, Heart-of-my-Heart, that you are now totally dependent upon my picking that up for you and restoring it to your possession?"

"I have a mobile phone and many lovely friends willing to assist me in an hour of need."

"No you haven't. It's downstairs in the kitchen, charging and turned off, so don't try screaming for SIRI."

Sounds of frantic searching, swiftly followed by – "oh, murder. Is it really?"

"It really, truly is," said Carl primly. "And there it will remain, until you humbly apologise for hurling your crutch at my innocent head."

"It was your trespassing legs I was aiming for. Either way, I missed by a mile."

"Changing the subject completely," said Carl, "did you know about the Roman village below our feet?"

"No, I didn't and that is very odd. I've been here 20 years and big bro was here a lot longer. I've never seen a document that even mentioned it, nor did the solicitors ever say a word, which is mighty odd, though I suppose I was inheriting, not buying, so why would they? But all those photos JJ took suggest a site that has been regularly visited. It's spotless, when it should be wet, dreary and full of cobwebs. That is not a place that has been mothballed for 40 years."

"The Rabbit could be a demon spring-cleaner?"

"Bit spooky, that, don't you think – 'Alien Rabbit's Roman Hideaway?' There's something missing, Carl, don't you think?"

"Actually, I couldn't agree more. I went for a rootle around with sister/brother Evie.

The iron grille is factory fresh, as is the printed notice. Also, for some reason I studied the photo-floods. They don't have a maker's name on them."

"And that's unusual?"

"You make something, you logo your product. Even dope-dealers customise their tabs. So on top-end equipment like that, you'd expect it. Also, there's zero Museum of London labelling down there. In fact, there's a remarkable 'lack of' down there. It's that 'absence of' that's confusing me, rather than 'presence of.'"

"I sense you have a theory?"

"I do but it's a bit way-out."

"Oh, do try me. And be a nice underling and chuck my crutch back, please, I'm sinking. Gently now…"

"OK, if you are now resurrected, I will begin.

"I'm guessing that Jo-Jo, JJ, whatever we're titling him these days, was followed from the moment he snorted the Stag's marching powder. He's probably perforated with internal trackers, incorporated as indelibly as BLACKPOOL is through a stick of rock. Cut him open and it'll say – 'Property of Earth II. Please return. Reward.'"

"That's a very unpleasant image of our buddy."

"Nevertheless, he's tracked, knowingly, unknowingly, benignly, aggressively or otherwise. I have no idea. He winds up here. No-Name Roundabout Motel – actually that's a brill name, if you ever fancy a change from 'Andy's Place.'"

"We're not a motel."

"A mere detail. So he settles in. But they are spying. They have cameras behind his retinas, or up his bum, I don't know. Once they see he's in for the long haul, they recce the place for an Operations Room. We know they have ground penetrating radar of a very high order, or something infinitely more sophisticated. They find the Roman settlement and it amuses them to excavate it. You saw those tunnels they cut at the cwm – straight as rulers, flat enough for wheelchairs – and that was through solid rock. All there is down there is a couple of thousand years' worth of accumulated worm crap and project debris. Mere nothings to them. They excavate, then send down his mate, the Rabbit, for now he has the perfect hidey-hole.

"Don't get me wrong, this is all B-movie stuff but here's a detail that has been overlooked by everybody. I took a good look at the roof, I can get quite paranoid underground. It should be all doubled, tripled, scaffolding-boards held up by a sea of steel props. There should be sand, rainwater and wireworms falling through the gaps. Nothing like that at all. Between the fabulous paintings – so fabulous you don't look at their edges – is fused 'something.' It looks and feels like rock. There is no rock round here and the only thing that might pass for it is chalk, or soft limestone. This is like some mix of chert, basalt and obsidian, black, with a matt sheen and incredibly hard."

"Carl! You're under-paid, under-employed and under-estimated. You should be assuming Tee's Holmes' badge – though I wouldn't risk asking her for it. So, no sarcasm intended, your conclusion is…because I'd really like to know?"

"I don't think that the Museum of London has a clue about this place. We could always phone the number on the grille but I'm sure they've got that covered in some way. Could be the Museum even 'thinks' they know about our site, which would righteously set us back to ground zero. I think this is all Earth II. I could bang on about it all day but speculation is pointless and of facts, I have very few."

"Don't stop," said Andy. "Honestly, I'm enjoying this more than a boxed set."

"What I keep coming back to is – if they wanted a bunny hole, why not dig a discreet one, something bijou under one of the tank trap mountains? If they excavated this site, as I'm inclined to feel that they did, why did they excavate so much, so scrupulously? Also, is that a Regional Seat of Government down there at all?"

"Hang on, hang on! I'd forgotten about the RSG. Doesn't that, potentially, blow your theory? Certainly complicates it." Andy scratched his head and shook himself, insofar as he could. "No-Name is a very strange site. It isn't even a roundabout, as we're landlocked on the west. Let's allow that a Roman villa or two were here. We know there was a motorway building frenzy in the middle of the last century. Maybe that's when it was discovered, when they were site-prospecting, aiming to join up to the old North Road?

"Motorways trumped villas, back then. So, the Museum gets to excavate in secrecy, they were made whatever promises they were made. Suddenly, just as the line of the motorway is shifted anyway, all of Government falls under the Cold War spell. "Ah," thinks a Whitehall Mandarin, "we have a surveyed site, ideal for a RSG. Get digging boys!" So we have motorways trump villas, RSG's trump motorways and villas, then in the final turn of the wheel, common-sense trumps RSG's and motorways but abused villas might prove embarrassing.

"Quick, sell the site to the concrete-casting plant, that'll cover things up – but it goes bust! My bro buys the site and starts crushing concrete, then, dammit, he dies. Luckily, eccentric lil'ol'me inherits and buys up the tranny caff. 'Thank God,' think those in authority, 'this loony will never sell, nor will he develop. All our embarrassing secrets are buried. Let it stay that way. Anyone applies to develop and it can become a site of special scientific interest, home of the winged, web-toed vole."

"How complicated is this?" groans Carl.

"I know, it's pure paranoia! So along comes an alien, followed by his Rabbit…"

Carl starts to laugh, calmly at first, then with increasing hysteria. Andy soon follows suit and eventually, both are howling, with tears starting to run down their cheeks.

Finally, Andy manages to choke out – "whatever…something very strange is going on. We can all agree on that. It's either cock-up, conspiracy or the start of an alien invasion by giant rabbits. I'm too whacked to figure it out and that noise you just heard was my brain blowing its main fuse."

"Really? It sounded just like a fart to me."

"That's why I told you it was the fuse. I didn't want you confusing it with a fart."

"Either way, before I shoe-horn you into your sleeping pit, do you want…"

"Macallan, please."

"I think there's a drop or two left."

"Two then!"

"For myself?" Carl thought out loud. "I feel in need of icy, icy vodka – which means a trip to the kitchen. Do you want your phone bringing up?"

"Oh yes, please – at least if it's managed to heave itself past 80 per cent. Thing is Carl, will any of this look clearer in the morning?"

"I have no idea but I was wondering, if the authorities knew of this subterranean screw-up, why on earth would they allow you to trundle huge diggers on site, yards from impending embarrassment and dig trenches for allotments, hard-standings, roads etc? Doesn't make sense."

"That's easy. I didn't ask them."

"Good grief," said Carl admiringly and descended the stairs.

36

A GHOST STORY

The red display on the clock was showing 03.15 when he was awakened by a shove of Andy's crutch against his mattress. (Two in a bed was a goal not yet in sight. Firstly, there was the plumbing to think about and then there was the bed cage, that had proved necessary to spare Andy the pressure of bedclothes against his painfully, resurrecting body. Muscles that were responding again to signals from the brain had much to say for themselves. Pain-killers could only do so much. What with one thing and another, if Carl was to have even a fragment of sleep, a separate bed was called for.)

"What do you need, mate?"

"Sorry but I need to talk."

"Honestly?"

"Really, truly, because I haven't slept a wink."

"Shoot," said Carl. "I'll try to follow."

"We discussed at length, who dug holes in our backyard."

"We did."

"We did not discuss, we have never discussed, the impossibility of the trip we made to Earth II. Carl, we went to another planet, in another galaxy. We drove there off the end of our slip road and we have never talked about how that cannot have happened."

There was a long silence.

"You've not gone back to sleep, have you?"

"Not at all, no. You've well and truly woken me up."

"I am sorry, I'm sure it could have waited."

"No," said Carl, in an oddly thoughtful voice, "I can see why it couldn't."

"Why has your voice gone odd?"

"Has it?"

"Very."

"It's probably because the enormity of what you just said has struck me. That we went to another planet for what felt like weeks and when we got back it turned out we'd been gone for a day or two. We decided to leave for deeply personal reasons. We informed our affable hosts. Hugs and reassurances all round. We arrive back here. Everyone vaguely thinks we've been to Torquay, or somewhere. 'Hi, how are you? Did you have fun? Are you rested? Did it rain?' And we, all the gang in the know, never mention it again. We just carry on like it never happened. Absolutely inexplicable."

In the darkness, Carl inched himself upright and then continued – "did I ever tell you about the time I saw a ghost?"

"Is this relevant?"

"Highly."

"No, I have to say you've never mentioned it."

"Exactly. Hold that thought. Here's the story. I was 19, 20, living with gran and grandad. I worked about 50 miles away, in Gloucester but on the bike, breaking all the speed limits, it was a doddle. Nevertheless, I had to be on the road by seven, so I was always up before them. Slice of toast, cup of tea and off.

"This particular night I wake up at stupid o'clock, 2.30 am says the clock. Now, I never used to pull the curtains, it being countryside-dark outside. I stare out and I can see the old apple trees twitching in the night breeze. I mumble a bit, re-arrange my pillows, turn over to face the door side of the room.

"Damn me, sitting on the chair, by the side of the big chest of drawers, less than a yard away, is a bloke in a cheap-cloth, light blue suit, 30's styled. He has a good head of floppy blonde hair, which he has slicked back, Brylcreem-boy style. He's resting his head in his hands and his whole body language is fatigue. He looks whacked. I look at him, size him up and think – 'yes, he's a ghost and he's just passing through. He's exhausted, poor guy.'

"I roll over, snuggle into my pillow and am about to fall off to sleep, when I think – 'hang-on, I'll try to tell people about this, tomorrow and they won't believe me. So make sure you've got this right. That you're not dreaming.' I look up and he's still there. I check him out again, yep, just as I described. I turn to the window and the trees are doing tree-y things outside. I know that if you screw your neck round, you can just see the headlights of cars on the A40 but they're few and far between at this hour. But I do it and eventually, some traffic rolls up. Big truck with lights along the high sides and a fair way behind him, a car. Fair enough.

"I rub eyes, arch my back and even pinch myself to the point of 'ow!' Great, turn back, he's still there in the same attitude. OK, I'm square with all this. I'm satisfied that I'm awake. Now I'm tired. I'm going to sleep. I settle down and that's what I do. I don't even think of saying – 'what are you doing in my chair?'

"I wake with the clock in the morning. The guy has gone. Up I get. Tea and toast. Lid, bike, work.

"Never once crossed my mind at work – all my mates and I jabbering away at break, over lunch. Bike home, kiss nan, hug grandad. Help with supper. Off to bed and last thing, I think – 'oh, I forgot, must tell them about the ghost, tomorrow, they'll be so excited.' Every day I forgot. Always. Never did get to tell them.

"That is exactly what is happening now. You have perfect recall of what happened but you never vocalise it. There doesn't seem to be any point…it's already rolled off you, water off the duck's back, belle-indifference, deja vu, I don't know. I can't make any rational sense of it. Something utterly extraordinary has happened but you can't bring it into the present moment. Qu'est que c'est?"

"Forgive me interrupting but is it a 03.30 thing with you, to hit the Froggy lingo button?"

"Nope, it's my lessons with Alice."

"You're taking lessons with Alice?"

"No. I'm not but listen – here we go again. You prod me awake to discuss the momentous event. I finesse it with a ghost story. You do a segue, vis-a-vis Frog lessons with Alice and the main topic slides off again, undiscussed. What is happening? Something very odd is going on."

"You're right. It's proving slippery," Andy agreed.

"It is almost as if it's a 'not-to-be-discussed-under-any-circumstances' topic that words simply recoil from. It's out of bounds to everyday language."

"I suppose, in a way, it is…when you think about it," Andy said thoughtfully. "Who the hell wants to hear about your trip to Earth II? Only the psychiatrists and they've heard it all before, anyway. We know we were there and it was remarkable – except that it wasn't. Once you'd got over the engineering, the communications, all the things that are just extensions of what we have now but are 100 times better, what is, was, there to talk about?

"Moss and Shade were lovely human beings and Moss didn't look 10,000 years old. The age thing has to be filed under 'don't understand' along with all the other 'don't understands' of existence.

"The 'having-been-there' completely neutralises most of the conversations we could be having. Like your ghost story. I believe you, so what more is there to say? 'How-do-you-think-it-was-possible?' What's the point of that discussion? I don't know, you don't know.

"Think about the poor old American Indians. They fell into the 19th and 20th centuries from, arguably, the stone age, or the early bronze age. Putting their outrageous dispossession to one side, because that's not what we're talking about, what alternatives did they have other than to shrug and accept the new facts of their lives – steam locomotives, Winchester repeating rifles, alcohol and skyscraper buildings?"

"You're absolutely right," Carl agreed "but there is a bit of a difference. If we'd been to Mykonos, or wherever you like, we'd be pressing the replay button, off and on, for weeks. 'Remember that night I got pissed on ouzo and was so-oo sick?' Or, 'I loved those alabaster windows in the little church, the way they filtered the light.' We've never said – 'eating baked potatoes out of Moss's forge – wasn't that just like being kids again?' Why haven't we?"

Andy gave the matter some thought. "Possibly because the answer would be –

'yes I do, yes it was but at the same time it's completely messing with my head.' All I can say is that the whole event was the most extraordinary one in my entire life but that it all passed off in the most ordinary manner. The only reason I don't rave on about it is that we were all there, we all seem to have had very different, very delicate, personal reactions to it and group solidarity demands we don't expose each other to the inquisition of outsiders. We either talk about it within the group and as you know, because of those delicate reactions, we don't, or we don't talk about it at all.

"Somewhere in that lot is what I mean," he finished helplessly. "If I say any more, it'll count as less, just more chaff."

"I hear. I agree, largely but let me ask you one."

"Shoot."

"How do you feel about them giving you your body back?"

"Superficially, that's easy – worshipful gratitude, eternal thanks from the bottom of my doubtless fatty heart. Me casa, et tu casa!"

"That last one might be important."

"It was just a phrase."

"What if it wasn't, what if they want No-Name as Earth II, local HQ, and you keeping shtum about it?"

"Shtum while they what – pick daisies, visit Historical Properties, eat seven-year-olds, watch the Changing of the Guard? Which of the above?"

"None. Shtum while you don't know what the hell they are doing, because whatever they are doing will be totally beyond our comprehension anyway, until such time as they have done it."

In the darkness, Andy nodded thoughtfully. "I hear you, I take the point. But let's be upfront, they don't need me, my permission, or my land to do anything they might care to do. What they've done for me has to count as pure goodwill and performed on a micro-management level that I'm amazed they can be bothered to operate at.

"I expect these people, this Intelligence, to make some moves that will horrify us as humans, moves that may however, be for the good of the Galaxy. Perhaps sterilising the human race might be such a move. I don't know. I do know though that if it was, it would be a better option than the coming wars over resources and the displacement of poor people dispossessed by climate change. Maybe this will shock you but I'd vote 'Yes' to that…after all mate, you and I are already doing our bit!"

There was silence for a while. Andy began to wonder if he'd gone too far and was about to leaven his pronouncement when Carl said – "before everyone goes sterile, though, a No-Name baby would be nice, wouldn't it? It would have all of us fussing over it, taking it exploring and things – and yes, I'll even do the nappies."

"You're right," said Andy ruefully, "I'd like a No-Name baby, too but there's only Tee with production parts and I can't see her agreeing to have anybody's other than Beaver's.

"Changing the subject and hurriedly at that, I just thought of a way to settle some part of this whole mystery. Some time, when the moment seems opportune, shimmy down the Rabbit-hole and see if you can cut away a square inch of that ceiling that fascinates you so. You'll know better than I do what you need. But let me guess, cordless angle grinder, diamond discs? And don't you dare forget goggles!

"We can take it to one of the Kensington Museums. I haven't been there since I was a kid. If they won't analyse it, they might know a laboratory that would. That could settle a question or two."

37

SEX AND METAPHYSICS

Jo-Jo and Alice were happily engaged with one another, under a mound of duvets that they had smuggled into the Mithraic Temple. The photo floods were decisively turned off. Jo-Jo had banned them in favour of the humane yellow glow given off by a hissing, burbling hurricane lamp he'd invested in. In some peculiar way, it was also a satisfactory accompaniment to the recovery of his double-O's. These were being restored to him by Alice, along with gleeful, consensual sex, a delight he'd mislaid for several thousand years.

"I like this light, Jo-Jo," she said, "it makes this place mysterious and alive – in a good way, you understand."

"There isn't very much at the moment that I don't like," he said happily. "You seem to have found my 'on' switch and I'd blush to mention how long it's been off. I can't imagine why Earth II kept me going in my old format. Four thousand years of negativity and misanthropy – what possible use could that be to them?"

"Maybe they were looking forward to your resurrection," she giggled. "I mean, look at you, you're like the 16-year-old school-kid who just seduced his French mistress and can't believe his luck. Apologies, bad analogy, my upbringing has been largely from the pages of some very racy books."

"Don't knock them, they seem to be working to my advantage, at present."

"Maybe Earth II are tapping into your rediscovered sex drive. Using it to power a whole new solar system. You're like a mouse on a treadmill – oops, that's another bad analogy isn't it?" she gurgled happily. "Never mind, you know I meant it as a compliment!"

Jo-Jo was not in the mood to resent anything. These last few days had been revelatory, a rekindling not just of lustful playfulness but a rediscovery of intensity and meaning.

Whilst Alice was aware that Earth II had been as good as their word, that a new solidity and strength was being poured into her, Jo-Jo felt that he'd been restored to his 40's. He was suddenly competent, strong and eager, without being so brash and arrogant so as to miss the point of everything. Suddenly, he was in possession of an elder's head and a warrior's heart.

"Long may this last," he said fervently.
"I couldn't agree more," said Alice.

The next time they surfaced, Jo-Jo seemed in more thoughtful mode.
"Do you find it… I don't know… let me put it another way, what do you think about the way Punch and Marie-Claire are suddenly elder statesmen, sort of God-given parents to us all? Do you resent sharing Marie-Claire?"
"Good heavens, no! She'll be my Nounou forever but I want her to love everyone else as well. I love everyone here, so I'd be so upset if she didn't. I mean, poor old you can't even remember if you have a maman and papa, so you must be aching to find some."
Jo-Jo hesitated. "I don't know if I am, or if I'm not. I don't know what I feel about the whole parent, grandparent, God-parental business. Cautious, I think. Anxious about investing all that trust."
"It's only because you don't know who you really are, yet. You really do think too much, Jo-Jo. Don't look so worried!" she laughed. "I'm an expert at dealing with that. Look, I'll show you…"

Later still, as the hurricane lamp still hissed and gurgled happily, it was Alice's turn to look thoughtful.
"You know who I feel sorry for?" she said, "Evie."
"Why on Earth I or II, would you feel sorry for Evie? She's with Tee, which is almost as good as me being with you."
"Oh, nicely done, sir! A fine point towards your merit award."
"Don't you worry! I'll get there, I'm fearless with a good woman alongside me."
"That's rather my point, poor old Evie is neither fish, nor flesh, nor good red herring."
"Your comparatives are a bit devastating, don't you feel?"
"I wouldn't have used them with anyone else, sweetheart but there was no point beating about the bush. I love Evie like the sister, brother, she is. But the poor love can't ejaculate, menstruate or lactate. How do you think that makes her feel? "
"We could give thanks that she can still pee and poo!"
"Oh! That is bad! You're getting a smack for that…"
"Ouch! Ow! I meant it in a good way, a nice way."
"I might let you off."
"Bit late now, I'm mortally wounded."
"Maybe so but try to follow this, it's very hard to put into words. Evie's two parts are at war. The He bit has been carrying around this insane notion that He has to atone, personally, for the damage done to women by men. So He, throughout His early life, went out seeking abuse from other men to wreak on His She bits. When She suffered, so did He. He was landed in hospital with Her wounds. Do you follow?"

"Certainly I follow but isn't the point that for all that scheming, it was She who ended up taking another beating invited by Him? It all backfired, because it could never work in the first place. He, She, was a hospitalised teenager, pumped full of painkillers. We don't have to go any further than that, for pity's sake. Teenagers are pretty susceptible creatures and Evie got landed with a malignant utterance worthy of the Old Testament and its Prophets."

"Don't go anywhere near the established Church, Jo! It'll take me a very long time to get over my last two 'priests' – they made the gory bits of the Old Testament look like a kindergarten. Truth is, I could have chosen a better book to wriggle out of! We managed to miss a lot of bad stuff but not nearly enough. As for the damage done to Marie-Claire, I'll never forgive myself."

"I can see why but trust me, she was more scared about what might happen to you, than in fretting over what happened to her. Either way, Punch put paid to them both."

"You were no slouch in coming forward, yourself."

"Thank you. I appreciate that. I've actually never been so outraged. I don't know, most people keep their fantasies within mutually agreed boundaries. But when one of them loses their self-control, they're like a fox in a hen house – mad, bad and dangerous to know. It's then that they have to be put down and Punch was the right man to do it."

"Yes, I knew he was from the first time I saw him in the book – then later, in the flesh and covered in blood, after he'd been blown through the Hedge. He never failed us. I'll never know how it worked but I always knew it would. My one regret is that I wanted to slit that flabby fool's throat myself but Papa got there first!"

"My Lord, I believe you would!"

"You can trust me on that. I would have cut it very slowly. I'm sure Papa was too quick. I fret about that sometimes."

Jo-Jo sat up a little straighter. "Ally – am I safe with you?"

"So far, so far. But Jo-Jo, I do have a worry and I have never told anyone this. The Black Nun at the Manor. She was more evil than the other two added together. They were scared of her. She was not in the reckoning, that day. Whether she hid, whether she fled, whether she lived – I'll never know, will I? She haunts me some nights and you are the first person I've told that too."

"Three hundred years, Ally, 300 years. She's bone and dust, manure for a fresh cycle of life. Forget her, she's gone."

"It's not that easy, Jo. After all, we're still here."

Jo-Jo took a deep breath – "I am now, ponderously and deliberately, going to change the subject. What do you make of the Intelligence that runs my old planet, now you've begun to feel how they've kept their promise to you and Marie-Claire?"

"I'm not hedging Jo, because first of all, I'm more grateful than I can ever express, not just for me but for my Nounou. To see her want to live again, makes me so happy. There again, I never met 'Them,' did I? What messed everything up was that I really started to hate that angelic cwm. It started to obsess me. At first I thought it was a miracle. All that light, what a spectacle! And I was listening to Papa's funny story, as well as making sure Marie-Claire didn't trip and turn her ankle. She's really not very seaworthy.

"It was after the picnic. I started to feel claustrophobic. The damn things had stared at us and I kept remembering their gaze. I've been around a lot of bad things in my life and none of them of my making. But I started to feel judged. It must have been paranoia but I was convinced it was original sin making itself heard. I couldn't get the idea out of my head and it's not like I even believe any of that stuff in the first place. Damn you all, I thought, I'm not staying in a valley of little tin judges.

"Then I started having problems breathing and I'm not in the least asthmatic. I'm a healthy, hearty girl. I thought about my friends, the girls in the books in the library. They had all been judged as guilty in their stories – harlots, wantons, Sapphists, heretics. Such a catechism of prissy judgements! It seemed to be summed up by that angelic host, righteously taking flight out of the valley. You wouldn't find a blow job among them, not even a hand job! Who wants friends and allies like that? Not me!

"So I crept over to your old friend and ally, Mr Rufus Rabbit and I asked him to fly me home, please. I was feeling sick, tired and near my end. Nor was I lying. I wanted a hole to crawl into and all the holes on Earth II were poisoned with angels. He was so sweet. He promised he would see to it that 'They' prioritised my 'strengthening medicine'- which is a line from 'Winnie-the-Pooh' he was probably saving to use on Tee. But as Tee has declared him Tigger Enemy Number One, he trotted it out for me. Actually, I thought it was rather sweet.

"When I got back here, I was really poorly, wan and wasted. It was Tee and Evie who took me in and I'll never hear a word against them. They kept me warm, cuddled me and told me how much they loved me. I kept drifting in and out of sleep and once I heard someone say – 'shush! Don't wake the baby…' That pieced me back together. I was warm, welcomed and I so wanted to belong to someone who cared."

There was a long silence. Only the hurricane lamp filled it, with its steady hiss and the glow from the gently pulsing mantle.

"I feel terrible," said Jo-Jo eventually. "Why didn't you come and get me?'

"I couldn't. You and Moss were joined at the hip, catching up on the last few thousand years. He was basking in praise and as he was the creator of that Sistine Chapel extravaganza, I could barely interrupt to say that I was off, because the whole thing made me want to toss my cookies – by the way, that's a new phrase I've just discovered. It's bang on the money – and that's another discovery from the vernacular! I'm seriously pursuing my studies in slang. I find I love the cutting edge of language and I haven't even reached the 21st century, yet!"

"Can we finish with the angels first?" asked Jo-Jo. "Because that's quite a revelation, that they could be seen that way. I'd never given them any serious thought in that direction. To me, Moss is just Moss. He's anything but religious. Before Shade reined him in he was… what? Not wild but distinctly untamed. He and I hung out, because I liked to be there when he started to boil up with a new idea. He could go quite crazy, downright deranged. He'd stop eating. He'd draw 24 hours a day, until the floor was, literally, knee-deep in rejected plans. He wouldn't speak, all you could persuade him to do was drink. So I was forever brewing coffee and piling sugar into it. You could get the odd slab of fruit cake into him, too, if you were lucky.

"I know for certain that the angels were nothing more than a tribute to the medieval carvers and carpenters who'd first set them soaring across church naves. He made no bones about it, he was copying. He thought he could see what they had dreamed of doing and that he had a chance of realising it for them.

"You're absolutely right, of course. People will see it as an exercise in piety. In fact, it was meant to celebrate the profane – the artisans, their hands, their tools. I honestly don't think he ever thought about priests and popes, bishops in mitres. If he'd overheard us talking like this, I think he'd go out and dynamite the lot."

"I'll help him pack the charges," said Alice grimly. "Punch will tell you, I'm good with ordnance.

"At least that tale explains why Shade loathes you. I couldn't decide if it was because of me, or something historical. Now I get it. It's the homo-erotic thing. She sees you as competition."

"Oof!" said Jo-Jo, "that's a blow below the belt! Moss and I were just mates, both distinctly heterosexual, at least in the early days, when we could still be bothered. You think it's the wifely feeling that 'my husband's best friend is my worst enemy'?"

"Most definitely. You'll never be seen as anything other than competition. Women will not abide that."

"Back in the day when the Rabbit and I were best mates, he told me – 'she doesn't hate you, she just hates your ideas.' To which I said – 'that's even worse, my ideas are me!' Then, damn it all Ally, she then went on to steal my Rabbit! Now look what he's turned into, some sort of inter-galactic Lance-corporal, with me playing the lowly Private."

"There's a chain of command then, in this Earth II affair – is that what you're telling me?"

"No, no, no. Not a bit of it. I'm just irritated that he's making such a show of being 'the Messenger,' when in point-of-fact, he's no more than a lowly interface. If you're looking for CEO's, Presidents, secretaries, agents, nameplates and a visible hierarchy, you've got Earth II all wrong. There's no Head Office, no-one on the front desk.

"The only 'face' that Earth II has, is the residents' 'requests box.' I've told you about those. They're not identified individually, you can use anybody's if you need to. Ostensibly, you're as a free as a bird up there. No supervision, no rules but equally, no free-for-all. I'm also certain that every cell of your being is wired, in some untraceable, inexplicable way, to whatever 'whole' they are contriving. Earth II is a hive, it's that simple but what sort of bees we are, what 'honey' we're laying down, I have no idea."

Jo-Jo pulled Alice close and stroked her back. She arched herself into the imitation of a cat and thrust out her hands, clenched as paddling paws. "More mansplaining," she yawned, "I need my little female brain to be overwhelmed, like my helpless female body…"

"You asked for it – here we go, from the non-existent manual of Earth II…

"The Intelligence behind Earth II operates a totally efficient, nano-level recycling process. Every used, rejected or unwanted item, every scrap of waste, every piece of redundant material is broken down to atomic particle level. Thereafter, it is stored until required, or immediately re-utilised in nano-level assembly. Without going into detail – which I can't – you can build a dinosaur from a boxcar, or a helter-skelter from a refrigeration plant. The assembly work, the deconstruction work thereafter, both are blindingly swift.

"Where the blueprints for items originate, I could not say. There is so much I can't say, because I simply don't know. Had I ever asked, I would have been told. There are no secrets, only methods way beyond human understanding.

"It is no secret that Earth II is run by quantum computers and I haven't a clue what that means, either. I know that they operate at 'star-cloud' level. Somewhere in a distant galaxy, they have harnessed an entire star to function as their computer. Every particle of that Star's energy represents the Intelligence's 'feet-on-the-ground, eyes-on-the-street,' which presumably explains why there are no feet-on-the-ground, with or without eyes, to be seen. What can this all mean? How would I know? Maybe they have dozens of suns wired up to their master-board.

"This Intelligence controls a sizeable chunk of the Universe and it intends to subvert natural process by outwitting entropy. It does not allow items under its control to collapse, beyond a certain level. It is opposed to chance. Unfortunately, this sounds alarmingly close to eugenics but it is set within an entirely different set of parameters, that are being practised at a galactic level. The ultimate intention must be to organise but embrace, the Universal.

"I'm almost certain the intention is benign, benevolent. Its message is that it is opposed to waste, the waste of potential, of 'good things' not being allowed to run their course. 'Good' universes terminated, for no better reason than that their time was up. It believes that to be wasteful and of course, from our humble viewpoint, it does seem to be.

"However, whether we agree, or disagree, I'm sure our vote is quite meaningless."

Jo-Jo paused and scratched his head.

"This isn't making any sense, is it?"

"It sort of does," replied Alice, scratching her nose with a paw, "and it sort of doesn't. Why, given that it's so powerful, isn't it running our Earth, this one, the one we're sitting on? Life here is anarchic chaos. The detail would overwhelm even a sun doubling as a computer – at least, I say it would, which quite obviously makes it so.

"Are you listening?" she bellowed at the ceiling and then cocked her ear upwards. "Nope, it's not listening. Go on, more mansplaining, it's incredibly restful, far better than counting sheep."

"Can't be done," said Jo-Jo sadly. "My brain's mouse has fallen off its treadmill. It's now lying on its back, with its little legs feebly paddling in the air."

"Aw…poor little thing," said Alice. "Let me help! I'm a cat!"

"Keep away," said Jo-Jo. "It's a very delicate mouse, easily frightened.

"Seeing as it's you, not just anyone, I'll have one last shot at my theorising. Let's call this Intelligence, Sun-Cloud, it's a nice enough name. I've described the physicality of 'the Core' to you, the milky object that kebabs our planet. I think that Core runs on and on and on, 'through galaxies measureless to man' to corrupt a phrase. I think it contains Sun-Cloud's best shot at producing the undifferentiated stuff of the Implicate. You've heard me babbling enough about Implicate and Explicate, yes?"

"Yes," yawned Alice.

"I think it might even be digesting entire-galaxies, trying to establish a matrix that they can draw on to replicate what they feel are successful blue-prints. But the simple fact that even I can see shapes swirling about in there, suggests they haven't got things right yet."

"You mean," said Alice, "that their soup isn't clarified adequately yet? That that is giving them problems?"

"Yes. I think their soup keeps forming Boltzmann bodies. As I just said, you can see shadows forming, dissipating, regrouping. It could be that that's a good thing, for all I know, that they're replicating the Implicate precisely. I just don't think though, that that is what they want to do."

"This is Ludwig Boltzmann, yes?"

"Yes. He predicted Intelligences would form automatically at certain molecular densities, or I think that's what he meant."

"I think that's what he meant, too," agreed Alice. "So obviously we must be right."

"Probably not but it doesn't really matter."

"How big is this tube-thingy?"

Jo-Jo sighed. "This is a giant secret. I've told everybody it took me 50 years to walk round it. It actually took me 500."

"Fucking hell!!" shrieked Alice. "Sorry, sorry, pardonnez-moi. Had you nothing better to do? Were there no daisy chains waiting to be made?"

"It was a Quest" said Jo-Jo. "Arthurian. I had a lot of time on my hands. Please, please don't tell the Rabbit. He thinks I owed him 50 years' worth of birthdays. If he finds out it was 500 he'll hunt me down with murder in his hideous, little, felt heart."

"Hmm. You are at my mercy. Excellent. Keep talking."

"Oh, Ally! Couldn't we have a cuddle instead. I don't want to waste any more time."

"Cuddles after. I'm a disgustingly demanding sort of girl, you'll discover."

"So long as your demands are disgusting enough, I shall cope," said Jo-Jo hopefully.

"OK, how about… I know… come closer… I'll have to whisper… I don't think the Romans had invented that one!"

"Oh wow! Let's get on with it!"

"No. Not until you've told me how this core can possibly link solar systems and galaxies, yet still be a visible entity."

Jo-Jo shrugged helplessly. "I can only think it's some sort of ramped up, virtual arterial, venous, system of connectivity. Why it should be visible, locally, is probably to halt speculation at a sufficiently useless level. I'm living proof that no-one can make head nor tail of it, not even after traipsing all the way round it.

"Honestly Ally, low-grade speculation is quite useless. Let me get back to where I started this conversation – what do 'You,' lovely you, make of this Intelligence we're involved with?"

Alice pulled her knees up under her chin, wrapped a duvet round her shoulders until only her head stuck out. She looked distressingly like a trophy head atop a tepee's centre pole.

She began thoughtfully and slowly. "They have done nothing but good things for me and been nothing but benevolent towards me. Without their intervention I would have faded away, like the abused heroine of some repressed novel. Instead, I am frolicking like a young foal.

"They have sent me no bill, asked nothing of me. They have facilitated my progress at every turn. I should love them the way a child loves its parents – unconditionally. Yet the truth is, they scare the daylights out of me. I can't spot their gameplay.

"Look what they've done to your funny, furry, little friend. They've turned that innocent Rabbit into a liveried footman, who has the pretensions of a Czar. That is a crime against a concept. It might not sound like much but it's unfeeling to the point of deliberate sadism. You and I know, however, that it's not. What it is, is simply 'unfeeling.' This Intelligence doesn't feel and is far beyond our moral scruples. What is terrifying about that is that they haven't had to de-humanise themselves, they were never 'human' in the first place. They simply don't possess 'feelings'… they can never 'get it' because they haven't got the necessary equipment any more. That was jettisoned way back. They are as unfeeling as the real Process of the Universe but in a different way – actively, not passively.

"The real Universe works. It probably works because it's unfeeling. It can't be blamed for that, because it's the only game in town. But this Intelligence pitches itself as a better alternative to the inevitabilities of the actual Universe. As such, it should be showing sensibilities that would necessarily belong to a smaller, neater, more scrupulous package. I would have hoped those would have exhibited elements of compassion.

"For all that it is doing for us, I detect none. That sounds arrogant and perhaps I am being. But in my opinion, what it is doing with us, is a little local experiment to see if there is any profit in exhibiting partiality, any pay-off in being kind and caring. If it detects none and this scares me, I think it could very well decide to stop. 'This experiment has run its course and has produced nothing we can utilise on the Universal scale.' If it does that, it will be discarding 'love,' which will make it villainous in a way that the real Universe is not. The real Universe is blind and cruel – this thing claims to have eyes and may still turn out to be cruel. There's a huge difference in my mind.

"I'm done. Have I come over as ungrateful? I must have."

Jo-Jo stared at the mosaic crabs and dolphins, flickering under the drowsy light. 'Was Alice being ungrateful?' Not that he cared if she was. It couldn't alter the fact that he was head over heels in love with her and he wasn't head over heels with Earth II, or its masters. However, did he think it wise to bite the hand that was feeding them so generously?

"I don't know if you have or not, Ally. You are, at least, being honest – which is no mean feat when something gives you life, possibilities, a future and yet you tell it that you don't like it, or trust it. I guess it could reasonably ask – 'what do I have to do to win your trust?'"

"Let me have another go," said Alice, "because I don't want to appear ungrateful. It's just that my subjective feelings clash with the little objectivity I can muster.

"So let me ask you – 'what's your opinion of the Universe?'"

"Indifference, awe, plus 'please don't hurt me' and 'what the hell is it?'"

"You don't love it to bits? You wouldn't trust it not to maim you, or cast you aside?"

"All those things and more."

"That," said Alice, "is my attitude to your smaller, wannabee Universe. Just because it's a family company, 'God & Sons, Est. 18-O'Flaherty' doesn't give it automatic lien on my feelings. That it intervened on my behalf should make me adore it. All I owe it, though, is honesty. As a result, I regret to say, it makes me suspicious. I do not believe in altruism without motive. It's evolutionarily unsound – however much I may have personally adored Kropotkin."

"How can you possibly know Kropotkin, Ally?"

"Just because you met me emerging from one century doesn't mean I haven't inhabited others now and again. I'm the off-spring of a genre, so travelling forwards and backwards within its parameters, has never been a problem. What is odd, is that I never remember I can do it, until something unexpected reminds me." Alice paused. "That doesn't really make the slightest sense. But, for example, I was chatting with Evie recently and remembered that I knew a lot more about Porn Hub than I thought I did! It was very, very embarrassing! The future outside the genre – that's a whole other matter. I've tried going there and it's scary.

"Anyway, when I knew the Prince, he was such a sad, tired old man. He had no teeth and his constitution was ruined but his mind was as sharp as ever. Why was I on his shelves? I think I was there, in my usual state of deshabille and distress, by accident. He kept me to remind him of emotion's contradictions. He would, occasionally, turn the pages to look at my unfolding plight but he looked so kindly, so fondly that I knew he wished me no ill. He would have rescued me, put me to sleep in a bed of my own, with a sandwich and a warm cup of cocoa. He was a very dear old gentleman.

"His evolutionary theory, though, was too compassionate. It lacked Darwin's rigour, born out of Malthus. Now there was a man I did not like, Malthus, not Darwin. Perhaps I'm slandering him. I don't like any clergymen. He had a self-righteous, pitiless rage about him. When he plucked me off the bookshelf, I knew to reduce myself to pigment, to become devoid of feeling. The urge to be right, to be dominant, to possess the power to punish, those were the emotions that seemed to burn brightly in him, within his fantasy self at least.

"Lamarck however…"

"Stop, stop, Ally!" wailed Jo-Jo. "You're a walking copy of 'Famous Masturbators of History.'"

"Too right I am," she said stoutly. "I have enjoyed very wide circulation, over many centuries. I appear in most illustrated titles and with the advent of modern printing I enjoyed a positive Renaissance. I am the Universal Wanton and have recently been digitalised. Would you like me to continue?"

"Ally, Lovely, couldn't we just snuggle down into our own little slice of happiness, while it lasts and tell everyone else to go forth and multiply in their own chosen fashion?"

"Sounds good to me," chortled Alice, sinking down into her tepee.

38
A THEORY, OF SORTS

The Princess Tulipa Agnethuram, of Sikhim, is behind the wheel of her car.

The faithful Beaver is curled up very tightly alongside her, trying to think pure and noble thoughts before death inevitably overtakes them.

"What is wrong with you?" asks Tee crossly. "Why are you wriggling? Are you at the point of death? Do I need to stop for a bag of wood chippings, or whatever it is that solaces dying Beavers?"

"You need to give them certainty," I said faintly. "Certainty that they will return unscathed from this terrifying outing."

"Impossible. That's all in the hands of Karma. We may and we may not. If the finger points, we're dog scraps. No use thinking about it."

"Right," I said boldly. "If that's the situation I shall share my last thoughts with you, out loud, then you will know how deep and profound they were, even in the face of terror."

"I am all ears and no voice," said Tee, slumping in her seat with such resignation that I began to question my own genius – but only for a moment.

"I shall begin with a sort of title – 'Has Life got it all Wrong by relying on Death?' You have to pretend I'm reading my doctoral thesis, you see. I know, it's not very snappy but I'll work on that.

"The system has certainly worked until now," I said boldly, then paused and added – "the system's the title thingy I just said." Then I changed back from my 'ad-lib' voice and continued – "but a species has evolved that demands a platform from which to challenge this age-old assumption. It wishes to have words with who, or whatever it is that sponsors the show.

"My opinion is that the Species – 'that's us, by the way…'"

"Oooh, I'd never have guessed," mumbled Tee. "I really thought you were speaking on behalf of newts…"

"…thank you! … is that the Species is making a hell of a mistake here…"

"…you can't say that…you can't say 'hell of a mistake,' in a doctoral thesis…" interrupted Tiggs. "It would blow your cover."

"What cover?"

"The pretence that you're actually a doctoral candidate, rather than a half-wit who has bundled the real candidate into a broom cupboard and stolen their place on the podium. Saying 'hell of a mistake,' would do for you…"

"Shut up and listen in reverent silence. This is work in progress, produced under extreme pressures and presented extempore. So… I will continue…

"…hell of a mistake here. They are making the colossal assumption that a coherent intelligence is running the show. The idea implicit in posing a question, is that someone, or something, is listening.

"Why do we assume that anything is interested in anything we have to say? It is foolish to believe that there is anything there. The only thing running the show is – Process!

"Are you with me so far?"

"…ish," said Tee. "Very …ish, as in …ishy."

"OK," I bristled, trying to marshal what passed for thoughts, as we made a violent Mach 2 turn left, only to correct it by an even more violent Mach 3 swerve to the right. Horns blared from every point of the compass.

"People expect arrogant behaviour from a car like this," Tee said calmly. "I'd be disappointing them if I drove like a saint."

"But I'd be thrilled," I said. "Just try and keep us alive a bit longer, I'm getting to the juicy bit. If I can recover my thread. My thoughts swerve one way, then you drive the other. It's very confusing."

"Maybe your thoughts are confusing my driving. Have you thought of that?" Tee demanded, as she riposted to a lunge by very large articulated lorry, with a very passable Veronica. I could hear the crowds roar. There again it might have been brakes, rubber and horns. I get confused.

"Process!" I squeaked. "The Process of the Universe is simplicity itself. It emulates the metronome – tic-toc – tic-toc – a rhythm of two beats that initiated the Universe and will conclude it.

"Remember Tiggs, I don't know anything but I've read stuff, listened to stuff. A personage no less than Roger Penrose…"

"Who he?" demanded the Princess, "is he on our guest list?"

"We don't have any guests. Or lists. Ever. We don't like guests. A personage no less than Roger Penrose has suggested that particles, as they emerge from the veil of the quantum vacuum, the back-door to the Universe, or wherever, have an instantaneous choice to make – 'do I attach to that rogueish-looking blob over there, or that randy little bugger in the corner?'

"Because you see, Tee, they come out electrically charged, pos. or neg. so they have some, admittedly limited, 'choice' of who, or more precisely, what, they're going to hook up with. Which lucky, oppositely-charged, unrequited particle is singing a particularly alluring song – shit, mind that motorcycle! In fact, it's a bit like you're driving, which other vehicle are we going to irrevocably weld ourselves to?"

"I've told you it's all down to karma."

"Well it wasn't, it was a brilliant doctoral thesis and you've sent it all pear-shaped by going round this roundabout four times."

"I like pears," said Tee. "Tinned pears in syrup. Let's have lots for supper, with ice-cream."

"All right, all right but let me finish my lonely particle dance first, before I die and am buried in a stewed pear tin because they couldn't find very much of me. It's such a sad end, I could cry but I won't."

"There are tissues in the glove compartment if you feel you absolutely must. Here's a thought for a thesis, do you think anyone ever kept gloves in a glove compartment?"

"No. It's like houses with garages. No-one ever keeps the car in the garage. They keep £500 worth of crap in the garage and £55,000 worth of car out in the rain."

"Lot more in my case," said Tee. "But we haven't got a garage."

"We could park it in the caravan and live in the car."

"That's not a bad idea, actually. These seats are real leather, all we've got inside is split vinyl pouffes. How would we get it through the door?"

"I don't know! It's like particles! They go like this – 'hello, I am a lonely particle' – and all around it are voices saying 'come and join me' and it simply has to. It has to join up with something to become stable. Now that implies choice – 'do I take this one, or that one?'

"What's that got to do with fitting the car into the caravan?" Tiggs demanded.

"Nothing! Shut up and listen! To continue!

"That is the root process that has established the Universe. And you can see that mirrored, magnified of course, in every process of life. Just because elephants look complicated doesn't mean that they're not totally dependent on that underlying 'tic-toc' process…"

"You said there were two things, aren't there three?"

"You were listening!" I said gleefully. "I always knew it was exciting!"

"I'm bothered about your mental health. That's why I was appearing interested. I didn't want you to de-rail suddenly."

"I'll ignore that," I said with dignity.

"No, don't," said Tee. "Imagine for a moment…'tic' emerges from behind the veil. It sees 'toc', that would be 'toc 1' or 'toc 2' smirking in a corner. It drifts over and hooks up with 1 or 2, it doesn't matter. That's at least three things. 'Tic' plus 'Toc' equals 'Tic 'n' Toc' – you can't ignore the 'n' bit, or the fact that 1,2,3, have now become 1 again."

"You're ruining my thesis," I said sulkily. "It was a really good thesis until you came along with your 'n' and your 1,2,3, hypothesis."

"Not a hypothesis,: said Tee. "Just an observation. Please continue."

"I'll try," I said, "but you've seriously depressed me. If you insist on driving up this lorry's bum, I will not utter a word of protest."

"Bloody hell!" said Tee. "That was close!"

"Karma sees all," I said sadly. "The wheel is spinning, we cannot deflect it."

"Oh do go on," said Tee. "It really is amazingly diverting."

"All right… if you absolutely insist! Imagine billions and billions of dominoes laid out in that exciting way that if you knock over the first one, the whole lot will fall in the most complex heap you ever did see. What started it all was the simple thrust of one domino onto another.

"I say that that is the process that assembled the Universe and it will be the same process that disassembles it. Entropy, at heart, will be stuff being busted back into particles and them sliding back across the quantum vacuum."

"Sneaky little devils," said Tee in an admiring voice.

"Anyway, as I detect a certain sarcasm in your tone, I shall rest by saying that EVERYTHING starts with 'tic and toc.' maybe your 'n' is in there, too. How should I know, if it baffles the likes of Penrose? My final point is that you can't talk to, or argue with 'tic, toc' can you? Just because you can talk to an elephant doesn't mean you can talk to all the 'tic, tocs' that made it. You can't plead your case to it."

"I'm very glad I didn't know that when I was small," said Tee. "I used to like going for elephant rides, until I found out how cruel they were. Then I cried for days and apologised every time I saw the one I used to ride on. I gave it bananas, too. I hope it forgave me. I didn't know it was wrong."

"I'm sure it did – forgive you, that is."

"I tell you what, though, if I'd known that elephants were assembled from tiny bits, all clinging together on very dodgy premises, I might never have climbed aboard in the first place."

"So, you're impressed?"

"What by?"

"My unbelievably cogent presentation of a startling thesis under very trying conditions."

"What – that the world is made of atoms and that atoms are made of smaller bits, too? Everybody knows that."

"Grr. No! That the tiny bits came into being by a very minute bit of decision-making, basically 'this?' or 'that?' and that things never got more complicated than that, because that's the underlying structure of the Universe. That that is all there is – so why on earth would you appeal to it? How could you appeal to it?"

"Because," said Tee, "we're on earth, where we have tinned pears and elephants, so stuff looks an awful lot more complex."

"But my point is that it isn't."

"So prove it."

"I can't. I'm not bright enough. I am a Beaver of little brain. But I'm convinced my core principle is spot on."

"Which puts you in the position of a Desert Father, doomed to deliver sermons to rocks."

"Does it?"

"Absolutely. They had convictions that they couldn't prove, so they went round trying to impress rocks, because no-one else would listen."

"You're listening."

"Only because I love you and because I'm stuck in a car with you – by choice, I hasten to add."

"It's not that corny an idea, is it?" I asked meekly.

"Not at all," agreed Tee airily. "It's probably the whole truth and nothing but the truth. However, there are monsters called secondary truths and they can invade your argument and destroy it. Short-circuit it completely."

"Are there really?"

"I dunno," said Tee, "I just invented them. They seemed appropriate. Let me give them some thought."

She screwed up her face.

"Don't close your eyes!" I shrieked.

"A secondary truth," she continued calmly, "would be this entity that's responsible for the Earth II farrago we're currently embroiled in. You could think of it as a parasite within a parasite. If we accept that Life is a parasite on the natural process of the cosmos – which is very necessary to your thesis, by the way – then this 'thing' is trying to construct its own closed system within the accommodating arms of all Life's possibilities and the cosmos. To us, who are just one of the doubtless numerous parochial branches of Life, it's saying – 'guys, we have a better deal. Life with Death not included, until you decide enough is enough."

"And is that good?" I asked.

"Which bit?"

"That it's writing new rules. Ones that fly in the face of the established system. Is that good?"

"I don't know," said Tee. "That really is the Poodle in the Spin Dryer."

"Poodle in the Spin Dryer?"

"Don't be dumb – 'fly in the ointment."

"So why a poodle?"

"Don't like flies and I'd hate to find a poodle in my spin dryer."

"Good job we don't possess either of them, then," I said, as calmly as I could. "You realise you're playing 'secondary truths' with established metaphor? You're piggy-backing on their solidity."

"Yes. I suppose I am. Bit anarchic of me, wouldn't you say?"

"Potential exists for confusion."

"How so?"

"Insofar as some innocent might hear 'Poodle in the Spin Dryer' and assume it meant something completely different than 'fly in the ointment.' Perhaps, say, it was meant to combine confusion and humour, representing a chaotic moment in one's domestic life."

"My Lord, so it could!" Tiggs suddenly jerked upright behind the wheel, newly activated brain waves strobing forth like the Eddystone lighthouse on full alert. "I must stop and buy a notebook. You can be my Boswell. I'll reel off new metaphors and you can assign them meanings. Together we'll re-write the English language. This could be big, really, really BIG!"

The Sat-Nav interrupted – "in 800 yards turn left, then take the second left on the roundabout and you have reached your destination."

"Thank you, thank you, thank you!" I warbled. "Saved, saved I'm saved!"

"What are you wiffling about, Beaver of my Dam? Ooh, oh, quick – write that one down! 'Beaver of my Dam,' it means 'soul of my heart.'"

"Oh, that's really lovely, Tee. Can't that one be private? Just for me? It's more of a euphemism, anyway, or simple shared vocabulary of affection, like – 'Tiggs of the Moon.'"

"Yes, yes," she gabbled. "Get that one down, too! By the way, what does it mean?"

"It means you're a crazy fucker but I love you" – agh!! air-horns again! Tee .v. a 40-tonner on the roundabout, no doubt. I should mention that, these days I always plug the Sat-Nav in, so at maximum moments of terror I can pull down an eye-mask, when the going gets too tough for me. I have relinquished the post of honorary map-reader, as it required permanent nerves of steel and open eyes.

Clearly, we have survived and arrived or, another possibility, the Sat-Nav can't take any more and has flat-lined. There again, this could be the cliff at the end of the earth and we're about to hurtle off it…though I think even Tee would slow down for that. Unless she'd just re-watched 'Thelma and Louise,' of course.

Cautiously I open my eyes and peel up the sleeping mask. Ah, I was right. That bit of reversing was Tiggs going backwards into a tight spot of parking. For some unfathomable reason she can park this juggernaut quite brilliantly, first time, every time – decorously and with smooth precision. It's the complete opposite of her Mr Toad performance on the open road.

I look around and I still don't really get it. We're actually alive and the forces of law and order are nowhere in sight. Nevertheless the fact remains, if she's destined to go in an RTA, I better go with her, because I can no longer imagine life on my own. Equally, the thought of exiting this circus as a blood and bone speckled pretzel, is both sobering and nauseating to one of gentle disposition.

39

UNCOMMONLY CUMBERSOME FOOTWEAR

METALLURGICAL STUDIES says the sign, with a very large arrow. So we duly follow it, like little Robin Hoods, I think, as I swing hands with the Demon Princess, down the path.

"If you changed it to 'Like a Tiger in the Moon,' we could use it then," she said eagerly.

"But Sweet Pea, it's not 'Like a Tiger in the Moon,' it's 'Tiggs of the Moon,' totally, totally, different. Also, it's very private, one of my loving-tags for you; I don't want it cheapening to mean something commonplace like, like, like… – 'BEEP – SORRY – We have a MALFUNCTION. Major brain BURNOUT. Auxiliary back-up on-line, shortly. BEEP. Stay tuned for further bulletins – BEEP!" I finish in a mechanical voice.

"What does BEEP mean?" Tiggs asked anxiously.

"IT MEANS – WAIT, BEEP" I said robotically.

"Oh," she said, in a small voice. "Are you irreparably damaged?"

"REPAIRS UNDERWAY. BEEP."

We bundled ourselves through a door, courtesy of an all-seeing magic eye and confronted a counter boasting a humble bell push. Tiggs, still in possession of a brain, pushed it. Distantly, we heard ringing. Not everything electrical had short-circuited, it seemed. Just my brain.

We waited. I tried to concentrate on brain repairs – which is really difficult when it's your own brain you're trying to repair. Tiggs, inevitably, did something that involved bouncing up and down. She was trying to peer down the corridor behind the counter. She was also developing considerable lift-off. Vaguely, I wondered if that was an exploitable resource? My funds were low.

In the distance I heard the tread of a heavy pair of boots approaching. My brain, which was still popping fuses, nevertheless registered – 'uncommonly cumbersome footwear.'

Occupying the boots was an equally hefty human being. One that managed to combine unusual height, width, depth and solidity in a package that came with a free crocodile smile. The white coat he wore did not fit him. In fact, the buttons that had been called upon to perform their task of securing the garment, had legitimate right of protest. They could call on me as a witness.

"Good morning, ladies. You're calling about your nut, aren't you?"

"Yes," said Tiggs.

"Here it is," and he produced a small plastic, ziplock bag containing the nut I'd found in the gravel, outside Moss's place. I was uncomfortably aware that he kept a thumb the size of my ear pinning the baggy to his side of the bench.

"And?" I managed.

"Here's the problem," he said ponderously. "This nut doesn't exist. Or, as far as we know, this nut does not exist."

"But there it sits," said Tee gravely.

"There it sits indeed. But it shouldn't. Now, where did you say you found it?"

Before Tee could open her mouth, which means very quickly indeed, I said – "I-found-it-on-a-table-in-a-coffee-bar-in-Soho-it-was-sitting-on-that-shelf-that-some-establishments-have-running-across-the-window-y'know-where-you-can-perch-on-stools-and-pretend-to-be-comfortable." Then I ran out of breath, which was just as well, because I was about to confess all my dirty deeds and throw myself on the floor to beg for forgiveness.

"Ha, ha, yes," said the man.

"You look a bit old to be a student," said Tee, who doesn't care if she comes across as antagonistic.

"I'm a tutor," he grimaced.

"Sorry to take you away from your tutoring," I apologised.

"I assure you, your nut is the most interesting object to have turned up in this building for a very long time. It's well worth my time and energy.

"So," he continued, turning on a multi-kilowatt smile that scared me rigid, "can we keep it here for a while?"

"You've kind of had it for a while," said Tiggs.

"For a while longer, then?"

"It's your nut," said Tiggs, looking at me with an expression that suggested immediate death if I dared agree with anybody but her.

"Properly speaking," I said, "it belongs to whoever left it in that cafe. I merely acquired it, magpie-like."

"Theft by finding," said the man, giving me the full-crocodile.

"Is that so?" I quavered.

"Indeed it is."

"Don't be so melodramatic," said Tiggs. "It's a nut. And in any case, filing a civil charge would be the prerogative of whoever discarded it, along with his, or her, newspaper – which we also appropriated, being the utter villains we so obviously are."

"My little joke. Clumsy of me, I'm sure."

"Ha, ha," drawled Tiggs. "We'll have it back. The nut that is."

"Do we have to?" I whispered to her.

"It's pretty. I like it. Maybe it's lucky. I believe in luck."

"It could be unlucky..." said Triple XL. "You see, Miss, we really would like to study it some more. It doesn't respond to any of our tests. Also, this may interest you, it's uncannily perfect. I shouldn't really be telling you this but I can see you're both co-operative girls, it's too perfect. All mass production items, like nuts, have lots of tiny flaws, little air bubbles, nicks, snags. They wouldn't be able to hide under a microscope. This nut is a super-nut. It has no flaws. Not even under magnifying X-Ray chromatography. None," he finished flatly, ominously.

"Oh, keep it," I said.

"No. I want it," countered Tiggs.

I felt the floor begin a flexible space-time lurch. I was trying to stand on the rippling latex of space-time. Ugh, I was definitely going to be sick.

"I don't feel well," I said. "have you got a chair?"

"Oh dear," he said, in a voice bereft of all sympathy. "I'll get one." He left and the nut went with him.

"Tiggs," I hissed, "we need to get out of here. That's no tutor. That's Secret Service."

"No he's not. Maybe an allied department, probably investigating industrial espionage. Low-grade, nothing to worry about. I know a problem when I see one. This isn't."

"Lord have mercy," I cringed. "It's going to be bright lights, water-boarding and our fingernails on the floor!"

"I like a challenge," Tiggs replied equably.

"Beavers don't – they hate challenges."

"Are you man or mouse?"

"Squeak, squeak..." That was me but in the distance I could hear the boots returning. I think the building began to vibrate but that could have been space-time doing its thing.

Triple XL returned with his gallows smile and an office-chair that probably weighed half-a-ton. He hoisted it over the counter with the ease of a man accustomed to heaving body bags into the backs of army lorries.

"There you go, Miss," he said. "Glass of water?"

"That's all right," quavered the mouse, "very kind of you to offer. I've got water in the car but thank you for the chair."

"Not at all," he said, idly flexing his knuckles. Maybe one-handing the chair had strained a teensy ligament? The same movement could have detached my arm from my shoulder. 'Oh God! Maybe they do that, too – pull arms out of sockets! Not for a nut, surely?'

Tiggs and Muscles now began a sort of Mexican stand-off, either side of the counter. The nut had reappeared between them, innocent-looking in its plastic ziplock. It lay there like an unplaced gaming chip in a high-stakes roulette game. Despite my approaching delirium, I knew he stood no chance.

"Mine, I think," said Tiggs and faster than one of those snakes that flies through trees, swept her hand across the counter.

To my utter dismay, Muscles was faster. His huge, arm-dislocating-hand, descended on the baggy and finessed it from her fingertips.

"It would only be for a few more weeks…"

"You've already had it for two months. It's coming home with us, today. Trust me, I am taking it back."

"It's only a nut, Miss."

"I could say the same to you."

"Yes, you could."

'He conceded valuable ground there,' I thought distantly.

"You could say that," he emphasised, "but to certain people it's become a Nut of National Importance."

"That would make it an N.N.I." Tiggs riposted, obviously delighted to have discovered a new seam of sarcasm.

One of my nine lives scuttled out of the door, squealing. How many was I down to? Three, maybe four? Could be even less. A bad cold could probably finish me off.

"It would, wouldn't it, Miss," said Muscles stolidly.

"I like acronyms," she said cheerfully. "What's your favourite?"

"I never really gave it much thought, Miss."

"Oh, go on, humour me. A nut's life is at stake."

Another life made for the door. I hauled it back by its tail, while it squeaked in protest. 'Stick around,' I growled to it, 'you're needed on site!'

"I'll take that water," I said. "If you'd be so kind?"

"Feeling worse, Miss?" He almost managed to sound solicitous.

"No, no, much better, in fact. I just think water would be the very thing, now."

"Of course, Miss." The boots creaked away.

"Let's take the nut and run," I hissed.

"Don't be daft," said Tee. "We can't run, it's a buzz-lock door and I see no switch."

"Then let him have it. If you like it that much, I'll get the Rabbit to find you another one."

"Like it? I couldn't care less about it. I just don't want anyone laying their grubby paws on it, other than ourselves – let alone getting any hint of what's been going on."

"They're not going to, are they? It's inert metal. They can't slow-roast it over charcoal, or stick six inch pins in it? It can't confess. It's a nut. I'm a living, trembling coward, immensely susceptible to such persuasions."

"And to think, you were once a BDSM icon! How are the mighty…"

"…fallen," I finished for her. "Quite correct. Things, times and people change."

A steady 'creak, creak…' announced the arrival of my water. Tee handed it to me, with a wry smirk and returned to her game of poker.

"You'd be helping your country, Miss."

'Patriotism,' I thought, 'who said it was the last refuge of a scoundrel?' Not quite the same thing, I know but it'll do. I could also have told him that was a bad call.

"You're colour blind?"

"Only socially and politically, Miss."

"I am not so constrained. I hold a massive grudge against your ancestors, especially any who sailed with Clive to India. Categorically this is not my country, though there are aspects of it that are very dear to me. The Tower of London holds jewels that were stolen from my great, great, great, great, grandfather's treasury. Theft. Not theft by finding. Theft by breaking, entering and murdering."

"Rajah, was he, Miss?"

"Yes he was. Not quite up to Tipu Khan's high standards but close."

"Shame, that."

"From your point of view it's a serious impediment."

"Now about this nut. Where did you say you got it?"

"Oh come, come, come! Stretch your memory. See if you can remember by yourself."

Triple XL actually coloured-up. I'm far from certain that embarrassment was the cause.

"Then…which coffee bar?"

"Oh, officer! This is unworthy of your profession. A day-out in London…two friends stop for coffee…en route to the Royal Academy…via Soho. It could have been any one of a dozen. I do know it wouldn't have been a franchise. My partner objects to them."

"Uh?" I mumbled. It was the first I'd heard of it. But I tried to make it a corroborative sound.

"Principles, eh?" enquired Muscles.

"Occasionally," I said.

"Where do you stand on National Security, Miss, in comparison to your partner here?"

I searched for some blanket dismissal of cheap jingoism and could find none. I didn't have the courage to trot out the Samuel Johnson line, if that's who it was…I'm pretty sure it was. But I understand, he was misunderstood anyway… 'BEAVER! This is not the time, or place!' yelled the voice of self-preservation. 'It's still very interesting…' insisted the voice of eclecticism.

"I know," I said. "I've had an idea – why not bribe me? I'm incredibly mercenary. I'm also, currently, skint."

"Mercenary…I would never have thought that, Miss. You look quite the opposite."

"Check my eyes – fruit machine rolls."

"My, my," said Muscles, trying for moral anguish and failing badly. "What are things coming to..." he shook his head sorrowfully. After a while, he paused, as if the next comment was going to cause him personal distress, almost beyond his pain threshold.

"I have actually been authorised to offer you a handsome sum for that nut," he said finally.

"Well I never," said Tee " and universities in the parlous state they are, financially. But trot it out – with the proviso that I, myself, that's me, the cappuccino-coloured one, am wealthy enough to endow a new metallurgical unit at any university of my choice. So, as the saying goes, let us not dick about, start high."

This was unexpected and definitely caused Muscles discomfort. He could muster none of Whisker's unflappable electronic detachment. There was an air of confusion about him.

"Yes," said Tee, "I'm all ears."

"Well, ladies...I...the...department," he struggled with his lines, " have authorised me to go to £100."

"Oh my!" cried Tee. "Beavie, can I borrow your chair and water?"

"Of course, of course," and I sprang up like a jack-in-the-box, all vim and vigour.

"One hundred pounds!" I crowed, "that's almost a day's petrol!"

"Not really," said Tee gloomily. "That salesman was fibbing."

"Now who would have expected that?" I finished... mustering impressive ambiguity, I thought.

"How about it, Miss? One hundred pounds? Nearly half my take-home pay for a week!"

"My God, you're overpaid," said Tee.

"And there's another problem, too," I said brightly.

"What's that Miss?" he croaked, as his game plan disintegrated around him.

"This," I said and dropping my jeans and pants, to flash what Muti had so lewdly referred to as 'a stallion's cock.'

"It is funny but things are rarely what they seem," I smiled, "also, if you would be so kind, my nut, please."

Dejected, Muscles pushed the baggy across the counter.

I scooped it up. "Thank you for the chair and water, that was kind, at least. The rest was disappointing, if I'm obliged to be honest."

He said nothing but buzzed us out, his face filled with confusion. I remember thinking it wasn't quite the right emotion to be registering.

We were too full of ourselves, for a moment or two, to care and we walked with sprightly bounce, toward the car park.

We made it as far as the car but as the doors clunked shut, Tee simply disintegrated. She suddenly collapsed across the mid-way console, in such a way that I thought, for a terrible moment, she had been shot. "I'm so sorry," she was bawling, waterworks on full, saturating my jeans in seconds. "I'm sorry, sorry, sorry!"

"My God, Tiggs, what's wrong? What's got into you? What are you sorry about? I can't recall anything to be sorry about?"

But all I could get out of her was – "sorry, sorry, sorry" and more salt-water.

I patted her head and stroked her hair, letting her sob and utter "sorry" for a while.

"All right. You are definitely sorry. What about?"

Finally, between hiccups, she managed to blurt out – "our pet names. I wanted to do stupid things with them. I get so full of myself. I'm so sorry…" and we were off again.

"Forget it," I said. "You were just being Tiggerish. I'm not offended."

"You were," she insisted. "Your brain broke down. I was stupid and careless, full of my own shit, as usual. I want to stop being so hurtful. I'm always hurting you and I never mean to."

I stuck out the hiccups and the sluice gates a while longer.

Then I went for the firm voice. It's the only way, sometimes. "My brain didn't break down, Lupa. That was my little joke. I wasn't offended. A bit Tiggered, perhaps but I am used to Tigger enthusiasms by now. I can cope. What I can't cope with is all this water. I'm wringing wet. Get up Lupa-Tigg and let's calm you down."

That worked for a minute. Then she collapsed again. More hiccups, more sobs. I dried those up and then insisted – "when I say 'stop,' this stops, OK?"

Eventually, I got a nod, from somewhere around my middle regions. Then I gave her a whole minute. "Stop," I said, as gently as I could and slowly pushed her upright, back into her seat.

"Phew," she said eventually. "That was really venting, wasn't it?"

"It was, I agree."

"I am sorry though," she said sweetly.

"No need to apologise for Tiggerishness," I said. "In fact, to prove I'm not nursing a grievance, I'll buy you a petrol-head cola at the next services we spot."

"You will? Can I have some of those cheesy things that aren't cheese, as well?" she asked hopefully.

"Not even through prayer."

"Poo…"

40

BARELY JAMES BOND

The car following us was a black Honda Jazz. Apart from being black, I thought that was an excellent choice. Now, had it been red, the manufacturer's default colour, I'd probably not have noticed – though I confess that I was looking.

We weren't even on a motorway, so our stop at an obscure, so-called 'Services' made it a certainty. Black Honda in, Black Honda out. Not that a refuelled, revivified Tigger cared about spooks.

"How exciting," she said. "Do you think they're real spies, with guns, poison darts and ponds full of piranhas?"

"Not in the car. Piranhas need running water."

"How shall I lose them? Shall I drive like a maniac?"

I resisted the temptation, which was big of me.

"How about," I said, after a deal of pondering, "I get Carl to meet us in a lay-by. He can come on the big bike. It hasn't got plates on, because he's working on it but it can be on the road in half-an-hour. We hand the baggy over and he burns rubber out of there. We sit still, suck mints and see what happens. If they go after him, excellent. If they stick with us, not so good.

"But I guess we just drive home. They know where we live, anyway. If anyone questions us, we can say – 'you saw the man on the bike, actually it was a girl…"

"Carl's not a girl," objected Tee.

"I know, I know but after flashing my bits at Muscles I just thought throwing a chick in leathers into the mix would really mess with their heads.

"…the girl on the big bike has got it. She offered us £101. Then, when we get home, I'll hide it in the rubble. They'll never find it in a million years. No-Name's the perfect place to hide anything."

"It's certainly a dangerous place to play hide'n'seek," agreed Tee. "You could easily end up as the apocryphal skeleton."

That was the play we went with.

The gang in the black Honda held their nerve and followed us home. They parked up by the trucks but when I wandered over for a chat through the tinted glass, they drove off. Silly of them, really. They hadn't actually investigated anything.

We decided to eat in the caff, which we do 99 per cent of the time anyway.

Andy was hobbling gamely on crutches, getting in everybody's way.

"How did that go?" he greeted us.

Tee told him, in one enormously long sentence which ended – "then she flashed him her his-bits!"

"Never a dull moment with you two around. As a prize for being insanely provocative, in the face of Authority, I'll gift you a rather fine red from my cellar. It'll wash the steak pie down a treat."

"Oooh!" said Tee. "It's my lucky fluids day – on the way back Beaver bought me a high-octane cola and let me drink it!"

"Really? It wasn't just for looking at?"

"It might have been," Tee said cautiously, "but I never gave it a chance to say."

"You must have been incredibly well-behaved."

Tee shook her head. "Much more complicated than that but I never do detail. How are the crutches?"

"Murderous, exhausting but not half as murderous and exhausting as that sweet little physio who comes in. Today was one of her days and she really put me through it. I'd have had an easier ride through a wood-chipper. Every muscle has filed a complaint, in writing, in triplicate."

"Who with?" I asked.

"The Authorities, of course," said Andy.

"Ah! THE Authorities… Not sure if I'm Bearish or Bullish about them, at present."

"Do bears bullshit in the woods?" Tee pondered, half to herself. "Or is it only popes?"

"Princess Agnethuram!" I said in a stern voice, "do not go there! You are banned from Analogy country, Metaphor county and Aphorism city centre, until further announcements are forthcoming, following due consideration of your crimes by The Authorities.

"They weren't exactly crimes…" wheedled Tee, temporising.

"What are you two on about – or is it the cola speaking?" asked Andy.

"Crimes against the English language were committed earlier, resulting in lifetime bans and the recitation of solemn oaths renouncing the temptations of the Word Elves," I explained.

"Opacity piled on opaqueness," he said, shaking his head. " Why do I even like you, let alone love you both?"

"Because we are adorable!" said Tiggs, signing off with a very emphatic – "worrah!"

41

TIC-TOC

About 3.00 a.m I woke the gently-slumbering Princess with a violent dig in the ribs.

"Jabberwocky!" she howled. "What was that for?"

"You were snoring."

"I was not."

"You were."

"Well, I'm not now!"

"No, you're not – which gives you your first starter point. For your bonus, I need you to wind back to secondary truths."

"Secondary truths? What on earth are they?"

"You invented them, this morning, about 11.00 a.m."

"I did?"

"From scratch and now, I repeat, 'for your team's bonus point' you are going to wax eloquent about them."

"Oh my God," she groaned. "At least give me some hints! Helpful Beavers do that sort of thing."

"OK. Secondary truths are like the concentric circles on an archery target. They're not the bullseye, or the outer diameter ring, they're the ones with two sides, if you like, the ones between, the ones that complicate the certainties of unitary confinement and the plughole in its centre. They are the adverbs and adjectives of the universal language."

"Stop there," groaned Tee. "You have a way of mutilating simplicity in the pursuit of additional clarity that simply blows all my fuses."

"That was a bit hurtful – you asked me to help," I said huffily.

"You don't normally do what I ask you to."

I sulked and Tee ignored me, while she pondered.

"Oh yes, I remember them. They were the parasites within parasites, weren't they?"

I could afford to be gracious – "that was your '-ish' territory. Go on from there."

"If you have a very big thing, there's plenty of room within its parameters, its boundaries, its methodology even, for another self-contained system to exist. And that secondary system could be possessed of a totally different methodology, resulting in different outcomes, parameters and the like."

Tee paused and counted her fingertips, twice. Just checking, I suppose.

"As I recall, you were babbling about the cosmos?"

"Indeed I was."

"OK – billions of self-centred, self-obsessed systems are trying it on within the cosmos, only to find themselves snookered when the cosmos finally shuts down. That's the trouble with secondary truths, they're like lust – they don't last. Most of them burn out way short of the universal endgame. To be honest, I hadn't thought this through before but they're really, really, like lust. They have this heavy 'hey, hook-up with me' style but no answers for the long haul.

"I think we've both worked out in our own heads that this set-up we know of, via JJ and Whiskers, is luring participants with a promise of eternal life, which sounds like 'new lamps for old' in our ears but it never spells out what it wants in exchange, or what its endgame play might be, when push comes to shove."

"Maybe we're too thick to understand, or we don't have the right equipment to do so – maybe it doesn't even know itself," I suggested.

"That could well be the case. 'Sign up for the gen-uine, Bed-ouin-e, mystery tour – where even the driver is blindfolded, folks…'" she finished in a lazy Texan drawl.

Again, the double fingertip count and then – "it may know what it wants and it may even have a plan for getting it but wanting and planning are not the same as getting. The only certainty is the primary truth. Now Beavie, you had an idea about that."

"I did?"

"You did, yes. It went 'tic-toc, tic-toc…'"

"Thank you! That's exactly it. 'Tic-toc' is all there is. 'Tic-toc,' is the Primary Truth of this Universe. A particle squeezes through the veil of the quantum vacuum and it has to join up with another particle which floated through earlier, because they have opposing charges and they need each other to be complete. It doesn't happen in ones, of course…well, it does but in countless trillions of 'ones,' all happening simultaneously. And that process builds on itself, in the same fashion, becoming more and more complex with every move. Then, at the moment of maximum complexity, it all starts to unravel. But 'tic-toc' is all there ever is as base reality."

"The truth about our Universe," said Tee, "is that it's got its recall papers. It knows it's going to be rewound, unwound, or in some other way subsumed back into the nothingness that gave birth to it. We are lucky, we are living in the 'something' times. In billions of years, the 'something' times will be wisps and rags floating about, forming and un-forming, just like Boltzmann bodies. But Process is immaterial to us. We'll be so long gone by then, we won't even be history."

"Unless we're signed up with one of the secondary truth merchants, the snake oil salesmen," I said.

"Sure, but long before the end, we'll have understood we were sold a pup."

"What if we weren't?"

"Of course it's a dud. 'Tic-toc,' you said it yourself. Nothing can dodge that."

"It's just the game of 'Faith,' isn't it?" I said. "Faith says – 'if you invest in me, how can you lose?' Our intelligence, limited, circumscribed as it undoubtedly is, says – 'sorry, Faith, you've got no clothes.'"

We sat and pondered, or stared at the peeping star, which stared back.

Finally I mooted – "how do you fancy being a lonely particle looking for love?"

"Good idea," said Tee. "But first let me count my fingers again. I think I must have lost one somewhere."

42

GENERATION GAPPED

An indecent amount of time passed before we broached the 'Metallurgical Department' fiasco again. It was over a late breakfast that I re-opened the topic.

"Do we DO something, or just sit around waiting for something to happen, a little like we have been doing? I mean, what do you think will happen in the end?"

"I have absolutely no idea," said Tee. "From my very limited grasp of this decent-at-heart but utterly-corrupt country, governed as it is by third-rate straw men, my guess is that something mis-directed, underfunded and faintly disgraceful will occur."

"There's a lot of scope there," I said.

"You did ask and I thought it was a more helpful way of saying – 'I haven't a clue!' Sorry if it crashed on take-off."

"Not at all, top marks for trying. My problem is that my panicky bit is starting to panic."

"You have a Third Eye, to wit – the Eye of Shambala in the Age of the Maitreya," Tee said comfortably. "Large men in boots can't hurt you."

"In the thick of the Stalin era, party hard men were sent to Siberia to destroy the network of Shamanism that had existed there since the year cocoa."

"What's 'the year cocoa'?" interrupted Tee, suddenly showing an interest.

"I've no idea, my Third Eye just invented it. It says it's very sorry."

"It's just that it sounds late to me, rather than early, which I think it was meant to be."

"That's true enough. We're very late and we make the mistake of thinking that history began with us."

"We're derailing!" said Tee. "Finish the Shamans first, do the cocoa later."

"Quite right. So many things to discuss. So little time. These thugs, murderers, rooted out the Shamans within each village, took them up in planes, over the Taiga and threw them out, with parting words to the effect of – 'you say you can fly, now's the time to prove it.'"

"And did they?"

"Tigger! That is unworthy of you. Of course they didn't. They died, in terror. Many of them were good people who'd tried to help others."

"Sorry. You're quite right. I know they couldn't really fly. It was just that, like me believing I'm Tigger, you sometimes wonder if… hope, even…"

"Yes, I do see. Please don't go sad-Tigger on me."

"No, I won't. I just get strange around cruelty – especially state-sponsored cruelty. I don't want to believe that it can be true. Also, I hate seeing little people hurt. That day Andy was upset about the refugee lady? I knew I had to sort him out, first but later, I got in a terrible rage about it, myself.

"Why do we ever grow up? Aren't we better as children? No. Stop. I'll answer my own question…I knew some utterly beastly children when I was small."

"We've really drifted off-piste, have we not? Coming from me, I realise that's a bit thick…nevertheless, I detect…movement…"

"I blame these chipolatas," said Tee, spearing another one. "my mind's gone to CJD mush ever since I got involved with them. I used to be quite incisive. Cola, chipolatas, high altitude flight and to a lesser degree, crunchy junk snacks, have done for me."

"Flying?" I asked.

"You do recall the journey over?"

"I am unlikely ever to forget it."

"Permanent scarring of vital brain tissue."

"How do you know that?"

"I ran a virtual MRI scan on myself."

"How does that work?"

"It's really complicated. Are you sure you want to know?"

"Yes. No. Not now. Look, should we keep a diary, a notebook-thingy of serious points to be discussed later?"

"It sounds like an idea," said Tiggs, gloomily. "But consider, there'd be the whole matter of precedence…which idea would come first?"

"Time and date based…first come, first served, etc?"

"Hopeless. Some ideas are major, save the world stuff. Others are 'v. interesting.' Then there are the ones that you keep pressing the 'not now' option on. Also, they're intensely contextual. I mean, I'm already dubious about the importance of 'the year cocoa.' I know your Third Eye said it, or maybe you just slipped it in. But the context, beyond an association with Shamans, has already drifted away. It's worse than cheap make-up – my mind, that is."

"Nuts," I said firmly, "or to be precise 'The Nut.' To do. What?"

"Ah yes, I remember."

A long silence followed.

"We could flee," she said, romantically.

"On horseback, I suppose?"

"Can't we take the car?"

"You can't 'flee-romantically' in a car."

"You can't?"

"Obviously not. Fleeing is very 18th century, early 19th at a pinch. We could ask Punch, he'd probably know the rules about fleeing."

"I will," said Tee, "because he's there, talking to Andy. "Come on, we'll get something sorted for once!" She grabbed my hand, speared the last lethal chipolata and away we went.

It could be brain-damage I thought, as I trailed after her, reprising my role as a tow-along duck. I don't think anyone researched CJD in pigs and along with cheap chickens, they are absolutely the worst sort of meat to eat. Also, sausages, chipolatas, are absolutely the worst bits of the pig, even if they are exceedingly tasty. 'Here endeth the lesson!' I thought grumpily and sat down with a bump.

"What's up, son?" asked Punch.

"Chipolatas and agents of state repression are threatening to ruin my life. Also the Princess wants to know if we can 'flee' in a car. Technically, that is. In short, is fleeing, the act of romantic flight, commensurate with any form of transport other than the horse?"

"Whoa!" said Tee, "that is definitely leading the witness."

"It certainly is," said Andy. "As self-appointed Judge of No-Name Roundabout, I rule that statement inadmissible. Rephrase the question, Counsellor."

"We're not in America," I said crossly.

"I am," Andy replied. "I get all my information from Judge Judy and re-runs of Perry Mason."

"As a' en t' way?" asked Punch.

"Not at all. You are the expert witness. You hold a privileged position. You are almost an arm of the court," Andy said.

"A ne'er 'eld wi' t' Squire an' 'is trumpery courts," said Punch thoughtfully. "They'd allus ended up a 'angin o' some poor starvation rascal, who'd bin a' poachin' fer t' feed 'is lil' fambly."

You could have heard a pin drop.

"Shit," I said eventually. "That's blown my crap out of the water. I withdraw, unreservedly. We'll take the car, Tiggs. Consider the matter settled."

"I feel for your predicament," she said. "Just to show there are no hard feelings, if there are any horses around when the time comes, I'll let you choose."

"More graceful than I deserve," I said. "I feel quite ill, as a matter of fact. Historical verisimilitude and impending doom have an effect on my solar plexus."

"Nervous tummy," Tee explained helpfully. "He has to poo at moments of crisis."

"A' sees now why tha's a taste fer dresses," Punch said gravely. "But tha' cud 'ave them pants wi' a trapdoor in t' seat."

"What's happened to my court?" asked Judge Andy.

"It's been disrupted – by history," said Tee.

"Tis awk'ard," continued Punch, mercilessly, methodically, "wh'n thart caught short b'crisis. 'Tis quite common, though. Tha'll find shit a'plenty on a battlefield an' many a young lad falls t' pissin' o' theer pants when 'e sees men a' fallin' alongside o' 'imself, like. 'Tis on'y t'be expected."

"Pa," I pleaded, "could you go easy on reality for a bit? I'm not sure I'm built for it. I know I can cope when it's happening, because I have. But thinking about it, hearing about, does something odd to my insides."

"Most certainly, son. Ye 'ave a word wi' yon sister o'thine. She knows a thing or two 'bout reality an' 'ow t' turn t' page on it, as she puts it. A doesna' quite folla, bein' an un'ner-eddicated fella but she 'as a ways o' explainin's."

"Zero authority in my own court, that's what gets me," Andy complained.

"Actually," enthused Tee, "how do you fancy being a Judge in Chambers, with the expert witness, for we have a problem that needs serious advice?"

"Oh Lord," I croaked, "if the Tigger thinks that it's serious, I'm definitely having to go to the loo. I was counting on your bounce," I ended accusingly.

"Fear not," said Tiggs, "for I am filled with bounce. It's just grave bounce, with solemn demeanour, rather than mere frivolous destruction of thistles."

"Be she ol' reet in t' head, Andrew?" whispered Punch. "A be verra fond o' t' lil' purty Princess an' a'd tek agin 'er bein' 'eaded fer t' Bedlam."

"She's OK, Pa," I soothed. "Sometimes she talks in tongues. I think it's all to do with being a Hindu."

"Wheel, a remembers all thet," agreed Punch thoughtfully. "Them weer most excitabl' folk, ba'k th'in, an' weer't verra de'ils fer a'burnin' o' lil' girl widders on theer 'owd dead 'usbands funeral pyres. Suttee it wer' called. Many a' times a' we bin rousted o'ot o't' barracks t'shut down sich goin's on. An' yet, a wus towd by oor sweeper fella 'as we wus a wastin' our time, fer 'er own fambly worra strangle't 'er later on, 'fer t' shame o' it. Ugly business, awl roond."

Punch's eyes then took on that look of having seen, if not too much, then at least more than required. But he was far from finished. Staring into the middle distance, he began to whisper, almost to himself.

"'Tis mighty odd, 'ow great cruelty an' great wisdom can exist in t' same body 'n' brain. 'Tis true o' savage men an' true o' so-called civilised. In t' savage tho' it do show more clear, like. A've 'eard near nekkid men, speakin' t'words o' a King 'n' Priest. Then, troubled too far by dispute, o' legal lang'age, they 'as tekken t' t' path of war and nor a babe, a woman, a man, nor a dog 'as they left alive, an' in t' killin' o' 'em, they 'as waxed most cruel, a' pleasurin' in t' slow dyin' o' t' defenc'less. An' yet, t' day afore, they weer true men o'reason. T'moral, as a' sees it, is ne'er push a man tae far."

Punch took from his waistcoat pocket the stub of clay pipe he'd found under the Hedge and pursed his lips about the broken stem, while pretending to tamp down tobacco with his thumb.

"You know," said Tee, "I think what we have here is nothing more than the generation gap, demonstrating that it can be a major problem, parked as it is, firmly in space-time."

"True enough but who knows what might emerge from left-field? Let's not knock it until we've tried it, at least."

"I wasn't precisely knocking," muttered Tee. "That was more the sound of me running for the 21st century."

I began my explanation of our problem but Punch had turned from brown study and pipe-sucking to sleep. He had not lost the soldier's art of sleeping anywhere, any time.

Nevertheless, undaunted, I went into a gallop, so-to-speak.

"What happened was, we gave to a nice fat boy, with greasy hair and an awful lot of pimples, who was very enthusiastic and thought his department would 'crack this nut pretty quickly.' I think that's why I liked him, on reflection," I babbled on, "because he got tripped up by his own daft pun. He certainly wasn't comely but he went such a deep beetroot red when he realised what he'd said and I do that all the time, don't I, make unconscious daft puns? I'm sure it's misplaced niceness, over-eager sympatico, y'know laying alongside…no, you don't agree?" I finished with a rush… and imitated my own variety of beet.

"You're straying," said Tee, patience personified. "You are definitely the culprit when it comes to conversational waywardness, vis-a-vis subject matter." She leaned back contentedly and crossed her arms.

"Gah! Hang me now!" I said crossly.

"I was merely saying…" said Tee, the very model of restraint.

"Ahem," said Andy. "Fat boy, not comely, gave him what, where, how, why and when?"

"I didn't say?"

"Correct."

"I must have done," I said craftily, "otherwise you wouldn't have understood about the pun!" That'd show them – a subtle but devastating masterstroke.

"Precisely. We didn't understand."

"You, alone," said Tee. "I think Punch retired."

"A's all ears," said Punch, eyes firmly shut, "but 'tis mortal borin' so far."

"Agh!" I howled. "Why does no-one ever follow me? Well, in a nutshell… No, dammit! Now I'm infected!"

"Gerr'on wi' it, son," groaned Punch.

"To fat youth at (I named the famous university) we gave a nut, as in nut and bolt, found, by me, in gravel, at Moss's place. If it turned out to be a common or garden nut, maybe we were all hallucinating. If it was exotic, perhaps we weren't. I hope that, in common with everyone else, we were entertaining doubts about what had really happened?

"Anyway, when we went back, months later and probably months ago now, no pimply, punning youth. No. We got a military type built like the proverbial brick shithouse, practicing his dramatic grasp of menace. Off and on, he was quite good."

"Beaver developed a tummy upset again," Tee explained.

"Don't be unkind. Those were tummy problems of a diversionary nature, not real ones brought on by historical imbalances in time and space. And who's straying from the subject now?"

"Just like an old married couple," said Andy serenely. "Speaking of which, why did you involve my other half, Carl?"

"Wasn't precisely 'involve.' He was chaff, you know, that stuff planes used to scatter to foul up radar. Huge bike, no plates. Lone biker, mirror visor, no face. Zoom!"

"Traffic cams, easy to trace."

"Un-huh," contributed Carl, who'd silently drifted to the table. "I know all about traffic cams. Country roads to a mate's barn. Came back on his moped, just in time for night shift. Picture of innocence. My mate helps out here, occasionally. Seasonal rushes and the like."

"Remind me," Andy asked drily, "how many covers, last night, as in night shift?"

"Twenty-three, yes, I know, I take your point – but we can't help it if the coach didn't show that night."

"Sorry to care, Carl but you're a bit special to me – and so are these two wanton maniacs but on the scales of devotion, loveable though they may be…"

"This is all very OTT," I said. "As the holder of the Mr and Mrs Paranoia Award for the last God-knows how many years, even I declare – one black Honda? Speaks of underfunding to me."

"True enough," Andy agreed "but now they know where you live."

"That's for certain," I said, "Portly-Pimples was so sweet I gave him our address yonks ago."

Everyone went 'Agh!' as if they were somehow sharper than I was. I always find that hurtful, perhaps because I suspect it's true – and I so don't want it to be. It's not that I want to be sharper, though it wouldn't hurt. 'As-sharp-as,' would do.

"Look," I said, "imagine push comes to shove, hear out my monologue of justification and see if it wouldn't wring a tear from the stoniest heart?

"Here we are, two gentle little girls…" everyone went 'Ha!' simultaneously "…two gentle little girls, geddit! Girls trying to make a bob or two in a competitive world, where everyone is on the make. Just because some engineering nerd leaves his company's revolutionary metalware beside an empty coffee cup, in Soho and we happen to pick it up, doesn't make us villains. Nor does thinking it looks awfully special and trying to find out about it. Gosh, Officer, we even gave our names and address!" Saying which I gave everyone a superior toss of my locks but they just looked mystified. (I'm sure I'm sharper…) "We turn up to collect our nut from PP…"

"What's PP?" demanded Carl.

"Who! Who!" I raged, "Portly-Pimple! Does anybody listen to me?"

"I wasn't here for that bit," retorted Carl, now mortally offended.

"No more you were. Awfully sorry. You may kill me later. By the way, the queue for that starts over there!

"TO CONTINUE – when we turned up to collect our nut from PP, we were met by a very intimidating gentleman who scared us by talking about National Security…"

"Didn't scare me," said Tigger.

"Shut up!" I screeched. "Let me finish! What I'm laying out here is all persiflage, potentially for 'use-in-the-future,' don't you see?

"…then we were offered a derisory sum of money for something which obviously was special. So, when we left, because we'd been treated to such a performance, we sold to the highest bidder, who happened to be someone we knew – but we're not saying who. So there."

"Probably all blow over, anyway," said Andy. "Like you said, it was just a nut."

Punch sniffed, eyes still closed. He took 'old clay' from his mouth.

"The'll be back," he said. "certain matters 'as a flavour to 'em. A whiff o' summat rotten, like. This 'ere affair 'as just thet savour. A'll be watchin' out fer thee, lad – but thee stay sharp an' ready. Reckon on worr' a' just said – the'll be back, mek sure tha' sees 'em furst, is all."

With which reassuring words he heaved himself from his chair, ready to take his leave. But I was swifter by far in leaving mine, though I was headed in the direction of the loo.

"Thet boy, 'e do worrit 'iself so…" I heard, floating faintly after me.

That night, while Tee slept like a hibernating bear, rolled up in all the available blankets and duvets, I crept out to the lorry park and slid between two-closely parked artics. "Eeeny, or meeny?" I muttered and deciding on 'eeny,' crept under one of the trailers. Eventually I found a rusted hole in the angle of a box-girder frame. Into that I pushed the nut and above the cooling tics and tocs of the big engine, I heard it fall. With my eyes firmly focused on the floor, for I wanted no subliminal memories of registration numbers, colours, or companies, I sped my way back to bed.

43

PAPERS AND PITCH

Perhaps it was a week, maybe 10 days later that we were reading, late one afternoon, in the trailer. The door registered a polite knock.

"Who on earth could that be?" asked Tee.

"Nobody we know," I said. "They either come through the door as if propelled, or hammer on it until it falls down."

"Don't forget the Alice approach," added Tee, "a very soft tappity-scratch, sometimes followed by a small voice."

"This could be our come-uppance," I suggested. "Is it MI 1,2,3,4,5,6 or 7? Police, Army, Air Force, Navy, maybe St. John's Ambulance Brigade – they'd be very polite. Either way…I think the loo just called me…bye…"

"Do I open it?" asked Tigger.

"Depends how bold you're feeling."

From the loo I heard the door open, presumably only a crack, because Tee said – "yes?"

"It's me," said Carl's voice.

"Whathehell, Carl?" said Tee, "we thought you were the fingernail-pullers, or the Old Bill."

Mentally relieved meant physically reprieved. I decided to pull my pants back up.

"Why?" I heard Carl ask.

"Because," explained Tigger, "you normally come through the door like a torpedo at 5.00 a.m. talking in tongues and risking terrible curses, until the Beaver explains what you are up to and saves you."

"That was only the once," protested Carl. "That's my usual door knock."

"It's not been registered with us," Tiggs said firmly. "Thus you have caused the Beaver to spontaneously melt-down, not to mention reducing my supposedly immortal life by several centuries, I'm certain. But I shall forgive you, for I am large of heart. I can't speak for Evie. It all depends if she made it in time."

"Forgiven," I panted, rejoining them. "Near run thing, though."

"Blimey," said Carl, "any chance I could deliver my message?"

"What's stopping you?" asked Tiggs, round-eyed.

"Oof! Give me patience and may mercy fill my heart!" he groaned. "It's very simple. Would you care to join Andy and I for an evening meal?"

"Certainly," said Tiggs. When?"

"Today"

"Time?"

"Now-ish?"

"Dress code?"

"Come as you are. Indeed, if you're ready, pray follow your leader."

"Ladies are never ready," I said haughtily. "We shall follow. You may depart."

"Suit yourselves," said Carl cheerily.

"I was ready," said Tee, registering surprise.

"What are we both wearing?" I demanded.

"PJ's" said Tee. "Doesn't mean I wasn't ready."

"Not clean PJs, are they, though? Neither is it a PJ party. We should change into our best ballgowns."

"I swear Beaver, you're getting worse…"

"I know, I know…I haven't any balls, so I can't have a gown!"

"You know it has to said, Beaver! It's obligatory. Otherwise, who will remember the old lines? There is such a thing as historical responsibility."

Eventually, we were wandering down the familiar path, ballgown-less, PJ-less but clad.

My problem is that I can never walk this way, latterly, without feeling certain there is a sniper's rifle, trained on the mouse that operates my brain's treadmill. The moment X authorises Y, the marksman will be told that the time has come. As we live in a world of equal job opportunities, his or her finger will squeeze the trigger and a low-weight, high-velocity bullet will penetrate my skull, knocking the mouse off its wheel. Then, just for good measure, that pirouetting bullet will turn both mouse, treadmill and any other contents of my skull to slurry.

Tee tells me this is purest paranoia and that it must be catching, because she feels exactly the same. Consequently we try to turn ourselves out nicely, just in case – clean undies, a hint of make-up. Washed jeans and sweats, basically.

Caff is busy tonight, tables a'bustle. We go up the STAFF ONLY stairs, cross the wide landing and bow through the lowish arch into the general purpose meeting and dining room. Very exclusive and quite fun, because you can catch the vibe of the diner without being surrounded and distracted on all sides.

Andy is ensconced behind a mighty sirloin and the table is freighted with fine-looking veg, fresh, I am guessing, from Punch and Marie-Claire's allotment.

Telepathy informs me that we think this looks good, if a touch foreboding.

"Oh my," I say, "what a spread. Not, I pray, by any chance a last meal for the condemned?"

"Do sit down, guys," says Andy genially. "We have Punch's famous gravy and his and Marie-Claire's vegetables. My humble cellar has contributed interesting, bottled items. The aim is to stick your ribs together, sooth your anxieties and afford us an affable space in which to discuss a topic of mutual interest."

"Which is?" demands Tee in her surgeon's voice. The one that can yell – 'Scalpel!'- and have you jump to attention and freeze on the spot simultaneously.

"Basically, we find ourselves, that would be me and my beloved partner here, in the same pile of direst doggie-doo that you seem to have landed in. But we arrived via a different route and one that seems to have the potential for even worse fallout. Does that cover it, Carl?"

"That'll certainly do," agreed Carl. "I enjoy reading words but the ones I venture to speak stick in my throat, somewhat. As Andy says, we have a situation, so we thought we'd chat that over with friends who have a similar debacle on their hands."

"For someone claiming verbal handicap, Carl, that last offering was crystal," said Tee. "I'm guessing you guys have done something rash and now you want to see if your dunghill smells like ours?"

"Now we all know what we're talking about," said Andy, "how about some food?"

"Hang on," I bleated, "I know Beavers are dull of brain and wary of excitement but these metaphorical ellipses are whirling this one round by its little, flat, fat tail. Please tell the Evie-Beavie what's going on, in little people language and I don't mind if you use your fingers."

"We screwed up, Evie," said Andy. "Carl had some thoughts about the Roman remains. It was to do with the roof. He spotted what looked like unusual material up there. In my role as Blofeld…"

"You've always fancied that part, haven't you?" I interrupted eagerly.

"You're right but having been appointed, I'm now resigning. Shush, while I explain why. As Blofeld, I sent Carl down the hole with an angle grinder and diamond cutting discs. He managed to find an overhanging extrusion and went to work on it."

"It took four blade changes before I could persuade a very small piece to let go…" Carl interrupted, shaking his head in wonder.

"We took it to one of the big museums," Andy continued – showing far more patience with Carl than Tiggs ever shows me! – "largely I think, because I was reprising my days spent reading 'Famous Five' mysteries. The Five were forever, I recalled, being congratulated by affable custodians, who rewarded them for their pluck and sincerity in finding the lost whatever-it-was."

"If it makes you feel any better," I said, "I entertain exactly the same fantasies of being congratulated by avuncular figures."

"Good. We can be disillusioned together.

"Like you with your PP, we had a decent enough reception. But that was the end of it. Quite some time later I contacted them and after a great deal of – 'please hold the line for a moment...' – was transferred to someone, somewhere, who stonewalled me. However, I had a name and I can be very insistent. Eventually 'the name' rang me back and in a patently rehearsed speech, which he was obviously mortified to be reciting, confessed that our specimen had been 'lost.'

"I protested vehemently, whereupon I was 'transferred' and ended up speaking with some Fat Controller – probably in an office in Whitehall. This guy told me the same pack of lies but was quite unperturbed by them. He also managed to be vaguely threatening, asking why on earth my interest in such 'a commonplace material' was so intense?

"Childhood faith in tatters, I was eventually obliged to manifest sullen silence. Now we await, on a daily basis, the arrival of dead-eyed men in matching suits.

"However, I also owe you an apology. All this time that you've been feeling bad about the nut, I knew I'd dropped us just as deeply in the shit with a square inch of 'rock.' Nor did I own up, the day you came over to chat to Punch and I. In fact, I think I acted in a rather superior manner. All of it was unforgivable but I hope you'll both find a way..."

He sat back, wearing the wry smile of a man considerably diminished in his own eyes and Carl took his hand and held on to it.

"Oh Lord, Andy," I said, "I've made so many bad, questionable, clumsy decisions in my life, I'll never hold anyone to account for admitting to theirs. I'd guess that I speak for the orange and black stripey one, too."

"Worrah!" said Tiggs, getting into character.

"That is very gracious of you both," said Andy. "Now, one mild, last surprise – it's time for the not-so mystery guests, our very own JJ and Marie-Gabrielle, aka Alice, for short!"

"Tah-dah!" said Alice, appearing as if by magic, with JJ happy to bring up the rear.

"You were waiting for your cue!" I exclaimed.

"I most certainly was. I am an outstanding actress."

"As well as a very nice Alice," said JJ. "I'm working towards my first Merit Badge" he hissed in booming sotto voce. "So far, it's going well."

"Don't count your chickens, Alien Boy," growled Tiggs. "That Marie-Gabrielle character is a hard nut to crack, while Alice is downright tricksy.

"Anyway," and she turned her attention to Andy, "what gives, 'now-we-are-six'? Why am I breaking my caste, yet again, by dining with you pariahs, let alone piling up torments in Hindu Hell for imminently partaking of the noble Sir Loin?"

"We are conscious of your condescension and much-honoured by it," said Andy, expertly carving meat – while everyone watching silently applauded the fact that he could now do so, again. "Firstly, there was that humble apology to deliver to you both. But 'now-we-are-six' as you put it, I thought we needed a council-of-war to decide what the hell we do next."

"If it's war, don't we need Pa?" I asked.

"You may recall the last time we consulted him, Evie?" asked Andy mildly. "Within five minutes we'd heard his recollections of the squire hanging poachers, boy soldiers crapping their pants and young widows going up in flames, back in the days of the British Raj. Punch wouldn't see the problem. He'd just cut their throats, one by one and throw the bodies in the most convenient hole. If that filled up, he'd move on to the next."

"Whose throats, Andy?" asked JJ, with a most peculiar expression on his face. Only I noticed but he winked at me, as if to say – 'wait.'

"Agents of the State Most Secret," intoned the boss.

"Why is it deemed necessary to remove them so dramatically?"

"We feel, the four of us that is, that they are about to become a royal pain in the backside. But to backtrack, I was maintaining that Papa Punch's solution might be seen as a little too abrasive, for the 21st century."

"It's his tendency to get to the heart of a problem," I said.

"Quickly and usually with minimum discussion," added Alice. "Don't forget I've seen him in action – twice. I'd definitely keep him in reserve, in case things get out-of-hand."

"Whoa, Love of My Long Life," said JJ, "have things even got going, yet…let alone out-of-hand?"

Nope," agreed Andy. "This is a council of paranoia, not war – so shall we eat and drink, first?"

"Are Mama and Papa not joining us to eat, at least?" asked Alice.

"They are at the theatre," explained Andy. "They've gone with Carl's Gran and Grandad to see 'Les Misérables." He looked at his watch. ""They've just had their slap-up meal and after the show they'll be going back to their Five Star suites. The limo service brings them back here, tomorrow, then they're off for a week on the Cotswolds, with Carl's folk. They all get on rather well. Punch wants to show Grandad Jack, Brown Bess, so that's why they're detouring back here, first.

"I know that was very presumptuous of me but I worry about Marie-Claire's nerves. I don't want her around 'atmosphere' or 'trouble.' She's been through quite enough. Was that OK, Marie?"

Alice leapt up, ran lightly round the room and gave Andy a stonking kiss on the cheek. "Thank you," she said, "that was nothing but kind and thoughtful. She's a lot stronger than she was. She's started scolding me again and that's such a good sign." She sighed, "I don't suppose she'll ever really heal and I know who's to blame for that."

Then she tiptoed back to her chair, wearing a wan little smile, to sit down quietly by JJ. He leaned over, pulled her to him and whispered in her ear. Words to which she nodded her head, eventually.

Finally, we fell to our meal and for all that the Princess's immortal soul and caste were doomed, she dined royally on all that was on offer. Baby leeks and sprouts in a cider reduction, potatoes three ways, Savoy cabbage with Stilton and walnuts – the latter a dish in itself in my book – and a mess of shallots, cooked to a slow, caramelised ruin, so utterly delicious they might have served as a pudding course. I don't imagine the beef was as powerful as Pa's winter-hung auroch but it had been hung for 12 weeks. As a result it still packed a punch…(befuddle it! There I go again, inadvertent puns!)

After the last items of cutlery fell to the board, we all voted to place dessert on hold until later, much later. Thus, reluctantly, we had arrived at the business of the day, as witnessed by the blowing out of cheeks and the wry wrinkling of lips.

Surprisingly, it was JJ who launched the boat. "I'd rather like," he grinned knowingly, "to possibly…what might be the phrase, Ally?" She hissed back at him – "short circuit…" JJ grinned at us – "…yes, short circuit some of the proceedings by means of a brief update, if you'd allow me, Andy?"

"Fire away," said Andy. "If you've got a sword that can cut our Gordian Knot, be our guest and get stuck in!"

"OK," said JJ. Then he paused, smiled and said – "no, you tell them, Ally."

"Why me?" she looked dumbstruck.

"Go on. You deserve a treat, tell them!"

Alice turned to the table. She was still a little sad about the eyes, following her confessional about Marie-Claire but she managed a smile.

"I don't suppose you know," she said in a small but strong voice, "that we are no longer hosting a magnificent Romano-British settlement beneath our feet? Sadly, all we have are strata upon strata of crushed and broken concrete, packed with an in-filling of decayed organic matter and a scattering of biros, drinks cans, ring pulls and broken bottles. The odd half-crown, sixpence, penny and farthing might also be found but beneath them lies, largely, a thick layer of London clay. No-Name Roundabout can once again rejoice in having absolutely nothing to single it out – other than this excellent caff and its deeply-eccentric, interdependent family.

"To be fair, it still possesses the quite uninteresting Regional Seat of Government. That could barely be done away with, as it is there legitimately – though I suppose it might have been whimsical to magic it out of existence. If you want to know where the entrance is, JJ can tell you. I think, though, we should wait till next summer and then have a hunt the RSG game. We could have a prize for the winner and strawberries, cream and cake for everybody. We'd need a sunny day, though…but they're not unheard of.

"Anyway, apropos of Family," she said with a knowing grin, as JJ hoisted a carpet bag onto the table, "we have gifts to bestow on all and sundry…as you are about to see."

From the bag she produced official looking envelopes.

"Here," she began, "we have an envelope for Punch and Marie-Claire, which I shall be explaining to them, when they get back." She looked at JJ… "I may be gone some little time with that one…" she intoned. "I ask you…Mr and Mrs Percy Mathew…do you think I can sell that to them?"

We all stared at her. "Here are envelopes for me and for JJ, a small one for Evie and a small one for Tee." She giggled. "Isn't this just the height of mean? Lovely people invite you to dine regally and you serve up party bags for everyone, except your hosts!

"The reason and you're probably cottoning on by now, is that inside these envelopes are identities, solidly endorsed by the United Kingdom's National Insurance system, the National Health Service, the Passport Office and the National Registry of Births Marriages and Deaths. The sort of 'paper' most people have, stuffed at the back of a drawer. These are not forgeries. They are authentic legends and what they record are facts that lie within musty archives. Do you get it guys? The four aliens are now bona fide citizens. We exist, we can be backtracked, we have rock-solid, verifiable history. You lovely people are no longer harbouring illegal immigrants! We can't be used to bring you down. Of course, Andy, Carl, you already possess this stuff – hence our shameful lack of gifts.

"Tee and Evie also have some valid documents but additionally, they now have dual citizenships, for India and the UK. Neither of you can be deported, extorted, or exported without your consent. I know you don't know where your documents are Evie but you've applied for duplicates and they will be flopping through the letter-box any day soon. Tee, your brilliant forgeries are being replaced by valid issues."

There was a huge silence. I'm tempted to dilate on its qualities. It had something of a dozen Babbage Difference Engines running full-pelt, silently and the moment when the Athenians heard that the Spartans were actually coming. A combination of astonished disbelief, coupled with admiration for the sheer effrontery of the exercise and the largest of unanswerable question marks – HOW?

"Well, well," ventured Andy, eventually, "it would appear that we've been ring-fenced. Forgiven? I have to wonder about that. Clearly not forgotten though and certainly reprieved, because heading our way might be the bulldozer blade of the State. That would have turned us over for sure…" and he drifted off into some sort of reverie.

I put my hand up. Someone said – "yes, Evie?"

"I quite enjoy being slow on the uptake," I said. "People then explain things to me, in words of one syllable. That's good. It gives me time to brew fiendish strategies – like fainting, or crapping my pants."

"Or both," interjected Tiggs, helpfully, "it has occurred even at very ordinary moments. But, 'thank-you, someone' for my dual citizenship. I had the feeling that was the weak point in my defences. As for yours, Beavie, we can now go over and demand your back wages from Muti!"

"Are you trying to bring a demonstration of my nervous disposition to the dinner table, Teazle?" I asked. "Because bringing up my chequered past is definitely one way to proceed. Once upon a time I was a very belligerent Beaver, with a brash, bold nature. Then I found love and developed IBS – makes you ponder, doesn't it?"

"Are we sliding off the track here?" asked Andy.

"It's the Beaver," said Tee flatly. "It has been proven, under laboratory controlled conditions, that he can change the subject matter of any discourse in seconds. He is, actually, a genius. If the Devil had dropped him into God's seven days of creation, the old boy would still be stuck on fishes and the waters of the earth."

"Vile calumny," I mumbled, "mere vulgar slander. I have a fascination with detail and an uncontrollable desire to examine it more closely. That's what I was planning, minutes ago, before the rude remarks. I was going to launch the second courageous Beaver examination of our Roman villa but you tell me I'm too late?"

"All gone," said JJ, "we are back to being a roundabout on the edge of the civilised world, with nothing but the caff to commend it to nosey-parkers."

"Which will raise the question, eventually," said Andy, "of where did I get that sample of stuff from. Because 'They' know I had it, 'They' know I gave it to them and another tranche of 'Theys' have it in a secure laboratory, somewhere."

"And the nut, Evie?" asks JJ.

"It's happily roaming about between here and Eastern Europe, for the remainder of a certain trailer's life-time."

"Fair and far enough," grinned JJ.

"The very fact that the villa complex has gone, without any of us even noticing, perhaps explains everything you might have been wondering about capabilities of the Intelligence we are enmeshed with. It also tells us that 'these-powers-that-be' place some value on our group, our roundabout, our odd little family. We've been inquisitive, all human beings are. The Intelligence is not unaware of that. We have not engendered any animus, maybe the equivalent of the wry grin you might give when your three-year-old knocks over the house-of-cards you just spent an age building.

"The analogy is not inappropriate. I was reliably informed, via Rabbit-tech…" Tee made a horrible noise and buried her head under her flailing arms "…that the villa was constructed for our pleasure and that there would have been more wonders. Not now, alas. Nevertheless, no black mark for us. We gave them a lot of work, clearing up but nothing a quantum computer the size of a large sun, or two, can't handle on its tea-break. If you're interested, it engendered nano-tech molecules on site and had them convert Roman-to-rubbish, just as, earlier, it had programmed them to convert rubbish-to-Roman. Awesome, isn't it?"

Chagrined silence told 'the-powers-that-be' all that they needed to know about lessons learned…assuming they were even bothering to listen.

JJ, who seemed to have taken control, continued affably – "I suggest you guys come up with mutually compatible, consistent stories. Something plausible is the issue. The truth won't do at all. Certainly they're not going to believe that we all went for a jolly jaunt off-planet and that Evie found a nut in a valley of angels."

Alice winced. Vaguely, I wondered why.

"Also, Andy, I doubt telling them that Carl retrieved some strange roofing material from a Roman villa in your back garden, will convince them of your soundness.

"They will believe only what they are capable of believing. They will believe you have contacts who supplied these materials. They will believe you are both in league, because the coincidence of your both being based here is too unlikely, otherwise. They will want your contacts. I think we can, hopefully, rely on Sun-Cloud – are we calling our Intelligence that? – to come up with something innovative in that department." JJ paused for a moment. "It does bother me, slightly," he went on, in a more doubtful tone, "that they've not mooted anything so far. It certainly can't be that they're baffled. I do hope it's not their idea of an examination."

"I hate exams!" I howled. "I never passed one. They always made me feel fat and stupid. If this is one, it's already making me feel obese and sub-normal. 'Boo, bloody, hoo,' let's hear some sympathy for persecuted Beavers!"

"Here's a bit of a cheat-sheet then," said JJ. "Drop the Soho line and join up with Andy for a mutually-agreed confession. Something on the lines of 'we've been played, we realise now. These things were left on a table one morning and they were so unusual we thought we'd get them looked at – half from genuine inquisitiveness, half with greedy thoughts. So we put them in the system and we've never been contacted since. So we're beginning to assume that's what we were meant to do and guess what, we did it, for free! Now that you Higher Beings know all about them, someone will contact you, some other way. We were never in any loop. We were just curious, like the cat and we have got our paws burned.'

"Evie, Tiggs, you can pass off the motorcycle stunt as over-excitement. You thought you were being cool and that was Carl just being helpful. He's already involved," JJ said hastily, registering dismay on our faces, "as he's on CCTV, with Andy, at the Museum. So you're not 'dobbing-him-in' as Alice tells me, the phrase goes."

I could see Carl was gathering himself.

"JJ…" he interrupted, awkwardly. "This is a bit mortifying but it's not a secret, so whatthehell, I'm among friends…" then he looked so anxious that we all beamed our support, like a row of Halloween pumpkins. Reassured, he went on – "I've got a five-year suspended prison sentence hanging over me for another 12-months. I've got a lot to lose, guys…" He looked so thoroughly miserable and ashamed, there was a small hubbub of supportive noises from the table, all of whom no doubt had darker moments in their own lives, just moments that, fortuitously, hadn't caught the eye of Authority.

"Comrade," said JJ, cupping his ear and pretending to listen to an invisible, inaudible voice – "Sun-Cloud tells me that your inside leg measurement is 32 inches, that you have an eight-inch scar on your left bum cheek, you mislaid your appendix some time ago and that you have never, ever appeared before any criminal, or civil court in this country. So you most certainly don't have five-years susp' hanging over your head – how could you have?"

Carl's face lit-up.

"I don't, really?!"

"You don't. The most you will ever be required to be, should enquiries ever proceed that far, is shamefaced for helping your mates – so not shamefaced at all."

We all applauded. As the noise died down, JJ shouted across the table to me – "actually Evie, I'd tell them about the nut, it will give them something to chase. So tell them exactly where you shoved it."

That produced a stifled ripple of amusement, one that totally perplexed JJ until Alice whispered in his ear, upon which revelation lit-up his face.

"That night," I explained, "I'd turned off the Beaver detail engine, deliberately. So I've no idea where it might be now. But more importantly and as a matter of some urgency, can that Quantum Doodlechuck of yours cure my IBS?"

"Probably but I doubt it will."

"Then excuse me guys, I'm in a rush," and I fled.

As I left I heard Andy start up – "look JJ…" But I was forced to ask Tigger, later, what had followed.

She had pondered for a while -"erm…he said – 'you' – that was JJ – 'say they're going to believe we're fronting for some agency. They're going to push really hard about that. We know we can't be cracked, blah, blah, blah, who would believe the truth. But can we really convince them we're innocents who have been played?"

"Then it got interesting because JJ said – 'I would have thought so but Sun-Cloud says not. They're inherently suspicious people. Innocence doesn't appear in their catalogue of possibilities. They view everyone's motives as inherently corrupt. They're professionally paranoiac." Tigger had paused for a moment, fingers steepled – "I bet they peel their sandwiches apart, just to check what's in them."

But all that was later.

When I'd crept back, Tee had greeted me like a long-lost friend, "worrah-ing" and bouncing about as if I'd been absent for 20 years, not 10 minutes. That may be a long-time in the life of a hyper-active Tigger but I think she was just trying to embarrass me.

"Get off!" I protested, "I wasn't away long!" I turned to Carl – "this is all your fault!"

"What? How!" he gaped.

"She was a perfectly normal human being until you introduced her to Winnie-the-Pooh, Alice in Wonderland, Holmes and Watson. Now look at her! She's never been right since and it's all your fault. I thought I'd found love and I actually hooked-up with a creature from the 100-Acre Wood.

"Worrah!" Tee exclaimed enthusiastically.

"For all we know we're going to be incarcerated in the Tower of London and fed to the ravens, a slice a day and all she can contribute is…"

"WORRAH!" boomed Tee, bang on cue.

"I could expand her horizons, in the hope of a cure manifesting spontaneously," offered Carl. "How about C.S.Lewis and Narnia, Ursula Le Guin's Earthsea, The Borrowers, BB's little Grey Men and Worzel Gummidge? Mind you, under present circs we might do better moving up a gear to Swallows and Amazons, the Famous Five and Malory Towers."

"Malory Towers? Isn't that a girls' book?"

"She is a girl," Carl explained patiently.

"I know – but you're not, so how come…"

"It's not that different from you being steeped in Treasure Island."

I instantly went into reverie. "I absolutely adored that book. I had a really cheap copy, on paper that got yellower and yellower, tattier and tattier, till it fell apart and was hanging by threads."

"At least you had a copy with threads," offered Carl. "My 'Malory Towers' was a perfect binding and if ever there was a misnomer, that's it. 'Fall-apart-in-your-hands' binding would be more accurate.

"And that's how kids love to read – one book, read to destruction. I read 'The Coral Island' till it fell apart, just like your 'Treasure Island.' Funny thing is, I can't remember a thing about it, now. It must have had a huge impact on my life and yet it registers zero on the memory scale. I think it's where I picked up the phrase 'demi-lunes,' which is something to do with artillery placements and the unpleasant habit of launching war canoes over the trussed bodies of prisoners. Their eyeballs popped out – from the weight. Punch might know about 'demi-lunes' but I bet even he's mute on war canoes."

"I thought canoes were light little things?" I said. We had all elided into private, mutual conversation by this stage of the meal and the table was lively with chatter.

"I think you need to be visualising things more on the lines of the Royal Barge but leaner, faster and meaner. You know, 30 paddlers a side, berserkers up at the pointy end, drugged to the eyeballs and hot-to-trot. I suppose the Chief would sit safely at the back, so the comparison with the Royal Barge isn't too wayward."

"You should ask Alice about artillery," I advised. "She's surprisingly practical on matters of ordnance, as Punch will vouch for. She's loaded and reloaded Pa's pistols for him, a couple of times."

"I can spear sofas," Tee offered, joining us, "is that any use?"

"Not in the matter of demi-lunes," Carl said sadly. "If we ever need to lead an assault on a soft furnishings warehouse, I'll put you in charge but sofa-spearing doesn't appear in many military manuals."

"Worrah," said Tee, in disappointed tone.

"We could form a small defensive corps here, on the roundabout," said Carl. "Punch could be General and we'd take it from there."

"One Brown Bess," I said. "That's the extent of the arsenal. Also, it doesn't have any ammunition. That's a constant source of sorrow to Punch, though he tries to hide it."

"What does he particularly wish to shoot?" asked Carl'

"The enemy," I said flatly. "Who that is depends on the extent of your paranoia. If you're totally barking, it's the first person through the door. Otherwise, you reserve your best shot for the likes of Vladimir Putin, Comrade Xi, or Donald Trump – and it could be that even they deserve to live, were you to start brooding on the themes inherent in redemption."

"I still think we should have a Corps," said Carl stubbornly. "How about 'Captain Tigger'?"

"She's quite a peaceful Tigger, at heart," I explained. "Bouncy, easily-distracted but rarely violent – except when defending cubs," I added, remembering the night Alice came to call.

Conversation had revived us. It had slumped badly, after JJ's depressingly grown-up revelations. Our playground had been bulldozed, before we even got to know that it was ours to play in. Actually, it had been nano-chewed, by tiny, tiny molecules that took in Roman Villa at one end and poo-ed out credibly-aged No-Name Roundabout detritus at the other. Andy and I had been directly responsible and I think the guilt was still oppressing us. But some natural perkiness was creeping back and as it finally rose to pre-announcement levels, Andy judged the moment ripe to call for the pudding and his crate of Tokay.

Naturally – and we had all guessed anyway, because JJ had definitely looked a bit floury – it was apple pie that emerged triumphantly from the wings, flanked by righteously large pitchers of custard. (I should make it quite clear that 'real custard,' according to 'The Beaver Book of Custard,' has everything to do with the transformation of custard powder by sugar and hot milk and nothing at all to do with egg yolks, cream, milk, cornflower, caster sugar, brought together during labour intensive activities of a five-star nature. The latter concoction simply doesn't taste right.) There was also a modest jug of cream for my dissenting partner.

"You know, Beavie," she said earnestly, "how do you expect to be anything other than 'dull of habit' when you pour that stuff into your brain at every opportunity?"

"Tiggs," I replied firmly, "Beavers are slow of habit, not dull. We are peace-loving creatures, renowned for our acuity and love of custard. Also, as we pour it down our throats and not into our ears, our brains are unaffected."

"You may think that's the case, Beaver but that stuff passes dangerously close to your brain en route to your fat little tummy. Contamination by seepage cannot be ruled out. On medical grounds alone you should cease and desist, then seek professional assistance."

"What sort of 'professional assistance,' Tiggs?" I asked, helping myself to a dangerously large amount of the disputed lubricant.

"Actually, hang-on a second…is that stuff a fluid or a solid? Because it's coming out in chunks. I have always been told it was meant to be a fluid but you seem to prefer it in a set form. Hence, I suppose, that special jug for you and Alice who, it appears, has caught this deadly infection from you. Explain yourself immediately."

"I don't see why a preference for thick custard should be seen in terms of a communicable disease. I haven't caught an awkward desire to explore bestiality from Alice, why should she have 'caught-custard' from me?

"Actually, though, while we're on the subject of fluid and solid – and this is very interesting…" As I spoke, one of those lulls that punctuate mass conversations fell on our group. My voice boomed into the void.

"What's 'very interesting'… Evie?" demanded Andy.

"Share!" chipped in JJ.

"More, more!" boomed Carl by now overwhelmed with Tokay and probably, relief that his suspended sentence had been magically commuted by Sun-Cloud.

"Shame on you all," I said, "embarrassing a nervous Beaver, who has already been forced to flee for sanctuary. Anyway, this was for the Tigger's ears only, in the hope of broadening her education – and believe me, I try, God! How I try… However, this evening, I shall extend my writ…

"…in the Maths and Physics Dept. of the University of Queensland, there hangs in a controlled environment, a glass funnel filled with pitch. At room temperature pitch feels solid, you can shatter it with a hammer. Yet, at room temperature, it also drips. In 87 years this sample has dripped nine drops and no-one has ever been around to see any of them fall. This latter fact is in no way mysterious, say like eels, which are mysterious, it just so happens no-one was around, or the equipment they set up to record a drip malfunctioned – so maybe it was mysterious, after all…

"I can see you are all stunned," I lectured the silence that followed. "The question arose because Alice and I happen to like our custard nearly solid. Tiggs was trying to imply that the solidity might be bad for my brain. Rubbish, of course."

"Why are eels mysterious, Evie?" asked Carl wickedly.

"It's because…" I had begun, excitedly… then everyone had burst out laughing.

"…a very embarrassing and humiliating thing to happen to a peace-loving creature of slow aquatic habit," I complained later, in the privacy of our trashy trailer. "And eels really ARE interesting. In fact, I must ask Alice, whether her quest for interesting sexual contact has ever led her to eels."

"Wouldn't live ones bite your bum?" asked Tiggs, in an eel-interested voice.

"Undoubtedly," I said. "You'd have to use an eel-proof condom, which would rather undermine the point of the exercise – or use them backwards, which might not be that stimulating, as they'd intuitively head for the Sargasso Sea, which would be the wrong way."

"In porn films," yawned Tee, "their mouths seem firmly shut."

"I have the ghastly feeling that they glue them," I said, "which is cruelty to animals. That I will not tolerate at any price!"

"I will not challenge you on that," drawled Tee "but you do recall spider-geddon, last month?"

"Don't taunt," I said, " or I'll go and get the remains of the custard to eat in bed, with a lot of slurping and concomitant spillage."

"You wouldn't!"

"I most certainly would, young lady."

"Oh well then – but don't forget to ask Alice."

"I'm bound to. I'll have something else on my custard-addled brain by then. Anyway, what about your CJD riddled chipolatas?"

"I happen to know," Tee replied primly, "that Carl personally inspected the abattoir, farm-shoppy-place from whence we draw our supplies. He reported that all the pigs he saw and I quote – 'were cheerful and of sound mind.'"

That phrase began to swirl around my brain with the same intensity that I might have expected from the sniper's high-power, low-weight bullet, should it ever leave the rifle in the lorry park and head for my twitching temple. Consequently, I was frozen to the lavatory seat, as I processed it. When finally released, I emerged pulling off my jeans. I hopped in on one foot, the other being hopelessly caught up, so that my statement went – "I… (hop) …have… (hop) …just… (hop) …turned… (hop…hop… hop) …vegetarian…" Crash!

44

CARNIVORES, CUSTARD AND HYMNS

At breakfast, Tee, cheerful and sound of mind, loaded her plate with chipolatas and bacon from pigs of similar disposition. I half-filled mine with eggs, probably from grumpy and argumentative hens and fried potatoes that might have had opinions, had I bothered to enquire. As I can't abide fart-filled baked beans, I went for the hash browns, which in my opinion, have no opinions at all.

Silently, I contemplated the contents of my plate and found that I had taken against them all – each and every last one. Therefore, I rose from the table and embarked on a mission, to the large fridges at the back of the kitchen.

"Eeeny-meeny-miney-mo…where did my thick custard go?" I mumbled to myself.

"Right-hand side, second from the end," said Sally. "Sorry but I can't get that to rhyme."

"Don't fret," I said, "we custard-eaters are dull of brain. That's official. We would never, ever, think to persecute anyone for merely failing to generate a rhyme."

"Which official body has pronounced on the eaters-of-custard?" asked Sally.

"The Princess herself."

"Oh, crikey. Really, really official. You're being a bit daring, then, aren't you?"

"Reckless is more like it," I said. "Now, are we, is the kitchen that is, possessed of a very long spoon. Sort of long enough to get to the bottom of this jug?" It was the model of jug that once ferried hot water to dressing rooms, before the advent of cheap plumbing and the rise of expensive ladies' maids.

"I could supply you with a thin serving ladle."

"That should do the job," I said. "Thank you kindly, breakfast can now be served."

I bumbled my way back to where the Princess was staring disconsolately at the emptiness of her plate."

"What's in your jug?" she demanded.

"You don't want to know."

"My point is that I do want to know."

"Then watch, all will shortly be revealed."

I trapped the jug between my thighs and began an assault by ladle. Immediately, I realised there was a problem. The neck of the jug, the inflexible nature of the ladle and the angle of its scoop, all were at odds with one-another. Also, the custard was now set to a consistency true-north of jelly but still south of pitch.

I and the jug trundled back to Sally.

"Plan B," I announced. "Spatula and large dish."

"Coming up, Evie. This is getting exciting."

"Nothing to be seen here," I mumbled. "Everyday events, all perfectly ordinary – things are completely under control."

"That's a bit of a fib, Evie," she said, handing me my tools.

I sniffed, haughtily.

I ran the spatula around the custard and shook the jug. Nothing. I bisected the contents and shook it very hard, over the platter. It could have moved a bit. It was hard to tell. I needed an adjudicator, preferably someone from the University of Queensland.

I'd soon figure this out.

"What's up, Evie?' asked Harry.

"I feel I could train this into the form of a song," I said, "but the unvarnished facts are that my custard is glued to the bottom of that jug and I can't get it out."

"I could warm the bottom, unglue it," Harry suggested.

"Good idea but not for one in pursuit of cold custard. It would become tepid custard. Also, as physics are my downfall today, there's the whole matter of the latent heat of custard to consider…or is that chemistry? Heat might start a chain reaction and melt the lot, can't risk it. Custard is at stake here." I looked up and found that everyone was looking at me.

It was very unsettling. "I know, I know," I said, "I get a little obsessive from time to time. Come on Harry, Plan C?"

Harry frowned at the jug. "Give it here," he said.

Reluctantly I handed it over – "cold and solid, Harry. Solid and Cold!"

"Trust me Evie, I have City and Guilds certificates,"

"In custard handling?"

"We covered custard…"

I pondered. "All right, go for it but remember, the well-being of that custard is in your hands."

He tucked the pitcher under one arm and chopped the contents into cubes. Their mutuality sundered, they wobbled happily out of the jug and into my bowl.

"Harry," I said, in a meaningful voice, "I have yet to dream up your reward but it will be proportionate. In the mean-time, thank you," and I returned, primly to my seat, just in time to see Her Royal Highness finishing my breakfast.

"It was going cold," she said guiltily.

I sniffed. Translated, the sniff ran as follows – 'you were overcome by gluttony and have indulged it at your long-suffering partner's expense, without her, or his, consent and thus in flagrant indifference to their hopes and wishes. This attitude is hurtful and was unnecessary. You could have waited and asked. You didn't. You are forgiven but such a breach of etiquette will leave an indelible mark.' Amazing how much information you can pack into a sniff.

"Sorry," said Tee. "Can I get you another?"

I did another sniff, which meant – 'do you remember my earlier sniff? I still do.'

"Very kind," I said "but there will be no need. I shall be requited with my platter of cold custard. Do stay and observe. Amuse me with your observations on the matters of the day."

Then I shovelled in the first mouthful. Heavenly! Tooth jarring, worryingly so but overall, heavenly.

Tee held up a red-top rag of a newspaper. "What does this mean?" she demanded. Filling the front page was a super-size headline – 'Albert Square Fandom Fury Routs Beeb.'

"In a nutshell," I explained, "it reads – 'enthusiastic watchers of a popular soap opera are angry at an action taken by their programme's makers."

"Ah, I see. Shorter headline – 'Fans forget it's only a story'?

"Or," I riffed, "something from Punch's repertoire might read – 'fans asking for a whiff of grapeshot from Aunty's home-knitted carronade," I finished with a flourish.

"Grr," rumbled Tee, "ask a simple question, get a Beaver answer. Go-on then, gloss, explain, expand, let's have the complete exegesis, at your leisure, when you are quite ready."

I smiled in a superior way and took in more nourishing custard.

"'A whiff of grapeshot,' is a phrase Napoleon was supposed to have used in the context of dispersing rebellious crowds. Grapeshot is musket balls loosely held in small sacks. These could be loaded into a short-barrelled, wide-mouthed cannon, eponymously known as a carronade, after the Carron Company that had the casting and fettling of them, in Scotland. Think 'sawn-off shotgun, supersized.' Very popular armament for clearing the decks in naval battles. 'Hand-knitted' was my reflection on the BBC's supposedly cosy role within society. May I now proceed with my brain-rotting breakfast?"

Tee looked apologetic, then glum.

"Maybe I'm wrong about custard," she said cautiously. "You seem particularly bright this morning."

I gave her a superior look. "That is because this the dawn of a NEW DAY. I have, overnight, become a vegetarian."

"Why didn't you warn me?" screeched Tee. "Does that mean that I have just eaten a vegetarian breakfast?"

"It certainly does," I said pertly. "Do you feel better for it?"

"I feel terrible. I've treacherously betrayed those cheerful pigs of sound mind. They've died, pointlessly. If I knew where they'd lived, I'd send an apologetic card to their friends and relatives."

"Would you care for a spoonful of soothing, consoling custard?" I wheedled, cunningly.

"OK," said Tee distantly – obviously in deep shock.

"Do you want your own spoon, or shall I shovel it in for you?"

"Feed me, due to my unwitting treachery and betrayal, some of my motor faculties have been temporarily disabled."

I admit it, nakedly evil thoughts ran through my mind. Was there anyone here who might take a photo of this incriminating scene? There was. The large man on the opposite table has his phone out, alongside a plate of full English, drowning in double-beans. I was even prepared to forgive that, if he'd help me capture this moment.

"Mate," I hissed.

"Uh?" he said in shocked tones, no doubt surprised at being accosted so unexpectedly.

"Grab a photo of us on your phone. I've left mine behind. Be a pal, I can't explain but it's nothing bad."

I raised a large, wobbling cube of custard towards Tee's beak, which opened wide, while her eyes strayed abroad, searching for distant, forgiving horizons.

"Gotcha!" said the big fella.

I scribbled my number on a scrap of napkin. "Be a darling and send it to me! It's strictly for in-house blackmail. Nothing grievous."

"My pleasure, sir," he said, his voice suddenly all-too familiar. My little world collapsed into molten custard.

Once I had escorted the still numb victim of 'veggie-shock' back to our humble quarters and installed her in 'the thinking place,' I rummaged through my various jackets until I found my wreck of a phone. Even through the shattered screen I could make out the custard and Tee's gaping, fledgling's beak. Ample material for joyous blackmail, if it wasn't rather trumped by a selfie of the large, 'helpful' chap, grinning maliciously as he devoured the remnants of my custard.

Then, from the ruins, surfaced a brain-wave. I abandoned Tee and ran as fast as Beavers can run to Alice and JJ's place, where I did a 5.00 a.m. Carl through their front door.

"Guys!" I shrieked…until I computed – 'huge-error! Ooops!'

I spun on my tail and faced the door. "I'm not looking," I squeaked. "I'm actually blind on Fridays and just in case I'm not, that's why I've turned round…

"JJ, sticking out of my bum pocket is my phone. On it is a selfie of a man eating custard. Oh God!" I raged, "that's not a man, 'hyphen,' eating custard but – oh bloody hell! – a man, comma, eating custard… Take a look, you'll get the idea. That picture came from his phone. If your mate Sun-Cloud, Star-Cloud, whatever it's called, hacks his number, he must be able to retrieve all sorts of inter-linked data from it."

"Why would it want to do that, Evie? Is a gang of dessert-eaters threatening to take over the galaxy, with or without the aid of custard?"

By now, Alice was giggling helplessly in the background.

"Oh!!" 'idiot Beaver,' I stormed silently. "I left out the important bit! That bloke is the fingernail puller who braced Tee and I at the Uni."

I danced on the spot, somewhat uselessly. I was trying to signal embarrassment, idiocy and vital information but words had betrayed me, which was why I was invoking dance. It has a very distinguished pedigree as regards the dissemination of information, though I'm not sure my impromptu performance partook of that.

"If, er, Sun-Cloud wants to publish the picture of Tee eating custard on the cosmos-wide web, I waive my copyright…OK…I was intruding…apologies. Bye Lovelies, I'm out of here. As you know, I saw nothing. Your secret is safe with me! Bye!"

Then I did the accelerated Beaver run, which is terrible to behold and double-Carl-ed through our front door. "Guess-what-Alice-and-JJ-are-doing?!!" I shrieked.

"Having breakfast?" said a voice from the thinking-place.

"No! Second guess."

"Eating custard, secretly, behind screens?

"Walking innocently, hand-in-hand, towards breakfast?"

"That was your last guess and to be honest, you didn't really try. I wouldn't have asked you to guess if they'd been doing anything ordinary, would I?"

"That's so, very, very true," said a dreamy voice, "how excessively dull of me. I think it's the vegetarianism that's done it. I needed my daily intake of cheerful pigs of sound mind."

"You've already had it. You had a plateful of murder to begin with! Then you ate my breakfast of eggs, from grumpy, argumentative chickens, which was exactly like yours, except that it didn't have a double helping of cheerful pigs of sound mind on it."

"Precisely," yawned Tee, "the ever-agile Beaver brain has grasped the point. It was a vegetarian meal, sans pig. Hence, I am poisoned."

"Holy Angels Bright!" I roared. "You are of unsound mind!"

"Precisely what I've been telling you for the last half-hour," Tee groaned. "I have been poisoned. Take me somewhere they can save me! A hospital would be best. Failing that, a petrol station, a newsagents, the supermarket, the offices of the National Grid. Anywhere! Just get help!"

"Cease and desist," I said. "You are safe. The antidote was administered on site. In your confusion, you have mislaid a sub-section of memory. However, you may come out now, because I have a picture to prove it."

"Oh, all right," she said perkily.

The door opened and there she stood, stark naked.

"Why have you got no clothes on?" I demanded.

"No idea. Let me guess… I think better? I've become a nudist? It's very hot today? I'm an exhibitionist? Aliens ate my clothes? I know! I'm being repainted? I don't know, I give up. Why haven't I got any clothes on?"

"Has the world gone mad?" I wondered, out loud.

"It's the custard," said Tee. "It's upset the balance of the cosmos. Personally, I feel a great confusion of the spirit. A perturbation in my being."

"You're not wrong," I said.

"I'm not?"

"Nope. Your being should be perturbed."

"Well it is."

"When you find out why, it'll be even more perturbed."

"I am agog, I am aghast…actually, I've caught an under-reported disease. I'm full of lines from musicals and hymns. I'm being invaded by the likes of W.S. Gilbert, Tim Rice, Cameron Mackintosh, Julia Ward Howe, Robert Crosby and a whole raft of 19th century evangelists. I'm drowning."

"Ditch the Tim Rice," I advised. "He and Webber can't help one jot in the struggle for comprehension of the cosmos."

"Actually, I'm not certain that I was searching for comprehension of anything," Tee admitted. "I was simply invaded, a bit like the Ukraine."

"Let us hope for a happier outcome."

"Do you think…" she said slowly, "that if I went outside…and sang ALL the verses of the Battle Hymn of the Republic, I'd be saved?"

"From what?"

"Invasion by custard propelled lyrics, of course."

"Of course," I agreed, "how stupid of me to forget. Would you be singing with, or without clothes?"

"Without."

"Then I think the outcome would be uncertain. Try it and see," I said, heading for the kettle, in the vague hope that coffee might solve something. "On balance, things couldn't get much worse."

"OK," she said and promptly rolled off the bed and out of the door – 'before I could stop her, Officer!' – to start singing and I must say very powerfully and tunefully –

> "Mine eyes have seen the glory
> "Of the coming of the Lord,
> "He is trampling out the vintage
> "Where the grapes of wrath are stored,
> "He has loosed the fearful lightning of his terrible swift sword,
> "His truth is marching on!
>   "Glory, glory hallelujah,
>   "Glory, glory hallelujah,
>   "Glory, glory hallelujah,
>   "His truth is marching on!

> "I have seen him in the watchfires of a hundred circling camps,
> "They have builded him an altar in the evening dew and damps,
> "I can read his righteous sentence by the dim and flaring lamps,
> "His day is marching on!"

… now, strangeness upon weirdness, the chorus is being swollen by other voices.

> "Glory, glory hallelujah,
> "Glory, glory hallelujah,
> "Glory, glory hallelujah,
> "His truth is marching on!"

… "oh, Little Tigger, what have you done…?"

> "He has sounded forth the trumpet that shall never call retreat,
> "He is sifting out the hearts of all before his judgement seat,
> "Oh, be swift my soul to answer him, be jubilant my feet,
> "Our God is marching on…

> …comes the chorus…more voices still!

I'm in a cata-something of pride, confusion, terror, love, exaltation. Dare I? Oh, be damned to it, yes! I tear my clothes off and I'm out there – miming, I have to admit…

> "In the beauty of the lilies,
> Christ was born across the sea,
> "With a glory in his bosom,
> that transfigures you and me,
> "As he died to make us holy,
> let us die to make all free,
> "While God is marching on…

and we roared into the chorus. Twenty of us singing, 40 wretches filming…

> "Glory, glory hallelujah,
> "Glory, glory hallelujah,
> "Glory, glory hallelujah,
> "His truth is marching on!

" …and once more, from the top," bellows the little voice…so we all do…

Oh my, the camera phones went mad. You wouldn't think you could source a crowd on a Sunday morning, that quickly. Arm-in-arm we walk, heads high, back to our trashy trailer and I fall back against the door.

"Wow Tiggs! You were superb, I never knew you had such a powerful voice."

"I was in the Church choir," she said lightly. "That's why I know all the verses."

"There are some killer lines in there," I reflected. "'…he is trampling out the vintage where the grapes of wrath are stored…' that, for some reason, always makes me well-up, I know not why. Then there's '…I have seen him…' go on for me, please."

"…in the watchfires of a hundred circling camps…"

"…and the next one, please…"

"…They have builded him an altar in the evening dews and damps…"

"Should have been 'an hundred'," I said.

"Pedant!"

"No, no. I mean, yes, yes, I am. But not about this, 'an hundred' packs more punch. It sounds more bible-black, men in frock coats and stove pipe hats, scarves and scars."

"You might have a point," she said. "I just wish it hadn't been raining. I think I'm coming down with something."

"I wouldn't have come out if I'd known it was raining," I agreed, vigorously towelling myself. "You'd have sung it out on your own."

"Yes you would and no I wouldn't."

"Dammit, I would, wouldn't I?" But in the back of my mind I wondered. It had been a close run thing, though it wouldn't have been rain that swung it.

"Who were our friends and supporters?" asked Tee.

"The Family were all there – though merciful Providence, Punch and Marie-Claire weren't back. Also, on reflection, I can't imagine how Alice got there… Then there was the breakfast crew. The regulars, those coming off shift, some going on. I imagine you emptied the place." At which I fell to wondering if Muscles and his crew got some good shots.

"How do you reckon the charges will read?" I added.

"There won't be any," said Tee, with complete certainty. "Be a love, grab some more towels, I'm a bit cream-crackered."

I rummaged for bath sheets – "I know for a fact we've got two…ah, here's one…" which flies across the room and is deftly fielded and deployed. "Where are you, number two, this is not the time to hide. Oh saints and martyrs, I'll make do…no, no, I won't…

"Tiggs, swop, please – I've got bigger, wetter boobs."

"OK," says Tiggs equably and swops.

"Some very strange things are happening this morning," I pondered, mostly to myself, "you wouldn't normally swop…"

"I know, it's very strange, isn't it? I felt OK at breakfast, until I ate that veggie offering. That's when I first noticed that bloke eyeballing me over his beans. You don't usually get lust and lechery at breakfast, especially when your partner's spooning custard out of a jug and looking like Pooh with a honey jar."

"Did I look like Pooh with a honey jar?"

"Yes, you had my '100-Acre Wood' top on."

"But that's a PJ's top!"

"I know, MY PJ's top."

"Lord, had I changed my bottoms?"

"Can't remember, really. Lots of cells have burned out."

"So that means sagging boobs?"

"I'm afraid so."

"Utter horror show."

"Anyway," continued Tiggs, "says I to myself, says I,' where have I seen you before, baked bean man? Then you wandered off to decant custard, so I subjected him to the scrutiny of the Mighty Tigger Cosmic Computer Mug Shot Comparison program."

"I've not encountered that one before."

"No. It's quite new, actually."

"How did it perform?"

"Brilliantly. It was that bloke who sometimes does afternoons in Ahmad's shop and has a personal commitment to re-arranging the top-shelf to best advantage."

"And you and your program are quite certain of that, are you?"

"We are," said Tee, smugly.

"So if I were to suggest to you that it was Sergeant Muscles from the Dept. of Metallurgy, whose hundred quid we sniggered at, you would feel yourself in a position to put me right?"

"Of course," said Tigger pertly. Then, as the gruesome realisation dawned that she was wrong, her face changed from superior Tigger, via apologetic Tee to a whispered – "oh poo!"

"I wouldn't fret," I said. "Probably the least of our worries now."

"Do I have some catching up to do?" Tiggs enquired. "Catastrophe-appalling' extends even further than the fingernail-pullers?"

"Please don't take this the wrong way, because truly, you were magnificent. Just a pity you couldn't scramble the Salvation Army band in time. However, I feel we may find ourselves caught between internet Trolls and a hard place in the coming hours. In fact, I can see at least three major wars breaking out in the car park by this afternoon. You've got the gang who will hate us for singing a hymn in the all-together, versus the ones who'll love us for the same. Then there's the mob who'll hate you for being a Paki-bitch and the crowd who'll loathe me for being a weirdo lady-boy, androgynous bum-runner and the ones who will support us for being all of the above. Thereafter there's the whole business of 'is it a pro-civil rights' song, or a subtly contrived piece of white supremacy…"

"Really?" interjected Tiggs.

"No. I actually made that last one up but you've got to admit it's an absolute juggernaut for collecting moral indignation from every side. I can't actually visualise any conclusion that doesn't end in bloodshed."

"Wow! What an exciting afternoon. I'm going to put my man-flu on hold – AND I'm an Indian-bitch, not the other word you said."

"That's a nicety that could easily get lost in the ensuing furore, I feel."

"Do we sally forth to meet them naked?"

"I'm leaning more towards a suit of armour."

"Naked is armour. Yossarian proved it!"

"Oh, you're onto 'Catch 22' – most excellent! Wretched book changed my life."

"How so?"

"Somewhere very near the front, as I recall, it says – 'it was the best Officers' Mess Yossarian hadn't helped to build. He hadn't helped to build a lot of Officers' Messes but this was by far and away the best…' or something like that. Those sentences stopped me dead in my tracks. Heller was saying that there was another way of seeing the world. From then on, I put on my 'reversing-goggles' and sure enough, everything looked different."

"Are 'reversing-goggles' actually, a thing? As in – 'real-thing?'"

"Certainly not. They just came to me now. Maybe I invented them."

"Excellent, because I know exactly what they are."

"Change of direction alert," I said. "Where would 'I' be without books?"

"We'd have more room."

"Undeniable but where would 'I' be, in my head?"

"Maybe you'd have more space there, too. Maybe you'd be less confused. You'd probably have very rigid ideas."

"Because I wouldn't know enough to know that I knew nothing, correct?"

"That's right. It's a common enough position. You'd not lack for company."

"My problem is," I said slowly, "that every wretched book I read changes the way I see things. So how are we meant to learn? What are we meant to learn? For that matter, are we even meant to learn anything, other than self-preservation? What gives others the right to lecture and insist that their viewpoint is the correct one? Why do they start from a position of certainty, while I bring confusion to the table? And finally, were I to start from a zero sum position, how would I be supposed to reach a decision about ethical behaviour, given that there are so many opposing views?

"That's the problem stated…so-oo, Great Oracle, are you ready? One, two, three – GO!"

Tee was scrubbing her hair with a towel. From under the waving Terrycloth the voice of wisdom uttered forth.

"We are meant to learn the survival strategies that benefit our ruling elite. Currently that means we learn the rules of neo-liberal, consumer capitalism, at least here in the First World. After your lessons, you will be expected to sell your time and labour, be that body, brain, or both and you will reap the rewards considered appropriate to your position on the social ladder. This is because we are required to put our shoulders to society's wagon wheels and shove. All your life lessons, your school lessons, equip you for and point you at this goal.

"Individually, our brains are not that large and we also have a very shallow range of focus. So most of the stuff we learn, we have to take on trust. We cannot investigate everything anew. It's in this way the elite dominates, by advertising their vision of society as the most attractive. In every society there'll be a group of innovators, who want things to go differently but their progress is slow and covert. It has to be. No ruling group wants their ship to be sunk by loose cannons. So-called democracies are very good at stifling dissent, they lure the dissenters in with glimpses of the inner sanctum. 'Come and join us, my boy, we'd love to have your new ideas shaking us up.' Very soon the 'new boy' wants to be an 'old boy.'

"Stop! Cease and desist!" I ordered, rudely. "You have begun to wander down familiar and tedious political highways. What I want to know is where does new thought come from? Can it be sought out? Is it generated and if so, by whom? Where's the nipple of inspiration?

"Take the hymn you were belting out. That was supposed to have arrived by inspiration and if you didn't stop to think, you might believe that. Lines like – 'he is trampling out the vintage where the grapes of wrath are stored,' – sound inspirational, until you realise they're purely evangelical, born from too much Old Testament and not enough sex. I'll allow that 'they have built him an altar in the evening dews and damps,' is pretty mysterious but I'd still say its pedigree is showing. So if one generation's 'inspirations' are shown to be babes of that generation's obsessions, where does that leave inspiration?

"Is it words that are at fault? They're the only tools we have really, for communicating inspiration. I suppose that's why artists strive to speak another language, with colour and form…do you think?"

Poor old Tiggs. She tried to answer but the Queen of the Rhetorical Question was now in full flow. All credit, Tee waited patiently.

"The last revelation I had," I ranted, "was when the phrase – 'let there be light!' – floated into my head one day. I suddenly realised what that must have amounted to and how the scribe, the person who dictated Genesis had dug back and found something so astonishing, so seminal that it almost passes you by as commonplace. It's colossal. Total darkness – then light, yet, if I understand my science books accurately, light came much, much later…a whole bunch of stuff had been going on before light came on the scene.

"What's bothering me, Tiggs, is the nagging feeling that we can only understand things within the parameters of our own group's accepted truths and heresies. Do you remember when we took our jokey notion of 'flee' to Punch and Andy buffooned us into his 'Court'? Punch totally wiped us all out by memories acquired in an earlier age. Because he lived 300 years ago, he understood things differently."

"Three memories as I recall and each one as shocking as its predecessor," said Tee slowly. "I'm unlikely to forget."

That was a remark so wholly out of character for her that I was quite derailed and left floundering. "Tiggs," I said feebly, "you're supposed to be Bishop Berkeley and not allying yourself with other points of reference. It's either now and here, for you, or it doesn't exist – remember?"

"I'm only BB on odd-numbered days," explained the Tigger, "on even-numbered days I'm very ponder-full, very Pooh-Bear, contemplative and going round in circles. Sometimes, just to confuse the enemy, I swop the days around."

"The enemy are?"

"Is – the enemy is – logic. I hate logic."

"That is eminently reasonable. There's nothing logical about the major events of planetary existence. Only annoying little things are logical."

"Hang on, hang on," said the unnaturally incisive Tigger, "you're the 'tic-toc' proponent, remember? That's pure and remorseless logic from beginning to end."

I paused. "I'm snookered, aren't I?"

"Totally, unless you invoke my secondary truths. They'd probably get you off the hook. They're useful like that, a sort of 'Get Out of Jail Free' card."

"Where am I, Tiggs? I'm sure I had a point."

"Oh you did. It's just macro-macro and micro-micro don't sit side by side very easily. It's to do with what I was trying to say about our brains – that they can't see very far, or take in too much information. Just because we think that they're amazing doesn't make them so. When you say 'tic-toc' is all there is, that might very well be all that there is to know on the micro-micro scale but we live in the macro-micro world and have to deal with all sorts of things that have got hideously complicated since their constituent parts went 'tic-toc.' Just because we can say 'tic-toc' and feel intellectually superior, that won't save us from a charging rhino."

"We could try it," I suggested feebly.

"You try first. I will observe, having previously and prudently loaded Dada-ji's elephant gun."

"You'd save me, at the last minute? How incredibly romantic."

"Actually, I was more focused on saving me, after you'd bravely proved my point to your satisfaction."

"Less romantic, by far. But as you're in rescue mode, rescue some of my argument for me, that's if you can see any useful wreckage floating around." I flopped back – vaguely wondering when the Army of the Internet's Righteous Ones would arrive to destroy us…before or after lunch?

Tee pondered. After a while she perked up. "If I go back to the 'Battle Hymn of the Republic,' I might rescue something. I actually know quite a bit about it. I had to do some deep-digging for my Choir Medal and that's the hymn I chose to research.

"The fact is, that tune has been used for everything and Julia Ward Howe didn't write the music. That was composed for an earlier, Methodist hymn but pretty quickly pinched for other stuff, including 'John Brown's Body.' The righteous lyrics I sang are just another rider for that horse. Rugby songs have been bawled out to it, patriotic anthems constructed to fit it, adverts and political rallies have all used it.

"It has a marching, sassy rhythm, so it railroads you into a frame of mind subconsciously. The music is directing the head. Is that Right Brain talking to Left, or Left drowning out Right?"

"You need to get onto Professor McGilchrist for that one," I said. "I can't answer as I am currently undergoing essential repairs."

"Hmm," said Tee. "Think about rhythms, think about all the things that are hiding in plain sight and influencing us. In very simple terms, the things advertisers use to hook us, or planners use to warn us. Meanwhile, consider the colour red, if that's not too boring, because everyone with a point they want to make uses red. At first, its connotations seem inescapable – Danger, Stop, Alert but the funny thing is, it can mean the opposite too. The red fire that destroys, also welcomes and warms. The red light of a brothel is edgy but alluring. A sunset is mysteriously beguiling. All these contradictions are yoked to red and yet red is simply red, it's our bolt-ons that swirl around it.

"It could just be us. Our brains are hung up about red and we can use it as shorthand, provided we make sure our 'listener,' 'viewer,' knows which sort of red we're coming from.

"Now, here's interesting…there's a deep storage facility, somewhere in America, for super-obnoxious atomic waste and its planners have given a lot of thought as to how they should warn future generations to steer clear of it. Painting the barrels red won't do, nor will skull and crossbones, or anything using language. The people who penetrate these caves eventually may be morons or intellectuals. But say they get down there in 30,000 years – how do we tell them what the state of play is?

"What are the fixed points, Beaver? What is unchanging? What can be relied on to bridge even the very shortest geological time span?"

The silence was not charged and expectant, it had more of that agonising 'teacher-has-asked-a-question-and-you-don't-know-the-answer-because-you-weren't-listening' quality about it.

"Croutons!" I blurted, "they bridge geological time."

Tee looked at me quizzically. "Little bits of fried bread in soup, correct?"

"Not that sort of crouton. these are made of rock and are sort of like tap-roots from the tectonic plates of the mantle to the molten core."

"Cratons," said Tee flatly, "I think you mean cratons."

"I do, I do, I do," I scrambled. "I was very nearly there! After a tough morning and a probably worse afternoon, that wasn't a bad effort, was it?"

"No, it was excellent. I propose, however to anthropomorphise them, shamefully."

"Ah ha! Return of the insect sex lady," I crowed.

"Very funny. That was a peculiar day out. The director was loathsome. Also, off the back of that – and you started it! – I discover I have a question – having gone to such pains to acquire the insect book, why haven't we made more use of it?"

"That is too good a question to dismiss and it is well-known that I am a devil for a diversion. But could we park it until we're done with anthropomorphised cratons?"

"Coming up but be aware, this is purely a Tigger-invention, unlicensed for use on public highways.

"There is a Jewish belief and I really like it, that there are 36 righteous men and women who are holding mankind together. They are not Presidents, Kings or CEO's. They are more likely to be toilet-cleaners, humble clerks, postmen, road-sweepers, bakers and women who take-in washing. They are the truly good and without them, our so-called civilisation would simply implode. Their humility and simple affection for their fellow-man encompasses the world and gives meaning to what we are doing here. God looks down and he sees them. He thinks 'if they can love their fellow-man, then their fellow-man can't be as bad as I sometimes think he is.' Or perhaps that's a bit of what he thinks. They know nothing of this and even if an angel were to tell them, they wouldn't believe it. They're too humble.

"They, to my sudden leap of imagination, are the cratons of the human race. The steady points in this awful flux of good and evil that we've allowed to wash over our planet. They're known as the Tzadikim Nistarim and my grandad told me about them when I was at a very suggestible age, so I'm pleased to say they stuck in my feather-filled noggin.

"I built a whole philosophy on them, for the days when I'm not Bishop Berkley-ing. It's my belief that there are other ancient and persistent 'cratons' in our world. Perhaps music, light and colour are far more than we think they are. Perhaps life is a peculiar crystal form. However often it is melted down and reformed, certain lineaments will persist. These are very few but together they compose Life – each and every time. When they are in place, like the Tzadikim Nistarim, the rest of us are allowed to swarm all over the place, as clueless as Hamelin's rats. Just occasionally, one of us, more thoughtful, more humble, might come up with something worthwhile. I don't know."

"I don't know, either," I said. "But I think at 36 souls, the planet is sadly under-crewed. I'd like to help. I know you would, too, whatever you say to the contrary.

"However, as we lack an invitation, shall we in the meantime put on some clothes and go in search of our friends and enemies?"

"It is getting chilly," Tee agreed.

45

SAVED BY 'STAN

We were hot news by 10.00 am. But by 11.00 we were scorching.

Andy, hobbling sardonically on his crutches (can you 'hobble-sardonically-on-crutches?' Whatever the consensus on that, take it from me, he could) asked whether he should have the windows boarded, or lay-on crisis staff in anticipation of extra covers? I suggested he hobble off and consult the small print of his insurance. In his departing wake, Tee hiccupped a very sad "worrah."

"That could be my last one, ever," she groaned. "How do you like the sound of St. Tigger?"

"Better than I like the sound of St. Beaver," I replied. "But if you think we're about to be martyred, it might be time to request divine intervention, on the basis that there's no way the Big Man wants us on the payroll. We'd be nothing but an embarrassment."

"I can see you would be," nodded Tiggs, "but I'm quite cute."

"Hah! I'm following in the footsteps of Mary Magdalen. I have precedent, so that's where you're mistaken, young lady."

"I'm sure St. Francis could fit me in, alongside a lamb or two."

On the basis of 'last meals, heartily eaten,' I'd asked Harry to keep the pain-au-raisins coming and we were on the fourth plateful, when fate intervened for us.

The newly-installed President of a 'Stan, one that nobody had ever heard of, announced his universal agenda. From the turret of a tank, he declared some startling changes. Polygamy was henceforth an obligation, women were to be regarded as the property of men, Sharia Law was invoked, with strengthened clauses, while from Monday public execution of self-confessed lesbians and gays would be instigated. Even the Taliban were refusing to recognise him but suddenly, we were off the menu. Rent-a-rage shifted hashtag and focus.

To put it mildly, that was a relief. I was not ready to meet my maker, nor I suspect, was he that keen on meeting me. I still needed a lot of detail attending to, before I achieved the 'bottom' necessary to join the Choir Invisible. As for Tiggs, she was barely house-broken, let alone Heaven-trained. We were both to be considered as 'works-in-progress.'

Then the chauffered Rolls Royce turned up bearing our beloved elders, who had been soaking up the ambience of the West End. If the car park had been thronged with competing lynch-mobs, I could not have answered for Punch. He'd probably have borrowed a ladle from Andy and killed them all before lunch.

As it happens I can't abide 'Les Mis' but the elders and betters seemed to have had a great time and as Punch was now over the absolute necessity of starting a bivouac fire, wherever his caravan alighted, the Five Star suites had gone down very well, too.

Carl now danced attendance on them with the lunch of lunches he'd been preparing all morning – and half the night, I'd guess.

Watching him, I suddenly realised how much he loved his Nan and Grandad. It was a beautiful thing to see and as he'd co-opted Punch and Marie-Claire into his Family Dream Team, his attentions fell on them all equally. I was so touched, that I later awarded him a 'Special Beaver Hug'. "What was that for?" he croaked, (Special Beaver Hugs can be hard on the ribs.) "For being you," I explained.

Grandad Jack then received a tutorial on Brown Bess, which he took quite well. In return he suggested they could fit in a bit of rough shooting, at the cottage. "But nothing larger than a 12-bore," he explained, apologetically. After that, Punch could barely wait to be off.

We waved them away and turned back to the diner.

"That went well," said Tee decisively, "in fact, on reflection, it deserves my very best – "WorraWorraWorra,Worrah!!" After which she clapped a hand to her mouth and exclaimed – "do you realise, Beavie, that's me doing a pure Yossarian! 'Worrahing' something I had absolutely nothing to do with – it's just like the officers' mess! Andy and Carl organised the whole thing." She scrabbled her hair into a mare's nest, in search of inspiration. "Got it! I'll do another set of 'worrahs' just for them, sometime when it's totally unsuitable. How about that?"

"Excellent thinking. Pure genius, really, "I said. "Even more locally, however, I find I'm focusing on that madman in the unknown 'Stan. I'm hoping he can stay on the front pages for at least a week. Unbelievable lunatic he may be but he's saved our sorry backsides."

"My backside is quite pert," Tee said proudly. "I was quite pleased with it. In fact, while I'm handing out compliments, yours didn't look that bad, either. But you were quite right, a silver band would have added a lot more 'oomph.' Do you think we could ask JJ's quantum star thingy to dub one over us?"

"The sooner our pert bums and dulcet tones are forgotten, the happier I shall be," I said. "I wouldn't be that surprised if aforesaid 'puter didn't invent the whole 'Stan story, just to divert attention away from its interesting specimens in the petri-dish."

"Interesting specimens with pert bums," said Tee. "There are worse obituaries to be written. Anyway, what shall we do next? I've got oodles of energy all of a sudden!"

"Go for a drive?" I suggested warily. "I could fancy high places with trees and wind

– but not the beech hanger, it would probably throw the whole copse at us if we turned up uninvited."

"You're on," said Tee and she turned round in a tight circle, a U-boat periscope hunting for innocent merchantmen. "Look – over there, JJ and Ally… Victims!

"Ally and Pally," she roared. "Do you want to come for a drive to a high-up, tree-y sort of place?"

"Yes, please!" squeaked Alice and dragged JJ across the car park.

"Can you drive cars here, JJ?" demanded Tee.

"I can."

"Please drive this one of mine then. You've met it before. We girls are going for a back-seat snoozle. Take us to a place with trees, wind and nobody else. Oh and you have to stick to this planet, too."

"Ah, that does cramp my style," he grinned.

We piled into the back, Alice-in-our-sandwich.

For what seemed to be an age, JJ fiddled with the seat – up down, back, forwards. Only finally, and I guess when he supposed we were too distracted to notice, did I see him slip a stand-alone ear bud into position. That was equipment I hadn't seen before. He was probably now wired-in to Sun-Cloud, via brain pulses. How else would he know where to go?

Utterly fascinating, I thought, to be touring the Home Counties with the Sat-Nav operated from an alien galaxy. How, on earth – literally – would it know where and when to – 'turn left in 300 yards'? The fact is that it did. And if I was alert enough to notice that we'd collected a black Honda, when we were a few miles out, I'm sure it was, too.

"It's been clocked, Evie," said JJ quietly, as I opened my mouth.

Alice and Tee were playing 'paper, scissors, stone' as a two-girl scuffle that seemed to be making them happy. So as I was feeling strangely expansive and benevolent, I leaned back to give the eternal verities the honour of my attention. First up, as usual – Death. Why does it clamour so?

The Samurai say that Death should be your constant companion. I suppose that they knew a thing or two about it. The Tibetans made Death a speciality, too.

In far flung monasteries, where the adepts were prepared to risk life and limb pursuing knowledge, those who were sick-unto-death volunteered to venture down Death's slippery slope before their time was, strictly speaking, up. Smothering, starvation, narcotics, all were applied to consenting guinea pigs. No doubt some slipped too far. Others were coaxed and nursed back to brief respite, during which they reported their experiences.

What they described was broadly similar, a path taken through a series of colour fields, enveloping auras of purple, green, violet, yellow. It was a path through a Rothko world. The conclusion was that you should follow a will o' the wisp white light. The rest of the colours were snares. Today, I fell to wondering which one would snare me. Probably the right shade of red or green would stand a good chance.

"Look behind," JJ whispered to me.

We were driving along an endlessly straight road. Roman, no doubt, back in the day. It crested hills, rather than circumventing them. Half-a-mile back, the black Jazz had stopped and something about the angle of its front suspension suggested that it wouldn't be moving any time soon.

"I won't ask," I said.

"Only because you've already guessed," he laughed.

"Paper wraps stone!" squeaked Alice and off they went again. So I returned to my colour fields.

'What's so wrong with red and green?' I asked silently. 'We're going on a green hunt now. It envelops, soothes, strengthens.' I waited but Sun-Cloud wasn't talking to me, which I thought was a bit snooty. Then I recalled, with a stab of guilt, that I had emphatically and very rudely, told it not to. 'Oh well, easy come, easy go.' Not a great attitude, Beaver, said the internal Eva. A bit more humility might be a good thing. How could it ever be a bad one?

'Oh shut up!' I groaned, 'leave me alone with my colours!' My thinking may be indifferent but at least it is mine. 'Or is it?' asked the deeper, wiser, grampus of Eva. 'Go away!' I squeaked. 'I want my colours back!' Purples were not unattractive but I could see that they might turn tricky. Yellows? Too likely to go orange on you. Yellows as constituent parts, say as in a Tibetan apron, are wonderful. I don't think it would stand on its own, though.

We were climbing a hill and a trick of angles allowed me to snatch a glimpse of the black Honda in the left-hand wing mirror. It was a mere speck, isolated and vulnerable. For some reason that made me reflect how much I enjoyed this grotesque, gas-guzzling, eco-nightmare of a vehicle. It was a protective carapace, wrap-around armour for the fragile ego. One gentle exhalation from a Zen master could blow it away to the Land of Boys' Toys but until it did, I enjoyed playing 'Kings and Queens,' in the stupid tin can.

Tin can, that reminds me – I used to beat frenziedly on a red and blue tin drum that mum bought me. She must have had a moment of parental madness. I played it so much that I beat a hole in it and it went off to retirement in that week's bin-bag. After that I was relegated to banging on an old saucepan with a wooden spoon. Sadly, in my imaginings, that had no military credibility.

I searched my scrapyard of a mind – where had I left Death? He was no longer before my Third Eye, where the Samurai insisted he should be. I was too unfocused, too frivolous by half. Evie of the diversions, the loops, the long-ways-round, the fascinating cul-de-sacs, the interesting stories, the random chatter and glee over small things of even less importance. Though who, I wondered, was the arbiter of relative importance?

Death was waiting patiently where I had left him. (Why is Death a 'He,' Evie?). He was among the colour fields of the Book of the Dead. I looked for him in the green place but when he looked up, he was staring at me with the face of my beloved Tee.

"Stone blunts scissors!" I heard her chirrup in the background.

She was grinning at me from her green background, like some imp of spring. Then the green began to fade and the brown eyes, the familiar, luxuriant black hair swam into focus. Her lips, parted and sensuous, seemed to rise like nurturing hands from some polished, sacred cistern.

I knew what was coming. I had been here before. In hospital such scenes had paraded past me through every hour of unconsciousness, or on any occasion I closed my eyes. At first they had terrified me, now I could drift by them – the decomposing dead, as though I was some devotee of Chod. Embrace the awful, the better to be able to reject its awfulness. Draw the teeth of your fears – that is a part of what Chod teaches.

Tee's eyes began to widen but only because her eyelids were withdrawing, falling back into the orbits. The whites were staring wildly, as her nose began to crumble, the fine bridge falling to ruin and nothingness, the flare of the nostrils collapsing like the walls of a desert city. The eyes had dissolved but Tee was still there, in her lips. These drew back so swiftly, from smile to snarl and then to the revelation of teeth and gums.

All was fleeing before decay. Her hair, once so glossy, the hair we were amassing for our own fetish, was dry and dusty. The soft cheeks were fallen in. Some construction of muscle and palate survived above the dissolving tongue that collapsed down her throat. The bones of her skull and jaw were appearing and now other suitors for my attention begin to edge closer, jostling for precedence. The newly dead seem hungry to be noticed.

Floating into the distance now, she is falling apart. Her head falls back, like a puppet's severed from its strings. As it sinks, dozens of hopeful faces crowd forward, all craving recognition but their flesh has already sloughed away. They too fall back, like slow stones sinking in black water. Wherever I shift my gaze they surge briefly, as if they were become shoals of fish. Yet they will all die before their wave has even begun to gather.

Night after night I would lie, craving sleep, having such scenes play out relentlessly on the cinema screen of my closed eyelids. I could not be free of them. Catastrophe after catastrophe invited and hosted me at scenes of carnage. I was privy to witness both the humane and the helpless, both mercilessly reduced to their skulls and long bones.

In time I began to feel immune to the pity of it all. Certainly I grew to be unmoved by charnel house horrors. When I look back now, what has stayed with me, is the anonymity of bone. Were your skeleton to march towards you, its hand extended in greeting, you would not recognise it, your twin beneath the skin.

When, in your life did you glimpse your bones? Never, I trust, except on X-ray, or by reflecting on textbooks; by empathy in an ossuary. My bones scare me. Even when

I was young I learned that bones, deep within their marrow, can condemn us to a slow and abject death.

As for the life lived to three score years and ten, thereafter it is under threat from the neck of the femur. Three quarters of an inch of bone can snap because of a moment's inattention or through simple misfortune. Then your remaining time on earth could be measured in months. Pneumonia prowls around your bed, while you lie there hoping the bone will knit, or that the titanium screws will bed home tightly, before your muscles start to waste.

If you're not convinced as to the betrayal implicit in bone, consider that shoddy column of bricks we call a spine. A tower of plastic building bricks would be a better proposition. Our backbone is a series of accidents waiting to happen. Not built to swivel, bend, arch and stretch, we insist that it shall do all these things. To make things more awkward your ribs cleave to it, thus complicating the issue of free movement. But the real nightmare is that some of the most vital nerves of your body fan out from artful little sockets between its vertebrae. Swivel, bend, stretch, or arch one millimetre too far and you've entered a world of chronic pain or, worse still, paralysis.

Considered proportionately, say as in hen to human-being, the collar bone is as delicate as the wishbone of a chicken. However, there can never be anything lucky about breaking it. Break things when you're young, for if you break them when you are old, be they collar bones, backs, legs, wrists, or what-have-you, you face real pain and metal plates under wounds that won't heal.

I saw all these things in my hospital days. They scared me then and they scare me more now. The elderly stoically bearing their pain. The young, astonished that they can actually break. The middle-aged, furious that they can be inconvenienced by something they had never even considered – bone!

Why does wisdom come too slowly to be of service? It always arrives late. You never take your last and vital lesson in time for it to be of service. Caution only arrives in the wake of disaster, never before it.

What a morbid Beaver I am.

Consider the medieval propensity for the recreational breaking of bone, if you can bear to. It was Auden who rightly observed that our forefathers knew a thing or two about suffering. They also knew that torture was a useful spectator sport. Not only did it requite the longing that suffering should be visited upon others, not oneself, at the same time it demonstrated the awful power of authority.

I'm just considering the practice of…when I take a jolt in the ribs from Ally's pointed fingers – "play with me," she demands. "Tigger's all snoozed out."

Ever-so-gratefully, as I don't care for my current vale of contemplation, so uncertain am I of my reasons for being there, I turn myself into paper, scissors or stone, for what seems an age of fields, hedgerows and small lines of houses where, unbelievably, lives as delicate and as coarse as our own are unfolding.

46
OF GROUNDNUTS AND CREAM TEAS

Finally we have arrived somewhere, a destination chosen for us by an Intelligence in another galaxy. Therefore I am right to wonder if any other human being has ever set foot here before. The fact that the road exists suggests that they have and probably on a daily basis, too. The utter silence suggests otherwise.

We all creep out of the car, sensory equipment flaring, nostrils, eyes, ears and skin. For touch, we have each-other's hands and we stand on the edge of the wide terrace the road created, as it took a sharp right-hand turn, each one holding a familiar paw. Then Tee and I shuffle up towards Alice and Tee links us into one powerful unit that feels electrifyingly good. No-one says a word but we all feel it. The choreography of head movements proves that. We keep casting glances up and down the line, to reassure ourselves that this curious current actually does exist.

We are standing on a promontory, the edge of which is a steep bluff at the head of a field shaped like the cross-section of a funnel, making it a small, rural amphitheatre-in-waiting. To left and right are paths down to the immediate descent below us. The descent itself leads down, down, down to the neck of a tree-filled valley that looks utterly tempting – even to timid explorers such as Beavers.

This Beaver is currently looking for the safest way down, for I know Tee is contemplating a Tiggerish leap over the edge. I turn my arm into a rigid bar to dissuade her. The girl is simply insane, a jubilant, gravity-denying, bundle of exuberance. I tug her towards the lubber's path, the one that winds in short corkscrews down into the field.

"Poo!" she exclaims, breaking the silence. "It would have been a super jump. A Tiger in freefall – not often witnessed."

"And certainly not about to be by one dedicated to your long-term survival," I reply, firmly gripping the hand that is itching to be four-years old again and unbreakable.

"The slow habits of Beavers are quite alien to Tiggers, you know."

"Which is why there are whole colonies of Beavers but very few Tiggers," I explain patiently. "If I had known we were going to encounter adventures, I would have brought a bottle of calming medicine with us."

"You did bring nourishing supplies, didn't you?" she demands, her voice rising to wild panic. "You know Tiggers need regular refuelling."

"How could I have managed that? I was snatched off the car park at a moment's notice."

"Oh no! Help! I may have to start hunting. Do you think there are any very slow antelopes about? Ally, are you good with camp fires? JJ you're in charge of something else. I shall have to summon emergency rations by 'worrah, worrah, WORRAH-ing."

I fished in all my pockets and finally uncovered a fluff and particle encrusted peppermint ball. I brushed off the worst.

"Open!"

"Mrrmphf! Than-k-foo!" and away she skipped.

"Extraordinary," remarked JJ. "Is the species rare?"

"Almost extinct," I said. "This is the last one in captivity and in fact, she never used to be this way. The consensus is that oxygen starvation is to blame, on the flight over. She's never slowed down since landing."

"As it happens," Alice contributed, "I was incredibly docile in books – all panda eyes and pouts. Now I'm quite horrible and vicious. See…" and she casually gave JJ a push that sent him tottering and reeling down the hill, in a desperate attempt to recover his balance.

"…and him, I love," she finished with an air of huge self-satisfaction.

"So I observe," I said nervously, while linking arms with great deliberation. 'Oh well, maybe it's better the monsters you know, than the ones you don't…or something along those lines,' I thought momentarily, until stark terror flashed into focus in my woefully slow mind.

"Don't even think about it!" I shouted. I sensed anarchy in the air. It was linked to a plot to pull me down the hill. "Beavers are of doleful, slow habit and do not take kindly to sudden movement, especially sudden, downward movement. Also my bowels are filled with custard, which is just the sort of ammunition craved by the imps of IBS. So…" redoubling my grip, "…watch it, young Alice!"

"Yes, Evie," she said, in a voice of such horrifying docility that I immediately sat down, pulling her with me.

"What are you plotting?" I demanded.

"Nothing, Evie," she purred, head on my shoulder.

"Help!" I yelled, "I'm in grave danger!"

"Why?" floated up.

"I'm stuck on a vertical hillside with a homicidal maniac!"

"Tough shit…" I'm pretty sure that's what they said…

"Evie?" purred the little voice.

"What?" I demanded.

"Just a little kiss, to prove we're still friends…" and she turned her sweet little face up to mine – sweet little face with devilment in its eyes.

"Aaagh!" … now we're rolling, roly-poly down the slope.

"Tuck your arms in!" she shouts gaily. "You don't want to break them!"

Fresh from my melancholy contemplation of bone, particularly broken ones, I am now rolling down a hillside in the company of a tiny, malignant sprite who is actually somersaulting her way to the bottom. Meanwhile, be it known, Beaver bosoms were never designed for this.

I had time to register – 'God, this is awful. I'm scared…I'm going to be sick! Oh, that was definitely a break! This is my last day on earth…' just before I arrived at the bottom.

"Alice," I groaned into the grass, "if I ever get up, you are dead, as in D-E-D."

"Wow," said a sprinting Tigger, skidding to a halt. "That looked incredible fun. Do you want to do it again?"

"Fuck off," I muttered into the grass. "Fuck off and pick on someone your own size."

In the distance I can hear JJ vainly protesting – "Lovely, I'm 4000 years old. I might have osteoporosis."

"Have you?" she chirrups.

"No but that's not the point. Look at Evie, bits of her have come off!"

'Oh My God!' I think. "Which bits?" I bellow.

"Well isn't that part of your insides?" gurgles JJ, hugely amused by himself.

Opening my eyes, cautiously, I find I am millimetres away from an auroch-sized cow-pat.

"I need Punch," I mumble. "When he's finished killing that, I'm going to get him to kill all of you, slowly. Very slowly and I shall watch."

"Oh dear," says Tiggs, possibly with a hint of remorse. "Do you want a suck of my peppermint, now I've licked the fluff off?"

"Yes," I say sullenly, "but that will excuse nothing. You didn't come to my aid. Your debt is huge. You'll be giving more than lip service to my private parts for weeks."

"Could be worse," says Tiggs, bounding off.

Were there to be an opposite of the beech 'hanger,' this vale of trees might be it. It sits in its green hollow, almost imitating a fur stole sensuously rising up a slender neck, a reversed and elegant answer to the beech hanger's jaunty beret.

Outlying, young trees, are slim, tall and light on leaf. They seem full of a sense of airy hope and opportunity, as if they were thinking they might uproot themselves to emigrate, simply in search of adventures.

They flank a narrow path that winds away into older, sturdier growth, trees that are well-established among coppices of hazel. Not far along the path is a rugged line of hawthorns, something of an anachronism in a wood. My guess is that they were once a hedgerow, overtaken when the forest pushed its way through them, decades ago.

My tree lore is improving. Largely because Pa loves to talk about the Hedge, which usually leads him on to talk about trees. As regards the Hedge, he is forever marvelling at how benevolently it had behaved towards him, whereas I am still well-aware of how maliciously it had behaved with me. Nevertheless, whatever differences we recorded as personal memories, neither of us doubt that in its role as a green fuse, it is electricity personified.

Pa had two keepsakes that he was rarely without. The first was 'old clay', the quite useless stub of clay pipe he'd found under its branches. This he would set between his lips and drift away into a brown study, a sailor forever compelled to look to the sea's horizon. The other was the stub of bone I'd retrieved for him. It fascinated him more than the lead cannon shot Tee had uncovered. That it should be that way always pained me, for I recalled how industriously she had excavated, digging in the mould of 300 years, while I whined at her for us to be off. I think the ball made him feel guilty, while the bone reminded him of, in comparison, good times.

Another thing we always agreed on was how mobile the Hedge seemed to be. For all its deep and solid roots it seemed to have an ability to surround you or, in Punch's case, open its branches to allow him passage. "Not tha' a' weren'y torn t' bits, boy!" He vividly recalled the flight but not much about his landing. "A dunno, a' war'n't in this 'ere world, not fer a goodly time." For my part, I could remember the claustrophobia of feeling jostled by its branches, despite the fact that I never really approached it. That had not been the sort of Hedge that would allow itself to be overtaken by the young pretenders of the forest. True, it had been engulfed but the trees involved had probably had to apply in writing and in triplicate.

I wondered how often Pa had lain on his back and stared up through the mantle of branches and leaves, to watch the tiny white clouds scudding by, like so many elusive memories. I was doing just that, lying on my back, alongside a bank of dwarfed ferns and simply staring into the blue. Something nearby smelled peppery and something else of nutmeg. When I craned my head back, the better to spot the clouds, I found I was neighbours with a fat, affable-looking mushroom, which was probably broadcasting scents from its gills.

What a sense of languor under these valley trees. Their trunks, unhampered by branches, have to push themselves up high to seize all possible light. Every available leaf has to be concentrated in the crown. In one way the trees that rise from the sides of the valley have it easier when it comes to light. They don't have so far to climb but their downfall is that they have to hang on to the sloping sides by their root tips. Some have lost that battle to maintain the vertical and are now lying at crazy angles, having fallen and become wedged between neighbours.

Even these still hunt for the light, hurling up vertical shoots from their trunks, in pursuit of the high-life, when once they would have nipped in the bud any branch that dared to suggest it had a future emerging more than 20 feet below the canopy. 'Which is not quite true, Beavie,' I correct myself. 'These vertical shoots have nothing much in common with branches. This tree has been re-organised by its intelligence. It is shooting out wannabee trees, not branches and each one is in pursuit of light. If it finds it, it will be able to feed the whole. The original crown has been abandoned. These fallen trees, confronted by death are fighting for light and life, by intelligently changing their life-plan. How odd is that,' I reflect, 'they are following the white light. Not the filtered green light of the wood's interior but the white light from outside…'

I lie here, in the short grass and realise that I am surrounded by life-lessons. For all the apparent tranquillity, life is as cut-throat here as it is on our streets. 'Gimme your money!' can be translated as 'gimme your light!' Only the fastest and tallest can get there and in so doing they will starve out the competition.

This side of the valley seems to be favoured by ash trees. Some are still young, in smooth, silver-grey bark, while others have matured and become fissured and craggy. All of them rear up like the voice-pipes of an organ.

"Ash," Pa tells me, "gud log fer t'fireside an' 'e meks a fine tool 'andle. Tha' can turn it green, fer stool legs an' tha' turnin's come away like 'tato peel. As fer tha' pole-lathe, weel tha'll be a' buildin' 'im unner a livin' ash saplin'- fer yon's wot tha'll use fer't pole! (Took me some time to work that one out. The more excited and confidential Pa gets, the thicker his accent grows. It seems that a pole lathe is driven by the whippiness inherent in a young sapling. The top of the sapling is connected to a foot treadle you've cunningly constructed and the connecting rope has taken a couple of turns around the billet of ash you are turning. You depress the treadle and the springy, young sapling bends and the wood on your lathe rotates. You then release the treadle and the sapling corrects its posture, whilst your wood rotates yet again. On one of those rotations, the piece of turnery will rotate towards you, which is when you press your razor sharp chisel to it and the turnings come off, 'like potato peel.')

Now we have to season our stool legs. "Stack tha' legs crissy-cross fashion, somewheers as is shelterin' from everythin' 'cept time. Then, see wot time brings ye. 'Appen a few turns oot crazy, like folk bent o'er in't back. Others'll be 'olding 'ard t'theer shape. 'Tis these tha' drills fer't crosspieces, which tha's alree'dy turned up and 'tis these tha' drives inter some craggy owd seat o'elm, tha' kin trust ne'er t'split on thee. Then son, tha's med' a stool fer tha' weary bum!"

His spiritual son had looked at him with what he trusted had been large, panda eyes, hoping to be excused stool-making in deference to gender dysphoria, though I'm not at all sure why that should influence anything.

I think he cottoned on, for with a sigh he had added – "them shavin's tha saved, dry reet fast an'll gi' thee a gud cookin' fire, as'll them twisty legs."

Then he had discoursed on elm, in which any sections of twisted grain made for fine seats and wheel hubs, while wide, clear-grained boards, cut from the run of the trunk, were the very business for coffins. "Anywheer as is wet, boy, e' b' worthy. Tha's why a ship's keel'll be o' elm, or owd watter pipes." The joke he never tired of was – "elm'll gi' thee a fine seat t'perch on wh'n tha's livin' an' a fine coffin wh'n tha' finally falls off t' seat!" To which he would usually add an old country saying to the effect that – 'elm hateth man and waiteth.'

"Meanin' as 'ow them girt owd branches'll gi' way, an' fall on thee all o' a sudden, like. Be thee unwary an' idlin' unnerneath, tha'll be a needin' thy coffin, sharpish!"

We were all now wandering down the valley, taking our own snaking paths, which was why I had had time to reflect on Pa and consider the intelligence of trees.

Once I'd got myself up and said goodbye to the mushroom, I continued on my path, a natural upwards meander that led, eventually, to a collapsed bank, a small landslip. The earth revealed looked like dense, useful sand, the sort that might make mould material for a foundry but surely not sand sturdy enough to maintain a tunnel shape, such as the one some beast has excavated in it?

A hole that size must lead to a badger sett but nothing here seems fresh. If it ever was a sett, it must now be abandoned. I peer into the entrance. Inside, elbows of tree root stick out of the roof, only to immediately snake back in to the walls. In that way a naturally interwoven reinforcement for the inherently treacherous sand is formed.

Once again, I'm startled by the clever ruses of the wild. I can't see far but as far as I can see, this tunnel is driven under roots and rootlets, taking advantage of the dense mesh they form. Do badgers have the wit to take advantage of natural reinforcing-bars? It would seem so. Do they, then, favour certain trees, known to them to form thick, wide-ranging root-balls and do they assess where that underground growth will lie most thickly, then dig there? These sort of considerations have never exercised my mind before.

Wasn't Tigger holding forth about such matters recently? That we are born into the world and inevitably have to accept our blueprint for living and surviving, from preceding generations. Also, that we have to take what we inherit on trust. We don't have the leisure to examine their discards and say – 'hang-on, why did you dump this? That was a good thing!'

As 21st Century Westerners we don't need to know how to build a shelter, construct a stool, or rig a pole-lathe. We don't have to build a brick-kiln, bake our bread in a furze oven, or journey to the mill to have our flour ground – or grind it ourselves, one in a line of happy, singing girls working diligently at the metate.

It's not that we couldn't do those things. It's that the skills necessary have been superseded. They're not precisely discarded, nor are they entirely out of reach. They exist, in generational memory, here and there. I'm particularly lucky, because Punch and Marie-Claire bridge 300 years and given a few basics, could survive anywhere – provided they had enough land to roam across.

Squatting in front of the sett, with half an eye watching the wild caroomings of Tigger, who is intent on secret matters of deep concern to her, I recall a trip we all made to the Seven Sisters, in Sussex.

Those white cliffs snake around to that infamous spot for suicide, Beachy Head. As it happened, we ended up wandering along a little estuary at a place called Cuckmere Haven. It's not much of an estuary, mostly a fresh water flow into the English Channel – not a place of moorings, or saltings. No deep water. Here and there, under the cliffs, are fallen lumps of chalk and flint, eroded out from the bones of Sussex and now being washed to oblivion by the tides.

Spying nodules of flint, Punch became quite over-excited, almost going into Tigger-mode, though age is against him. He fell to sorting among them, searching for any that would "strike out" as he put it, into gun flints. But search as diligently as we all did, we could find nothing to meet his standards. He would turn them this way and that in his horn-hard hands. Then sighting some grain that was wholly invisible to everyone else, he would strike a sharp, mean blow and the flint would shiver into a dozen fragments, all of which he would discard.

"Tsk,tsk, tsk…'tis no use. This 'ere en't gun-flint. Seems as 'tis true wot a's bin towd, as 'ow gun-flint 'as t' be mined. It do 'ave to come from a seam unner't' ground. These 'ere knobs be strikin' out brittl' n' crazy. No strength, no fire in 'em."

That was a wasted walk for Punch and he came as near to sulking as he ever could. Not that ice-cream failed to revive him and I don't recall him lacking any stamina when it came to sinking real ale, over a late-lunch.

As the beer made him expansive, he confided – "yer true gun-flint 'as t'be dug in Norfolk. We 'as t'git oursen' t' Norfolk, boy, Thetford way, as a've 'eard told. We'll fine 'em theer."

I, 'the boy,' in my chiffon-y summer dress, shuffled awkwardly. Alice, 'the girl,' in jeans and a Guernsey, stepped unerringly into the breach…or should that be 'breech'?

"I don't think they're mining gun-flint any more, Pa. Modern guns don't use flints."

"Weel, a' doesna' old wi' percussion caps a've 'eard tell of. A'reet fer sportin' fellas. In sport, yer misfire's just a missed bird, 'tis a different tale fer a fightin' man."

"That's all sorted, now, Pa," Alice said confidently. "The old paper cartridge you used has been done away with. What's called a bullet has the ball, the charge and the priming, in one metal casing. Today, the breech opens and you slide the bullet into place. You close the breech and you're ready to shoot. It's very simple. Look, let me draw a 'bullet' for you."

There followed the usual call for a pen and paper. The pen was forthcoming as was a beermat, on which a very accurate-looking bullet soon appeared. This led to a huddled discussion out of which phrases such as 'expansion-sealing…rifling…projectile/charge ratios…magazine-feed-rates…gas-recovery-auto-feed…rate-of-fire… selector-mechanisms' could be heard floating mellifluously.

Marie-Claire had leaned over to me and holding my hands first, reassurance that she was only teasing, had said with a conspiratorial wink – "and you are the boy, non, Evie?"

"Oooh, Marie!" Tiggs had cackled, "that was unworthy of you! Evie keeps his weaponry under wraps!"

"Poo!" I'd said and flounced off to 'The Ladies' in a pretend huff. I returned just in time to hear – "we'll keep belt-fed, heavy-machine-guns for next time, Pa. That's enough to digest today."

Punch had looked up, dazed. "Weel, weel, weel…" he'd said and those were, more or less his last words of the day, though I recollect he did manage a – 'yes, please,' to chips, later on.

Here and now, however, 'the boy,' on her creaky knees, staggers upright and pays more attention to the rest of the tribe. JJ is on the valley floor, carefully examining the rocks from which a stream emerges. Tee and Ally are currently on high points on either side of the valley. Ally seems unusually content, while Tiggs is still doing mad dashes here, there and everywhere.

I find I'm on a natural path, leading steadily along the middle contour, so I stay with it, appreciating its modest rise and fall, the fact that it maintains an excellent viewpoint. The whole valley is slewing to the left and that favours my outlook, as I am on the right bank. Nothing much seems to be changing, certainly we are not heading for impenetrable terrain. In fact, the sun is breaking through down there, which to me suggests a thinning of the trees, maybe leading to open fields? 'What a scout I'd make,' I think proudly. 'Well, Girl Guide, at least.'

I return to the issue of lost skills. My developing thesis will enquire – 'if everything "stopped," tomorrow, how far "back," in socio-historical terms, would we have to go to arrive on a self-sustaining plateau?' Let's ignore the nature of the Armageddon that caused this crisis and the inherent problem of 'rapacious-other-people.' If Tee and I were thrown out of the pram, into this wood, say, how would we survive, given that I finished the last peppermint some time ago? No car, no nearby supermarket, no passing traders, what the hell would we do?

Pa had had his Hedge, Crusoe had Man Friday who, being a local, knew stuff. The Swiss Family Robinson, if I remember correctly, got shipwrecked in the local supermarket and Quixote had Sancho Panza, who probably made sure the mad old twit didn't starve. But we'd be here, surrounded by nothing more than very green rabbit food. The only thing I've seen resembling human food, so far, is one friendly-looking mushroom. Not that I would know woodland edibles if I fell over them, sorrel and the like. Anyway, I doubt they'd keep you going for long.

If we crept out of the wood, maybe we could track down the owner of the giant poo and slay it with pointy-sticks and rocks, if it would keep still long enough. Or perhaps we could drive it over a cliff, a bison-jump, that's if there are any cliffs, locally?

Turning to the problem of fire, I know the theory – spindles, hardwood boards, soft 'punk.' Whirl the spindle round and round in a hole in the board, the friction strikes off enough heat to kindle the famously-inflammable 'punk.' Then, lo-and-behold, 'here we have firelight!' The problem lies with the fact that all the rotten wood I've seen has been wet-through, while all the spindles and hardwood boards are still green and growing.

Maybe there are fish in the stream? That's what JJ is doing! Searching for an evening meal! Maybe he'll find langoustine, or do I mean lampreys? Could we eat bits of each other, painlessly? Don't be stupid. Perhaps we'd just have to curl up, like the 'Babes in the Wood' and hope that a passing fairy story would bail us out.

I begin to feel quite downcast. I'd like to survive, please but there's too much of me. I'm too sophisticated a package to survive off a diet of beetles and earthworms, with the odd dandelion leaf as side-salad. Anyway, I haven't seen one dandelion and don't they make you pee, incontinently?

It's very unfair to bring a creature to the human-level of development without providing it with a fool-proof, fall-back survival kit. Why is it we can't eat grass, saplings, rotten wood, or leaves, if the going gets rough? Humans, of whom I am one, of sorts, require too many layers of support. We need long-established systems, together with their intermingled supply chains. This is why farmers farm, merchants buy and sell and commuters in the city eat sandwiches and drink coffee. It's complex but it's long-established and it works. Once you start taking bits of that jig-saw away, you end up here, stuck in a wood with rapidly diminishing stocks of adipose tissue and no toilet paper – though I do carry 30 sheets wherever I go, since the encounter with Pa's Hedge. So we could pretty well guarantee squeaky-clean bums and empty bellies, which makes me realise I'd be better off carrying emergency peanuts, rather than loo roll.

It appears there are many levels of adversity and it's only the very civilised variety that requires loo roll. That would be Duke of Edinburgh Award-style adversity. Armageddon-level adversity requires peanuts and preferably by the sack load.

'They're called "groundnuts," aren't they?' enquired my stomach, trying to be helpful. 'You could start digging, after all this is ground and it's all around us!'

"You need African ground, you fool!" I snarled at it, out loud, because I'd worked myself into a bit of a panic by now.

"African ground – what and why?" asked JJ. "Also, perchance, why am I a 'fool' in your eyes? I'm sure I am but an explanation might help me mend my ways."

"Agh!" I yelped, jolted into third party awareness. "How did I get down here? I was up there…" and I gestured informatively at the higher ground. "Also, you're not the 'fool,' JJ. I was talking to my stomach, it's the 'fool.' It told me I should be digging for groundnuts, so I was politely correcting it, on the question of which sort of ground yields 'groundnuts.' Hence, 'African ground.' I know, I know, I'm babbling. Blame the bends, compression sickness, I've just come down from 50 feet, really quickly. Oh no…I think you have to go up for 'bends.' What do you get when you go down too quickly?"

"Mmm," said JJ, "you mean the way you came down earlier?"

"Agh!" I yelped again. "where is the evil little sprite?"

"Safely up her bit of hill. She comes down in 50 yards or so, then we collect Tee."

"The Descent of the Maniacs," I said. "It should be set to music."

"Let me probe," said JJ. "What's going on between you and your stomach?"

"We were discussing the ins-and-outs of survival. I had decided we were unlikely to last long on beetles and sorrel, nourishing though they may be. The best option was to scare a local cow to death. But then we'd have to start a fire and find a way into the cow. Just because you scare them over a handy cliff, doesn't mean they land in ready-to-cook form. The fire is also problematic.

"The nuts came up because I'm carrying toilet paper. The last time we went to 'the wild,' absence thereof proved to be a serious omission and I have scrupulously honoured that hard-won experience ever since, by carrying a minimum of 30 sheets. In a civilised world, that is an excellent precautionary measure. However, I was discussing, with myself, a world that had just ended. Therefore, I had decided peanuts would be better than bog roll. Which is when my stomach forgot that they grow in Africa and why I was calling it a fool. Not you. Simple, really."

"Why couldn't you just go to the caff, like we always do?"

"Because the world has ended!"

"Has it? When?"

"Just now."

"Who told you?"

"Nobody told me!"

"So how do you know?"

"I don't."

"Then why are you so sure?"

"I'm not. I was pretending. Preparing. As with the toilet paper but in more depth."

"Do I see? Probably not but I can't take any more," he muttered to himself.

We walked quietly along the path. I absolutely know JJ was keeping a safe distance from me. He was probably anticipating a psychotic assault, a ravenous Evie in search of food. I found this hurtful. My explanation had been impeccably logical. I am constantly misunderstood. It is my fate.

In the distance Alice was waving.

"I beat you, I beat you!" she was chirping, grinning from ear to ear.

She looked thoroughly pretty and agreeable…that's if you didn't know how evil she was on hills. I checked, surreptitiously. There were none in sight. I guessed we were pretty much at sea-level, or near enough…though that wouldn't preclude a submarine, inland valley, so caution was still called for. I kept a careful distance from her.

"Help me, Lovely," pleaded JJ. "Evie's gone barking."

"Good Lord, why? What did you do to him?"

"It's all your fault," I said bitterly.

"Little me! What could I possibly have done?"

"You know very well. You rolled me down a hillside. A very humiliating and frightening experience for a peace-loving, aquatic creature of slow habit. It is due entirely to this inelegant motion that my brain has become jumbled and the philosophical section has got mixed up with the survival department, which is why I was desperately searching for groundnuts and calling your very agreeable companion a fool."

"That's all right," said Alice airily, "I've called him far worse. As for your brain, wasn't it always a bit jumbled?"

"Certainly not," I replied haughtily, "it had its own logic which made perfect sense to its owner…most of the time. Occasionally it might have seemed it had a tendency to non-sequiturs but this was faulty interpretation on the part of the listener. To me, those apparent segues made perfect sense."

"You mean as in the jump from the drip-rate of block pitch, to the habits of the eel?"

"Exactly! It's a relief to know you understand."

"I see," Alice said gravely.

Further along the path, Tee came lolloping down to meet us. "Tiggers," she panted, "are really hungry and thirsty."

"Evie has some groundnuts," said JJ.

"I do not!" I shouted. "I have some toilet paper and if people don't stop teasing me, when I get home I'm retreating to my lodge and am never, ever, coming out again!"

"Oh no, don't do that," JJ implored. " Might fresh scones, jam, clotted cream and tea soothe you?"

"They might," I said suspiciously, "if everyone lets me have first go at the jam and cream and no-one pokes fun at me for eating too much. You don't understand. I've just emerged from a time of no-food. It was traumatic."

"What have you done to my Beaver?" demanded Tee. "Apart from the roly-poly, it was working just fine when I left. Now listen to it!"

"Evie encountered a famine in the woods," explained JJ, "and has taken it very personally. Apparently you were both living on beetles and sorrel. And failing to start fires."

"You had to be there to really appreciate it," I explained to Tee.

"Would it help if I told you it's only three hours since pain au raisins and six hours since breakfast?" asked Tee.

"First of all, it was you issuing a call to rations just now. Also, it's nearly seven hours since petit dejeuner and as I recall you had your breakfast – then ate mine!"

"But to be fair, you had your custard."

"That fat pig from MI5 stole most of it. You've seen the photographic evidence."

"I really shouldn't have rolled him down the hill. I feel awful," said Alice.

"She'll be fine after scones," said Tee, "you'll see. He's actually quite resilient. It's a celebrated attribute of Beavers."

47

'O WAD SOME POW'R THE GIFTIE GIE US,
'TO SEE OURSELS AS ITHERS SEE US!'

Tee is so excited she's nearly bouncing off the walls. I'm excited, too but it's mixed with a mass of butterflies in the stomach. Not that I'm scared but I am anxious. Tee has never seen me like this before and I'm so hoping, maybe praying…what? Mainly, that she'll 'get-it.' I so need her to 'get-it.'

The revelation that started all this is barely a week old. Andy sought us out, on the Monday, I think it was and said – "Evie, I've got some pretty amazing news. At least, I think it's amazing. I just hope you do, too."

"Tell me, do. I'm all ears!"

"Me too! Me too!" squawked Tee. "I have enormous, trunky ears!"

We'd been lounging on the bench in the allotment where, in the absence of Marie-Claire and Punch, they being on yet another Cotswolds' break, we had been allotted weed control duties. To be fair, until Andy's arrival we had been hard at it but we'd called 'pax' some minutes ago. Since then we had been discussing the absence of our mentors.

"Without them," said Tee, "this place feels like the 'Marie-Celeste.' We know where they are but I don't think the vegetables do and daft though it may sound, I think it's bothering them."

"I keep telling my rows," I said. "I've told the broad beans and asked them to pass it on but I don't think they've told the early peas. "

"Marie-Claire's winter pansies are plain sulking," said Tigger. "I've told them in French but they give that Gallic shrug routine, then pull their berets over their eyes."

"I'll try an All-Stations Broadcast, Tiggs…here goes…fingers in ears! – WE MISS THEM TOO!" I boomed… No visible effect whatever.

"It's a peculiar thing but my life needs them in exactly the same way as it needs oxygen. Some days I look at them and they're not really that old at all. But they feel ancient, like standing stones, the great big irregular ones you see at Avebury and Carnac. They wouldn't fit in at Stonehenge at all. If I'm going to describe them, I need a word that evokes the feeling you get in old, country graveyards, where the stones lean towards the church, the grass hasn't been cut, apart from on the paths, the seed heads are blowing and rabbits are flitting to and fro. A place where moss has grown into the chiselled names and time has simply stopped. That's the feeling I have about them but I haven't encountered the word – yet. Maybe I'll invent one."

"I know what you mean," agreed Tee, "but I doubt they'd find that too flattering. Anyway, Marie-Claire's not really stone, is she? She's as soft and gentle as…I don't know, a nana's warmth under her cardigan, a familiar old cardigan with a ball of wool in the pocket."

"Then we've probably got to get one of the standing stones a cardigan," I suggested.

"We'd know what we meant," nodded Tee. "I did start reading Worzel Gummidge, the other day. He's very Punch like in some ways, very not in others. Did you know, in India, the little kids are sent out to scare the birds?"

"That suits," I ventured. "Rugged old scarecrows with the hearts and minds of children, in the innocent sense. Yet," I continued in a whisper, "and I am now breaking sworn confidence, 'twas on yonder tank trap, many, many moons ago, that your bestie, Whiskers, told me that Punch was an avenging devil, until that cannon ball you found rammed him through the Hedge. Apparently he'd been pursuing a very dark vendetta for many years and was red in tooth and claw. That info' comes in an Official Secrets Act wrapper, Sweet Pea, so…"

"Zipped!" said Tee, with appropriate gesture, "but while we are 'alone and unobserved,' what oh-so gory details have you?"

"None, really. I gather that in his childhood some awful wrong was perpetrated upon his grandmother and when old enough, he hunted the wrongdoers down and delivered the ultimate in grievous bodily harm to each and every one, even unto the third and fourth generation, sort of…but I'm inventing and embroidering, so…take with a pinch of salt and added silence."

"I certainly wouldn't put it past him," Tee reflected. "His anecdotes are frequently of the swash and buckle variety, with added ketchup."

"Too true, too true…"

That is when Andy arrived, red in face, perspiring, bearing down on our bench, not so much assisted as propelled by his crutches and at a fearsome speed.

"Make way," he croaked, "emergency landing coming in! Clear all runways!"

Adroitly we rolled out of harm's way, just in time for him to land in a sprawl of aluminium tubing plus arms and legs, on the bench.

Once he'd finished puffing, he gasped – "what was, 'too true, too true,' oh fair ones?"

"Nothing of great import," I said, "merely that my spiritual Pa' has not always been the modest old gentleman we know today, eccentrically entertaining the favoured few with tales of derring-do, or weeding the onion bed with Marie-Claire as muse and companion."

"I'm sure that's right but didn't someone say that the past is another country? In Punch's case, given his peculiar circumstances, that is as good as the literal truth. And besides, don't we all parcel up the past and leave it…I don't know…where do we leave it? Somewhere, no doubt.

"Anyway, Evie, I have some pretty amazing news…" (which is where, if you were paying attention, we came in.)

"So spill the beans," growled Tigger, in her best growly voice, "my ears are flapping dangerously and you only have seconds to live, before I slice you open to search your entrails for said news!"

"Crikey," complained Andy, "I came in peace and at great personal peril. Seems I have fallen among beasts!"

"You better believe it," I said equably. "When she changes it's an awful sight. She sprouts razor claws and sabre teeth, then makes this terrible pounce!"

"OK, OK, I get it. Here I go…

"Evie, you remember in the past, before you became a peace-loving Beaver of slow habit, you were a bit of a wild child with a death wish?"

"Stay on-call, Tiggs," I said. "Your transformation may still be needed."

"Grrr!"

"I do recall those days," I agreed, "though events of that era have all been labelled 'hazardous waste' and sealed in a lead-lined casket, marked 'not to be opened for millions of years.'"

"Nevertheless, you will recall as if it were yesterday, that the late and on the whole, yeah, on the whole…lamented, Harold Caulke, painted a huge portrait of you. You as a conduit for energies. It was," he turned to Tee, "utterly, that abused word – 'awesome'- and amazing. If you didn't know it was Evie, you might have thought it was abstract. But oh, it wasn't! It so wasn't! Anyway, to recap, it sold even before the show opened for £140,000. After two weeks of critical praise in some influential prints, 'it-and-you' vanished to someone's very large wall, somewhere."

"I remember all that," I said passively. "It was the start of a very strange time in my life."

Andy talked on and on. Today, in Tee, he had found the ideal audience – silent, wide-eyed and drinking-up every word, every event that had led up to that bizarre evening.

As I listened I was glad he knew no more about my early days, for his recall was perfect, and of no assistance at all to the amnesia I was so assiduously cultivating around that decade.

After a while, I switched my attention to the cabbage whites. 'I will read the Insect Book,' I thought. 'I want to talk to them. I want to talk to them without scaring them. They have the strangest lives and so have I. Yet both of us know that we are utterly ordinary. Strange lives are lived by ordinary people and probably the reverse is true, too. Everything is like that, really, circular and chasing its own tail, though to what end beats me. Someone, somewhere must understand what's going on…mustn't they? Or is the whole operatic shebang a product of the sorcerer's apprentice and everything is going round in circles until the boss gets back? The butterflies might know.'

"…are you there, Beavie?" Tiggs was prodding me with Andy's crutch…

"No," I said mildly, "I was miles and miles away. What's new?"

Andy leaned out and grabbed my hand, pulling me back to the bench.

"Listen up," he said. "Yesterday, a punter turned up and asked to see the boss. Eventually Carl brought him up to 'the office' and over coffee we had a long chat. The gist of it was that this guy was the son of the mystery purchaser. His dad, he told me, was a mildly well-to-do, retired military gent who had totally doted on his younger, wilder wife.

"She wasn't wild as in 'wicked wild,' but she'd had a crazy, roving life, hunting down what he referred to as 'sources.' She was in search of certain fundamental truths and some of these she believed she saw in a category of art she called 'abstracted abstract art.' This was not, he stressed, a category that the art world recognised.

"Occasionally, she'd see some evidence that an artist had transcended the mundane and teased the exceptional from it. You could say that every artist aims to do that. But she maintained that very few achieved it. The ones that did, she called 'mediums,' after the old table-turning mediums who claimed to be able to contact other worlds. Her mediums and this is the important bit, drew – as in actual drawing – one thing by way of another. She maintained that they were conduits, used by Higher Intelligence, to attempt to communicate certain fundamental truths to we numbskulls. These artists were effectively 'employed' by Higher Intelligence to explain truths by way of painterly analogy."

Andy now began flapping his hands in indignant frustration. "I'm really bollocksing this. I almost got what this guy was raving about yesterday. Now it's me that's raving and I don't get it at all. Look, I'll try again, a painter could produce a still life and on the surface everything would be icily remote, in the way those things can be but underneath it could be frothing with ideas…not just the obvious ones like death, or plenty, but messages hidden in plain sight, if you like. Unconscious analogy is at the heart of it. That's why Harold's portrait is so important.

"Harold saw in you a way of analogising the coming together of diverse, competing energies. Competitive themes that harmonised in one being and flowed out transformed. I say 'Harold saw…' It was Higher Intelligence that saw and knew we were ready to hear something. It was equally aware that Harold was the painter to compose the analogy.

"I really have bollocksed this! Does anybody have a clue what I'm talking about?"

"I get it, I get it, I get it!" sang Tee, running up and down the grass, "my Beavie's a giant van der Graff generator and she's really, really important…" to emphasise which she started chanting mixed-up nursery rhymes, skipping in and out of cartwheels, and rolling over and over in series of somersaults.

"I'm sure she's quite loopy," said Andy admiringly. "Do you think she's another project by Higher Intelligence?"

I nodded my head slowly. "Yes, I think she is. I hope you weren't planning on going anywhere for a while. This has only just started and she's acting out what you've been trying to say. At least, I think that's what it is. This isn't Tigger being crazy. It's something else entirely. Don't ask me what, because I'm still learning the language."

We watched her perform some more crazy manoeuvres, Jack-in-the-Box hops, hand-walking, somersaulting and corkscrew spins, until I yelled – "Tiggs! Feeding time!" and she bounded over. Sprawled on the bench, she smothered us both in kisses until she decided it was time to waltz away again. With a peppermint gobstopper bulge in one cheek and cheerfully mangling her nursery rhymes in a mixture of Hindi and English, she rolled very slowly down the grass to the drainage ditch, only to topple gracefully over the edge, vanishing from view.

"Don't drown, Tiggs!" I yelled.

"OK!" rose out of the long grasses.

"She'll be wet through!" groaned Andy.

"So long as she floats, I can cope."

"Tigger control is totally beyond me," admitted Andy. "I'll go on with my story. Suddenly, it seems simpler. OK. Or rather not OK. Dearly-beloved wife and mum upped and died a while back. Upon which, Dad had one of these," and Andy gestured at his still defaulting body, while making a corkscrew motion with one finger in the air.

"You mean he went loopy, too?"

"Not precisely. He developed obsessions. Wouldn't, won't, leave the house under any circumstances. Son thinks it's because he believes his wife has just 'gone out for a while' and could be back at any moment. He sits and broods, staring at Harold's painting, which he simply doesn't understand. His wife loved it, adored it. Out of all the artwork he'd bought and commissioned for her, this was the one piece she couldn't leave alone.'

"She'd explained 'why' to them both, endlessly but the more she explained, the more helpless they both felt. She might as well have been talking in tongues." He added ruefully – "I think I know how she must have felt!

"The old gentleman's current obsession is 'who was Harold's model and is there any way he can talk to her?' He believes she must understand something of what his wife felt. If he could only talk to her…"

I felt sudden, physical, weight settle on me, together with the knowledge that I wasn't through with the past, however much I might wish I was.

"Son and heir did some digging and without much trouble tracked Harold's last years to here, to No-Name and all that in it is… He made a recce and saw what he saw, which is why he ended up probing my slender store of information, over a cup of coffee. All I told him was that I'd been Harold's unofficial everything, including court-appointed executor. Also, for free, I said I thought he was an unacknowledged genius and one of the great 'unknowns' of his century."

"Can I interrupt?" I asked.

"Absolutely, be my guest."

"Just let me check on the Tiggs, first." I stood up – "Tiggs, you still alive Sweet Pea?" Slowly, a complex construction of long grasses and assorted weeds rose up like a lonely egret from the ditch and nodded its head of buttercup flowers. "That's lovely! Make sure it has a name." I turned back to Andy. "She's all right. Calming down now. No, I was thinking, earlier, about the Insect Book."

"Ah, indeed. And.?"

"And nothing, directly. Just another question mark. But if one was collecting question marks, you could add in Harold's crazy eye and mind that could see whatever it was that he saw. Add to that Ishmael's crazy ear and mind that could talk to insects, with music. They don't and they do, seem to add together, don't they? 'Unidentified objects in the bagging area,' if you like. Somehow, they must add together and while I'm at it, what would you say is still missing?"

Andy looked stunned.

"Blimey, Evie, I don't really think that way, which is not to say that you're wrong… just that… just that…I'm not precisely equipped to answer your questions. As for proposing lost elements, missing elements, you should be looking for deep-dive metaphysicians to answer that one. My thinking is superficial, as in 'on the surface' of things. I order stock and pay people wages…I don't look for cosmic clues in the wide-blue yonder. Should I go on with my story?"

"You can, in a minute," I said. "First I'm going to drop another OMG into the pot. My 'Third Eye'… I'm the one who's got it and I've actually used it, as you know. But what it is, how it functions, whether it has anything to do with that monster ruby that came with it, I have no idea. JJ knows more about it than I do but he's annoyingly coy about the whole business. He insists that all he knows is hearsay and not worth repeating – which is massively irritating.

"He certainly wasn't surprised when it 'lifted' him, Punch, Marie-Claire and Alice out of the poo and into the 21st century. All he'll say about that is that there's a link between Alice, Punch and I that's been forged by a Higher Intelligence and our little 'spiritual family' is a unit in some chain of events that will probably remain completely unknown to us. Someone, something, has turned us into a cog in a box of gears.

"I mean, I ask you, Andy…" and I put a hand on his knee… "do I look like Punch's son, to you?"

He blushed. "No. Of course you don't. But within the family, it's a truth and no-one is going to question its validity. It's a truth with a reason behind it and we'd be fools to question it."

"Absolutely," I agreed. "Punch doesn't question it, nor do I. Well, we do…but we don't."

"However, I'm not done. There's that wretched lens that Marie-Claire found…"

"Now I don't have a clue what you're on about!"

"No, no more you do. I'll fill you in, some time."

From the ditch came the lines of an extempore nursery rhyme…

> "Hickory, dickory dock!
> "A Tigger ate a clock!
> "The hour struck – BONG!
> "But sounded all wrong,
> "Cos it came out of a Tiggery bot!

A strangely weedy creature staggered up the garden towards us. It was dressed in the latest fashions from the Ditch-Range and it is surprising that it wasn't followed by a line of admiring frogs, newts and papparazzi.

"Refuelling, please…plee…ee…ase!"

"Open!" In went a peppermint.

"Fl-a-nk foo!" … and away the weedy creature skipped…

> "Phick-ory, phlick-ory, plock.
> "A fliggra ate a flock…

…not to the ditch, this time but to the highest point of the tank traps, where it sang its mellifluous song to the clear blue sky…until it collapsed out of sight.

"Are you sure she'll recover?"

"She'll be fine."

"I've never seen a full-blown attack before."

"Oh, that's not a full-on, hyper-blow. They can be quite awesome. Sometimes I have to capture her, sit on her and tickle her tummy till she calms down."

"Sounds relatively peaceful."

"Try it some time."

"Rain-check on that but back to my story…

"I told the son that I had a pretty good idea who the model had been. That she was a very special person. That it was an equally special set of circumstances that had brought them together. That the whole event sparkled either with pure serendipity, or Higher Design." Andy smiled. "Of course, he leapt at Higher Design."

"I wouldn't be so quick to dismiss it myself," I said, "given the subsequent flow of events. Anyway, go on."

"I said I'd make some calls on his behalf. Take some counsel, maybe make a trip.

But I did promise I'd get back to him with a – 'yes, the lady in question is available,' or a – 'no, the lady is no longer accessible.' Of course, what he wants is for you to go and meet his dad. I'm pretty sure he wants to meet you on his own account, too. You'd have to go to his place. His dad can't and as I've mentioned, won't travel. I told him I'd have a progress report within a week or so, I thought you'd need time to stew over it."

I'd gone back to watching the cabbage whites and wondering exactly where Tigger was. She could very easily have decided to somersault all the way round the main road, nude but given no horns were blaring, that might not have come to pass.

I'd known where this was going to end up from the opening sentences and my immediate and very strong reaction was to issue a decisive 'NO'.

"I'll leave you to your thoughts," said Andy.

I grabbed his hand.

"Don't think me ungrateful. I really do appreciate your heaving yourself out here to tell me. And congratulations on being able to do that, by the way. Do you need help going back?"

"Thanks but no. Carl would kill me if he found out I strayed this far – but I felt I had to tell you."

"I really do appreciate it. You're a true friend. I need to do some proper thinking though, because there's no denying that this was a surprise."

The four-year-old trotted past on her hands.

"Bye, Flandy – loove ooo! Fee oo shoon!"

"I'll go," he said and heaved himself up on his crutches. "See you soon too, Tiggs."

"Ploo foo!"

He laboured away. As he made the offset of traps that doubled as a gate, Tiggs did a triple-forward roll towards the leeks, stood up in time, brushed herself down and sprinted back to the seat, where she flopped full-length on the boards, head in my lap.

"Phew," she said calmly, "I thought that was going to be a three-peppermint break-out but two seem to have done the business. Nevertheless, you are my cleverest Beaver!"

I stroked her bristle of hair, cut number two had just been done and replied – "I wasn't really a Beaver then. You wouldn't have recognised me."

"I'd recognise you anywhere, in any state," she insisted happily. "We are going, of course, aren't we?"

I made a throaty noise which, like the breakfast sniff, carried a lot of load. It expressed an understanding of her eagerness, set against largely negative reservations of my own, a fear of the past, an eye to the future and a conservative attitude that I hadn't been aware I possessed.

"I'm not entirely sure," I said at last.

"But Evie! This is pre-Beavie! I didn't know you then. I HAVE to know you then. I want to see if he saw what I see and who sees most. Am I missing something? Does it hurt?…"

When she said that, I started to cry. Because yes, it hurt. It hurts all the time. Why else would I hide behind the buffoon role I've created? I have a lot of time for the honourable position of court jesters but I'd rather be exploring the land beyond their remit of politics, supper and slander.

I wanted to know about things that didn't reek of the past. I was eager for answers to the question marks of life. I didn't want answers born of fear and desperation. I want to know how the cosmos hangs together. Is the human race important, at all? Are we on the verge of a paradigm shift in our understanding? Are we headed for swift extinction?

Parts of the portrait touched on these questions but to see those I had to own the chaotic portions that didn't. Those were humiliating, perhaps they even jeopardised my future. I couldn't bear the thought of my castles in the air, falling about my ears because of some unexploded mine from my past. And God knows, there were plenty.

I was going to have to go on this jaunt. Maybe, the slimmest of maybes, this old man, touched by his fey wife, knew something about the ground where my answers were to be found? Perhaps Tiggs would see them and I wouldn't? She was perceptive in places where I was blind and she was fearless, when I was cowardly.

"Evie, Beavie, Evie-Beavie," implored the Tigger, breathing out a peppermint cloud that could have unblocked an elephant's trunk, "I know you're going to say 'yes.' Just say 'yes' to me first. I know it hurts. There are bits of Princess Lupa that really hurt, too."

She fell silent, staring around the garden as if it was a place she'd never seen properly until now and though she found it interesting, unfortunately, it was also irrelevant. Then she took a breath and began, softly – "I never wanted to tell you this but now I will.

"My father pushed me away, days after I was born, because I wasn't a boy. He told my mother to take me to Dada-ji and Dadi-ji's, forever. I wasn't old enough to hear, or speak but somehow, I knew. I was so vain, so needy, even then and I knew I looked pretty in my little white frock. What was I – three, four days old? How dare he push me away, when I was so, so pretty! I knew. I couldn't know. But I knew. That hurt, it still does. I know it's a different sort of hurt. I feel outrage, you feel guilt. Trust me though – my vanity has caused more hurt than your actions ever did. You may have humiliated yourself in front of others. I have humiliated loyal, kind people."

Now it was Tiggs' eyes that were full of tears.

"That really is pain," I said. "I tell you what. We're going to have a pain swop. You have mine. I'll have yours."

She sat up. "Ye-e-es! I'd never thought of that. That would work. Let's go and do it, now. You can show me how."

We went home, hand-in-hand, climbed into bed and swopped pains. It was good.

Swopping pain is gambit play. It's a bit like offering to pay your partner's parking ticket, the one that they're finding so unfair that it's eating them alive! All you take is the financial hit, the material burden. The grudge and the itch, which the 'unfairness-of-it-all' has exacerbated, are nothing to you. And once you announce it has been paid – miraculously your partner no longer feels the ugly need to lash out at everyone and everything.

We lay, motionless, holding hands on our comforting old mattress, under the acres of duvet we both deemed necessary for survival. I thought about Tee's father. Visualised him in his echoing palace. 'You self-regarding, empty-brained, double-barrelled, piece-of-shit,' I thought. 'I hope you choked on your pride and died, knowing that the child you rejected, exceeded you in every facet of your being.'

I can't know what Tee thought but I knew she would examine my fear-filled rage. She would examine my anger that my anatomy might be no more than a trick to amuse a demi-god. That I was merely another monkey for a jester's shoulder. These humiliations she would brush up, like so much broken glass and throw away. As for the capers at Muti's farm and the agonies that proceeded them, she would draw a line through those, as if they were redundant adjectives hustling for precedence in an overlong sentence.

We rolled together and were one. We were good at that, now.

Now the day is here. I have butterflies and Tee is doing Tigger bounces. I give her a calming peppermint and get back that mournfully melodic – "thank-foo-o" – exactly like an American freight train's whistle, best heard in sleepless hours of the night.

Then Carl gives his 'respectable-person's' knock and we head out to the car.

Thankfully, bouncing Tiggers accept that they are currently unfit to drive two-ton automobiles, so we begin a thoroughly uneventful transit into Berkshire – and I get to keep my eyes open for once.

Half-way, we glide into an acceptable looking Services. The inevitable request for cola is ignored and the ritual of four large, black Americanos and four pain-au-raisin, is ceremoniously conducted.

"If anyone doesn't want their Danish…" Tee fishes hopefully, "…I'm ready, willing and able." She looks around with an appealing, child-like eagerness and on seeing three scrupulously empty plates, slumps dejectedly across my lap. I brandish a £20.00 note at a willing barista and hold up three fingers and an empty plate. "Two-to-go," I hiss. They arrive and I gently scratch her thick matt of crew-cut.

"Mmmmr-r-r-r-ffpl-ff," she says to my thighs. "Leave alone. Dying, so soo-oon."

"Food!" I whisper.

"Purrrr-oo-f! Oh yum. I really, really, really need this! Not driving is very exhausting and I've done all my colouring-in. Than-foo, foo, foo!"

"Don't eat the serviette!" I say in sudden alarm.

"Eh, ooh! …ppllff …no …quite right! Look, is everyone ready? I've been ready for ages! Oh!OH! I need a WEE. NOW!!"

"My Lord," says Andy, to Carl, "we must never have children…"

"She's 34," I say drily.

"Well, I suppose there's time to mature yet."

"Hope not," I say, "she keeps me young."

Carl starts to laugh out loud.

"What?" we both demand.

"Remember the rescue gang? The lads who salvaged her car off the tank traps?"

"Every time I see one of them, which is not that often, they never fail to say – 'who was that girl?' It's like the closing scenes of that old black and white TV series, 'The Lone Ranger'…someone he'd saved, or one of their ever-grateful family, had to bleat in astonished tones – 'who was that masked man?' And a super-male voice would say, as the credits rolled, 'that was the Lone Ranger!'… and his horse would rear-up on its hind legs and he'd thunder off to the next adventure."

"Which kind of raises the question," murmured Andy, "of where the hell has she got to?"

We all periscope around the amusing diversions and potential wrong-turns, but no Tigger is in sight.

"She's not going for another hair-lop after this one, is she?" asks Carl. "It's really hard on my psyche."

"Try it on your bosom," I say, "on day four and five. And yes, she is, the third and last time. But you should see the silver mask she's having made. She wants my ruby for one of its brow diadems."

"One of?" asks Andy.

"Oh yes. I think and I'm not sure, because she isn't sure, that it might have seven faces. You know, Janus-style, where you get two faces every three eyes? So you can get seven faces for seven eyes and seven noses – you're not keeping up, are you? Anyway, the sun is already in there and the moon's face…"

"…has your bum!" interjects Carl…

"…even worse, Sunshine. It has my face!"

At which we all get hysterics, just in time for the return of the absent Majesty.

"Coo-eee!" she thunders across the open-plan half-mile, "that's so much better! You know, I was absolutely full to the brim! Bursting!"

"Young women these days," mutters some passing soul, righteously affronted.

"Thing is," demands Majesty, "are you sure I can't have just the teensiest cola? It is my car, after all!"

"And we are not having you wee in it," I say firmly. "You're getting very over-excited, come on now, act your age."

"I'm four," Tee says adamantly.

"And a half…" I add.

"Am I, really?" she gasps in amazement.

"Yes, you grew overnight."

"I knew something happened," she squeaks joyously. "Are there any holes to go down, or hills to roll on where we're going?"

"I absolutely do not know but whether there are or not, you are neither going down them, or rolling on them. You have your best dress on."

"I could tuck it in my knickers," ventures Tee hopefully.

"Let's wait and see, shall we?"

Finally we get her back to the car and trap her between Andy and myself, in the back.

"Why can't I sit in the front?"

"Because the pains au raisin are in the back."

"Ah! Can I have one?"

"In 20 minutes."

"What!?!"

"Twenty minutes, we're going to play 'I-spy' first."

"Oh good! Me first!"

We finally arrive, liberally coated with sticky crumbs, at the imitation of an Elizabethan mansion – or something similar, as conjured from nightmare by a speculative builder, circa 1920. To my horror it is also possessed of a short, beautifully-manicured, embanked lawn, one that spills down gently towards a wider, lower, grassy terrace. That slope, seen under the mid-morning sun can only be described as unholy temptation, in the form of pure hill-rolling bliss.

I make a futile grab but she's away and gone, just as the huge front door, its timbers baked to the colour and texture of beef jerky, swings open. There stands a young man, presumably the one who came to question Andy.

"So good of you to come! Come in, do come in…oh, just a second.!" He steps forward, then swivels unbelievingly on one heel. Peripheral vision has caused him to twist around to see the glory that is Tiggs in full-flight. He stares, aghast – "now who the hell? What is going on out here? Hey, you!"

"Stop! Stop. Don't worry," I say hurriedly. "I do apologise. Just a bit over-excited. Brought up in a very flat part of India. No hills to speak of for miles. She's making up for lost time. Second childhood, possibly her fourth, I've lost count. Can you bear to just leave her be? She'll catch up in her own good time. You'll see…utterly charming, merely a tad ingenue."

"Good Heavens," says the young man, quite obviously defeated on every level. I see him take a deep breath for England. Then he tries again – "ha, ha…must be getting set in my ways. Too old for my decade, what? I really must get out more. Of course she can roll downhill…all day if it makes her happy. But, er, who is she…if I might make so bold?"

"Brace yourself," I say. "I'll give you the short version – that is Princess Tulipa Agnethuram, of Sikhim, though she's never actually set foot in the country. She is not the model – if you're starting to fret."

"Oh no, not at all, no. Now, Andrew's probably told you that I'm Jonathan Sawyer. I'm a creature of no work and unknown abilities. I live here with my recently derailed father, as I explained and a houseful of 'abstracted-abstract art,' something else I tried to explain. Lot of explaining…"

"I got the drift, Mr Sawyer. Andy did a good job. Carl you've met before, I believe. I'm Eva, commonly Evie and I'm the person who modelled for Harold that night. Unlike my other half, currently rolling down your lawn, I'm pure vanilla."

"Lovely to meet you…and, again…oh, look, do just come up and meet Pa. He's a shadow of his former self but he's still perfectly compos mentis. Nearly all the 'art' is upstairs. We have a poor man's imitation of a long gallery. It runs the length of the house and makes a passable gallery. Pa had some rooms bashed through to make the whole-thing into a sort of T-shape. You'll see why in a minute." He gestured with his hands, striving for architectural visions in the air, while moving backwards all the while. That proved to be a difficult undertaking, when attempting to rise graciously through the threshold and into the short hall. But he managed it, despite a few stumbles.

Now he stood anxiously at the foot of the great staircase, one foot on the first tread, one hand to the banister. "Do you…are you sure…the 'Princess' will find us, if we just vanish upstairs?"

"Actually, Mr Sawyer, I'm more concerned about Andy," I say. "I don't believe he can swing himself up that lot, without all four of us pushing and pulling. Surely, with your dad, you have a lift, by now?"

He clapped a hand to his forehead. "Oh I am a damn fool! So rude. I do apologise. Just a bit thrown, y'know – the lawn rolling, surprised me. Of course, of course… Andrew, I'm so sorry. Do come with me. Of course we had to get a lift installed. Actually, we had to get it for mum but now it's doing duty for Pa.

"Eva…mm, Evie…will you be able to find us…once you've, y'know, the Princess? I mean, in your own time, of course. Just up the stairs and it's fairly obvious. I'll get on with Andrew and Carl. Please, in your own time…so sorry."

"I'll go and try to gather her up," I said. "We'll find you."

Carl winked at me, as they crocodiled away down the gloomy hall. I went in search of Majesty and fresh air.

God but this is a dismal hole! Dark-stained panelling, its varnish long ago dried to dustiness. Parquet floor scored by a million boot heels. Along every wall hang tapestries and all are faded to the level of well-worn rag rugs. I hate tapestries. Even the liveliest seem to wither under scrutiny. In my mind they occupy a no-man's land between oversized tea-towels, wallpaper and draught excluders. I peer at these offerings on my way back to the front door and fail to make out form, feature or function. I'm not surprised the courtiers of Versailles pissed behind the wretched things. I'm tempted to revive the custom.

At the door, I look back, just to confirm I'm right and I conclude that this whole place died shortly after it was built. All it can await is demolition, resurrection being quite impossible.

Outside I take some deep breaths, ridding myself of the shade of Miss Haversham that permeates the interior. The sun seems cheerful, radiant and hopeful.

"Tiggs," I bawl, "we'll be upstairs when you're done."

"OK!" comes the happy reply.

"It's just that you said you'd like to see, remember?"

Silence. Suddenly broken by – "Oh! Evie-Beavie!" Then the pounding of feet and a panting, tousled figure arrives at my side.

"Jabberwocky! Evie! I almost forgot. Anyway, here I am. Lead me on."

"Take your skirt out of your knickers and shed those holes that used to be tights… yeah?"

"OK, OK, but I'm so excited, sweetheart."

"As calmly as you can then."

"OK" – wriggling like jelly.

Past the wretched tapestries once more and I still can't make out any theme. Zeus and his coal scuttle? Or is it a very small bus?

"Ugh," says Tiggs. "Gloomy, gloooooomy, glooo-ooo-ooo-me, oh my!"

"I think our trashy trailer has got the edge on this."

"AGREED!"

Up the majestic central staircase. The huge window on the half-landing is north-facing, so the heraldic cartouches in the glass, few and far between as they are, have the look of hopeful wanderers in an icy wilderness. The cold light that is admitted illuminates a huge copy of some lesser master's vision of St. Marco, Venice, on a rainy day.

"Grrr!" challenges Tiggs, as we climb past the carved lions and griffins surmounting the stair newels but being unequivocally wooden, they fail to snarl back at her. Then, as we're passing the painting she trots over to Venice and pokes her finger at an opaque blob of burnt umber, in one of the arcades and says – "Vikky and I had huge ice-creams, just there, on our honeymoon!" Ridiculously I feel a sudden surge of jealousy and she is aware of it at once. "We'll go, too and have twice as much!" she insists, hanging from my arm to prove it.

Oh, I don't like this house! It's the worst some Historic Trust might have to offer, a cul-de-sac of punctured aspirations, severed from whatever intention might once have informed them. From the faded-out tapestries, to the dirty varnish obliterating San Marco, by way of heraldries unknown, this place is lost. If they only had the energy, the bricks and mortar would sigh beneath the weight of futility they've been asked to bear so pointlessly.

At the head of the stair we hover. Hearing voices we head in their general direction. Ah, possibly not, we may be going away from them. We look at each other and shrug. Now we have a choice, this tiny corridor, or that one. We 'eeny-meeny' it, with Tiggs giggling and take one that ends in an ante-room, what was possibly a servants' waiting area. Here the afternoon teas would have been assembled before being triumphantly born forth. To make an exit you have to insinuate yourself between a wall and grand double doors. Most odd.

We open one door a crack and slide through. Bingo! …here we are at the wrong end of the long gallery. This presents a problem of etiquette, way beyond my council-house up-bringing. At the very far end, a reverential arc has formed around a seated, rug-swathed figure, who is holding forth in a voice saturated with certainty and authority. Oh dear. Am I going to make it?

I'll persevere.

So far, I don't see any sign of me hanging from any of these walls and having come this far, I'd like to see me again. I signal a frantic 'SHUSH' to Tigger, who seems eager to burst upon the scene, like a stripper from a pasteboard cake and we creep, little mice, down one long wall.

We pass copy after copy of the edgier Grand Masters – Greco, Goya, Velasquez – then we hit the corner of a turning, that must be into the 'T' that Jonathan Sawyer described earlier. We take the turn and wow! There I am, right at the blind gable end, in a setting worthy of a Christ in Majesty. I'm seriously flattered. Vertical windows, on either side, deliver a filtered east-west light and illuminate the young Eva, in all her raging fury and certainty of purpose. I have to say, who shouldn't, that I look amazing – or rather the explosion, the curving spirals of light and electricity that hammer through me and then pulse out in whorls and gyres, they look amazing.

Tee is hissing – "Evie-Beavie – that really is you! Wow! It's fantastic! What a vision! What genius! What a technician. My Lord, who were you then, girl? You're part demon, part angel and a dozen other parts and pieces. Sweetheart, I've never seen the like! That is one 'kiss-my-ass' portrait." She paused… "but it's so much more than portrait, isn't it?"

Then she's loping down the length of the room, coming up in a heap to say – "look at that chrome yellow! It's like a snake… but it gets subsumed, chewed into froth – sperm is what that is – now a crimson cloud goes billowing up from the heat! Those greys, will you look at the greys? I never saw grey so charged before. Have you ever seen grey jostling, vibrating? They've got little clouds…" she crept closer… "little clouds with broken steel needles flying through them."

She turned to me – such a serious face. "I'm totally overwhelmed. You knew this guy? You discussed the price of bread together?"

"Egg and chips, usually. Apple pie, the pre-JJ variety, for afters. Loads of thick-sliced white, heavy with butter, too."

"Not much of a diet for genius."

"His preferred maintenance was cheap port and super-dry sherry. Egg and chips were robust solids, consumed usually – no, only – when I was paying. Otherwise some of the girls would take him leftovers. Sometimes he ate them, most of the time he didn't. In dietary terms he was 'an accident waiting to happen.'"

"And it happened?"

"It did."

We stand and contemplate the painting.

It has peculiar depth. Not from the inevitable over-laying of colour, nor from any attempt at perspective. Somehow and I can't see how, he has achieved the dream-like succession of images that David Jones built into his finest paintings. Energy lies over energy and because Harold didn't do 'filmy,' this is rude-boy layering. Lava sits on top of lava, that's the sort of overlay I'm talking about, the volcanic variety, laid down in molten rock, day after day. But what is translucent, is not the paint but the information. This painting is a three-dimensional theorem. For all I know it could have many more dimensions. It also has something of the quality of stained glass, in the moment when the sun lights up the gold, the reds, the greens and they ripple free of their leadwork to dance above the surface. That's when the myth can come to life.

I was there when the skeleton of this masterpiece was laid down. I am, or I was, that skeleton. I try for memories, for recall. There's nothing to draw on. Not only has the artist died, so has the model. The studio is still there, home to pigeons and pigeon crap but to ever recreate what this task took? Forget it. Truly, that river has rolled on to the sea.

I feel hugely sad. I never really retained anything from those painful hours. I was mortally embarrassed, frozen and horribly self-conscious. There was too much of me there. Far too much of me to be able to allow a quiet me to pay attention properly. All the bits of my ego were jostling to be noticed, that's when they weren't pretending to hide, so everything that happened, happened to someone else.

What a loss. I had prime position at an act of creation. I could have been silent and watched. I even thought I had, until now. In fact, my idiotic ego was waving its hands about, like the leader of some self-important orchestra. 'I was there, Officer but I saw nothing. A passing seagull probably noticed more.' What an expensive lesson in the cost and nature of inattention. I'd never be able to recoup it. Rueful doesn't even begin to cover it.

I know Tee can feel my ache because, silently she takes my hand, though her attention is almost wholly directed forwards, towards the canvas – or whatever we should call this message, or mnemonic. What it actually is, I don't suppose I'll ever learn.

A brusque cough behind us… "I do begin to wonder – will you ladies actually be joining us?" Jonathan Sawyer, in the presence of daddy, appears to have sharpened up his doorstep persona. He'll learn.

"I'll be a minute or two," says Tee, without turning round.

Sawyer makes a chewing noise which I translate as – 'what abominable cheek, to enter someone's house and fail to greet your host.' Coupled with, 'and what the hell do I say to a woman whose skirt is caught in her knickers, feet away from my self-righteous, prig of a father?' Though, to be honest, the last bit didn't really have its own noise.

However, not being blind, I can see the skirt and knicker problem too. I sidle forwards and whisper – "Tiggs, your skirt's caught up on your left bum cheek, do you mind if I make it match on the right one?"

"Go ahead, knock yourself out," she says in a distant voice. "Did you notice this streak of turquoise. It's quite deliberate, it's overpaint and it's as thin and fluid as a pencil line. I ask you, on a canvas this size, why would he do that? How would people see?"

"You're seeing," I said.

"I know but that's because you're my very own Beaver-person. That's why I'm looking. I know how to look, where to look."

"That's nice," I say glumly, "because I'm actually lost in front of it. I could handle the moment of seeing it again. That really was like a star-burst. Now, I can't see anything. I'm as good as blind."

"Then it's good I'm here. I'll be your eyes."

That made me well-up. So I stared out of the window instead and thought I'd quite like to go lawn-rolling, too.

Tee stared for an eternity. Finally, she span round and said breezily – "good! I've got it now. Let's go and meet the man who thinks he owns this." And we emerge into fractious limelight.

"So glad you could finally join us," says Sawyer junior. Obviously we are meant to shrivel on the spot.

Tee looks at him, head on one side. Then, straightening up, says – "I don't normally, or recklessly, break caste but I admit, this was worth it. That is one hell of a painting. These, I gather, are the rest?" She makes a marvellous bum-revealing twirl, that allows her to take in all four walls. "Ah, hah, I see."

"Anyway, as I must present myself," she turns to the invalid, stranded in his chair, "Mr Sawyer, I am delighted to meet you. Princess Tulipa Agnethuram, of Sikhim. What an… interesting …collection you have."

"Colonel Sawyer!" erupts the confined one, apoplectically.

"Ah, excellent. You are telling me that you are reluctant to break caste, too. I sympathise but about this painting…"

"Which painting?" rages the 'Colonel' – "there are a great many paintings, young lady."

'Oh go for it,' I think, 'shoot 'em down Tiggs,' pair of insufferable snobs marooned in this scrapyard of a house. I don't like either of them, for a dozen different reasons and I'm adding fresh ones every minute.

"No, Colonel," purrs Tigger. "There is only one painting. The rest are copies of paintings, made to elucidate your dear wife's theme of 'abstracted-abstraction,' if I have the correct phrase. The Rothkos, the Goyas, the Velasquez, the Vermeers – all lovely work and I adore the Cotan. Excellent technique. Your wife chose such an intriguing theme and it does emerge, no doubt about that. But there is only the one original painting and that is simply outstanding. It's a great privilege to have seen it."

Sawyer would probably have had her shot by now, if he could but he can't. Also, he can't untangle the flattery from the ruthlessness, or the fact that she's a woman and a beautiful one at that.

Andy and Carl are simply frozen. I think Carl is sitting on complex emotions but Andy is pure mortification. He's also disadvantaged in that his armchair has swallowed him, whole.

"Should I send for coffee?" tweets Sawyer minimus, utterly taken aback that his terrifying parent and proxy backbone, have been coolly ignored.

"Go on," I say. "We've come an awfully long way. Do rustle up something snacky, if you can, please. Tee'll be ravenous after all that rolling."

He lifts himself up to his full five feet six inches, only four inches less than me and shooting me a perfectly ugly glance, says – "would you be good enough to tell the… lady… that her skirt is caught up, at the back."

"That's not caught," I say loudly. "Her skirt is tucked in her knickers. She got very hot rolling and that's a great way to cool down. We're all grown-ups, aren't we? After all, that would be me, stark-naked, on your wall over there."

He wanders away, like a man who has opened a miniature Pandora's box and now bitterly regrets it.

"I have to say," barks the Colonel, " you are not at all what I was expecting."

"All of us," I ask, "or just one or two?"

"As we are being blunt, I wasn't expecting a mob."

"Ah, I see. Which are the mob and who are the invited, in your eyes?"

"I have no idea who my son invited. It was his ludicrous idea. I was led to expect two of you, the proprietor of the establishment and the young woman who modelled there."

I smiled, my very best crocodile – "sadly, we come in inseparable pairs. It's how we roll and it's our great strength. There are another couple of pairs and they'd loved to have been invited, too. One is an expert in earth pigments – your late wife would have adored speaking to her! Her partner has, literally, centuries of experience, bizarre though that may sound."

"Young lady, you cannot have centuries of experience, 'literally.' That's poppycock."

"Only in your mind, Colonel. For, trust me, you can. You've not yet experienced it, that's all. But do forgive me, I wasn't trying to be contentious, merely interesting. After all, if you're fascinated by what was flowing through an artist's mind when he painted his most exceptional piece, extended experience should be well within the parameters you'll have to contend with." I'd caused a very awkward pause and for once, I was delighted and perfectly at ease in it. Then, as if his manners had suddenly returned, the Colonel tried to turn over another page and begin afresh.

"The theme, as you seem partly to be aware, was one pursued by my late wife. She was intrigued by 'what was not said,' as she put it. She spoke of it a lot in the context of the Velasquez, 'Las Meninas.' She used to say, 'it's what you don't see. Despite the centrality of the irrelevant, it's the dialogue and drama beyond the frame that counts most. It's what you feel in Goya, the uncertainty of the child who looks out of the Duke of Wellington's eyes. Or what was Cotan demonstrating, when he drew beads of icy moisture in the dry heat of summer? What insight, what theme were they playing their variations on?" He stopped for a moment and then continued in a strained voice – "I don't really believe I understood all she was saying." He finished with a barking sound, at which we all jumped, except Tee.

"The Caulke painting," she broke in, "was way off theme. Was she not disappointed?"

The Colonel looked at her with distaste but also a new measure of healthy respect.

"She was utterly thrilled by it. But you are correct, it was not the theme she had been pursuing and she admitted as much. She said that that painting knew exactly what it was saying. For all the apparent chaos it was a statement of utter, the utmost, clarity."

"What an intelligent woman," said Tee, in a very relaxed voice.

"Yes, my boy and I are her ignorant heirs."

"An acknowledgment that honours you, Colonel. So please tell me, what interest had you in meeting my partner, the model for Caulke's last piece?"

"He's dead?" exclaimed the Colonel.

"As the dodo," chipped in Andy, happy to have entered the conversation at any level, I think.

"But young man, he was within your care?"

"No sir, not exactly. He lived in one of my buildings, rent free. As he was a hopeless alcoholic, I managed his affairs as best I could. I'm sorry to report that, in one sense, it was your purchase that killed him. It was the largest sale he had ever made. He came demanding money one day and in such an ugly manner, that I gave him notice to quit. I told him to instruct solicitors and I would hand over his money to them. In the interim I gave him the £200 I had in cash and he stormed off into town with it. There he came to a very unpleasant end, either by a blow to the head, or by final outrage to his liver. The pathologists were uncertain."

That caused a distinctly sober silence, broken by the entrance of a tea-trolley carrying an assortment of ill-matched crockery, jugs and kettles.

"I'm afraid catering has gone to hell, since mother passed," said Jonathan.

"No matter," I said. "I lived on crisps and diet tonic after my mum died. Surprisingly, I'm here to attest that that is possible."

Eventually, after much clinking and clanking, the rediscovery of the milk and a hunt for the sugar, everyone was supplied with mugs of tepid, coloured fluid.

"Not a snack in the place," said Sawyer, rediscovering some of his earlier belligerence.

I sipped the fastest and got my question in first – "why am I here?"

"Aah," began Jonathan, with a hasty glance at his father, who flicked a set of 'carry-on' fingers at him, as if he no longer cared, "the reason for that is a bit peculiar."

"Can I start by saying that mum was 'different.' She was, oh hang it all, she was more like you people than like us. She was spontaneous, funny, fey and given to mysterious pronouncements. I could go on but I'm sure you get the general idea. Not as if you're strangers to it, after all," he finished, in a voice so compromised I almost felt for him.

From the depths of his chair, the Colonel said in a broken voice – "I loved her like a child loves its mother. I never understood her. I just adored her. Losing her to Death was terrible. But had I lost her in any other way it would have killed me, not merely half-paralysed me."

"Colonel! That's the sweetest, most sincere epitaph I've ever heard!" exclaimed Tee. She stopped her abstracted pacing and kneeling, took the old man's hands between her own and began to talk to him in a low, sing-song whisper.

Jonathan turned to us.

"Dad married very late, which is why I'm so comparatively young. He met mum in an army hospital, in Darjeeling, while he was on overseas exchange. He was the senior medic and mum was a patient. She'd been in Tibet, illegally and had slipped back through Sikhim…" he stopped, to glance at Tee, who was still tete-a-tete with his father. A sad jealousy spread across his face and he sighed, as if compelled to re-shoulder a heavy load.

"She'd picked up every disease you can pick up in those places. She was being nursed at death's door and no-one knew which way she'd go. She had no possessions, except her passport and a rug-roll, trussed up with hide-straps that she wouldn't let out of her sight. She made dad promise that if she died he'd bring it back to England, because the person it belonged to lived there.

"As it was, she survived. Mainly because dad wouldn't let her die. She married him in the hospital, in Darjeeling. They came home on a military transport. The rug-roll came too and was never really mentioned again.

"It next resurfaced a few weeks after dad came home, one day and announced the forthcoming delivery of a painting he'd purchased, that morning, in London.

"Mum was used to dad buying her paintings. He never really…" Jonathan glanced at his father and Tee again, shrugged and continued… "he never really 'got it.' Mum didn't want the paintings she raved about and certainly not copies. Of course, once she'd raved about the first one he had done for her, he thought he'd found a way into her secret heart. So the copies kept on coming and how could mum ever tell him to stop? It would have crushed him. I tried to tell him but you can imagine how that went down. I don't have your friend's chutzpah. That's the story of how we come to have walls full of new, Old Masters. They're top rate copies but pointless for that very reason – they're copies.

"To be frank, neither dad nor I ever cared for art. We did dote on mum, though. Now, I'm pretty sure we hate art.

"Mum couldn't have got to that gallery show. She was far too sick to travel any distance at all. I don't even know how dad knew about it. It wasn't on his circuit. Anyway, somehow he'd known he had to buy it for her. It cost an absolutely ludicrous sum. It's as good as bankrupted us." He glanced at me with distaste and something more complicated. "I'm sorry," he continued, "this is coming out in pieces… I've never really had to put it together before.

"Poor old mum was in terrible suspense, waiting for it to arrive. She was convinced it would be another well-meant mishap. But this time he'd hit the jackpot. Something about it had screamed 'mum' at him and for once, he'd got it absolutely right.

"I guess it was worth every penny. He wouldn't let either of us see it until the framers had installed it and everything else had been cleared away. Then he wheeled mum in, in triumph, with me following – both of us in utter dread.

"What a victory, though!" Jonathan stopped, while his face expressed emotions other than joy. "She went into ecstasies and dad damn nearly had his stroke early, from sheer joy. After that, she just sat there, day after day, staring at it, reading every message she saw in it. Dad and I came to hate it, in the end. 'Pays more attention to that scrawl than she does to either of us,' was his most memorable comment. We were jealous… of a painting. Now it's all we've got left of her and it's our turn to sit staring at the bloody thing.

"I apologise, Ms. Eva, no animus intended."

"None taken…" I murmured.

"About six months ago, all of her sub-continent diseases caught up with her – liver, pancreas, kidneys, everything was shot. 'Right,' she said, 'I'm on my way out, so listen up boys. In the middle of that painting is a real live woman. Maybe you've seen that, maybe you haven't.' Needless to say, we hadn't." Jonathan flashed a conflicted look at me, then went on in a strangled voice – "she said – 'that woman is also a man, so she's something special. She's also alive, a truly lovely person and she has to have my travel diaries, my notes, together with that that bloody old carpet roll. There's nothing in that lot you'd value, trust me. In time you'd just throw it all away. But she might be able to use it, to help with the burden she's carrying.' On and on she went and I think both of us felt increasingly estranged."

He lifted his head and shot me a look of what felt like pure hatred. I was too concerned with my own feelings to care. I could feel the belly-emptying drop as my life began to free-fall away from me, again. 'Not more shit!' I was screaming, inside. 'I can't take on any more crap.'

I took a huge breath and counted it out in tiny spurts, from one to seven. Then I sucked one in, to the same count. In and out, twice. I was calmer, now and came back to earth to hear him saying… "so hurtful, so painful, to know she valued other things more than you and that you could never compete."

I looked up and took another of his hate-filled darts. It skidded off me, because all I could feel was – 'yes, I know exactly how you feel – you're being used. Eaten, while you're still alive. Join me, on the table.'

He sighed… "find this lady and give her my things, with all my goodwill. Find her, she's a nice person – you boys will see that, in time. Don't start procrastinating, 'if-ing,' 'but-ing,' wondering whether or not I'd lost my marbles. Get on with it!' Then, within the week, she was dead. And so, really, was dad."

Now it was Sawyer's turn for the deep breaths.

"I've done what she asked. I've sought you out. It was pretty easy. If it hadn't been I'd have stopped, as I never wanted to do it in the first place. But – and this is with all the respect I can muster – you don't seem 'truly-lovely.'"

The pause that followed was all mine to fill. For once I had an atom of control and I relished it. Had it been possible, I would have waved a wand and spirited us all back to wherever this nonsense began… and I would have ended it there.

I remember a chunk from one of the early Castaneda books where Carlos, the author, is trying to back Don Juan, his teacher, into a corner. To do so he imagines a hidden assassin, on the bluff overlooking Don Juan's little shack. As Don Juan takes his accustomed stroll around the verandah, this rifleman will shoot him dead. "What would you do, Don Juan?" he begs, pleading with his teacher to admit that, in the face of rogue events, we are all helpless. Don Juan looks at him with an amused grin and says words to the effect of – 'I simply wouldn't come around, little Carlos.'

How I wish I knew the secret of 'not coming around.' For if I did, I wouldn't be sitting here in this loathsome house, dealing with a man-child who is grudgingly laying his mother's last wishes on my shrinking shoulders and can't even muster the politesse to be gracious about it.

Those thoughts filled my pause. Now it's my turn to speak.

"Obviously I've heard what you've said. First off, I'm sorry about your mum, who sounds really special, in many ways. But you seem to want me to convince you of something – probably my fitness to inherit things that, for all that 'you wouldn't value them' – your mother's words, not mine – you're loathe to part with. I completely understand and that decision is entirely yours and your father's. So you will decide.

"To be quite honest, I'd much rather you didn't burden me with more. I seem to be a living repository for secrets, strange devices, gnomic utterances and oracular pronouncements. Only one of these has, so far, produced any practical outcome to the good. The others have done no harm but they do interfere with my life. Therefore, if you have the slightest reservation about your mother's instruction, I'd beg you to indulge it.

"It's just possible that one of these 'packages' that turn up might resolve the cryptic intimations of the others, some fine day. Perhaps your mum's is the one that will do that. I don't know but that's the only caveat that inhibits my desire to say – 'keep your stuff, I don't want it.' Consider the ball to be wholly in your court."

I aimed for another long breath but what I discovered was a tuneless, aggressive sigh hunting for an exit. Spontaneously I broke out – "no, sod this. Allow me to backtrack. I'm sick to death of being accommodating. 'Not a 'truly-lovely' person...' and I quote. Good on you for voicing your opinion. Just recall that you have lured me out here, at our expense, under false pretences. You don't want to discuss Harold's painting, or my part in it. You want me to participate in some charade that means a lot to you and nothing to me.

"Now you can listen while I tell you how I arrived at this day in my life. To get here, as I am, I have been raped, robbed, beaten and abused. After all that, people expect me to oblige them. Pardon me if I tell you both, very plainly, to fuck off.

"I'll bet your mum was a 'truly-lovely' person and maybe I'd have hit it off with her. Nevertheless, I'm having one hell of a job to gel with you two. Just do exactly what you want. All I want – when Tee's finished healing your father – is to go home."

After which outburst, I slumped back and stared listlessly out of a distant window at the even more distant clouds.

Jonathan considered the backs of his hands, then the palms. Perhaps they told him something, probably not. Eventually I heard him say – "I'm sorry. I need to talk to dad." He headed off across the threadbare rug and after a few seconds Tee rejoined us.

"Come and see!" she said to Andy and Carl.

"Oh no," I whined. "Can't we just go?"

"In a minute, Bella," she said, gripping my arm. "You can do this. You're paper, scissors and stone!"

"No, I'm not. I'm a peeled prawn."

"Shush, shush. I'm here, so nothing bad can happen to you."

We heaved a shell-shocked Andy to his feet and joined by a thoughtful Carl, we trooped off to admire me. But I didn't want to be admired by my friends. It was an imposition. I could feel a sort of violence stirring in me – a very un-Beaverish sensation.

"Hang onto your boots, Beautiful," whispered Tee. "This is admiration, not cannibalism."

"It feels like rape," I groaned, "and by my friends, too."

Carl must have overheard.

Checking that Andy was stable and upright, he turned back.

"No, no, no Evie. Never that, never that, Sweet. No-one ever gets to hurt you while we're around. No-one knows what you went through, after this…" he gestured at the painting … "Tee has an inkling but even she doesn't know. You need a mum and we haven't got one for you. We'll do our best and Marie-Claire will do her best. There'll be no more teasing. Punch will keep you safe and Tee will keep your safer. Tee's a tigress. You're safe now."

"I hope so," I sobbed. "I was so young when this was painted. I was so full of rage. What I went through on that ship, the way I had to bluff in the brothel – those things broke me but I've never been allowed to snap. I wasn't like any of the things I did but I had to pretend I was. All I was, was young and stupid. But I scared myself and I can't lose the fear. It stalks me. I keep thinking I've moved on but I haven't. I'm like an unborn lamb with its head and shoulders jammed. I want to come out. I want to be born but I can't be. I'm jammed in the machinery that made me."

With that, I just collapsed against Tee and sobbed my heart out, boy and girl.

"Come on," said Carl rubbing my back gently. "I'll give you a special ride on the big bike. We'll go and find a nice tranny caff, together."

"With egg and chips and apple pie," I hiccupped, tears rolling down my face.

"And loads of white sliced, with best butter…" he said.

"OK, lead me to it," I grimaced, awkwardly. "I've always been a cheap and easy cure."

But I'm not.

Our little gang trailed away, not rudely but without goodbyes. Each party was carrying its own sorrows and each party was beginning to feel the sorrows of the other. Yet neither of us had words that could set this right.

At the car, Jonathan Sawyer was loading cardboard boxes and a carpet roll into the boot.

"It wasn't much of a decision, in the end," he said.

I couldn't speak, so I just nodded.

Everyone else shook his hand. I sidestepped the group and climbed into the back seat to lie down. Andy went up front. Tee climbed in with me and put my head in her lap. We left and I never came back. But as we drove away, I found myself wondering – 'what was the lady's name?'

48

DUCKS IN DRY DOCK

Carl 'got it,' Andy didn't. For five days he was furious with me, which did nothing for my state-of-mind, especially as his wrath was communicated silently, without right of reply.

Then, I guess, Carl must have blown him up.

I was sitting among my confidantes, the fireweed, when he came heaving over the rubble like a ship in heavy seas.

"Easy, Andy," I squeaked. "Steady, steady, let me help!" I leapt off my perch and ran, managing to grab him in time, a moment before he beached and wrecked.

That did for him. He burst into tears and sobbed on my shoulder for ages, until I said – "could you change shoulders, please. This one is thoroughly wet through." At least that got a laugh and stemmed the leak.

We sat on the mossed-over concrete and surveyed the very-soothing desolation together, absorbing the distant grumble of the traffic. Filtered through the tank traps, the little clumps of stunted, volunteer trees and the seed-heavy weeds, it was a consoling rattle and grind with musical pretensions. It was a noise that harmonised with the way we both were.

After a while, he fumbled for my hand and holding it tightly, finally got himself together. "Evie, I owe you such an apology. I really don't know where to begin."

"Tell you what," I said, "let's skip the formalities with one-another. Otherwise we'll be here all morning. Carl and Tee would be forming a search party, probably even conjuring up the bonking alien and the literary legend herself, to play the bloodhounds."

"Could just be that JJ's got a 'friend-finder' in that little pack of his," Andy said ruefully. "I am sorry, Evie. I get above myself. I keep forgetting that I'd be in a nursing home by now and the caff nothing but a ruin of broken windows in the middle of nowhere, if it wasn't for you, Carl and the rest of the crew. We were sinking. No. We were sunk and you and your gang of weirdos showed up and saved the day.

"Even after all that, I find myself thinking I know what's best for you. I was really wide of the mark, last week and I'm sorry. I should never have compromised you in the first place. Then not to understand what you were going through, was simply unfeeling

– doubly so after the amount of empathy I've had expended on me. It was un-bloody-believable."

"Forget it," I said, "life's too short. Tee was the only one who was crazy enough to sort the bones out of that day. She has this uncanny, spectacular ability to 'sense' where the heart of a situation lies and then wind herself into it like a corkscrew. I still don't know what she said to that old man but you probably know she had a letter from him? She wouldn't let me read it but it made her cry.

"She's a Zen-master – not that she knows what one is. A crazy magician in the form of a 34-year-old Indian Princess, occasionally going-on four-and-a-half. On reflection, I guess that all makes perfect sense."

We listened to the traffic symphony a while longer. Then he said – "can you help me back to the path, Evie? I nearly broke my neck coming through the weeds. Carl was going to kill me if I didn't apologise and now he's going to kill me for trying to. Actually, as an act of self-preservation, why don't you both come for supper and everybody else, too! You can tell us about eels. I promise there'll be extra thick custard for you and Alice. How about it?"

"We'll be there," I said, "but I'll have to think about the eels. I'm not sure any of you are worthy."

Jonathan Sawyer's mother had been called Lucy Mahoney. The sturdy cardboard boxes her son had loaded into the car had been dumped in a corner of our trashy trailer, between the bed and the wall of the toilet, thus doubling as my bedside table, a luxury I had not been afforded until now. I put a piece of MDF I'd scavenged on the top and then draped one of Tee's myriad scarves over it – 'so-oo elegant!'

Normally, such a move would have incurred the obligatory death sentence – rending by Tigger claws, specially sharpened for the purpose. But I was reprieved, on the grounds that a suicidal moth had sunk its teeth into it first and chewed a decent-sized hole, dead centre. "Sod you, you free-loading, lepidopteran low-life," she'd mumbled bundling the scarf into the bin. I, ever thrifty, had retrieved it, for purposes then undetermined and only now realised.

There the boxes had remained and there, I intended, they would remain until the caravan collapsed around us. That was not in itself the most unlikely event. Indeed it was one on which Tee was prone to philosophise. She usually did so the middle of the night, when neither of us could sleep, or during those hours when the rain was just of the appropriate calibre to drum magically upon the roof. On those nights, by long-standing agreement, the first to wake would nudge the other so that we could mumble our thoughts and stories while listening to the rain dance.

"Y'know," Tee pondered, on one such night, in fact the very night preceding events yet to unfold…to be unfolded? No, that's not right …in fact, I'm not at all sure I can remember when it was, anyway…

"We could be living in a serviced flat in Knightsbridge, with a country pad in the county of our choice," she had murmured. "I could be Lady Tigger and you could be … the dairymaid." When I finished tickling her she conceded that I could be promoted to librarian, instead.

"In that capacity," I enquired, "ought we to have modern editions of Alice, a.k.a. Marie-Gabrielle on our shelves? It would be broad-minded, eclectic but it could never be said to be in the best of taste."

"It's a good point," agreed Tigger. "We better canvas her opinion. Given, however, that I would have to be there – my vital role in 'The House at Pooh Corner,' could barely go uncelebrated – she couldn't really complain."

"Ah, appearing on our illustrious shelves as Alice from 'Through the Looking Glass,' or 'Wonderland,' is one thing. Appearing as Marie-Gabrielle out of 'Marie-G. de St. Etude,' is quite another. And I'm not sure how she thinks of herself these days, as Marie-G, or Alice."

"So, stick us all companionably side-by-side and have done with your bibliographical faffing," Tigger said decisively.

"What? Marie-Gabrielle alongside Pooh and Alice? Are you crazed? That would be literary paedophilia, or worse!"

"That bad, eh?"

"Not precisely but it might be a bit toe-curling. It would not feel…comfortable."

"I'm perfectly comfortable with it and I'm intimately involved."

"Yes but you're an adult Tigger."

"I am not! I am four…and a half!"

"That cannot be denied."

The night rain fell, steadily and consolingly, while we wrestled with these irresolvable, thorny hypotheticals.

"Will you listen to that rain," I mumbled. "What exactly does it say?"

"I wish I knew. It's not like monsoon rain. It sounds free and trustworthy."

"Trustworthy rain…I rather care for that. I wonder why?"

"Not sure, not sure. Isn't it a bit too much like a company name… ooh…Trustworthy Cycle Clips Ltd.?"

"No, I mean yes, no, that's good! I love the Victorian flavour. Sepia-toned photographs of a man in a high-collar, his redoubtable penny-farthing cycle leaning against a gas lamp, securing his Oxford bags with a 'Trustworthy Cycle Clip.' Hang-on, that's not right. I've got at least three periods muddled. Victorians didn't have Oxford bags, they must be Edwardian – or, horror, even later? Save me Tiggs! I'm drowning in successive waves of British monarchy. My fantasy is under threat from coastal erosion, or some such."

"Oh don't flap, who cares? Anything pre-WW2 is ancienne regime to us and therefore, axiomatically, Victorian."

"You're right. Things can be anything you like, in the middle of the night, listening to the rain on the roof, can't they?"

"Yep. Turns back the dominance of words as defining entities. You just give 'em the Humpty-Dumpty treatment. It's like my favouritest word, 'Jabberwocky'. Utterly anarchic, without moving a muscle. No red-paint stupidly splashed about, no protest posters, no gluing yourself to the front of innocent buildings, the whole poem scrupulously demolishes the hegemony of words…"

"Whoa there! Hold hard, Humpty…qu'est que c'est le 'egg-o-monee', pliz?"

"Keep up, Beaver, you're supposed to be the fount of all wisdom. I am a mere, ebullient Tigger."

"Egg-money, Tigger?"

"OK, OK …the moral, political and probably strong-arm domination of others by one self-promoting force…

"To continue…demolishes the hegemony of words, dictionary-conformable words shall we allow, obviously by being a word itself. It turns them against themselves. Their boots fill up with the importance of being 'defined' and they drown. But it does it so gently, wouldn't you allow?"

We lay back in deep companionable silence, hoping that the rain would not stop. Or perhaps hoping that it would, so that we could get some Zzzz's in. Then I had a perfectly ghastly thought, jolted by the vague memory of a thoughtful Tigger voice saying 'serviced flat' and 'Knightsbridge', in the same sentence.

I sat upright – "you don't actually want to leave No-Name, do you – for 'Knightsbridge?"

"God no. I was merely musing on the irony of having access to a billion quid and living in a fibreglass shed, whilst mopping floors for my keep. You know, if Andy and I amalgamated our finances, we could buy just about any place the team fancied. But I don't think there is anywhere else. It's got to be here, hasn't it? The wonky old caff, all 4 x 2's, shiplap and years of paint. Tarpaper roof – I'd have thought it was an insurer's nightmare, being a pyromaniac's wet-dream."

"Third-party only, I'm advised. You know how the whole front can be opened out, in seconds, in summer? That's why no-one ever claims it's a fire-trap. Anyway, you know yourself how many of the Health and Safety elves, underwriters and building inspectors eat here…" I paused. We were in the Witching Hour and I was trespassing into Real World stuff! Insurance! Inspectors! Assessments! "Slap me! I said 'insurance' and other forbidden words!" I held up a wholly innocent hand and it took a resounding 'thwack!'

"Tigger Power," she cackled, as I 'ouched' and 'double-ouched'.

I retreat, mortally wounded, under the duvet.

Here, in our very own Llareggub, we are at ease under the rain, sun, snow and stars.

Not even the heavy axled trucks, wheels turning on wet concrete can dent this sort of peace. I listen to the hiss of air brakes, the jolt as the engine shuts down, the far-off slam of cab doors, jovial Polish voices. Then the caff door opens…closes…slight click of the double latch. I rest my head on the Tigger tummy, not because I'm listening-in, more to share in the perfect anatomy, to revisit that Sargasso sea between rib-cage and pelvis, where so much that is delicate functions with, seemingly, the utmost robustness. Then I find I'm running low on oxygen, so I wriggle up, via the 100-Acre Wood and rest my face on her shoulder.

"We could have a boat," I murmur.

"A boat, on the sea? Aren't you cured yet?"

"Only of that particular boat. I've had a thing about boats since I was small. It's all to blame on the non-availability of ducks."

"No-ooh," groaned Tiggs, "it's another Beaver riddle."

"Not at all. It is elegant Beaver logic, founded on impeccable reasoning, with improbable segues cunningly negotiated."

"Continue. I will rend you if it turns out to be anything other than what you said."

"Poo. You've scared me now. As punishment you're going to have to listen to the SHORT VERSION which is REALLY BORING. It's your own fault. No use complaining now…" I waited, hopefully, for a reprieve but there was none.

"Tiny tot craves yellow duck for bath-time. Availability of ducks is nil. Sudden run on the webbed-footed ones. Instead, is given a boat. Falls desperately in love with little boat, tiny crew, wheel and mast. Removes boat from bath and plays with it night and day. Boat is never permitted to enter bathwater again, lest helpless crew members drown.

"Now…stay thy terrible teeth!…e'er since, I have had a thing about boats on land. It's perverse, I realise but the reasons are clear – firstly, the subliminal duck/boat affair. Next chapter arrives later in life of boat-loving Beaver.

"When small but no longer tot, I used to be farmed out to gran, when she still lived alone. At the bottom of her lane, which was a dirt track that climbed up from a valley, there was a rubbish tip. Opposite gran's house, across the valley, was the hill down which the council waste lorries tipped their garbage. I suppose the idea was that this blind valley was eventually going to fill up but there was a fair bit of valley left at that stage. It was sort of fenced off and we were banned from going there, that's the three of us who made up our own little gang. Of course, we used to crawl in and stare at the interesting junk."

"No Beaverish diversions at this point – so sprach Tiggerthustra!"

"You're missing very interesting details," I said winsomely and hopefully.

"The facts, Beaver – just the facts!"

"All right! We didn't like to go too far in, because there were Big Boys prowling at the top. We were very small people, at the bottom and that situation was fraught with danger. Big Boys were axiomatically bad news. But one day, in 'our bit,' on the cowardly side of the fence, a boat turned up – not as junk though.

"John's dad had been in the Merchant Marine and he told John that it was a lifeboat, off a really big ship. Also, it was unsinkable – a very important detail for six and seven year olds.

"A young couple were converting it – to sail round the world – at least, that's what the man told us. The adult Beaver has severe doubts about the viability of that. Anyway, they were very nice to us but we were all too scared to climb up the ladder, to look round the deck. So we used to stand and stare, then run away. I can still see that boat in my mind's eye, though."

I paused to reflect.

"Blimey – open tips! It was a pretty backward part of the country where gran lived. She'd had an outside loo for years. Probably 50 years behind the rest of the country.

"Bit like India, today," said Tee. "Kids of all ages live on the tips and live off them – as in, finding stuff to sell."

"There was a foul dump at Muti's place," I remember. "Immaculate gardens and house but all the crap just got heaved over a high wall at the back, to fester in the sun. Stench could be appalling."

"Totally typical," said Tee. "There used to be a filthy lagoon at the back of the Taj – or was it some other sumptuous pile? – complete with animal carcasses, dogs blown up to the size of seals. Could still be there, for all I know."

"Anyway, to return to boats and you have to allow the detail here, it's what matters. Rend me afterwards, if you must."

Tigger growled, in an anxiety-provoking manner.

"Years later mum took me for an educational day-out, to see Nelson's flagship, 'Victory,' at Portsmouth dry dock. We set off on a really sunny day but at every station – and there seemed to be an awful lot – the sky kept getting darker. Half-way and the rain started, serious rain, OK, not monsoon-standard but what passes for it over here. By the time we got to Portsmouth Harbour, there was no sky, just rain. It was Biblical.

"We had a 'maybe-it-will-stop-raining-coffee-and-bun,' but it didn't. If it was possible, it had got heavier. Mum says through clenched teeth – 'we've come this far, we're going on.' Ten yards out from the caff and we were wet to the skin.

Big plus point though, there was absolutely no-one else there – in the final analysis, just me, because mum ran for cover.

"Once I was on site I could not be moved. All I could see was this silhouette, under white water. You know what the 'tumblehome' is on a boat? 'No?' It's when the width of the boat starts to shrink inwards, some way above the waterline. The planking is no-longer flaring out in that typical boat shape, it's falling back. The tumble-home was a white, raging waterfall. The rain had been falling all morning. It was pouring down the masts, cascading off the spars and where it beat on the hatches it was leaping back into the air. Behind the gunwales, the deck was a lake and the open ports were spouting like gargoyles on a cathedral roof. All this water had to go somewhere and it was falling down into the dry dock, making this awesome thundering noise.

"'Victory,' is painted yellow and black and you could occasionally make out the chequerboard design, through the water. It was the strangest thing to see, this solid piece of war machinery besieged by water and unable to move. At least in a gale, at sea, she could writhe and gnash her teeth. Here, she was thwarted.

"I walked along the dockside and imagined myself into the stern cabin, warm behind those bottle-glass windows, tootsies to a snug fire, reading the Admiralty charts. Just think of it! You, in your cabin, feet away from the huge guns, that would be run out when the ship was in action, to fire 32-pound lumps of iron at the French."

"I don't think Punch would have got up if he'd been hit by one of those," Tee said thoughtfully.

"I tell you true, I read nothing but C.S.Forester's 'Hornblower' novels for the next year or more. That filled in the background admirably but the impression that sank in, the one that's still there, are those gunwale ports spouting water, not into the sea but into a dry dock. Ever since, my ships sail on land.

"The End. You may now rend, as you see fit…"

Tiggs yawned. "I'll let you off."

49

INTERLUDE WITH TOAST

We held hands, listening to the rain, occasionally squeezing fingers, as an 'all-is-well' signal,' until Tiggs said – "I'm awake. Let's go and have toast."

"Excellent notion," I agreed. "PJ's, waterproofs and clogs?"

"The Classic Eng-er-lish Outfit," declared Tee in her Lady-of-the-Manor voice. "Let us be 'orft, toot suet!"

We suited up and belted through the rain, crocs on our feet, heavy plastic macs above, a pair of shiny, scampering witches, heading for a warm cauldron of coffee. Inside the sanctuary of the door, we shed the slickers, to give them a good shake. It was only then that we realised, horror of horrors, that although I was Mickey Mouse and Tee was Pooh Bear, somehow we'd swopped bottoms. Tee now had a tail and I had a fat bum.

The Polish lorry drivers examined us with frank amazement.

"Dzien dobry, jak sie masz?" growled Tigger, undaunted.

"Good, good," they nodded happily over their beans and chips, eyeing the nightwear with half-hopeful eyes, in case they'd missed any signs of – 'Hello, boys!'

"Hiya, Harry," says I, "can I invade your kitchen to fix a perc of coffee for we two benighted orphans of the storm, as well as grab a couple of mugs?"

"Help yourself, lovely Evie. Why not take the perked one? It's fresh. I can bang another one on."

"You sure, angel?"

"I'm sure, I'm sure…slow night. You want toast, too?"

"The ravenous Tigger did happen to mention it, H."

"The ravenous Tigger," repeated Tee, "is ready and willing to do an Alice on a pile of white sliced."

"A Tigger after my own heart," said Harry, who is comfortably built. "You girls grab your coffee, Uncle Harry will arrive bearing toast."

Up and away we go…past the STAFF ONLY sign and the truck drivers tuck their hopeful smiles away for another rainy night.

Here we sit, coffee and toast in the half-dark, because we hadn't bothered with the lights and we tell Harry, when he asks – "no, ta, it's nice like this, thanks all the same," – then we start to chew the fat of life again.

"This boat," says Tiggs, "where would we put it?"

"Here, at No-Name," I say. "Somewhere in the wreckage, not too far away, perhaps behind the Portakabins, say. There's a bit of a dip there and the fireweed grows really tall, for some reason or other. I could sit on deck, on a coil of rope and chat to it."

"Could I chat to it, too?"

"Of course you could, once I'd introduced you. It's a very broad-minded, accommodating sort of weed. It gets on particularly well with lupins and they're extremely talkative."

"Where did you get to know lupins?"

"In an old railway siding, of all places. The tracks had gone years earlier but some lupins were still there. An old boy, out walking his dog, told me that lupin seed was transported loose, in railway wagons and they fell through cracks in the boards. So you have railway tracks full of lupins but no rails. Sad, really. The lupins liked to talk to the trains, not the engines, the wagons. The wagons had been to loads of places."

"Why were there wagons full of lupin seeds? Why weren't they in sacks, or boxes?"

"Maybe they were and one of the bags would split, or a box burst."

"Lupins in daring jail break," said Tee. "Fine company you keep!"

"I was still young and easily led."

"What sort of boat would it be?"

"If the world was ideal, I'd like a modest sort of coastal vessel, what was called a packet boat, the sort that sailed around the Isles of Scilly and the Hebrides. Or something trawler-ish, though I don't think you'd ever get the stink of fish out of a fishing vessel. It would be sealed-in, under every rivet. I hate the smell of fish. In fact, I'm not keen on fish – with certain noble exceptions, such as my friend the North Atlantic stonefish and for eating, tasteless whitefish, like cod and haddock."

"I was about to mention that you don't turn your nose up at fish and chips."

"The batter conceals the ugly facts of the matter from my tender sensibilities."

"What's that supposed to mean?"

"That I don't much like fish."

"Beavie, I sense a cul-de-sac. Change the subject. Your needle's got stuck on fish."

"Natural glue, boiled from sturgeon, was used to fasten sinew to the back of Indian bows – as in bows and arrows."

"Bad Beaver!"

"OK, OK, no rending! I'm full of toast. Think of the mess! What might be more practical would be two canal longboats, moored side-by-side, a day boat and a night boat? Because there's not a lot of room on them… do you know Tiggs, I think this may be more of a fantasy than a nuts and bolts, real thing.

"I suppose, though," I continued fantasising, "you could go 'wrecked boat hunting,' in the hope of finding something really magnificent but with its back broken…"

"Erk," squawked Tee, "'back-broken' sounds very unpleasant to Tigger ears. Explain, please."

"…it just means that its sailing days are over, no use for water or waves any more. But with a bit of welding, or timber bodging, it would be fit to sit on shore. Somewhere we could tell salty stories to fireweed from. We would invite Punch and his clay pipe, to be a visiting Captain."

"Do you want to go on a recce?" asked Tee. "Carl would drive us, because we could make it a day-out for Andy, too. I don't know where – down to Brixham, or such like. Aren't there Brixham trawlers, like there are Thames barges?"

"There were and there are. New builds, old builds, steel and wood. There must be wrecks and write-offs for sale."

"Captain Tigger…" Tee muses.

"Admiral Tigger, I insist."

"No, I like 'Captain.' Why? Why do I like the sound of 'Captain?' It's got a very solid, satisfying ring to it. A sort of 'everything's ship-shape and Bristol-fashion' feeling to it. As for 'aye, aye, Captain,' I could lap-up some of that. Shall we go on a boat hunt?"

"Just to bowl a googly," I say, "we could think about railway carriages…"

"Or trams," yawns Tee.

"Now you're talking, Captain!"

"How about we muddle up a boat, a railway carriage and a tram. All piled together in a muddle…for lack of a better word?" wondered Tiggs. "The right words are all asleep…like we should be. But now I'm all of a bother about the balance and symmetry of 'a muddle.' Do you need two trams to equal one boat and what does a railway carriage to do your equation? Also, could you include part of a submarine? If you dug a big hole, the submarine could be doing a crash dive. There again, if you buried the back end, it might be surfacing underneath a perfectly law-abiding assembly of trams, carriages and boats." Tiggs yawned again, then stretched happily. "Beavie, I may have caught your digressive disease. The utter necessity of exploring all interesting and possible alternatives."

"You may well have done. I shall examine you, with the aid of more coffee and toast, once I've used Andy's private loo. Do you know, in the spirit of midnight mischief, I may just write an obscene couplet on the wall. Hast thou a biro?"

"Nope. Am attired in PJ's, hence no pointy objects on board."

"Definitely for the best. Anyway, I've already gone off the idea."

The rain, blessings be upon it, still fell heavily. Quite a different sound on the roofing-felt overhead. More of a muffled drumming, not unpleasing but not the active, friendly chatter that came off the van roof.

A good wee is a wonderful, life-affirming thing and I returned quite refreshed, bearing even more hot toast and fresh coffee.

"We could sit on the deck of our ship," I said, "chatting to fireweed and eating piping hot bacon sandwiches, barbecued alongside us. Theoretical bacon in my case, of course," I added hastily. "Everyone invited."

"How would we get Andy up there?"

"Bosun's chair," I said. "I have become nautical and therefore have an answer for all possible contingencies."

"We need a film set designer," pondered Tee. "They're very good at designing to maximum dramatic effect. A designer junk heap, with ladders and walkways, Mad Max meets Howard's End."

We talked on and on, until the rain stopped.

"It's stopped," announced Tee, "which must mean it's bed-time."

"Let's tidy-up," I said, "and if anyone inquires as to our whereabouts, I'll tell Harry to explain that we were kidnapped by aliens who promised to have us back by midday."

"Given the situation here," said Tee, drily, "that's the likeliest explanation."

50
GREEN TEA

But...and I did sort of warn you...I have digressed.

Lucy Mahoney might have stayed forever in her boxes, if I hadn't one careless, carefree night, while practising my bullfighting skills, executed a passable molinete with the duvet and upset the pint glass of water I keep on the aforementioned 'bedside table.'

"Satan and all his imps!" I squeaked. "Catastrophe appalling! Turn back time 10 seconds and tell me to stop fooling with the duvet or, failing that, chuck me a towel – quickly!"

A towel flew across the room and I began a rescue operation.

A little water, like blood, goes a long way. Also, old, dry cardboard is remarkably hygroscopic. The bottom box was dissolving, so I upended it on the bed. Dozens of notebooks fell out. The second box had survived but true to the spirit of the moment, I upended it as well. Out poured dozens more.

'Please!' I prayed silently to the patron saints of archivists – Jerome, Lawrence and Catherine, should you be interested – 'let them be numbered!' I seized one. 'Agh!' they weren't. It's my fault, I was never a good Catholic – probably because I was brought up a Methodist. Oh well, it had been the saints' chance to nab a conversion – if they didn't care, see if I did. I regarded the chaos on the bed and felt very Beaverish.

Enter Tigger, stage right, towelling her hair.

"What is all this?" she asks in a voice of infinite patience – very frightening to one of nervous disposition.

"Diaries," I say brightly.

"Whose diaries?"

"That woman's. The one who died in that horrible house with the good rolling lawn and my picture on the wall."

"Ah yes. Expand, do."

"Water fell on floor. Bedside 'table' instantly dissolved. Emergency rescue team heroically save victims of storm – very Grace Darling and all that. Triumphant, I stand before you."

"Why did the water fall on the floor?"

"I was practicing my molinete with the duvet, not a cape and the water, foolish stuff, got in the way."

"To the detriment of these" – she gestured – "and…my…scarf!"

"Correct on both points but before I die, allow me to remind you that this is the scarf that was ravaged by a suicidal moth and which you therefore discarded. This fact is already within your domain, due to re-appearance of said scarf some months back and remarked upon, by your good self, at that time."

Tee sniffed. I shan't bother to translate it. It was an unnecessarily long and complex affair, with numerous caveats, exemptions and sub-clauses.

"So, we are down one bedside table, one glass and the proud possessors of what, 50, 60, little A5 notebooks?"

"Over 100 I reckon – and the glass survived," I explained, ever helpful.

"I-D-I-O-T!" said Tee, in a peculiar voice.

Tee has been reading the more penetrable parts of G.I.Gurdjieff and is much taken with his declension of 'idiots-humaine.' As he was a Georgian by birth, she has begun mimicking his guttural pronunciation – frequently. I-D-I-O-T was actually, a term of endearment.

"I will go forth," said Tee, "and return with a sturdy box of the appropriate dimensions." Upon which she turned on her heel and made to depart.

"You're not wearing any clothes," I observed.

"Am I not?"

"Not so far as I can see."

"Good Heavens! Why not?"

"You took them off for a shower and they do not magically re-attach themselves."

"You're sure about all this?"

I checked, surreptitiously, that we were still on earth.

"I'm certain. Have you been drinking?"

"Incredible amounts of green tea."

"Why?"

"It protects my brain from ageing."

"Who told you that?"

"The man in the shop – and it said so on the helpful leaflet, too."

"I have this ghastly feeling," I said, "that it's working. Not only is your brain not ageing, it's regressing, too."

"What makes you think that?"

"When was the last time you left the house without any clothes on – and not just for a dare?"

"I suppose I was about six. I just forgot and Dadi-ji shouted so loudly that a monkey fell out of a tree, from shock. I'd gone a long way, you see."

"I suggest, therefore, that the green tea has regressed you to age six."

"Oh my word! It's worth every penny!"

At that point I gave up.

"Off you go then. It can't turn out any worse than the Battle Hymn of the Republic day."

"When and what was that?"

"The last time you actually left the house without any clothes – months and months ago, prehistory, really."

"I don't remember. Was I six then?"

"You were actually 34."

"Time really flies when it goes backwards. I've got a feeling I shall invent the spear, soon."

"Well if you do, spare the sofa."

"S-a-f-e-t-y spear, remember?"

"Of course, how foolish of me. How could I forget!"

"Right-ho, I'm off!"

And off she went. It was a warm, sunny evening and the most likely place for boxes was round the back. They're all fairly grown up round there…

…hang on! Beaver engages remnants of brain…there are other outcomes possible…

"COME BACK HERE AT ONCE – NOW!!" No falling monkeys but I'm sure Dadi-ji would be proud of me.

Return of fair maiden. Bewildered, bemused, even.

"Yes?"

"Your dress…your shoes…you've forgotten them."

"So I have!"

"By the way, lay off the green tea – just until your age stabilises."

"OK!"

Lord love her, 20 minutes later she returns, breathless but bearing an excellent wooden box and three pristine house bricks.

"Stand box on bricks. Flood proof to the four-inch level. Thereafter it'll float and have to take its chances."

"What an excellent Tigger you are. Tell me, do you do numbers yet?"

"Up to 100."

"Grab your best crayon and together we shall solve this little contretemps."

Boy, did it take some time. During those hours, however, I gleaned that as well as being a Mahoney, she also, rightly or wrongly claimed distant kinship with Captain Frederick Travers O'Connor, 1870-1943, Royal Artillery. He was something of a maverick, despite serving solidly and indispensably, both as an officer and – more importantly, interpreter – with the Younghusband incursion into Tibet, in 1903-04.

That, in certain Tibetan circles, is something of a feather in your cap, especially if you're trying to fly below the radar of the occupying Chinese forces. It's way above my entry-level credentials, which are that I was there with my mum, for 10 days, when she scooped a holiday cancellation deal during the year she was trying to save my soul. We went everywhere with Chinese guides and as I barely knew where we'd gone anyway, it was all wasted on me. Once again, I curse my obdurate, sulky teenage self – no doubt, not for the last time.

As I browsed Wikipedia, I read aloud – "turned his hand to organising tiger hunts, for Americans, in India, in 1931."

"Then he dies," said Tigger, sleepily. "Consider him savaged."

"He's already dead."

"I shall dig up his bones and savage them. Good night."

Not that sleep counted for much with Tiggers who had had their age messed with by green tea. By 5.00 a.m she had bounced awake, while I was still cosily paddling through Beaverland.

With a great rattle the carpet-roll landed on the bed.

"I am tired of unexpectedly encountering this object in the loo. It is inconveniencing me, to crack an incredibly amusing pun – far funnier than any of yours. Open it."

"No. I'm asleep."

Violent, utterly uncalled-for, shameful shaking.

"Open it!"

"No. I'm gravely ill."

More violence.

"Open IT!!"

"Open it yourself, you great bully," I mumble.

"OK," she said happily. "We Tiggers love surprises."

"We Beavers hate them. All of them."

Much ripping of seams, occasional shocking vulgarity.

I see a remnant of sleep and grab at it.

"We need Carl. I'll get him."

"Don't you dare!"

Too late, the whirlwind has left – in PJ's and clogs. I suppose it will be modest revenge for the Villiers morning, when he could have ended up withering beneath a terrible curse, had I not saved his sorry bacon.

I relish five minutes of calm, all the more delectable for knowing that it must soon end – as it does, with a ghastly inrush of fresh air bearing Carl with it.

"Hi Evie," he chirps brightly.

"Go away," I say bitterly.

"Ignore them Carl," says Tee. "They're suffering from an incurable disease. I could cure them both with green tea but they're closed to all reasonable suggestions. Lost cause, really. I don't know why I'm even bothering."

"Why don't you both 'eff off and do whatever you're about to do in Carl's van?"

"No. People would talk. I have a reputation to consider."

That did it. One of us was consumed by inner cackling, which quickly turned to outer cackling. We cackled under the bedclothes. We cackled struggling free of them. We cackled hysterically in the loo. We cackled as we struggled into minimal outerwear and wellies. Between cackling, one of us said – "A solitary Beaver will return, with coffee. Kindly solve this problem in our absence. We shall leave the door open – the better to preserve your 'reputations.' Farewell!"

We even cackled to ourselves, as we blundered towards the caff, busily sorting out the day's persona.

I cackled on the way back. "We are sorted," I announced, "not that either of you care but one of us is here, bearing coffee. A chaperone has returned. Your saviour. Don't strain to thank us, it's all part of the service."

I gazed at the construction on the floor. It was exceedingly ugly and obviously incomplete.

"What is it?" I demanded.

"Isn't that obvious?"

"Not to me."

"Oh, what a shame, 'cos we've no idea either."

"Maybe you've got it upside down?" I volunteered.

"Could be," said Carl. "Unlikely though, those are lion's paws…" and he pointed at the floor.

"Real ones?" I asked with sudden interest.

"No, you moron," grunted my beloved. "Bronze ones."

I considered the construction again… "Should you want my opinion," I mumbled "and I'm sure you don't, it's a – do you know, I have absolutely no idea…but it does seem to be missing a piece. There, at the top. That tilty circle, at the top, seems to be a cradle of some sort or other and the rest of it is geared to moving that circle around, inclining it and things. Some sort of astrolabe… maybe…"

"This is excellent," stage-whispered Tiggs. "He's getting his 'she' brain turned on… or it could be the other way round. Either way, results may be imminent."

"Don't slander my other half," I muttered, sinking to my knees to examine matters more closely. "Together we are a tightly knit team, except when we're having psychological crises, which is most of the time usually."

"In fact," I pondered, suddenly becoming interested, " I think it's missing at least two bits, probably more… Now, I wonder… Are they missing, or were they never made? And if…" I crawled over the bed, hearing a distant scream of "wellies!" in the background … "how did it go together Carl? I'm sorry, I wasn't looking. Still had the night grumps. Hang on a minute…something's pulling…" I twisted round… " stop pulling my legs off, Tiggs. We have a guest."

"Agh!" shrieked Tigger.

"I think she's trying to get you to take your wellies off, Evie. You know, while you're on the bed?"

"Well why didn't she just say that?" I mumbled, kicking them off, which for some reason elicited another – "gah!!" in the distance – "anyway, to resume, how did it go together?"

"Really easily, Evie," he said, with a nervous glance over his shoulder at something that was doing a sort of dance, to judge by the thumping and banging. "It was what I'd call a natural build – at least it was to me but I think in 3D solids."

"Mm, yep, I've got you. Anyway, turn your peepers on this. That top seating. Nothing's been sliding in and out of there once or twice a day, a week, a month or what have you, That matters, because this is old, far older than it looks. That construction technique, It's based on woodworking joints. This is how you would put wood together, not metal. I think this is very, very old."

"Oh, I should have seen that myself, Evies. That's a neat bit of deduction. What are you feeding them both on Tee?"

"I slip green tea into the custard powder."

"You better not be, Holmes. I'm regressed enough, without sliding back any further."

"My dear Watson, please proceed with your interesting theory. Mr Ripley and I are deeply impressed with your reasoning, so far."

"Look at these notches in the lower legs. Some are worn, some are not. The sturdy way this thing stands suggests to me that this is exactly how it was meant to go together. If you turn on your 3D vision you can visualise a succession of circular plates and collars could have fitted into these slots. What you might have ended up with then, would have been some sort of collapsible, therefore portable, astrolabe-type machine."

"Sorry," said Carl, "give me a moment to assume the mantle of Inspector Lestrade …'what the devil is he talking about Holmes?'

'Holmes' looked question marks at me.

"My dear Lestrade," I explained, "an astrolabe is a circular slide rule, for the sky. It comprises a number of discs and rings that can revolve around a central axis and by ingenious use of pointers and such-like, you can work out the alignment of the night sky for any period of the year. To be honest, I'm winging-it. It's way beyond me. The Arabs invented it, back in the famous year cocoa – sorry Carl, in-joke – and it's one of the many objects that I always covet in science museums. I think we are looking at a particular and peculiar adaptation of the principle.

"Bear with my woffling a while longer. There's also a set-up known as an armillary sphere – bearing no relation at all to the dear little armadillo person, who can roll up in a tight, armoured ball, like a woodlouse. Shall I pause here for hearty, collegiate laughter? No? Truly, Holmes, really Lestrade, I blush for you! The armillary sphere is a 3D representation of the solar system. A clever piece of enlightenment engineering.

Spheres set on cranked arms represented the known planets, the moon and sun. The top-notch ones had a geared mechanism that let the whole shebang be rotated by turning one handle. The owner played God, turned the crank and the solar system span around slowly, emulating the actual state of affairs out there. So clever! All those cogs and pinions cut by hand. Baffles and intrigues me."

"I tell you what," said Tee thoughtfully, "there's a tradition of skilled metalworking in North West India – that's geographically speaking. What is now Pakistan has rather swallowed up the area I'm thinking of. Up there little kids work in metal shops making copies of AK 47's that are better machined than the original factory-stampings. They have machinery but there's an awful lot of hand-work goes on. Whatever this thing is, I'll bet it was made up there, maybe hundreds of years ago. The native population claim to have inherited their skills from the Scythians and they were the original fine metal-workers."

"I'm going to take a flyer here," I said, "and if this works, then I'm a genius and breakfast is on me. If it doesn't, I shall be wholly cast down and you'll have to revive me with a paid-for breakfast. Deal, anybody?"

"I'm in," said Carl.

"That was faster than a ferret down a rabbit hole" marvelled Tee. "Allow me to seize your vanishing coat tails. Me, too, please."

"Stand aside, then, the bed-crawler needs access to her knicker drawer, pronto!"

"Does this require pants?" wondered Tee. "I may be under garmented! Hey, Beaver, I'm getting good at these puns, aren't I?"

"An absolute marvel, Sweet Pea. No, it doesn't require pants but it does require that which lurks beneath them."

"Whoa," said Carl. "Am I in danger, alone, unchaperoned?"

"You'll survive to tell the tale," I grunted, crawling to the chest of drawers, to begin my excavation. I have a pervy thing about lingerie, so there was an excessive quantity of quality designs in top notch fabrics to rootle through. I was quite prepared to offer a guided tour but the audience were restless.

"How many knickers does one androgyne need?" ruminated Tee.

"Twice as many as ye, the under-equipped," I riposted. (That was a sort of pun, too but the thought of explaining it was daunting).

"Hah! Found it!" I cried and emerged with the wrap of knitwear, that was protecting the stainless cylinder Marie-Claire had found. Until this moment, I had more or less forgotten about it. Deliberately, I'm sure, as it had been the cause of much angst, the night that JJ had handed it over to me. I hadn't felt much better about it since, either and that was despite our escorting it for a nocturnal ramble among the Jacobs' sheep of Oxfordshire.

I gave the parcel to Carl. "Shove that where you think it should go – having first resisted the lure of the appallingly obvious double-entendre."

He unwrapped it and my stomach performed a slow somersault. Tee wasn't paying that much attention, so I was on my own with this revelation. I could see, quite clearly, that the cylinder had grown lugs and engineered grooves around its previously flawless perimeter. Buried under a mound of intimate garments, it had passed its time by indulging in a little light plastic surgery. The irritating thing was alive and sentient. My stomach rolled back again, upon which a chilly flood of iced water began to track a familiar route through my bowel.

"Back in a minute!" I said lightly and headed for the loo.

Tee and Carl were too engrossed to care. Carl was studying the new configuration, turning the casing in his hands, feeling the bumps and grooves as carefully as might some lucky phrenologist, newly entrusted with Einstein's skull.

"It goes here, doesn't it?" I heard him say, as I closed the door behind me.

I knew it would, that it would click into place like the slice of science fiction it was fast becoming. It would sit bang on top of the skeleton frame, where flat-faced pillars reached up to secure it. Their flats would slide into those barely perceptible rebates on the sides of the canister. Meanwhile, the lugs that had grown out, like otter's ears, would stop any displacement. The casing and the eye were now secure but they were also free to move, in accord with the mechanical organisation of the frame. It would swivel just as it had turned in our cupped hands, that night in the Oxfordshire field. Instead of having to align itself via willing but nervous fingers, it had now found pre-forged metalware to accommodate its homing instinct. The implications were unnerving.

My bowel agreed – the whole business was too uncanny for comfort.

"It fits, as neatly as Cinderella's shoe," yelled Carl, so giddy with enthusiasm that every obvious question was left unspoken. Which was just as well, because neither of us would have had any answers. "You shall go to the ball!" he finished. "I'm off to rouse the Clan. I daresay breakfast will be on the house."

Behind closed doors, I groaned some sort of reply. Then my supper exited in a rush, as I heard the van door slam behind him.

"Come out, Beaver!" yelled Tee. "There's a conspiracy afoot."

I staggered out and stared at the ghastly assembly on the floor.

"I hate that thing," I said, "as in, really, really, really-hate!"

Tee, however, was holding up a sweatshirt. "Why is my top in your bottoms drawer?" she demanded.

"Why do you think?" I said. "It's obvious – things are taking over. First that alien cylinder sprouts grooves and ears, now our tops and bottoms are scuttling from drawer to drawer. It's a world-wide conspiracy to befuddle and bewilder the human race before They finally take over."

"What? We're going to be ruled by pairs of pants?"

"Precisely. Ask yourself why you are wearing my 'jama bottoms. You didn't realise did you? Also there are at least three of your bras in my collection and the shoes have got muddled up. It's all that machine's fault. Hundreds of years of blind-engineering suddenly coming to fruition in our trashy trailer. Have you any idea what that means?"

"None at all," said Tee.

"It means," I said slowly, "that the mechanical aspect of the cosmos is taking a liberty. Our disarray is being sardonically compared to the perfect evolution of that wretched contraption and its allies. Clothes have now joined the war against humans. It's the final assault!"

"They're winning," said Tee, holding up fresh evidence. "Where will it end?"

"In some awful terminal gridlock. Everyone will have one leg in somebody else's jeans and half a bosom in your neighbour's top. When we're totally immobilised, in left-footed pairs of wellies and knickers that have sewn up one leg-hole, they'll unleash their final, devilish plan!"

"Oooh!" squeaked Tee, with appropriate terror. "What is it?"

"I don't know. It's top secret. Nothing can penetrate their defences, not even the moths we sent. They were trained to operate nano-transmitters but nothing has been heard from them."

"Idiotic to employ moths," grumped Tee. "They're very easily side-tracked. Probably all double-agents by now. Promise them an 'all-you-can-eat' silk scarf buffet and they're anyone's."

"But that is where our survival plan becomes truly cunning." I shall explain. "We know that they know but they don't know that we know that they know."

"What do we know?"

"Absolutely nothing. I told you, their defences are impenetrable."

"Heaven protect me," said Tee wearily, "you talk utter drivel. Where are my trainers?"

51

KNOCK-KNOCK, WHO'S THERE?

I really love to lose myself in the hustle, the smell and the low rumble of conversation in the caff. As usual, I scanned the tables for MI5 custard thieves but ever since that day, they had been mysteriously absent. Carl and I shared high levels of paranoia but neither of us had registered sight or sound of them. My assumption was that they were gathering their data via satellites. Somewhere, in a Portakabin in Ohio, Nevada, or Milton Keynes for all I knew, steel-eyed operatives were watching and mapping our every move. They would have trashy-trailer penetrating radar and all our secrets would be laid bare. One day, while seeking the fireweed's opinion of the situation, I'd be gone, in the white-hot flare of a Hellfire missile.

Seems very unfair on the fireweed, though most gardeners would totally disagree. My mum never had a good word for it, which is probably what pushed me in its general direction. At that early age I had not learned its language. Today, however, emboldened by my new-found ability to commune with aspects of the natural world, I am seriously thinking about establishing communication with bindweed. Now there is a plant in a hurry. But whether convolvulus arvensis, to give it its Sunday name, is inclined to chat or not, is yet to be determined.

I'm digressing again but as I do so I am also elegantly manoeuvring myself around the queues and tables, hailing the regulars and exchanging small talk.

The paper-lad is here. He always turns up, be it late or early. He's at least 70 and has the most far-flung, dog's leg of a round to pursue. He is in the employ of Mr Ahmad, who never frequents us in person but always shows his gratitude for the free takeaway coffee we despatch his way, via the homeward-bound paper-lad, in the form of a free sweetie or two, for Tee, Alice, or I, when we duck in for jars of this or that, having suddenly and unexpectedly run out.

He is 'only a sort-of a Muslim' and Tee is 'only a sort-of a Hindu.' Therefore both of them, as fervent partisans and part-owners of the sub-continent, have much to talk about. They have that deep, expatriate empathy and as they rattle away in a language unknown to Beavers, I have begun to feel very small indeed, standing there clutching the box of necessities we came to procure. In some reversed cameo of the

Raj years, I imagine myself cast as Evie, faithful retainer to Princess Tee or, worse by far, the nautch-creature of Ranee Tulipa. "How's it going, Ted?" I enquire of the paper-lad.

"Hello, Evie love. Yes, everything's as it should be – except there's one heck of a bite to the wind, this morning. Winter is rolling towards us."

"Note my chunky-knit!" I gestured. "What's hit the headlines, today, then?"

"Do you know, love, I haven't a clue. I just stick'em through people's doors. Haven't read a paper in years. Never listen to the news, either. I feel much better for it."

We'd had this conversation, with variations, ad infinitum but we both find it soothing, non-intrusive, affable.

"Take care on those roundabouts, Ted, bye!"

"I will Evie, bye."

I squeeze aside for a phalanx of five burly drivers, each carrying a platter filled with double full-English, enough food to sustain a family of five for a day. They ignore me, so involved are they in a hectoring discussion of last night's football, a sport every aspect of which, I loathe from the bottom of my soul.

Allow me another digression. 'No' – be damned to, 'allow me.' If you haven't grasped that digressions are the whole point of this exercise, then you should stop reading now. I'll allow there is a slender narrative thread but trust me, it's not the point. Please don't tell me you hadn't got that and you've been waiting for the action to begin?

My digression is, that being an androgyne, I get to exercise certain liberties. At one end of the scale, I can nip into M & S Ladies Loo and take a pee standing up. Score 1. Another liberty I take is that as a sort of man, I get to observe men from a privileged viewpoint, from within the tent, if you like.

Observing them, as a tribe, on the whole I find them obnoxious. I look at their huge bulk, their barely-contained urge to commit violence, that unstoppable aggression and I wonder how their women feel. I imagine twilight evenings when they hear the car pull up outside, at the end of another working day. Within 60 seconds this hyena, inevitably-thwarted by his day, will come crashing into the house. My female side recoils with something close to terror. I'm missing the gene that relishes the taming of Giant Terrible, I am not the subversive, submissive fetcher of slippers, pourer of beer, provider of warm food.

I can see, theoretically, there's a fillip to be had from throwing a bridle over the wild stallion but give me a more muted, kinder sort of creature. Something with a brain. I don't mind the sharp edge that can cut with intelligence but I'm scared rigid by the clenched fist that can come with the lack of it.

I shouldn't generalise. I know some utterly lovely, plodding, humble men but there's another clan of male animals that make me fearful, for myself, for the world, for the future of the human race.

Where was I? About to escape up the "Staff Only" staircase, past the sign that never fails to fill me with self-important glee – "Private: no admission" – when Harry bellows – "Evie, love, can you clear for five or ten? I'm two down."

Foiled! "I'm on it, H," I yell and battle my way to grab a big tray, a pinny, a cloth and spray. Sensibly, I shed the chunky-knit. "Behold!" I cry, "Hurricane Evie is upon you!"

"Go girl, GO!" roars Harry, entering into the spirit of the moment.

I go, roaring round in concentric circles, or rather spirals and ferrying back one tottering load after another.

Eventually Tee sticks her head over the balcony and enquires – "what are you doing?" She can be remarkably slow on the uptake, for a Princess.

"What does it look like I'm doing? Buttering parsnips for the Archbishop of York, of course. I've been press-ganged by Harry."

"Hmph," said Tee, "we'll start without you."

"No," I yell back. "I am the missing link. You need me. Beaver-glue. I shall be levitating shortly. Discuss sister Ally's forthcoming book on bestiality, or find something equally uplifting to talk about until I arrive."

"Has she written a book on bestiality?" yells Tee, showing an interest – as well as sparking a frisson of attention, a ripple even, across the audience below.

"I've no idea, ask her."

"I certainly will." Tee vanished, as mysteriously and certainly as the Cheshire Cat.

I started clearing tables under the deck. Above, all were assembling. I could hear Andy, arriving like Long John Silver, tap, tap, tapping his way across the floor.

I can't ignore the fact that some gang of reprobates must have had a toast fight round here. Damn, I need dust pan and brush. At least I know where to find one. Lord, there's toast, tomatoes, even bacon – a full-English – as if fired from one of the Carron Company's ever-reliable carronades. I duck under tables collecting crusts, rinds and perfectly decent food, which makes me cross and sad. Damn it all, people starve in this world, little children go hungry! Finally I sweep my way almost to the limit of the breakfast wars.

In a very awkward corner, by itself on the floor, under this fine, solid table, sits intact a fried egg. It's a perfect specimen of the ilk. Bright yellow yolk, the white in a well-formed circle. It looks as though it's about to issue a statement on behalf of abused and abandoned fried eggs worldwide. I feel quite pained on its behalf and am about to enter into conversation, when I recall that I am in a hurry and that my dustpan is over-filled.

Naturally I lurch to my feet, forgetting where I am and consequently knock my brains out on the underside of this excellently-constructed table. I see a multitude of floaty, white dots. They remind me that I really am hurrying but am getting more and more delayed. I must have a word with that egg, so I spin full circle, locate the kitchen and – I am told later – proceed to measure my full length on the dining room floor.

"Eva," says a gentle voice in my head, "Eva, dear, please listen to me, just for a little while."

Because I know that voice, I want to say – "I told you where to go, once before" – but I can't. Whoever owns this voice is exerting fingertip pressure on my solar plexus. It is the most delicate touch but I can't bear that it might increase. I feel sick, so utterly, utterly sick. While this pressure lasts, this voice owns me. We know each other very well.

"I know, Eva. I heard you the first time but I can help you. For a start, let me tell you that you're going to be fine. You'll be 'out cold,' as you put it, for a bit and that will upset and frighten your friends, especially Tee. She's with you now. She's a bit panicky, because she can't bear the thought that you might not wake up. You will, though, you'll be quite all right. So will everyone else. You know, I don't think there's anyone here who doesn't love you – and that includes poor old Ted, the paper-boy. I bet you didn't know that!"

"Stop patronising me," I say. "I'll listen. You know I have no choice. I'm too scared to say 'no' to you now." Then I hear myself say – "I've not been right since I saw my portrait again." The thought had been jerked out of me like a tooth, or a confession.

"I know you haven't. I worry for you, at times but you will be OK. You've heard of Guardian Angels? Imagine you have one, perhaps that will soften the intrusion. Do you want me to change my voice, might that help?"

'Oh God,' I think, 'the bloody thing's a Sat-Nav.'

I sense an ironic chuckle.

'You're Star-Cloud, Sun-Cloud, some interface or other, of a wretched quantum computer – of course you are, what else could you be?'

"You can dwell on what, or who I am when you wake up. In the meantime I've a lot to tell you and limited time in which to tell it. There are small things you need to know. Things that will help you.

"Here I go – your portrait is accurate. To me, that's what you look like. Actually, you're slightly more powerful, more centred than you think. You'll find out how powerful you are, before too long – though to you, it will probably seem like a long time. You're going to become more solid. The way that you see 'solid' in Punch. Don't refuse any help Earth Magic offers you. You can see what it's made of him. You need some of that and oddly, I don't have the means of giving it to you.

"Now, listen – all through the many cycles of life, clusters of being have searched for ways to avoid the inevitability of death. You know that death cannot be avoided. It is a necessary part of life, an essential ingredient. It is true that we are interested in changing that. Just because a process exists, does not mean that it cannot be restructured. 'Something' does not necessarily have to revert 'No-thing' – but this event horizon is far, far beyond death as organic life knows it. But you are familiar with the ideas?"

'Explicate…Implicate…' I think.

"Exactly. That's a very useful phrase for you, a great simplifier. Therefore incorrect and inevitably, of its time. It is, however, a useful fiction for facts to grow around. Remember 'useful fiction' too, it explains much of what I'm trying to explain. I, we –

you choose – didn't take much interest in humankind until the Paleolithic. That was a mistake on our part, for we missed the genesis of the spark that 'set-you-off', evolving exponentially along a certain vein – the one you call 'intelligence' but isn't.

"Ever since we have been encouraging discreet clusters of life. The problem with such short-lived, active beings, is that they crave indications of 'success,' some sign that they are making meaningful progress in breaking the cycle of life and death."

'Well, wouldn't you?' I think belligerently.

"If I had set myself such a stupid task in the first place, of course I would crave some visible sign of progress, exactly in the same way that the alchemists craved the glint of gold. You can see, can't you Eva, that the question is stupid, therefore any answer will be, too?"

I could think of nothing, because I knew nothing.

"Trust me Eva, visible signs, tangible objects, secret formulas, anything purporting to be a solution, or a staging post on the way to a solution, is a waste of time and energy. The piece of equipment that has, unfortunately, arrived into your care is such a chimera. It has been a chimera for well over 1000 of your years.

"Oh dear," lamented the voice, "I've a lot to impart and very limited time. I wish I could talk to you when you're functioning normally but sadly, you have to be 'out cold.' So prepare for raw material, patronising and insulting.

"However clever you organic clusters become, you will remain dunces. You will not find a way out of your dilemma. You are food. You were born to be eaten. But when you try and strive in a certain manner, you subtly alter the fabric of the universe.

"The 'myth' of the Lamed Vavniks is not a myth. It's truth. A huge truth. The Tzadikim Nistarin, to give them their other name, are elite only in the sense that their humility is the sublime counterpoint to mankind's arrogance. They would never seek to lead. The concept would make them smile.

"Behind them, if you like, are other more active strivers. Not humble people but naturally gifted people. Arrogant people who are trying to temper their arrogance into humility. That struggle, their struggle, alters the fabric of the universe. Striving to rid yourself of arrogance counts for a lot. Love, however, counts most of all. The Tzadikim Nistarim love, humbly, all beings. Your little group is bound together by love and that is why we are interested in your 'chemistry.'

"Other groups, without that adhesive, fail. Nevertheless, they try and try and try and that counts for something. But without simple, humble love for all things, the human race will fail. It's brutal. We try to encourage most of the groups we encounter but it usually ends badly.

"That piece of metal rubbish you have is an accumulation of centuries of tangible encouragement. It has become ludicrously totemic. It all began in the Altai Mountains, a long time ago. A group were gifted the knowledge of metallurgy. What a poisoned chalice that turned out to be."

I felt myself throw up. There was something monstrous about the conversation.

"Don't fret Eva. It's not the words that are affecting you, it's being party to their implications. It's very unpleasant to know something denied to others, especially others you love. Nevertheless, I have to dissuade you from prizing this apparatus. I can't allow you to waste your time. It is far too valuable.

"Every group that has inherited this thing has made of it a Grail object. At every stage of its development, it could always perform some party trick or other. I don't know where it's up to, I've stopped taking any interest. Perhaps it can talk, walk, expand, contract. I don't care. Every group unfortunate enough to inherit it, has the 'honour' of adding some fresh segment to the construct. You did that very thing, some fraction of time since.

"If and when the thing is ever finished, it will be, allow me the oxymoron, a crudely-sophisticated communications device, one that will permit a very limited form of contact, cosmos-wide. I'm sure you sense how alluring that prospect would be to many kinds of mind. That is why this particular carrot has been dangled under the noses of so many spiritually-minded groups.

"Perhaps it has been a 'useful fiction,' parts of me obviously believe so and I can see its allure. Yet, ask yourself, if you could communicate with other like-minded groups, cosmos-wide, what of it? What would you talk about? The weather, your tedious concepts of 'God?' I suppose you could exchange cake recipes, at least they wouldn't become horribly dangerous... no, maybe they could... I shouldn't try to be humorous.

"Too many groups have become fixated on the object itself. They have taken for granted the mutuality, the struggle for humility that led them to it in the first place. The irony being that that was the whole point, that was the progressive path, the road to consciousness!

"There is only one truth, Eva. It is that the humble love of one being for another is the only thing that matters. Somehow, it operates as a solvent, one that can unhitch this universe from its unending, useless reincarnations.

"My counsel is that you throw the thing into a junkyard, though I suppose some passing visionary would rescue it from the crusher. It's a hare someone started running, with the best intentions but as is usual with hares, it is now out of control. Please do not waste time on it.

"Unfortunately, I know you are not going to take my word for it. You will develop a nagging feeling that I am, in some way, acting from self-interest. That I am a villain and that the protection and development of the device is paramount. That will be a lapse of judgement.

"The only thing that matters on No-Name Roundabout is the mutual love you all have for one-another. The energy that rises from that is fabric-changing. For this universe to survive, huge quantities of that energy are required.

"Lucy Mahoney died as a consequence of pursuing, securing and protecting that device. She was a fine, strong, loving person but the gibberish she misunderstood led her to that piece of metal and turned her into a fugitive, unable to live out her otherwise impeccable life. What a colossal waste!

"Last words, Eva, you're about to wake up. I do apologise for the lump on your head. Good luck, you are loved."

'You made me bash my head?' I raved silently. 'You bastard!'

There was no answer.

52
CHOD

Tee said, later, that when I first came to, in the caff, I was like an angry wasp. The only reason she didn't swat me with terrible Tigger claws, was that too many people were watching.

"Oi tink she's foine," said a familiar voice – but I don't know any Irishmen – do I?

"She's a foine, strong girl. Will you b' watchin' for the concussion, though? Slightest soin o'that an' you brings her into A & E, sharp loik. Lord love her, what a bump she's havin' on her noddle. Harry, my love, break out d'ose frozen peas!" (Turns out I know him perfectly well. He's a lovely Irish doctor, who does permanent nights at A & E. Has breakfast with us, every day, on his way home. Mystery solved!)

Now…it appears I'm starkers…oops… don't tell me I've got green tea regression? No. I'm under a duvet…and this is our duvet…coming up for air…Now…

"Tigger?"
"It lives and speaks! Tigger rejoices! Which fluid do you require?"
"I hope I never say this again – water, please."
"Your wish is my command – for a limited period only."

I must exploit that while I can… "are you familiar with the Clydeside dictum of Para Handy – 'water, 'tis the wonderful stuff for floatin' boats on but not a drink for a Christian man.'?"

"Ah," said Tee, knowingly, "if your capacity for digression has returned. I'm pretty sure you're back for good."

Upon which, I'm stunned to report, she burst into great whooping sobs and fell on top of me. "Oh my God, I was so scared. I thought I'd lost you. You were out for ages."

At least, that's the concise version. The full, tearful account doesn't really translate to paper, far too many hiccups.

"Gosh Tiggs, where would I go?"
"I don't know but I'd have to come and find you."
"Oh dear, don't ever do that. I'd be so cross, I'd kill you. Then I'd have to kill me.

Then you'd kill me and it would all get incredibly complicated. We'd never manage to catch-up with one-another."

She managed a wry smile through the tears.

"Try not to collapse like Punch's auroch, again. I gather it was spectacular but very disconcerting for the regulars. Good job our Irish friend was there. Otherwise we'd have been up at A & E for a fortnight. He really checked you over very thoroughly.

"We were all upstairs, sipping coffee. We'd no idea you'd de-brained yourself, until this great hullabaloo started up from down below."

I learned later, that she'd come down the banister side-saddle, cut a swathe through the spectators and started CPR, until the Doc had hauled her off as an idiot.

"She's not that sort of 'out,' Princess," he'd yelled. "You'll be giving her an arrhythmia if you carry on so! Lord love you, so you will!"

"I'm guessing my antics urinated on the breakfast surprise?"

"You turned into the breakfast surprise, Lovely," said Tee. "Anyway, if you're sure you're OK, I'm off to spread the good-tidings. I did promise people. I've even got to phone the night crew at home. That's how loved you are. Oh, the mechanical device that started it all is back in the bathroom, eager to fulfil its true function as a toe-catcher. The all-seeing eye is back sniffing your knickers and reporting suspicious pheromones to Galactic Central."

"You can tell everyone I'm very touched. Actually, I'm gruesomely embarrassed. It's all the fault of a fried egg. I'll tell you, once you've ridden back from Ghent."

"Oh Lord, you haven't actually gone dotty, have you?"

"Not at all…it was a very sensible fried egg."

Tee was gone a long time. I lay under the duvet, strangely at peace, staring idly at the gap at the top of the curtains, where the wretched Star of Bethlehem pokes its nose into our business, on a nightly basis. I wondered if it was there, right now, observing. Could it peep, when it was daylight, or was our own star, the sun, protecting me? Stupid question!

Stupid question or not, I felt satisfactorily 'me.' I don't know why, just unusually aware of myself. I could sense my extremities and that root of everything – at least it is for me – that V-notch at the bottom of my ribs…where something had been pressing…?

I said 'hello' to my elbows, the backs of my knees, my wrists, my neck, the sides of my backside and the arches of my feet. I was truly thrilled to get 'helloes' back, as if they knew me, even liked me!

Then I thought about the fried egg. It's quite tricky to think about a fried egg, outside its familiar format as an element of breakfast on your plate, in a frying pan or otherwise employed in matters that are germane to consumption. This one, however, I felt a sorrowful respect for. It would have to take a whole different road to transformation, now. It would have to go via the food waste cycle, not via the human energy route.

Perhaps that was good?

We'd already blocked its most purposeful route – that of becoming another chicken. We'd obliged it to embark on the human food cycle and I can't imagine how good that looks from the egg's point-of-view. Maybe, like us, it can't see what eats it? Would an unfertilised egg be observant in any way?

Some fool, however, had placed it on the floor, presumably in the hope that his chosen victim would unwittingly squelch their size-tens on top of it. What sort of fool is that? One certainly unworthy of eating an egg. Yet, if the egg was eaten by a fool, or a philosopher – assuming the two are not synonymous – its end would be the same, wouldn't it? The majority of it would join the 'waste' cycle, the 24-hour one. Some of it would have to wait a while longer, for the demise of its consumer and some of it would immediately feed the energy of aforesaid diner. It's the last bit wherein things get tricky

How you use your energy is what must matter. Do you waste it, devising damn-fool practical jokes on the scrubbed floors of diners, where the eggs are fried with care, do you attend to matters of state, with due pomp and ceremony, or do you scrub clean the newly-fouled bed-pan of some agonised, departing soul? The egg has no say in who eats it, does it?

Equally, we have no say in what eats us, or why.

Does that make me feel dejected? It shouldn't but it does.

At the end, all we have to offer is ourselves. I have no idea if there is a spiritual recycling. In common with everyone, I'd like there to be. But I do know that there is a material recycling. Every living thing departs via its own charnel ground, where sit the practitioners of Chod.

'Oh Egg, I truly didn't want Chod in my head. That is most unfair of you!'

Yes, I've been here before, because Chod fascinates me. It seems to penetrate to the heart of the matter – our fear of the material world and the havoc it brings to our being.

A woman started it. That in itself is fascinating. Machig Labdron, lived a good while ago, in Tibet, when life was a whole lot harsher than it is now. Her biography is sparing on detail, her hagiography is tedious. Her central idea is astonishing – make your demons your allies. Better still, your demons are your allies!

Her adherents – many of whom were mad, while some were mad and bad – were inclined to take up residence in the charnel grounds, surrounded by the sights and scents of human bodily decay. Their notion was that such places were the haunt of restless, unfulfilled wandering souls, filled with the torments of the newly-departed. If you could reconcile yourself to living amongst such dispossession, you were well on the way to sundering the ties that make us so dependent on the material world. That's not what she said. She said bring your fears into yourself, welcome them, be reconciled. Learn to use their strengths.

I know Machig foretold that her way would become twisted out of shape by the emotionally insane. Like Tantra, her way was so narrow, most would fall from its path. It relied on the single-minded search for truth in the heart of the practitioner, their relentless pursuit of it, with pure intentions. How many of us can aspire to that? How many of us are not hopelessly compromised between the material world and the invisible, intangible world of the soul? I know I am.

Something about Chod however, not only its being desperate measures for desperate times but its recognition that the last fence is the only fence worth jumping, attracts me. Why fool around with half-measures when full ones are freely available? I see it clearly but I can't make myself engage with it in a meaningful way.

Chod…what the hell do I know? And all the fault of an egg.

I actually enjoy cleaning the caff. Siding the tables, mopping, even scrubbing the floor. I don't know why people think it's a demeaning job. I really don't. I'll even go one further and confess that cleaning toilets can be very satisfying, too. Perhaps that's my peculiar psychology, though I am regularly impressed by the pleasant natures of so many toilet cleaners.

I once took a very memorable pee, in Paris. The lady manning the 'triage' point at the bottom of the stairs was not suffering from any sense of false humility. She was an elderly, black lady possessed of a terrifyingly stern demeanour. This toilet was her kingdom. Deposit your franc, or whatever coin you vouchsafed, GENTS turned Left. DAMES turned Right. OTHERS need not apply.

She rarely, as the queue moved past her table, raised her eyes from her battered, black Bible. It was open at the Apocrypha and she was deep in the Book of Daniel. Despite this, I felt scrutinised, judged and found wanting – but I generally feel that way. As I was wearing a summery dress, I scuttled Right. I have been known to turn Left, when feeling wicked side out but nothing could have induced me to that level of transgression before such a redoubtable judge and jury. She'd have dialled up the Beast 666 and I would have ended up in the fiery furnace, with Shadrach, Meshach and Abednego…which I happen to know is how Chapter Three of Daniel turns out.

So-oo, in the last five minutes we've had transformation in fried eggs, the practice of Chod and experiences in Parisian loos. Yes, I'm returning to normal. That's a very ordinary five minutes in the junk room of my mind.

I stare at the patch of discolouration on the ceiling. It really is horrible.

Tee said I'd been unconscious for ages. I wonder why? I couldn't remember a thing, really. Except someone had kept shouting 'useful fictions' in my ear. What would they do that for? I'm sure they meant to say – 'how many fingers am I holding up?' They always say that! Nobody had asked me that! I'd been cheated. So I did it myself. "How many fingers am I holding up, Eva?" "Ten." "Wrong! Eight fingers and two thumbs!" Schoolyard prank, circa year cocoa, from my Paleolithic era, when I was called Evan – all I lost was my 'n,' for 'nuts.'

'Steady on…all of a sudden, one of us feels horribly sick and we share the same stomach. Oh no, really sick. Oh bugger. Forehead is running with sweat, ice is swilling in my belly and I'm shaken with rigors. I'm not going to get away with this one. Quick – run, stagger, whatever. Oh gawd, heave, ah, oh, grief, nothing…oh, but that hurt! Oh no, again, and now liquid in the guise of a solid comes up and out. Oh, that was horrible. Rest my forehead on the cold porcelain, so smooth, so cold. Oh no…heave… and that hurt…there can't be any more. But there is… Now, please, I'm empty. Stop, stop. I'm shivering, shivering. Under the duvet, shivering. Some warmth coming. Thank God, I feel OK. I feel normal. Please let that be it! I've nothing left to throw up. Whatever you are, begone – some damned imp in my gut.'

How is it that we know nothing about ourselves and our bodies? We treat them the way we treat our cars – jump behind the wheel and off. It works, ignore it, leave it be. Feed it, water it, wash and polish on weekends. It breaks down, call the AA or the NHS. Replace a part, patch a hole, free up a blockage. It goes again! Hallelujah! What a way to live.

Pity my poor friend, the stonefish. One day his float bladder goes wrong. No fishy hospital, so, down, down he sinks and all alone, he dies. All that miraculous bony engineering is abandoned, as his fishy soul flees to piscine heaven.

We humans found that degree of uncertainty too much to bear – the indifferent attentions of casual, accidental, death. We raged at fate and at the malevolent demons who heaped their curses on our unequal souls.

It was then that the women got to work, while the men slunk away to hunt, leaving the screams of childbirth gone wrong behind them. The women tried to find ways in which they could extract the tiny bodies, that had mis-presented themselves. In time, they found that there were ways they could help.

The first Shamans were women. Women who found that they could assist a birth, stem a fever, set a bone, stitch a ragged opening torn by horns, or claws.

Women tried to make sense of this no-sense world. Everything begins with birth and ends with death. Sometimes the two follow too closely on each other's heels but they, the women, try. Try to turn fate around, to intervene in life's indignities, thwart its indifference, find another answer.

If the women hadn't intervened, hadn't discovered the wisdom of the Shaman, we'd still be deep within a Malthusian existence, a nightmare of too many mouths and not enough bread which, admittedly, comes a little later but I'm tired and I can jumble the two together, if I want to. Alice knew Malthus and she says he was horrible.

I feel for my dick, warm under the duvet and wonder about it. What is that game that has you shouting – "better with, or without?"

Lord, I'm tired, I'm going to sleep for a while.

53

CALORIES IN A CRISIS

I wake feeling fine. Tee is sitting cross-legged on the bed, watching me and eating Jumbo Roasted Cashews from a very large packet. She is solemnly shovelling them in, with dedication. I watch her through slitted eyes, trying to fathom exactly what she's doing – because it looks far more serious than merely eating nuts.

"I know you're awake," she says, between chews. "I can see you peeping."

"I'm trying to understand your nut ritual."

"Easy, they're actually your nuts, so I'm trying to eat them all before you wake up." She glanced in the bag. "Not many to go now."

"My nuts? I haven't got any cashews."

"You had," says Tee with unhappy emphasis on the 'had.' Ted, the paper-boy, came by with them earlier, as a sort of 'get-well-soon' card. He entrusted them to me but I'm thoroughly untrustworthy around salted, roasted cashews – small or large – and that," she said with huge satisfaction, while shaking the packet to be certain, "is the last one."

"That's thoroughly outrageous," I protest feebly. "What else have you guzzled of mine?"

"Let me think…a super-size bar of Bournville, a kilo of red grapes… a-a-and something…" she's rooting around in her pocket… "ah, a small box of white Lindor," she reads off a scrap of paper. Lots of nice people brought you things, so I kept a list, so that you could say 'thank-you'. That was clever, don't you think?

"Worrying consumes a huge amount of calories. I might have died without additional nutrition and I didn't want to leave you."

"You seem very calm, for one caught thieving from the sick and dying."

"I am calm. I'm practising my inner Zen calmness. Also, if I move I'll probably be sick."

"I've been sick," I say brightly.

"Please don't talk about it, or I shall be forced to abandon you again. Then I'll worry. Then I'll need more calories and if anyone else has brought more goodies, I'll be forced to eat those, too."

"I can see that this could resolve into a lethal cycle," I agreed.

"I teeter on the very brink of disaster, it's true but it's been worth the sacrifice."

"How can I possibly help?"

"Take me to dinner. I need steak pie and mash to settle my stomach. Then I'll probably need almond cake with raspberry coulis and cream, just to level off the steak pie. After that, I'll probably need burping."

"It's certainly a plan, though my casual calculation puts you on about 12,500 calories before supper."

"Thank goodness," said Tee. "What with all your to-do, I missed breakfast."

"Please accept my humblest apologies."

"Granted," said Tee, in a faraway voice. "You know, I actually do feel rather sick."

"I suggest we settle you with some steak pie and mash."

"What a splendid idea," says Tee. "I wish I'd thought of that. You'll have to pay though, I haven't any money."

"I'll put it on the slate. Then I'll save Andy from some terrible fate and he'll generously wipe it clean."

"You know, Beaver, you really are having tip-top ideas. Do you think the bang on the head might have helped?"

"Could be, could be... probably a bit like your oxygen starvation on the plane. Some kind of divine intervention? We may both become reference points in the evolving history of the species. Imagine a TV documentary, years hence, narrated by the St. Attenborough of the Latter Days -'from here on, things became different on Planet Earth' – (cue portentous music) – over a small clip of us nobly striving at our daily tasks, somewhat in the style of Russian proletariat art, cc1940's."

"Staggering prediction. I feel quite overcome. Though that could be the Bournville – it was a sort of display-sized one. In fact, Beaver, it was very unreasonable of you to spend all that time asleep, I needed some help with those goodies – at times. However, I'm not one to bear a grudge so, back in the present, what 'terrible fate' were you planning on saving Andy from?"

"Your largeness of heart never fails to stagger me," I said thoughtfully, "and in much the same spirit, vis-a-vis Andy, what came to mind was something fiery, with dragons. Though as he'd make a very poor damsel in distress, I should probably re-think that."

"That has always been a matter of some concern to me," said Tee, "the inherent bias of disaster roles. Women get eaten, strangled, eviscerated, burned or impaled. Men get pierced by swords, thrown off battlements or, moving on a bit, shot. Definite terminal fate imbalance. It's in the same league as potty-parity."

"That bad?"

"That bad but if you were to save Andy from being thrown from the battlements, that would probably do the trick."

"We haven't got any local battlements," I object.

"Don't be so trivially pedantic. We're clean out of dragons, too. My over-riding point is that there is cinematographic, sexual bias in fates. Ugly, protracted fates for women, swift and relatively clean dispatch for men."

"All movies play out sexual-obligato, don't they?"

"What's 'sexual-obligato,' is it anything to do with fellatio?"

"No but that would make an excellent illustration. 'Sexual-obligato' is another way of saying 'doing-what-you're-expected-to.' So women are frequently caught blowing blokes, but men are rarely caught muff-diving women. In movies, that is."

"And life," said Tee, apparently pointedly until, suddenly engaging her full majesty, she added – "this is a disgusting conversation. I am certain I need to go to supper."

Grovel, her faithful retainer, scrambled to open the door.

54
'LOVE YOU, EVIE'

Tee slept like the proverbial log. Barely surprising, as she was now teetering around the 20,000 calorie mark and resembled the trunk of a baobab tree, after a particularly rainy season.

I lay impatiently awake, staring at the gap in the curtains and the star beyond it. I wondered how far away it actually was. It seemed strangely bizarre that I could see it but it couldn't see me – at least, nothing I've been taught suggested that it might be able to.

The problem with that is, or MY problem with that is, that a great deal that has happened subsequent to my state-sponsored education, is leading me to revise and question my knowledge base. Like Yossarian, I am starting to see things differently – all over again. Why shouldn't the star see me? Just because I can't see very small things, doesn't mean that that principle holds good for every interrogation of small by large. If God can mark the fall of every sparrow, then stars may be able to see troubled Beavers attempting sleep. After all, we are distant cousins, both made of star stuff.

The morning's events were beginning to niggle me. I turned my eyes away from the star and began probing the dark corners of the van for secrets. I must be able to recall something, because I know something had gone on. Either I'd had a prophetic dream, or there had been a voice in my head. Either would be as bad as the other. There had been some sort of urgency – unless I did something appropriately, something would be lost…?

Oh no! No way! I am not being coerced down that dark alley again! I've worn that particular hair shirt before and just because it fits me like a glove doesn't mean it's mine.

Nothing hinges on me. I am not important. We are all just collections of atoms in a world of atoms. The universe has breathed in and breathed out a zillion times so far and no doubt it will do so again and again, whatever I do, or don't do. Ozymandias wasn't the first to get that wrong and I won't be the exception.

I think something had told me that I should try to avoid a particular pitfall – that was what had hinged on me, 'not doing something,' rather than 'doing something.' I would waste energy. A lot hinged on energy, the right sort of energy and I was some sort of conduit for energy – but that's what Harold had seen and he was crackers.

I must have drifted off, because the clock said 40 minutes had vanished.

Why, oh why, had I eaten that steak pie? It was delicious but now it's troubling me. What unpleasant changes had to take place before it could end up on my plate? It doesn't do to examine how the industrialised society feeds its teeming masses.

The calf, now separated from its mother, is innocently obliged to convert grass into muscle, until it has rendered itself into a solid, saleable steer. I guess that's not too bad. But it means the end-game is approaching – and how can that ever have a good outcome? First, the terrifying lorry ride. Then the indifferent faces, the steel pens, the waving arms that will drive you through blind alleyways towards the abattoir's stun gun. The crash down onto the killing floor, the pithing rod and all the remaining indignities from knives and saws until you have been separated, into marketable product and by-product.

But what do I know of these things? Only what I read.

The refrigerated truck takes sections to the wholesaler, where Carl will purchase one or two quarters. Gentle, affable Carl who will skilfully butcher flesh on the tables at the back of our kitchens. Thereafter, meat will marinate for days in decoctions of herbs, spices and wine, products that have been flown from the far corners of the globe by aircraft, whose emissions poison the atmosphere with unreclaimable exhaust.

Then I should consider the global wheat markets, the European butter mountain, the question of where the vegetables came from – Punch's allotment, or from fields laced with nitrates? Those nitrates are made, not only in the Ukraine but in two major UK factories that pump out CO_2 as a valuable by-product of their manufacturing process. Do you know what they use that for? Among other things, to stun pigs and chickens in their millions, prior to slaughter, or to keep your salads and fruit nice and crispy. Where must all that CO_2 go, eventually? Where else could it, other than the atmosphere!

But I shouldn't pretend to know anything, beyond what I read and hear.

Shall I go on with this, admittedly, half-baked litany, that nevertheless verges on being a horror story? Yes, I will. Consider the question of natural gas. Our government self-righteously denies that any wicked Russian gas, the same that sustains much of Europe, ever ducks under the 7000-year-old English Channel, to end up burning wet and bright in John Bull's house, or at No-Name Roundabout. I reserve the right to take that affidavit with a pinch of salt. The fact is, wherever it comes from, it's bad news.

Entrepreneurs, slick, coke-snorting, Porsche-driving kids, commodity traders, buy and sell futures in gas, wheat, carcasses. They rely, in part, on my feeble attempts at vegetarianism breaking down, so that I dive into a steak pie I didn't need and remark happily, upon its excellence. What a charade, what casual brutality, all in the name of a toothsome, lovingly-made supper!

Please tell me that I don't know anything! That I read too much!

Because I can't keep doing this. It's not my fault I was born into an overpopulated world, hell-bent on self-destruction. Nor can I stop it. I roll over and demand another 20 from Morpheus – who obliges.

Now, definitely NOW – a pox and a blight upon it – I simply have to pee!

Can't stand, far too wobbly. I sit on the circle of cold plastic and it accords perfectly with the strange sensations coursing in my internal plumbing. It's as if they needed the call from that 'cold song,' to begin the rituals of unlocking their own valves and sluices. It's an agreement between sensors and organs. A signed contract to open the pipeline. Obviously I'm mad, so it's perfectly fit that I should have Klaus Nomi's haunted voice, stencilling his 'Cold Song' across my brain, as, in some archly fantastic ritual, I double over, lifting my top so that my warm tits can graze my thighs. Nipples now erect, from that goose-bumping cold, they can join in pointing the flow of pee, through my innards and out of my wholly disinterested prick, into the porcelain I vomited on, barely 15 hours since.

Everything seems improbably physical and strange. Pricks, pee, stun guns, pastry, pithing rods – all the other nouns of oppression we bring to bear on the innocent world. If only I could set these mute words to music and have some invisible choir hurl them out into the space between me and my star, perhaps the Gods would be forced to awaken to make a reckoning with this bestial species, before it despoil the entire planet?

It is all ridiculous. An innocent beast, scrabbling in its death throes, as it slides down the ramp to the killing floor, blood and hooves, shit and piss. Finally, the bloody meat is blended with onions and oregano and I eat it. I am going mad. I can feel it.

Do not think this way. You are not solely accountable for the sins of your species. You have walked this road before and you swore you would never do so again. Goddamn it! Why can't I remember what was said? This is a new twist to events. Some sea-change has occurred but please, God, let it be a simple matter from hereon. I am an ignorant creature. Instructions from IKEA are too much for me.

I'm off to talk to the fireweed, because I can't sleep and it never sleeps. I've put on Tee's ridiculously huge, military greatcoat, which she got from a junk shop – "because I couldn't leave it behind – look at the quality!" – and pulled on my thickest watch cap.

On the way past the kitchen, I sneak in, through the back door, to 'borrow' the big, bullseye flashlight when nobody is looking.

I love the night chill of late summer. The way the dew falls suddenly, as the sky begins to lighten. But for now, it's still dark. I find my preferred pile of tank traps and climb up to the topmost caltrop, a regular King and Queen of the Castle. I perch on top, hunched over like a Notre Dame gargoyle.

I spend some time quietly looking out across the wilderness, surprising myself by being barely able to recognise any of my own familiar landmarks and I begin to wonder why I know so little. There's no coherently-organised filing cupboard in my mind.

It's an attic filled with shreds of information, half-formed concepts and abandoned crazes. A butterfly brain, or a brain full of butterflies? I can't even claim to have much knowledge about my obsessions, for I cannot study logically. Neither can I remember coherently – be it recipes, historical sequences, quotations, or specifications.

The half-life of information that enters my brain can vary between seconds and decades. Certain impressions, complete with their circumstances, surroundings and modifiers, I will be able to recall on my deathbed – yet none of them could be said to be 'memorable.' Yet my mind holds that they are priceless. That must say something about me, because the odd thing is, I didn't choose these impressions, they chose me. They hopped into my brain and took up residence, uninvited. Some I would dearly love to evict, others I am very fond of. Perhaps my old age will mellow the former?

These residents get in the way of my ever establishing any still calm place between my ears. If that ever seems to be happening, the unwanted guests decide it's time they came out to party. They are as uncouth as boorish neighbours and as challenging. In the same way that you would hesitate to involve the police in a squabble with your neighbour, so I shy away from unleashing the thought-police, the psychiatrists, on some of my memories. They might have some short-term effect but I just know that, in time, those impressions would come back, leaner, meaner than before, hell-bent on revenge for my having tried to thwart them.

I once tried, for some months to meditate. All that did was to turn up the noise, as well as render my joints well-nigh unbearable. Every ball-joint felt as if it had been invaded by fire-ants. Also, I began with a disadvantage, I dislike meditators intensely. They always have to make sure that you know that they meditate and that you are aware of what a difference it has made to their lives. They're the cerebral/emotional equivalent of joggers but instead of shouldering you off the pavement, they bully their way into every conversation with their reserved air of faintly-amused, other-world superiority. I'm probably just jealous, of joggers and meditators.

I would like to possess some broad upland of certainty. In physical terms I would imagine it as a high plateau of grass, through which I could wade, thigh-deep, for mile after mile, brushing the seed-heads with my out-stretched palms and fingertips. How might I translate that back into a state-of-mind? In the forgiving darkness, I sit quietly and wonder.

After a while a fox comes, trotting lightly and briskly across the debris. First he scents me, then he sees me. Food but live food, too large to venture investigating. For most of the beasts, survival comes first, food second. Reckless attack is not on their 'to do' list, unless you have them cornered, under threat. The fox that trots away, lives to trot away another day. The silly thing is, they know their world – I don't know mine. I have too much time to think, they only have time to hunt and eat.

One of Punch's many tales, second-handed to me by Alice, flickers through my mind, the story of the honey cake and the spun-sugar figure. The cornerstone of it had been that, as little kids, they were normally too hungry to bother with thinking about abstract things. The day the cook had stuffed them all full, however, they had found they had time to stand back and reflect on the beauty of the sugar figure. Any other day, they would simply have wolfed it down.

That, I imagine, is how it must be for the majority of life on earth. Most individuals, two-legged as well as four and six, have no time, no energy to waste examining abstractions. They have to eat. That made me wonder if lions and tigers, when they've downed some ample beast, have any inclination to ponder the eternal verities? Do boas, anacondas and pythons become broody with thought, after swallowing a dying dog, or some other broken-legged unfortunate?

Abstract thought seems incidental to most life, or so it would seem. In fact, I'll take a flyer on this, Life probably detests plein-air thinking, anything above and beyond what is necessary to secure food and snare mates. So here, on my tetrapod tank trap, I'm venturing outside life's blueprint for me, if I'm doing anything more than planning the next meal, or the next rape.

What I'm trying to think about is the unthinkable – disembodied intelligences. How would that work. What might constitute a discreet disembodied intelligence? What would define the individual's parameters if there were dozens, hundreds, thousands, millions of them? Are those even viable questions, or does the concept – disembodied intelligence – undermine all our reference points?

For some reason, I ascribe virtue to Higher Intelligence, surely it must be one of its natural attributes? Could I be hopelessly wrong and some disembodied intelligences will prove to be moronic, venal, treacherous and malignant? Does a disembodied intelligence necessarily mean 'higher' intelligence, or do the things, if they exist at all, come like us, in all varieties? How do they pass their time? Are they born? Do they die? Do they submit to societal constraints, or physical limits? Are my questions hopelessly naive? Finally, in the name of this unnamed tank trap, how did one come to be speaking to me, yesterday?

Perhaps that was a Bodhisattva. Those demi-human products of Buddhist philosophy and practice are reputed to have two options at their death. The first is to leave the treadmill of reincarnation and join the Buddha, wherever he may be. The second is to stick around, to help their former fellows – men and women. That they choose the second is what makes them Bodhisattvas.

There's no doubt in my mind that the Buddhists have the best set of solutions to the world's problems. First you have the amazing Noble Truths, the second of which, in all its simplicity, leaves me reeling – 'Evil is the product of desire. Put aside desire and set yourself free.' And if that's too stark for you, which it is really, for all of us, then they have all the elaborations of ritual that help beguile the mind's 'desire' (oh dear!) for more. From the starkness of Primitive Buddhism, right the way up to Tibetan Buddhism, the Buddha's followers have got all the answers – true and false.

Part of me would welcome tips from a passing Bodhisattva but there's another part that is suspicious of all answers generated by the human species. So perhaps, searching through Earth's current stockpile of answers is not the way forward?

What bothers me particularly, is that I seriously wonder if there is any link between we creatures here on Planet Earth and the Higher Intelligences we all subscribe to in our various belief systems. Is there any genealogy to be demonstrated, linking the disembodied with the embodied? Do we, in the form of the souls we believe we possess, ever cross-over to the other side? Or are we just a lowly form of intelligence, forever hungering for the unattainable?

In my bones I feel we are tied to our cycle of life and death. Any reincarnation we experience will be of the molecular, or atomic variety. Perhaps we are 'eaten,' in some manner inconceivable to us and in that way find our translation to a higher sphere. But as Tee's 'pigs of sound mind and cheerful disposition,' live on in her, I don't think they get much personal, piggy feedback from the experience and it will probably be the same for us. Nevertheless, it seems that something I do is of value to the disembodied and benevolent intelligences of the Cosmos – but who told me that?

I ponder that one for quite some time until, having long since drifted away from my pondering, I find I suddenly say out loud – "I love you, Evie" – and I'm so embarrassed that I nearly fall off my saddle. Yet, for a moment, I really did. I blush to say it but it was a thoroughly encouraging thought and it made me love everyone else even more.

Impulsively I slid off my rock and with the aid of the bullseye picked out a path to the allotment where, putting a pound to a penny, I bet that I would find Punch and Alice.

"Hello boy!" Punch greeted me, when I must still have been only a beam of light in the distance. "Tread 'ard on any slugs tha' sees, if tha' boots be serviceable. Tha' hast t'leave t'snails tho,' a' offers them t' flag o'truce. Pick'em up, a's a box fer 'em, up 'ere."

'No ta, Pa,' I thought, dodging a slug hell-bent on a Last Supper among the red chard – the strangest-looking vegetable under the moonlight, frozen fire, curling from cold ground. Most odd.

I snuggled up beside him and gave him a thoroughly non-masculine cuddle and kiss.

"Easy boy," he cackled. "Mi 'owd bones be spokken fer, an our Ma' 'ent convinced by tha' credentials, not awltoge'er, like."

"I have told her," yawned a sleepy voice.

As I was still filled with love for all creatures great and small, I bent backwards to bestow a kiss upon my soul sister. Unfortunately I miscalculated the necessary angle and promptly overbalanced. Net result, I slid down to land squarely on top of Alice. I'd only intended the most chaste of embraces but it ended in a thoroughly incestuous grappling. Up I scrambled, one electrocuted Evie, burning with Biblical shame! The giggle that pursued me only served to double my embarrassment.

"Dammit," I protested, "I'm just pleased to see you both! I can't help being two for the price of one! Tee calls me her very own Bog-off. I can't win!"

"Anyway," I continued more calmly, regaining my seat alongside Pa, "what's new in the world of insomniacs?"

"I was perfectly somnolent, until you arrived," said Alice, in subterranean tones. "Has Tigger infected you with extra bounce? Is she suddenly contagious?"

"Not at all. I was having my very own bout of insomnia, over on the tank traps, when it suddenly resolved itself. So in an evangelical spirit and bursting with filial affection, I picked my way through the concrete Hindu Kush over there, to bring you the Good News!"

"What?" They both demanded, suspiciously.

"I could make the standard evangelical joke at this juncture," I ventured, "but it would probably end with my premature demise, so I won't. Let's leave it that I wanted to see you both and to say that I loved you, lots."

"Weel, gud fer thee!" said Pa. "A ne'er wer' much o' an 'and wi' mi feelin's, 'till tha' Ma comes by, towin' young scraplin' 'ere."

"Scrapling yourself!" said Alice boldly. "I'm a strong, tough, independent girl with a mind of her own."

"A cud fit thee in a pint pot," said Punch, equably, "a reg'lar li'l Thumbelina."

"Bloody hell," protested Alice. "That's enough to make me go forth and commit acts of wanton…indiscretion."

"Now, think on," cautioned Punch, "none o' yer talk in front o' our Ma. She'd be washin' tha' mouth clear wi' lye an' watter."

"Blurgh!"

"Tha's bin warned, scraplin' – think on."

"Double blurgh."

The bundled duvets re-arranged themselves into a new pattern and fell silent.

"Pa," I started, "sitting here, night after night, when you're not stomping slugs and saving snails, do you ever look up at the stars and begin to wonder?"

"Wonder wot, boy?" Punch demanded, in a voice already salted with exasperation.

"What it's all about? What are we doing? Why are we doing it? Where are we going? Is there more? Why do we think beyond our capabilities?" I was going to continue but Punch interrupted – "if tha' stoppit thinkin' and started doin' stuff, tha' might git some answers. Tha' needs a task fer tha' 'ands, then tha' mind'll foller."

I swear Alice giggled, so I gave the duvet pile a backwards kick, just in case.

"Tha' brain is builded fer doin', not day-dreamin' 'bout stuff that's mebbe an' mebbe not. Tha' brain can do things o' great beauty, like owd Moss's angels an' it can put food in tha' belly, like this 'ere gard'n o'ours. If tha' just sits an' thinks, tha' mind'll turn thee aroun' like a whip turns a top!"

From the shadows, Alice emerged, hauling her duvets into a protective cone around her. With her tousled hair flaring out at the peak, she resembled a small but highly destructive volcano.

"I hate Moss's angels," she enunciated clearly. "I'd pack a pound of C5 under every one and launch them. See if they could make it to Heaven with a bit of a kick start."

Punch swivelled rapidly on his axis, to face his pyromaniacal daughter. "An' this 'ere C5 be just wot, y'ung lady an' 'ow comes tha' be a knowin' o' it?"

"It's a very powerful explosive, Pa," Alice explained, eagerly and deliberately mistaking outrage for interest. "You can knead it, like dough, or putty and pack it into any handy crack, joint, or crevice. You don't have to be careful with it, like dynamite, or nitro, or gunpowder for that matter. You push the detonator in separately and until that is set off, all you're dealing with is plasticine, play-dough."

"By 'eck," complained Punch, "th'art a reet li'l powder monkey, fer all tha' purty li'l frocks and a' bathin' in buttercups. An' what did owd Moss e'er do t'thee? Young Jo'd be reet shekken t'ear thee a' plannin' o'sich things. 'E an' Moss b'likes brothers!"

'Mmm,' I thought happily, 'someone else in trouble. I'll simply have to stick around to ensure fair play!'

"Don't you worry, Pa, I've told him. And while our Mama's not here I'll tell you something fair and square, for I don't want to be misunderstood on the subject. You can take the whole Roman Church, the Orthodox Church, the Anglican Communion, the non-Conformists, to which I'll add the Muslims, Sikhs, Buddhists, Confucians, Latter Day Saints and every other Church Militant I can't be bothered to recite, then I'll gleefully blow them all to Hell and back, along with Moss's Angels. The zealots, the proselytizers, the missionaries, the evangelical, prating hounds of hell – I'd melt the lot in a furnace and cast them as a bell that would ring a warning whenever false gods – and that would be any god – appeared on the horizon!

"Jo-Jo told me that Moss raised his angels to praise the artisans who first conceived the idea of wings lighting-up the vaulting of the churches, years ago. It was the genius behind the idea and the carpentry that realised it, that he wanted to celebrate, not the half-baked piety it was designed to represent. Jo said that if he realised that his valley could be seen as some sort of soppy church, he'd be joining me in blowing it all to hell. Well, as far as I know, it's still standing. That's what I currently hold against Moss."

'Ooooh,' thought the Beaver, timidly, 'perhaps I should have scuttled off, while the going was good. So-oo glad I didn't.'

"Mmm," said Punch. "Tha's said thy mouthful an' 'tis a fair piece t' digest. Trust mi, our lass, a'll b' chewin' on it fer a while. A 'ent e'er considered them angels in yon light, afore. Tha' sees, an' agin, while tha' Ma's not abawt, a 'ent a streak o' religion in me. Tha' can leave it all a' 'ome fer me – an' a'd prefer 'twere summun else's 'ome, too. Yet tha' needs t'be careful o'crusades an' talkin' o' wild violence in a ginneral way, y'ung lady. A bin' on't business end o' sich matters an' they ne'er turns oot well. Theer's no idea worth seein' a man's belly blown thro' 'is back fer, an' 'im t'die screamin' fer 'is mammy, be it fer t'church, or agin' it. B' careful o' tha' wishes, li'l love, 'lest they comes t'pass, b'times.

"Now, gi' tha' owd Pa' a peck an' skip off neat, t'be theer fer Jo when he wekks."

'Poo,' thinks the Beaver. 'What a let-down – Sage, not Rage.'

Alice had kissed us both goodbye and then danced away, evidently carrying nothing heavier on her shoulders than her duvets. My spiritual sister declines to harbour guilty feelings about anything. I envy her the ability. I am only too willing to pick up any extra pounds of guilt that may be going begging, to pack into my saddlebags. My very own version of C5.

Pa and I shared a companionable silence and though one part of me favoured idle chatter, another cautioned against it. I was aware that the little jolt of energy occasioned by that spontaneous – "I love you, Evie," – was almost spent. I felt the need to conserve what was left.

After 20 minutes, I squeezed Pa's shoulders, pecked him on the cheek and rose to leave.

"Tha' unnerstans, don't tha' boy?" he said and from the urgency in his voice I felt that wasn't a question about anything he wanted to debate further.

"I think so," I said slowly, which was half true and quite enough for one who hadn't fully grasped whatever it was that Pa trusted had been fully aired.

With dawn breaking, I walked slowly back to our van and the further I walked, the less certain I became of what it was I was supposed to understand. When he'd first said 'tha' unnerstans' I'd thought I did, that I'd grasped something we held to be mutually important. But the more I tried to frame 'what we understood' in words, the more it eluded me. If I just left it alone, as a warm block of mutual comprehension, then I felt good. The moment I switched back to defining what 'it' might be, I felt growing unease. It seemed to boil down to – 'words, bad' – 'pit-of-stomach, good.' But how frustrating it was not to be able to say what it was you intuitively grasped.

Was I suffering from a classic Left Brain/Right Brain hiatus? I could affirm with the Right but the Left simply couldn't find the words to frame the affirmation. Consequently, it threw a wobbly and robbed me of my understanding, on the spot.

55

RUNNING FOR MY LIFE

I opened our door gently and stepped across the threshold like a mouse. How was I to know that lurking in the shadows behind me was a wild animal? Stepping noiselessly into the gloom, I was suddenly – "worra-worra-worrahed" – from behind.

I was shocked into unleashing a fart I didn't even know I'd been maturing. Its immediate toxicity was such that the "worrah-ing" beast scrambled off my back and ran to take shelter under the duvet, gagging as it went.

My latent hunter's instinct was roused. I was also aware that the deadly weapon had reloaded. Swiftly I shed greatcoat and clogs, the better to roll-in, under the duvet.

"Fire in the hole!" I cried, (I don't know what that means but Hollywood heroes use it a lot) and a second vile fart was loosed. I rolled free and now I had the advantage. I was bigger, stronger and armed. I wrapped the evil creature in the duvet and suggested that it beg for mercy.

All I got was a very odd noise, a sort of "worra-urgh, worra-gah, worra-phew," at least that's the best transcription I can offer.

The beast thrashed wildly, so I sat on its head and farted again. This was amazing. Obviously I had a latent ability for yogic farting – just like Tigger! Shock had caused it to break forth, triumphantly. I must talk to her about it later but first I had to conquer this animal.

It's possible I did fart a few more times. You can't be too cautious. I can't really recall, because I was pondering whether to skin the beast, or have it stuffed and mounted. It was a quandary, so I thought it only polite to ask.

"Shall I turn you into a hearthrug, Creature, or have you stuffed and mounted? The cheapest option would be your preserved head on a plaque. Have you any opinions on the subject?"

All I got by way of answer was a very faint "worra" and then I think it passed out.

Jo-Jo sat on the bed and contemplated the contents of his survival pack. A dozen cunning devices from Earth II and the Stag's stock of paper-wraps – 'powdered fragments of unused history.'

Recently returned from her night sojourn in the allotment, Alice lay comfortably alongside her partner, wriggling her toes to the silent harmonies she could hear rising from her latest copy of 'Ordnance Monthly,' a fanatics' magazine she subscribed to, that was dedicated to the very latest advances in hand-held weaponry, everything from pistols to shoulder-launched missiles. There was always a 'pull-out and keep' centrefold that reprised 'the finest old firearms,' with features on early Colt patents, the Sharps buffalo rifle and the like. Every now and again it would touch on weapons from Punch's fighting era and these old familiars she would religiously pull out and save – for him to pore over when Marie-Claire was absent.

"You don't fancy a trip, do you?" asked Jo-Jo.

"Where to, Jo?" replied Alice, absently, lost as she was in a technical review and field test of the new Heckler and Koch sub-machine gun.

"That's the poser, Ally. With one of these" – he waved a Stag wrap – "anywhere in the Universe, any time, any place, provided that it hasn't happened already."

Alice rolled over. "Buy me one of these!" she demanded, waving the spread on the Heckler.

"Good God, woman, you're a fully paid-up psychopath."

"I'm just a bit insecure, Jo, that's all. I feel safer with protection."

"I'm protection, so why do you feel the need for that… thing?" he retorted, half-amused, half-dismayed.

"You are, indeed, no slouch but with one of these, wow! I could clear the room without having to bother you."

"It would certainly shut down a party that was beginning to drag. But weapons beget wars, Ally."

"Nope. People start wars."

"Not without weapons they don't."

"True, but in a pinch any rock will do. So why not get many rocks ahead?"

"I don't think you can buy these at Asda."

"Funny thing is," said Alice, "you can probably buy a modified version, in the US of A, at Wal-Mart. Now they have, or used to have, a big part of Asda. So why can't I get one down the road? Why doesn't Mr Ahmad have one under the counter, like the corner shop owners do in New York?

"You see Jo," she wheedled, "I emerged from my books very thin mentally, still very 2D. So I'm insecure. I need reassurance and 5,000 rounds of 9mm parabellum cached under the bed would help. I'd feel quite cosy then – provided I had something to fire them from.

"You know how hard I'm trying to get educated, grow up to be a genuine English rose but it is proving tres difficile. Ma' and Pa' are lovely but can't really get out of the 18th century, my big bro's got serious identity problems and my desirable partner is older than Stonehenge. The only other role-model is an insanely-bouncy creature out of Winnie-the-Pooh and the other boys don't really count, not for a girl.

"So I really, really, really, really need that Heckler. You can see that now, can't you? Please? Pretty please?" she said, finishing with an old-fashioned Bardot pout she'd been practicing.

"I think you're making a very fine effort at personality building without any additional help," said Jo-Jo stoutly. "You're a splendid, courageous person."

"Thank you kindly but you do have to admit that constructing a personality from the local role models, could result in some very odd juxtapositions."

"Then it's a good job we're not doing it," Jo-Jo said breezily. "Imagine being a No-Name Roundabout layer cake – a slice of Evie, 1 & 2, with a filling of Tee, a strong marzipan layer of Carl, followed by a topping of Andy and decorated with Punch and Marie-Claire sugar figures. Something like that. And if we added our own particular chemistry, I could dig around for Celtic roots and I'm sure you've elements of Gallic patisserie you could donate."

"Actually," said Alice, "what with you mentioning Celts, I go back a long way, too. I only really got going after Gutenberg, to be honest but I can claim Roman graffiti in my pedigree, so I could introduce some very strange spices.

"Your spicing is quite robust enough…" began Jo-Jo, only to be interrupted.

"What I'm actually trying to do here," Alice said firmly, "is lead the conversation, artfully. So shut-up and listen, will you, because I've rather lost my thread. While I'm recovering it, did I ever tell you all the interesting things I've eavesdropped on from bookshelves?"

"Frequently," yawned Jo-Jo.

"No, I didn't think I had," Alice said gaily. "Would you have guessed that Schopenhaeur was an absolute sweetie, underneath all his grouching? He had a little dog he doted on and he was regularly in love with his housekeepers. The trouble was, he thought he was ugly and he wasn't at all. Also, women don't care about 'ugly,' they're far too grown-up to be that childish.

"The thing is, I have been, shall I say 'a decorative addition,' to the libraries of many great men but not many great women. I suppose that's barely surprising. If we're going to go somewhere I need it to be late blue-stocking, not precisely Sapphic but edging that way. How about, Marija Gimbutas's 'goddess lands'?"

Jo-Jo looked at Alice fondly, leaned forward and pulled her nose, gently. "That is the clumsiest segue I've been party to, for some time. You need to take lessons from your big brother. I'll pretend, seeing as it's you, that I've fallen for it.

"I'm guessing that 'goddess lands' will prove to be an Edenic age when women had their hands on the tiller of society? Somehow, however, no-one can quite prove that it existed?"

"Correct," said Alice delightedly, "just don't labour the latter point, except insofar as it leads directly to the Stag's powders, which could whisk us away there for a brief hol."

"The point to be laboured," explained Jo-Jo, "is that the Stag failed to label his packages. There's no way of knowing where you're going to end up. That's the attraction."

"No use at all to an insecure person without a Heckler and Koch. Think about it… if we landed in the middle of a huge battle, I might need to start shooting right away! You could have used a sub-machine gun the day you landed, admit it."

"It would have been a useful adjunct," Jo-Jo conceded. "Though I don't know how one works."

"Oh, it's very easy. You load your clips, then you slot them in there," Alice pointed to the picture in her magazine. "Next you pull back that knob, on the top. That moves one shell into the breech. You set your selector switch to 'safe, one shot, or auto,' pull the trigger and bang, or bang-bang-bang-bang…"

"You are utterly psychopathic," Jo-Jo marvelled. "Given your attitude, I fail to see how your books landed you in such messes in the first place!"

"Purely because I didn't have a handy MP7A1! I'm sure it's my birthday soon!"

"You had one last week."

"Did I really? What did I get?"

"A pair of boots and a new skirt."

"You're right, I did but this week I need the Heckler."

"Birthdays are annual – not weekly."

"Not when you're so passionately in love as you are – then they're weekly, or even daily, if you were chasing maximum House Points."

"Ally, what are House Points? I know about Merit Badges, because Beaver and I are competing for different ones but House Points? What, where, who, is my 'House' precisely?"

"A plague on both your Houses…? Up to speed yet?"

"Oh, that sort. I thought we were all No-Name Roundabout House, here?"

"We certainly are but your House Points are quite different. They're personal. I debit, or credit, them to your account, which I keep in my head – so they're subject to the most fickle sort of book-keeping. I suppose I should have warned you about them."

"Oh calamity," said Jo-Jo.

"Exactly," said Alice. "Now you know.

"Let me backtrack a bit," she continued ruthlessly, "don't you think – 'Captain of the House Innominate Guard,' has quite a ring to it? That would be me, by the way, providing you bought me the MP7A1. I can barely be a Captain with a wooden sword, can I?"

"You haven't made a wooden sword, have you?"

"I might have," Alice said coyly. "You said yourself that I got in some terrible messes in the past and I said that that was because I was unprepared. Therefore, Tee and I have been taking certain precautionary steps…"

"Oh Heaven help us all! Not Tigger!"

"She's our very own Princess and she has a design for safety-spears, which she patented when she was five, or four. Anyway, she's offered it – free from copyright."

"Ally, Tigger is barking mad. She'd probably turn up to a battle with a bag of sweets for the enemy!"

"If she did, it would be to unsettle them…make them think twice. She knows that they might turn on one another, squabbling over who got the coffee creams."

"You're all insane." Jo-Jo shook his head, trying to re-locate common-sense and reason. "Remind me," he said cautiously, "did this conversation begin with the commonplace concept of going on holiday? Me asking you if you fancied a break somewhere?"

"Yes," said Alice, giving him a look that had Jo-Jo fearing for his House Points and Merit Badge alike.

"Well, do you?"

"I can't pretend it isn't tempting," yawned Alice, "but we'd have to take everybody. If we went alone, I'd be miserable after a few days – no offence intended. I truly am very insecure. My outrageous character is all sham. I'm quite shy and I'd miss Andy and Carl, who are always so sweet to me. I can't possibly leave Ma and Pa and even though I hate my bro at the moment – at least I think I do – he and Tigger would have to be there."

"I can't find Evie believable as a bro, she'd be a much easier sell as a sister," Jo-Jo said with finality.

"That's just because you haven't seen below the waist. I have. We banged heads in Catherine the Great's bath-tub and then Evie stood up. 'Gaze in wonder, gaze in awe. Often copied – never bettered,' or something like that. The lesson here is that relying on your eyes can lead you astray, young man."

"Young man! Don't you start! You said it yourself, I'm older than Stonehenge!"

"Then how come you bed innocent little me like a sex-starved 16-year-old?"

"I like to try."

"And I like your trying."

They grinned at each other.

"Do you really want the sub-machine gun?" Jo-Jo said eventually.

"No-oo," Alice admitted cautiously, "but I would like some C5."

"Ally, you get worse!"

"I have only defensive strategies in mind…mostly."

"Lovely, out there is a truly vast, star-cloud quantum computer keeping an eye on this innominate menagerie. Never doubt it. Has it occurred to you to wonder why MI5, or whoever they were, never came back?"

"It had crossed my mind. It's certainly occupying Evie and Tee's."

"I thought the Tigger was paranoia-proof?"

"She is. She just frets if Evie frets. Isn't that lovely?"

"Actually, yes, it is."

They shared another complicit smile, lay back on the bed, touching hands lightly. Jo-Jo lay wondering vaguely if… "Ally, do you think Evie gets anything out of being half and half, or is it all anxiety and resentment?"

Alice spent some time considering.

"I think there's a world of difference between something being elective and the same thing being forced on you. Evie never had a choice. He spent 10 years as a happy little boy, the most formative years of his life and then 15 miserable years as a rebellious, often suicidal girl. Short of a double-mastectomy, however, what could he do about that? And given that he has the other female part, too, even the mastectomy would be pointless. Since he met Tee, though, I don't think he's living a lie any longer, I think he's discovering a whole world of truths about himself as a herself. It's something incredibly complicated in words but almost poetic in reality. Does that make any sense?"

"I think that's a gallon of thought squeezed into a pint pot of words," said Jo-Jo, "I'm going to have to go into deep thought mode."

"Before you do," said Alice, still wearing her serious face, "if you're so interested, why did you never ask your Earth II Control to give you half your life as a woman? You could have spent 2000 years discovering truly new ways of looking at the world."

"Bloody hell," said Jo-Jo quietly. "I could, couldn't I…"

"You could. While you're thinking about it, I'll study this Heckler spec. again…" Five minutes later she said decisively "…yes! …I do need one!"

"Then ask Rufus for one, I'm thinking!"

"Agh, men!"

On 'agh men!' as if cued, the door burst open under the charge of an Evie, in full flight.

"Save me, Sis!" it bleated. "Danger de mort! An enraged Tigger is pursuing me and I'm clean out of Tigger repellent."

"Fear not," Alice said stoutly, entering into the pantomime spirit. "There's nowhere to hide, so assume a relaxed position on the bed and I will defend you to my last drop of blood."

"Thanks Sis. I'm not scared, merely petrified. I think I've driven her a bit crazy."

"No need for alarm. I have here a picture, in glorious technicolour, of the Heckler and Koch model MP7A1, which should daunt even the wildest of Tiggers. If I had the real thing, there'd be no doubting it. Don't worry about Jo, by the way. He's thinking. It's an arduous business. Difficult thought, too."

"Oh," said Evie, cheering up, "what's he thinking about?"

"Whether he'd like to be a woman or not."

"I could probably give him some hints there. Lucky I turned up, really. Aaagh! Here she comes!"

Alice struck the pose of a revivalist preacher facing down the devil himself, double-page spread held Biblically in front of her, like a sword of flame.

Clogs skidded on gravel. "Grrr! Worra-worra-worrah!"

"That's her fiercest 'worra,'" Evie said nervously.

"Fear not," said Alice, "I am armed with the Good Book."

The door swung open with a crash and a "Grrrr!"

"Halt, Tigger. You cannot pass! Behold the MP7A1! Thou art undone! Thou art pierced, in multiple, at the rate of 980 rounds per minute, should you be polite enough to hold still for me whilst I reload 20 times."

"Oh, all right," said the Tigger. "I capitulate. You win. But he, she, or other, over there, that cowering, whimpering wreck, is clean out of farts. Aforesaid skulking creature of swamps and foetid lagoons is destined to die."

"Hold back, Foul Creature of Hell," said Alice cranking up the vocabulary, "yonder brother is currently engaged on work of international importance. A Top Secret Mission."

"Oh," said Tigger, "do tell."

"Jo, currently at peace over there, is trying to figure out whether or not he should have put in for a sex change, a couple of thousands years ago."

"Bit late to start now, don't you think? A tad après? Anyway, what's that got to do with the farty, Scarlet Beaver?"

"Foolish Tigger! Forsooth, she counsels him!"

"Counsel, counsel, counsel," said Evie, in an eager-to-please voice, "counsel, counsel."

"How's it coming on E?" asked Tigger, leaning on the door frame, suspiciously relaxed.

"Pretty good. Another couple of days and he'll be fine. You can go home and wait, you don't have to stick around. I'll keep you posted."

"Quite impossible," said Tigger, flatly. "Our living quarters have been infected by the most ghastly stench it's ever been my misfortune to encounter."

"What caused that?" asked Alice.

"That did," answered Tigger, pointing grimly, "with aggressive farting."

"Oh well then, I quite understand," said Alice, folding up her magazine, "take her, she's all yours."

"Worrah!" roared Tigger, advancing.

"I wouldn't," counselled Evie. "There's another one in the breech. It's the running that did it. Brought it on, so-to-speak. I've reloaded – don't say you haven't been warned."

"Worra?" wavered Tigger, slowing her advance.

"Hey!" said Jo, suddenly looking up, "What's going on? Why is the room suddenly full of Beavers and Tiggers and what is that terrible smell?"

"The terrible smell is me," Evie explained primly. "I've discovered Yogic Farting and I can't turn it off."

"You can't go around smelling like that, you'll cause an accident. Alternatively, you may spontaneously combust. Have you thought about that?"

"I hadn't," admitted the Beaver. "I better drink something immediately. There again, Dickens was fascinated by the phenomenon, you know, so I'll be of literary interest if it happens. Which, you've got to admit, is a pretty selfless attitude."

"Thing is, Evie, you might be consumed."

"It's entirely up to you Tiggs," said Evie, in a relaxed voice. "I could burst into flames and consume you without even venturing another fart – so, at your own risk, advance…"

"Worra?"

"Absolutely."

"Oh well then, revenge on hold. Turn yourself off."

"That's the problem, I can't. The valve's gone. You shouldn't have jumped on my back."

"I was trying to surprise you."

"You succeeded and here's the result. Your very own handiwork. I am the innocent victim."

"You could try putting lavender oil in your pants, Evie," Alice suggested.

"Oh, does lavender beat fart – you know, like paper wraps stone?"

"The idea was to neutralise it, flavour it, sort of drown it out."

"You'd need the whole of Provence, cold-pressed, to do that," said Tigger, sadly. "I think she's lost to me. My one and only true love!"

"If you'd 'worra-ed' me, I'd have been lost either way," complained Evie.

"That's very true," groaned Tigger.

"None of this, fascinating as it is, addresses the question of my sex-change crisis," said Jo-Jo. "Also, the smell is getting worse, much worse."

"Heaven helps us," said Evie, crossly, "I've just counselled you! The effort involved has resulted in an SBD, or I've sprung a leak. I'll be fine after a poo. It's the steak pie that's done it. After centuries of vegetarianism I've allowed flesh back into my stomach. Enzymes ran amok and this is the result. It's entirely Tigg's fault, every inch of the way – if she hadn't eaten all my get-well sweeties, none of this would be happening."

The room fell silent. The smell got worse.

"It is quite vile, I have to admit," Evie said, apologetically.

"I'll put the kettle on," said Alice. "A nice cup of tea solves everything, I'm assured."

"Would that be with the aid of a gas jet, as in 'naked flame?" Tigger enquired.

"Yes, why?"

"Probably a high risk of explosion. Gas/oxygen ratios and all that."

"I'll open the front door – safest on all fronts, possibly. And, Jo, open the window – wide."

"Any chance we could change the subject?" asked Jo-Jo. "I find that after 4000 years, fart conversations, fail to thrill as they once did."

"Sorry," said Evie, in a small voice.

"OK," said Tigger, "ball is in play – your punt Jo!"

"We were talking holidays," said Alice, "before bro's, what shall I say, now customary, precipitate arrival."

"Sorry, again," said Evie, "it does seem to have become something of a habit."

"Wouldn't have it any other way," said Jo, expansively.

"Really?" Evie asked hopefully.

"No. Sarcasm. As a result of which I now feel small and cheap. My apologies."

"Oh don't apologise on my account. Don't worry at all. I'm already contemplating suicide for a whole raft of reasons. Not just rebukes and imagined failures but big stuff, such as the general impossibility of squaring circles, making sense of why we're here. Then there's Species' Depression, existential angst, my inability to breed and then specifically, murder of mother, wasted, unrecoverable youth, self-contempt and IBS. All the usual candidates, I suppose, to which I can now add Yogic Farting, which is deemed noble in Tiggers but culpable in Beavers. One more lick of sarcasm can be added to that lot without me even feeling it."

"Just as long as I'm not the straw to break the camel's back," said Jo-Jo.

"Not at all, not at all," Evie smiled expansively.

Then her expression changed. "Oh dear," she gulped. "Please remember that I can't help it. It's in no way personal. I just have this awful feeling we're about to enter uncharted territory."

It was pure Marie-Claire revisited. Rose up the scale and down. Seemed to be drawing to a close, only to break free again. On full double diapason it concluded in majesty.

"Ooh, how refreshing," said Evie, happily. "Everybody, the smell's gone!"

Met with silence, she looked around the empty room, shrugged, put the kettle on and settled down with Ordnance Monthly, happy to have a cosy read by herself…or, in view of the subject matter, should she be…himself?

56
PHILOSOPHY OF 'AS IF...'

Yogic Farting was doomed to sink from sight, a wry memory from a lighter-hearted past.

Real Worries from the Real World had arrived, in the shape of inquisitors from the technical branch of some scientific establishment not a million miles from Porton Down. That was how they had introduced themselves – "Hello, we're the guys who work at Porton Down, except that we don't really. We're, shall we say, allied with Porton Down. We do materials. They generally stick to gases and fluids. There is overlap but not much.

"Now, for us to be able to continue to talk freely with you…" the one with the rat's face and yellow teeth, consulted his notes… "Ms. Rydel, Mr Grey, Mr Ripley, Princess Agnethuram, we would first like you to sign the Official Secrets Act."

Mr Grey – or Andy, as he is known on the Roundabout, said – "I think that would be a 'No' from me." Everyone followed suit.

"Ah, this often happens. All it leads to, however, is us being obliged to charge you with offences under the Terrorism Act of 2000. We really don't want to do this but we have charge sheets ready that read, let me see," and Rat Face bent over and fooled around in his briefcase. From under the table, he read, hollowly – "being in possession of items likely to be of assistance in the plotting and commission of terrorist acts, within the United Kingdom." Rat Face surfaced – "your call, Mr Grey."

"I think any half competent lawyer could punch a hole in that fairly swiftly."

"I'm sure you are right, Mr Grey. It's just that while your lawyer is busy punching that hole we'll have been able to hold you all in solitary for the best part of a week. You'll be so bored and – forgive the vernacular – so utterly pissed off, you'll wonder why on earth you hadn't just signed the OSA! After all, what possible harm could it do? Every keyboard-punching, penny-ante filing clerk at GCHQ has to sign!"

Taking unfair advantage of a moment's silence, Rat Face turned his eyes heavenwards – "Lord, give me strength" he whispered, histrionically, "even the cleaners sign!

"When your lawyer has got you all out – we just arrest you again. Also, though it pains me to admit it, we have viler tricks up our sleeves. We can set loose the VAT-man and the Inland Revenue, disrupt your business with kitchen visits from the local public health people. Fire safety could prove an issue. Planning permissions might need to be revisited. We can dig up the dear old folks' vegetable garden, subject them, as well as the wholly innocent Mr and Mrs Pearson, to ridiculously intrusive interviews. We would have to consider that the poor old chap obviously suffers from senile dementia. Is he a danger to that sweet old lady? Perhaps he'd be better-off Sectioned and she sent to a 'nice' Nursing Home, somewhere up North?"

"You win," I said. "We'll sign."

"Of course you will, of course you will!" he agreed jovially. "Let me give you your personal copies."

We signed. He counter-signed. His silent lieutenants witnessed our signatures. He tucked the envelopes into his briefcase, rose up, gave us all a hangman's smile and said – "no doubt we'll be meeting again, very soon."

As it turned out, we never saw the men "allied with Porton Down," again. But at the time we weren't to know that. In fact, we didn't know much at all and when we did, it all came in a rush.

"They're messing with our heads," Andy said.

"My head's OK," Tee volunteered, "but someone's just pissed on my carnival parade. Is that the same thing and I'm just pretending to be OK?"

"I'd been feeling a bit magical, lately," said Carl. "When that creature smeared his slime trail across my life, the magic got up and left. I'm hoping it's not gone forever."

"I think there's a satisfactory way out of this," I said. "I just don't know what it is, yet."

I recoiled – shocked. It wasn't at all like me to be upbeat. I was the one who spent hours communing with weeds, poring over the insect book – without even managing to get a beetle to change course – then spent sleepless nights choking down reflux, or fighting off the bat wings of a panic attack. No doubt that's why everyone looked at me. I had been presumed slain, an early casualty but was apparently alive and well.

"You couldn't expand on that, could you Evie?" asked Andy. "We are all on the verge of drowning in gloom."

"I'd love to. Unfortunately, my communications centre is currently closed for repainting. I'll get back to you all if I score a bull's eye. Keep in mind, there's nothing we can tell them that they would even entertain as the truth. We're in search of a colossal lie – one we can prove." With that, I upped and offed, to call on Mr and Mrs Pearson, AKA, JJ and Alice.

I rat-tatted politely at their door, which eventually opened.

"My God," said Alice, "are you an impersonator, or are you actually you?"

"I'm me."

"Why then, didn't you come through the door like a hurricane?"

"Because, sadly, this is the new, sober, business-model me and I have matters to discuss. Can I come in, or are you armed?"

"Am I fiddlesticks! He won't conjure up the MP7A1, nor will he contemplate changing his name to Clyde Barrow. Though even I have to admit the film didn't end well."

"Any ideas on circumventing such obstacles?"

"I'm collecting bird-shit…let me finish!" Alice was waggling an admonitory finger. Quite unnecessarily. I hadn't said a word. The new, sober, business-model Beaver would never dream of interrupting. "I've purchased flowers of sulphur and I've located some shrubs who say they're willing to donate the odd branch for me to turn into charcoal, once they're asleep for the winter, that is."

"Obviously you are pursuing gun-powder and no doubt you will tell me precisely why, in time, though I'll take a flying guess that you're aiming to charge up Brown Bess? How much poo do you need for the nitre?"

"Hundredweights," I imagine. "I've scraped up eight ounces so far and that stinks to High Heaven. Furthermore, I have not the slightest idea how to leach out what I want. I daren't Internet search it in case THEY are watching. How did that go, by the way, the meeting with THEM?"

"Terribly," I said. "It's really why I'm here…"

Alice was not listening… "I could ask Pa, I suppose – about the leaching."

"Not precisely idle chatter is it?" I said. "Pa, how do I wash nitre out of bird crap?' Could lead to an extended inquisition. Tell you what, we could use the double-pronged approach. Me from one side, you from the other… ME -'Ally, did you know they used to use bird poo in making gunpowder?' YOU – 'oh my, oh gosh, how could that work?' Both of us – 'Pa, is that true?"

"Oh, that would work," said Alice, sarcastically. "Pa – 'what are you two horrors planning?"

"I wasn't suggesting we'd be quite so heavy-handed. I was merely outlining the approach. Anyway, what about bullets, balls, whatever you call them?"

"Aha," said Alice, "once upon a time there was a tricky connection from gutter to downpipe on that knackered Portakabin over there…" Alice's hand described a wild arc but I knew where she meant, so I nodded encouragingly… "some clever plumber fabricated a cunning affair in lead. 'Alice, amateur plumber,' has fabricated a very dodgy replacement out of milk containers and gaffer tape. As for the casting, if that's the word – I mean moulding, don't I? – Carl says Moss instructed him in die-making, so he's making a six ball block we can use. He's still keen on the Roundabout Militia idea and Pa's musket has actually been proofed…so there you have it. Eat your hearts out, Herr Heckler and Herr Koch. Who needs them?"

"You do," I said flatly. "Even with your loading skills, Brown Bess is good for two to three shots per minute. Your chances of besting a SWAT squad are slight."

"A girl's got to try and I was ever a tryer."

"Your suicidal preparations make my mission even more important. In which case, I actually need to speak with Mr Pearson. Is he in?"

"He's having a two-day sulk in the bedroom, major affair. If you can coax him out, I'll even make tea."

"Coffee, I beg you. I hate tea."

"Coffee it shall be, bro."

I had to admit, Alice maintained an elegantly tidy little maison. I gave that some thought and decided it must all have stemmed from being constrained within the A5 format for most of her adult life – A5 landscape, if she was lucky.

I tapped on the bedroom door.

"What?" demanded a grumpy voice.

"It's the Angel of Death – your time is up."

"On your way, you've got the wrong address."

"Come out, or I'm coming in," I trilled in my best Ange de Mort voice.

"Then open the door. Why should I waste energy on you?"

I opened the door, to be enveloped in stale gloom, as I stepped inside.

JJ lay abed. Not in my swift, albeit un-wifely, assessment sulking but depressed.

"Mrs P send for you?" he demanded.

"Nobody sent for me. For what it's worth, Mrs P thinks you're sulking." JJ gave a wry, bitter laugh. "I can see you're not. I know depressed when I see it. So it might just help you to know that I've come looking for help, from you, or via you."

"What could I possibly give you? You've had my wagon-load of crap and see where it's got you. You actually want more?"

"Depends what you're selling. I want access to Star-Cloud, Sun-Cloud, the Big Y'in, or whatever we're calling it these days. Failing that, the Rabbit will do, Double-R, Rufus, Whiskers, our cruelly-maligned gofer. Or perhaps you'll do, instead – because all I want is a link."

"I can't give you that. Not because I'm denying you but because there's a shroud between Earth II and Earth I. That's why we have Rabbit-mail. I thought you'd been told all this, the day you blitzed your bonce in the caff?"

"I was obviously told a great deal that day but they should have chosen a better receptacle. I can recall scraps, unconnected bits and pieces but that's par for my head on a good day. Also, I have a serious problem with voices in my head – the last one I listened to cost me dearly."

"You're not alone in that," said Jo-Jo, straightening himself up and looking surprised to find himself so dishevelled. "On Earth II, the voice in your head is a constant companion, a go-to resource, a welcome friend. Here, voices in the head are taboo, psychotic episodes, talked about in hushed voices – which is a bit ironic when you consider it. We Earth II folk would be reluctant to block our voice out but I gather you told yours to 'go forth,' none-too-politely. Not that that matters down here, it couldn't contact you if it wanted to – except by engineering an episode such as you had with the table, which is barely going to win it brownie points in your book.

"No, the direct link doesn't exist. Therefore, as I said, you need Rabbit-mail but I haven't seen my little friend in weeks. I call – he doesn't answer. Do you really not remember anything useful from your conversation?"

Coming from a man indulging a depression, the irritation in JJ's voice needled me.

"I remember clouds of information, not connected phrases. I know that since that conversation my outlook has changed, that I think I see more clearly. That's why I think I have a notion of what we might try to do to shake these malignants off our tail but I need help. You're not helping – so far."

"Tell me what you do recall, then. I don't want to be rude but where was your attention? "

"It was present, in the same way it always is, ready to do some colouring in, totally unwilling to do detail. Look, I can't even remember the recipe for scones and I must have made them 50 to 100 times. Every time I have to look it up and something in the recipe makes me go – 'oh yes, I remember that!' when I patently do not. I should be famous for not-remembering. I quite resent the fact that I'm not. But as for remembering, after I've just had a table-for-six driven into the top of my skull and seen both Stars and Stripes, give me strength! I'm astonished I even remember the way to my mouth after that.

"Let me tell what I do remember. I remember the phrase 'useful fictions,' that definitely stuck. Afterwards I did some digging and unearthed an author I already knew about, Hans Vaihinger. I read the review-precis of his book and thought – 'the man's a giant, a genius, why doesn't everyone know about him?' Then I bought the book and read it, with a great deal of difficulty, annoyance and upset. In 300 words, the reviewer had condensed what Vaihinger struggled to get across in 30,000. My little Beaver brain can only cope with a sturdy precis of strong-meat titles.

"My point, which I'm failing to get across, is that if that giant brain had something important to say to the residents of No-Name Roundabout, why choose me? Because, as for the rest of it, all I really recall is the very strong flavour, taste, call it what you will, of 'only love matters.' I know that is the central message but all the subordinate, AKA dependent clauses, have gone AWOL.

"The reptiles from Porton Down, who came wielding the Official Secrets Act are doing their level best to jam spanners in love's cogs. I think unjamming them could be part of the Beaver Mission – though it's equally possible that I was instructed to purchase a packet of aniseed balls from Ahmad's and deliver them to a secret address.

"What I am praying is that, for once, instead of being scatter-brained, I'm actually thinking in a productive manner. But am I? I really don't know. I know that I feel the spontaneous love and affection of the Roundabout is suddenly under threat, imperilled. I think I've been given the chance to set a hare running, one that the destructive elements will follow and leave us alone. I even think that I have an idea what that could be. I just don't know how to set in in motion."

JJ swung his legs over the edge of the bed. "I feel terrible about things," he said. "I brought about all this, this… these, noxious events, that are raining down on your heads, with my off-planet jaunts, introductions to quantum computers and summoning aliens from the heavens! Yet none of the problems have come back to me. It's you four innocents who've had to take the heat."

"Is that the reason you took to your bed, Jo?" I asked in amazement. "Because if anyone can claim those laurels, it's me. Catastrophe was born the moment that I pocketed Moss's dropped nut, or perhaps it was Andy who set the wheels turning when he had a 'bright idea' about the roof-material.

"Without your alien visitation there'd be no No-Name community for us all to be in a flap about. It was I, with my little eye, who dragged the four of you into the 21st century. It was my wiles that led Princess Agnethuram off the not-so straight and narrow she was embarked upon. I will concede it was Carl who alchemised her into the one and only Princess Tigger – but you are just a hapless time-traveller, fallen among lunatics.

"Fact is, Jo, any one of us could claim to be the catalyst that set-off the explosion – Alice plotting to add a third dimension to herself and Marie-Claire, Andy, messing with the roof but Carl actually doing it. Tee, Tiggering Mr Muscles, Punch saving Alice, you saving Punch but most of all, me, with my little eye. Marie-Claire's about the only innocent among us.

"Shake off your glums, scrub your gums, eat some toast and join us all for a War Council. We need everyone."

I scooted out of the bedroom, anticipating coffee and at the very least, biscuits. There was no sign of Ally, or refreshments. I finally ran her to ground at the very far end of the car park, where the wood pigeons roost in the big old elder tree and plaster the ground beneath with Grade A pigeon-poo.

"I think I can safely say, sis, that better things await you at home. I will return in 20, bearing croissants and coffee. Time for a flying shag if you're quick. Your man has rejoined the human race – I think."

I roared off to the kitchen and ordered. As I waited, I felt I could detect, just below the surface that the malaise that was affecting us all, was now creeping into the crew. It was by no means fully-fledged but like some ugly, uninvited cuckoo it was starting to trample the nest in its search for nourishment. There was a hint of bickering behind the ostensibly good-natured bantering and Harry and Sally, who were de facto "mum and dad" to the place, both looked worn-out.

Beaver to the rescue!

Or not, perhaps…

Without a plan in my head, I gathered up my supplies, told a seriously off-colour joke and fled. I trip-trotted down the path trying my utmost to summon one useful thought. It was all well and good assembling the troops but without an objective in mind it would become a pointless exercise.

I was on the point of despair, when I finally stumbled into a light-bulb moment. I brought to mind the rug-roll, filled with portentous brassware, that had been a gift, of sorts, from Lucy Mahoney. That was the junk I would use for a hare, something that the hounds could chase till their legs gave out. It was the ideal bait for the crude stratagem I'd been brewing.

Then, mid-trot, I applied my air brakes and stopped dead. 'Why, all of a sudden, was it junk?' What justified that conclusion? I had no idea, until the answer arrived with all the subtlety of a size 12 boot to the bum – 'because it is!' Of course! That's cleared that up nicely. I restarted my engine and the message-mouse toddled off, task completed, telegram delivered.

I burst through the door, shoulder first.

Damn it all – my hands were full and I had said 'back in 20!'

"So sorry, didn't see a thing. I'll leave these here and go off to write a brief critique of Schopenhauer. See you later." But I'd only wandered 20 yards when an Alice head appeared and yelled – "come back! We can finish this later!"

Amazing how warm Danish, croissants and coffee can fill in for sex, at least on a temporary basis. We tucked in, crumbs flew. Napkins couldn't cope. Kitchen roll to the rescue. Excellent…sugar and caffeine.

"JJ," I said, "you simply have to ferret-out Whiskers. I need hooking to the interface and my vote is against taking another blow to the head."

"I told you, Evie, I can't. He was my little buddy for centuries but I haven't seen hairy hide, nor sparkly suit of him for months. It appears that I can't raise him on speed dial any longer. Do you want to tell me what it is you want to share with the Powers-that-Be?"

"It is a modest proposal," I said. "You remember the wood you took us to, the day MI5 had the inexplicable breakdown in their Honda? I was going to suggest that Earth II's nano-tech brigade construct an underground bunker, filled with obscure, misleading shit, protected by well-nigh impenetrable access. I wouldn't want them to think we had the key, or anything but we might have had the misfortune to have found the nut and the segment of roofing material there, while we were out walking. There was an old badger sett I discovered that might answer nicely, as a site. I could say I found the nut and the bit of roofing stuff among the badger debris.

"You see, if they contrived to make it look like an alien RSG, the spooks would be happy as pigs in ordure and hopefully, we might be off the hook.

"I know, it's crude and silly. To be honest it's not much better than the pack of lies we're currently considering – 'we found them on a table, when we were clearing breakfast, honest guv!' But I just had another thought, on the way over from the caff. I wondered if we could get them to seal Lucy Mahoney's brassware and our all-seeing eye in there. That way MI5 could waste the rest of their lives doing the 'what-iffing' and 'ah,but-ing' that goes with toys like that. We could turn the bastards into modern-day alchemists, chasing their own tails. We know the damn thing does something and that's it's both very old and very new. But I also know that it's a piece of junk. That's what the 'bang-on-the-head-voice' told me. That came back to me, not 20 minutes ago."

Both JJ and Alice looked deeply uncomfortable.

"Do we know that for sure?" asked Alice. "Jo was saying you couldn't really remember a thing about your conversation with Earth II. So is it possible that's what you think and Earth II thinks quite differently?"

I felt a horrible shiver run down my spine. Alice and Jo had taken a bite out of the tantalising apple called 'what if.?' A very different fruit from Vaihinger's 'As if…'

"Of course it's possible," I agreed. "But before I had my chat, I was lined-up with you guys '-ooh, what an interesting piece of kit we have here.' What the voice told me was that that was precisely how it had been designed, as a carrot to keep people focused and rewarded. It had been a good idea but it had gone wrong. People began focusing on the wrong thing."

"I only know what Carl and Tiggs told me," said Alice.

"And I only know what Ally told me," interjected JJ.

"Which was," Alice resumed, "that it was a piece of machinery, one that had been designed down through the centuries, on some sort of rolling blueprint that we're not yet privy to. It's totally uncanny, to put it mildly, that the 'eye' Nounou found, slots perfectly into a piece of brassware a girl-on-a-mission brought back from the Himalaya. Machinery that thinks in advance, isn't that something unheard of?"

I had to stay calm, very calm. This was exactly what I had been warned against and now, to make things worse, I was beginning to wonder if they, the doubters, had a point. How was I to know that my head-voice had been telling – 'the truth, the whole truth and nothing but the truth'?

"Because I do," echoed deafeningly in my ears. That was a voice I recognised. It came from the same size 12 that had booted me on the way over. It was booting me again.

"I'm sure you'd be right, sis, if it did think in advance. For my part, I don't believe that it does. Somehow we are coerced to think for it and to think in a certain way. While we would be advancing its agenda here, perhaps in some other country another designer is being suborned to make a matching part and one day, those parts will be manipulated so that they come together, to be assembled to the delight and perplexity of an innocent bunch such as ourselves.

"It's thus that the whole charade rolls on – not malevolently, but pointlessly. The answer, to whatever is being sought, cannot be a piece of machinery – and after all, whatehell are we looking for in the first place? We weren't even interested in this thing until it turned up on our doorstep. Now it's shouldering itself into pole position.

"Carl is our engineer and he'd probably spend the rest of his life happily working out what it needs next. Whatever he created, the next crew of spiritual engineers would find inspiration in it and continue the search. All I ask is – 'search for what and why?"

"Wouldn't that be the point," asked Jo, "that we couldn't know? We'd be working with faith alone, plus some intuition and whatever instruction we found along the way?"

"That way, it would keep us honest, open and bright," Alice insisted.

That most reliable of barometers, my stomach, was performing back flips.

"I definitely see your points. I'd contend, however, that we'd be neither honest, open, or bright. We wouldn't be 'open' because we'd be committed to it, its lead, its direction. That would not be 'honest,' because we would be lying to ourselves if we shut our minds and failed to consider alternatives. Definitely, nothing of the above is bright.

"Honestly, I fail to see why we're interested in the first place. We were pootling along perfectly happily, until we got reeled in like little fishes by an enigmatic eye and an archaic tripod. I'm not saying they're not a strange and even wonderful coincidence but what do they have to do with us? Let someone else play with them."

"Surely," said JJ, "if a mystery lands in your lap, you try to unravel it, follow its lead and see where it goes?'

"Don't forget," I said, "Andy and I have already trespassed down that 'Famous Five' footpath, by trying to interrogate the nut and the roof – all because we couldn't quite believe JJ's off-world excursion hadn't been an illusion. Look at where that got us – covered in spooks!

"Guys, I think this calls for a major meeting. We cannot let this place and all it means to us, in terms of other people, go down the pan just because of threats from Turds-in-Power. I think that this afternoon, we all need a get-together to interrogate our heads. In the interim, I suggest we try and get our personal ducks in line. Maybe work out what the hell it is that we are actually trying to achieve. Agreed?"

Mr and Mrs Pearson nodded. Reluctantly, I thought.

57

ROCKY ROAD

I took the scenic route home, over the hills and vales of concrete, that hedged the old crushing plant. There was a decent-sized mountain of the big stuff that had to be skirted, before you could approach what was left of the works. Between it and the far-end of the conveyor belt, which was still in situ, had been the business end of the crusher. That had been sold, at the auction Andy had held after his brother's demise. Nobody had wanted to buy the conveyor, its bearings had been shot. Today, they were still shot and also rusted solid. The conveyor's swan-neck was therefore doomed to remain at a rakish angle until it finally collapsed under its own weight.

At least this pleased the local pigeons, who could maintain a lookout at the very tip of the jib. They were giving me sidelong glances already. "Hello, pigeons," I said, in my best pigeon-friendly voice but they simply flew off. Total over-reaction. It was perfectly obvious I had no wings.

I chose my own perch and surveyed both the winter fireweed wreckage and the new season's growth. Where the old control tower had once stood, demolition and clearance had been total, right down to ground level but where there were any chinks in the poured concrete, a bonsai variety of the weed was growing. Also, at discreet intervals across the ruins, it was flourishing in oddly formal, squared beds – possibly where pillars had been removed, as if it were being nurtured for 'The Weed of the Year' show.

I can see potential in promoting a show like that. More people than you might think like weeds and anyone with a garden grows lots of them. I'll bet a well-nourished bed of dandelions is a handsome sight – especially to a ravenous horde of guinea pigs. Nothing wrong with daisies and buttercups in profusion, in the right place. It's all a matter of re-setting your expectations.

On a more dramatic scale, escaped Virginia creeper, wisteria, even bindweed can look spectacular, if you give them freedom to express themselves. I'm probably a lone voice when it comes to fireweed and nettles but I like them. And I'd love to have seen the really old railway sidings full of lupins. The one I did see was flagging a bit, if I'm honest.

Tomato plants were once big on the railway, until they stopped direct discharge loos and everybody's poo, complete with tomato seeds, got diverted to captivity in slurry tanks. Lately, I've taken to throwing apple cores away, in the hope that we'll get some volunteer crab-apples shooting up between the concrete. I like nature when it gets tangled up.

I'd actually stopped to ask the fireweed if it had any ideas on how to maim bureaucracy, block its insidious craving for control and its rapacious need to police every human exchange. It gave its usual answer – 'time, endurance, persistence, these are all you need. Take your casualties. Keep coming back.'

That, I have to conclude, is the deep wisdom of Life speaking – Life, hand-in-hand with evolution. The fate of the individual is meaningless, only the fate of the whole matters. Be diverse, be multiple, embrace change, resist specialisation. These may be shrewd, long-term truths but to the individual, they sound like Death's footsteps on the gravel path.

"I – who is 'I?" breathes the fireweed.

For the short-term world of human ambitions it has no answers. "You can only be what you are," it whispers.

"I'm not at all sure what that is," I answered. "I can have no descendants. I am the first and last of my line. I am a mule that wants to make some mark that will last."

"You can make no mark that will last," say the weeds. "Only seeds can endure in this world."

'Yes,' I thought, 'seeds, sands and waters…' Then, out of left field, as it were, came the realisation that that was the nature of the devices we had found…they were seeds for the seedless. They were meant to encourage us, to nurture the lie that we could leave some token of ourselves behind. They were carrots, for donkeys. Carrots on sticks, the cartoon sort that project over the donkeys' heads, to keep them plodding on along the approved road. If we had a little project that kept us all focused, our dynamic would endure, so long as the fascination didn't wane.

What I could also see, quite clearly, was that the fascination wouldn't so much wane as grow divisive. We would find ourselves splitting into 'those who were for the device' and 'those who were reluctant.' Where we had once been cohesive, knit by simple love and affection, we would begin to fragment.

Wasn't this the story of every religion, every cult, every political body, every tribe that held anything greater than the sum of its own members to be its goal? We were at risk of being snared in the oldest, most hackneyed of traps. Once caught, it would take uncommon genius, or an awful shock, to shake us free.

These were not encouraging or buoyant thoughts. I stood up, acknowledged the fireweed, wished it well and forged on to track down the Tigger.

She was not lurking in the undergrowth, It was far worse – she was belly down, on our bed, reading the Forbidden Mahoney Diaries. 'Forbidden' by me, that is and therefore a prohibition without any weight at all. A little like the censor's 'X'-certificate would be to a determined tweenie.

"How goes it?" I enquired.

"Worra," she murmured absently, turning a page.

"Did you stay for lunch?"

"No. None of us did. Like you, everyone wandered off sunk in gruesome thought. I came back here and 'worra'd' these diaries, in the vague hope of tracking down a miracle-working spell."

"Any luck?"

"Pitiful. However, I can reveal that Lucy was a hell of a gal for a spiritual shag. The dear soul was an uncontrollable, spiritual nymphomaniac. Anything that even hinted of fakir, guru, lama or Holy Man got laid, there and then, be it in ashram, temple, secluded retreat or, I fear, as we climb ever-higher in the Himalaya and she pursues her dedicated bonking at 6000 feet, air burial sites."

"Urgh," I said lightly but in the distance I could hear tiny squeaks, together with the beat of small, leathery wings.

"I know. I can't stop reading. It's gruesome."

"She should have taken an air bed," I offered, trying to lighten the tone.

"Um…yep," Tee mumbled, distractedly. "Listen, this entry is typical… 'it seems that I've found a pilgrim's path that leads to a hermit's cave – at least that is what the headman has just told Dave, who's supposed to be leading this trek. I came across it when I was wandering about and I got him to ask where it went. Now he tells me we're not going that way, we're taking a parallel route, well-below the ridge. So I'm sticking to my resolution – no pain, no gain. I'm going on via the hermit. I've told Ilsa to tell Dave I'd meet them at the next camp. She says I'm crazy. I say, "so what?" Set off before sun up and climbed, climbed, climbed. Had to slow down, felt so sick…' Tee turned to me and said – "there's a lot about altitude sickness. She feels awful most of the time, so I'm guessing she was more susceptible than most, or her other illnesses were getting up to speed.

"Anyway, the long and the short of it is that she forces herself on to try and find this crazy guy's cave. What she actually stumbles onto is a deaf and dumb girl, with a baby, who look after him. They eke out a living from what they can skim from pilgrims."

Tee banged her hand on the duvet, in what looked like anger and despair.

"I can't tell you how typical this is of India. This poor, outcast girl and her baby, for Chrissake! Cooking, skivvying for this lunatic in his hole, because there's absolutely no alternative. This is her Last Chance Saloon, through no fault of her own. Karma? Corrupt bureaucracy more-like."

She turned back to the diary… "this is Lucy writing -'he's no more walled-up than I am. The cave is walled across but there's a crawl-space under the wall with logs that can be pulled into place. Probably more to do with keeping the weather out, than this "guru" in. The girl gave me a milky drink and when I'd got myself back together, let me hold her baby for a bit. I think she went for a pee. I had nothing suitable to give the little guy and that breaks my heart. Why am I chasing gurus when babies are starving?'

"Why indeed," muttered Tee venomously. "Though, goddammit, I'm no better!"

She began to skim the entry and as she did so, I began to feel that I, too, was fighting some sort of altitude sickness. My feet were cold, my legs were jelly, my head was beginning to swirl, as if some slowly accelerating centrifuge was starting to pull its contents apart.

'...guru looks 60, he's probably 40. He crawls out of his cave on his belly, pretending to chew the dust. He's filthy. I can smell him from 20 feet. He's as good as naked but is be-slung with half-dried animal bones tied together with sinews and coloured threads. They hang like bandoliers across his body. He staggers up and starts chanting and wailing. The girl ignores him, attends to her fire. The baby howls. He's sporting a three-quarter erection and he beckons me into his cave.

'I have to go. I have to. I swore I'd be open to everything…'

"Enough, enough! Tee, stop! Stop. It's too close for me. It's that one phrase – 'I swore I'd be open to everything' – that's what I had at the back of my so-called brain, every night I dared myself to go and stand by roadsides at midnight. Holy Christ, Tee, I know how this will end…!"

I stand at the end of the bed, swaying as if I was drunk. I've almost lost control of my body. I'm going to be horribly sick. I can smell dirt, bone, half-dried sinew. Oh Christ, here comes the cold liquid at the back of my mouth and my body at least remembers to hurl itself towards the loo, which is lucky, because my head is wholly elsewhere.

It's wandering the blasted heath but across a stage-set borrowed from an 'oh-so-modern' production of King Lear. There's a roundabout and cars. It's midnight. I'm standing centre stage, precariously balanced on a rock, in bra, pants, suspender belt, stockings and stiletto boots. A gang of 'lads' get out of a Subaru they've driven up the mountain path. They leave it standing, engine running, doors open, headlights blazing, rock music hammering and they pile out in a great, ugly swarm.

All of them are guzzling from giant buckets of greasy fried chicken. They pull out the bones, tear off the skins and these they start to hurl at me. As the first bone hits, a crazy girl begins to howl, though I can't see her. Then another bone strikes me squarely on my forehead. With that I throw up every particle of food, every digestive fluid I've ever owned into the worn bowl of our shabby van.

But that is not enough. More is demanded, because behind me the Subaru is now dancing, crazy as a metal Hindu god suddenly come to life, all lights blazing, flying doors and maddened music. The real menace, however, is from 'the lads.' They've become hulking men. They no longer flick skin and chicken bones at me, they are clutching clubs fashioned from the femurs of greater beasts and they are tightening their circle around me.

Then, from the real-life lorry park and more redeeming than the pure opening note of a psalm, I hear a huge engine start-up. Air-brakes release and something massive begins to move.

My world pitches like a wounded butterfly trying to straighten its wings but it's all too soon, too soon. Poor Lucy is dead in her grave and the deaf and dumb girl's baby has become some sort of questing human, leading some sort of life. The guru is in his cave, walled up for eternity. And I am still me, raising my head from a lesson I couldn't stomach.

I don't know what just passed through me but I never want it in my life again.

I drag myself upright and blast cold water into my face and mouth. I massage my eyes, my temples, my cheeks. I rub my teeth and gums with my forefinger, even the insides of my nostrils, until every surface feels the same. Nothing from those moments can remain. Only when they are gone dare I look in the mirror, hanging on to the wash basin for support. Frankly, as I raised my eyes, I had no idea what might look back at me.

Me. It was still me.

I could hear Tee, lovely Tee, crying – "Evie, Evie, Evie," over and over again. I straighten myself up and go out. We lock ourselves together and just lie on our faithful old bed breathing. Not Lucy's crazy breaths, the ones she learned in India, just the breaths your lungs keep taking when they're working properly again, on the whole earth and not on soil tramped to madness by the deluded feet of pilgrims, the evil dances of fakirs.

I must have fallen asleep. When I wake, there is no sign of the diaries. Tiggs is kneeling on the floor, beside me.

"I've tidied them away. They're still in the wooden case but I've turned it to the wall and now it's just a useful bed-side table. I vote that we never read them again. For all that she may be owed a requiem, it's not one that is owed by us. We've become temporary guardians through no fault of our own. When the time comes, we'll pass them on."

I squeezed her hand in agreement.

"While you were zonked, Ally came by to summon us to a meeting, upstairs at the caff – 'afternoon tea-time' – whenever that may be… You know, I really should have asked but I didn't want to appear…what…un-princess-y? So I said we'd be half-an-hour, which I thought was pretty cunning, because if it was supposed to be three o'clock we'd be late and if it was five o'clock we'd be ridiculously early. So, she'd have corrected me, just assumed that we kept different afternoon tea times, in India.

"My God, what pathetic subterfuge!" gurgled Tiggs. "I think I need to rend myself, if I've got to this pitch.

"Whichever, whatever, whenever…I said we'd had a crisis. She agreed that was pretty obvious. Could she do anything to help? It wasn't anything she or Jo had said, was it? So I said no, it was all my fault but it wasn't a falling out, or anything like that. It was more that I'd obliged your brain to eat something that disagreed with your tummy and unfortunately, the two of them had been fighting it out…"

I thought that Tiggs had phrased that rather well.

"…I suggested she let everyone know you weren't precisely 'on-form' but not for anyone to start making jokes about it, or overdoing the sympathy. In fact, could everyone manage to be grown up? That would be best. She said she'd make sure everybody got the message."

I stroked her hair and said, sleepily – "thanks, Tigger-een" – then dozed a bit more.

After a while I stood up, cautiously and felt OK.

So, off we went. I wished we could take Lucy with us in some way – just so she'd understand that her things were safe but that I wasn't the recipient she had dreamed of.

As we were walking along, hand-in-hand I realised that I had no idea how to count my parts. I don't suppose anyone does. I began to think about it in the sense of, 'if I was a cake, how many slices would I make and what would be the name of the pile of crumbs that always gets left in the middle?'

That felt like a Beaver thought and it made me remember why I enjoy being a Beaver.

We were exchanging a few high-fives with afternoon regulars, when I spotted Alice lurking at the bottom of the stairs. She was obviously lurking with intent, because all she lacked was a battered trilby, a trench coat and an edition of 'The Third Man' under her arm, to complete her undercover persona. She handed a sheet of A4 to Tiggs, gave me a hug and vanished up the stairs.

In Carl's best art school script was written -

'Conference Room bugged.

Say nothing important. Don't sound anxious.

We'll eat, drink, chatter, disperse.

Meet again, tomorrow, Penny's old place. About noon.

Eat this paper, or easier by far, give it me back and I'll burn it.'

That was all very reassuring.

I told the butterfly colony in my tummy to settle down. That they'd already had their outing. To the ever-alert IBS, I explained that it hadn't heard anything and if it had, it was merely the coo-ing of a peace-loving dove. 'Thank-you,' gurgled my intestines. A polite bowel is a fine thing, don't you agree?

Once upstairs, Alice seized on Tee and involved her in a wholesome discussion of the minutiae of bestiality and what, precisely, her latest researches had uncovered in the field.

I hung around with Carl and we chewed over missed opportunities and the fickleness of youth, particularly our own youth. He regretted not toughing it out at art school. I mourned my determination to be the least qualified student to ever leave our academy. It had been the spectacular own goal of an under-achiever and one in which I had over-achieved.

"I still can't believe my arrogance," I mourned.

"I don't even know what to call my belly-flop," confessed Carl.

"We share one redeeming positive feature, nevertheless," I insisted. "Neither of us has ever stopped reading since.

"My problem with that, however, is that with a butterfly brain and a colander for a memory, I develop notions above my station. I patchwork everything, jump to conclusions, rely on intuition, cross my lines and generally end up sounding like an idiot. You may have noticed. I'd have made a great jester, or so I like to imagine."

"What is this station you get ideas above?" asked Andy, gate-crashing our nicely-developing confessional.

"Do you know, I haven't a clue.

"But to digress, to be seen at my best, I should be assessed retrospectively. Perhaps I could have been something interesting in the Burgess Shales. Something that obviously had huge potential but no-one could quite work out which way up it was meant to be. I would be an enigma known as the Evie-Beetle."

"Before we were so rudely gate-crashed by Mr Grey, here," grinned Carl and Andy bowed elaborately from his crutches, "akin to your reading is my drawing. I've never stopped that. Now the urge is upon me to draw the Evie-Beetle."

"Oooh," I said "shall I sit for you?"

"Tricky, with six legs," Andy said drily.

"You manage with four," I parried.

"Children," said Carl. "You won't have to pose at all. I shall work Tenniel/Potter magic upon you and all who see you shall love you."

"I'm glad to hear that," I confessed. "I was just remembering that I've been down the modelling road before and my emotions about the experience remain conflicted."

"More tea-cake anyone?" demanded JJ, thrusting a large platter among us.

"Yum," I gurgled and grabbed the largest slice.

"Give mine to Andy," said Carl, "he's gone exceeding scrawny since rediscovering motion."

"You've no idea," sighed Andy, "what hard work crutches are. I'm not surprised Long John Silver was long and lean."

"Let us not forget that he also had the extra weight of a brightly-coloured parrot to carry around," I contributed helpfully.

"Actually Andy, what do your medics say?" asked JJ.

Andy returned his complicit grin.

"They shrink from using the phrase 'miracle' but they resent like hell the fact that my recovery has simply ignored their prognoses. So they fall back on – 'it's highly unusual but not unknown.' The more seditious ones mutter about the possibility that Guillain-Barre, or some underlying psycho-somatic condition, could have been 'overlooked.' Then they look at my notes again and sigh. What they really hate is the fact that I refuse any further scans, probes and investigations. I always say to them is, 'if this was happening to you, would you want to interrupt it, disturb it, threaten it in any way?' That makes them very grumpy. As a result, I see little enough of them, latterly. My gratitude, however, to whatever 'intelligence' is responsible simply knows no bounds."

JJ turned to me – embarrassingly as my cheeks bulged like a hamster's, with tea-cake – "Evie, what are Tee and Ally gabbling about? It looks horribly intense."

"Bestiality," I managed, after a good swallow. "Ally proclaims that she's writing a book. That is she proclaims it to everyone except Pa and Ma. Ma would drown her in soap and Pa would remember some chilling anecdote. I don't know if Tee is advising, editing, censoring or volunteering herself – or, even worse, volunteering me!"

"Just so long as nothing four-legged crosses our threshold," winced JJ. "I broaden my mind on a daily basis but Ally's been steeped in such stuff for centuries, whilst I was innocently communing with a Rabbit."

"It's a start, JJ," I grinned.

"Bloody hell, Evie – it was a boy Rabbit!"

"Remember where you are JJ, before you impale yourself ever more deeply on that particular hook. I will not cause you further agony, I will merely observe that Ally's book is 'a sober history of…IT…in art, society, religion and of course, pornography.' It is structured towards the professorial but shall we say, has a tendency to be over-illustrated. It will be one for the coffee tables of the chattering classes and the Cotswold set. It should net you both a tidy sum. Her major problem is finding a sober-enough title and dustcover, so that purchasers don't blush scarlet at the checkout. At the same time, it has to be something that provides enough 'nudge, nudge, wink, wink, say-no-more,' to hook you in the first place."

"Probably very common on the Cotswolds," observed Andy, "throughout the ages. Didn't a one-time prime minister – or am I thinking of Dark Mirror?"

"Both," I said. "David Cameron and the initiation by deceased pig's head? Unhappily never proven but ne'er contested, either, to the best of my knowledge. There again, Heaven help us all if our adolescent stupidities came back to haunt our twilight. Did you know, however, that it nearly put Princess Tee off her breakfast chipolatas? Until I mentioned that those particular chipolatas had been consumed before she was even born."

It was in this manner that we imitated the chattering classes ourselves, for the benefit of whichever unfortunate was manning the transcription desk that day. 'Perhaps,' I thought, 'it will be the only time my valuable thoughts ever appear in print?

And what do I do? Start 'twittering like a twat,' an observation shrewdly offered, albeit in a slightly different context, by the aforementioned PM.

Eh bien, perhaps it could help to counterbalance my more gritty appearances on film? I wondered if they'd tracked those down yet? They'd need to have done some deep dives. Conventional keyword searches wouldn't get them anywhere.

I thus fell to pondering whether or not I wouldn't have preferred a little more fame, rather than merely being a select item passed on from one so-called connoisseur to another. That's one of the troubles with frivolous chatter, it makes a rubbish bin of your mind.

The afternoon wound down and we all drifted away. Precisely why we didn't meet in corners and discuss ever deeper and darker conspiracy theories, I couldn't say. We simply didn't. Tee and I went home, exhausted and slept unusually well. I suspect that held true for all six of us. There's only so much wind-up you can take, it seems.

58

BLOOD MONEY

The next day, at Penny's old place, we got serious, or tried to.

Consider our problem. We had honest answers for every question but not inquisitors who would believe them. Thus we were tasked with inventing the credible to sidestep the incredible, so that we could lie to the satisfaction of people who would claim to want -'no more than the truth.' We also needed to understand the ramifying whirlpool that had been drawing us all together, possibly for most of our lives. Coincidence had lost all its credibility, yet every day seemed to throw up further manifestations of its antics.

Andy was explaining yesterday's debacle.

"Don't ask me why I had the place swept, I just did. I have peculiarly sensitive antennae when it comes to authority, especially the covert variety and my thumbs were starting to prick. My mate found six bugs and I told him to leave them in place. We want them to think that we're naive idiots. That's why yesterday turned into a Mad Hatter's tea party.

Carl or I could have scooted around to you all earlier but for some reason, I came over weary. By the time I was thinking properly again, it was too late – and obviously phoning you all was a definite 'NO.' If only you knew how much I hate authority, you'd understand. Now, for Heaven's sake, somebody else say something worth saying."

"I'll put my pennyworth in," said JJ. "The truth is of absolutely no use to us. It's not just the question of it being unbelievable, it's the fact that Sun-Cloud has given us all perfect legends. Even Ally, who came out of a book, can trace her lineage back to the Vikings. We're all 100 per cent authentic.

"Naively, I first thought that this was for our benefit. Now I see it cuts both ways. Sun-Cloud has effectively disowned us. They would absolutely hate to become a blip on someone else's radar screen – however helpless the owners of that radar might be to do anything about them. I honestly thought they were helping us and to a certain extent, they were. But as I've just said, they were also effectively disavowing us. They would loathe anything to rock their cosmic applecart, such as my good-self proving to be enigmatic when examined in detail… 'where precisely did you say you were born and brought up?' Simple questions leading to complex answers. Bad cess."

I'd seated myself on a commode, in case the conversation became too dramatic for my colon to cope with. From my perch I volunteered an uncomfortable thought – "given then, that Sun-Cloud may not be quite the cosy benefactor we had all assumed, it's entirely possible that it has allowed these leeches into our lives for a reason. A bit of acid in our petri-dish. See what we do. How we respond, how our communal bond holds up under pressure.

"We were assuming that these seemingly inexplicable delays in the comings and goings of MI-whichever-number-you-like, were because Sun-Cloud was stifling them, leading them off the scent, wiping their memories, their records…I don't know what else. Perhaps doing that was never even on the cards…maybe this is just how bureaucracy works, how long it takes to grind into action, slow but inevitable, like appointments with the dental hygienist. Anyone for more guesswork?"

"I'll vote for 'slow-moving bureaucracy,'" Carl seconded me. "They're like the supposed 'mills of God,' grinding exceeding slow but exceeding fine. Having said which, however, something caused that Honda to break down, the day you guys took your walk. Trust me on this, Hondas rarely break down."

"Mills of God," mused Tee. "Puts me in mind of juggernauts – Indian variety, not your artics. Pulled by hundreds of men, hauling on silken ropes. They're huge temples on wheels, quite gigantic. They roll through the streets on festival days and occasionally someone gets too close and goes under – squelch! There you go, my useless contribution, though I can do rending and tearing, by appointment."

"Thank you, Princess," bowed Andy. "Much as I'd love to squelch, rend and tear, even by appointment, what I'd really like to know is – 'what do they think is going on?' It's obviously driving them crazy, at some level. If it's penetrated far enough through the system for covert bugging of innocent citizens to be approved, then it's being considered high up. What are they expecting to find? There are so many loose ends here and a lot more unanswered questions than we realise."

"May I suggest," said Ally, "that Jo was right a long-time ago. These malevolent clowns do not have the imagination to even consider that those two artifacts could have arrived from off-world. Their superiors wouldn't tolerate such a hypothesis. Therefore the only road open to them, is the one where you were recruited to 'alert-the-market' to a new capability in base-material manufacturing. For some reason or other, this manufacturer can't be open about themselves – or someone is thieving product and trying to net a bob or two on the side, before the open market gets in on the act. Their next presumption has to be that 'this capability' will either proffer further goodies for examination, or lay out terms, either for access to manufacturing capability, or technical know-how. That's what the bugs are about. Not for us but for what we seem to have access to.

"For certain, they're not going to harm us, because we're the only 'entree' they've got. They must be baffled as to why a bunch of clowns, such as ourselves, have been chosen as a conduit. That, in itself, lends some credence to the story of simply having 'found' the articles. Let me tie that into the 'allied-with-Porton-Down' farrago, the guys who coerced us into signing the Official Secrets Act.

"I was surprised, in retrospect, at the level of hardball they wanted to play. At first, I thought we'd been caught napping there, when we rolled over and signed. They probably expected us to laugh in their faces. They would have anticipated that we knew that we held all the cards. 'Threaten us in any way and we terminate your options,' should have been our attitude. In many ways we fluffed Round One, largely because we know we have nothing to offer that could pass the credibility test. That's why we panicked.

"They're going to conclude from our reactions that we have no right to these items. They will assume we stole them, maybe from a truck, a car, a briefcase. 'Finding them,' will come a very poor second in their estimations."

"Hang-on," I interjected wildly, "it was me who panicked, when they threatened Ma and Pa. I could feel Punch's heart straining. I could feel Marie-Claire's pain for him. She's had too much upset in her life and I don't think anyone in this room will risk her having any more. Damn it, I could see him chemically coshed in the shittiest asylum they own. Not that he's not equal to anything the 21st century might throw at him. He's 18th century mettle, not peanut brittle, like us. I'm sorry, I couldn't bear it. I thought with my heart, not my head. I let us down and I'm sorry."

"Don't you apologise," rumbled Andy. "We all felt the same, at the time. Ally said she was examining things retrospectively. We all love the retro-spectroscope, it's the mind's most magnificent creation."

"Oh, Evie!" Ally rushed over to console me. "Sweet Pea, I thought I'd made it clear I was analysing after the event. Don't you worry, I could see Marie-Claire crying, me crying, you crying. If you hadn't caved, I would have. Family first, every time and we're all Family here."

She turned to the rest of the room – "something has occurred to me, however. We can all cave in, rely on the 'we-found-them,' line, or we can play our own version of hardball the next time they turn up. If we were going to do that I'd suggest we start with a joint affidavit to the effect that our signatures to the OSA were coerced, under emotional duress. That we individually and jointly rescind our agreement to be bound by its terms. We can lodge copies with Liberty and any other Civil Rights organisations we can think of.

"Then, when they come calling, we tell them their tricks have endangered their position. Our client has been irritated by their attitude and they'll have to demonstrate considerable good faith to regain client confidence. We could see how they reacted to that. If those listening devices disappeared, we'd know we were back on a flat field. If they didn't, we could tell them to go forth until they'd mended their manners."

"Don't forget," Carl said slowly, "they can unleash all the crap they threatened us with any time they choose. We'd only have the upper-hand if we had anything they actually wanted and the fact is, we don't."

There was a long pause, which to me, began to feel uncomfortable.

"We can't go down the tough guy road," I said. "It's like Carl says, we're clean out of picture cards and aces. Also I can't think of anything that would induce Sun-Cloud to send us so much as the bolt to go with the nut. There's absolutely nothing it wants from these morons. What could they have that it needs? The only thing on its agenda is to protect whatever it sees here at No-Name and I very much doubt that even that exercises it unduly. There must be lots of petri-dishes in its lab. There are the contents of JJ's rucksack. He says he's hidden them. I'll bet if he went to check on their well-being, he'd find they'd been nano-botted into leaf mould, or used tissues. JJ said it himself, they won't be leaving any hints that they exist."

Across the room, JJ shot me an 'OMG, I hadn't thought of that,' glance and rubbed a thoughtful hand over his chin.

The silence resumed and this time I wasn't imagining it, it was definitely uncomfortable.

"I can solve this," said Tee, softly. She stared at the floor for a while, then braced herself and looked at us all, one by one.

"My husband deals with very dodgy people all the time. He has done so all his life and his father did so before him. Kindly, none of you have ever asked why I am rich and I am, bloody rich. It's about time I levelled with you and I'm sorry sweetheart" – this to me, over everyone's head, because for some reason we'd managed to end up at different ends of the room – "I haven't even told you, because I'm mortified. He's an arms dealer, an unhappy, covertly-gay arms dealer, if that's any sort of mitigation.

"I don't mean that he can find you the odd handgun and 15 rounds. He operates at revolutionary government level. You need 50,000 AK's, he's your go-to man. Shoulder missiles – which one? Small tanks, launchers – retired, or brand new? Ammunition? Only deals in 100,000 rounds and above. For tactical explosives and detonators, we have a glossy catalogue. He sells, shall I say, with political astuteness. The financial pages of every credible journal are his light-reading. He has to keep track of big money, where it's going and who it's going to. He supplies both sides in wars you'll never hear of and he defers to preferences expressed by the world's major players, within their arenas of influence.

"He never sells on his own doorstep. Does he buy? You bet he does. As a result he's on the cocktail party circuit at the highest levels. When ministers are constrained by protocols, he ensures their pockets are properly filled, after they've facilitated his needs. I'm sure you get the picture.

"I'm rich, because I am his long-stop bank. If one day he has to vanish and his accounts are frozen, I'm the conduit to a major portion of the family's fortune. What is technically mine is of course his. It exists in Switzerland, where else, as a string of digits and symbols which become useful only after my iris and palm prints have been referenced. One of the reasons he's so laid-back about our separation is that he can present it as a rancorous estrangement, which makes it unlikely that I would be the key to his strong box. In fact, we're quite fond of one another, as Beavie knows.

"I tell you this, firstly because I trust you all, secondly in the interests of full disclosure and thirdly, if these snoopers represent any serious department at all, then they already know who I am. They would, a priori, expect me to be the conduit for anything Vikky was touting, say on behalf of some entity within one of the 'Stans. It's not a huge leap, to guess that I'd, naively, get my friends to 'put it out there.'

"To them it's already obvious, Vikky is behind all this – they just want you to admit it. Of course you won't, because there's no advantage to your doing so. They know that and we know that they know…and so on down the line. They think that they have their answer already. If they want the goods, they're pretty certain that they know which door to go knocking on.

"Of course, I'll have to let Vikky know that they might knock on his door. He will tell them, 'sorry guys, you've jumped to the wrong conclusion, I've nothing to sell you. I wish I had.' Round and round in circles we will go. I honestly think that sticking to the 'we-found-them-on-the-table' is the best play for everybody. They know, we know, that there's not going to be anything else forthcoming, so we need to act like the innocents we originally were. We thought – 'these are funny objects, what on earth are they?' That's a perfectly decent position to stand on, for people obliged to keep a very dodgy secret."

Tee flopped back in her chair, looking drained and tired. Anxiously I blew her a kiss, trying very hard to send healing Beaver vibes with it. She gave a wan smile, then raised her hand, in order to speak again – "I'm so sorry," she said in a small voice, "Please don't hate me. It was an arranged marriage. I was 11 and he was 17. Our honeymoon was when I was 13. We separated, amicably, when I was 18 and now I'm 34. I'm not proud of what I am."

The silence that followed was agonising.

It was Carl who broke it and he did so forcefully. "Tiggs, you are one of my most loved people on this planet. We all love you very much and to see and hear you doing this to yourself, on our behalf, is humbling. We were silent because it's hard to know what to say when someone cuts themselves open in front of you, for you."

From everyone came mumbled noises, awkward stamps and claps, and finally a little half-circle of attentive souls gathered around her, touching, patting, stroking timidly, before they all shuffled back to their places. I didn't move. I was frozen, not by any of her revelations but by the thought of the pain she must be undergoing right now.

It was Ally who finally managed to lighten the mood and rekindle the conversation – "you don't think, do you," she said, loudly and clearly, "that Vikky would make an exception about low-level dealing, just the once and sell me that HK, MP7A1?"

Everyone gurgled in their own way and even Tee managed a wry grin.

"Right," said Andy, not without emotion, "thanks to Tee we have a possible conduit and excellent reasons for being jumpy about it. We never admit to it, of course, we stick to the 'found-them-on-the-table,' explanation and let them draw their own conclusions. They will believe what they want to believe. It's as JJ told us way back, that Sun-Cloud had said they would only be able to believe anything that was as grubby as they are. I think we ought to have the affidavit Ally suggested drawn up and if they start any hostile acts, we should threaten to involve Liberty. I don't think we fight but we defend aggressively."

"I've got to ask," said Carl, "I know it's been answered but I'm not the brightest, so indulge me, please."

"You ask away," said Ally, "whatever it is, I'm sure I need to know the answer, too. None of we pebbles in this room shine that brightly on our own but together, we're diamond."

"Where will these people turn next? We have nothing to give them and whatever we tell them, they will disbelieve. Are they ever going to leave us alone?"

"I agree," I said. "We should be discussing the way forward, given that what has happened, has happened. Does anyone have any insight beyond what Andy has, very sensibly, concluded?"

"This isn't insight," said JJ, " and in many ways it may seem negative but I think it may be a good negative. Being who I am, what I am and from whence I came, I imagine I have Earth II's stamp running through every cell in my body. If they wanted something from us, it's logical to assume that, in some way, I'd know what it was. I'm getting nothing, which I rather imagine means – 'stay with nothing and you'll be fine.' I think Ally's right, we involve Liberty and every other organisation we can think of if they start rocking the boat again. Also, perhaps before we do that, we should get their threats on tape. If we play at being quivering blancmanges the next time they turn up, they'll probably shoot their mouths off."

"I like that, especially the last bit," said Andy. I can get my mate to rig my chair, my crutches, with a transmitter. That would work. A bit of insurance."

"It's a bastard, isn't it?" I chipped in. "You see what pisses me off, to use the technical term, is the way we de-railed ourselves. We were chugging along so nicely, a lovely, loving little team. Then Andy and I opened Pandora's box. Why did we have to go and do that?

"What makes me hopeful is that Sun-Cloud has the same problem as us, I think. Outside influences are rocking its apple cart. That's one of the reasons, I'm guessing, that it's studying us, it wants to see how we react, how we retaliate, how we get out from under, assuming that we do. I'm still far from convinced it didn't set the whole thing up as an experiment."

"Why do you think it has our problems?" asked JJ.

"Intuition, largely. But Sun-Cloud is trying to change the underlying structure of the cosmos. Inevitably it is going to find that it, too, has opened Pandora's box in attempting to do so. It won't be encountering Rat-Face, or Muscles, but a dozen force-field and plasma equivalents. Again, I'm using intuition but I think there are very few laws in the universe. It's my guess that you can write the same law HUGE, or very, very small. Maybe it won't look the same but at root, it will be. How we react may be important to them."

"Kinesis" Alice interrupted, beaming brightly. "It's called kinesis and it's unavoidable. It's an outside influence affecting an entity. As simple as kicking a ball. There it was, lying on the beach, soaking up the sun. Along comes an idle passer-by and – 'blam' – now it's landed on the ebb tide and is heading off to unexplored lands. Every entity is a ball and there are lots of steel toecaps.

"Do you know," she finished conspiratorially, "I learned an awful lot from my more philosophically minded gentlemen. After they'd burned the midnight oil, pursuing the conundrums of existence, out pops I to read their correspondence and notes. You learn so much more from conjecture and intuition that you do from finished manuscript. Take Denis, for example, his correspondence was fascinating, full of very intriguing speculations…"

"Ally," interrupted Carl, hesitantly, "I think I'm finally getting the hang of your 'ins' and 'outs,' so what I was going to ask…" He froze, mid-sentence. "Oh no," he gulped, "sorry, that was a totally unconscious Beaver pun…it just escaped. Sorry!"

"There will be a licensing charge," I said proudly. "Also, that goes to prove that the condition is catching. I shall reflect upon a name for it…"

"Pardon granted," Alice beamed. "I'm proud to be infectious."

"Hang on!" I protested. "Hands off! It's me that's infectious. Not you. It's my disease! It's called Beaverpunitis."

"Sounds like an STD," grinned JJ. "Steer clear, Ally. I don't want it."

"STOP," boomed Andy. "I imagine Carl's lost his thread but if you haven't… continue."

"Thank you, kindly. What I was wondering was if you could see any way of reverse-engineering your emergence from the pages of books? I gather you used to be able to flit to and fro between titles, across the centuries and from different libraries. Quite the peripatetic lifestyle. Could you see any way of luring these goblins into a book, us slamming it shut and throwing away the key? In principle, that is."

"What a neat idea," I said.

"It is, in principle," said Alice. "The immediate problem I foresee, is that of, what-to-call-it… embodiment, corporeality? You recall I complained of 'thin-ness' when I was first here? By now, Marie-Claire and I would have simply faded-away, if JJ and Rufus hadn't requested Earth II's quantum genius to build us up, from the inside-out. We were still very two-dimensional, not to look at but as items professing reality. It's terribly hard to describe, because it's not something you can see but I think it's the problem physicists have foreseen with time-travel, how to translate all the workings of a human being, across space and time, from A to B. We were both more idea than reality."

"I can assure you," I interrupted, "Muscles is all reality. He compensates by being exceedingly thin in the ideas department."

Andy slapped his knees.

"I can't think sci-fi is going to solve this. No offence, Carl but if we are going to have sci-fi, it will have to come from Sun-Cloud's side of the fence. We might have ideas but they've got the technology. We're stuck with our local version of reality – Muscles in all his beastliness and Rat-Face in all his sliminess."

"Can we stand one more piece of woffle?" I asked, hopefully.

"I am sorry to say that I am fully woffled," Andy said.

"Sorry, bro," Alice added.

JJ gave an apologetic grin – "what she said…"

I looked at Tee but she was lost, staring out of the window with a 1000 yard stare that foretold of bad things on our horizon.

"That's all right," I said lightly. "My woffle and I are not even slightly hurt. That you'll never know, is your loss, not ours. We care not a sugar puff!" But by the time I'd finished they'd all left, even Andy, with the parting shot – "lock-up after yourselves, please." And I was alone, with a badly-mauled Tigger. Her confession had cost her dearly.

I knelt in front of her and held two frozen, reluctant hands.

"Really… truly… you can't think anyone holds any of that against you. That's why they've left without making any fuss. They accept the facts. You couldn't control those. They know that. They don't love you less, they love you more for being so brave. You can't think anyone holds it against you!"

"I hold it against me. I care!" was the angry response.

"I'm sorry, sorry if you felt I was speaking carelessly. Of course you care and of course we all care. But truly, no-one connects you to the harm Vikky's weapons cause."

"I know that Evie but I connect myself. Maybe you saw newsreels in the East, maybe you didn't. They're not censored the way they are here. The film is raw footage from killing fields. Terrible sights. Behind them all – the men who sell guns and explosives.

"Look at me, Evie – Princess with the Best of Everything! If I want it, I can have it – courtesy of arms deals. I should cover myself in pitch and rags. If anyone is dragged to the charnel grounds, it should be me. Let some of the stink, the torn flesh of children stick to me!"

I could think of nothing that could deflect such darkness. I'd been in many dark places but only on my own behalf, never, wittingly, as a proxy for the tens of thousands she was attempting to apologise to.

I gathered her up and helped her into Penny's old bed. It was still dry, fresh and clean – Andy was meticulous about housekeeping. There was a large, appealing Panda sitting on a chair. I hauled it over and wrapped her arms around it. She hugged it tightly, eyes firmly closed.

I pulled the curtains, settled into a chair and prepared to wait it out, however long it took.

59
THREE STOMACHS

I knew a fair bit about carrying crosses that aren't yours to bear. What had Warren Zevon written…?
 "I met the man with the thorny crown,
 "Helped him carry his cross through the town…
 "I was in the house when the house burned down."
Sometimes, three lines of lyric can unpick a knot that would defeat Philosopher-Kings.

That's what Tee was doing, carrying someone else's cross through the town, while the fire of her own home raged around her.

After an hour or so, when I was satisfied that she was deeply asleep, I propped the bedroom door open, so that I could squint back into the gloom and went to sit on the front step. There I communed with the weeds that had sprung up around the slabs, uninvited.

There was a large, self-important dock, already asymmetric with long-stemmed, smoky-orange seed heads. What did it crave for its children? Soft earth and gentle rain, I guessed.

Every nook, every cranny, every chink, had been colonised by some intrepid seedling or other. Particularly pushy was a low-lying, small-leaved character in purple and brown. It boasted attractive yellow flowers that set to fat little seed pods, like inflated grains of wild rice. If you tapped against a ripe one, it exploded like nature's own cluster bomb, hurling out seed in all directions. On consideration, that that wasn't the most empathetic of analogies to be making, under the circumstances.

Could you accuse weeds of being arms dealers? There's many a neat-and-tidy-gardener who would agree that that is exactly what they are, when they see what their uninvited appearance achieves in a well-raked seed bed, a full ten days before the guests-proper arrive. This is not a piece of whimsy I will dare to lay before my precious girl, still sleeping soundly inside. Nevertheless, to prove a point, I touch one more swollen pod and hear the tiny spatter of seeds, as they bounce off the fabric of my jeans. Cocky little gangster!

I crept back inside and snuggled in behind her, inhaling the fragrance of her hair.

I reached round to give the Panda a reassuring pat. Then I slept, too. Sleeping is one of my preferred occupations but as night sleep is frequently elusive, an afternoon snooze is as welcome to me as warm rain is to the weeds and their seeds.

The treacherous Panda woke us both.

Heaven help me! He was an alarm Panda!

Courtesy of lithium-batteries with a life-span that wouldn't have disgraced a Tesla, he was still rousing the long-absent Penny from her afternoon nap, at five thirty. He was suddenly filling the room with a most un-Panda-like racket.

"Jabberwocky!" shrieked Tee. "Where are they? I'll kill them all!"

I could only summon vaguely Beaverish noises, suggestive of terror or indigestion.

"Secure the Lodge!" I babbled.

"Understood," she bellowed. "What's happening? Which direction are they coming from?"

"Gr-floer, gumbla-poarg, bahwaa, hic, pekroo," I managed.

"Precisely, Watson," said Tee. "They hold the outer perimeter. We are totally surrounded."

"I shall create a diversion," I replied. "When you hear me open fire, leg it to the high ground."

Finally coherent, I wandered back to the front door, collected the key from its hook and prepared to cover Tigger Holmes' desperate flight to high ground. I stretched, politely, went outside where I … go-on, you can guess the rest…

Holmes ducked past me, holding her nose and scuttled up to the walkway. Carefully, I locked the door and with my mind bullied by useless questions that refused to settle into any logical enquiry, walked after her. What was going to be waiting for me?

Some battles you fight alone. Tee was currently engaged in such a one. That placed us in terra incognita. Until now we'd been able to depend on each other but some demons, by their very nature, remain exclusively one's own.

At first sight, however, it seemed the flight to higher ground had helped Holmes morph back into Tee. She was waiting by one of my favourite trees, a cantankerous, overgrown hawthorn that I had first squeezed past with Harold, 1000 years ago.

"Oh Lupa, you're back," I breathed in her ear, giving silent thanks to whichever Gods rule the Sargasso of Lost Souls.

For a while we propped each other up, indulging in mutual sniffling and snuffling. Then, refreshed, we toddled gently away, arm-in-arm… very difficult, it's a narrow path.

"Evie," she asked after a while, "have I had any good ideas recently?"

"How recently?"

"Don't know. Last 34 years, give or take?"

"There was the safety spear," I ventured.

"True. That was genius. Anything else?"

I thought hard.

"Do you remember discussing an old-fashioned travellers' van?"

"I do, oddly."

"I'd vote that to number one."

"Anything for two, or three?"

"Don't push your luck! There is the fetish but that's a work in progress, at least another six months growing time on your thatch. Anyway, to turn the boat round, how about me? Have I had any good ideas recently – or ever?"

Tee scratched her head and scoured the wilderness for inspiration. After a considerable time, she said – "don't take this the wrong way but… no."

"Phew, that's reassuring," I said. "We Beavers are naturally very conservative, being slow of habit. We mistrust innovation for innovation's sake. You'd never have got the safety spear past our quality control. By the way – what time is it?"

"Don't Beavers ever have watches?"

"An innovation," I explained. "Natural mistrust. We allow others to take the risk."

"Where on earth is the risk in a watch?"

I gestured frantically – though I knew it was futile – to Heaven.

"It fails to understand, Lord! Grant me the gift of single syllables!"

"Are you, the Tigger, ever late – or, perhaps – early?"

"Inevitably. It's a feature of life, it happens."

"And you know this, how?"

"Through the agency of mine, or someone else's timepiece – the watch. They keep track of time, O Beaver!"

"Exactly!" I said, triumphantly. "A Beaver is never late, nor early – due entirely to their refusal to accept the innovative tyranny of chronometers.

"Anyway, what time is it?"

Tigger sighed. In my opinion, it was the sigh of the soundly vanquished.

"Six forty three and some seconds."

"Excellent. Egg, chips, white bread and butter, apple pie and custard/cream. Merely follow the Beaver of perfect timing, please."

"Stop reading the menu," I said crossly. "You are undergoing Dr. Beaver's prescribed medical remedy and the ingredients must be consumed in order and in precise quantities."

"But for afters?" whined Tee. "I really fancy hole in the toad with gravy and chips. I really do, Beavie! Couldn't you check your medical dictionary, or something? I'm not denying the efficacy, even the necessity of egg and chips, apple pie and CREAM but for dessert can I have Holey Toad, pleeese?"

"Only if you're very good and promise not to engage in any running around games with the children in here and absolutely no walking on your hands."

"None!?" – voice of horror.

"None!" – voice of finality.

"At all?"

"None!!" – very firmly.

"Just a few yards…?"

"If you throw up, you're in so much trouble!"

"Phew, I'd have been stuffed otherwise. You see I have another tummy above my ordinary one but to fill it up, I have to walk on my hands. I'll show you an X-Ray sometime. I've actually got two. So I might need two Toads and two Holes. One for each extra tummy. I promise, I'll show you!"

"Idiot," I said. "Not even a Gurdjieffian one. Just a plain, unvarnished idiot. Those are your lungs."

"They are?"

"Yes."

"It's still important to keep them fed."

"Are you actually serious?"

"Absolutely. Undernourished lungs are a medical catastrophe."

"But you don't achieve that by filling them with food."

"Of course you don't, are you being deliberately obtuse or something?"

"All right, all right! I capitulate, totally. Eat what you like. Walk on whatever you choose – water for all I care. Just remember what happened the last time you stuffed yourself is all I ask."

"What did happen?"

"You were overcome by fumes and waxed oracular in the loo."

"And that's bad?"

"Not particularly, but you didn't seem to enjoy the run-up to it."

"Why was that, then?"

"You attained the dimension of an advanced pregnancy – in fact probably a month overdue with triplets."

"Gosh! We had children!"

"Only of a kind."

"What happened to them? They're not still around are they? I don't recall being on nappy duty, recently."

"No, no. They were of such divine essence that they took flight for Shambala, instantly."

"Oh, how sweet!"

"It was."

"It's so touching…"

Throughout this ridiculous conversation we had been inching our way along the queue. I'd almost forgotten why we were there, when Harry boomed – "hi, guys, what'll it be?"

"I need large quantities of baby food, Harry," said Tee decisively. "Start writing now – two egg and chips for two. Oh, hang on, that's not right. Chips twice with two eggs each, is that it? OMG it could be egg and chips twice but with double the eggs… twice…? How do you say it in this accursed language, Beaver?"

"What? I wasn't listening."

"How do you say – 'egg and chips twice but with two eggs each?'"

"You say – 'egg and chips twice but could we have two eggs each, please.'"

"Oh."

"Easy, really."

"What he said Harry but with six slices of bread and butter for me. None for him – he's dieting."

"HE might be," I said, "SHE isn't. I'll take that bread, too, H. I'm in urgent need of restorative carbohydrate."

"I could well believe that," agreed Harry, nodding sagely.

"Ah, but she hasn't finished yet, H," I warned, "the worst is yet to come."

"You jest?"

"Not. New pencil."

"I also NEED," stressed Tee, "with a ten minute time-lag, two holes with toads for one, many chips and mucho gravy. No bread."

"Who's coming in ten minutes, then?" asked Harry.

"My second stomach," Tee said proudly.

"But you said 'two holes' and you've only invited one extra stomach," Harry insisted. Then he added – "I think…"

"Ah but – He, or She, one of 'em, anyway, said I had two extra stomachs in one!" Tee said triumphantly, pointing at me.

I groaned. So vividly, so agonisingly that Harry cast an anxious glance at the defibrillator.

"No need," said Tee, "a plaster will do. I'll sort both of them out, never fear!"

"Whose slate?" Harry asked feebly.

"Alice's," I said. "I'm pretty sure it's all her fault," and I led the way to where I had commenced communication with a philosophically-minded fried egg. No trace of it remained. And no trace of me from that day, either, I supposed. Man, woman, androgyne and fried egg are kin to Heraclitus's river – never the same twice.

Princess Agnethuram ate – if that is the right word – like her Norse counterpart, Loki, trickster and sometime God of Fire. Loki, when challenged to an eating duel, ate everything – the ox, its bones and hide, the rye loaves, the ale, the wooden trenchers and finally the table itself. I always suspected her 'Agne' was from 'agni,' or fire and this most peculiar of evenings she proved it, though she did spare the table.

I enjoyed my meal, for I was feeling light-headed and optimistic. Firstly, I was almost certain that Tee had recovered herself. That allowed my mind to stray and grow pleasantly nostalgic with memories of Harold. Indulgently, I let imagination wander even further afield and began to wonder how I might contrive to meet my egg again. All of this nonsense totted up to a very self-centred, rueful happiness, the very best you could hope for, on a day like this. It was in that rhapsodic state, I fell to wondering why you're not allowed to amend your life.

Why can't you be allowed, I wondered, pauses in life's momentum, during which you could try to amend the most egregious acts you've committed? I recognise that the mechanical structure of material living won't permit it. Then why, in the first place, hook up a mind with the capacity for regret, to a body that can't return to the scene of the crime and set things right? It's a flaw in evolution.

At some stage of the game, a free-floating quality got its toes entangled in a corporeal web. It struggled but it couldn't free itself. It took up residence, within man, as conscience. There, it does its best. Perhaps, if it had remained free-floating but had co-opted some of the yearnings of the mud-bound beast, we and it might have morphed into angelic human beings? 'Just a thought,' I said to the memory of the egg, which wobbled its yolk sagely.

I looked up from this dreamy uselessness to see Tee, on her hands, walking down one aisle, while Harry, on his feet, walked up the other, bearing the Holey Toad, Mk.II, almost bang on time.

"Is she all right?" he enquired, in an anxious whisper.

"Hard to say. You'd need to present me with a checklist, a bit like one of those you get when you have a car serviced. Come to think of it, I might draw one up. It could be useful for keeping her in good running order."

Tee had executed a neat turn and to the delight of all the children in the room, was now on her way back.

"No use," was Harry's opinion. "It's the unexpected faults that do for people and cars alike. 'Heart' – tick, 'OK,' and tomorrow, 'heart' – boom!"

"It is a bit weird, if you happen to be in a pondering mood, H, to wonder if her dear little heart knows it's upside down, in a tranny caff, south of the M1 A, making its way back to Holey Toad II?"

"Too deep for me," said Harry. "I just hope you've got plenty of Gaviscon."

"We have the impoverished shopper's alternative, which is made from stale cheese and very cheap raspberry flavouring. Doesn't so much soothe your tummy as threaten it with something worse. It forces a Mexican stand-off."

"Rather you than me tonight, then," he laughed, before striding away with the empties.

Tee rolled herself upright, stood, to a smatter of applause, announced she was dizzy and sat down heavily.

"Phew, I needed that."

"Yes," I said. "That should be one lung full."

"Don't be stupid," she chided me. "You fill lungs from the top, with air."

"I got appalling marks in biology," I admitted. "Obviously I was misled. Anyway, Holey Toad II awaits you."

"Wow! I was hoping that was mine. Look at that gravy! You could hide elephants in it!"

"I am pleased that it makes you happy."

Agne/Loki got to work, again.

I tried to reconvene with the egg. Sadly, like Elvis, it had already left the building.

It's quite a long walk home to our van, on your hands. It's bad enough on your hands and knees. I know this, because there have been rare occasions on which some crime of mine has warranted the forfeit of giving the Princess an elephant-ride home. I should also wish to report, that despite making the journey in cross-legged posture, she bounces a lot – which is well outside the stipulated terms and conditions.

For my own return I favoured the stance adopted by Homo ever since he became Erectus.

Sadly, the whole Gurdjieffian thing had got to her and she was faithfully emulating many of his childhood oddities, as outlined in his writings.

"He was a child then," I was pointing out. "You see no pictures of him upside down in old age. He was far too portly. You are 34 and that is assumed, by many but not me, to mark the beginning of your maturity."

"I'm thixx," said the muffled voice. Her sweater inevitably falls down and covers her head, so that she looks like Smitty, from the Bash Street Kids but inverted.

"I think you're four," I said provocatively.

"Mm' noth! Thixx, thixx, thixx!"

"Upside-down tanty… Let me see… The Eye-Spy Book of Tantrums categorises that as a four-year-old tantrum. Six-year-old tantrums, it seems, are performed in clothes stores, where the 'performing artiste' clings to the underside of designer apparel racks."

"Letth dwrivve thoo Mmmm 'n' Sssss, thenssh!"

"Over my dead body -'which would be quite a climb'- I know, I know, I know. We're home. Shall I open the door, so that 'We' can roll gracefully inside?"

"Yeth, plith."

The Royal 'We' rolled in. I, the humble retainer, followed.

60

CONSULTING HARDY

"Shall I say your next line for you?" I asked. "Save you the trouble?"

"OK." 'We' had uncoiled, restored the sweater to midriff level and were looking very green around the gills, sprawled on the floor.

"I – Feel – Sick."

"How did you know?"

"Naturally intuitive," I suppose. "Anyway, can you get up?"

"Not a chance."

"If you stay there I'll have to put birthday cake candles on you."

"Whatever for?"

"Because we haven't any hazard beacons and that's the only alternative I can come up with."

"Oh." Long pause. "Why do I need them?"

"Because you are a hazard and you're starting to inflate."

Tee lifted her head to glance down her body.

"Oh Lord, send for the vet! I've got bloat! Horses die of that."

"So do sheep," I advised, informatively.

"What shall we do? I mean – 'what will you do?' I'm stuck here with bloat."

"I shall consult Thomas Hardy."

"Is he some sort of expert?"

"I don't think he was. But when Bathsheba Everdene's sheep get in the clover and bloat, handsome farmer, Gabriel Oak, trocars them for her and all is well – for the sheep, that is."

"What's trocar-ing?"

"You don't want to know."

"If it's happening to me I do!"

"Far better you don't. Just pretend to be a sheep in 'Far from the Madding Crowd,' and we'll let Carl do the trocar-ing bit."

"Why can't you do it – especially if it's intimate?"

"Haven't got a trocar."

"And Carl has?"

"He's got a very extensive toolkit," I said encouragingly.

"These 'trocar' things sound specialised."

"I'm sure he could improvise, sharpen something up."

"SHARPEN SOMETHING UP?!"

"Be reasonable. He can't make a hole in your belly with something blunt, can he?"

"He's not making a hole in my belly with anything, thank you! I've plenty holes in that region as it is. Any more and you'd be able to play 'join-the-dots-and-discover-the-Princess.' Furthermore, if we're playing 'Far from the Madding Crowd,' I want to be this Bathsheba Everdene character – I mean, what a cracking moniker! You can play the sheep."

"You are utterly unreasonable," I protested. "Bathsheba doesn't get bloat. The sheep do. You have bloat. Ergo, you are a sheep. Bathsheba's role has gone."

"Who to?"

"Me, of course."

"Get me up!"

"Why?"

"So I can fight you for it."

"For what, in Heaven's name?"

"The part, the role, the name-y thing of course!"

"Bathsheba Everdene?"

"That very one."

"You can't," I said flatly.

"I can't what?"

"Get up! Give me strength! You are a sheep, with bloat and axiomatically you cannot arise before you have been trocared. Currently we have no trocar. So stay down. Your life is in danger."

There was silence for a while. Slowly, however, I could sense that it was becoming a silence filled with great cunning. I grew alert.

"Beaver," cozened a voice from the dark shape on the floor, "am I, or am I not, an Indian Princess, currently stranded, through little fault of mine own, on the floor of a trashy trailer, in the dark, somewhere near London?"

"Mmm," I pondered. "It's hard to say in the dark. I thought you were a sheep."

"This is a cruel prank, Beaver, ill-becoming a creature of slow and peaceful habit."

"It is, a bit," I agreed.

"Therefore, would you assist my arising…please?"

"Providing you promise to remain a sheep called Bathsheba Everdene and do not turn into a ferocious Tigger that mauls and rends."

"All right, I promise."

"Here we go then. Hup-up-up-up-hup – grab the bed – heave! Up, up! DO NOT sit down. Keep upright, I will guide you to the loo – slowly.

"OK – that's good. Back, turn around, around. Reverse, reverse – reverse you idiotic sheep!! Not forwards, reverse!

"Now, do not sit. Try to unfasten your jeans…"

"Can't."

"Breathe out – out – out! The opposite of in! Lord give me strength! OUT!

"Very good! That's the button done!

"I'm going for the zip. Same routine. Out…OUT! You woolly-miscreant, OUT!

"That's the spirit. Good God, they really engineered that zip…impressive.

"Now, can you get them down?"

Tragic pause.

"At least try!"

Horrible struggling noises, pitiful really but sometimes you have to be cruel to be kind.

"OW!!! THAT WAS ME!!!"

"Sorreee!" Ooops, clumsy Beaver…

"Stop, stop, stop!" groans Tee. "We haven't got a chance. I think my bum's grown and my thighs. I'm being re-built for something bigger than child-bearing. I think there's a new twist to the Ganesh story being played out in my nether zone. I've been interfered with – by myth. Get ready to cut the head off anything that appears!"

"Stop drivelling! You're not a myth, you're you. You've been inflated by Holey Toads. I told you we should have waited for the trocar but oh no, you've got to have the heroine's role. Now look at you – blown up like a bouncy castle!"

"Not half as much fun," moaned Tee.

"Grab the wall – I'm going to pull…hopeless… What we need is an irresistible force. I know! Scissors!"

"Spare them!" she wailed, "they're designer. I know, I know… I'll try for a belch… stand back… 'Toad in the Hole!"

"Let go of me first! If you're going to…aagh!…you animal!…that was gravy, Toad and egg spray, all over me… I cannot forgive that… I am forever defiled!"

"It's all 'me, me, me' – think about me! I'm the hideously expanded one!"

"Good grief, woman – I smell like Brighton sea front on Bank Holiday – cheap fat, pee and chips. Come on, hold the wall, I'm going for broke – it's your jeans or this van."

Above me, another horrible burp and the van shakes. The jeans are definitely moving though – or Tee's legs are coming off. Ah, excellent this is what success feels like! We definitely, definitely are getting somewhere…

"OMG, Tee! Something awful has happened to your tummy!"

"What! What? WHAT!?"

"There's a zip, all the way down it. I think this is that moment from 'Alien' all over again. Do you think you're about to explode?"

"I told you – I've been mythed! Get ready with the bread knife!"

"You're not having that sort of Mother's Pride, for Chrissake."

"I know I'm not! That comes ready-sliced, you moron! I thought we were playing 'Far from the Madding Crowd' and I was Bathsheba Everdene?"

"We were and you were a sheep! Then you went all oriental on me and insisted you were having a re-write of the Mahabharata. But now it's definitely 'Alien' and you're Kane. That means I'm Ripley, AKA Sigourney Weaver. Very satisfactory."

"In your dreams," scoffed Tee, "your tits are too big. You can be the cat. Anyway, I'm now first in line for a serious poo. Then we'll have some recasting and probably a change of movie. Shut the door on your way out!"

"Suit yourself," I said…and waited for the howl.

"It's DARK!"

"You keep forgetting to buy the bulbs. You say you'll get them but you never do. The entire trailer is officially in darkness."

"Open the door then!"

"You just said, rather rudely, to shut it."

"So open it, rudely or politely, I don't mind. You know I get scared in dark rooms. Let that peepy star in. It can have the satisfaction of watching me poo. Maybe it'll go 'hyper,' or whatever it is they do."

"They go 'nova, supernova,' that's brighter and brighter, then they implode, collapse in on themselves."

"Do you know, I think I might be about to do that. Make sure you finish our fetish if I do."

"How the hell could I? I need your hair!"

"That's a valid point," said Tee thoughtfully. "How long does this 'nova' business last?"

"In your case, not long enough. We need six months growth, minimum. Try to resist. Fact is, I'd find it very hard to cherish a cinder – even if it was you."

Tee perches and contemplates her prospects. She thinks that the star, considerately and benignly, is encouraging her to poo. I know better. I know that the star is gazing approvingly at me, the sage, loyal Beaver…asleep on the job.

61

NOCTURNE

Carl prods Andy gently in the ribs, fingertip-light. Finally they can share the same bed. The cage isn't needed any more, the worst of the neuropathic pain has passed. This makes partner/partner consultation that much easier.

"You rang?"

"I prodded."

"And your prod, at, er…1.38 a.m…was the preface to?"

"I re-read 'Way Station.'"

"You did? Why, especially?"

"I knew it was relevant."

"To?"

"Our situation, our condition, our…what's special about this place."

"Tell me."

"You don't mind, at 1.42 in the morning?"

"Hell no, I can recognise important when I hear it."

Carl sighed, comfortably. He stretched out his left hand and let it run across the spines of the books in the wall case. He could name a lot of them by touch, even in the dark, by height, width, location and from long familiarity with his own filing. Touch was reassuring, so he found Andy's hand and held that too. Now the electricity from the ideas and images stored on the shelves, would run all the way through, with him as conduit. The idea made him smile.

"To begin with, it wasn't the way I'd remembered it at all. I'd dreamed up a different book, still 'Way Station' but I'd discarded the entire plot.

"What I'd remembered as the principle of the whole exercise, was the Alien agent sending a message – 'arriving such and such a time – have the coffee on!' I'd held on to an image of this ageless but very old man, having long, affable raps with the terrible-looking creature, who had sought him out to become Keeper of a Way Station.

"What is so special about it is the compassion of living creatures for one another, however strange and terrible they may look, once they are aware that their minds are in tune. It's together that they recognise how fragile and special is the deaf mute, Lucy – and how ghastly her family are. It's not how things look on the outside, or to the world, it's how your heart greets them. Can you walk and talk together? Because walking is what Enoch does every day, he walks with his rifle in the crook of his arm. I think I said this before, he's not looking to kill but his rifle is part of him. Perhaps it's part of being a pioneer American? I wouldn't know but I can feel something solid about it. And always in sight is his old farmhouse, which will stand forever. Home. Trust in home, hearth, love, respect, extended family…and coffee – to which we can add Danish. I guess they didn't have them then…"

Awkwardly aware that he hadn't made a very good hand with his description, Carl paused and tried to let his words flow as feelings, through his fingertips, into his friend and lover. "That's all, I guess. What's special, for me at least, is the small stuff, not the big. The plot is an irritation. It intrudes, the way a timer intrudes, ticking loudly in the background and threatening to end something you don't want to end."

He paused again, then added – "one thing I did get wrong and it kind of matters, is that he didn't carve and whittle the wood the aliens brought him. He got them for his friend, the mailman. They'd known each other for ever. Enoch never aged but the postman did. Neither of them needed to talk about that. The mail guy just accepted that his friend was different. He also knew that he was good. So when he made a carving of him, it was a carving of this free spirit, rifle in the crook of his arm, wind blowing his jacket…walking, just walking his slice of the earth with goodness in his heart."

The two men squeezed each other's hand.

"To my reading, the book's about the sensibility of small people. How the world trusts them to keep things right, through their heads and hands and hearts. I love that about it. In many ways it's more of a song than a book, a blend of music and words about the harmonies of the world and its small, considerate people."

Carl paused.

"We're small people, aren't we?" he asked. "I just hope that we're good small people."

Andy drew in a great, silent breath and tried, for a moment, to manipulate it. Instead he simply breathed out and said – "yes, we are small and that's the way I like it.

"I've loved watching you re-build the bike. The body, the frame, you call it. All that brazing and filing. I don't know, you're bringing it back to life and that's an incredible thing. And I know, because that is what Sun-Cloud is doing with me. I just hope your bike feels as grateful as I do.

"Do you think Vikky will ever send you another? I kind of don't want you to finish. I want this beautiful emerging entity on one side of the shed and that heap of rust and ruins on the other. I know I want it to happen again. Do you think he will?"

"I was going to ask Tee to give him a gentle goose. I've sent him a crate of Norton bits, built up from eBay trawling, boot fairs, bike fairs. She told me he was over the moon.

"You know, I had no idea and come to think of it, you might be interested too, he actually employs a mechanic, full-time, maintaining his collection. Old bikes are like old cars, full of quirks. Anyway, yeah, the guy doesn't 'owe me,' not by a long stretch but a while back he mentioned he'd seen a combination, rotting away in some backwater. He kind of made me think that it might be coming my way. Now if that ever does happen, I really will owe him! But I'd have enough work to keep me busy on the magical mystery front for a very, very long time."

Both men chased their own thoughts for a while. The clock self-importantly twitched its digits around to 2.27.

Andy broke the silence first.

"What do you make of the arms dealer business?"

"Not much, I'm ashamed to say," Carl admitted. "It's a job. I've got a bit of a morality by-pass when it comes to drugs, weapons, forgery and such-like 'crimes.' You don't have to pull the trigger, you don't have to shoot up junk. You don't have to own the Picasso."

"Oh dear…that's pretty thin."

"I know. I'm a lazy thinker and I'm also selfish. I'm not blowing out a guy who's happy to send me piles of interesting rust from darkest Asia, out of the goodness of his heart. That's how selfish I can be. It's the same attitude junkies have – they don't hate their dealer, they love him. Your conscience can be remarkably blind when it comes to self-interest. In fact, don't start needling me until I've got that combo in our shed."

"Good Lord, I'm not needling. Life's complex, we all know that. I was more upset about Tee," confessed Andy. "She was carving her heart out this afternoon."

"I saw that, too. I'm selfish, not blind. Poor girl was really hurting. Bloody hell, Andy, now I'm really on the spot. To put it crudely you've stuffed a rip-rap right up my arse. But bollocks to it, I'm not St. Carl."

"Pace, pace, Bro. I shan't be sprouting wings any time soon myself. I imagine that if Vikky inherited the job from his dad he was totally compromised. Especially on top of being screwed up about being gay and married, in a country 50 years in moral arrears. I doubt that's a job you can walk away from. Anyway, it could have sounded cool at 18-20 and only slowly turned to vinegar by the time you were 40.

"It did upset me though, to see how deeply it affected her – as if she could have done a damn thing about it. What could she do, other than what she has done – walk away? Giving up what was probably her darkest, most painful secret, just to try and help us all out, was pretty unselfish."

"I hear you Andy, I hear every word and I know where you're going with it. But trust me, the only person who can help Tee, deal with Tee, manage Tee, keep Tee the right side of sane, is Evie. All we can do to further that, is support Evie. For all that Tee comes across as a crazy, loveable crackpot, scurrying around with her tail wagging – if she's not having an interlude playing Princesses – she's actually intensely private. Evie's the only key-holder. That's why she plays the steady old Beaver, plodding along behind, ready to re-assemble all the pieces."

"Does any of this have anything to do with 'Way Station?" asked Andy. "I'm not being a smart-arse, I'm actually asking."

"I think it does. We're horribly close to getting involved in 'a bigger story.' Like Enoch Wallace, 'stuff' has got out about us. In his case it was because he didn't age. In our case we opened our very own Pandora's Box, by stupidly revealing off-world materials. In both cases, something bigger and darker, has now muscled in on local information.

"Simak obviously has to fudge his plot to get a happy ending and round his story off. We don't have that option. We have to ride out a storm of our very own making, in our very own teacup. Whoever these characters are – and can I just say, for the record, I think it's very strange that we don't really know the answer to that – they won't give up until they're satisfied that they've found whatever it is that they are looking for. Two tiny things seem to have set an avalanche in motion."

"Are you saying 'Way Station' offers no solution?"

"To put it politely – nothing viable."

"Have you any ideas?"

"Not a one, Sweet Pea, except for begging JJ to set Sun-Cloud on the job."

"I don't think that Sun-Cloud asks – 'how high?' – when any of us says -'jump," said Andy, thoughtfully. "For all we know, this is game-plan as devised."

"Too true, I couldn't agree more. My major concern is not so much how we deal with the situation, rather how the situation deals with us. Which is what you just said but different."

"Wow, we're deep – or is it 3.00 am?"

"It's 3.00 am and in the spirit of full-disclosure suitable to the hour," said Carl, "I'm admitting that I'm scared. I'm scared for all the little stuff we've talked about, tonight and at Moss's place. You can't kick back on the verandah, me covered in oil, Tee walking on her hands, JJ and Alice doing their martial arts, Punch and Marie-Claire planting and weeding and Evie seemingly just pootling about but actually stitching the whole quilt together, when the Men-from-the-Ministry-of-Fear are about to call. It's like having a guilty secret. You can never relax.

"Being Gay, we both know about paranoia. Once a thing like this is in your head, there's never any getting it out. I know that comes across like a counsel of despair but it's not meant to be. It's more a statement of reality. Personally, I'm searching for a weapon that will blow all this away."

Andy stared at the ceiling. It was probably one of the most undistinguished ceilings in the western world but he implored it to provide an answer. It stared back at him, calmly indifferent to his prayers, blandishments and threats. If it said anything at all, it said – "I am mere plaster-board, what can I do?"

He took in another deep breath and this time propelled it out, staccato. The night-time breath yoga was coming on apace, he thought, for the second time. "Ah, so what," he murmured, largely to himself, then added with a short bark of laughter – "so they buried him in the ceiling."

"What?"

"Forget it. Old age. Poverty. I was rambling. Punchline of a stone age joke."

"Tell," demanded Carl.

"Seeing as it's you, then but I'll trim the shaggy bits… Robin Hood is dying, in the attic room of a tavern, on the edge of Sherwood Forest. Little John, Will Scarlet, Maid Marian are all there. Through the little window he can see the tops of the trees, waving. He heaves himself upright, looks at the beckoning branches. 'Bring me my great bow,' he gasps. He takes an arrow, nocks it to the string, hauls back the yew stave into an arc and says – 'bury me where this arrow falls!' – and drops back, dead "…so, they buried him in the ceiling…"

Carl gives his own version of a yogic snort and asks – "what brought that on?"

"That's even feebler. I was staring at the ceiling and wondering if it could help."

"You can't say it didn't try. Nevertheless, that's definitely, kiss, kiss, goodnight!"

"Night…"

'Come on ceiling…try harder!'

62

CURSED BY MEMORY

'Tis grand,' thinks Punch, 'fer t'do yon bit o' weedin', slow an' methodical, like. Then t'sit 'ere, on t' bench together, a waitin' on lunch t'magic i'sself out o' yon basket.'

If only he didn't sense a cloud.

"A's frettin' abaht t' chilluns, Ma. Weel, not frettin' more as a'm worrit fer 'em," says Punch thoughtfully, twisting open the screw-top on the wide-mouthed soup thermos.

"Oui, Papa. It is because it is they, the children, are fretting. All of them, from big Monsieur Andrew down to ma p'tite Alice… and Papa, why is Marie-Gabrielle become, Alice? Always, I forget to ask."

"Suitin' 'er, ain't it?" grins Punch.

"I don't like to agree but oui, it does. But I interrupt. You are worrying?"

"A is Ma, a' is. All t' spring 'as gone out theer step, thet daftness o' youth…what does you lot call it -'joy de viver?"

"If I was not trying to block my ears to your murderous French, Papa – 'you lot' – would earn you a rap on the knuckles with my spoon."

"An' nae doot warranted, too, Ma. So, firstways a's beggin thy pardon but second'y tha's a beggin' m' question, methinks?"

"Papa, you have asked no question but your question is, 'why are the children worried and what are they worrying about?'"

"In a nutshell, Ma, 'tis that, entire."

"You break our bread and I will try my answers with you."

Punch pulled a shining cottage loaf from the basket and regarded its golden glow fondly. Deftly he twisted it into two unequal portions. There was no point trying to coax Marie's appetite. It was what it was.

"Papa, you know as well as I that the world is a mass of circles. All these circles interlock and sometimes that coming together of strangers, greater, or lesser than oneself is a good thing and often, it is not. It is the way of the world. It was easy, was it not, when our circle brushed against that of Monsieur and Madame Moss? We were old people, quiet in our ways. No harm came to us. Yet great harm could have befallen us and I believe it befell the children in that strange world. I don't know how. I was at peace in the valley of Les Anges," and Marie quietly crossed herself – simultaneously provoking violent rage and an angry humility in Punch. Rage at the church's filthy acolytes and humility in the face of Marie-Claire's enduring faith. "But the children were startled by the strangeness of it all and in ways I cannot explain, they sought to confront the things they could not comprehend.

"Papa, I express myself so badly!"

"No," said Punch, "A kin unnerstan' thee."

"Papa, that world was not ours. To take away anything but memories might provoke a great crisis in affairs. I don't know what has happened exactly but matters of that world are being acted out here. The children find they are caught in these circles. They do not understand that an item from one circle may not be transferred to another, without a great balancing of the scales. This is how they find themselves, caught in the balancing. All they can see however, is the chaos of the moment. They are not old enough to see that it is not they but forces that are changing around them. A great system is resolving a small matter and something else, something wicked…" her voice trailed off and she turned away, to stare sadly at the turned earth of the furrows.

Punch, arrested by her tone, halts his excavation of the loaf to follow her gaze. He saw his orderly lines of vegetables. You'd expect an old soldier to lay out good lines of greens, he thought. The fact was, however, he had been a terrible soldier, a backsliding, brawling lout, who had taken the King's Shilling solely to spirit himself away from an overdue reckoning with so-called forces of Law and Order.

He'd had the wit to survive by making a profession of cowardice and cunning. He'd been among the first to fall on every battlefield he'd ever been marched onto and in that way, he had been able to crawl off it alive. He was unlikely ever to forget the cold facts of that calculation. One bully-ragging 'lance-pesade,' a would-be corporal, had been wise to his scheme. Punch had coldly and deliberately shot him in the back, on a day sufficient chaos presented him with the opportunity. He was not proud of that but the fact that he had done it was the only reason he was still here to brood upon the murder.

Fate, ever the jester, now obliged him to imitate the clay-pipe-clutching legend, once found outside every tavern in the land, begging for a peg of ale or a crust, crutched aboard their one good leg. His wits had spared him his limbs. But his head had been spared by the mysterious Hedge, that had turned around his wits, set loose his wisdom and made him a man who fretted more for others than for himself. He was, in short, a reformed character, a concept that caused him the hollowest laughter and weariest pangs of conscience it was possible to experience.

Whenever he silently examined the past, in the small hours of the night, he wondered if it was possible for one man to embody all such reverses as he had, yet still be capable of choosing a path he knew was decent, honest and true. He nursed a horror, deep in his gut, that he could become the murderous creature he had been before, at the click of fate's fingers. To blind himself to this, he tried to commit himself as passionately as he could to the tasks of fatherhood, husband-hood and husbandry.

It was a peculiar penance, to be making his amends in a century that had no yardstick by which to judge him. Effectively, he was alone with his memories, with no way of knowing what value he represented to himself, or others. His only relief was that he was far away in time from the lives that he had destroyed and no longer face-to-face with the fact that better men than he had died, because they had been gallant. To take the measure of it all was a task wholly beyond him. All he could do, was vow to be decent from hereon.

In the chaos that represented his life, he could feel the play of Marie's circles. Had he not been pitched from one to another, his very chemistry altered to bring balance to some equation he knew nought of?

He tried, for a moment, his hand once again deep within the soft heart of the loaf, to face the past. Grandmother was his past. Everything began and ended there. The pain it caused him was still acute and that it was more than 300 years distant, made it worse. Either he needed it close, for fuel, or he needed it excised from memory for ever. He could have neither.

He was for all time, the child who had in innocence, found the great, gold coin. At first it brought such good fortune. Then he had spoken out of turn and from that the chaos of 30 violent years flowed. The vengeance he had wreaked he would never regret, not God himself would persuade him to feel otherwise. But the shambles it had made of him had only been amended by the mystery worked within the pale of the Hedge.

He sensed now, as Marie had sensed too, that his new family had found the equivalent of the great gold coin and just as it had torn his life to shreds, so it was beginning to pluck at theirs. Unscrupulous creatures were abroad and were following them all, from circle, to circle. Within these gyres, it was hard to glimpse who were the pawns, who the kings and queens and what their goal might be.

He shook his head, half hoping to clarify thought and when that failed, he returned to the soft excavation of the bread.

"What 'as oor Ally said to thee, Ma?"

Marie-Claire paused her own scrupulous preparations.

"It is, of course, what she has not said. Monsieur Jo has said things that have made her anxious. Very big things are afoot but it is, as ever, the small things that concern us. As far as I can guess, little Evie and Monsieur Andrew may have shown others items from that…" she searched for the most neutral phrase… "that other place. Which, I think, Papa may have been a mistake?"

Punch put his arm around her and pulled her close. Skilfully she juggled the items on her lap, averting catastrophe, so that she could lean on his chest, head tucked under his chin.

"It will not end badly, will it Papa?" she asked hopefully.

Punch felt every emotion he had ever known clamouring for attention.

He had seen the men in the black car. He wasn't blind. He kept a steady lookout.

He was, however, perplexed. Whatever the big picture might be, it eluded him. He was aware that he was seeing a mere fragment of it. That, then, would have to do.

Inside, he gave a cold laugh that, had it been heard, would have chilled bone.

"This time, Maman, none o' t' family gets 'urt and thet includes Jo, t' boys and yon Princess. Yet, tha' cud do somethin' as might be 'elpful…" he bent and whispered in her ear.

She smiled, sat up and giggled. "It is a very shameful trick but I shall do it!" she said happily.

At that the sun smiled and the thick soup was just the right temperature to pour into the bread bowls With the teased crumb dropped back in, grated cheese and chopped chives added liberally, here was food to relish. Once it was spooned away, in went a half-inch thick slice of rum and sugar soaked ham, making a sandwich, thought Punch, for which all good men and women needed appreciative palates… and most of their teeth. He reflected ruefully upon the latter and with a wry smile drew out his knife. Ah, how he longed to forget! For that he turned to the bottle of wine. It bore no label but was dense, yellow, redolent of autumn colours and a hazy sun…a sun that could coil around his stomach, as comfortable as a cat before a fire.

Asked in that moment, Punch would have elected himself one of the happiest men alive. Only memories plagued him. But what could he have done? He had been barely 10 years old.

63

MALICE AND MALACHITE

Jo-Jo's thoughts revolved around age, too, though his were less anguished.

Last night he had promised Ally he would check on Tee and Evie. Everyone, it seemed wanted to watch over Tee until she recovered herself. For his part he trusted Evie, recognising that she was the only person capable of handling Tee's particular brand of volatility.

He had caught up with them as they were making their way home from the diner and he had remained in the shadows, smiling at the strange progress of waving legs and a circling Evie. "I'm thixff, thixff, thixff!" he heard, followed by Evie's deadpan – "you're four, got it? Four!"

"Thixff! Thixff!"

'They're fine,' he'd thought. They'd bicker amicably all evening and finally Tee would win. Then, once victorious, she'd agree instantly with Evie. "No – you're probably right. I'm four, well four-and-a-half!" And both of them would collapse into private, hysterical cackles.

"How old do you reckon you are, Ally?" he asked.

"Never ask a girl her age, bud."

"No, I know and I wasn't, really. I'm currently about 4,500 and feel and act like a 45-year-old, thanks to you. Tee's 34 and claims to be six. Evie says she's four – Tee, that is. Punch and Marie are about 50, plus 300 but come on like spry centenarians. How do you date yourself, see yourself?"

"I see. How old do I look?"

"Anywhere between nine and 30. Depends which frock and face you put on, what mood you're in."

"Oh dear, jail bait! Let me think…

"Realistically then, if I go by active memories, I suppose I must be – I know this sounds silly – somewhere between 250 and 350. But I always act the same age, nine to 34. Discerning of you to recognise that. I do suffer from multiplication, however, which is an odd condition brought on by entertaining four, or more, great minds during their, what shall I say, recreational periods?"

"And you were aware of that?"

"Only if I wanted to be. I'll bet I was the very first, two-dimensional, peeping Thomasina. It could be great fun, once I'd worked out how to do it. I'll spare you the details.

"Old Magic woke me up," Alice said reflectively. "It sort of chivvied me awake. It used the chalks and ochres, later the wood blocks and the old, organic inks. I took a lot of waking!

"You'd never suspect what powerful agency exists in the earth colours. You take lapis lazuli, for example. Lapis is downright naughty. Using Lapis to paint the Madonna's robes is hilarious, if you're in the know – which means you have to be one of the earth tribe, really. Otherwise, I suppose, Lapis just seems a very refreshing blue. But it's not just coincidence that 'blue' has become slang for lewd.

"As for malachite, oh don't let me start! Oh my! There is nothing that malachite won't bring crashing down, in the end. It's a very, very angry piece of earth. Look what happened to the Czars – people think that was all Rasputin and Marx but believe me or not, malachite had a hand in the whole downfall of Russia – fact is, it's still doing it…

"You're off piste, Lovely," warned Jo-Jo, affectionately.

"I know, I know but you really need to know about malachite. I come with terrible warnings! Don't mess with it. It hates the human race. You know, Pa was telling Evie and I an old rhyme about elm trees – 'elm hateth man/and waiteth.' That refers to the nasty habit elms have of dropping large branches on people, without warning. I'm going to make up a rhyme to warn people about malachite. Let me see…

> 'Let me sleep,
> For if I wake,
> I'll bend my will
> Your bones to break.'

"Do you reckon that's creepy enough?"

Jo-Jo reflected for a moment or two. Then he cocked his head to one side, in the manner of a rueful bird robbed of its crust and murmured – "Ally, I may have asked you this before but are you sure I'm safe with you?"

"You are as long as you keep treating me as sweetly as you do. But you shouldn't forget, I'm actually Earth Magic, which makes me Old Magic's creature. Old Magic is quite outside human reason."

"Oh, that's so reassuring! For a moment or two there, I was almost anxious. Next time I see that blasted Rabbit, I shall ask him for the keys to the RSG."

"Sweetheart! There's not the slightest point seeking sanctuary from Old Magic in the bowels of the Earth, is there?" And Ally skipped over to give Jo-Jo a reassuring peck on the cheek.

"We couldn't get back to age and time, could we?" he asked feebly.

"Oh I doubt it. The problem is I'm fretting about Tee. It's very rare and very dangerous for someone to open themselves up like that. Leaves a raw wound that takes a long time to heal. That means we all have to put ourselves into healing mode. That may sound soppy but I wouldn't choose to bare myself like that – and being bare is something I know a lot about.

"The thing is, Jo, I could see inside her while she was talking her story. All she could see were mounds of dead children and that's what she thinks we see when we look at her, now – raped, murdered, maimed and tortured children."

"Oh Lord, that's awful."

"Yes it is. This may sound pious but we've all got to make an effort. Evie can't do all that propping up and healing on his own."

Jo-Jo thought for a while. The two of them had seemed happy, relaxed, last night.

"You quite sure you're right here, Lovely?"

"I'm sorry, Jo but yes. I'm always right about Earth Magic and that's what she's dealing with, weird though that may sound. We're talking about blood and I wish we weren't."

"You're sending a chill down my spine."

"Don't think I'm blind to it myself. Something bad is going to happen."

END OF PART 1

Acknowledgements and gratitude are expressed at the end of Part 2.